MW00571136

The Science Fiction Century, volume One

Edited by **DAVID G. HARTWELL**

The Science Fiction Century, Volume One

ORB

A Tom Doherty Associates Book

New York

To Maron Waxman, Susan Ann Protter, Les Pockell, and Kathryn Cramer, without whom this book would never have been completed.

I would like to acknowledge the significant presence of John W. Campbell, Isaac Asimov, Robert A. Heinlein, and Arthur C. Clarke, and all the other science fiction writers who are not re-printed in this book. I used their work to support my argument for the consideration of science fiction as a worthwhile literature in *The World Treasury of Science Fiction*. I used many of them again to illuminate and uphold the value of the hard SF tradition in *The Ascent of Wonder*. In this book, I chose the work of other major writers, some of them less familiar, some of them equally famous, so as not to allow my argument to get lost in the particular aesthetic of SF that is so dominant in their work. But their presence is here anyway, anyhow, even in the absence of representative examples of their work.

The stories collected in *The Science Fiction Century, Volume One*, and the forthcoming *The Science Fiction Century, Volume Two*, were previously published together in hardcover as a single volume under the title *The Science Fiction Century*.

THE SCIENCE FICTION CENTURY, VOLUME ONE

Book design by Fritz Metsch

An Orb Book
Published by Tom Doherty Associates, LLC
175 Fifth Avenue
New York, NY 10010

www.tor.com

ISBN 0-312-86484-1
EAN 978-0-312-86484-2

First Hardcover Edition: November 1997
First Trade Paperback Edition: March 2006

Printed in the United States of America

0 9 8 7 6 5 4 3 2 1

Copyright Acknowledgments

Contents

Rooted as they are in the facts of contemporary life, the phantasies of even a second-rate writer of modern Science Fiction are incomparably richer, bolder, and stranger than the Utopian or Millennial imaginings of the past.

—ALDOUS HUXLEY

Science fiction is no more written for scientists than ghost stories are written for ghosts. Most frequently, the scientific dressing clothes fantasy. As fantasies are as meaningful as science, the phantasms of technology now fittingly embody our hopes and anxieties.

—BRIAN W. ALDISS

Introduction

David G. Hartwell

Science fiction is the characteristic literary genre of the century. It is the genre that stands in opposition to literary Modernism. It is the paraliterary shadow of Modernism.

The twentieth century is the science fiction century. By the middle of the 1990s, we are living in the world of the future described by genre science fiction of the 1930s and '40s and '50s, a world of technologies we love and fear, sciences so increasingly complex and steeped in specialized diction and jargon that fewer and fewer of us understand science on what used to be called a "high school level." These are the days, as Paul Simon sings, of miracles and wonders.

Science fiction is a literature for people who value knowledge and who desire to understand how things work in the world and in the universe. In science fiction, knowledge is power and power is technology and technology is good and useful in improving the human condition. It is, by extension, a literature of empowerment. The lesson of the genre megatext, that body of genre literature that in aggregate embodies the standard plots, tropes, images, specialized diction, and clichés, is that one can solve problems through the application of knowledge of science and technology. By further extension, the SF megatext is an allegory of faith in science. Everyone knows there are SF addicts—I am one— and this is why: it expresses, represents, and confirms faith in science and reason.

Life is never so neat that abstract patterns, such as centuries, are more than arbitrary dividers. In the case of science fiction, this century really began about 1895, with the first stories of H. G. Wells, the greatest writer in a vigorous literary tradition now superseded, called the Scientific Romance. Wells had many contemporaries writing Scientific Romances, such as George Griffith and M. P. Shiel; predecessors include Jules Verne and Sir Edward Bulwer-Lytton. But the tradition did end in Wells's lifetime, although Brian Stableford, in *Scientific Romance in Britain, 1890–1950* (1985), revives the term, which fell out of usage by World War II, to emphasize the differences between the evolution of American and British science fiction. Olaf Stapledon, S. Fowler Wright, Aldous Huxley, and George Orwell, for instance, might properly be considered as having written late examples of Scientific Romance.

But Wells, especially in his works between 1895 and 1911, was the primary model for a variety of other writers, in many languages, to explore the explosion of ideas and technologies that the advent of the new century promised. Not the only model, I hasten to add. I have included a fine story by J. H. Rosny *aîné*, from the French, in this anthology and examples from Rudyard Kipling and Jack London. And as the genre of science fiction began to coalesce in the teens and twenties of the new century, it became evident that a number of earlier writers, first of all Jules Verne but also many others from Mary Shelley and Edgar Allan Poe to Fitz-James O'Brien and Sir Edward Bulwer-Lytton might provide variant models for science fiction. Wells, however, was that spark that ignited the genre.

But the fires of science fiction did not blaze in the United States until April 1926, when editor and publisher Hugo Gernsback launched *Amazing Stories*, the first magazine devoted to the new genre and which provided, as it were, a fireplace. To give examples of the new literature he proposed to support and publish, Gernback filled parts of his issues with "classic reprints" of Wells and many of the others named above. And in his oft-quoted first editorial, in which he defined *scientifiction* (the term *science fiction* was not coined until 1929), he said it was in the manner of Poe, Verne, and Wells: "charming romance intermingled with scientific fact and prophetic vision."

In addition to this relative confusion, Gernsback, an eccentric immigrant and technological visionary, was tone-deaf to the English language, printing barely literate stories, often by enthusiastic teenagers, about new inventions and the promise of a wondrous technological future cheek by jowl with fiction by Wells, Poe, Edgar Rice Burroughs, and a growing number of professional pulp writers who simply wanted to break into the new market. Gernsback was the man who first saw science fiction as the ordinary pleasure reading of the new technological world. But his standards were not the standards of a literary man, of a modernist. They were the standards of a publisher of popular entertainment in pulp magazines, low-class, low-paying, low-priced popular entertainment serving the mass market.

So genre science fiction became, was founded to be, antimodernist. It rapidly developed a loyal readership, literary conventions, and a body of specialized writers who, converted by the evangelical pitch of Gernsback and the other early editors—chief among them John W. Campbell, Jr., who took over the helm of *Astounding* in the late 1930s and set higher stylistic standards for the genre (his was for decades the highest-paying market)—set about improving themselves.

Of all the pulp magazine genres, science fiction was the most socially unacceptable for decades, so it attracted the alienated of all stripes, some of them extremely talented writers. By the early 1940s the SF field had come into being. And it decided to rule the world. "Science fiction is the central literature of our time. It is not part of the mainstream. It is the mainstream," says Ray Bradbury, and such grandiose claims are part of the essence of the SF field. Bradbury was a teenager who published a fanzine in the late 1930s and became a writer in the 1940s under the tutelage of such established SF professionals as Leigh Brackett (who coauthored the script for *The Big Sleep* with William Faulkner, and later wrote the screenplay for *The Empire Strikes Back*). Science fiction did not aspire to take over literature, but reality.

The field (an aggregation of people) as opposed to the genre (a body of texts) was originally a closely knit international group of passionate readers and writers of science fiction in the 1930s and 1940s, people who knew each other for the most part only through correspondence and rarely met. They published fanzines and sent them to one another. They developed and evolved their own practical literary criticism and their own literary standards. Most of them were teenagers at the start—including the writers. Practically speaking, none of them had the benefit of a literary or humanist education. They read a lot. Some of them had technical training, some a scientific education—like Wells. But they were organized, and when the economy and publishing opportunities expanded after World War II, the SF field was ready to expand.

In its own view, science fiction had already grown up, in Campbell's *Astounding*: the 1940s were the Golden Age of SF. But by any sensible calculation, the SF field really began to grow up after the war and blossom with the first publications of genre science fiction in hardcover books; the founding of major new magazines, such as *Galaxy* and *Fantasy & Science Fiction* in 1949; and the growth of the mass market paperback publishing industry in the early 1950s, which discovered science fiction right away. Most of the stories in this book are post-WWII mainly because that was the time at which the idea of revision took hold in the SF writing community, with a concomitant improvement in the fiction; it was a time when the money improved, although not enough for any but five or six of the highest paid writers to make a living without "a day job"; and most of all it was a time of optimism in the West after the terrible war.

The international SF field grew with the sudden influx of American science fiction, and a dialogue began among literatures that grows and continues today. In Russia in the 1940s, one of the key texts is a story written in response to a Murray Leinster story in *Astounding*. In France, Boris Vian translated A. E. van Vogt's uneven English (*The World of Null-A*) into literate French and launched van Vogt as the most important SF writer of the period in France. American science fiction, in translation or in the original, dominated the discourse world-wide. It still does; even though there have been major writers in other languages who have made major contributions. American science fiction is still the dominant partner in all the dialogues. I have attempted, in this anthology, to provide some translations that give evidence of the growth of other traditions, but the overwhelming evidence is that American science fiction and the American marketplace drive the SF world.

It is a source of both amusement and frustration to SF people, writers and readers, that public consciousness of science fiction has almost never penetrated beyond the first decade of the field's development. Sure, *Star Wars* is wonderful, but in precisely the same way and at the same level of consciousness and sophistication that science fiction from the late twenties and early thirties was: fast, almost plotless stories of zipping through the ether in spaceships, meeting aliens, using futuristic devices, and fighting the bad guys (and winning). SF people generally call this sci-fi (affectionately, "skiffy"), to distinguish it from the real, grown-up pure quill.

Science fiction is read throughout the English language–reading world, and in many other languages for pleasure and entertainment. But it is not read with much comprehension or pleasure by the dominant literary culture, the writers and academics who, on the whole, define literary fashions and instruct us in the values and virtues of fashionable literatures. This is understandable given the literary history of the genre, which has now outlasted all the other counterculture or outsider literary movements of the century. Science fiction is read with ease and comprehension by the teenage children of educated adults who can derive little or no pleasure from it. I have written an entire book, *Age of Wonders* (1984, 1996), devoted to elucidating the nature of the field and the problems of understanding it, and the literature associated with it, for outsiders, but one particular point needs to be repeated each time the subject arises. Science fiction is read properly, as an experienced reader can, only if the givens of the story are granted as literal, so that if the story is set on Mars in the future, that is the literal time and place. It might secondarily be interpretable as "only" a metaphor for the human condition, or for some abnormal psychological state of the character or characters, but with rare exceptions in science fiction, the literal truth of the time and place and ideas is a necessary preconditon to making sense of the story. This is because only through this literality (the real world is pared away and reduced to an imaginable invented world, in which we can focus on things happening that could not happen in the mainstream world of everyday reality) can the emotional significance of totally imaginary times and places and events be felt.

Kingsley Amis, in *New Maps of Hell* (1960), quotes his friend Edmund Crispin as saying, "Where an ordinary novel or short story resembles portraiture or at widest the domestic interior, science fiction offers the less cosy satisfaction of a landscape with figures; to ask that these distant manikins be shown in as much detail as the subject of a portrait is evidently to ask the impossible"; he then goes on himself to say: "This is perhaps partisan in tone, but it does indicate a scale of priorities which operates throughout the medium and which, of course, is open to objection, though this is not often based on much more than an expectation that science fiction should treat the future as fiction of the main stream treats the present, an expectation bound to be defeated" (p. 128).

Tom Shippey, in his introduction to *The Oxford Book of Science Fiction Stories*, comments, "What, then, has science fiction had to offer its human readers? Whatever it is, it has been enough for the genre to make its way into a prominent, if not dominant place in popular literary culture despite every kind of literary misunderstanding or discouragement. A very basic answer must be, Truth. Not every science fiction story, of course, can 'come true,' indeed . . . probably none of them do, can, or ever will. Just the same, many of them (perhaps all of them, in some way or another) may be trying to solve a question for which many people this century have had no acceptable answer."

In the end this anthology is a collection of attempts to get at the truth of the human condition in this century, so contoured and conditioned by science and technology. Overall, perhaps, you can see the big picture, surely a bigger picture than any other. One might even get some intimations of the scope of the future—which of course leads us always back to the ground of the present. And perhaps we return illuminated.

—PLEASANTVILLE, N.Y.
1996

James Tiptree, Jr.

James Tiptree, Jr. was the pseudonym of Alice B. Sheldon (1915–87), an ex-employee of the CIA who became a psychologist and then, secretly, an SF writer. Unlike the pseudonymous Cordwainer Smith, a writer who remained silent and mysterious, Tiptree was vociferous, opinionated, passionate, and involved in the SF field. Thus it was a substantial shock to the social system of science fiction in the late 1970s when the Tiptree pseudonym was penetrated, when in the midst of a rising tide of feminist consciousness he was discovered to be a feminist she.

Tiptree made her essential impact with a continuing stream of powerful short stories. Many of her best stories appeared in her first four collections (*Ten Thousand Light Years from Home* [1973], *Warm Worlds and Otherwise* [1975], *Star Songs of an Old Primate* [1978], and *Out of the Everywhere and Other Extraordinary Visions* [1981]). Her two novels, *Up the Walls of the World* (1978) and *Brightness Falls from the Air* (1985), are underappreciated. Perhaps the shock of her suicide in 1987 has made it difficult for many readers to gain perspective on her later, darker stories.

The closest parallel to her work in impact, in attitude, in attention to craft and art, is Theodore Sturgeon's writing of the 1950s. Also like him, when she erred it was in the direction of too much sentiment. She was obsessed with the theme and the imagery of the alien biologically and emotionally. Yet at least one of her stories, "The Girl Who Was Plugged In" (1973, one of her several award-winners), is acknowledged by William Gibson as one of the sources of cyberpunk.

Tiptree continually challenged the idea of the coldness of the universe, portraying that coldness as a negative aspect of human character rather than an affect existing somehow in external reality—until her last stories. *Crown of Stars* (1988) gathers most of her final tales, suicide-filled and full of the idea of honorable death. She was a deeply moral writer, even when embracing death.

In the 1990s, friends and especially a younger generation of woman SF writers have created an award in her memory, the annual James Tiptree, Jr., Award "for gender-bending science fiction." A collection of her nonfiction pieces and a biography have been announced as forthcoming. This story, one of Tiptree's earliest, refers to the influence of a certain television show popular among the young in the 1960s, *Star Trek* (though the name is never mentioned in the text). Joanna Russ, the feminist critic and a correspondent of Tiptree's, sometimes tells this story aloud, and then weeps.

BEAM US HOME

Hobie's parents might have seen the first signs if they had been watching about eight-thirty on Friday nights. But Hobie was the youngest of five active bright-normal kids. Who was to notice one more uproar around the TV?

A couple of years later, Hobie's Friday-night battles shifted to 10 P.M. and then his sisters got their own set. Hobie was growing fast then. In public he featured chiefly as a tanned streak on the tennis courts and a ninety-ninth percentile series of math grades. To his parents, Hobie featured as the one without problems. This was hard to avoid in a family that included a diabetic, a girl with an IQ of 185 and another with controllable petit mal, and a would-be ski star who spent most of his time in a cast. Hobie's own IQ was in the fortunate 140s, the range where you're superior enough to lead, but not too superior to be followed. He seemed perfectly satisfied with his communications with his parents, but he didn't use them much.

Not that he was in any way neglected when the need arose. The time he got staph in a corneal scratch, for instance, his parents did a great job of supporting him through the pain bit and the hospital bit and so on. But they couldn't know all the little incidents. Like the night when Hobie called so fiercely for Dr. McCoy that a young intern named McCoy went in and joked for half an hour with the feverish boy in his dark room.

To the end, his parents probably never understood that there was anything to understand about Hobie. And what was to see? His tennis and his model rocket collection made him look almost too normal for the small honors school he went to first.

Then his family moved to an executive bedroom suburb where the school system had a bigger budget than Monaco and a soccer team loaded with National Merit Science finalists. Here Hobie blended right in with the scenery. One more healthy, friendly, polite kid with bright gray eyes under a blond bowl-cut and very fast with any sort of ball game.

The brightest eyes around him were reading *The Double Helix* to find out how to make it in research, or marking up the Dun & Bradstreet flyers. If Hobie stood out at all, it was only that he didn't seem to be worried about making it in research or any other way, particularly. But that fitted in, too. Those days a lot of boys were standing around looking as if they couldn't believe what went on, as if they were waiting for—who knows?—a better world, their glands, something. Hobie's faintly aghast expression was not unique. Events like the installation of an armed patrol around the school enclave were bound to have a disturbing effect on the more sensitive kids.

People got the idea that Hobie *was* sensitive in some indefinite way. His usual manner was open but quiet, tolerant of a put-on that didn't end.

His adviser did fret over his failure to settle on a major field in time for the oncoming threat of college. First his math interest seemed to evaporate after the special calculus course, although he never blew an exam. Then he switched to the precollege anthropology panel the school was trying. Here he made good grades and acted very motivated, until the semester when the visiting research team began pounding on sampling techniques and statistical significance. Hobie had no trouble with things like Chi square, of course. But after making his A in the final he gave them his sweet, unbelieving smile and faded. His adviser found him spending a lot of hours polishing a six-inch telescope lens in the school shop.

So Hobie was tagged as some kind of an underachiever, but nobody knew what kind because of those grades. And something about that smile bothered them; it seemed to stop sound.

The girls liked him, though, and he went through the usual phases rather fast. There was the week he and various birds went to thirty-five drive-in movies. And the month he went around humming "Mrs. Robinson" in a meaningful way. And the warm, comfortable summer when he and his then-girl and two other couples went up to Stratford, Ontario, with sleeping bags to see the Czech multimedia thing.

Girls regarded him as different, although he never knew why. "You look at me like it's always good-bye," one of them told him. Actually, he treated girls with an odd detached gentleness, as though he knew a secret that might make them all disappear. Some of them hung around because of his quick brown hands or his really great looks, some because they hoped to share the secret. In this they were disappointed. Hobie talked and he listened carefully, but it wasn't the mutual talk-talk-talk of total catharsis that most couples went through. But how could Hobie know that?

Like most of his peer group, Hobie stayed away from heavies and agreed that pot was preferable to getting juiced. His friends never crowded him too much after the beach party where he spooked everybody by talking excitedly for hours to people who weren't there. They decided he might have a vulnerable ego-structure.

The official high school view was that Hobie had no real problems. In this they were supported by a test battery profile that could have qualified him as the ideal normal control. Certainly there was nothing to get hold of in his routine interviews with the high school psychologist.

Hobie came in after lunch, a time when Dr. Morehouse knew he was not at his most intuitive. They went through the usual openers, Hobie sitting easily, patient and interested, with an air of listening to some sound back of the acoustical ceiling tiles.

"I meet a number of young people involved in discovering who they really are. Searching for their own identities," Morehouse offered. He was idly trueing up a stack of typing headed *Sex Differences in the Adolescent Identity Crisis*.

"Do you?" Hobie asked politely.

Morehouse frowned at himself and belched disarmingly.

"Sometimes I wonder who *I* am," he smiled.

"Do you?" inquired Hobie.

"Don't you?"

"No," said Hobie.

Morehouse reached for the hostility that should have been there, found it wasn't. Not passive aggression. What? His intuition awoke briefly. He looked into Hobie's light hazel eyes and suddenly found himself slipping toward some very large uninhabited dimension. A real pubescent preschiz, he wondered hopefully? No again, he decided, and found himself thinking, What if a person is sure of his identity but it isn't his identity? He often wondered that; perhaps it could be worked up into a creative insight.

"Maybe it's the other way around," Hobie was saying before the pause grew awkward.

"How do you mean?"

"Well, maybe you're all wondering who you are," Hobie's lips quirked; it was clear he was just making conversation.

"I asked for that," Morehouse chuckled. They chatted about sibling rivalry and psychological statistics and wound up in plenty of time for Morehouse's next boy, who turned out to be a satisfying High Anx. Morehouse forgot about the empty place he had slid into. He often did that too.

It was a girl who got part of it out of Hobie, at three in the morning. "Dog" she was called then, although her name was Jane. A tender, bouncy little bird who cocked her head to listen up at him in a way Hobie liked. Dog would listen with the same soft intensity to the supermarket clerk and the pediatrician later on, but neither of them knew that.

They had been talking about the state of the world, which was then quite prosperous and peaceful. That is to say, about seventy million people were starving to death, a number of advanced nations were maintaining themselves on police terror tactics, four or five borders were being fought over, Hobie's family's maid had just been cut up by the suburban peacekeeper squad, and the school had added a charged wire and two dogs to its patrol. But none of the big nations were waving fissionables, and the U.S.-Sino-Soviet détente was a twenty-year reality.

Dog was holding Hobie's head over the side of her car because he had been the one who found the maid crawling on her handbones among the azaleas.

"If you feel like that, why don't you do something?" Dog asked him between spasms. "Do you want some Slurp? It's all we've got."

"Do what?" Hobie quavered.

"Politics?" guessed Dog. She really didn't know. The Protest Decade was long over, along with the New Politics and Ralph Nader. There was a school legend about a senior who had come back from Miami with a busted collarbone. Sometime after that the kids had discovered that flowers weren't really very powerful, and that movement organizers had their own bag. Why go on the street when you could really do more in one of the good jobs available Inside? So Dog could offer only a vague image of Hobie running for something, a sincere face on TV.

"You could join the Young Statesmen."

"Not to interfere," gasped Hobie. He wiped his mouth. Then he pulled himself together and tried some of the Slurp. In the dashlight his seventeen-year-old sideburns struck Dog as tremendously mature and beautiful.

"Oh, it's not so bad," said Hobie. "I mean, it's not *unusually* bad. It's just a stage. This world is going through a primitive stage. There's a lot of stages. It takes a long time. They're just very very backward, that's all."

"They," said Dog, listening to every word.

"I mean," he said.

"You're alienated," she told him. "Rinse your mouth out with that. You don't relate to people."

"I think you're people," he said, rinsing. He'd heard this before. "I relate to you," he said. He leaned out to spit. Then he twisted his head to look up at the sky and stayed that way a while, like an animal's head sticking out of a crate. Dog could feel him trembling the car.

"Are you going to barf again?" she asked.

"No."

But then suddenly he did, roaringly. She clutched at his shoulders while he heaved. After a while he sagged down, his head lolling limply out at one arm.

"It's such a mess," she heard him whispering. "It's such a s——ting miserable mess mess mess MESS MESS—"

He was pounding his hand on the car side.

"I'll hose it," said Dog, but then she saw he didn't mean the car.

"Why does it have to go on and on?" he croaked. "Why don't they just *stop* it? I can't bear it much longer, please, please, I can't—"

Dog was scared now.

"Honey, it's not that bad. Hobie honey, it's not that bad," she told him, patting at him, pressing her soft front against his back.

Suddenly he came back into the car on top of her, spent.

"It's unbearable," he muttered.

"What's unbearable?" she snapped, mad at him for scaring her. "What's unbearable for you and not for me? I mean, I know it's a mess, but why is it so bad for *you?* I have to live here too."

"It's your world," he told her absently, lost in some private desolation.

Dog yawned.

"I better drive you home now," she said.

He had nothing more to say and sat quietly. When Dog glanced at his profile, she decided he looked calm. Almost stupid, in fact; his mouth hung open a little. She didn't recognize the expression, because she had never seen people looking out of cattle cars.

Hobie's class graduated that June. His grades were well up, and everybody understood that he was acting a little unrelated because of the traumatic business with the maid. He got a lot of sympathy.

It was after the graduation exercises that Hobie surprised his parents for the first and last time. They had been congratulating themselves on having steered their fifth offspring safely through the college crisis and into a high-status Eastern. Hobie announced that he had applied for the United States Air Force Academy.

This was a bomb, because Hobie had never shown the slightest interest in things military. Just the opposite, really. Hobie's parents took it for granted that the educated classes viewed the military with tolerant distaste. Why did their son want this? Was it another of his unstable motivational orientations?

But Hobie persisted. He didn't have any reasons, he had just thought carefully and felt that this was for him. Finally they recalled that early model rocket collection; his father decided he was serious, and began sorting out the generals his research firm did business with. In September Hobie disappeared into Colorado Springs. He reappeared for Christmas in the form of an exotically hairless, erect and polite stranger in uniform.

During the next four years, Hobie the person became effectively invisible behind a growing pile of excellent evaluation reports. There seemed to be no doubt that he was working very hard, and his motivation gave no sign of flagging. Like any cadet, he bitched about many of the Academy's little ways and told some funny stories. But he never seemed discouraged. When he elected to spend his summers in special aviation skills training, his parents realized that Hobie had found himself.

Enlightenment—of a sort—came in his senior year when he told them he had applied for and been accepted into the new astronaut training program. The

U.S. space program was just then starting up again after the revulsion caused by the tragic loss of the manned satellite lab ten years before.

"I bet that's what he had in mind all along," Hobie's father chuckled. "He didn't want to say so before he made it." They were all relieved. A son in the space program was a lot easier to live with, statuswise.

When she heard the news, Dog, who was now married and called herself Jane, sent him a card with a picture of the Man in the Moon. Another girl, more percipient, sent him a card showing some stars.

But Hobie never made it to the space program.

It was the summer when several not-very-serious events happened all together. The British devalued their wobbly pound again, just when it was found that far too many dollars were going out of the States. North and South Korea moved a step closer to reunion, which generated a call for strengthening the U.S. contribution to the remains of SEATO. Next there was an expensive, though luckily nonlethal, fire at Kennedy, and the Egyptians announced a new Soviet aid pact. And in August it was discovered that the Guévarrista rebels in Venezuela were getting some very unpleasant-looking hardware from their Arab allies.

Contrary to the old saying that nations never learn from history, the U.S. showed that it had learned from its long agony in Vietnam. What it had learned was not to waste time messing around with popular elections and military advisory and training programs, but to ball right in. Hard.

When the dust cleared, the space program and astronaut training were dead on the pad and a third of Hobie's graduating class was staging through Caracas. Technically, he had volunteered.

He found this out from the task force medico.

"Look at it this way, lieutenant. By entering the Academy, you volunteered for the Air Force, right?"

"Yes. But I opted for the astronaut program. The Air Force is the only way you can get in. And I've been accepted."

"But the astronaut program has been suspended. Temporarily, of course. Meanwhile the Air Force—for which you volunteered—has an active requirement for your training. You can't expect them just to let you sit around until the program resumes, can you? Moreover you have been given the very best option available. Good God, man, the Volunteer Airpeace Corps is considered a superelite. You should see the fugal depressions we have to cope with among men who have been rejected for the VAC."

"Mercenaries," said Hobie. "Regressive."

"Try 'professional,' it's a better word. Now—about those headaches."

The headaches eased up some when Hobie was assigned to long-range sensor recon support. He enjoyed the work of flying, and the long, calm, lonely sensor missions were soothing. They were also quite safe. The Guévarristas had no air strength to waste on recon planes and the U.A.R. SAM sites were not yet operational. Hobie flew the pattern, and waited zombielike for the weather, and flew again. Mostly he waited, because the fighting was developing in a steamy jungle province where clear sensing was a sometimes thing. It was poorly mapped. The ground troops could never be sure about the little brown square men who gave them so much trouble; on one side of an unknown line they were Guévarristas who should be obliterated, and on the other side they were legitimate national troops warning the blancos away. Hobie's recon tapes were urgently needed, and for several weeks he was left alone.

Then he began to get pulled up to a forward strip for one-day chopper duty when their tactical duty roster was disrupted by gee-gee. But this was relatively peaceful too, being mostly defoliant spray missions. Hobie, in fact, put in several months without seeing, hearing, smelling, or feeling the war at all. He would have been grateful for this if he had realized it. As it was he seemed to be trying not to realize anything much. He spoke very little, did his work, and moved like a man whose head might fall off if he jostled anything.

Naturally he was one of the last to hear the rumors about gee-gee when they filtered back to the coastal base, where Hobie was quartered with the long-range stuff. Gee-gee's proper name was Guairas Grippe. It was developing into a severe problem in the combat zone. More and more replacements and relief crews were being called forward for temporary tactical duty. On Hobie's next trip in, he couldn't help but notice that people were acting pretty haggard, and the roster was all scrawled up with changes. When they were on course, he asked about it.

"Are you kidding?" his gunner grunted.

"No. What is it?"

"B.W."

"What?"

"Bacteriological weapon, skyhead. They keep promising us vaccines. Stuck in their zippers—look out, there's a ground burst."

They held Hobie up front for another mission, and another after that, and then they told him that a sector quarantine was now in force.

The official notice said that movement of personnel between sectors would be reduced to a minimum as a temporary measure to control the spread of respiratory ailments. Translation: you could go from the support zone to the front, but you couldn't go back.

Hobie was moved into a crowded billet and assigned to Casualty and Supply. Shortly he discovered that there was a translation for respiratory ailments too. Gee-gee turned out to be a multiform misery of groin rash, sore throat, fever, and unending trots. It didn't seem to become really acute; it just cycled along. Hobie was one of those who were only lightly affected, which was lucky because the hospital beds were full. So were the hospital aisles. Evacuation of all casualties had been temporarily suspended until a controlled corridor could be arranged.

The Gués did not, it seemed, get gee-gee. The ground troops were definitely sure of that. Nobody knew how it was spread. Rumor said it was bats one week, and then the next week they were putting stuff in the water. Poisoned arrows, roaches, women, disintegrating canisters, all had their advocates. However it was done, it was clear that the U.A.R. technological aid had included more than hardware. The official notice about a forthcoming vaccine yellowed on the board.

Ground fighting was veering closer to Hobie's strip. He heard mortars now and then, and one night the Gués ran in a rocket launcher and nearly got the fuel dump before they were chased back.

"All they got to do is wait," said the gunner. "We're dead."

"Geegee doesn't kill you," said C/S control. "You just wish it did."

"They say."

The strip was extended, and three attack bombers came in. Hobie looked them over. He had trained on AX92's all one summer; he could fly them in his sleep. It would be nice to be alone.

He was pushing the C/S chopper most of the daylight hours now. He had gotten used to being shot at and to being sick. Everybody was sick, except a couple of replacement crews who were sent in two weeks apart, looking startlingly healthy. They said they had been immunized with a new antitoxin. Their big news was that gee-gee could be cured outside the zone.

"We're getting reinfected," the gunner said. "That figures. They want us out of here."

That week there was a big drive on bats, but it didn't help. The next week the first batch of replacements were running fevers. Their shots hadn't worked and neither did the stuff they gave the second batch.

After that, no more men came in except a couple of volunteer medicos. The billets and the planes and the mess were beginning to stink. That dysentery couldn't be controlled after you got weak.

What they did get was supplies. Every day or so another ton of stuff would drift down. Most of it was dragged to one side and left to rot. They were swimming in food. The staggering cooks pushed steak and lobster at men who shivered and went out to retch. The hospital even had ample space now, because it turned out that gee-gee really did kill you in the end. By that time, you were glad to go. A cemetery developed at the far side of the strip, among the skeletons of the defoliated trees.

On the last morning Hobie was sent out to pick up a forward scout team. He was one of the few left with enough stamina for long missions. The three-man team was far into Gué territory, but Hobie didn't care. All he was thinking about was his bowels. So far he had not fouled himself or his plane. When he was down by their signal, he bolted out to squat under the chopper's tail. The grunts climbed in, yelling at him.

They had a prisoner with them. The Gué was naked and astonishingly broad. He walked springily; his arms were lashed with wire and a shirt was tied over his head. This was the first Gué Hobie had been close to. As he got in he saw how the Gué's firm brown flesh glistened and bulged around the wire. He wished he could see his face. The gunner said the Gué was a Sirionó, and this was important because the Sirionós were not known to be with the Gués. They were a very primitive nomadic tribe.

When Hobie began to fly home, he realized he was getting sicker. It became a fight to hold onto consciousness and keep on course. Luckily nobody shot at them. At one point he became aware of a lot of screaming going on behind him, but couldn't pay attention. Finally he came over the strip and horsed the chopper down. He let his head down on his arms.

"You okay?" asked the gunner.

"Yeah," said Hobie, hearing them getting out. They were moving something heavy. Finally he got up and followed them. The floor was wet. That wasn't unusual. He got down and stood staring in, the floor a foot under his nose. The wet stuff was blood. It was sprayed around, with one big puddle. In the puddle was something soft and fleshy-looking.

Hobie turned his head. The ladder was wet. He held up one hand and looked at the red. His other hand too. Holding them out stiffly, he turned and began to walk away across the strip.

Control, who still hoped to get an evening flight out of him, saw him fall and called the hospital. The two replacement parameds were still in pretty good shape. They came out and picked him up.

When Hobie came to, one of the parameds was tying his hands down to the bed so he couldn't tear the IV out again.

"We're going to die here," Hobie told him.

The paramed looked noncommittal. He was a thin dark boy with a big Adam's apple.

" 'But I shall dine at journey's end with Landor and with Donne,' " said Hobie. His voice was light and facile.

"Yeats," said the paramed. "Want some water?"

Hobie's eyes flickered. The paramed gave him some water.

"I really believed it, you know," Hobie said chattily. "I had it all figured out." He smiled, something he hadn't done for a long time.

"Landor and Donne?" asked the medic. He unhooked the empty IV bottle and hung up a new one.

"Oh, it was pathetic, I guess," Hobie said. "It started out . . . I believed they were real, you know? Kirk, Spock, McCoy, all of them. And the ship. To this day, I swear . . . one of them talked to me once; I mean, he really did . . . I had it all figured out; they had me left behind as an observer." Hobie giggled.

"They were coming back for me. It was secret. All I had to do was sort of fit in and observe. Like a report. One day they would come back and haul me up in that beam thing; maybe you know about that? And there I'd be back in real time where human beings were, where they were human. I wasn't really stuck here in the past. On a backward planet."

The paramed nodded.

"Oh, I mean, I didn't really *believe* it; I knew it was just a show. But I did believe it, too. It was like *there*, in the background, underneath, no matter what was going on. They were coming for me. All I had to do was observe. And not to interfere. You know? Prime directive . . . Of course after I grew up, I realized they weren't; I mean, I realized consciously. So I was going to go to them. Somehow, somewhere. Out there . . . Now I know. It really isn't so. None of it. Never. There's nothing . . . Now I know I'll die here."

"Oh now," said the paramed. He got up and started to take things away. His fingers were shaky.

"It's clean there," said Hobie in a petulant voice. "None of this shit. Clean and friendly. They don't torture people," he explained, thrashing his head. "They don't kill—" He slept. The paramed went away.

Somebody started to yell monotonously.

Hobie opened his eyes. He was burning up.

The yelling went on, became screaming. It was dusk. Footsteps went by, headed for the screaming. Hobie saw they had put him in a bed by the door.

Without his doing much about it, the screaming seemed to be lifting him out of the bed, propelling him through the door. Air. He kept getting close-ups of his hands clutching things. Bushes, shadows. Something scratched him.

After a while the screaming was a long way behind him. Maybe it was only in his ears. He shook his head, felt himself go down onto boards. He thought he was in the cemetery.

"No," he said. "Please. Please no." He got himself up, balanced, blundered on, seeking coolness.

The side of the plane felt cool. He plastered his hot body against it, patting it affectionately. It seemed to be quite dark now. Why was he inside with no lights? He tried the panel, the lights worked perfectly. Vaguely he noticed some yelling starting outside again. It ignited the screaming in his head. The screaming got very loud—loud—LOUD—and appeared to be moving him, which was good.

He came to above the overcast and climbing. The oxy-support tube was hitting him in the nose. He grabbed for the mask, but it wasn't there. Automatically, he had leveled off. Now he rolled and looked around.

Below him was a great lilac sea of cloud, with two mountains sticking through it, their western tips on fire. As he looked, they dimmed. He shivered, found he was wearing only sodden shorts. How had he got here? Somebody had screamed intolerably and he had run.

He flew along calmly, checking his board. No trouble except the fuel. Nobody serviced the AX92's any more. Without thinking about it, he began to climb again. His hands were a yard away and he was shivering but he felt clear. He reached up and found his headphones were in place; he must have put them on along with the rest of the drill. He clicked on. Voices rattled and roared at him. He switched off. Then he took off the headpiece and dropped it on the floor.

He looked around: 18,000, heading 88-05. He was over the Atlantic. In front of him the sky was darkening fast. A pinpoint glimmer ten o'clock high. Sirius, probably.

He thought about Sirius, trying to recall his charts. Then he thought about turning and going back down. Without paying much attention, he noticed he was crying with his mouth open.

Carefully he began feeding his torches and swinging the nose of his pod around and up. He brought it neatly to a point on Sirius. Up. Up. Behind him a great pale swing of contrail fell away above the lilac shadow, growing, towering to the tiny plane that climbed at its tip. Up. Up. The contrail cut off as the plane burst into the high cold dry.

As it did so, Hobie's ears skewered and he screamed wildly. The pain quit; his drums had burst. Up! Now he was gasping for air, strangling. The great torches drove him up, up, over the curve of the world. He was hanging on the star. Up! The fuel gauges were knocking. Any second they would quit and he and the bird would be a falling stone. "Beam us up, Scotty!" he howled at Sirius, laughing, coughing—coughing to death, as the torches faltered—

—And was still coughing as he sprawled on the shining resiliency under the arcing grids. He gagged, rolled, finally focused on a personage leaning toward him out of a complex chair. The personage had round eyes, a slitted nose, and the start of a quizzical smile.

Hobie's head swiveled slowly. It was not the bridge of the *Enterprise*. There were no viewscreens, only a View. And Lieutenant Uhura would have had trouble with the freeform flashing objects suspended in front of what appeared to be a girl wearing spots. The spots, Hobie made out, were fur.

Somebody who was not Bones McCoy was doing something to Hobie's stomach. Hobie got up a hand and touched the man's gleaming back. Under the mesh it was firm and warm. The man looked up, grinned; Hobie looked back at the captain.

"Do not have fear," a voice was saying. It seemed to be coming out of a globe by the captain's console. "We will tell you where you are."

"I know where I am," Hobie whispered. He drew a deep, sobbing breath.

"I'm HOME!" he yelled. Then he passed out.

C. S. Lewis

C. S. Lewis (1898–1963) is important both as a writer and as a critic of science fiction. He is indeed one of the significant literary men of the century, whose scholarship and criticism of medieval and Renaissance literature were unsurpassed. Such critical works as *The Allegory of Love* (1936) and his volume in the *Oxford History of English Literature* are rich and illuminating. Lewis's Christian fantasy fiction, including *The Screwtape Letters* (1942) and most especially his Narnia series of fantasy tales for children, is enormously influential. Nearly fifty books on Lewis and his works have been published, and a film has been made on his life.

He was a member, with Charles Williams, J. R. R. Tolkein, and Dorothy Sayers, of a casual literary society in Oxford called The Inklings, at whose meetings they read each other's works in progress. His science fiction novels, also Christian allegories, *Out of the Silent Planet* (1938), *Perelandra* (1943) and *That Hideous Strength* (1945), overshadow the few SF short stories he published in the 1950s and '60s. They were only collected after his death (*Of Other Worlds*, 1966), along with his critical pieces examining and providing an eloquent defense of genre science fiction—which are generally overshadowed by his more famous critical work in other areas. Those, together with his learned and sensible *An Experiment in Criticism,* which includes perhaps the single best argument ever constructed on the appeal of science fiction, did not appear until the 1960s and have not, in the main, been given much notice. Perhaps the SF and fantasy novels and stories of R. A. Lafferty from the 1960s to the 1980s are the body of work after Lewis most centrally in that Christian tradition.

This story originally appeared in *Fantasy and Science Fiction.* It shows how the ordinary tropes of genre SF can be applied with wit and humor to spiritual concerns. It is also uproariously politically incorrect.

MINISTERING ANGELS

The Monk, as they called him, settled himself on the camp-chair beside his bunk and stared through the window at the harsh sand and black-blue sky of Mars. He did not mean to begin his "work" for ten minutes yet. Not, of course, the work he had been brought there to do. He was the meteorologist of the party, and his work in that capacity was largely done; he had found out whatever could be found out. There was nothing more, within the limited radius he could investigate, to be observed for at least twenty-five days. And meteorology had not been his real motive. He had chosen three years on Mars as the nearest modern equivalent to a hermitage in the desert. He had come there to meditate: to continue the slow, perpetual rebuilding of that inner structure which, in his view, it was the main purpose of life to rebuild. And now his ten minutes' rest was over. He began with his well-used formula. "Gentle and patient Master, teach me to need men less and to love thee more." Then to it. There was no time to waste. There were barely six months of this lifeless, sinless, unsuffering wilderness ahead of him. Three years were short—but when the shout came he rose out of his chair with the practised alertness of a sailor.

The Botanist in the next cabin responded to the same shout with a curse. His eye had been at the microscope when it came. It was maddening. Constant interruption. A man might as well try to work in the middle of Piccadilly as in this infernal camp. And his work was already a race against time. Six months more—and he had hardly begun. The flora of Mars, these tiny, miraculously hardy organisms, the ingenuity of their contrivances to live under all but impossible conditions—it was a feast for a lifetime. He would ignore the shout. But then came the bell. All hands to the main room.

The only person who was doing, so to speak, nothing when the shout came was the Captain. To be more exact, he was (as usual) trying to stop thinking about Clare, and get on with his official journal. Clare kept on interrupting from forty million miles away. It was preposterous. *"Would have needed all hands,"* he wrote. Hands . . . his own hands . . . his own hands, hands, he felt, with eyes in them, travelling over all the warm-cool, soft-firm, smooth, yielding, resisting aliveness of her. "Shut up, there's a dear," he said to the photo on his desk. And so back to the journal, until the fatal words *"had been causing me some anxiety."* Anxiety—oh God, what might be happening to Clare now? How did he know there was a Clare by this time? Anything could happen. He'd been a fool ever to accept this job. What other newly married man in the world would have done it? But it had seemed so sensible. Three years of horrid separation but then . . . oh, they were made for life. He had been promised the post that, only a few months before, he would not have dared to dream of. He'd never need to go to Space again. And all the by-products; the lectures, the book, probably a title. Plenty of children. He knew she wanted that, and so in a queer way (as he began to find) did he. But damn it, the journal. Begin a new paragraph—and then the shout came.

It was one of the two youngsters, technicians both, who had given it. They had been together since dinner. At least Paterson had been standing at the open door of Dickson's cabin, shifting from foot to foot and swinging the door, and Dickson had been sitting on his berth and waiting for Paterson to go away.

"What are you talking about, Paterson?" he said. "Who ever said anything about a quarrel?"

"That's all very well, Bobby," said the other, "but we're not friends like we used to be. You know we're not. Oh, *I'm* not blind. I *did* ask you to call me Clifford. And you're always so stand-offish."

"Oh, get to hell out of this!" cried Dickson. "I'm perfectly ready to be good friends with you and everyone else in an ordinary way, but all this gas—like a pair of schoolgirls—I will not stand. Once and for all—"

"Oh look, look, look," said Paterson. And it was then that Dickson shouted and the Captain came and rang the bell and within twenty seconds they were all crowded behind the biggest of the windows. A spaceship had just made a beautiful landing about a hundred and fifty yards from camp.

"Oh boy!" exclaimed Dickson. "They're relieving us before our time."

"Damn their eyes. Just what they would do," said the Botanist.

Five figures were descending from the ship. Even in space-suits it was clear that one of them was enormously fat; they were in no other way remarkable.

"Man the air-lock," said the Captain.

Drinks from their limited store were going round. The Captain had recognized in the leader of the strangers an old acquaintance, Ferguson. Two were ordinary young men, not unpleasant. But the remaining two?

"I don't understand," said the Captain, "who exactly—I mean we're delighted to see you all of course—but what exactly . . . ?"

"Where are the rest of your party?" said Ferguson.

"We've had two casualties, I'm afraid," said the Captain. "Sackville and Dr. Burton. It was a most wretched business. Sackville tried eating the stuff we called Martian cress. It drove him fighting mad in a matter of minutes. He knocked Burton down and by sheer bad luck Burton fell in just the wrong position: across that table there. Broke his neck. We got Sackville tied down on a bunk but he was dead before the evening."

"Hadna he even the gumption to try it on the guinea-pig first?" said Ferguson.

"Yes," said the Botanist. "That was the whole trouble. The funny thing is that the guinea-pig lived. But its behaviour was remarkable. Sackville wrongly concluded that the stuff was alcoholic. Thought he'd invent a new drink. The nuisance is that once Burton was dead, none of us could do a reliable post-mortem on Sackville. Under analysis this vegetable shows—"

"A-a-a-h," interrupted one of those who had not yet spoken. "We must beware of oversimplifications. I doubt if the vegetable substance is the real explanation. There are stresses and strains. You are all, without knowing it, in a highly un-stable condition, for reasons which are no mystery to a trained psychologist."

Some of those present had doubted the sex of this creature. Its hair was very short, its nose very long, its mouth very prim, its chin sharp, and its manner authoritative. The voice revealed it as, scientifically speaking, a woman. But no one had had any doubt about the sex of her nearest neighbour, the fat person.

"Oh dearie," she wheezed. "Not now. I tell you straight I'm that flustered and faint, I'll scream if you go on so. Suppose there ain't such a thing as a port and lemon handy? No? Well, a little drop more gin would settle me. It's me stomach reelly."

The speaker was infinitely female and perhaps in her seventies. Her hair had been not very successfully dyed to a colour not unlike that of mustard. The powder (scented strongly enough to throw a train off the rails) lay like snow drifts in the complex valleys of her creased, many-chinned face.

"Stop!" roared Ferguson. "Whatever ye do, dinna give her a drap mair to drink."

" 'E's no 'art, ye see," said the old woman with a whimper and an affectionate leer directed at Dickson.

"Excuse me," said the Captain. "Who are these—ah—ladies and what is this all about?"

"I have been waiting to explain," said the Thin Woman, and cleared her throat. "Anyone who has been following World-Opinion-Trends on the problems arising out of the psychological welfare aspect of interplanetary communication will be conscious of the growing agreement that such a remarkable advance inevitably demands of us far-reaching ideological adjustments. Psychologists are now well aware that a forcible inhibition of powerful biological urges over a protracted period is likely to have unforeseeable results. The pioneers of space-travel are exposed to this danger. It would be unenlightened if a supposed ethicality were allowed to stand in the way of their protection. We must therefore nerve ourselves to face the view that immorality, as it has hitherto been called, must no longer be regarded as unethical—"

"I don't understand that," said the Monk.

"She means," said the Captain, who was a good linguist, "that what you call fornication must no longer be regarded as immoral."

"That's right, dearie,' said the Fat Woman to Dickson, "she only means a poor boy needs a woman now and then. It's only natural."

"What was required, therefore," continued the Thin Woman, "was a band of devoted females who would take the first step. This would expose them, no doubt, to obloquy from many ignorant persons. They would be sustained by the consciousness that they were performing an indispensable function in the history of human progress."

"She means you're to have tarts, duckie," said the Fat Woman to Dickson.

"Now you're talking," said he with enthusiasm. "Bit late in the day, but better late than never. But you can't have brought many girls in that ship. And why didn't you bring them in? Or are they following?"

"We cannot indeed claim," continued the Thin Woman, who had apparently not noticed the interruption, "that the response to our appeal was such as we had hoped. The personnel of the first unit of the Woman's Higher Aphrodisio-Therapeutic Humane Organization (abbreviated WHAT-HO) is not perhaps . . . well. Many excellent women, university colleagues of my own, even senior colleagues, to whom I applied, showed themselves curiously conventional. But at least a start has been made. And here," she concluded brightly, "we are."

And there, for forty seconds of appalling silence, they were. Then Dickson's face, which had already undergone certain contortions, became very red; he applied his handkerchief and spluttered like a man trying to stifle a sneeze, rose abruptly, turned his back on the company, and hid his face. He stood slightly stooped and you could see his shoulders shaking.

Paterson jumped up and ran towards him; but the Fat Woman, though with infinite gruntings and upheavals, had risen too.

"Get art of it, Pansy," she snarled at Paterson. "Lot o' good your sort ever did." A moment later her vast arms were round Dickson; all the warm, wobbling maternalism of her engulfed him.

"There, sonny," she said, "it's goin' to be OK. Don't cry, honey. Don't cry. Poor boy, then. Poor boy. I'll give you a good time."

"I think," said the Captain, "the young man is laughing, not crying."

It was the Monk who at this point mildly suggested a meal.

Some hours later the party had temporarily broken up.

Dickson (despite all his efforts the Fat Woman had contrived to sit next to him; she had more than once mistaken his glass for hers) had hardly finished his last mouthful when he said to the newly arrived technicians:

"I'd love to see over your ship, if I could."

You might expect that two men who had been cooped up in that ship so long, and had only taken off their space-suits a few minutes ago, would have been reluctant to reassume the one and return to the other. That was certainly the Fat Woman's view. "Nar, nar," she said. "Don't you go fidgeting, sonny. They seen enough of that ruddy ship for a bit, same as me. 'Tain't good for you to go rushing about, not on a full stomach, like." But the two young men were marvellously obliging.

"Certainly. Just what I was going to suggest," said the first. "OK by me, chum," said the second. They were all three of them out of the air-lock in record time.

Across the sand, up the ladder, helmets off, and then:

"What in the name of thunder have you dumped those two bitches on us for?" said Dickson.

"Don't fancy 'em?" said the Cockney stranger. "The people at 'ome thought as 'ow you'd be a bit sharp set by now. Ungrateful of you, I call it."

"Very funny to be sure," said Dickson. "But it's no laughing matter for us."

"It hasn't been for us either, you know," said the Oxford stranger. "Cheek by jowl with them for eighty-five days. They palled a bit after the first month."

"You're telling me," said the Cockney.

There was a disgusted pause.

"Can anyone tell me," said Dickson at last, "who in the world, and why in the world, out of all possible women, selected those two horrors to send to Mars?"

"Can't expect a star London show at the back of beyond," said the Cockney.

"My dear fellow," said his colleague, "isn't the thing perfectly obvious? What kind of woman, without force, is going to come and live in this ghastly place—on rations—and play doxy to half a dozen men she's never seen? The Good Time Girls won't come because they know you can't have a good time on Mars. An ordinary professional prostitute won't come as long as she has the slightest chance of being picked up in the cheapest quarter of Liverpool or Los Angeles. And you've got one who hasn't. The only other who'd come would be a crank who believes all that blah about the new ethicality. And you've got one of that too."

"Simple, ain't it?" said the Cockney.

"Anyone," said the other, "except the Fools at the Top could of course have foreseen it from the word go."

"The only hope now is the Captain," said Dickson.

"Look, mate," said the Cockney, "if you think there's any question of our taking back returned goods, you've 'ad it. Nothing doing. Our Captain'll 'ave a mutiny to settle if he tries that. Also 'e won't. 'E's 'ad 'is turn. So've we. It's up to you now."

"Fair's fair, you know," said the other. "We've stood all we can."

"Well," said Dickson, "we must leave the two chiefs to fight it out. But discipline or not, there are some things a man can't stand. That bloody school-marm—"

"She's a lecturer at a redbrick university, actually."

"Well," said Dickson after a long pause, "you were going to show me over the ship. It might take my mind off it a bit."

The Fat Woman was talking to the Monk. " . . . and oh, Father dear, I know you'll think that's the worst of all. I didn't give it up when I could. After me brother's wife died . . . 'e'd 'ave 'ad me 'ome with 'im, and money wasn't that short. But I went on, Gawd 'elp me, I went on."

"Why did you do that, daughter?" said the Monk. "Did you *like* it?"

"Well not all that, Father. I was never partikler. But you see—oh, Father, I was the goods in those days, though you wouldn't think it now . . . and the poor gentlemen, they did so enjoy it."

"Daughter," he said, "you are not far from the Kingdom. But you were wrong. The desire to give is blessed. But you can't turn bad bank-notes into good ones just by giving them away."

The Captain had also left the table pretty quickly, asking Ferguson to accompany him to his cabin. The Botanist had leaped after them.

"One moment, sir, one moment," he said excitedly. "I am a scientist. I'm working at very high pressure already. I hope there is no complaint to be made about my discharge of all those other duties which so incessantly interrupt my work. But if I am going to be expected to waste any more time entertaining those abominable females—"

"When I give you any orders which can be considered *ultra vires*," said the Captain, "it will be time to make your protest."

Paterson stayed with the Thin Woman. The only part of any woman that interested him was her ears. He liked telling women about his troubles; especially about the unfairness and unkindness of other men. Unfortunately the lady's idea was that the interview should be devoted either to Aphrodisio-Therapy or to instruction in psychology. She saw, indeed, no reason why the two operations should not be carried out simultaneously; it is only untrained minds that cannot hold more than one idea. The difference between these two conceptions of the conversation was well on its way to impairing its success. Paterson was becoming ill-tempered; the lady remained bright and patient as an iceberg.

"But as I was saying," grumbled Paterson, "what I do think so rotten is a fellow being quite fairly decent one day and then—"

"Which just illustrates my point. These tensions and maladjustments are bound, under the unnatural conditions, to arise. And provided we disinfect the obvious remedy of all those sentimental or—which is quite as bad—prurient associations which the Victorian age attached to it—"

"But I haven't yet told you. Listen. Only two days ago—"

"One moment. This ought to be regarded like any other injection. If once we can persuade—"

"How any fellow can take a pleasure—"

"I agree. The association of it with pleasure (that is purely an adolescent fixation) may have done incalculable harm. Rationally viewed—"

"I say, you're getting off the point."

"One moment—"

The dialogue continued.

They had finished looking over the spaceship. It was certainly a beauty. No one afterwards remembered who had first said, "Anyone could manage a ship like this."

Ferguson sat quietly smoking while the Captain read the letter he had brought him. He didn't even look in the Captain's direction. When at last conversation began there was so much circumambient happiness in the cabin that they took a long time to get down to the difficult part of their business. The Captain seemed at first wholly occupied with its comic side.

"Still," he said at last, "it has its serious side too. The impertinence of it, for one thing! Do they think—"

"Ye maun recall," said Ferguson, "they're dealing with an absolutely new situation."

"Oh, *new* be damned! How does it differ from men on whalers, or even on windjammers in the old days? Or on the North-west Frontier? It's about as new as people being hungry when food was short."

"Eh mon, but ye're forgettin' the new light of modern psychology."

"I think those two ghastly women have already learned some newer psychology since they arrived. Do they really suppose every man in the world is so combustible that he'll jump into the arms of any woman whatever?"

"Aye, they do. They'll be sayin' you and your party are verra abnormal. I wadna put it past them to be sending you out wee packets of hormones next."

"Well, if it comes to that, do they suppose men would volunteer for a job like this unless they could, or thought they could, or wanted to try if they could, do without women?"

"Then there's the new ethics, forbye."

"Oh stow it, you old rascal. What is new there either? Who ever tried to live clean except a minority who had a religion or were in love? They'll try it still on Mars, as they did on Earth. As for the majority, did they ever hesitate to take their pleasures wherever they could get them? The ladies of the profession know better. Did you ever see a port or a garrison town without plenty of brothels? Who are the idiots on the Advisory Council who started all this nonsense?"

"Och, a pack o' daft auld women (in trousers for the maist part) who like onything sexy, and onything scientific, and onything that makes them feel important. And this gives them all three pleasures at once, ye ken."

"Well, there's only one thing for it, Ferguson. I'm not going to have either your Mistress Overdone or your extension lecturer here. You can just—"

"Now there's no manner of use talkin' that way. I did my job. Another voyage with sic a cargo o' livestock I will not face. And my two lads the same. There'd be mutiny and murder."

"But you must, I'm—"

At that moment a blinding flash came from without and the earth shook.

"Ma ship! Ma ship!" cried Ferguson. Both men peered out on empty sand. The spaceship had obviously made an excellent take-off.

"But what's happened?" said the Captain. "They haven't—"

"Mutiny, desertion, and theft of a government ship, that's what's happened," said Ferguson. "Ma twa lads and your Dickson are awa' hame."

"But good Lord, they'll get hell for this. They've ruined their careers. They'll be—"

"Aye. Nae dout. And they think it cheap at the price. Ye'll be seeing why, maybe, before ye are a fortnight older."

A gleam of hope came into the Captain's eyes. "They couldn't have taken the women with them?"

"Talk sense, mon, talk sense. Or if ye hanna ony sense, use your ears."

In the buzz of excited conversation which became every moment more audible from the main room, female voices could be intolerably distinguished.

As he composed himself for his evening meditation the Monk thought that perhaps he had been concentrating too much on "needing less" and that must be why he was going to have a course (advanced) in "loving more." Then his face twitched into a smile that was not all mirth. He was thinking of the Fat Woman. Four things made an exquisite chord. First, the horror of all she had done and suffered. Secondly, the pity—thirdly, the 'omicality—of her belief that she could still excite desire; fourthly, her bless'd ignorance of that utterly different loveliness which already existed within her and which, under grace, and with such poor direction as even he could supply, might one day set her, bright in the land of brightness, beside the Magdalene.

But wait! There was yet a fifth note in the chord. "Oh, Master," he murmured, "forgive—or can you enjoy?—my absurdity also. I had been supposing you sent me on a voyage of forty million miles merely for my own spiritual convenience."

Edgar Pangborn

Edgar Pangborn (1909–76) attended Harvard and The New England Conservatory of Music and then published his first novel, a mystery (*A-100*, under the pseudonym Bruce Harrison). Two decades later, he turned to writing science fiction and wrote several SF novels and a number of stories from the 1950s through the 1970s. Damon Knight, describing Pangborn's first story, "Angel's Egg," and his novels *West of the Sun* (1953) and *A Mirror for Observers* (1954), says, "The style is leisurely and reflective; the mood is one of blended sorrow and delight. . . . It is as if [Pangborn's] eye sees only certain moral and emotional colors . . . we can only assume that he has blinded himself in half the spectrum in order to see more radiantly in the rest. Certainly nothing is lacking in these stories for want of skill. It may well be that this is the only song Pangborn was made to sing; and a mournfully beautiful one it is—very like the thing that Stapledon was always talking about but never managed to convey: the regretful, ironic, sorrowful, deeply joyous—and purblind—love of the world and all in it."

Davy (1964) is generally considered his masterpiece. Critics generally find it hard to articulate the virtues of this novel that Robert A. Heinlein compared to *Huckleberry Finn*. Perhaps this is in part because there was little discourse about gay fiction until recently. *Dictionary of Literary Biography* (volume 8), for instance, says it "reads like a collaboration between Mark Twain, Dylan Thomas, and André Gide." There is more warmth than illumination in such statements. It is an intensely sensual book. His later works include two collections of stories, *Good Neighbors and Other Strangers* (1972) and *Still I Persist in Wondering* (1978).

This story is from his 1950s advent, the mournfully beautiful period that so impressed Knight and others.

THE MUSIC MASTER OF BABYLON

For twenty-five years no one came.

In the seventy-sixth year of his life Brian Van Anda was still trying not to remember a happy boyhood. To do so was irrelevant and dangerous, although every instinct of his old age tempted him to reject the present and live in the lost times. He would recall stubbornly that the present year, for example, was 2096 according to the Christian calendar, that he had been born in 2020, seven years after the close of the civil war, fifty years before the last war, twenty-five years before the departure of the First Interstellar. The First and Second Interstellar would be still on the move, he supposed. It had been understood, obvious, long ago, that after radio contact faded out the world would not hear of them again for many lifetimes, if ever. They would be on the move, farther and farther away from a planet no longer capable of understanding such matters.

Brian sometimes recalled his place of birth, New Boston, the fine planned city far inland from the old metropolis which a rising sea had reclaimed after the earthquake of 1994. Such things, places and dates, were factual props, useful when Brian wanted to impose an external order on the vagueness of his immediate existence. He tried to make sure they became no more than that, to shut away the colors, the poignant sounds, the parks and the playgrounds of New Boston, the known faces (many of them loved), and the later years when he had experienced a curious intoxication called fame.

It was not necessarily better or wiser to reject these memories, but it was safer, and nowadays Brian was often sufficiently tired, sufficiently conscious of his growing weakness and lonely unimportance, to crave safety as a meadow mouse craves a burrow.

He tied his canoe to the massive window which for many years had been a port and a doorway. Lounging there with a suspended sense of time, he hardly knew he was listening. In a way, all the twenty-five years had been a listening. He watched Earth's patient star sink toward the rim of the forest on the Palisades. At this hour it was sometimes possible, if the sun-crimsoned water lay still, to cease grieving at the greater stillness.

There must be scattered human life elsewhere, he knew—probably a great deal of it. After twenty-five years alone, that also often seemed irrelevant. At other times than mild evenings—on hushed noons or in the mornings always so empty of human commotion—Brian might lapse into anger, fight the calm by yelling, resent the swift dying of his own echoes. Such moods were brief. A kind of humor remained in him, not to be ruined by any sorrow.

He remembered how, ten months or possibly ten years ago, he had encountered a box turtle in a forest clearing, and had shouted at it: "They went that-away!" The turtle's rigidly comic face, fixed in a caricature of startled disapproval, had seemed to point up some truth or other. Brian had hunkered down on the moss and laughed uproariously until he observed that some of the laughter was weeping.

Today had been rather good. He had killed a deer on the Palisades, and with bow and arrow, not spending a bullet—irreplaceable toy of civilization.

Not that he needed to practice such economy. He could live, he supposed, another ten years at the outside. His rifles were in good condition, his hoarded ammunition would easily outlast him. So would the stock of canned and dried food stuffed away in his living quarters. But there was satisfaction in primitive effort, and no compulsion to analyze the why of it.

The stored food was more important than the ammunition; a time was coming soon enough when he would no longer have the strength for hunting. He would lose the inclination to depart from his fortress for trips to the mainland. He would yield to such timidity or laziness for days, then weeks. Sometime, after such an interlude, he might find himself too feeble to risk climbing the cliff wall into the forest. He would then have the good sense, he hoped, to destroy the canoe, thus making of his weakness a necessity.

There were books. There was the Hall of Music on the next floor above the water, probably safe from its lessening encroachment. To secure fresh water he need only keep track of the tides, for the Hudson had cleaned itself and now rolled down sweet from the lonely uncorrupted hills. His decline could be comfortable. He had provided for it and planned it.

Yet now, gazing across the sleepy water, seeing a broad-winged hawk circle in freedom above the forest, Brian was aware of the old thought moving in him: *If I could hear voices—just once, if I could hear human voices . . .*

The Museum of Human History, with the Hall of Music on what Brian thought of as the second floor, should also outlast his requirements. In the flooded lower floor and basement the work of slow destruction must be going on: Here and there the unhurried waters could find their way to steel and make rust of it; the waterproofing of the concrete was nearly a hundred years old. But it ought to be good for another century or two.

Nowadays the ocean was mild. There were moderate tides, winds no longer destructive. For the last six years there had been no more of the heavy storms out of the south; in the same period Brian had noted a rise in the water level of a mere nine inches. The windowsill, his port, stood six inches above high-tide mark this year. Perhaps Earth was settling into a new amiable mood. The climate had become delightful, about like what Brian remembered from a visit to southern Virginia in his childhood.

The last earthquake had come in 2082—a large one, Brian guessed, but its center could not have been close to the rock of Manhattan. The Museum had only shivered and shrugged—it had survived much worse than that, half a dozen times since 1994. Long after the tremor, a tall wave had thundered in from the south. Its force, like that of others, had mostly been dissipated against the barrier of tumbled rock and steel at the southern end of the submerged island—an undersea dam, man-made though not man-intended—and when it reached the Museum it did no more than smash the southern windows in the Hall of Music, which earlier waves had not been able to reach; then it passed on up the river enfeebled.

The windows of the lower floor had all been broken long before that. After the earthquake of '82 Brian had spent a month in boarding up all the openings on the south side of the Hall of Music—after all, it was home—with lumber painfully ferried over from mainland ruins. By that year he was sixty-two years old and not moving with the ease of youth. He deliberately left cracks and knotholes. Sunlight sifted through in narrow beams, like the bars of dusty gold Brian could remember in a hayloft at his uncle's farm in Vermont.

That hawk above the Palisades soared nearer over the river and receded. Caught in the evening light, he was himself a little sun, dying and returning.

The Museum had been finished in 2003. Manhattan, strangely enough, had never taken a bomb, although in the civil war two of the type called "small clean fission" had fallen on the Brooklyn and New Jersey sides—so Brian recalled from the jolly history books which had informed his adolescence that war was definitely a thing of the past. By the time of the next last war, in 2070, the sea, gorged on melting ice caps, had removed Manhattan Island from current history.

Everything left standing above the waters south of the Museum had been knocked flat by the tornadoes of 2057 and 2064. A few blobs of empty rock still demonstrated where Central Park and Mount Morris Park had been: not significant. Where Long Island once rose, there was a troubled area of shoals and small islands, probably a useful barrier of protection for the receding shore of Connecticut. Men had yielded their great city inch by inch, then foot by foot; a full mile in 2047, saying: "The flood years have passed their peak, and a return to normal is expected." Brian sometimes felt a twinge of sympathy for the Neanderthal experts who must have told each other to expect a return to normal at the very time when the Cro-Magnons were drifting in.

In 2057 the Island of Manhattan had to be yielded. New York City, half-new, half-ancient, sprawled stubborn and enormous upstream, on both sides of a river not done with its anger. Yet the Museum stood. Aided by sunken rubble of other buildings of its kind, aided also by men because they still had time to move it, the museum stood, and might for a long time yet—weather permitting.

The hawk floated out of sight above the Palisades into the field of the low sun.

The Museum of Human History covered an acre of ground north of 125th Street, rising a modest fifteen stories, its foundation secure in that layer of rock which mimics eternity. It deserved its name; here men had brought samples of everything man-made, literally everything known in the course of human creation since prehistory. Within human limits it was definitive.

No one had felt anything unnatural in the refusal of the Directors of the Museum to move the collection after the building weathered the storm of 2057. Instead, ordinary people donated money so that a mighty abutment could be built around the ground floor and a new entrance designed on the north side of the second. The abutment survived the greater tornado of 2064 without damage, although during those seven years the sea had risen another eight feet in its old ever-new game of making monkeys out of the wise. (It was left for Brian Van Anda, alone, in 2079, to see the waters slide quietly over the abutment, opening the lower regions for the use of fishes and the more secret water-dwellers who like shelter and privacy. In the '90s, Brian suspected the presence of an octopus or two in the vast vague territory that had once been parking lot, heating plant, storage space, air-raid shelter, etc. He couldn't prove it; it just seemed like a decent, comfortable place for an octopus.) In 2070 plans were under consideration for building a new causeway to the Museum from the still expanding city in the north. In 2070, also, the last war began and ended.

When Brian Van Anda came down the river late in 2071, a refugee from certain unfamiliar types of savagery, the Museum was empty of the living. He spent many days in exhaustive exploration of the building. He did this systematically, toiling at last up to the Directors' meeting room on the top floor. There he observed how they must have been holding a conference at the very time when a new gas was tried out over New York in a final effort to persuade the Western Federation that the end justifies the means. (Too bad, Brian sometimes thought, that he would never know exactly what had become of the Asian Empire. In the little splinter state called the Soviet of North America, from which Brian had fled in '71, the official doctrine was that the Asian Empire had won the war and the saviors of humanity would be flying in any day now. Brian had inadvertently doubted this out loud and then stolen a boat and gotten away safely under cover of night.)

Up in the meeting room, Brian had seen how that up-to-date neurotoxin had been no respecter of persons. An easy death, however, by the look of it. He observed also how some things endure. The Museum, for instance: virtually unharmed.

Brian often recalled those moments in the meeting room as a sort of island in time. They were like the first day of falling in love, the first hour of discovering that he could play Beethoven. And a little like the curiously cherished, more than life-size half-hour back there in Newburg, in that ghastly year 2071, when he had briefly met and spoken with an incredibly old man, Abraham Brown. Brown had been President of the Western Federation at the time of the civil war. Later, retired from the uproar of public affairs, he had devoted himself to philosophy, unofficial teaching. In 2071, with the world he had loved in almost total ruin around him, Brown had spoken pleasantly to Brian Van Anda of small things—of chrysanthemums that would soon be blooming in the front yard of the house where he lived with friends, of a piano recital by Van Anda back in 2067 which the old man still remembered with warm enthusiasm.

Only a month later more hell was loose and Brian himself in flight.

Yes, the Museum Directors had died easily. Brooding in the evening sunlight, Brian reflected that now, all these years later, the innocent bodies would be perfectly decent. No vermin in the Museum. The doorways and the floors were tight, the upper windows unbroken.

One of the white-haired men had had a Ming vase on his desk. He had not dropped out of his chair, but looked as if he had fallen asleep in front of the vase with his head on his arms. Brian had left the vase untouched, but had taken one other thing, moved by some stirring of his own never-certain philosophy and knowing that he would not return to this room, ever.

One of the Directors had been opening a wall cabinet when he fell; the key lay near his fingers. Their discussion had not been concerned only with war, perhaps not at all with war. After all, there were other topics. The Ming vase must have had a part in it. Brian wished he could know what the old man had meant to take from the cabinet. Sometimes he dreamed of conversations with that man, in which the Director told him the truth of this and other matters, but what was certainty in sleep was in the morning gone like childhood.

For himself Brian had taken a little image of rock-hard clay, blackened, two-faced, male and female. Prehistoric, or at any rate wholly savage, unsophisticated, meaningful like the blameless motion of an animal in sunlight. Brian had said: "With your permission, gentlemen." He had closed the cabinet and then, softly, the outer door.

"I'm old, too," Brian said to the red evening. He searched for the hawk and could no longer find it in the deepening sky. "Old, a little foolish—talk aloud to myself. I'll have some Mozart before supper."

He transferred the fresh venison from the canoe to a small raft hitched inside the window. He had selected only choice pieces, as much as he could cook and eat in the few days before it spoiled, leaving the rest for the wolves or any other forest scavengers which might need it. There was a rope strung from the window to the marble steps leading to the next floor of the Museum, which was home.

It had not been possible to save much from the submerged area, for its treasure was mostly heavy statuary. Through the still water, as he pulled the raft along the rope, the Moses of Michelangelo gazed up at him in tranquillity. Other faces watched him; most of them watched infinity. There were white hands that occasionally borrowed motion from ripples made by the raft. "I got a deer, Moses," said Brian Van Anda, smiling down in companionship, losing track of time.... "Good night, Moses." He carried his juicy burden up the stairway.

Brian's living quarters had once been a cloakroom for Museum attendants. Four close walls gave it a feel of security. A ventilating shaft now served as a chimney for the wood stove Brian had salvaged from a mainland farmhouse. The door could be tightly locked. There were no windows. You do not want windows in a cave.

Outside was the Hall of Music, a full acre, an entire floor of the Museum, containing an example of every musical instrument that was known or could be reconstructed in the twenty-first century. The library of scores and recordings lacked nothing—except electricity to make the recordings speak. A few might still be made to sound on a hand-cranked phonograph, but Brian had not bothered with that toy for years; the springs were probably rusted.

Brian sometimes took out orchestra and chamber music scores to read at random. Once, reading them, his mind had been able to furnish ensembles, orchestras, choirs of a sort, but lately the ability had weakened. He remembered a day, possibly a year ago, when his memory refused to give him the sound of oboe and clarinet in unison. He had wandered, peevish, distressed, unreasonably alarmed, among the racks and cases of woodwinds and brasses and violins. He tried to sound a clarinet; the reed was still good in the dust proof case, but he had no lip. He had never mastered any instrument except the pianoforte.

He recalled—it might have been that same day—opening a chest of double basses. There was a three-stringer in the group, old, probably from the early nineteenth century, a trifle fatter than its more modern companions. Brian touched its middle string in an idle caress, not intending to make it sound, but it had done so. When in use, it would have been tuned to D; time had slackened the heavy murmur to A or something near it. That had throbbed in the silent room with finality, a sound such as a programmatic composer, say Tchaikovsky, might have used as a tonal symbol for the breaking of a heart. It stayed in the air as other instruments whispered a dim response. "All right, gentlemen," Brian said, "that was your A. . . ."

Out in the main part of the hall, a place of honor was given to what may have been the oldest of the instruments, a seven-note marimba of phonolitic schist discovered in Indo-China in the twentieth century and thought to be at least 5,000 years of age. The xylophone-type rack was modern. Brian for twenty-five years had obeyed a compulsion to keep it free of cobwebs. Sometimes he touched the singing stones, not for amusement but because there was comfort in it. They answered to the light tap of a fingernail. Beside them on a little table of its own he had placed the Stone Age god of two faces.

On the west side of the Hall of Music, a rather long walk from Brian's cave, was a small auditorium. Lectures, recitals, chamber music concerts had been given there in the old days. The pleasant room held a twelve-foot concert grand, made in 2043, probably the finest of the many pianos in the Hall of Music, a summit of technical achievement. Brian had done his best to preserve this beautiful artifact, prayerfully tuning it three times a year, robbing other pianos in the Museum to provide a reserve supply of strings, oiled and sealed against rust. When not in use his great piano was covered by stitched-together sheets. To remove the cover was a somber ritual. Before touching the keys, Brian washed his hands with needless fanatical care.

Some years ago he had developed the habit of locking the auditorium doors before he played. Yet even then he preferred not to glance toward the vista of empty seats, not much caring whether this inhibition derived from a Stone Age fear of finding someone there or from a flat civilized understanding that no one could be. It never occurred to him to lock the one door he used, when he was absent from the auditorium. The key remained on the inside; if he went in merely to tune the piano or to inspect the place, he never turned it.

The habit of locking it when he played might have started (he could not remember) back in the year 2076, when so many bodies had floated down from the north on the ebb tides. Full horror had somehow been lacking in the sight of all that floating death. Perhaps it was because Brian had earlier had his fill of horrors, or perhaps in 2076 he already felt so divorced from his own kind that what happened to them was like the photograph of a war in a distant country. Some had bobbed and floated quite near the Museum. Most of them had the gaping obvious wounds of primitive warfare, but some were oddly discolored— a new pestilence? So there was (or had been) more trouble up there in what was (or had been) the short-lived Soviet of North America, a self-styled "nation" that took in east central New York and most of New England. So . . . Yes, that was probably the year when he had started locking the doors between his private concerts and an empty world.

He dumped the venison in his cave. He scrubbed his hands, showing high blue veins now, but still tough, still knowing. Mozart, he thought, and walked, not with much pleasure of anticipation but more like one externally driven, through the enormous hall that was so full and yet so empty and growing dim with evening, with dust, with age, with loneliness. Music should not be silent.

When the piano was uncovered, Brian delayed. He exercised his hands unnec- essarily. He fussed with the candelabrum on the wall, lighting three candles, then blowing out two for economy. He admitted presently that he did not want the emotional clarity of Mozart at all, not now. The darkness of 2070 was too close, closer than he had felt it for a long time. It would never have occurred to Mozart, Brian thought, that a world could die. Beethoven could have entertained the idea soberly enough, and Chopin probably; even Brahms. Mozart, Haydn, Bach would surely have dismissed it as somebody's bad dream, in poor taste. Andrew Carr, who lived and died in the latter half of the twentieth century, had endured the idea deep in his bloodstream from the beginning of his childhood.

The date of Hiroshima was 1945; Carr was born in 1951. The wealth of his music was written between 1969, when he was eighteen, and 1984, when he died among the smells of an Egyptian jail from injuries received in a street brawl.

"If not Mozart," said Brian Van Anda to his idle hands, "there is always the Project."

To play Carr's last sonata as it should be played—as Carr was supposed to have said he couldn't play it himself: Brian had been thinking of that as the Project for many years. It had begun teasing his mind long before the war, at the time of his triumphs in a civilized world which had been warmly appreciative of the polished interpretive artist (once he got the breaks) although no more awake than in any other age to the creative sort. Back there in the undestroyed society, Brian had proposed to program that sonata in the company of works that were older but no greater, and to play it—well, beyond his best, so that even music critics would begin to see its importance in history.

He had never done it, had never felt the necessary assurance that he had entered into the sonata and learned the depth of it. Now, when there was none to hear or care, unless the harmless brown spiders in the corners of the audi- torium had a taste for music, there was still the Project. *I hear*, Brian thought. *I care, and with myself for audience I wish to hear it once as it ought to be, a final statement for a world that was (I think) too good to die.*

Technically, of course, he had it. The athletic demands Carr made on the performer were tremendous, but, given technique, there was nothing impossible about them. Anyone capable of concert work could at least play the notes at the required tempi. And any reasonably shrewd pianist could keep track of the dynamics, saving strength for the shattering finale. Brian had heard the sonata played by others two or three times in the old days—competently. Competency was not enough.

For example, what about the third movement, the mad scherzo, and the five tiny interludes of quiet scattered through its plunging fury? They were not alike. Related, but each one demanded a new climate of heart and mind—tenderness, regret, simple relaxation. Flowers on a flood—no. Window lights in a storm—no. The innocence of a child in a bombed city—no, not really. Something of all those. Much more, too, defying words.

What of the second movement, the largo, where in a way the pattern was reversed, the midnight introspection interrupted by moments of anger, or longing, or despair like the despair of an angel beating his wings against a prison of glass?

It was a work in which something of Carr's life, Carr's temperament, had to come into you, whether you dared welcome it or not; otherwise your playing was no more than reproduction of notes on a page. Carr's life was not for the contemplation of the timid.

The details were superficially well-known; the biographies were like musical notation, meaningless without interpretation and insight. Carr was a drunken roarer, a young devil-god with such a consuming hunger for life that he choked to death on it. His friends hated him for the way he drained their lives, loving them to distraction and the next moment having no time for them because he loved his work more. His enemies must have had times of helplessly admiring him if only because of a translucent honesty that made him more and less than human. A rugged Australian, not tall but built like a hero, a face all forehead and jaw and glowing hyperthyroid eyes. He wept only when he was angry, the biographic storytellers said. In one minute of talk he might shift from gutter obscenity to some extreme of altruistic tenderness, and from that perhaps to a philosophic comment of cold intelligence. He passed his childhood on a sheep farm, ran away on a freighter at thirteen, was flung out of two respectable conservatories for drunkenness and "public lewdness," then studied like a slave in London with single-minded desperation, as if he knew the time was short. He was married twice and twice divorced. He killed a man in a silly brawl on the New Orleans docks, and wrote his First Symphony while he was in jail for that. He died of stab wounds from a broken bottle in a Cairo jail, and was recognized by the critics. It all had relevancy; relevant or not, if the sonata was in your mind, so was the life.

You had to remember also that Andrew Carr was the last of civilization's great composers. No one in the twenty-first century approached him—they ignored his explorations and carved cherrystones. He belonged to no school, unless you wanted to imagine a school of music beginning with Bach, taking in perhaps a dozen along the way, and ending with Carr himself. His work was a summary as well as an advance along the mainstream into the unknown; in the light of the year 2070, it was also a completion.

Brian was certain he could play the first movement of the sonata as he wished to. Technically it was not revolutionary, and remained rather close to the ancient sonata form. Carr had even written in a double bar for a repeat of the entire opening statement, something that had made his cerebral contemporaries sneer with great satisfaction; it never occurred to them that Carr was inviting the performer to use his head.

The bright-sorrowful second movement, unfashionably long, with its strange pauses, unforeseen recapitulations, outbursts of savage change—that was where Brian's troubles began. ("Reminiscent of Franck," said the hunters for comparisons whom we have always with us.) It did not help Brian to be old, remembering the inner storms of forty years ago and more.

His single candle fluttered. For once Brian had forgotten to lock the door into the Hall of Music. This troubled him, but he did not rise from the piano chair. He chided himself instead for the foolish neuroses of aloneness—what could it matter? Let it go. He shut his eyes. The sonata had long ago been memorized; printed copies were safe in the library. He played the opening of the first movement as far as the double bar, opened his eyes to the friendly black-and-white of clean keys, and played the repetition with new lights, new emphasis. Better than usual, he thought—

Yes. Good. . . . Now that naïve-appearing modulation into A major, which only Carr would have wanted just there in that sudden obvious way, like the opening of a door on shining fields. On toward the climax—*I am playing it, I think*—through the intricate revelations of development and recapitulation. And the conclusion, lingering, half-humorous, not unlike a Beethoven *I'm-not-gone-yet* ending, but with a questioning that was all Andrew Carr. After that—

"No more tonight," said Brian aloud. "Some night, though . . . Not competent right now, my friend." He replaced the cover of the piano and blew out the candle. He had brought no torch, long use having taught his feet every inch of the small journey. It was quite dark. The never-opened western windows of the auditorium were dirty, most of the dirt on the outside, crusted windblown salt.

In this partial darkness something was wrong.

At first Brian found no source for the faint light, dim orange with a hint of motion. He peered into the gloom of the auditorium, fixing his eyes on the oblong of blacker shadow that was the doorway into the Hall of Music. The windows, of course!—he had almost forgotten there were any. The light, hardly deserving the name of light, was coming through them. But sunset was surely past. He had been here a long time, delaying and brooding before he played. Sunset should not flicker.

So there was some kind of fire on the mainland. There had been no thunderstorm. How should fire start, over there where no one ever came?

He stumbled a few times, swearing petulantly, locating the doorway again and groping through it into the Hall of Music. The windows out here were just as dirty; no use trying to see through them. There must have been a time when he had looked through them, enjoyed looking through them. He stood shivering in the marble silence, trying to remember.

Time was a gradual, continual dying. Time was the growth of dirt and ocean salt, sealing in, covering over. He stumbled for his cloakroom cave, hurrying now, and lit two candles. He left one by the cold stove and used the other to light his way down the stairs to his raft; once down there, he blew it out, afraid. The room a candle makes in the darkness is a vulnerable room. Having no walls, it closes in a blindness. He pulled the raft by the guide-rope, gently, for fear of noise.

He found his canoe tied as he had left it. He poked his white head slowly beyond the sill, staring west.

Merely a bonfire gleaming, reddening the blackness of the cliff.

Brian knew the spot, a ledge almost at water level, at one end of it the troublesome path he usually followed in climbing to the forest at the top of the Palisades. Usable driftwood was often there, the supply renewed by the high tides.

"No," Brian said. "Oh, no! . . ."

Unable to accept or believe, or not believe, he drew his head in, resting his forehead on the coldness of the sill, waiting for dizziness to pass, reason to return.

It might have been a long time, a kind of blackout. Now he was again in command of his actions and even rather calm, once more leaning out over the sill. The fire still shone and was therefore not a disordered dream of old age. It was dying to a dull rose of embers.

He wondered about the time. Clocks and watches had stopped long ago; Brian had ceased to want them. A sliver of moon was hanging over the water to the east. He ought to be able to remember the phases, deduce the approximate time from that. But his mind was too tired or distraught to give him the data. Maybe it was somewhere around midnight.

He climbed on the sill and lifted the canoe over it to the motionless water inside. Useless, he decided, as soon as the grunting effort was finished. That fire had been lit before daylight passed; whoever lit it would have seen the canoe, might even have been watching Brian himself come home from his hunting. The canoe's disappearance in the night would only rouse further curiosity. But Brian was too exhausted to lift it back.

And why assume that the maker of the bonfire was necessarily hostile? Might be good company . . . He pulled his raft through the darkness, secured it at the stairway, and groped back to his cave.

He locked the door. The venison was waiting; the sight made him ravenous. He lit a small fire in the stove, one that he hoped would not still be sending smoke from the ventilator shaft when morning came. He cooked the meat crudely and wolfed it down, all enjoyment gone at the first mouthful. He was shocked to discover the dirtiness of his white beard. He hadn't given himself a real bath in—weeks, was it? He searched for scissors and spent an absentminded while in trimming the beard back to shortness. He ought to take some soap— valuable stuff—down to Moses' room, and wash.

Clothes, too. People probably still wore clothes. He had worn none for years, except for sandals. He used a carrying satchel for trips to the mainland. He had enjoyed the freedom at first, and especially the discovery that in his rugged fifties he did not need clothes even for the soft winters, except perhaps a light covering when he slept. Later, total nakedness had become so natural it required no thought at all. But the owner of that bonfire could have inherited or retained the pruderies of the lost culture.

He checked his rifles. The .22 automatic, an Army model from the 2040's, was the best—any amount of death in that. The tiny bullets carried a paralytic poison: graze a man's finger and he was almost painlessly dead in three minutes. Effective range, with telescopic sights, three kilometers; weight, a scant five pounds. Brian sat a long time cuddling that triumph of military science, listening for sounds that never came. Would it be two o'clock? He wished he could have seen the Time Satellite, renamed in his mind the Midnight Star, but when he was down there at his port, he had not once looked up at the night sky. Delicate and beautiful, bearing its everlasting freight of men who must have been dead now for twenty-five years and who would be dead a very long time—well, it was better than a clock, if you happened to look at the midnight sky at the right time of the month when the man-made star caught the moonlight. But he had missed it tonight. Three o'clock? . . .

At some time during the long dark he put the rifle away on the floor. With studied, self-conscious contempt for his own weakness, he unlocked the door and strode out noisily into the Hall of Music, with a fresh-lit candle. This same bravado, he knew, might dissolve at the first alien noise. While it lasted, it was invigorating.

The windows were still black with night. As if the candle flame had found its own way, Brian was standing by the ancient marimba in the main hall, the gleam slanting carelessly away from his gaunt hand. And nearby sat the Stone Age god.

It startled him. He remembered clearly how he himself had placed it there, obeying a half-humorous whim. The image and the singing stones were both magnificently older than history, so why shouldn't they live together? Whenever he dusted the marimba, he dusted the image respectfully, and its table. It would not have needed much urging from the impulses of a lonely mind to make him place offerings before it—winking first, of course, to indicate that rituals suitable to a pair of aging gentlemen did not have to be sensible in order to be good.

The clay face remembering eternity was not deformed by the episode of civilization. Chipped places were simple honorable scars. The two faces stared mildly from the single head, uncommunicative, serene.

A wooden hammer of modern make rested on the marimba. Softly Brian tapped a few of the stones. He struck the shrillest one harder, waking many slow-dying overtones, and laid the hammer down, listening until the last murmur perished and a drop of wax hurt his thumb. He returned to his cave and blew out the candle, never thinking of the door, or if he thought, not caring.

Face down, he rolled his head and clenched his fingers into his pallet, seeking in pain, finding at last the relief of stormy childish weeping in the dark.

Then he slept.

They looked timid. The evidence of it was in their tense squatting pose, not in what the feeble light allowed Brian to see of their faces, which were blank as rock. Hunkered down just inside the doorway of the dim cloakroom cave, a morning grayness from the Hall of Music behind them, they were ready for flight, and Brian's intelligence warned his body to stay motionless. Readiness for flight could also be readiness for attack. He studied them through slit eyelids, knowing he was in deep shadow.

They were very young, sixteen or seventeen, firm-muscled, the boy slim but heavy in the shoulders, the girl a fully developed woman. They were dressed alike: loincloths of some coarse dull fabric, and moccasins that were probably deerhide. Their hair grew nearly to the shoulders and was cut off carelessly, but they were evidently in the habit of combing it. They appeared to be clean. Their complexion, so far as Brian could guess it in the meager light, was brown, like a heavy tan. With no immediate awareness of emotion, he decided they were beautiful, and then within his own poised and perilous silence Brian reminded himself that the young are always beautiful.

The woman muttered softly: "He wake."

A twitch of the man's head was probably meant to warn her to be quiet. He clutched the shaft of a javelin with a metal blade which had once belonged to a breadknife. The blade was polished, shining, lashed to a peeled stick. The javelin trailed, ready for use at a flick of the young man's arm. Brian sighed deliberately. "Good morning."

The man, or boy, said: "Good morning, sa."

"Where do you come from?"

"Millstone." The man spoke automatically, but then his facial rigidity dissolved into astonishment and some kind of distress. He glanced at his companion, who giggled uneasily.

"The old man pretends to not know," she said, and smiled, and seemed to be waiting for the young man's permission to go on speaking. He did not give it, but she continued: "Sa, the old ones of Millstone are dead." She thrust her hand out and down, flat, a picture of finality, adding with nervous haste: "As the Old Man knows. He who told us to call him Jonas, she who told us to call her Abigail, dead. They are still-without-moving the full six days, then we do the burial as they told us. As the Old Man knows."

"But I don't know!" said Brian, and sat up on his pallet too quickly, startling them. But their motion was backward, a readying for flight. "Millstone? Where is Millstone?"

They looked wholly bewildered and dismayed. They stood up with animal grace, stepping backward out of the cave, the girl whispering in the man's ear. Brian caught two words: "—is angry."

He jumped up. "Don't go! Please don't go!" He followed them out of the cave, slowly now, aware that he might be an object of terror in the half-dark, aware of his gaunt, graceless age, and nakedness, and dirty hacked-off beard. Almost involuntarily he adopted something of the flat stilted quality of their speech. "I will not hurt you. Do not go."

They halted. The girl smiled dubiously. The man said: "We need old ones. They die. He who told us to call him Jonas said, many days in the boat, not with the sun-path, he said, across the sun-path, he said, keeping land on the left hand. We need old ones, to speak the—to speak . . . The Old Man is angry?"

"No. I am not angry. I am never angry." Brian's mind groped, certain of nothing. No one came, for twenty-five years.

Millstone?

There was red-gold on the dirty eastern windows of the Hall of Music, a light becoming softness as it slanted down, touching the long rows of cases, the warm brown of an antique spinet, the clean gold of a twentieth century harp, the gray of singing stones five thousand years old and a two-faced god much older than that. "Millstone." Brian pointed in inquiry, southwest.

The girl nodded, pleased and not at all surprised that he should know, watching him now with a squirrel's stiff curiosity. Hadn't there been a Millstone River in or near Princeton, once upon a time? Brian thought he remembered that it emptied into the Raritan Canal. There was some moderately high ground there. Islands now, no doubt. Perhaps they would tell him. "There were old people in Millstone," he said, trying for peaceful dignity, "and they died. So now you need old ones to take their place."

The girl nodded vigorously many times. Her glance at the young man was shy, possessive, maybe amused. "He who told us to call him Jonas said no marriage without the words of Abraham."

"Abr—" Brian checked himself. If this was religion, it would not do to speak the name Abraham with a rising inflection. "I have been for a long time—" He checked himself again: A man old, ugly, and strange enough to be sacred should never stoop to explain anything.

They were standing by the seven-stone marimba. His hand dropped, his thumbnail clicking against the deepest stone and waking a murmur. The children drew back, alarmed. Brian smiled. "Don't be afraid." He tapped the other stones lightly. "It is only music. It will not hurt you." They were patient and respectful, waiting for more light. He said carefully: "He who told you to call him Jonas—he taught you all the things you know?"

"All things," the boy said, and the girl nodded three or four times, so that the soft brownness of her hair tumbled about her face, and she pushed it back in a small human motion as old as the clay image.

"Do you know how old you are?"

They looked blank. Then the girl said: "Oh—summers!" She held up her two hands with spread fingers, then one hand. "Three fives." She chuckled, and sobered quickly. "As the Old Man knows."

"I am very old," said Brian. "I know many things, but sometimes I wish to forget, and sometimes I wish to hear what others know, even though I may know it myself."

They looked uncomprehending and greatly impressed. Brian felt a smile on his face and wondered why it should be there. They were nice children. Born ten years after the death of a world; twenty, perhaps. *I think I am seventy-six, but what if I dropped a decade somewhere and never noticed the damned thing . . . ?* "He who told you to call him Jonas—he taught you all you know of Abraham?"

At the sound of the name, both made swift circular motions, first at the forehead, then at the breast. "He taught us all things," the young man said. "He, and she who told us to call her Abigail. The hours to rise, to pray, to wash, to eat. The laws for hunting, and I know the Abraham-words for that: Sol-Amra, I take this for my need."

Brian felt lost again, and looked down to the clay faces of the image for counsel, and found none. "They who told you to call them Jonas and Abigail, they were the only ones who lived with you?—the only old ones?"

Again that look of bewilderment and disappointment. "The only ones, sa," the young man said. "As the Old Man knows."

I could never persuade them that, being old, I know very nearly nothing. . . .

Brian straightened to his full great height. The young people were not tall. Though stiff and worn with age, Brian knew he was still overpowering. Once, among men, he had gently enjoyed being more than life-size. As a shield for loneliness and fright within, he now adopted a phony sternness. "I wish to examine you for your own good, my children, about Millstone and your knowledge of Abraham. How many others live at Millstone, tell me."

"Two fives, sa," said the boy promptly, "and I the one who may be called Jonason and this girl who may be called Paula. Two fives and two. We are the biggest. The others are only children, but the one who may be called Jimi has killed his deer; he sees after them now while we go across the sun-path."

Under Brian's questioning, more of the story came, haltingly, obscured by the young man's conviction that the Old Man already knew everything. Sometime, probably in the middle 2080's, Jonas and Abigail (whoever they were) had come on a group of twelve wild children who were keeping alive somehow in a ruined town where their elders had all died. Jonas and Abigail had brought them all to an island they called Millstone. Jonas and Abigail came originally from "up across the sun-path"—the boy seemed to mean north—and they were very old, which might mean, Brian guessed, anything between thirty and ninety. In teaching the children primitive means of survival, Jonas and Abigail had brought off a brilliant success: Jonason and Paula were well-fed, shining with health and the strength of wildness, and clean. Their speech, limited and odd though it was, had not been learned from the ignorant. Its pronunciation faintly suggested New England, so far as it had any local accent. "Did they teach you reading and writing?" Brian asked, and made writing motions on the flat of his palm, which the two watched in vague alarm.

The boy asked: "What is that?"

"Never mind." *I could quarrel with some of your theories, Mister-whom-I-may-call-Jonas.* But maybe, he thought, there had been no books, no writing materials, no way to get them. What's the minimum of technology required to keep the human spirit alive? . . . "Well—well, tell me what they taught you of Abraham. I wish to hear how well you remember."

Both made again the circular motion at forehead and breast, and the young man said with the stiffness of recitation: "Abraham was the Son of Heaven who died that we might live." The girl, her obligation discharged with the religious gesture, tapped the marimba shyly, fascinated, and drew her finger back, smiling up at Brian in apology for naughtiness. "He taught the laws, the everlasting truth of all time," the boy gabbled, "and was slain on the wheel at Nuber by the infidels; therefore since he died for us, we look up across the sun-path when we pray to Abraham Brown who will come again." The boy Jonason sighed and relaxed.

Abraham—Brown? But—

But I knew him. I met him. Nuber? Newburg, temporary capital of the Soviet of—oh, damn that . . . Met him, 2071—the concert of mine he remembered . . . The wheel? The wheel? "And when did Abraham die, boy?"

"Oh—" Jonason moved fingers helplessly, embarrassed. Dates would be no part of the doctrine. "Long ago. A—a—" He glanced up hopefully. "A thousand years? I think—he who told us to call him Jonas did not teach us that."

"I see. Never mind. You speak well, boy." *Oh, my good Doctor, ex-President—after all! Artist, statesman, student of ethics, agnostic philosopher—all that long life you preached charity and skepticism, courage without the need of faith, the positive uses of the suspended judgment. All so clear, simple, obvious—needing only that little bit more of patience and courage which your human hearers were not ready to give. You must have known they were not, but did you know this would happen?*

Jonas and Abigail—some visionary pair, Brian supposed, full of this theory and that, maybe gone a bit foolish under the horrors of those years. Unthinking admirers of Brown, or perhaps not even that, perhaps just brewing their own syncretism because they thought a religion was needed, and using Brown's name—why? Because it was easy to remember? They probably felt some pride of creation in the job; possibly belief even grew in their own minds as they found the children accepting it and building a ritual life around it.

It was impossible, Brian thought, that Jonas and Abigail could have met the living Abraham Brown. Brown accepted mysteries because he faced the limitations of human intelligence; he had only contempt for the needless making of mysteries. He was without arrogance. No one could have talked five minutes with him without hearing a tranquil: "I don't know."

The *wheel* at Nuber?—but Brian realized he would never learn how Brown actually died. *I hope you suffered no more than most prophets. . . .*

He was pulled from the pit of abstraction by the girl's awed question: "What is that?"

She was pointing to the clay image in its dusty sunlight. Brian was almost deaf to his own words until they were past recovering: "Oh, that—that is very old. Very old and very sacred." She nodded, round-eyed, and stepped back a pace or two. "And that was all they taught you of Abraham Brown?"

Astonished, the boy asked: "Is it not enough?"

There is always the Project. "Why, perhaps—"

"We know all the prayers, Old Man."

"Yes, yes, I'm sure you do."

"The Old Man will come with us." It was not a question.

"Eh?" *There is always the Project . . .* "Come with you?"

"We look for old ones." There was a new note in the young man's fine firm voice, and it was impatience. "We traveled many days, up across the sun-path. We want you to speak the Abraham-words for marriage. The old ones said we must not mate as the animals do without the words. We want—"

"Marry, of course," Brian grumbled. *Poor old Jonas and Abigail, faithful to your century, such as it was!* Brian felt tired and confused, and rubbed a great long-fingered hand across his face so that the words might have come out blurred and dull. "Naturally, kids. Beget. Replenish the earth. I'm damned tired. I don't know any special hocus-pocus—I mean, any Abraham-words—for marriage. Just go ahead and breed. Try again—"

"But the Old Ones said—"

"Wait!" Brian cried. "Wait! Let me think . . . Did he—he who told you to call him Jonas—did he teach you anything about the world as it was in the old days, before you were born?"

"Before—the Old Man makes fun of us."

"No, no." Since he now had to fight down a certain physical fear as well as confusion, Brian spoke more harshly than he intended: "Answer my question! What do you know of the old days? I was a young man once, do you understand that?—as young as you. What do you know about the world I lived in?"

The young man laughed. There was new-born suspicion in him as well as anger, stiffening his shoulders, narrowing his innocent gray eyes. "There was always the world," he said, "ever since God made it a thousand years ago."

"Was there? . . . I was a musician. Do you know what a musician is?"

The young man shook his head lightly, watching Brian, too alertly, watching his hands, aware of him in a new way, no longer humble. Paula sensed the tension and did not like it. She said worriedly, politely: "We forget some of the things they taught us, sa. They were Old Ones. Most of the days they were away from us in places where we were not to go, praying. Old Ones are always praying."

"I will hear this Old Man pray," said Jonason. The butt of the javelin rested against Jonason's foot, the blade swaying from side to side, a waiting snake's head. A misstep, a wrong word—any trifle, Brian knew, could make them decide he was evil and not sacred. Their religion would inevitably require a devil.

He thought also: *It would merely be one of the ways of dying, not the worst.*

"You shall hear me make music," he said sternly, "and you shall be content with that. Come this way!" In fluctuating despair, he was wondering if any good might come of anger. "Come this way! You shall hear a world you never knew."

Naked and ugly, he stalked across the Hall of Music, not looking behind him, though he sensed every glint of light from that bread-knife javelin. "This way!" he shouted. "Come in here!" He flung open the door of the auditorium and strode up on the platform. "Sit down!" he roared at them. "Sit down over there and be quiet, be quiet!"

He thought they did—he could not look at them. He knew he was muttering between his noisy outbursts as he twitched the cover off the piano and raised the lid, muttering bits and fragments from the old times and the new: "They went thataway. . . . Oh, Mr. Van Anda, it just simply goes right through me—I can't express it. Madam, such was my intention, or as Brahms is supposed to have said on a slightly different subject, any ass knows that. . . . Brio, Rubato, and Schmalz went to sea in a—Jonason, Paula, this is a pianoforte; it will not hurt you. Sit there, be quiet, and I pray you listen. . . ."

He found calm. *Now, if ever, when there is living proof that human nature, some sort of human nature, is continuing—now if ever, the Project—*

With the sudden authority that was natural to Andrew Carr, Andrew Carr took over. In the stupendous opening chords of the introduction, Brian very nearly forgot his audience. Not quite. The children had sat down out there in the dusty region where none but ghosts had lingered for twenty-five years, but the piano's first sound brought them to their feet. Brian played through the first four bars, piling the chords like mountains, then held the last one with the pedal and waved his right hand at Jonason and Paula in a furious downward motion.

He thought they understood. He thought he saw them sit down again. But he could pay them no more attention, for the sonata was coming alive under his fingers, waking, growing, rejoicing.

He did not forget the children. They were important, too important, terrifying at the fringe of awareness. But he could not look toward them any more, and presently he shut his eyes.

He had never played like this in the flood of his prime, in the old days, before audiences that loved him. Never.

His eyes were still closed, holding him secure in a world that was not all darkness, when he ended the first movement, paused very briefly, and moved on with complete assurance to explore the depth and height of the second. This was true statement. This was Andrew Carr; he lived, even if after this late morning he might never live again.

And now the third, the storm and the wrath, the interludes of calm, the anger, denials, affirmations . . .

Without hesitation, without awareness of self, of age or pain or danger or loss, Brian was entering on the broad reaches of the last movement when he glanced out into the auditorium and understood the children were gone.

Too big. It had frightened them away. He could visualize them, stealing out with backward looks of panic, and remembering apparently to close the exit door. To them it was incomprehensible thunder. Children—savages—to see or hear or comprehend the beautiful, you must first desire it. he could not think much about them now, when Andrew Carr was still with him. He played on with the same assurance, the same sense of victory. Children and savages, so let them go, with leave and goodwill.

Some external sound troubled him, something that must have begun under cover of these rising, pealing octave passages—storm waves, each higher than the last, until even the superhuman swimmer must be exhausted. It was some indefinable alien noise, a humming. Wind perhaps. Brian shook his head in irritation, not interrupting the work of his hands. It couldn't matter—everything was here, in the labors his hands still had to perform. The waves were growing more quiet, subsiding, and he must play the curious arpeggios he had never quite understood—but for this interpretation he understood them. Rip them out of the piano like showers of sparks, like distant lightning moving farther and farther away across a world that could never be at rest.

The final section at last. Why, it was a variation—and why had he never quite recognized it?—on a theme of Brahms, from the German Requiem. Quite plain, simple—Brahms would have approved. *Blessed are the dead . . .* Something more remained to be said, and Brian searched for it through the mighty unfolding of the finale. No hurrying, no crashing impatience any more, but a moving through time without fear of time, through radiance and darkness with no fear of either. *That they may rest from their labors, and their works do follow after them.*

Brian stood up, swaying and out of breath. So the music was over, and the children were gone, but a jangling, humming confusion was filling the Hall of Music out there—hardly a wind—distant but entering with some violence even here, now that the piano was silent. He moved stiffly out of the small auditorium, more or less knowing what he would find.

The noise became immense, the unchecked overtones of the marimba fuming and quivering as the smooth, high ceiling of the Hall of Music caught them and flung them about against the answering strings of pianos and harps and violins, the sulky membranes of drums, the nervous brass of cymbals.

The girl was playing it. Brian laughed once, softly, in the shadows, and was not heard. She had hit on a primeval rhythm natural for children or savages and needed nothing else, banging it out on one stone and another, wanting no rest or variation.

The boy was dancing, slapping his feet and pounding his chest, thrusting out his javelin in time to the clamor, edging up to his companion, grimacing, drawing back in order to return. Neither one was laughing, or close to laughter. Their faces were savage-solemn, grim with the excitement and healthy lust. All as spontaneous as the drumming of partridges. It was a long time before they saw Brian in the shadows.

Reaction was swift. The girl dropped the hammer. The boy froze, his javelin raised, then jerked his head at Paula, who snatched at something—only moments later did Brian understand she had taken the clay image before she fled.

Jonason covered her retreat, stepping backward, his face blank and dangerous with fear. So swiftly, so easily, by grace of great civilized music and a few wrong words, had a sacred Old One become a Bad Old One.

They were gone, down the stairway, leaving the echo of Brian's voice crying: "Don't go! Please don't go!"

Brian followed them. Unwillingly. He was slow to reach the bottom of the stairway; there he looked across the shut-in water to his raft, which they had used and left at the windowsill port. Brian had never been a good swimmer, and would not attempt it now, but clutched the rope and hitched himself hand over hand to the windowsill, collapsing awhile until he found strength to scramble into his canoe and grope for the paddle.

The children's canoe was already far off. Heading up the river, the boy paddling with deep powerful strokes. Up the river, of course. They had to find the right kind of Old Ones. Up across the sun-path.

Brian dug his blade in the quiet water. For a time his rugged, ancient muscles were willing. There was sap in them yet. Perhaps he was gaining. He shouted hugely: "Bring back my two-faced god! And what about my music? You? Did you like it? Speak up!"

They must have heard his voice booming at them. At least the girl looked back, once. The boy, intent on his paddling, did not. Brian roared: "Bring back my little god!"

He was not gaining on them. After all they had a mission. They had to find an Old One with the right Abraham-words. Brian thought: *Damn it, hasn't MY world some rights? We'll see about this!*

He lifted his paddle like a spear, and flung it, knowing even as his shoulder winced with the backlash of the thrust that his action was at the outer limit of absurdity. The children were so far away that even an arrow from a bow might not have reached them. The paddle splashed in the water. Not far away. A small infinity.

It swung about, adjusting to the current, the heavy end pointing downstream, obeying the river and the ebb tide. It nuzzled companionably against a gray-faced chunk of driftwood, diverting it, so that presently the chunk floated into Brian's reach. He flung it back toward the paddle, hoping it might fall on the other side and send the paddle near him, but it fell short. In his unexpectedly painless extremity Brian was not surprised, but merely watched the gray face floating and bobbing along beside him out of reach, and his irritation became partly friendliness. The driftwood fragment suggested the face of a music critic he had once met—New Boston, was it? Denver? London?—no matter.

"Why," he said aloud, detachedly observing the passage of his canoe beyond the broad morning shadow of the Museum, "why, I seem to have killed myself."

"Mr. Van Anda has abundantly demonstrated a mastery of the instrument and of the"—*Oh, go play solfeggio on your linotype!*—"literature of both classic and contemporary repertory. While we cannot endorse the perhaps overemotional quality of his Bach, and there might easily be two views of his handling of the passage in double thirds which—"

"I can't swim it, you know," said Brian. "Not against the ebb, that's for sure."

"—so that on the whole one feels he has earned himself a not discreditable place among—" Gaining on the canoe, passing it, the gray-faced chip moved on benignly twittering toward the open sea, where the canoe must follow. With a final remnant of strength Brian inched forward to the bow and gathered the full force of his lungs to shout up the river to the children: "Go in peace!"

They could not have heard him. They were too far away, and a new morning wind was blowing, fresh and sweet, out of the northwest.

H. G. Wells

H. G. Wells (1866–1946) is the Shakespeare of science fiction: not the first SF writer but, thus far, the best. H. G. Wells is simply the most important writer to influence—both directly, through his works, and indirectly, through the other major writers in his tradition—the course of science fiction in its formative decades. His influence transformed, in the long run, all later science fiction, and his shadow grows longer as the century ends.

The implications of Darwinian evolution and social criticism are the major themes of his works and his principal novels, *The Time Machine* (1895), *The Island of Dr. Moreau* (1896), *The Invisible Man* (1897), *The War of the Worlds* (1898), *When the Sleeper Wakes* (1899), and *The First Men in the Moon* (1901), as well as five collections of short stories later combined as *The Short Stories of H. G. Wells* (1927). A popular and influential intellectual throughout the first half of the twentieth century, he was devoted to the idea of progress. He became arguably the most famous living writer in the English language, but at the cost of his literary reputation as a modernist artist, which he ceded to Henry James after years of argument, in favor of bestseller popularity.

Although Wells lived until 1946, he was never personally associated with genre science fiction; nonetheless, many of his stories were reprinted in the early years of *Amazing Stories* as paradigms of the new kind of fiction that editor Hugo Gernsback wished to bring forth. Wells called himself a Scientific Romancer early in his career, and his fiction was certainly the pinnacle of that genre that preceded science fiction and existed parallel to it into the 1940s in the works of Olaf Stapledon, Aldous Huxley, Evgeny Zamiatin, Karel Čapek, and George Orwell (to name only the five most important writers influenced by Wells's early works).

Kingsley Amis, in his literate, opinionated, and now somewhat neglected study of science fiction, *New Maps of Hell* (1960), comments on the (quite surprising) virtual exclusion of some of Wells's work from the SF canon, including "A Story of the Days to Come," which Amis calls "an early and lively piece . . . it forecasts the modern satirical utopia with fantastic exactness." He summarizes the many accurate prophecies of the story, concluding that "quite likely Wells will soon get all, instead of part, of the recognition as a pioneer he clearly deserves."

"A Story of the Days to Come" is actually a kind of compressed novel by Wells, and yields many unexpected pleasures. Zamiatin calls it "the sharpest, most ironic of Wells's grotesques." It is the story of two young lovers who reject the technological future for pastoral bliss, and learn better.

A STORY OF THE DAYS TO COME

I. THE CURE FOR LOVE

The excellent Mr. Morris was an Englishman, and he lived in the days of Queen Victoria the Good. He was a prosperous and very sensible man; he read *The Times* and went to church, and as he grew towards middle age an expression of quiet contented contempt for all who were not as himself settled on his face. He was one of those people who do everything that is right and proper and sensible with inevitable regularity. He always wore just the right and proper clothes, steering the narrow way between the smart and the shabby, always subscribed to the right charities, just the judicious compromise between ostentation and meanness, and never failed to have his hair cut to exactly the proper length.

Everything that it was right and proper for a man in his position to possess, he possessed; and everything that it was not right and proper for a man in his position to possess, he did not possess.

And among other right and proper possessions, this Mr. Morris had a wife and children. They were the right sort of wife, and the right sort and number of children, of course; nothing imaginative or highty-flighty about any of them, so far as Mr. Morris could see; they wore perfectly correct clothing, neither smart nor hygienic nor faddy in any way, but just sensible; and they lived in a nice sensible house in the later Victorian sham Queen Anne style of architecture, with sham half-timbering of chocolate-painted plaster in the gables, Lincrusta Walton sham carved oakpanels, a terrace of terra cotta to imitate stone, and cathedral glass in the front door. His boys went to good solid schools, and were put to respectable professions; his girls, in spite of a fantastic protest or so, were all married to suitable, steady, oldish young men with good prospects. And when it was a fit and proper thing for him to do so, Mr. Morris died. His tomb was of marble, and, without any art nonsense or laudatory inscription, quietly imposing—such being the fashion of his time.

He underwent various changes according to the accepted custom in these cases, and long before this story begins his bones even had become dust, and were scattered to the four quarters of heaven. And his sons and his grandsons and his great-grandsons and great-great-grandsons, they too were dust and ashes, and were scattered likewise. It was a thing he could not have imagined, that a day would come when even his great-great-grandsons would be scattered to the four winds of heaven. If any one had suggested it to him he would have resented it. He was one of those worthy people who take no interest in the future of mankind at all. He had grave doubts, indeed, if there was any future for mankind after he was dead.

It seemed quite impossible and quite uninteresting to imagine anything happening after he was dead. Yet the thing was so, and when even his great-great-grandson was dead and decayed and forgotten, when the sham half-timbered house had gone the way of all shams, and *The Times* was extinct, and the silk hat a ridiculous antiquity, and the modestly imposing stone that had been sacred to Mr. Morris had been burnt to make lime for mortar, and all that Mr. Morris had found real and important was sere and dead, the world was still going on, and people were still going about it, just as heedless and impatient of the Future, or, indeed, of anything but their own selves and property, as Mr. Morris had been.

And, strange to tell, and much as Mr. Morris would have been angered if any one had foreshadowed it to him, all over the world there were scattered a multitude of people, filled with the breath of life, in whose veins the blood of Mr. Morris flowed. Just as some day the life which is gathered now in the reader of this very story may also be scattered far and wide about this world, and mingled with a thousand alien strains, beyond all thought and tracing.

And among the descendants of this Mr. Morris was one almost as sensible and clear-headed as his ancestor. He had just the same stout, short frame as that ancient man of the nineteenth century, from whom his name of Morris— he spelt it Mwres—came; he had the same half-contemptuous expression of face. He was a prosperous person, too, as times went, and he disliked the "new-fangled," and bothers about the future and the lower classes, just as much as the ancestral Morris had done. He did not read *The Times*: indeed, he did not know there ever had been a *Times*—that institution had foundered somewhere in the intervening gulf of years; but the phonograph machine, that talked to him as he made his toilet of a morning, might have been the voice of a reincarnated Blowitz when it dealt with the world's affairs. This phonographic machine was the size and shape of a Dutch clock, and down the front of it were electric barometric indicators, and an electric clock and calendar, and automatic engagement reminders, and where the clock would have been was the mouth of a trumpet. When it had news the trumpet gobbled like a turkey, "Galloop, galloop," and then brayed out its message as, let us say, a trumpet might bray. It would tell Mwres in full, rich, throaty tones about the overnight accidents to the omnibus flying-machines that plied around the world, the latest arrivals at the fashionable resorts in Tibet, and of all the great monopolist company meetings of the day before, while he was dressing. If Mwres did not like hearing what it said, he had only to touch a stud, and it would choke a little and talk about something else.

Of course his toilet differed very much from that of his ancestor. It is doubtful which would have been the more shocked and pained to find himself in the clothing of the other. Mwres would certainly have sooner gone forth to the world stark naked than in the silk hat, frock coat, grey trousers and watch-chain that had filled Mr. Morris with sombre self-respect in the past. For Mwres there was no shaving to do: a skilful operator had long ago removed every hair-root from his face. His legs he encased in pleasant pink and amber garments of an airtight material, which with the help of an ingenious little pump he distended so as to suggest enormous muscles. Above this he also wore pneumatic garments beneath an amber silk tunic, so that he was clothed in air and admirably protected against sudden extremes of heat or cold. Over this he flung a scarlet cloak with its edge fantastically curved. On his head, which had been skilfully deprived of every scrap of hair, he adjusted a pleasant little cap of bright scarlet, held on by suction and inflated with hydrogen, and curiously like the comb of a cock. So his toilet was complete; and, conscious of being soberly and becomingly attired, he was ready to face his fellow-beings with a tranquil eye.

This Mwres—the civility of "Mr." had vanished ages ago—was one of the officials under the Wind Vane and Waterfall Trust, the great company that owned every wind wheel and waterfall in the world, and which pumped all the water and supplied all the electric energy that people in these latter days required. He lived in a vast hotel near that part of London called Seventh Way, and had very large and comfortable apartments on the seventeenth floor. Households and family life had long since disappeared with the progressive refinement of manners; and indeed the steady rise in rents and land values, the disappearance of domestic servants, the elaboration of cookery, had rendered the separate domicile of Victorian times impossible, even had any one desired such a savage seclusion. When his toilet was completed he went towards one of the two doors of his apartment—there were doors at opposite ends, each marked with a huge arrow pointing one one way and one the other—touched a stud to open it, and emerged on a wide passage, the centre of which bore chairs and was moving at a steady pace to the left. On some of these chairs were seated gaily-dressed men and women. He nodded to an acquaintance—it was not in those days etiquette to talk before breakfast—and seated himself on one of these chairs, and in a few seconds he had been carried to the doors of a lift, by which he descended to the great and splendid hall in which his breakfast would be automatically served.

It was a very different meal from a Victorian breakfast. The rude masses of bread needing to be carved and smeared over with animal fat before they could be made palatable, the still recognisable fragments of recently killed animals, hideously charred and hacked, the eggs torn ruthlessly from beneath some protesting hen,—such things as these, though they constituted the ordinary fare of Victorian times, would have awakened only horror and disgust in the refined minds of the people of these latter days. Instead were pastes and cakes of agreeable and variegated design, without any suggestion in colour or form of the unfortunate animals from which their substance and juices were derived. They appeared on little dishes sliding out upon a rail from a little box at one side of the table. The surface of the table, to judge by touch and eye, would have appeared to a nineteenth-century person to be covered with fine white damask, but this was really an oxidised metallic surface, and could be cleaned instantly after a meal. There were hundreds of such little tables in the hall, and at most of them were other latter-day citizens singly or in groups. And as Mwres seated himself before his elegant repast, the invisible orchestra, which had been resting during an interval, resumed and filled the air with music.

But Mwres did not display any great interest either in his breakfast or the music; his eye wandered incessantly about the hall, as though he expected a belated guest. At last he rose eagerly and waved his hand, and simultaneously across the hall appeared a tall dark figure in a costume of yellow and olive green. As this person, walking amidst the tables with measured steps, drew near, the pallid earnestness of his face and the unusual intensity of his eyes became apparent. Mwres reseated himself and pointed to a chair beside him.

"I feared you would never come," he said. In spite of the intervening space of time, the English language was still almost exactly the same as it had been in England under Victoria the Good. The invention of the phonograph and such like means of recording sound, and the gradual replacement of books by such contrivances, had not only saved the human eyesight from decay, but had also by the establishment of a sure standard arrested the process of change in accent that had hitherto been so inevitable.

"I was delayed by an interesting case," said the man in green and yellow. "A prominent politician—ahem!—suffering from overwork." He glanced at the breakfast and seated himself. "I have been awake for forty hours."

"Eh dear!" said Mwres: "fancy that! You hypnotists have your work to do."

The hypnotist helped himself to some attractive amber-coloured jelly. "I happen to be a good deal in request," he said modestly.

"Heaven knows what we should do without you."

"Oh! we're not so indispensable as all that," said the hypnotist, ruminating the flavour of the jelly. "The world did very well without us for some thousands of years. Two hundred years ago even—not one! In practice, that is. Physicians by the thousand, of course—frightfully clumsy brutes for the most part, and following one another like sheep—but doctors of the mind except a few empirical flounderers there were none."

He concentrated his mind on the jelly.

"But were people so sane—?" began Mwres.

The hypnotist shook his head. "It didn't matter then if they were a bit silly or faddy. Life was so easy-going then. No competition worth speaking of—no pressure. A human being had to be very lopsided before anything happened. Then, you know, they clapped 'em away in what they called a lunatic asylum."

"I know," said Mwres. "In these confounded historical romances that every one is listening to, they always rescue a beautiful girl from an asylum or something of the sort. I don't know if you attend to that rubbish."

"I must confess I do," said the hypnotist. "It carries one out of oneself to hear of those quaint, adventurous, half-civilised days of the nineteenth century, when men were stout and women simple. I like a good swaggering story before all things. Curious times they were, with their smutty railways and puffing old iron trains, their rum little houses and their horse vehicles. I suppose you don't read books?"

"Dear, no!" said Mwres. "I went to a modern school and we had none of that old-fashioned nonsense. Phonographs are good enough for me."

"Of course," said the hypnotist, "of course"; and surveyed the table for his next choice. "You know," he said, helping himself to a dark blue confection that promised well, "in those days our business was scarcely thought of. I daresay if any one had told them that in two hundred years' time a class of men would be entirely occupied in impressing things upon the memory, effacing unpleasant ideas, controlling and overcoming instinctive but undesirable impulses, and so forth, by means of hypnotism, they would have refused to believe the thing possible. Few people knew that an order made during a mesmeric trance, even an order to forget or an order to desire, could be given so as to be obeyed after the trance was over. Yet there were men alive then who could have told them the thing was as absolutely certain to come about as—well, the transit of Venus."

"They knew of hypnotism, then?"

"Oh, dear, yes! They used it—for painless dentistry and things like that! This blue stuff is confoundedly good: what is it?"

"Haven't the faintest idea," said Mwres, "but I admit it's very good. Take some more."

The hypnotist repeated his praises, and there was an appreciative pause.

"Speaking of these historical romances," said Mwres, with an attempt at an easy, off-hand manner, "brings me—ah—to the matter I—ah—had in mind when I asked you—when I expressed a wish to see you." He paused and took a deep breath.

The hypnotist turned an attentive eye upon him, and continued eating.

"The fact is," said Mwres, "I have a—in fact a—daughter. Well, you know I have given her—ah—every educational advantage. Lectures—not a solitary lecturer of ability in the world but she has had a telephone direct, dancing, deportment, conversation, philosophy, art criticism. . . ." He indicated catholic culture by a gesture of his hand. "I had intended her to marry a very good friend of mine—Bindon of the Lighting Commission—plain little man, you know, and a bit unpleasant in some of his ways, but an excellent fellow really—an excellent fellow."

"Yes," said the hypnotist, "go on. How old is she?"

"Eighteen."

"A dangerous age. Well?"

"Well: it seems that she has been indulging in these historical romances—excessively. Excessively. Even to the neglect of her philosophy. Filled her mind with unutterable nonsense about soldiers who fight—what is it?—Etruscans?"

"Egyptians."

"Egyptians—very probably. Hack about with swords and revolvers and things—blood-shed galore—horrible!—and about young men on torpedo catchers who blow up—Spaniards, I fancy—and all sorts of irregular adventurers. And she has got it into her head that she must marry for Love, and that poor little Bindon—"

"I've met similar cases," said the hypnotist. "Who is the other young man?"

Mwres maintained an appearance of resigned calm. "You may well ask," he said. "He is"—and his voice sank with shame—"a mere attendant upon the stage on which the flying-machines from Paris alight. He has—as they say in the romances—good looks. He is quite young and very eccentric. Affects the antique—he can read and write! So can she. And instead of communicating by telephone, like sensible people, they write and deliver—what is it?"

"Notes?"

"No—not notes. . . . Ah—poems."

The hypnotist raised his eyebrows. "How did she meet him?"

"Tripped coming down from the flying-machine from Paris—and fell into his arms. The mischief was done in a moment!"

"Yes?"

"Well—that's all. Things must be stopped. That is what I want to consult you about. What must be done? What *can* be done? Of course I'm not a hypnotist; my knowledge is limited. But you—?"

"Hypnotism is not magic," said the man in green, putting both arms on the table.

"Oh, precisely! But still—!"

"People cannot be hypnotised without their consent. If she is able to stand out against marrying Bindon, she will probably stand out against being hypnotised. But if once she can be hypnotised—even by somebody else—the thing is done."

"You can—?"

"Oh, certainly! Once we get her amenable, then we can suggest that she *must* marry Bindon—that that is her fate; or that the young man is repulsive, and that when she sees him she will be giddy and faint, or any little thing of that sort. Or if we can get her into a sufficiently profound trance we can suggest that she should forget him altogether—"

"Precisely."

"But the problem is to get her hypnotised. Of course no sort of proposal or suggestion must come from you—because no doubt she already distrusts you in the matter."

The hypnotist leant his head upon his arm and thought.

"It's hard a man cannot dispose of his own daughter," said Mwres irrelevantly.

"You must give me the name and address of the young lady," said the hypnotist, "and any information bearing upon the matter. And, by the bye, is there any money in the affair?"

Mwres hesitated.

"There's a sum—in fact, a considerable sum—invested in the Patent Road Company. From her mother. That's what makes the thing so exasperating."

"Exactly," said the hypnotist. And he proceeded to cross-examine Mwres on the entire affair.

It was a lengthy interview.

And meanwhile "Elizebeθ Mwres," as she spelt her name or "Elizabeth Morris," as a nineteenth-century person would have put it, was sitting in a quiet waiting-place beneath the great stage upon which the flying-machine from Paris descended. And beside her sat her slender, handsome lover reading her the poem he had written that morning while on duty upon the stage. When he had finished they sat for a time in silence; and then, as if for their special entertainment, the great machine that had come flying through the air from America that morning rushed down out of the sky.

At first it was a little oblong, faint and blue amidst the distant fleecy clouds; and then it grew swiftly large and white, and larger and whiter, until they could see the separate tiers of sails, each hundreds of feet wide, and the lank body they supported, and at last even the swinging seats of the passengers in a dotted row. Although it was falling it seemed to them to be rushing up the sky, and over the roof-spaces of the city below its shadow leapt towards them. They heard the whistling rush of the air about it and its yelling siren, shrill and swelling, to warn those who were on its landing-stage of its arrival. And abruptly the note fell down a couple of octaves, and it had passed, and the sky was clear and void, and she could turn her sweet eyes again to Denton at her side.

Their silence ended; and Denton, speaking in a little language of broken English that was, they fancied, their private possession—though lovers have used such little languages since the world began—told her how they too would leap into the air one morning out of all the obstacles and difficulties about them, and fly to a sunlit city of delight he knew of in Japan, half-way about the world.

She loved the dream, but she feared the leap; and she put him off with "Some day, dearest one, some day," to all his pleading that it might be soon; and at last came a shrilling of whistles, and it was time for him to go back to his duties on the stage. They parted—as lovers have been wont to part for thousands of years. She walked down a passage to a lift, and so came to one of the streets of that latter-day London, all glazed in with glass from the weather, and with incessant moving platforms that went to all parts of the city. And by one of these she returned to her apartments in the Hotel for Women where she lived, the apartments that were in telephonic communication with all the best lecturers in the world. But the sunlight of the flying stage was in her heart, and the wisdom of all the best lecturers in the world seemed folly in that light.

She spent the middle part of the day in the gymnasium, and took her midday meal with two other girls and their common chaperone—for it was still the custom to have a chaperone in the case of motherless girls of the more prosperous classes. The chaperone had a visitor that day, a man in green and yellow, with a white face and vivid eyes, who talked amazingly. Among other things, he fell to praising a new historical romance that one of the great popular story-tellers of the day had just put forth. It was, of course, about the spacious times of Queen Victoria; and the author, among other pleasing novelties, made a little argument before each section of the story, in imitation of the chapter headings of the old-fashioned books: as for example, "How the Cabmen of Pimlico stopped the Victoria Omnibuses, and of the Great Fight in Palace Yard," and "How the Piccadilly Policeman was slain in the midst of his Duty." The man in green and yellow praised this innovation. "These pithy sentences," he said, "are admirable. They show at a glance those headlong, tumultuous times, when men and animals jostled in the filthy streets, and death might wait for one at every corner. Life was life then! How great the world must have seemed then! How marvellous! There were still parts of the world absolutely unexplored. Nowadays we have almost abolished wonder, we lead lives so trim and orderly that courage, endurance, faith, all the noble virtues seem fading from mankind."

And so on, taking the girls' thoughts with him, until the life they led, life in the vast and intricate London of the twenty-second century, a life interspersed with soaring excursions to every part of the globe, seemed to them a monotonous misery compared with the dædal past.

At first Elizabeth did not join in the conversation, but after a time the subject became so interesting that she made a few shy interpolations. But he scarcely seemed to notice her as he talked. He went on to describe a new method of entertaining people. They were hypnotised, and then suggestions were made to them so skilfully that they seemed to be living in ancient times again. They played out a little romance in the past as vivid as reality, and when at last they awakened they remembered all they had been through as though it were a real thing.

"It is a thing we have sought to do for years and years," said the hypnotist. "It is practically an artificial dream. And we know the way at last. Think of all it opens out to us—the enrichment of our experience, the recovery of adventure, the refuge it offers from this sordid, competitive life in which we live! Think!"

"And you can do that!" said the chaperone eagerly.

"The thing is possible at last," the hypnotist said. "You may order a dream as you wish."

The chaperone was the first to be hypnotised, and the dream, she said, was wonderful, when she came to again.

The other two girls, encouraged by her enthusiasm, also placed themselves in the hands of the hypnotist and had plunges into the romantic past. No one suggested that Elizabeth should try this novel entertainment; it was at her own request at last that she was taken into that land of dreams where there is neither any freedom or choice nor will. . . .

And so the mischief was done.

One day, when Denton went down to that quiet seat beneath the flying stage, Elizabeth was not in her wonted place. He was disappointed, and a little angry. The next day she did not come, and the next also. He was afraid. To hide his fear from himself, he set to work to write sonnets for her when she should come again. . . .

For three days he fought against his dread by such distraction, and then the truth was before him clear and cold, and would not be denied. She might be ill, she might be dead; but he would not believe that he had been betrayed. There followed a week of misery. And then he knew she was the only thing on earth worth having, and that he must seek her, however hopeless the search, until she was found once more.

He had some small private means of his own, and so he threw over his appointment on the flying stage, and set himself to find this girl who had become at last all the world to him. He did not know where she lived, and little of her circumstances; for it had been part of the delight of her girlish romance that he should know nothing of her, nothing of the difference of their station. The ways of the city opened before him east and west, north and south. Even in Victorian days London was a maze, that little London with its poor four millions of people; but the London he explored, the London of the twenty-second century, was a London of thirty million souls. At first he was energetic and headlong, taking time neither to eat nor sleep. He sought for weeks and months, he went through every imaginable phase of fatigue and despair, over-excitement and anger. Long after hope was dead, by the sheer inertia of his desire he still went to and fro, peering into faces and looking this way and that, in the incessant ways and lifts and passages of that interminable hive of men.

At last chance was kind to him, and he saw her.

It was in a time of festivity. He was hungry; he had paid the inclusive fee and had gone into one of the gigantic dining-places of the city; he was pushing his way among the tables and scrutinising by mere force of habit every group he passed.

He stood still, robbed of all power of motion, his eyes wide, his lips apart. Elizabeth sat scarcely twenty yards away from him, looking straight at him. Her eyes were as hard to him, as hard and expressionless and void of recognition, as the eyes of a statue.

She looked at him for a moment, and then her gaze passed beyond him.

Had he had only her eyes to judge by he might have doubted if it was indeed Elizabeth, but he knew her by the gesture of her hand, by the grace of a wanton little curl that floated over her ear as she moved her head. Something was said to her, and she turned smiling tolerantly to the man beside her, a little man in foolish raiment knobbed and spiked like some old reptile with pneumatic horns—the Bindon of her father's choice.

For a moment Denton stood white and wild-eyed; then came a terrible faintness, and he sat before one of the little tables. He sat down with his back to her, and for a time he did not dare to look at her again. When at last he did, she and Bindon and two other people were standing up to go. The others were her father and her chaperone.

He sat as if incapable of action until the four figures were remote and small, and then he rose up possessed with the one idea of pursuit. For a space he feared he had lost them, and then he came upon Elizabeth and her chaperone again in one of the streets of moving platforms that intersected the city. Bindon and Mwres had disappeared.

He could not control himself to patience. He felt he must speak to her forthwith, or die. He pushed forward to where they were seated, and sat down beside them. His white face was convulsed with half-hysterical excitement.

He laid his hand on her wrist. "Elizabeth?" he said.

She turned in unfeigned astonishment. Nothing but the fear of a strange man showed in her face.

"Elizabeth," he cried, and his voice was strange to him: "dearest—you *know* me?"

Elizabeth's face showed nothing but alarm and perplexity. She drew herself away from him. The chaperone, a little grey-headed woman with mobile features, leant forward to intervene. Her resolute bright eyes examined Denton. "What do you say?" she asked.

"This young lady," said Denton,—"she knows me."

"Do you know him, dear?"

"No," said Elizabeth in a strange voice, and with a hand to her forehead, speaking almost as one who repeats a lesson. "No, I do not know him. I *know*—I do not know him."

"But—but . . . Not know me! It is I—Denton. Denton! To whom you used to talk. Don't you remember the flying stages? The little seat in the open air? The verses—"

"No," cried Elizabeth,—"no. I do not know him. I do not know him. There is something . . . But I don't know. All I know is that I do not know him." Her face was a face of infinite distress.

The sharp eyes of the chaperone flitted to and fro from the girl to the man. "You see?" she said, with the faint shadow of a smile. "She does not know you."

"I do not know you," said Elizabeth. "Of that I am sure."

"But, dear—the songs—the little verses—"

"She does not know you," said the chaperone. "You must not . . . You have made a mistake. You must not go on talking to us after that. You must not annoy us on the public ways."

"But—" said Denton, and for a moment his miserably haggard face appealed against fate.

"You must not persist, young man," protested the chaperone.

"*Elizabeth!*" he cried.

Her face was the face of one who is tormented. "I do not know you," she cried, hand to brow. "Oh, I do not know you!"

For an instant Denton sat stunned. Then he stood up and groaned aloud.

He made a strange gesture of appeal towards the remote glass roof of the public way, then turned and went plunging recklessly from one moving platform to another, and vanished amidst the swarms of people going to and fro thereon. The chaperone's eyes followed him, and then she looked at the curious faces about her.

"Dear," asked Elizabeth, clasping her hand, and too deeply moved to heed observation, "who was that man? Who *was* that man?"

The chaperone raised her eyebrows. She spoke in a clear, audible voice. "Some half-witted creature. I have never set eyes on him before."

"Never?"

"Never, dear. Do not trouble your mind about a thing like this."

And soon after this the celebrated hypnotist who dressed in green and yellow had another client. The young man paced his consulting-room, pale and disordered. "I want to forget," he cried. "I *must* forget."

The hypnotist watched him with quiet eyes, studied his face and clothes and bearing. "To forget anything—pleasure or pain—is to be, by so much—*less*. However, you know your own concern. My fee is high."

"If only I can forget—"

"That's easy enough with you. You wish it. I've done much harder things. Quite recently. I hardly expected to do it: the thing was done against the will of the hypnotised person. A love affair too—like yours. A girl. So rest assured."

The young man came and sat beside the hypnotist. His manner was a forced calm. He looked into the hypnotist's eyes. "I will tell you. Of course you will want to know what it is. There was a girl. Her name was Elizabeth Mwres. Well . . ."

He stopped. He had seen the instant surprise on the hypnotist's face. In that instant he knew. He stood up. He seemed to dominate the seated figure by his side. He gripped the shoulder of green and gold. For a time he could not find words.

"*Give her me back!*" he said at last. "Give her me back!"

"What do you mean?" gasped the hypnotist.

"Give her me back."

"Give whom?"

"Elizabeth Mwres—the girl—"

The hypnotist tried to free himself; he rose to his feet. Denton's grip tightened.

"Let go!" cried the hypnotist, thrusting an arm against Denton's chest.

In a moment the two men were locked in a clumsy wrestle. Neither had the slightest training—for athleticism, except for exhibition and to afford opportunity for betting, had faded out of the earth—but Denton was not only the younger but the stronger of the two. They swayed across the room, and then the hypnotist had gone down under his antagonist. They fell together. . . .

Denton leaped to his feet, dismayed at his own fury; but the hypnotist lay still, and suddenly from a little white mark where his forehead had struck a stool shot a hurrying band of red. For a space Denton stood over him irresolute, trembling.

A fear of the consequences entered his gently nurtured mind. He turned towards the door. "No," he said aloud, and came back to the middle of the room. Overcoming the instinctive repugnance of one who had seen no act of violence in all his life before, he knelt down beside his antagonist and felt his heart. Then he peered at the wound. He rose quickly and looked about him. He began to see more of the situation.

When presently the hypnotist recovered his senses, his head ached severely, his back was against Denton's knees and Denton was sponging his face.

The hypnotist did not speak. But presently he indicated by a gesture that in his opinion he had been sponged enough. "Let me get up," he said.

"Not yet," said Denton.

"You have assaulted me, you scoundrel!"

"We are alone," said Denton, "and the door is secure."

There was an interval of thought.

"Unless I sponge," said Denton, "your forehead will develop a tremendous bruise."

"You can go on sponging," said the hypnotist sulkily.

There was another pause.

"We might be in the Stone Age," said the hypnotist. "Violence! Struggle!"

"In the Stone Age no man dared to come between man and woman," said Denton.

The hypnotist thought again.

"What are you going to do?" he asked.

"While you were insensible I found the girl's address on your tablets. I did not know it before. I telephoned. She will be here soon. Then—"

"She will bring her chaperone."

"That is all right."

"But what—? I don't see. What do you mean to do?"

"I looked about for a weapon also. It is an astonishing thing how few weapons there are nowadays. If you consider that in the Stone Age men owned scarcely anything *but* weapons. I hit at last upon this lamp. I have wrenched off the wires and things, and I hold it so." He extended it over the hypnotist's shoulders. "With that I can quite easily smash your skull. I *will*—unless you do as I tell you."

"Violence is no remedy," said the hypnotist, quoting from the "Modern Man's Book of Moral Maxims."

"It's an undesirable disease," said Denton.

"Well?"

"You will tell that chaperone you are going to order the girl to marry that knobby little brute with the red hair and ferrety eyes. I believe that's how things stand?"

"Yes—that's how things stand."

"And, pretending to do that, you will restore her memory of me."

"It's unprofessional."

"Look here! If I cannot have that girl I would rather die than not. I don't propose to respect your little fancies. If anything goes wrong you shall not live five minutes. This is a rude makeshift of a weapon, and it may quite conceivably be painful to kill you. But I will. It is unusual, I know, nowadays to do things like this—mainly because there is so little in life that is worth being violent about."

"The chaperone will see you directly she comes—"

"I shall stand in that recess. Behind you."

The hypnotist thought. "You are a determined young man," he said, "and only half civilised. I have tried to to my duty to my client, but in this affair you seem likely to get your own way. . . ."

"You mean to deal straightly."

"I'm not going to risk having my brains scattered in a petty affair like this."

"And afterwards?"

"There is nothing a hypnotist or doctor hates so much as a scandal. I at least am no savage. I am annoyed. . . . But in a day or so I shall bear no malice. . . ."

"Thank you. And now that we understand each other, there is no necessity to keep you sitting any longer on the floor."

II. THE VACANT COUNTRY

The world, they say, changed more between the year 1800 and the year 1900 than it had done in the previous five hundred years. That century, the nineteenth century, was the dawn of a new epoch in the history of mankind—the epoch of the great cities, the end of the old order of country life.

In the beginning of the nineteenth century the majority of mankind still lived upon the countryside, as their way of life had been for countless generations. All over the world they dwelt in little towns and villages then, and engaged either directly in agriculture, or in occupations that were of service to the agriculturist. They travelled rarely, and dwelt close to their work, because swift means of transit had not yet come. The few who travelled went either on foot, or in slow sailing-ships, or by means of jogging horses incapable of more than sixty miles a day. Think of it!—sixty miles a day. Here and there, in those sluggish times, a town grew a little larger than its neighbours, as a port or as a centre of government; but all the towns in the world with more than a hundred thousand inhabitants could be counted on a man's fingers. So it was in the beginning of the nineteenth century. By the end, the invention of railways, telegraphs, steam-ships, and complex agricultural machinery, had changed all these things: changed them beyond all hope of return. The vast shops, the varied pleasures, the count-less conveniences of the larger towns were suddenly possible, and no sooner existed than they were brought into competition with the homely resources of the rural centres. Mankind were drawn to the cities by an overwhelming attrac-tion. The demand for labour fell with the increase of machinery, the local mar-kets were entirely superseded, and there was a rapid growth of the larger centres at the expense of the open country.

The flow of population townward was the constant preoccupation of Victorian writers. In Great Britain and New England, in India and China, the same thing was remarked: everywhere a few swollen towns were visibly replacing the ancient order. That this was an inevitable result of improved means of travel and trans-port—that, given swift means of transit, these things must be—was realised by few; and the most puerile schemes were devised to overcome the mysterious magnetism of the urban centres, and keep the people on the land.

Yet the developments of the nineteenth century were only the dawning of the new order. The first great cities of the new time were horribly inconvenient, darkened by smoky fogs, insanitary and noisy; but the discovery of new methods of building, new methods of heating, changed all this. Between 1900 and 2000 the march of change was still more rapid; and between 2000 and 2100 the continually accelerated progress of human invention made the reign of Victoria the Good seem at last an almost incredible vision of idyllic tranquil days.

The introduction of railways was only the first step in that development of those means of locomotion which finally revolutionised human life. By the year 2000 railways and roads had vanished together. The railways, robbed of their rails, had become weedy ridges and ditches upon the face of the world; the old roads, strange barbaric tracks of flint and soil, hammered by hand or rolled by rough iron rollers, strewn with miscellaneous filth, and cut by iron hoofs and wheels into ruts and puddles often many inches deep, had been replaced by patent tracks made of a substance called Eadhamite. This Eadhamite—it was named after its patentee—ranks with the invention of printing and steam as one of the epoch-making discoveries of the world's history.

When Eadham discovered the substance, he probably thought of it as a mere cheap substitute for india-rubber; it cost a few shillings a ton. But you can never tell all an invention will do. It was the genius of a man named Warming that pointed to the possibility of using it, not only for the tires of wheels, but as a road substance, and who organised the enormous network of public ways that speedily covered the world.

These public ways were made with longitudinal divisions. On the outer on either side went foot cyclists and conveyances travelling at a less speed than twenty-five miles an hour; in the middle, motors capable of speed up to a hun-dred; and the inner, Warming (in the face of enormous ridicule) reserved for vehicles travelling at speeds of a hundred miles an hour and upward.

For ten years his inner ways were vacant. Before he died they were the most crowded of all, and vast light frameworks with wheels of twenty and thirty feet in diameter, hurled along them at paces that year after year rose steadily towards two hundred miles an hour. And by the time this revolution was accomplished, a parallel revolution had transformed the ever-growing cities. Before the development of practical science the fogs and filth of Victorian times vanished. Electric heating replaced fires (in 2013 the lighting of a fire that did not absolutely consume its own smoke was made an indictable nuisance), and all the city ways, all public squares and places, were covered in with a recently invented glasslike substance. The roofing of London became practically continuous. Certain short-sighted and foolish legislation against tall buildings was abolished, and London, from a squat expanse of petty houses—feebly archaic in design—rose steadily towards the sky. To the municipal responsibility for water, light, and drainage, was added another, and that was ventilation.

But to tell of all the changes in human convenience that these two hundred years brought about, to tell of the long foreseen invention of flying, to describe how life in households was steadily supplanted by life in interminable hotels, how at last even those who were still concerned in agricultural work came to live in the towns and to go to and fro to their work every day, to describe how at last in all England only four towns remained, each with many millions of people, and how there were left no inhabited houses in all the countryside: to tell all this would take us far from our story of Denton and his Elizabeth. They had been separated and reunited, and still they could not marry. For Denton—it was his only fault—he had no money. Neither had Elizabeth until she was twenty-one, and as yet she was only eighteen. At twenty-one all the property of her mother would come to her, for that was the custom of the time. She did not know that it was possible to anticipate her fortune, and Denton was far too delicate a lover to suggest such a thing. So things stuck hopelessly between them. Elizabeth said that she was very unhappy, and that nobody understood her but Denton, and that when she was away from him she was wretched; and Denton said that his heart longed for her day and night. And they met as often as they could to enjoy the discussion of their sorrows.

They met one day at their little seat upon the flying stage. The precise site of this meeting was where in Victorian times the road from Wimbledon came out upon the common. They were, however, five hundred feet above that point. Their seat looked far over London. To convey the appearance of it all to a nineteenth-century reader would have been difficult. One would have had to tell him to think of the Crystal Palace, of the newly built "mammoth" hotels—as those little affairs were called—of the larger railway stations of his time, and to imagine such buildings enlarged to vast proportions and run together and continuous over the whole metropolitan area. If then he was told that this continuous roof-space bore a huge forest of rotating wind-wheels, he would have begun very dimly to appreciate what to these young people was the commonest sight in their lives.

To their eyes it had something of the quality of a prison, and they were talking, as they had talked a hundred times before, of how they might escape from it and be at last happy together: escape from it, that is, before the appointed three years were at an end. It was, they both agreed, not only impossible but almost wicked, to wait three years. "Before that," said Denton—and the notes of his voice told of a splendid chest—*"we might both be dead!"*

Their vigorous young hands had to grip at this, and then Elizabeth had a still more poignant thought that brought the tears from her wholesome eyes and down her healthy cheeks. *"One* of us," she said, *"one* of us might be—"

She choked; she could not say the word that is so terrible to the young and happy.

Yet to marry and be very poor in the cities of that time was—for any one who had lived pleasantly—a very dreadful thing. In the old agricultural days that had drawn to an end in the eighteenth century there had been a pretty proverb of love in a cottage; and indeed in those days diamond-windowed cottages of thatch and plaster, with the sweet air and earth about them, amidst tangled hedges and the song of birds, and with the ever-changing sky overhead. But all this had changed (the change was already beginning in the nineteenth century), and a new sort of life was opening for the poor—in the lower quarters of the city.

In the nineteenth century the lower quarters were still beneath the sky; they were areas of land on clay or other unsuitable soil, liable to floods or exposed to the smoke of more fortunate districts, insufficiently supplied with water, and as insanitary as the great fear of infectious diseases felt by the wealthier classes permitted. In the twenty-second century, however, the growth of the city storey above storey, and the coalescence of buildings, had led to a different arrangement. The prosperous people lived in a vast series of sumptuous hotels in the upper storeys and halls of the city fabric; the industrial population dwelt beneath in the tremendous ground-floor and basement, so to speak, of the place.

In the refinement of life and manners these lower classes differed little from their ancestors, the East-enders of Queen Victoria's time; but they had developed a distinct dialect of their own. In these underways they lived and died, rarely ascending to the surface except when work took them there. Since for most of them this was the sort of life to which they had been born, they found no great misery in such circumstances; but for people like Denton and Elizabeth, such a plunge would have seemed more terrible than death.

"And yet what else is there?" asked Elizabeth.

Denton professed not to know. Apart from his own feeling of delicacy, he was not sure how Elizabeth would like the idea of borrowing on the strength of her expectations.

The passage from London to Paris even, said Elizabeth, was beyond their means; and in Paris, as in any other city in the world, life would be just as costly and impossible as in London.

Well might Denton cry aloud: "If only we had lived in those days, dearest! If only we had lived in the past!" For to their eyes even nineteenth-century White-chapel was seen through a mist of romance.

"Is there *nothing*?" cried Elizabeth, suddenly weeping. "Must we really wait for these three long years? Fancy *three* years—six-and-thirty months!" The human capacity for patience had not grown with the ages.

Then suddenly Denton was moved to speak of something that had already flickered across his mind. He had hit upon it at last. It seemed to him so wild a suggestion that he made it only half seriously. But to put a thing into words has ever a way of making it seem more real and possible than it seemed before. And so it was with him.

"Suppose," he said, "we went into the country?"

She looked at him to see if he was serious in proposing such an adventure. "The country?"

"Yes—beyond there. Beyond the hills."

"How could we live?" she said. "*Where* could we live?"

"It is not impossible," he said. "People used to live in the country."

"But then there were houses."

"There are the ruins of villages and towns now. On the clay lands they are gone, of course. But they are still left on the grazing land, because it does not pay the Food Company to remove them. I know that—for certain. Besides, one sees them from the flying machines, you know. Well, we might shelter in some one of these, and repair it with our hands. Do you know, the thing is not so wild as it seems. Some of the men who go out every day to look after the crops and herds might be paid to bring us food. . . ."

She stood in front of him. "How strange it would be if one really could. . . ."

"Why not?"

"But no one dares."

"That is no reason."

"It would be—oh! it would be so romantic and strange. If only it were possible."

"Why not possible?"

"There are so many things. Think of all the things we have, things that we should miss."

"Should we miss them? After all, the life we lead is very unreal—very artificial." He began to expand his idea, and as he warmed to his exposition the fantastic quality of his first proposal faded away.

She thought. "But I have heard of prowlers—escaped criminals."

He nodded. He hesitated over his answer because he thought it sounded boyish. He blushed. "I could get some one I know to make me a sword."

She looked at him with enthusiasm growing in her eyes. She had heard of swords, had seen one in a museum; she thought of those ancient days when men wore them as a common thing. His suggestion seemed an impossible dream to her, and perhaps for that reason she was eager for more detail. And inventing for the most part as he went along, he told her how they might live in the country as the old-world people had done. With every detail her interest grew, for she was one of those girls for whom romance and adventure have a fascination.

His suggestion seemed, I say, an impossible dream to her on that day, but the next day they talked about it again, and it was strangely less impossible.

"At first we should take food," said Denton. "We could carry food for ten or twelve days." It was an age of compact artificial nourishment, and such a provision had none of the unwieldy suggestion it would have had in the nineteenth century.

"But—until our house," she asked—"until it was ready, where should we sleep?"

"It is summer."

"But . . . What do you mean?"

"There was a time when there were no houses in the world; when all mankind slept always in the open air."

"But for us! The emptiness! No walls—no ceiling!"

"Dear," he said, "in London you have many beautiful ceilings. Artists paint them and stud them with lights. But I have seen a ceiling more beautiful than any in London. . . ."

"But where?"

"It is the ceiling under which we two would be alone. . . ."

"You mean . . . ?"

"Dear," he said, "it is something the world has forgotten. It is Heaven and all the host of stars."

Each time they talked the thing seemed more possible and more desirable to them. In a week or so it was quite possible. Another week, and it was the inevitable thing they had to do. A great enthusiasm for the country seized hold of them and possessed them. The sordid tumult of the town, they said, overwhelmed them. They marvelled that this simple way out of their troubles had never come upon them before.

One morning near Midsummer-day, there was a new minor official upon the flying stage, and Denton's place was to know him no more.

Our two young people had secretly married, and were going forth manfully out of the city in which they and their ancestors before them had lived all their days. She wore a new dress of white cut in an old-fashioned pattern, and he had a bundle of provisions strapped athwart his back, and in his hand he carried—rather shamefacedly it is true, and under his purple cloak—an implement of archaic form, a cross-hilted thing of tempered steel.

Imagine that going forth! In their days the sprawling suburbs of Victorian times with their vile roads, petty houses, foolish little gardens of shrub and geranium, and all their futile, pretentious privacies, had disappeared: the towering buildings of the new age, the mechanical ways, the electric and water mains, all came to an end together, like a wall, like a cliff, near four hundred feet in height, abrupt and sheer. All about the city spread the carrot, swede, and turnip fields of the Food Company, vegetables that were the basis of a thousand varied foods, and weeds and hedgerow tangles had been utterly extirpated. The incessant expense of weeding that went on year after year in the petty, wasteful and barbaric farming of the ancient days, the Food Company had economised for ever more by a campaign of extermination. Here and there, however, neat rows of bramble standards and apple trees with white-washed stems, intersected the fields, and at places groups of gigantic teazles reared their favored spikes. Here and there huge agricultural machines hunched under waterproof covers. The mingled waters of the Wey and Mole and Wandle ran in rectangular channels; and wherever a gentle elevation of the ground permitted a fountain of deodorised sewage distributed its benefits athwart the land and made a rainbow of the sunlight.

By a great archway in that enormous city wall emerged the Eadhamite road to Portsmouth, swarming in the morning sunshine with an enormous traffic bearing the blue-clad servants of the Food Company to their toil. A rushing traffic, beside which they seemed two scarce-moving dots. Along the outer tracks hummed and rattled the tardy little old-fashioned motors of such as had duties within twenty miles or so of the city; the inner ways were filled with vaster mechanisms—swift monocycles bearing a score of men, lank multicycles, quadricycles sagging with heavy loads, empty gigantic produce carts that would come back again filled before the sun was setting, all with throbbing engines and noiseless wheels and a perpetual wild melody of horns and gongs.

Along the very verge of the outermost way our young people went in silence, newly wed and oddly shy of one another's company. Many were the things shouted to them as they tramped along, for in 2100 a foot-passenger on an English road was almost as strange a sight as a motor car would have been in 1800. But they went on with steadfast eyes into the country, paying no heed to such cries.

Before them in the south rose the Downs, blue at first, as they came nearer changing to green, surmounted by the row of gigantic wind-wheels that supplemented the wind-wheels upon the roof-spaces of the city, and broken and restless with the long morning shadows of those whirling vanes. By midday they had come so near that they could see here and there little patches of pallid dots—the sheep the Meat Department of the Food Company owned. In another hour they had passed the clay and the root crops and the single fence that hedged them in, and the prohibition against trespass no longer held: the levelled roadway plunged into a cutting with all its traffic, and they could leave it and walk over the greensward and up the open hillside.

Never had these children of the latter days been together in such a lonely place.

They were both very hungry and footsore—for walking was a rare exercise—and presently they sat down on the weedless, close-cropped grass, and looked back for the first time at the city from which they had come, shining wide and splendid in the blue haze of the valley of the Thames. Elizabeth was a little afraid of the unenclosed sheep away up the slope—she had never been near big unrestrained animals before—but Denton reassured her. And overhead a white-winged bird circled in the blue.

They talked but little until they had eaten, and then their tongues were loosened. He spoke of the happiness that was now certainly theirs, of the folly of not breaking sooner out of that magnificent prison of latter-day life, of the old romantic days that had passed from the world for ever. And then he became boastful. He took up the sword that lay on the ground beside him, and she took it from his hand and ran a tremulous finger along the blade.

"And you could," she said, "*you*—could raise this and strike a man?"

"Why not? If there were need."

"But," she said, "it seems so horrible. It would slash. . . . There would be"—her voice sank—"*blood.*"

"In the old romances you have read often enough . . ."

"Oh: I know in those—yes. But that is different. One knows it is not blood, but just a sort of red ink . . . And *you*—killing!"

She looked at him doubtfully, and then handed him back the sword.

After they had rested and eaten, they rose up and went on their way towards the hills. They passed quite close to a huge flock of sheep, who stared and bleated at their unaccustomed figures. She had never seen sheep before, and she shivered to think such gentle things must needs be slain for food. A sheep-dog barked from a distance, and then a shepherd appeared amidst the supports of the wind-wheels, and came down towards them.

When he drew near he called out asking whither they were going.

Denton hesitated, and told him briefly that they sought some ruined house among the Downs, in which they might live together. He tried to speak in an offhand manner, as though it was a usual thing to do. The man stared incredulously.

"Have you *done* anything?" he asked.

"Nothing," said Denton. "Only we don't want to live in a city any longer. Why should we live in cities?"

The shepherd stared more incredulously than ever. "You can't live here," he said.

"We mean to try."

The shepherd stared from one to the other. "You'll go back to-morrow," he said. "It looks pleasant enough in the sunlight. . . . Are you sure you've done nothing? We shepherds are not such *great* friends of the police."

Denton looked at him steadfastly. "No," he said. "But we are too poor to live in the city, and we can't bear the thought of wearing clothes of blue canvas and doing drudgery. We are going to live a simple life here, like the people of old."

The shepherd was a bearded man with a thoughtful face. He glanced at Elizabeth's fragile beauty.

"They had simple minds," he said.

"So have we," said Denton.

The shepherd smiled.

"If you go along here," he said, "along the crest beneath the wind-wheels, you will see a heap of mounds and ruins on your right-hand side. That was once a town called Epsom. There are no houses there, and the bricks have been used for a sheep pen. Go on, and another heap on the edge of the root-land is Leatherhead; and then the hill turns away along the border of a valley, and there are woods of beech. Keep along the crest. You will come to quite wild places. In some parts, in spite of all the weeding that is done, ferns and bluebells and other such useless plants are growing still. And through it all underneath the wind-wheels runs a straight lane paved with stones, a roadway of the Romans two thousand years old. Go to the right of that, down into the valley and follow it along by the banks of the river. You come presently to a street of houses, many with the roofs still sound upon them. There you may find shelter."

They thanked him.

"But it's a quiet place. There is no light after dark there, and I have heard tell of robbers. It is lonely. Nothing happens there. The phonographs of the story-tellers, the kinematograph entertainments, the news machines—none of them are to be found there. If you are hungry there is no food, if you are ill no doctor. . . ." He stopped.

"We shall try it," said Denton, moving to go on. Then a thought struck him, and he made an agreement with the shepherd, and learnt where they might find him, to buy and bring them anything of which they stood in need, out of the city.

And in the evening they came to the deserted village, with its houses that seemed so small and odd to them: they found it golden in the glory of the sunset, and desolate and still. They went from one deserted house to another, marvelling at their quaint simplicity, and debating which they should choose. And at last, in a sunlit corner of a room that had lost its outer wall, they came upon a wild flower, a little flower of blue that the weeders of the Food Company had overlooked.

That house they decided upon; but they did not remain in it long that night, because they were resolved to feast upon nature. And moreover the houses became very gaunt and shadowy after the sunlight had faded out of the sky. So after they had rested a little time they went to the crest of the hill again to see with their own eyes the silence of heaven set with stars, about which the old poets had had so many things to tell. It was a wonderful sight, and Denton talked like the stars, and when they went down the hill at last the sky was pale with dawn. They slept but little, and in the morning when they woke a thrush was singing in a tree.

So these young people of the twenty-second century began their exile. That morning they were very busy exploring the resources of this new home in which they were going to live the simple life. They did not explore very fast or very far, because they went everywhere hand-in-hand; but they found the beginnings of some furniture. Beyond the village was a store of winter fodder for the sheep of the Food Company, and Denton dragged great armfuls to the house to make a bed; and in several of the houses were old fungus-eaten chairs and tables—rough, barbaric, clumsy furniture, it seemed to them, and made of wood. They repeated many of the things they had said on the previous day, and towards evening they found another flower, a harebell. In the late afternoon some Company shepherds went down the river valley riding on a big multicycle; but they hid from them, because their presence, Elizabeth said, seemed to spoil the romance of this old-world place altogether.

In this fashion they lived a week. For all that week the days were cloudless, and the nights, nights of starry glory, that were invaded each a little more by a crescent moon.

Yet something of the first splendour of their coming faded—faded imperceptibly day after day; Denton's eloquence became fitful, and lacked fresh topics of inspiration; the fatigue of their long march from London told in a certain stiffness of the limbs, and each suffered from a slight unaccountable cold. Moreover, Denton became aware of unoccupied time. In one place among the carelessly heaped lumber of the old times he found a rust-eaten spade, and with this he made a fitful attack on the razed and grass-grown garden—though he had nothing to plant or sow. He returned to Elizabeth with a sweat-streaming face, after half an hour of such work.

"There were giants in those days," he said, not understanding what wont and training will do. And their walk that day led them along the hills until they could see the city shimmering far away in the valley. "I wonder how things are going on there," he said.

And then came a change in the weather. "Come out and see the clouds," she cried; and behold! they were a sombre purple in the north and east, streaming up to ragged edges at the zenith. And as they went up the hill these hurrying streamers blotted out the sunset. Suddenly the wind set the beech-trees swaying and whispering, and Elizabeth shivered. And then far away the lightning flashed, flashed like a sword that is drawn suddenly, and the distant thunder marched about the sky, and even as they stood astonished, pattering upon them came the first headlong raindrops of the storm. In an instant the last streak of sunset was hidden by a falling curtain of hail, and the lightning flashed again, and the voice of the thunder roared louder, and all about them the world scowled dark and strange.

Seizing hands, these children of the city ran down the hill to their home, in infinite astonishment. And ere they reached it, Elizabeth was weeping with dismay, and the darkling ground about them was white and brittle and active with the pelting hail.

Then began a strange and terrible night for them. For the first time in their civilised lives they were in absolute darkness; they were wet and cold and shivering; all about them hissed the hail, and through the long neglected ceilings of the derelict home came noisy spouts of water and formed pools and rivulets on the creaking floors. As the gusts of the storm struck the worn-out building, it groaned and shuddered, and now a mass of plaster from the wall would slide and smash, and now some loosened tile would rattle down the roof and crash into the empty greenhouse below. Elizabeth shuddered, and was still; Denton wrapped his gay and flimsy city cloak about her, and so they crouched in the darkness. And ever the thunder broke louder and nearer, and ever more lurid flashed the lightning, jerking into a momentary gaunt clearness the steaming, dripping room in which they sheltered.

Never before had they been in the open air save when the sun was shining.

All their time had been spent in the warm and airy ways and halls and rooms of the latter-day city. It was to them that night as if they were in some other world, some disordered chaos of stress and tumult, and almost beyond hoping that they should ever see the city ways again.

The storm seemed to last interminably, until at last they dozed between the thunderclaps, and then very swiftly it fell and ceased. And as the last patter of the rain died away they heard an unfamiliar sound.

"What is that?" cried Elizabeth.

It came again. It was the barking of dogs. It drove down the desert lane and passed; and through the window, whitening the wall before them and throwing upon it the shadow of the window-frame and of a tree in black silhouette, shone the light of the waxing moon.

Just as the pale dawn was drawing the things about them into sight, the fitful barking of dogs came near again, and stopped. They listened. After a pause they heard the quick pattering of feet seeking round the house, and short, half-smothered barks. Then again everything was still.

"Ssh!" whispered Elizabeth, and pointed to the door of their room.

Denton went half-way towards the door, and stood listening. He came back with a face of affected unconcern. "They must be the sheep-dogs of the Food Company," he said. "They will do us no harm."

He sat down again beside her. "What a night it has been!" he said, to hide how keenly he was listening.

"I don't like dogs," answered Elizabeth, after a long silence.

"Dogs never hurt any one," said Denton. "In the old days—in the nineteenth century—everybody had a dog."

"There was a romance I heard once. A dog killed a man."

"Not this sort of dog," said Denton confidently. "Some of those romances—are exaggerated."

Suddenly a half bark and a pattering up the staircase; the sound of panting. Denton sprang to his feet and drew the sword out of the damp straw upon which they had been lying. Then in the doorway appeared a gaunt sheep-dog, and halted there. Behind it stared another. For an instant man and brute faced each other, hesitating.

Then Denton, being ignorant of dogs, made a sharp step forward. "Go away," he said, with a clumsy motion of his sword.

The dog started and growled. Denton stopped sharply. "Good dog!" he said.

The growling jerked into a bark.

"Good dog!" said Denton. The second dog growled and barked. A third out of sight down the staircase took up the barking also. Outside others gave tongue—a large number it seemed to Denton.

"This is annoying," said Denton, without taking his eye off the brutes before him. "Of course the shepherds won't come out of the city for hours yet. Naturally these dogs don't quite make us out."

"I can't hear," shouted Elizabeth. She stood up and came to him.

Denton tried again, but the barking still drowned his voice. The sound had a curious effect upon his blood. Odd disused emotions began to stir; his face changed as he shouted. He tried again; the barking seemed to mock him, and one dog danced a pace forward, bristling. Suddenly he turned, and uttering certain words in the dialect of the underways, words incomprehensible to Elizabeth, he made for the dogs. There was a sudden cessation of the barking, a growl and a snapping. Elizabeth saw the snarling head of the foremost dog, its white teeth and retracted ears, and the flash of the thrust blade. The brute leapt into the air and was flung back.

Then Denton, with a shout, was driving the dogs before him. The sword flashed above his head with a sudden new freedom of gesture, and then he vanished down the staircase. She made six steps to follow him, and on the landing there was blood. She stopped, and hearing the tumult of dogs and Denton's shouts pass out of the house, ran to the window.

Nine wolfish sheep-dogs were scattering, one writhed before the porch; and Denton, tasting that strange delight of combat that slumbers still in the blood of even the most civilised man, was shouting and running across the garden space. And then she saw something that for a moment he did not see. The dogs circled round this way and that, and came again. They had him in the open.

In an instant she divined the situation. She would have called to him. For a moment she felt sick and helpless, and then, obeying a strange impulse, she gathered up her white skirt and ran downstairs. In the hall was the rusting spade. That was it! She seized it and ran out.

She came none too soon. One dog rolled before him, well-nigh slashed in half; but a second had him by the thigh, a third gripped his collar behind, and a fourth had the blade of the sword between its teeth, tasting its own blood. He parried the leap of a fifth with his left arm.

It might have been the first century instead of the twenty-second, so far as she was concerned. All the gentleness of her eighteen years of city life vanished before this primordial need. The spade smote hard and sure, and cleft a dog's skull. Another, crouching for a spring, yelped with dismay at this unexpected antagonist, and rushed aside. Two wasted precious moments on the binding of a feminine skirt.

The collar of Denton's cloak tore and parted as he staggered back; and that dog too felt the spade, and ceased to trouble him. He sheathed his sword in the brute at his thigh.

"To the wall!" cried Elizabeth; and in three seconds the fight was at an end, and our young people stood side by side, while a remnant of five dogs, with ears and tails of disaster, fled shamefully from the stricken field.

For a moment they stood panting and victorious, and then Elizabeth, dropping her spade, covered her face, and sank to the ground in a paroxysm of weeping. Denton looked about him, thrust the point of his sword into the ground so that it was at hand, and stooped to comfort her.

At last their more tumultuous emotions subsided, and they could talk again. She leant upon the wall, and he sat upon it so that he could keep an eye open for any returning dogs. Two, at any rate, were up on the hillside and keeping up a vexatious barking.

She was tear-stained, but not very wretched now, because for half an hour he had been repeating that she was brave and had saved his life. But a new fear was growing in her mind.

"They are the dogs of the Food Company," she said. "There will be trouble."

"I am afraid so. Very likely they will prosecute us for trespass."

A pause.

"In the old times," he said, "this sort of thing happened day after day."

"Last night!" she said. "I could not live through another such night."

He looked at her. Her face was pale for want of sleep, and drawn and haggard. He came to a sudden resolution. "We must go back," he said.

She looked at the dead dogs, and shivered. "We cannot stay here," she said.

"We must go back," he repeated, glancing over his shoulder to see if the enemy kept their distance. "We have been happy for a time. . . . But the world is too civilised. Ours is the age of cities. More of this will kill us."

"But what are we to do? How can we live there?"

Denton hesitated. His heel kicked against the wall on which he sat. "It's a thing I haven't mentioned before," he said, and coughed; "but . . ."

"Yes?"

"You could raise money on your expectations," he said.

"Could I?" she said eagerly.

"Of course you could. What a child you are!"

She stood up, and her face was bright. "Why did you not tell me before?" she asked. "And all this time we have been here!"

He looked at her for a moment, and smiled. Then the smile vanished. "I thought it ought to come from you," he said. "I didn't like to ask for your money. And besides—at first I thought this would be rather fine."

There was a pause.

"It *has* been fine," he said; and glanced once more over his shoulder. "Until all this began."

"Yes," she said, "those first days. The first three days."

They looked for a space into one another's faces, and then Denton slid down from the wall and took her hand.

"To each generation," he said, "the life of its time. I see it all plainly now. In the city—that is the life to which we were born. To live in any other fashion . . . Coming here was a dream, and this—is the awakening."

"It was a pleasant dream," she said,—"in the beginning."

For a long space neither spoke.

"If we would reach the city before the shepherds come here, we must start," said Denton. "We must get our food out of the house and eat as we go."

Denton glanced about him again, and, giving the dead dogs a wide berth, they walked across the garden space and into the house together. They found the wallet with their food, and descended the blood-stained stairs again. In the hall Elizabeth stopped. "One minute," she said. "There is something here."

She led the way into the room in which that one little blue flower was blooming. She stooped to it, she touched it with her hand.

"I want it," she said; and then, "I cannot take it. . . ."

Impulsively she stooped and kissed its petals.

Then silently, side by side, they went across the empty garden-space into the old high road, and set their faces resolutely towards the distant city—towards the complex mechanical city of those latter days, the city that had swallowed up mankind.

III. THE WAYS OF THE CITY

Prominent if not paramount among world-changing inventions in the history of man is that series of contrivances in locomotion that began with the railway and ended for a century or more with the motor and the patent road. That these contrivances, together with the device of limited liability joint stock companies and the supersession of agricultural labourers by skilled men with ingenious machinery, would necessarily concentrate mankind in cities of unparalleled magnitude and work an entire revolution in human life, became, after the event, a thing so obvious that it is a matter of astonishment it was not more clearly anticipated. Yet that any steps should be taken to anticipate the miseries such a revolution might entail does not appear even to have been suggested; and the idea that the moral prohibitions and sanctions, the privileges and concessions, the conception of property and responsibility, of comfort and beauty, that had rendered the mainly agricultural states of the past prosperous and happy, would fail in the rising torrent of novel opportunities and novel stimulations, never seems to have entered the nineteenth-century mind. That a citizen, kindly and fair in his ordinary life, could as a shareholder become almost murderously greedy; that commercial methods that were reasonable and honourable on the old-fashioned countryside, should on an enlarged scale be deadly and overwhelming; that ancient charity was modern pauperisation, and ancient employment modern sweating; that, in fact, a revision and enlargement of the duties and rights of man had become urgently necessary, were things it could not entertain, nourished as it was on an archaic system of education and profoundly retrospective and legal in all its habits of thought. It was known that the accumulation of men in cities involved unprecedented dangers of pestilence; there was an energetic development of sanitation; but that the diseases of gambling and usury, of luxury and tyranny should become endemic, and produce horrible consequences was beyond the scope of nineteenth-century thought. And so, as if it were some inorganic process, practically unhindered by the creative will of man, the growth of the swarming unhappy cities that mark the twenty-first century accomplished itself.

The new society was divided into three main classes. At the summit slumbered the property owner, enormously rich by accident rather than design, potent save for the will and aim, the last *avatar* of Hamlet in the world. Below was the enormous multitude of workers employed by the gigantic companies that monopolised control; and between these two the dwindling middle class, officials of innumerable sorts, foremen, managers, the medical, legal, artistic, and scholastic classes, and the minor rich, a middle class whose members led a life of insecure luxury and precarious speculation amidst the movements of the great managers.

Already the love story and the marrying of two persons of this middle class have been told: how they overcame the obstacles between them, and how they tried the simple old-fashioned way of living on the countryside and came back speedily enough into the city of London. Denton had no means, so Elizabeth borrowed money on the securities that her father Mwres held in trust for her until she was one-and-twenty.

The rate of interest she paid was of course high, because of the uncertainty of her security, and the arithmetic of lovers is often sketchy and optimistic. Yet they had very glorious times after that return. They determined they would not go to a Pleasure city nor waste their days rushing through the air from one part of the world to the other, for in spite of one disillusionment, their tastes were still old-fashioned. They furnished their little room with quaint old Victorian furniture, and found a shop on the forty-second floor in Seventh Way where printed books of the old sort were still to be bought. It was their pet affectation to read print instead of hearing phonographs. And when presently there came a sweet little girl, to unite them further if it were possible, Elizabeth would not send it to a *creche*, as the custom was, but insisted on nursing it at home. The rent of their apartments was raised on account of this singular proceeding, but they did not mind. It only meant borrowing a little more.

Presently Elizabeth was of age, and Denton had a business interview with her father that was not agreeable. An exceedingly disagreeable interview with their moneylender followed, from which he brought home a white face. On his return Elizabeth had to tell him of a new and marvellous intonation of "Goo" that their daughter had devised, but Denton was inattentive. In the midst, just as she was at the cream of her description, he interrupted. "How much money do you think we have left, now that everything is settled?"

She stared and stopped her appreciative swaying of the Goo genius that had accompanied her description.

"You don't mean . . . ?"

"Yes," he answered. "Ever so much. We have been wild. It's the interest. Or something. And the shares you had, slumped. Your father did not mind. Said it was not his business, after what had happened. He's going to marry again. . . . Well—we have scarcely a thousand left!"

"Only a thousand?"

"Only a thousand."

And Elizabeth sat down. For a moment she regarded him with a white face, then her eyes went about the quaint, old-fashioned room, with its middle Victorian furniture and genuine oleographs, and rested at last on the little lump of humanity within her arms.

Denton glanced at her and stood downcast. Then he swung round on his heel and walked up and down very rapidly.

"I must get something to do," he broke out presently. "I am an idle scoundrel. I ought to have thought of this before. I have been a selfish fool. I wanted to be with you all day . . ."

He stopped, looking at her white face. Suddenly he came and kissed her and the little face that nestled against her breast.

"It's all right, dear," he said, standing over her; "you won't be lonely now— now Dings is beginning to talk to you. And I can soon get something to do, you know. Soon . . . Easily . . . It's only a shock at first. But it will come all right. It's sure to come right. I will go out again as soon as I have rested, and find what can be done. For the present it's hard to think of anything . . ."

"It would be hard to leave these rooms," said Elizabeth; "but—"

"There won't be any need of that—trust me."

"They are expensive."

Denton waved that aside. He began talking of the work he could do. He was not very explicit what it would be; but he was quite sure that there was something to keep them comfortably in the happy middle class, whose way of life was the only one they knew.

"There are three-and-thirty million people in London," he said; "some of them *must* have need of me."

"Some *must*."

"The trouble is . . . Well—Bindon, that brown little old man your father wanted you to marry. He's an important person. . . . I can't go back to my flying-stage work, because he is now a Commissioner of the Flying Stage Clerks."

"I didn't know that," said Elizabeth.

"He was made that in the last few weeks . . . or things would be easy enough, for they liked me on the flying stage. But there's dozens of other things to be done—dozens. Don't you worry, dear. I'll rest a little while, and then we'll dine, and then I'll start on my rounds. I know lots of people—lots."

So they rested, and then they went to the public dining-room and dined, and then he started on his search for employment. But they soon realised that in the matter of one convenience the world was just as badly off as it had ever been, and that was a nice, secure, honourable, remunerative employment, leaving ample leisure for the private life, and demanding no special ability, no violent exertion nor risk, and no sacrifice of any sort for its attainment. He evolved a number of brilliant projects, and spent many days hurrying from one part of the enormous city to another in search of influential friends; and all his influential friends were glad to see him, and very sanguine until it came to definite proposals, and then they became guarded and vague. He would part with them coldly, and think over their behaviour, and get irritated on his way back, and stop at some telephone office and spend money on an animated but unprofitable quarrel. And as the days passed, he got so worried and irritated that even to seem kind and careless before Elizabeth cost him an effort—as she, being a loving woman, perceived very clearly.

After an extremely complex preface one day, she helped him out with a painful suggestion. He had expected her to weep and give way to despair when it came to selling all their joyfully bought early Victorian treasures, their quaint objects of art, their antimacassars, bead mats, repp curtains, veneered furniture, gold-framed steel engravings and pencil drawings, wax flowers under shades, stuffed birds, and all sorts of choice old things; but it was she who made the proposal. The sacrifice seemed to fill her with pleasure, and so did the idea of shifting to apartments ten or twelve floors lower in another hotel. "So long as Dings is with us, nothing matters," she said. "It's all experience." So he kissed her, said she was braver than when she fought the sheep-dogs, called her Boadicea, and abstained very carefully from reminding her that they would have to pay a considerably higher rent on account of the little voice with which Dings greeted the perpetual uproar of the city.

His idea had been to get Elizabeth out of the way when it came to selling the absurd furniture about which their affections were twined and tangled; but when it came to the sale it was Elizabeth who haggled with the dealer while Denton went about the running ways of the city, white and sick with sorrow and the fear of what was still to come. When they moved into their sparsely furnished pink-and-white apartments in a cheap hotel, there came an outbreak of furious energy on his part, and then nearly a week of lethargy during which he sulked at home. Though those days Elizabeth shone like a star, and at the end Denton's misery found a vent in tears. And then he went out into the city ways again, and—to his utter amazement—found some work to do.

His standard of employment had fallen steadily until at last it had reached the lowest level of independent workers. At first he had aspired to some high official position in the great Flying or Windvane or Water Companies, or to an appointment on one of the General Intelligence Organisations that had replaced newspapers, or to some professional partnership, but those were the dreams of the beginning. From that he had passed to speculation, and three hundred gold "lions" out of Elizabeth's thousand had vanished one evening in the share market. Now he was glad his good looks secured him a trial in the position of salesman to the Suzannah Hat Syndicate, a Syndicate dealing in ladies' caps, hair decorations, and hats—for though the city was completely covered in, ladies still wore extremely elaborate and beautiful hats at the theatres and places of public worship.

It would have been amusing if one could have confronted a Regent Street shopkeeper of the nineteenth century with the development of his establishment in which Denton's duties lay. Nineteenth Way was still sometimes called Regent Street, but it was now a street of moving platforms and nearly eight hundred feet wide. The middle space was immovable and gave access by staircases descending into subterranean ways to the houses on either side. Right and left were an ascending series of continuous platforms each of which travelled about five miles an hour faster than the one internal to it, so that one could step from platform to platform until one reached the swiftest outer way and so go about the city. The establishment of the Suzannah Hat Syndicate projected a vast *façade* upon the outer way, sending out overhead at either end an overlapping series of huge white glass screens, on which gigantic animated pictures of the faces of well-known beautiful living women wearing novelties in hats were thrown. A dense crowd was always collected in the stationary central way watching a vast kinematograph which displayed the changing fashion. The whole front of the building was in perpetual chromatic change, and all down the *façade*— four hundred feet it measured—and all across the street of moving ways, laced and winked and glittered in a thousand varieties of colour and lettering the inscription—

SUZANNA! 'ETS! SUZANNA! 'ETS!

A broadside of gigantic phonographs drowned all conversation in the moving way and roared *"hats"* at the passerby, while far down the street and up, other batteries counselled the public to "walk down for Suzannah," and queried, "Why *don't* you buy the girl a hat?"

For the benefit of those who chanced to be deaf—and deafness was not uncommon in the London of that age, inscriptions of all sizes were thrown from the roof above upon the moving platforms themselves, and on one's hand or on the bald head of the man before one, or on a lady's shoulders, or in a sudden jet of flame before one's feet, the moving finger wrote in unanticipated letters of fire " 'ets r chip t'de," or simply " 'ets." And spite of all these efforts so high was the pitch at which the city lived, so trained became one's eyes and ears to ignore all sorts of advertisement, that many a citizen had passed that place thousands of times and was still unaware of the existence of the Suzannah Hat Syndicate.

To enter the building one descended the staircase in the middle way and walked through a public passage in which pretty girls promenaded, girls who were willing to wear a ticketed hat for a small fee. The entrance chamber was a large hall in which wax heads fashionably adorned rotated gracefully upon pedestals, and from this one passed through a cash office to an interminable series of little rooms, each room with its salesman, its three or four hats and pins, its mirrors, its kinematographs, telephones and hat slides in communication with the central depôt, its comfortable lounge and tempting refreshments. A salesman in such an apartment did Denton now become. It was his business to attend to any of the incessant stream of ladies who chose to stop with him, to behave as winningly as possible, to offer refreshment, to converse on any topic the possible customer chose, and to guide the conversation dexterously but not insistently towards hats. He was to suggest trying on various types of hat and to show by his manner and bearing, but without any coarse flattery, the enhanced impression made by the hats he wished to sell. He had several mirrors, adapted by various subtleties of curvature and tint to different types of face and complexion, and much depended on the proper use of these.

Denton flung himself at these curious and not very congenial duties with a good will and energy that would have amazed him a year before; but all to no purpose. The Senior Manageress, who had selected him for appointment and conferred various small marks of favour upon him, suddenly changed in her manner, declared for no assignable cause that he was stupid, and dismissed him at the end of six weeks of salesmanship. So Denton had to resume his ineffectual search for employment.

This second search did not last very long. Their money was at the ebb. To eke it out a little longer they resolved to part with their darling Dings, and took that small person to one of the public *creches* that abounded in the city. That was the common use of the time. The industrial emancipation of women, the correlated disorganisation of the secluded "home," had rendered *creches* a necessity for all but very rich and exceptionally-minded people. Therein children encountered hygienic and educational advantages impossible without such organisation. *Creches* were of all classes and types of luxury, down to those of the Labour Company, where children were taken on credit, to be redeemed in labour as they grew up.

But both Denton and Elizabeth being, as I have explained, strange old-fashioned young people, full of nineteenth-century ideas, hated these convenient *creches* exceedingly and at last took their little daughter to one with extreme reluctance. They were received by a motherly person in a uniform who was very brisk and prompt in her manner until Elizabeth wept at the mention of parting from her child. The motherly person, after a brief astonishment at this unusual emotion, changed suddenly into a creature of hope and comfort, and so won Elizabeth's gratitude for life. They were conducted into a vast room presided over by several nurses and with hundreds of two-year-old girls grouped about the toy-covered floor. This was the Two-year-old Room. Two nurses came forward, and Elizabeth watched their bearing towards Dings with jealous eyes. They were kind—it was clear they felt kind, and yet . . .

Presently it was time to go. By that time Dings was happily established in a corner, sitting on the floor with her arms filled, and herself, indeed, for the most part hidden by an unaccustomed wealth of toys. She seemed careless of all human relationships as her parents receded.

They were forbidden to upset her by saying good-bye.

At the door Elizabeth glanced back for the last time, and behold! Dings had dropped her new wealth and was standing with a dubious face. Suddenly Elizabeth gasped, and the motherly nurse pushed her forward and closed the door.

"You can come again soon, dear," she said, with unexpected tenderness in her eyes. For a moment Elizabeth stared at her with a blank face. "You can come again soon," repeated the nurse. Then with a swift transition Elizabeth was weeping in the nurse's arms. So it was that Denton's heart was won also.

And three weeks after our young people were absolutely penniless, and only one way lay open. They must go to the Labour Company. So soon as the rent was a week overdue their few remaining possessions were seized, and with scant courtesy they were shown the way out of the hotel. Elizabeth walked along the passage towards the staircase that ascended to the motionless middle way, too dulled by misery to think. Denton stopped behind to finish a stinging and unsatisfactory argument with the hotel porter, and then came hurrying after her, flushed and hot. He slackened his pace as he overtook her, and together they ascended to the middle way in silence. There they found two seats vacant and sat down.

"We need not go there—*yet?*" said Elizabeth.

"No—not till we are hungry," said Denton.

They said no more.

Elizabeth's eyes sought a resting-place and found none. To the right roared the eastward ways, to the left the ways in the opposite direction, swarming with people. Backwards and forwards along a cable overhead rushed a string of gesticulating men, dressed like clowns, each marked on back and chest with one gigantic letter, so that altogether they spelt out:

PURKINJE'S DIGESTIVE PILLS.

An anæmic little woman in horrible coarse blue canvas pointed a little girl to one of this string of hurrying advertisements.

"Look!" said the anæmic woman: "there's yer father."

"Which?" said the little girl.

" 'Im wiv his nose coloured red," said the anæmic woman. The little girl began to cry, and Elizabeth could have cried too.

"Ain't 'e kickin' 'is legs!—*just!*" said the anæmic woman in blue, trying to make things bright again. "Looky—*now!*"

On the *façade* to the right a huge intensely bright disc of weird colour spun incessantly, and letters of fire that came and went spelt out—

DOES THIS MAKE YOU GIDDY?

Then a pause, followed by

TAKE A PURKINJE'S DIGESTIVE PILL.

A vast and desolating braying began. "If you love Swagger Literature, put your telephone on to Bruggles, the Greatest Author of all Time. The Greatest Thinker of all Time. Teaches you Morals up to your Scalp! The very image of Socrates, except the back of his head, which is like Shakespeare. He has six toes, dresses in red, and never cleans his teeth. Hear HIM!"

Denton's voice became audible in a gap in the uproar. "I never ought to have married you," he was saying. "I have wasted your money, ruined you, brought you to misery. I am a scoundrel . . . Oh, this accursed world!"

She tried to speak, and for some moments could not. She grasped his hand. "No," she said at last.

A half-formed desire suddenly became determination. She stood up. "Will you come?"

He rose also. "We need not go there yet."

"Not that. But I want you to come to the flying stages—where we met. You know? The little seat."

He hesitated. "*Can* you?" he said, doubtfully.

"Must," she answered.

He hesitated still for a moment, then moved to obey her will.

And so it was they spent their last half-day of freedom out under the open air in the little seat under the flying stages where they had been wont to meet five short years ago. There she told him, what she could not tell him in the tumultuous public ways, that she did not repent even now of their marriage—that whatever discomfort and misery life still had for them, she was content with the things that had been. The weather was kind to them, the seat was sunlit and warm, and overhead the shining aeroplanes went and came.

At last towards sunsetting their time was at an end, and they made their vows to one another and clasped hands, and then rose up and went back into the ways of the city, a shabby-looking, heavy-hearted pair, tired and hungry. Soon they came to one of the pale blue signs that marked a Labour Company Bureau. For a space they stood in the middle way regarding this and at last descended, and entered the waiting-room.

The Labour Company had originally been a charitable organisation; its aim was to supply food, shelter, and work to all comers. This it was bound to do by the conditions of its incorporation, and it was also bound to supply food and shelter and medical attendance to all incapable of work who chose to demand its aid. In exchange these incapables paid labour notes, which they had to redeem upon recovery. They signed these labour notes with thumb-marks, which were photographed and indexed in such a way that this world-wide Labour Company could identify any one of its two or three hundred million clients at the cost of an hour's inquiry. The day's labour was defined as two spells in a treadmill used in generating electrical force, or its equivalent, and its due performance could be enforced by law. In practice the Labour Company found it advisable to add to its statutory obligations of food and shelter a few pence a day as an inducement to effort; and its enterprise had not only abolished pauperisation altogether, but supplied practically all but the very highest and most responsible labour throughout the world. Nearly a third of the population of the world were its serfs and debtors from the cradle to the grave.

In this practical, unsentimental way the problem of the unemployed had been most satisfactorily met and overcome. No one starved in the public ways, and no rags, no costume less sanitary and sufficient than the Labour Company's hygienic but inelegant blue canvas, pained the eye throughout the whole world. It was the constant theme of the phonographic newspapers how much the world had progressed since nineteenth-century days, when the bodies of those killed by the vehicular traffic or dead of starvation, were, they alleged, a common feature in all the busier streets.

Denton and Elizabeth sat apart in the waiting-room until their turn came. Most of the others collected there seemed limp and taciturn, but three or four young people gaudily dressed made up for the quietude of their companions. They were life clients of the Company, born in the Company's *creche* and destined to die in its hospital, and they had been out for a spree with some shillings or so of extra pay. They talked vociferously in a later development of the Cockney dialect, manifestly very proud of themselves.

Elizabeth's eyes went from these to the less assertive figures. One seemed exceptionally pitiful to her. It was a woman of perhaps forty-five, with gold-stained hair and a painted face, down which abundant tears had trickled; she had a pinched nose, hungry eyes, lean hands and shoulders, and her dusty worn-out finery told the story of her life. Another was a grey-bearded old man in the costume of a bishop of one of the high episcopal sects—for religion was now also a business, and had its ups and downs. And beside him a sickly, dissipated-looking boy of perhaps two-and-twenty glared at Fate.

Presently Elizabeth and then Denton interviewed the manageress—for the Company preferred women in this capacity—and found she possessed an energetic face, a contemptuous manner, and a particularly unpleasant voice. They were given various cheques, including one to certify that they need not have their heads cropped; and when they had given their thumb-marks, learnt the number corresponding thereunto, and exchanged their shabby middleclass clothes for duly numbered blue canvas suits, they repaired to the huge plain dining-room for their first meal under these new conditions. Afterwards they were to return to her for instructions about their work.

When they had made the exchange of their clothing Elizabeth did not seem able to look at Denton at first; but he looked at her, and saw with astonishment that even in blue canvas she was still beautiful. And then their soup and bread came sliding on its little rail down the long table towards them and stopped with a jerk, and he forgot the matter. For they had had no proper meal for three days.

After they had dined they rested for a time. Neither talked—there was nothing to say; and presently they got up and went back to the manageress to learn what they had to do.

The manageress referred to a tablet. "Y'r rooms won't be here; it'll be in the Highbury Ward, Ninety-seventh way, number two thousand and seventeen. Better make a note of it on y'r card. *You,* nought nought nought, type seven, sixty-four, b.c.d., *gamma* forty-one, female; you 'ave to go to the Metal-beating Company, and try that for a day—fourpence bonus if ye're satisfactory; and *you,* nought seven one, type four, seven hundred and nine, g.f.b., *pi* five and ninety, male; you 'ave to go to the Photographic Company on Eighty-first way, and learn something or other—I don't know—thrippence. 'Ere's y'r cards. That's all. Next! *What?* Didn't catch it all? Lor! So suppose I must go over it all again. Why don't you listen? Keerless, unprovident people! One'd think these things didn't matter."

Their ways to their work lay together for a time. And now they found they could talk. Curiously enough, the worst of their depression seemed over now that they had actually donned the blue. Denton could talk with interest even of the work that lay before them. "Whatever it is," he said, "it can't be so hateful as that hat shop. And after we have paid for Dings, we shall still have a whole penny a day between us even now. Afterwards—we may improve,—get more money."

Elizabeth was less inclined to speech. "I wonder why work should seem so hateful," she said.

"It's odd," said Denton. "I suppose it wouldn't be if it were not the thought of being ordered about. . . . I hope we shall have decent managers."

Elizabeth did not answer. She was not thinking of that. She was tracing out some thoughts of her own.

"Of course," she said presently, "we have been using up work all our lives. It's only fair—"

She stopped. It was too intricate.

"We paid for it," said Denton, for at that time he had not troubled himself about these complicated things.

"We did nothing—and yet we paid for it. That's what I cannot understand."

"Perhaps we are paying," said Elizabeth presently—for her theology was old-fashioned and simple.

Presently it was time for them to part, and each went to the appointed work.

Denton's was to mind a complicated hydraulic press that seemed almost an intelligent thing. This press worked by the sea-water that was destined finally to flush the city drains—for the world had long since abandoned the folly of pouring drinkable water into its sewers. This water was brought close to the eastward edge of the city by a huge canal, and then raised by an enormous battery of pumps into reservoirs at a level of four hundred feet above the sea, from which it spread by a billion arterial branches over the city. Thence it poured down, cleansing, sluicing, working machinery of all sorts, through an infinite variety of capillary channels into the great drains, the *cloacae maximae*, and so carried the sewage out to the agricultural areas that surrounded London on every side.

The press was employed in one of the processes of the photographic manufacture, but the nature of the process it did not concern Denton to understand. The most salient fact to his mind was that it had to be conducted in ruby light, and as a consequence the room in which he worked was lit by one coloured globe that poured a lurid and painful illumination about the room. In the darkest corner stood the press whose servant Denton had now become; it was a huge, dim, glittering thing with a projecting hood that had a remote resemblance to a bowed head, and, squatting like some metal Buddha in this weird light that ministered to its needs, it seemed to Denton in certain moods almost as if this must needs be the obscure idol to which humanity in some strange aberration had offered up his life. His duties had a varied monotony. Such items as the following will convey an idea of the service of the press. The thing worked with a busy clicking so long as things went well; but if the paste that came pouring through a feeder from another room and which it was perpetually compressing into thin plates, changed in quality the rhythm of its click altered and Denton hastened to make certain adjustments. The slightest delay involved a waste of paste and the docking of one or more of his daily pence. If the supply of paste waned—there were hand processes of a peculiar sort involved in its preparation, and sometimes the workers had convulsions which deranged their output—Denton had to throw the press out of gear. In the painful vigilance a multitude of such trivial attentions entailed, painful because of the incessant effort its absence of natural interest required, Denton had now to pass one-third of his days. Save for an occasional visit from the manager, a kindly but singularly foul-mouthed man, Denton passed his working hours in solitude.

Elizabeth's work was of a more social sort. There was a fashion for covering the private apartments of the very wealthy with metal plates beautifully embossed with repeated patterns. The taste of the time demanded, however, that the repetition of the patterns should not be exact—not mechanical, but "natural"—and it was found that the most pleasing arrangement of pattern irregularity was obtained by employing women of refinement and natural taste to punch out the patterns with small dites. So many square feet of plates was exacted from Elizabeth as a minimum, and for whatever square feet she did in excess she received a small payment. The room, like most rooms of women workers, was under a manageress: men had been found by the Labour Company not only less exacting but extremely liable to excuse favoured ladies from a proper share of their duties. The manageress was a not unkindly, taciturn person, with the hardened remains of beauty of the brunette type; and the other women workers, who of course hated her, associated her name scandalously with one of the metal-work directors in order to explain her position.

Only two or three of Elizabeth's fellow-workers were born labour serfs; plain, morose girls, but most of them corresponded to what the nineteenth century would have called a "reduced" gentlewoman. But the ideal of what constituted a gentlewoman had altered: the faint, faded, negative virtue, the modulated voice and restrained gesture of the old-fashioned gentlewoman had vanished from the earth. Most of her companions showed in discoloured hair, ruined complexions, and the texture of their reminiscent conversations, the vanished glories of a conquering youth. All of these artistic workers were much older than Elizabeth, and two openly expressed their surprise that any one so young and pleasant should come to share their toil. But Elizabeth did not trouble them with her old-world moral conceptions.

They were permitted, and even encouraged to converse with each other, for the directors very properly judged that anything that conduced to variations of mood made for pleasing fluctuations in their patterning; and Elizabeth was almost forced to hear the stories of these lives with which her own interwove: garbled and distorted they were by vanity indeed and yet comprehensible enough. And soon she began to appreciate the small spites and cliques, the little misunderstandings and alliances that enmeshed about her. One woman was excessively garrulous and descriptive about a wonderful son of hers; another had cultivated a foolish coarseness of speech, that she seemed to regard as the wittiest expression of originality conceivable; a third mused for ever on dress, and whispered to Elizabeth how she saved her pence day after day, and would presently have a glorious day of freedom, wearing . . . and then followed hours of description; two others sat always together, and called one another pet names, until one day some little thing happened, and they sat apart, blind and deaf as it seemed to one another's being. And always from them all came an incessant tap, tap, tap, tap, and the manageress listened always to the rhythm to mark if one fell away. Tap, tap, tap, tap: so their days passed, so their lives must pass. Elizabeth sat among them, kindly and quiet, gray-hearted, marvelling at Fate: tap, tap, tap; tap, tap, tap; tap, tap, tap.

So there came to Denton and Elizabeth a long succession of laborious days, that hardened their hands, wove strange threads of some new and sterner substance into the soft prettiness of their lives, and drew grave lines and shadows on their faces. The bright, convenient ways of the former life had receded to an inaccessible distance; slowly they learnt the lesson of the under-world—sombre and laborious, vast and pregnant. There were many little things happened: things that would be tedious and miserable to tell, things that were bitter and grievous to bear—indignities, tyrannies, such as must ever season the bread of the poor in cities; and one thing that was not little, but seemed like the utter blackening of life to them, which was that the child they had given life to sickened and died. But that story, that ancient, perpetually recurring story, has been told so often, has been told so beautifully, that there is no need to tell it over again here. There was the same sharp fear, the same long anxiety, the deferred inevitable blow, and the black silence. It has always been the same; it will always be the same. It is one of the things that must be.

And it was Elizabeth who was the first to speak, after an aching, dull interspace of days: not, indeed, of the foolish little name that was a name no longer, but of the darkness that brooded over her soul. They had come through the shrieking, tumultuous ways of the city together; the clamour of trade, of yelling competitive religions, of political appeal, had beat upon deaf ears; the glare of focused lights, of dancing letters, and fiery advertisements, had fallen upon the set, miserable faces unheeded. They took their dinner in the dining-hall at a place apart. "I want," said Elizabeth clumsily, "to go out to the flying stages—to that seat. Here, one can say nothing. . . ."

Denton looked at her. "It will be night," he said.

"I have asked,—it is a fine night." She stopped.

He perceived she could find no words to explain herself. Suddenly he understood that she wished to see the stars once more, the stars they had watched together from the open downland in that wild honeymoon of theirs five years ago. Something caught at his throat. He looked away from her.

"There will be plenty of time to go," he said, in a matter-of-fact tone.

And at last they came out to their little seat on the flying stage, and sat there for a long time in silence. The little seat was in shadow, but the zenith was pale blue with the effulgence of the stage overhead, and all the city spread below them, squares and circles and patches of brilliance caught in a mesh-work of light. The little stars seemed very faint and small: near as they had been to the old-world watcher, they had become now infinitely remote. Yet one could see them in the darkened patches amidst the glare, and especially in the northward sky, the ancient constellations gliding steadfast and patient about the pole.

Long our two people sat in silence, and at last Elizabeth sighed.

"If I understood," she said, "if I could understand. When one is down there the city seems everything—the noise, the hurry, the voices—you must live, you must scramble. Here—it is nothing; a thing that passes. One can think in peace."

"Yes," said Denton. "How flimsy it all is! From here more than half of it is swallowed by the night. . . . It will pass."

"We shall pass first," said Elizabeth.

"I know," said Denton. "If life were not a moment, the whole of history would seem like the happening of a day. . . . Yes—we shall pass. And the city will pass, and all the things that are to come. Man and the Overman and wonders unspeakable. And yet . . ."

He paused, and then began afresh. "I know what you feel. At least I fancy. . . . Down there one thinks of one's work, one's little vexations and pleasures, one's eating and drinking and ease and pain. One lives, and one must die. Down there and everyday—our sorrow seemed the end of life. . . .

"Up here it is different. For instance, down there it would seem impossible almost to go on living if one were horribly disfigured, horribly crippled, disgraced. Up here—under these stars—none of those things would matter. They don't matter. . . . They are a part of something. One seems just to touch that something—under the stars. . . ."

He stopped. The vague, impalpable things in his mind, cloudy emotions half shaped towards ideas, vanished before the rough grasp of words. "It is hard to express," he said lamely.

They sat through a long stillness.

"It is well to come here," he said at last. "We stop—our minds are very finite. After all we are just poor animals rising out of the brute, each with a mind, the poor beginning of a mind. We are so stupid. So much hurts. And yet. . . .

"I know, I know—and some day we shall *see*.

"All this frightful stress, all this discord will resolve to harmony, and we shall know it. Nothing is but it makes for that. Nothing. All the failures—every little thing makes for that harmony. Everything is necessary to it, we shall find. We shall find. Nothing, not even the most dreadful thing, could be left out. Not even the most trivial. Every tap of your hammer on the brass, every moment of work, my idleness even. . . . Dear one! every movement of our poor little one. . . . All these things go on for ever. And the faint impalpable things. We, sitting here together.—Everything. . . .

"The passion that joined us, and what has come since. It is not passion now. More than anything else it is sorrow. *Dear.* . . ."

He could say no more, could follow his thoughts no further.

Elizabeth made no answer—she was very still; but presently her hand sought his and found it.

IV. UNDERNEATH

Under the stars one may reach upward and touch resignation, whatever the evil thing may be, but in the heat and stress of the day's work we lapse again, come disgust and anger and intolerable moods. How little is all our magnanimity—an accident! a phase! The very Saints of old had first to flee the world. And Denton and Elizabeth could not flee their world, no longer were there open roads to unclaimed lands where men might live freely—however hardly—and keep their souls in peace. The city had swallowed up mankind.

For a time these two Labour Serfs were kept at their original occupations, she sat at her brass stamping and Denton at his press; and then came a move for him that brought with it fresh and still bitterer experiences of life in the underways of the great city. He was transferred to the care of a rather more elaborate press in the central factory of the London Tile Trust.

In this new situation he had to work in a long vaulted room with a number of other men, for the most part born Labour Serfs. He came to this intercourse reluctantly. His upbringing had been refined, and, until his ill fortune had brought him to that costume, he had never spoken in his life, except by way of command or some immediate necessity, to the white-faced wearers of the blue canvas. Now at last came contact; he had to work beside them, share their tools, eat with them. To both Elizabeth and himself this seemed a further degradation.

His taste would have seemed extreme to a man of the nineteenth century. But slowly and inevitably in the intervening years a gulf had opened between the wearers of the blue canvas and the classes above, a difference not simply of circumstances and habits of life, but of habits of thought—even of language. The underways had developed a dialect of their own: above, too, had arisen a dialect, a code of thought, a language of "culture," which aimed by a sedulous search after fresh distinction to widen perpetually the space between itself and "vulgarity." The bond of a common faith, moreover, no longer held the race together. The last years of the nineteenth century were distinguished by the rapid development among the prosperous idle of esoteric perversions of the popular religion: glosses and interpretations that reduced the broad teachings of the carpenter of Nazareth to the exquisite narrowness of their lives. And, in spite of their inclination towards the ancient fashion of living, neither Elizabeth nor Denton had been sufficiently original to escape the suggestion of their surroundings. In matters of common behaviour they had followed the ways of their class, and so when they fell at last to be Labour Serfs it seemed to them almost as though they were falling among offensive inferior animals; they felt as a nine-teenth-century duke and duchess might have felt who were forced to take rooms in the Jago.

Their natural impulse was to maintain a "distance." But Denton's first idea of a dignified isolation from his new surroundings was soon rudely dispelled. He had imagined that his fall to the position of a Labour Serf was the end of his lesson, that when their little daughter had died he had plumbed the deeps of life; but indeed these things were only the beginning. Life demands something more from us than acquiescence. And now in a roomful of machine minders he was to learn a wider lesson, to make the acquaintance of another factor in life, a factor as elemental as the loss of things dear to us, more elemental even than toil.

His quiet discouragement of conversation was an immediate cause of of-fence—was interpreted, rightly enough I fear, as disdain. His ignorance of the vulgar dialect, a thing upon which he had hitherto prided himself, suddenly took upon itself a new aspect. He failed to perceive at once that his reception of the coarse and stupid but genially intended remarks that greeted his appearance must have stung the makers of these advances like blows in their faces. "Don't understand," he said rather coldly, and at hazard, "No, thank you."

The man who had addressed him stared, scowled, and turned away.

A second, who also failed at Denton's unaccustomed ear, took the trouble to repeat his remark, and Denton discovered he was being offered the use of an oil can. He expressed polite thanks, and this second man embarked upon a pene-trating conversation. Denton, he remarked, had been a swell, and he wanted to know how he had come to wear the blue. He clearly expected an interesting record of vice and extravagance. Had Denton ever been at a Pleasure City? Denton was speedily to discover how the existence of these wonderful places of delight permeated and defiled the thought and honour of these unwilling, hope-less workers of the underworld.

His aristocratic temperament resented these questions. He answered "No" curtly. The man persisted with a still more personal question, and this time it was Denton who turned away.

"Gorblimey!" said his interlocutor, much astonished.

It presently forced itself upon Denton's mind that this remarkable conversa-tion was being repeated in indignant tones to more sympathetic hearers, and that it gave rise to astonishment and ironical laughter. They looked at Denton with manifestly enhanced interest. A curious perception of isolation dawned upon him. He tried to think of his press and its unfamiliar peculiarities. . . .

The machines kept everybody pretty busy during the first spell, and then came a recess. It was only an interval for refreshment, too brief for any one to go out to a Labour Company dining-room. Denton followed his fellow-workers into a short gallery, in which were a number of bins and refuse from the presses.

Each man produced a packet of food. Denton had no packet. The manager, a careless young man who held his position by influence, had omitted to warn Denton that it was necessary to apply for this provision. He stood apart, feeling hungry. The others drew together in a group and talked in undertones, glancing at him ever and again. He became uneasy. His appearance of disregard cost him an increasing effort. He tried to think of the levers of his new press.

Presently one, a man shorter but much broader and stouter than Denton, came forward to him. Denton turned to him as unconcernedly as possible. "Here!" said the delegate—as Denton judged him to be—extending a cube of bread in a not too clean hand. He had a swart, broad-nosed face, and his mouth hung down towards one corner.

Denton felt doubtful for the instant whether this was meant for civility or insult. His impulse was to decline. "No, thanks," he said; and, at the man's change of expression, "I'm not hungry."

There came a laugh from the group behind. "Told you so," said the man who had offered Denton the loan of an oil can. "He's top side, he is. You ain't good enough for 'im."

The swart face grew a shade darker.

"Here," said its owner, still extending the bread, and speaking in a lower tone; "you got to eat this. See?"

Denton looked into the threatening face before him, and odd little currents of energy seemed to be running through his limbs and body.

"I don't want it," he said, trying a pleasant smile that twitched and failed.

The thickset man advanced his face, and the bread became a physical threat in his hand. Denton's mind rushed together to the one problem of his antagonist's eyes.

"Eat it," said the swart man.

There came a pause, and then they both moved quickly. The cube of bread described a complicated path, a curve that would have ended in Denton's face; and then his fist hit the wrist of the hand that gripped it, and it flew upward, and out of the conflict—its part played.

He stepped back quickly, fists clenched and arms tense. The hot, dark countenance receded, became an alert hostility, watching its chance. Denton for one instant felt confident, and strangely buoyant and serene. His heart beat quickly. He felt his body alive, and glowing to the tips.

"Scrap, boys!" shouted some one, and then the dark figure had leapt forward, ducked back and sideways, and come in again. Denton struck out, and was hit. One of his eyes seemed to him to be demolished, and he felt a soft lip under his fist just before he was hit again—this time under the chin. A huge fan of fiery needles shot open. He had a momentary persuasion that his head was knocked to pieces, and then something hit his head and back from behind, and the fight became an uninteresting, an impersonal thing.

He was aware that time—seconds or minutes—had passed, abstract, uneventful time. He was lying with his head in a heap of ashes, and something wet and warm ran swiftly into his neck. The first shock broke up into discrete sensations. All his head throbbed; his eye and his chin throbbed exceedingly, and the taste of blood was in his mouth.

"He's all right," said a voice. "He's opening his eyes."

"Serve him—well right," said a second.

His mates were standing about him. He made an effort and sat up. He put his hand to the back of his head, and his hair was wet and full of cinders. A laugh greeted the gesture. His eye was partially closed. He perceived what had happened. His momentary anticipation of a final victory had vanished.

"Looks surprised," said some one.

" 'Ave any more?" said a wit; and then, imitating Denton's refined accent: "No, thank you."

Denton perceived the swart man with a blood-stained handkerchief before his face, and somewhat in the background.

"Where's that bit of bread he's got to eat?" said a little ferret-faced creature; and sought with his foot in the ashes of the adjacent bin.

Denton had a moment of internal debate. He knew the code of honour requires a man to pursue a fight he has begun to the bitter end; but this was his first taste of the bitterness. He was resolved to rise again, but he felt no passionate impulse. It occurred to him—and the thought was no very violent spur—that he was perhaps after all a coward. For a moment his will was heavy, a lump of lead.

" 'Ere it is," said the little ferret-faced man, and stooped to pick up a cindery cube. He looked at Denton, then at the others.

Slowly, unwillingly, Denton stood up.

A dirty-faced albino extended a hand to the ferret-faced man.

"Gimme that toke," he said. He advanced threateningly, bread in hand, to Denton. "So you ain't 'ad your bellyful yet," he said. "Eh?"

Now it was coming. "No, I haven't," said Denton, with a catching of the breath, and resolved to try this brute behind the ear before he himself got stunned again. He knew he would be stunned again. He was astonished how ill he had judged himself beforehand. A few ridiculous lunges, and down he would go again. He watched the albino's eyes. The albino was grinning confidently, like a man who plans an agreeable trick. A sudden perception of impending indignities stung Denton.

"You leave 'im alone, Jim," said the swart man suddenly over the blood-stained rag. "He ain't done nothing to you."

The albino's grin vanished. He stopped. He looked from one to the other. It seemed to Denton that the swart man demanded the privilege of his destruction. The albino would have been better.

"You leave 'im alone," said the swart man. "See? 'E's 'ad 'is licks."

A clattering bell lifted up its voice and solved the situation. The albino hesitated. "Lucky for you," he said, adding a foul metaphor, and turned with the others towards the press-room again. "Wait for the end of the spell, mate," said the albino over his shoulder—an afterthought. The swart man waited for the albino to precede him. Denton realised that he had a reprieve.

The men passed towards an open door. Denton became aware of his duties, and hurried to join the tail of the queue. At the doorway of the vaulted gallery of presses a yellow-uniformed labour policeman stood ticking a card. He had ignored the swart man's hæmorrhage.

"Hurry up there!" he said to Denton.

"Hello!" he said, at the sight of his facial disarray. "Who's been hitting *you?*"

"That's my affair," said Denton.

"Not if it spiles your work, it ain't," said the man in yellow. "You mind that."

Denton made no answer. He was a rough—a labourer. He wore the blue canvas. The laws of assault and battery, he knew, were not for the likes of him. He went to his press.

He could feel the skin of his brow and chin and head lifting themselves to noble bruises, felt the throb and pain of each aspiring contusion. His nervous system slid down to lethargy; at each movement in his press adjustment he felt he lifted a weight. And as for his honour—that too throbbed and puffed. How did he stand? What precisely had happened in the last ten minutes? What would happen next? He knew that there was enormous matter for thought, and he could not think save in disordered snatches.

His mood was a sort of stagnant astonishment. All his conceptions were overthrown. He had regarded his security from physical violence as inherent, as one of the conditions of life. So, indeed, it had been while he wore his middle-class costume, had his middle-class property to serve for his defence. But who would interfere among Labour roughs fighting together? And indeed in those days no man would. In the Underworld there was no law between man and man; the law and machinery of the state had become for them something that held men down, fended them off from much desirable property and pleasure, and that was all. Violence, that ocean in which the brutes live for ever, and from which a thousand dykes and contrivances have won our hazardous civilised life, had flowed in again upon the sinking underways and submerged them. The fist ruled. Denton had come right down at last to the elemental—fist and trick and the stubborn heart and fellowship—even as it was in the beginning.

The rhythm of his machine changed, and his thoughts were interrupted.

Presently he could think again. Strange how quickly things had happened! He bore these men who had thrashed him no very vivid ill-will. He was bruised and enlightened. He saw with absolute fairness now the reasonableness of his unpopularity. He had behaved like a fool. Disdain, seclusion, are the privilege of the strong. The fallen aristocrat still clinging to his pointless distinction is surely the most pitiful creature of pretence in all this clamant universe. Good heavens! what was there for him to despise in these men?

What a pity he had not appreciated all this better five hours ago!

What would happen at the end of the spell? He could not tell. He could not imagine. He could not imagine the thoughts of these men. He was sensible only of their hostility and utter want of sympathy. Vague possibilities of shame and violence chased one another across his mind. Could he devise some weapon? He recalled his assault upon the hypnotist, but there were no detachable lamps here. He could see nothing that he could catch up in his defence.

For a space he thought of a headlong bolt for the security of the public ways directly the spell was over. Apart from the trivial consideration of his self-respect, he perceived that this would be only a foolish postponement and aggravation of his trouble. He perceived the ferret-faced man and the albino talking together with their eyes towards him. Presently they were talking to the swart man, who stood with his broad back studiously towards Denton.

At last came the end of the second spell. The lender of oil cans stopped his press sharply and turned round, wiping his mouth with the back of his hand. His eyes had the quiet expectation of one who seats himself in a theatre.

Now was the crisis, and all the little nerves of Denton's being seemed leaping and dancing. He had decided to show fight if any fresh indignity was offered him. He stopped his press and turned. With an enormous affectation of ease he walked down the vault and entered the passage of the ash pits, only to discover he had left his jacket—which he had taken off because of the heat of the vault—beside his press. He walked back. He met the albino eye to eye.

He heard the ferret-faced man in expostulation. " 'E reely ought, eat it," said the ferret-faced man. " 'E did reely."

"No—you leave 'im alone," said the swart man.

Apparently nothing further was to happen to him that day. He passed out to the passage and staircase that led up to the moving platforms of the city.

He emerged on the livid brilliance and streaming movement of the public street. He became acutely aware of his disfigured face, and felt his swelling bruises with a limp, investigatory hand. He went up to the swiftest platform, and seated himself on a Labour Company bench.

He lapsed into a pensive torpor. The immediate dangers and stresses of his position he saw with a sort of static clearness. What would they do tomorrow?

He could not tell. What would Elizabeth think of his brutalisation? He could not tell. He was exhausted. He was aroused presently by a hand upon his arm.

He looked up, and saw the swart man seated beside him. He started. Surely he was safe from violence in the public way!

The swart man's face retained no traces of his share in the fight; his expression was free from hostility—seemed almost deferential. " 'Scuse me," he said, with a total absence of truculence. Denton realised that no assault was intended. He stared, awaiting the next development.

It was evident the next sentence was premeditated. "Whad—I—was—going—to say—was this," said the swart man, and sought through a silence for further words.

"Whad—I—was—going—to say—was this," he repeated.

Finally he abandoned that gambit. *"You're* aw right," he cried, laying a grimy hand on Denton's grimy sleeve. *"You're* aw right. You're a ge'man. Sorry—very sorry. Wanted to tell you that."

Denton realised that there must exist motives beyond a mere impulse to abominable proceedings in the man. He meditated, and swallowed an unworthy pride.

"I did not mean to be offensive to you," he said, "in refusing that bit of bread."

"Meant it friendly," said the swart man, recalling the scene; "but—in front of that blarsted Whitey and his snigger—well—I'ad to scrap."

"Yes," said Denton with sudden fervour: "I was a fool."

"Ah," said the swart man, with great satisfaction. *"That's* aw right. Shake!"

And Denton shook.

The moving platform was rushing by the establishment of a face moulder, and its lower front was a huge display of mirror, designed to stimulate the thirst for more symmetrical features. Denton caught the reflection of himself and his new friend, enormously twisted and broadened. His own face was puffed, one-sided, and blood-stained; a grin of idiotic and insincere amiability distorted its latitude. A wisp of hair occluded one eye. The trick of the mirror presented the swart man as a gross expansion of lip and nostril. They were linked by shaking hands. Then abruptly this vision passed—to return to memory in the anæmic meditations of a waking dawn.

As he shook, the swart man made some muddled remark, to the effect that he had always known he could get on with a gentleman if one came his way. He prolonged the shaking until Denton, under the influence of the mirror, withdrew his hand. The swart man became pensive, spat impressively on the platform, and resumed his theme.

"Whad I was going to say was this," he said; was gravelled, and shook his head at his foot.

Denton became curious. "Go on," he said, attentive.

The swart man took the plunge. He grasped Denton's arm, became intimate in his attitude. " 'Scuse me," he said. "Fact is, you done know 'ow to scrap. Done know 'ow to. Why—you done know 'ow to *begin.* You'll get killed if you don't mind. 'Ouldin' your 'ands—*There!*"

He reinforced his statement by objurgation, watching the effect of each oath with a wary eye.

"F'r instance. You're tall. Long arms. You got a longer reach than anyone in the brasted vault. Gobblimey, but I thought I'd got a tough on. 'Stead of which . . . 'Scuse me. I wouldn't have '*it* you if I'd known. It's like fighting sacks. 'Tisn't right. Y'r arms seemed 'ung on 'ooks. Reg'lar 'ung on 'ooks. There!"

Denton stared, and then surprised and hurt his battered chin by a sudden laugh. Bitter tears came into his eyes.

"Go on," he said.

The swart man reverted to his formula. He was good enough to say he liked the look of Denton, thought he had stood up "amazing plucky. On'y pluck ain't no good ain't no brasted good—if you don't 'old your 'ands.

"Whad I was going to say was this," he said. "Lemme show you 'ow to scrap. Just lemme. You're ig'nant, you ain't no class; but you might be a very decent scrapper—very decent. Shown. That's what I meant to say."

Denton hesitated. "But—" he said, "I can't give you anything—"

"That's the ge'man all over," said the swart man. "Who arst you to?"

"But your time?"

"If you don't get learnt scrapping you'll get killed,—don't you make no bones of that."

Denton thought. "I don't know," he said.

He looked at the face beside him, and all its native coarseness shouted at him. He felt a quick revulsion from his transient friendliness. It seemed to him incredible that it should be necessary for him to be indebted to such a creature.

"The chaps are always scrapping," said the swart man. "Always. And, of course—if one gets waxy and 'its you vital . . ."

"By God!" cried Denton; "I wish one would."

"Of course, if you feel like that—"

"You don't understand."

"P'raps I don't," said the swart man; and lapsed into a fuming silence.

When he spoke again his voice was less friendly, and he prodded Denton by way of address. "Look see!" he said: "are you going to let me show you 'ow to scrap?"

"It's tremendously kind of you," said Denton; "but—"

There was a pause. The swart man rose and bent over Denton.

"Too much ge'man," he said—"eh? I got a red face. . . . By gosh! you are— you *are* a brasted fool!"

He turned away, and instantly Denton realised the truth of this remark.

The swart man descended with dignity to a cross way, and Denton, after a momentary impulse to pursuit, remained on the platform. For a time the things that had happened filled his mind. In one day his graceful system of resignation had been shattered beyond hope. Brute force, the final, the fundamental, had thrust its face through all his explanations and glosses and consolations and grinned enigmatically. Though he was hungry and tired, he did not go on directly to the Labour Hotel, where he would meet Elizabeth. He found he was beginning to think, he wanted very greatly to think; and so, wrapped in a monstrous cloud of meditation, he went the circuit of the city on his moving platform twice. You figure him, tearing through the glaring, thunder-voiced city at a pace of fifty miles an hour, the city upon the planet that spins along its chartless path through space many thousands of miles an hour, funking most terribly, and trying to understand why the heart and will in him should suffer and keep alive.

When at last he came to Elizabeth, she was white and anxious. He might have noted she was in trouble, had it not been for his own preoccupation. He feared most that she would desire to know every detail of his indignities, that she would be sympathetic or indignant. He saw her eyebrows rise at the sight of him.

"I've had rough handling," he said, and gasped. "It's too fresh—too hot. I don't want to talk about it." He sat down with an unavoidable air of sullenness.

She stared at him in astonishment, and as she read something of the significant hieroglyphic of his battered face, her lips whitened. Her hand—it was thinner now than in the days of their prosperity, and her first finger was a little altered by the metal punching she did—clenched convulsively. "This horrible world!" she said, and said no more.

In these latter days they had become a very silent couple; they said scarcely a word to each other that night, but each followed a private train of thought. In the small hours, as Elizabeth lay awake, Denton started up beside her suddenly—he had been lying as still as a dead man.

"I cannot stand it!" cried Denton. "I *will* not stand it!"

She saw him dimly, sitting up; saw his arm lunge as if in a furious blow at the enshrouding night. Then for a space he was still.

"It is too much—it is more than one can bear!"

She could say nothing. To her, also, it seemed that this was as far as one could go. She waited through a long stillness. She could see that Denton sat with his arms about his knees, his chin almost touching them.

Then he laughed.

"No," he said at last, "I'm going to stand it. That's the peculiar thing. There isn't a grain of suicide in us—not a grain. I suppose all the people with a turn that way have gone. We're going through with it—to the end."

Elizabeth thought grayly, and realised that this also was true.

"We're going through with it. To think of all who have gone through with it: all the generations—endless—endless. Little beasts that snapped and snarled, snapping and snarling, snapping and snarling, generation after generation."

His monotone, ended abruptly, resumed after a vast interval.

"There were ninety thousand years of stone age. A Denton somewhere in all those years. Apostolic succession. The grace of going through. Let me see! Ninety—nine hundred—three nines, twenty-seven—*three thousand* generations of men!—men more or less. And each fought, and was bruised, and shamed, and somehow held his own—going through with it—passing it on. . . . And thousands more to come perhaps—thousands!

"Passing it on. I wonder if they will thank us."

His voice assumed an argumentative note. "If one could find something definite. . . . If one could say, 'This is why—this is why it goes on. . . .'"

He became still, and Elizabeth's eyes slowly separated him from the darkness until at last she could see how he sat with his head resting on his hand. A sense of the enormous remoteness of their minds came to her; that dim suggestion of another being seemed to her a figure of their mutual understanding. What could he be thinking now? What might he not say next? Another age seemed to elapse before he sighed and whispered: "No. I don't understand it. No!" Then a long interval, and he repeated this. But the second time it had the tone almost of a solution.

She became aware that he was preparing to lie down. She marked his movements, perceived with astonishment how he adjusted his pillow with a careful regard to comfort. He lay down with a sigh of contentment almost. His passion had passed. He lay still, and presently his breathing became regular and deep.

But Elizabeth remained with eyes wide open in the darkness, until the clamour of a bell and the sudden brilliance of the electric light warned them that the Labour Company had need of them for yet another day.

That day came a scuffle with the albino Whitey and the little ferret-faced man. Blunt, the swart artist in scrapping, having first let Denton grasp the bearing of his lesson, intervened, not without a certain quality of patronage. "Drop 'is 'air, Whitey, and let the man be," said his gross voice through a shower of indignities. "Can't you see 'e don't know 'ow to scrap?" And Denton, lying shamefully in the dust, realised that he must accept that course of instruction after all.

He made his apology straight and clean. He scrambled up and walked to Blunt. "I was a fool, and you are right," he said. "If it isn't too late . . ."

That night, after the second spell, Denton went with Blunt to certain waste and slime–soaked vaults under the Port of London, to learn the first beginnings of the high art of scrapping as it had been perfected in the great world of the underways: how to hit or kick a man so as to hurt him excruciatingly or make him violently sick, how to hit or kick "vital," how to use glass in one's garments as a club and to spread red ruin with various domestic implements, how to anticipate and demolish your adversary's intentions in other directions; all the pleasant devices, in fact, that had grown up among the disinherited of the great cities of the twentieth and twenty-first centuries, were spread out by a gifted exponent for Denton's learning. Blunt's bashfulness fell from him as the instruction proceeded, and he developed a certain expert dignity, a quality of fatherly consideration. He treated Denton with the utmost consideration, only "flicking him up a bit" now and then, to keep the interest hot, and roaring with laughter at a happy fluke of Denton's that covered his mouth with blood.

"I'm always keerless of my mouth," said Blunt, admitting a weakness. "Always. It don't seem to matter, like just getting bashed in the mouth—not if your chin's all right. Tastin' blood does me good. Always. But I better not 'it you again."

Denton went home to fall asleep exhausted and wake in the small hours with aching limbs and all his bruises tingling. Was it worth while that he should go on living? He listened to Elizabeth's breathing, and remembering that he must have awaked her the previous night, he lay very still. He was sick with infinite disgust at the new conditions of his life. He hated it all, hated even the genial savage who had protected him so generously. The monstrous fraud of civilisation glared stark before his eyes; he saw it as a vast lunatic growth, producing a deepening torrent of savagery below, and above ever more flimsy gentility and silly wastefulness. He could see no redeeming reason, no touch of honour, either in the life he had led or in this life to which he had fallen. Civilisation presented itself as some castastrophic product as little concerned with men—save as victims—as a cyclone or a planetary collision. He, and therefore all mankind, seemed living utterly in vain. His mind sought some strange expedients of escape, if not for himself then at least for Elizabeth. But he meant them for himself. What if he hunted up Mwres and told him of their disaster? It came to him as an astonishing thing how utterly Mwres and Bindon had passed out of his range. Where were they? What were they doing? From that he passed to thoughts of utter dishonour. And finally, not arising in any way out of this mental tumult, but ending it as dawn ends the night, came the clear and obvious conclusion of the night before: the conviction that he had to go through with things; that, apart from any remoter view and quite sufficient for all his thought and energy, he had to stand up and fight among his fellows and quit himself like a man.

The second night's instruction was perhaps less dreadful than the first; and the third was even endurable, for Blunt dealt out some praise. The fourth day Denton chanced upon the fact that the ferret-faced man was a coward. There passed a fortnight of smouldering days and feverish instruction at night; Blunt, with many blasphemies, testified that never had he met so apt a pupil; and all night long Denton dreamt of kicks and counters and gouges and cunning tricks. For all that time no further outrages were attempted, for fear of Blunt; and then came the second crisis. Blunt did not come one day—afterwards he admitted his deliberate intention—and through the tedious morning Whitey awaited the interval between the spells with an ostentatious impatience. He knew nothing of the scrapping lessons, and he spent the time in telling Denton and the vault generally of certain disagreeable proceedings he had in mind.

Whitey was not popular, and the vault disgorged to see him haze the new man with only a languid interest. But matters changed when Whitey's attempt to open the proceedings by kicking Denton in the face was met by an excellently executed duck, catch and throw, and completed the flight of Whitey's foot in its orbit and brought Whitey's head into the ash-heap that had once received Denton's. Whitey arose a shade whiter, and now blasphemously bent upon vital injuries. There were indecisive passages, foiled enterprises that deepened Whitey's evidently growing perplexity; and then things developed into a grouping of Denton uppermost with Whitey's throat in his hand, his knee on Whitey's chest, and a tearful Whitey with a black face, protruding tongue and broken finger endeavouring to explain the misunderstanding by means of hoarse sounds. Moreover, it was evident that among the bystanders there had never been a more popular person than Denton.

Denton, with proper precaution, released his antagonist and stood up. His blood seemed changed to some sort of fluid fire, his limbs felt light and supernaturally strong. The idea that he was a martyr in the civilisation machine had vanished from his mind. He was a man in a world of men.

The little ferret-faced man was the first in the competition to pat him on the back. The lender of oil cans was a radiant sun of genial congratulation. . . . It seemed incredible to Denton that he had ever thought of despair.

Denton was convinced that not only had he to go through with things, but that he could. He sat on the canvas pallet expounding this new aspect to Elizabeth. One side of his face was bruised. She had not recently fought, she had not been patted on the back, there were no hot bruises upon her face, only a pallor and a new line or so about the mouth. She was taking the woman's share. She looked steadfastly at Denton in his new mood of prophecy. "I feel that there is something," he was saying, "something that goes on, a Being of Life in which we live and move and have our being, something that began fifty—a hundred million years ago, perhaps, that goes on—on: growing, spreading, to things beyond us—things that will justify us all. . . . That will explain and justify my fighting—these bruises, and all the pain of it. It's the chisel—yes, the chisel of the Maker. If only I could make you feel as I feel, if I could make you! You *will*, dear, I know you will."

"No," she said in a low voice. "No, I shall not."

"So I might have thought—"

She shook her head. "No," she said, "I have thought as well. What you say— doesn't convince me."

She looked at his face resolutely. "I hate it," she said, and caught at her breath. "You do not understand, you do not think. There was a time when you said things and I believed them. I am growing wiser. You are a man, you can fight, force your way. You do not mind bruises. You can be coarse and ugly, and still a man. Yes—it makes you. It makes you. You are right. Only a woman is not like that. We are different. We have let ourselves get civilised too soon. This underworld is not for us."

She paused and began again.

"I hate it! I hate this horrible canvas! I hate it more than—more than the worst that can happen. It hurts my fingers to touch it. It is horrible to the skin. And the women I work with day after day! I lie awake at nights and think how I may be growing like them. . . ."

She stopped. "I *am* growing like them," she cried passionately.

Denton stared at her distress. "But—" he said and stopped.

"You don't understand. What have I? What have I to save me? *You* can fight. Fighting is man's work. But women—women are different. . . . I have thought it all out, I have done nothing but think night and day. Look at the colour of my face! I cannot go on. I cannot endure this life. . . . I cannot endure it."

She stopped. She hesitated.

"You do not know all," she said abruptly, and for an instant her lips had a bitter smile. "I have been asked to leave you."

"Leave me!"

She made no answer save an affirmative movement of the head.

Denton stood up sharply. They stared at one another through a long silence.

Suddenly she turned herself about, and flung face downward upon their canvas bed. She did not sob, she made no sound. She lay still upon her face. After a vast, distressful void her shoulders heaved and she began to weep silently.

"Elizabeth!" he whispered—"Elizabeth!"

Very softly he sat down beside her, bent down, put his arm across her in a doubtful caress, seeking vainly for some clue to this intolerable situation.

"Elizabeth," he whispered in her ear.

She thrust him from her with her hand. "I cannot bear a child to be a slave!" and broke out into loud and bitter weeping.

Denton's face changed—became blank dismay. Presently he slipped from the bed and stood on his feet. All the complacency had vanished from his face, had given place to impotent rage. He began to rave and curse at the intolerable forces which pressed upon him, at all the accidents and hot desires and heedlessness that mock the life of man. His little voice rose in that little room, and he shook his fist, this animalcule of the earth, at all that environed him about, at the millions about him, at his past and future and all the insensate vastness of the overwhelming city.

V. BINDON INTERVENES

In Bindon's younger days he had dabbled in speculation and made three brilliant flukes. For the rest of his life he had the wisdom to let gambling alone, and the conceit to believe himself a very clever man. A certain desire for influence and reputation interested him in the business intrigues of the giant city in which his flukes were made. He became at last one of the most influential shareholders in the company that owned the London flying-stages to which the aeroplanes came from all parts of the world. This much for his public activities. In his private life he was a man of pleasure. And this is the story of his heart.

But before proceeding to such depths, one must devote a little time to the exterior of this person. Its physical basis was slender, and short, and dark; and the face, which was fine-featured and assisted by pigments, varied from an insecure self-complacency to an intelligent uneasiness. His face and head had been depilated, according to the cleanly and hygienic fashion of the time, so that the colour and contour of his hair varied with his costume. This he was constantly changing.

At times he would distend himself with pneumatic vestments in the rococo vein. From among the billowy developments of this style, and beneath a translucent and illuminated head-dress, his eye watched jealously for the respect of the less fashionable world. At other times he emphasied his elegant slenderness in close-fitting garments of black satin. For effects of dignity he would assume broad pneumatic shoulders, from which hung a robe of carefully arranged folds of China silk, and a classical Bindon in pink tights was also a transient phenomenon in the eternal pageant of Destiny. In the days when he hoped to marry Elizabeth, he sought to impress and charm her, and at the same time to take off something of his burthen of forty years, by wearing the last fancy of the contemporary buck, a costume of elastic material with distensible warts and horns, changing in colour as he walked, by an ingenious arrangement of versatile chromatophores. And no doubt, if Elizabeth's affection had not been already engaged by the worthless Denton, and if her tastes had not had that odd bias for old-fashioned ways, this extremely *chic* conception would have ravished her. Bindon had consulted Elizabeth's father before presenting himself in this garb— he was one of those men who always invite criticism of their costume—and Mwres had pronounced him all that the heart of woman could desire. But the affair of the hypnotist proved that his knowledge of the heart of woman was incomplete.

Bindon's idea of marrying had been formed some little time before Mwres threw Elizabeth's budding womanhood in his way. It was one of Bindon's most cherished secrets that he had a considerable capacity for a pure and simple life of a grossly sentimental type. The thought imparted a sort of pathetic seriousness to the offensive and quite inconsequent and unmeaning excesses, which he was pleased to regard as dashing wickedness, and which a number of good people also were so unwise as to treat in that desirable manner. As a consequence of these excesses, and perhaps by reason also of an inherited tendency to early decay, his liver became seriously affected, and he suffered increasing inconvenience when travelling by aeroplane. It was during his convalescence from a protracted bilious attack that it occurred to him that in spite of all the terrible fascinations of Vice, if he found a beautiful, gentle, good young woman of a not too violently intellectual type to devote her life to him, he might yet be saved to Goodness, and even rear a spirited family in his likeness to solace his declining years. But like so many experienced men of the world, he doubted if there were any good women. Of such as he had heard tell he was outwardly sceptical and privately much afraid.

When the aspiring Mwres affected his introduction to Elizabeth, it seemed to him that his good fortune was complete. He fell in love with her at once. Of course, he had always been falling in love since he was sixteen, in accordance with the extremely varied recipes to be found in the accumulated literature of many centuries. But this was different. This was real love. It seemed to him to call forth all the lurking goodness in his nature. He felt that for her sake he could give up a way of life that had already produced the gravest lesions on his liver and nervous system. His imagination presented him with idyllic pictures of the life of the reformed rake. He would never be sentimental with her, or silly; but always a little cynical and bitter, as became the past. Yet he was sure she would have an intuition of his real greatness and goodness. And in due course he would confess things to her, pour his version of what he regarded as his wickedness—showing what a complex of Goethe, and Benvenuto Cellini, and Shelley, and all those other chaps he really was—into her shocked, very beautiful, and no doubt sympathetic ear. And preparatory to these things he wooed her with infinite subtlety and respect. And the reserve with which Elizabeth treated him seemed nothing more nor less than an exquisite modesty touched and enhanced by an equally exquisite lack of ideas.

Bindon knew nothing of her wandering affections, nor of the attempt made by Mwres to utilise hypnotism as a corrective to this digression of her heart; he conceived he was on the best of terms with Elizabeth, and had made her quite successfully various significant presents of jewellery and the more virtuous cosmetics, when her elopement with Denton threw the world out of gear for him. His first aspect of the matter was rage begotten of wounded vanity, and as Mwres was the most convenient person, he vented the first brunt of it upon him.

He went immediately and insulted the desolate father grossly, and then spent an active and determined day going to and fro about the city and interviewing people in a consistent and partly-successful attempt to ruin that matrimonial speculator. The effectual nature of these activities gave him a temporary exhilaration, and he went to the dining-place he had frequented in his wicked days in a devil-may-care frame of mind, and dined altogether too amply and cheerfully with two other golden youths in the early forties. He threw up the game; no woman was worth being good for, and he astonished even himself by the strain of witty cynicism he developed. One of the other desperate blades, warmed with wine, made a facetious allusion to his disappointment, but at the time this did not seem unpleasant.

The next morning found his liver and temper inflamed. He kicked his phonographic-news machine to pieces, dismissed his valet, and resolved that he would perpetrate a terrible revenge upon Elizabeth. Or Denton. Or somebody. But anyhow, it was to be a terrible revenge; and the friend who had made fun at him should no longer see him in the light of a foolish girl's victim. He knew something of the little property that was due to her, and that this would be the only support of the young couple until Mwres should relent. If Mwres did not relent, and if unpropitious things should happen to the affair in which Elizabeth's expectations lay, they would come upon evil times and be sufficiently amenable to temptation of a sinister sort. Bindon's imagination, abandoning its beautiful idealism altogether, expanded the idea of temptation of a sinister sort. He figured himself as the implacable, the intricate and powerful man of wealth pursuing this maiden who had scorned him. And suddenly her image came upon his mind vivid and dominant, and for the first time in his life Bindon realised something of the real power of passion.

His imagination stood aside like a respectful footman who has done his work in ushering in the emotion.

"My God!" cried Bindon: "I will have her! If I have to kill myself to get her! And that other fellow—!"

After an interview with his medical man and a penance for his overnight excesses in the form of bitter drugs, a mitigated but absolutely resolute Bindon sought out Mwres. Mwres he found properly smashed, and impoverished and humble, in a mood of frantic self-preservation, ready to sell himself body and soul, much more any interest in a disobedient daughter, to recover his lost position in the world. In the reasonable discussion that followed, it was agreed that these misguided young people should be left to sink into distress, or possibly even assisted towards that improving discipline by Bindon's financial influence.

"And then?" said Mwres.

"They will come to the Labour Company," said Bindon. "They will wear the blue canvas."

"And then?"

"She will divorce him," he said, and sat for a moment intent upon that prospect. For in those days the austere limitations of divorce of Victorian times were extraordinarily relaxed, and a couple might separate on a hundred different scores.

Then suddenly Bindon astonished himself and Mwres by jumping to his feet. "She *shall* divorce him!" he cried. "I will have it so—I will work it so. By God! it shall be so. He shall be disgraced, so that she must. He shall be smashed and pulverised."

The idea of smashing and pulverising inflamed him further. He began a Jovian pacing up and down the little office. "I will have her," he cried. "I *will* have her! Heaven and Hell shall not save her from me!" His passion evaporated in its expression, and left him at the end simply histrionic. He struck an attitude and ignored with heroic determination a sharp twinge of pain about the diaphragm. And Mwres sat with his pneumatic cap deflated and himself very visibly impressed.

And so, with a fair persistence, Bindon set himself to the work of being Elizabeth's malignant providence, using with ingenious dexterity every particle of advantage wealth in those days gave a man over his fellow-creatures. A resort to the consolation of religion hindered these operations not at all. He would go and talk with an interesting, experienced and sympathetic Father of the Huysmanite sect of the Isis cult, about all the irrational little proceedings he was pleased to regard as his Heaven-dismaying wickedness, and the interesting, experienced and sympathetic Father representing Heaven dismayed, would with a pleasing affection of horror, suggest simple and easy penances, and recommend a monastic foundation that was airy, cool, hygienic, and not vulgarised, for viscerally disordered penitent sinners of the refined and wealthy type. And after these excursions, Bindon would come back to London quite active and passionate again. He would machinate with really considerable energy, and repair to a certain gallery high above the street of moving ways, from which he could view the entrance to the barrack of the Labour Company in the ward which sheltered Denton and Elizabeth. And at last one day he saw Elizabeth go in, and thereby his passion was renewed.

So in the fullness of the time the complicated devices of Bindon ripened, and he could go to Mwres and tell him that the young people were near despair.

"It's time for you," he said, "to let your parental affections have play. She's been in blue canvas some months, and they've been cooped together in one of those Labour dens, and the little girl is dead. She knows now what his manhood is worth to her, by way of protection, poor girl. She'll see things now in a clearer light. You go to her—I don't want to appear in this affair yet—and point out to her how necessary it is that she should get a divorce from him. . . ."

"She's obstinate," said Mwres doubtfully.

"Spirit!" said Bindon. "She's a wonderful girl—a wonderful girl!"

"She'll refuse."

"Of course she will. But leave it open to her. Leave it open to her. And some day—in that stuffy den, in that irksome, toilsome life they can't help it—*they'll have a quarrel. And then*—"

Mwres meditated over the matter, and did as he was told.

Then Bindon, as he had arranged with his spiritual adviser, went into retreat. The retreat of the Huysmanite sect was a beautiful place, with the sweetest air in London, lit by natural sunlight, and with restful quadrangles of real grass open to the sky, where at the same time the penitent man of pleasure might enjoy all the pleasures of loafing and all the satisfaction of distinguished austerity. And, save for participation in the simple and wholesome dietary of the place and in certain magnificent chants, Bindon spent all his time in meditation upon the theme of Elizabeth, and the extreme purification his soul had undergone since he first saw her, and whether he would be able to get a dispensation to marry her from the experienced and sympathetic Father in spite of the approaching "sin" of her divorce; and then . . . Bindon would lean against a pillar of the quadrangle and lapse into reveries on the superiority of virtuous love to any other form of indulgence. A curious feeling in his back and chest that was trying to attract his attention, a disposition to be hot or shiver, a general sense of ill-health and cutaneous discomfort he did his best to ignore. All that of course belonged to the old life that he was shaking off.

When he came out of retreat he went at once to Mwres to ask for news of Elizabeth. Mwres was clearly under the impression that he was an exemplary father, profoundly touched about the heart by his child's unhappiness. "She was pale," he said, greatly moved; "She was pale. When I asked her to come away and leave him—and be happy—she put her head down upon the table"—Mwres sniffed—"and cried."

His agitation was so great that he could say no more.

"Ah!" said Bindon, respecting this manly grief. "Oh!" said Bindon quite suddenly, with his hand to his side.

Mwres looked up sharply out of the pit of his sorrows, startled. "What's the matter?" he asked, visibly concerned.

"A most violent pain. Excuse me! You were telling me about Elizabeth."

And Mwres, after a decent solicitude for Bindon's pain, proceeded with his report. It was even unexpectedly hopeful. Elizabeth, in her first emotion at discovering that her father had not absolutely deserted her, had been frank with him about her sorrows and disgusts.

"Yes," said Bindon, magnificently, "I shall have her yet." And then that novel pain twiched him for the second time.

For these lower pains the priest was comparatively ineffectual, inclining rather to regard the body and them as mental illusions amenable to contemplation; so Bindon took it to a man of a class he loathed, a medical man of extraordinary repute and incivility. "We must go all over you," said the medical man, and did so with the most disgusting frankness. "Did you ever bring any children into the world?" asked this gross materialist among other impertinent questions.

"Not that I know of," said Bindon, too amazed to stand upon his dignity.

"Ah!" said the medical man, and proceeded with his punching and sounding. Medical science in those days was just reaching the beginnings of precision. "You'd better go right away," said the medical man, "and make the Euthanasia. The sooner the better."

Bindon gasped. He had been trying not to understand the technical explanations and anticipations in which the medical man had indulged.

"I say!" he said. "But do you mean to say . . . Your science . . ."

"Nothing," said the medical man. "A few opiates. The thing is your own doing, you know, to a certain extent."

"I was sorely tempted in my youth."

"It's not that so much. But you come of a bad stock. Even if you'd have taken precautions you'd have had bad times to wind up with. The mistake was getting born. The indiscretions of the parents. And you've shirked exercise, and so forth."

"I had no one to advise me."

"Medical men are always willing."

"I was a spirited young fellow."

"We won't argue; the mischief's done now. You've lived. We can't start you again. You ought never to have started at all. Frankly—the Euthanasia!"

Bindon hated him in silence for a space. Every word of this brutal expert jarred upon his refinements. He was so gross, so impermeable to all the subtler issues of being. But it is no good picking a quarrel with a doctor. "My religious beliefs," he said. "I don't approve of suicide."

"You've been doing it all your life."

"Well, anyhow, I've come to take a serious view of life now."

"You're bound to, if you go on living. You'll hurt. But for practical purposes it's late. However, if you mean to do that—perhaps I'd better mix you a little something. You'll hurt a great deal. These little twinges . . ."

"Twinges!"

"Mere preliminary notices."

"How long can I go on? I mean, before I hurt—really."

"You'll get it hot soon. Perhaps three days."

Bindon tried to argue for an extension of time, and in the midst of his pleading gasped, put his hand to his side. Suddenly the extraordinary pathos of his life came to him clear and vivid. "It's hard," he said. "It's infernally hard! I've been no man's enemy but my own. I've always treated everybody quite fairly."

The medical man stared at him without any sympathy for some seconds. He was reflecting how excellent it was that there were no more Bindons to carry on that line of pathos. He felt quite optimistic. Then he turned to his telephone and ordered up a prescription from the Central Pharmacy.

He was interrupted by a voice behind him. "By God!" cried Bindon; "I'll have her yet."

The physician stared over his shoulder at Bindon's expression, and then altered the prescription.

So soon as this painful interview was over, Bindon gave way to rage. He settled that the medical man was not only an unsympathetic brute and wanting in the first beginnings of a gentleman, but also highly incompetent; and he went off to four other practitioners in succession, with a view to the establishment of this intuition. But to guard against surprises he kept that little prescription in his pocket. With each he began by expressing his grave doubts of the first doctor's intelligence, honesty and professional knowledge, and then stated his symptoms, suppressing only a few more material facts in each case. These were always subsequently elicited by the doctor. In spite of the welcome depreciation of another practitioner, none of these eminent specialists would give Bindon any hope of eluding the anguish and helplessness that loomed now close upon him. To the last of them he unburthened his mind of an accumulated disgust with medical science. "After centuries and centuries," he exclaimed hotly; "and you can do nothing—except admit your helplessness. I say, 'Save me'—and what do you do?"

"No doubt it's hard on you," said the doctor. "But you should have taken precautions."

"How was I to know?"

"It wasn't our place to run after you," said the medical man, picking a thread of cotton from his purple sleeve. "Why should we save *you* in particular? You see—from one point of view—people with imaginations and passions like yours have to go—they have to go."

"Go?"

"Die out. It's an eddy."

He was a young man with a serene face. He smiled at Bindon. "We get on with research, you know; we give advice when people have the sense to ask for it. And we bide our time."

"Bide your time?"

"We hardly know enough yet to take over the management, you know."

"The management?"

"You needn't be anxious. Science is young yet. It's got to keep on growing for a few generations. We know enough now to know we don't know enough yet. . . . But the time is coming, all the same. *You* won't see the time. But, between ourselves, you rich men and party bosses, with your natural play of the passions and patriotism and religion and so forth, have made rather a mess of things; haven't you? These underways! And all that sort of thing. Some of us have a sort of fancy that in time we may know enough to take over a little more than the ventilation and drains. Knowledge keeps on piling up, you know. It keeps on growing. And there's not the slightest hurry for a generation or so. Some day—some day, men will live in a different way." He looked at Bindon and meditated. "There'll be a lot of dying out before that day can come."

Bindon attempted to point out to this young man how silly and irrelevant such talk was to a sick man like himself, how impertinent and uncivil it was to him, an older man occupying a position in the official world of extraordinary power and influence. He insisted that a doctor was paid to cure people—he laid great stress on *"paid"*—and had no business to glance even for a moment at "those other questions." "But we do," said the young man, insisting upon facts, and Bindon lost his temper.

His indignation carried him home. That these incompetent imposters, who were unable to save the life of a really influential man like himself, should dream of some day robbing the legitimate property owners of social control, of inflicting one knew not what tyranny upon the world. Curse science! He fumed over the intolerable prospect for some time, and then the pain returned, and he recalled the made-up prescription of the first doctor, still happily in his pocket. He took a dose forthwith.

It calmed and soothed him greatly, and he could sit down in his most comfortable chair beside his library (of phonographic records), and think over the altered aspect of affairs. His indignation passed, his anger and his passion crumbled under the subtle attack of that prescription, pathos became his sole ruler. He stared about him, at his magnificent and voluptuously appointed apartment, at his statuary and discreetly veiled pictures, and all the evidences of a cultivated and elegant wickedness; he touched a stud and the sad pipings of Tristan's shepherd filled the air. His eye wandered from one object to another. They were costly and gross and florid—but they were his. They presented in concrete form his ideals, his conceptions of beauty and desire, his idea of all that is precious in life. And now—he must leave it all like a common man. He was, he felt, a slender and delicate flame, burning out. So must all life flame up and pass, he thought. His eyes filled with tears.

Then it came into his head that he was alone. Nobody cared for him, nobody needed him! At any moment he might begin to hurt vividly. He might even howl. Nobody would mind. According to all the doctors he would have excellent reason for howling in a day or so. It recalled what his spiritual adviser had said of the decline of faith and fidelity, the degeneration of the age. He beheld himself as a pathetic proof of this; he, the subtle, able, important, voluptuous, cynical, complex Bindon, possibly howling, and not one faithful simple creature in all the world to howl in sympathy. Not one faithful simple soul was there— no shepherd to pipe to him! Had all such faithful simple creatures vanished from this harsh and urgent earth? He wondered whether the horrid vulgar crowd that perpetually went about the city could possibly know what he thought of them. If they did he felt sure *some* would try to earn a better opinion. Surely the world went from bad to worse. It was becoming impossible for Bindons. Perhaps some day . . . He was quite sure that the one thing he had needed in life was sympathy. For a time he regretted that he left no sonnets—no enig- matical pictures or something of that sort behind him to carry on his being until at last the sympathetic mind should come. . . .

It seemed incredible to him that this that came was extinction. Yet his sym- pathetic spiritual guide was in this matter annoyingly figurative and vague. Curse science! It had undermined all faith—all hope. To go out, to vanish from theatre and street, from office and dining-place, from the dear eyes of womankind. And not to be missed! On the whole to leave the world happier!

He reflected that he had never worn his heart upon his sleeve. Had he after all been *too* unsympathetic? Few people could suspect how subtly profound he really was beneath the mask of that cynical gaiety of his. They would not un- derstand the loss they had suffered. Elizabeth, for example, had not sus- pected. . . .

He had reserved that. His thoughts having come to Elizabeth gravitated about her for some time. How *little* Elizabeth understood him!

That thought became intolerable. Before all other things he must set that right. He realised that there was still something for him to do in life, his struggle against Elizabeth was even yet not over. He could never overcome her now, as he had hoped and prayed. But he might still impress her!

From that idea he expanded. He might impress her profoundly—he might impress her so that she should for evermore regret her treatment of him. The thing that she must realise before everything else was his magnanimity. His magnanimity! Yes! he had loved her with amazing greatness of heart. He had not seen it so clearly before—but of course he was going to leave her all his property. He saw it instantly, as a thing determined and inevitable. She would think how good he was, how spaciously generous; surrounded by all that makes life tolerable from his hand, she would recall with infinite regret her scorn and coldness. And when she sought expression for that regret, she would find that occasion gone forever, she should be met by a locked door, by a disdainful stillness, by a white dead face. He closed his eyes and remained for a space imagining himself that white dead face.

From that he passed to other aspects of the matter, but his determination was assured. He meditated elaborately before he took action, for the drug he had taken inclined him to a lethargic and dignified melancholy. In certain respects he modified details. If he left all his property to Elizabeth it would include the voluptuously appointed room he occupied, and for many reasons he did not care to leave that to her. On the other hand, it had to be left to some one. In his clogged condition this worried him extremely.

In the end he decided to leave it to the sympathetic exponent of the fashionable religious cult whose conversation had been so pleasing in the past. "*He* will understand," said Bindon with a sentimental sigh. "He knows what Evil means— he understands something of the Stupendous Fascination of the Sphinx of Sin. Yes—he will understand." By that phrase it was that Bindon was pleased to dignify certain unhealthy and undignified departures from sane conduct to which a misguided vanity and an ill-controlled curiosity had led him. He sat for a space thinking how very Hellenic and Italian and Neronic, and all those things, he had been. Even now—might one not try a sonnet? A penetrating voice to echo down the ages, sensuous, sinister, and sad. For a space he forgot Elizabeth. In the course of half an hour he spoilt three phonographic coils, got a headache, took a second dose to calm himself, and reverted to magnanimity and his former design.

At last he faced the unpalatable problem of Denton. It needed all his newborn magnanimity before he could swallow the thought of Denton; but at last this greatly misunderstood man, assisted by his sedative and the near approach of death, effected even that. If he was at all exclusive about Denton, if he should display the slightest distrust, if he attempted any specific exclusion of that young man, she might—*misunderstand*. Yes—she should have her Denton still. His magnanimity must go even to that. He tried to think only of Elizabeth in the matter.

He rose with a sigh, and limped across to the telephonic apparatus that communicated with his solicitor. In ten minutes a will duly attested and with its proper thumb-mark signature lay in the solicitor's office three miles away. And then for a space Bindon sat very still.

Suddenly he started out of a vague reverie and pressed an investigatory hand to his side.

Then he jumped eagerly to his feet and rushed to the telephone. The Euthanasia Company had rarely been called by a client in a greater hurry.

So it came at last that Denton and his Elizabeth, against all hope, returned unseparated from the labour servitude to which they had fallen. Elizabeth came out from her cramped subterranean den of metal-beaters and all the sordid circumstances of blue canvas, as one comes out of a nightmare. Back towards the sunlight their fortune took them; once the bequest was known to them, the bare thought of another day's hammering became intolerable. They went up long lifts and stairs to levels that they had not seen since the days of their disaster. At first she was full of this sensation of escape; even to think of the underways was intolerable; only after many months could she begin to recall with sympathy the faded women who were still below there, murmuring scandals and reminiscences and folly, and tapping away their lives.

Her choice of the apartments they presently took expressed the vehemence of her release. They were rooms upon the very verge of the city; they had a roof space and a balcony upon the city wall, wide open to the sun and wind, the country and the sky.

And in that balcony comes the last scene in this story. It was a summer sunsetting, and the hills of Surrey were very blue and clear. Denton leant upon the balcony regarding them, and Elizabeth sat by his side. Very wide and spacious was the view, for their balcony hung five hundred feet above the ancient level of the ground. The oblongs of the Food Company, broken here and there by the ruins—grotesque little holes and sheds—of the ancient suburbs, and intersected by shining streams of sewage, passed at last into a remote diapering at the foot of the distant hills. There once had been the squatting-place of the children of Uya. On those further slopes gaunt machines of unknown import worked slackly at the end of their spell, and the hill crest was set with stagnant wind vanes. Along the great south road the Labour Company's field workers in huge wheeled mechanical vehicles, were hurrying back to their meals, their last spell finished. And through the air a dozen little private aëropiles sailed down towards the city. Familiar scene as it was to the eyes of Denton and Elizabeth, it would have filled the minds of their ancestors with incredulous amazement. Denton's thoughts fluttered towards the future in a vain attempt at what that scene might be in another two hundred years, and, recoiling, turned towards the past.

He shared something of the growing knowledge of the time; he could picture the quaint smoke-grimed Victorian city with its narrow little roads of beaten earth, its wide common-land, ill-organised, ill-built suburbs, and irregular enclosures; the old countryside of the Stuart times, with its little villages and its petty London; the England of the monasteries, the far older England of the Roman dominion, and then before that a wild country with here and there the huts of some warring tribe. These huts must have come and gone and come again through a space of years that made the Roman camp and villa seem but yesterday; and before those years, before even the huts, there had been men in the valley. Even then—so recent had it all been when one judged it by the standards of geological time—this valley had been here; and those hills yonder, higher, perhaps, and snow-tipped, had still been yonder hills, and the Thames had flowed down from the Cotswolds to the sea. But the men had been but the shapes of men, creatures of darkness and ignorance, victims of beasts and floods, storms and pestilence and incessant hunger. They had held a precarious foothold amidst bears and lions and all the monstrous violence of the past. Already some at least of these enemies were overcome. . . .

For a time Denton pursued the thoughts of this spacious vision, trying in obedience to his instinct to find his place and proportion in the scheme.

"It has been chance," he said, "it has been luck. We have come through. It happens we have come through. Not by any strength of our own. . . .

"And yet . . . No. I don't know."

He was silent for a long time before he spoke again.

"After all—there is a long time yet. There have scarcely been men for twenty thousand years—and there has been life for twenty millions. And what are generations? What are generations? It is enormous, and we are so little. Yet we know—we feel. We are not dumb atoms, we are part of it—part of it—to the limits of our strength and will. Even to die is part of it. Whether we die or live, we are in the making. . . .

"As time goes on—*perhaps*—men will be wiser. . . . Wiser. . . .

"Will they ever understand?"

He became silent again. Elizabeth said nothing to these things, but she regarded his dreaming face with infinite affection. Her mind was not very active that evening. A great contentment possessed her. After a time she laid a gentle hand on his beside her. He fondled it softly, still looking out upon the spacious gold-woven view. So they sat as the sun went down. Until presently Elizabeth shivered.

Denton recalled himself abruptly from these spacious issues of his leisure, and went in to fetch her a shawl.

Hal Clement

Hal Clement (the pen name of Harry Clement Stubbs [1922–]) is a retired science teacher who has published science fiction since 1942, and whose work has become a paradigm for that branch of science fiction that delights in careful extrapolation from a scientific principle or idea. *Science Fiction Writers* (1996) says, "Clement and his classic fiction are mentioned whenever the discussion of science in the genre comes up . . . their distinguishing characteristic is that a problematic condition in physical reality, or simply a condition of difference such as an increase or decrease in heat or gravity, must be elaborated upon, explained, and taken through certain plot changes so that the reader can simply understand the problem or the difference. This is a literature of total mimesis, in which the facts of the universe are mimed." It is commonly referred to as hard science fiction (think of hard rock or the hard sciences—physics, chemistry, astronomy).

Clement's mastery of the astronomy, physics, and chemistry in stories set in space and on other worlds became famous with the publication of the *Astounding* serial, "Heavy Planet" (later published as *Mission of Gravity*, 1954), but especially with the immediately subsequent publication of a nonfiction article in the same magazine, detailing the process by which he had figured out the physics, astronomy, and biochemistry of the world of Mesklin. With the publication of *Mission of Gravity*, Clement in effect redefined the game of hard SF as an exercise in interrelating the sciences to achieve a created world that would plausibly withstand rigorous examination from many angles. Of such conceptual breakthroughs are scientific revolutions accomplished, and this was a revolution in science fiction, a slow and subtle one that took more than a decade to take hold. Gradually Clement gained a worldwide reputation as a quintessential hard SF writer whose works in later years more or less defined the term.

"Hot Planet" builds a consistent and detailed world for its alien characters to operate in, a world radically distanced from our own by its physical nature but also clearly, through our knowledge of science, connected to it: it is plausible. The story has the beauty of science at its heart, the awe-inspiring vistas of universal truth made manifest. Clement's work is presently the most influential model for hard science fiction writers.

HOT PLANET

The wind which had nearly turned the *Albireo*'s landing into a disaster instead of a mathematical exercise was still playing tunes about the fins and landing legs as Schlossberg made his way down to Deck Five.

The noise didn't bother him particularly, though the endless seismic tremors made him dislike the ladders. But just now he was able to ignore both. He was curious—though not hopeful.

"Is there anything at all obvious on the last sets of tapes, Joe?"

Mardikian, the geophysicist, shrugged. "Just what you'd expect . . . on a planet which has at least one quake in each fifty-mile-square area every five minutes. You know yourself we had a nice seismic program set up, but when we touched down we found we couldn't carry it out. We've done our best with the natural tremors—incidentally stealing most of the record tapes the other projects would have used. We have a lot of nice information for the computers back home; but it will take all of them to make any sense out of it."

Schlossberg nodded; the words had not been necessary. His astronomical program had been one of those sabotaged by the transfer of tapes to the seismic survey.

"I just hoped," he said. "We each have an idea why Mercury developed an atmosphere during the last few decades, but I guess the high school kids on Earth will know whether it's right before we do. I'm resigned to living in a chess-type universe—few and simple rules, but infinite combinations of them. But it would be nice to know an answer sometime."

"So it would. As a matter of fact, I need to know a couple right now. From you. How close to finished are the other programs—or what's left of them?"

"I'm all set," replied Schlossberg. "I have a couple of instruments still monitoring the sun just in case, but everything in the revised program is on tape."

"Good. Tom, any use asking you?"

The biologist grimaced. "I've been shown two hundred and sixteen different samples of rock and dust. I have examined in detail twelve crystal growths which looked vaguely like vegetation. Nothing was alive or contained living things by any standards I could conscientiously set."

Mardikian's gesture might have meant sympathy.

"Camille?"

"I may as well stop now as any time. I'll never be through. Tape didn't make much difference to me, but I wish I knew what weight of specimens I could take home."

"Eileen?" Mardikian's glance at the stratigrapher took the place of the actual question.

"Cam speaks for me, except that I could have used any more tape you could have spared. What I have is gone."

"All right, that leaves me, the tape-thief. The last spools are in the seismographs now, and will start running out in seventeen hours. The tractors will start out on their last rounds in sixteen, and should be back in roughly a week. Will, does that give you enough to figure the weights we rockhounds can have on the return trip?"

The *Albireo*'s captain nodded. "Close enough. There really hasn't been much question since it became evident we'd find nothing for the mass tanks here. I'll have a really precise check in an hour, but I can tell right now that you have about one and a half metric tons to split up among the three of you.

"Ideal departure time is three hundred ten hours away, as you all know. We can stay here until then, or go into a parking-and-survey orbit at almost any time before then. You have all the survey you need, I should think, from the other time. But suit yourselves."

"I'd just as soon be space-sick as seasick," remarked Camille Burkett. "I still hate to think that the entire planet is as shivery as the spot we picked."

Willard Rowson smiled. "You researchers told me where to land after ten days in orbit mapping this rockball. I set you just where you asked. If you'd found even five tons of juice we could use in the reaction tanks I could still take you to another one—if you could agree which one. I hate to say, 'Don't blame me,' but I can't think of anything else that fits."

"So we sit until the last of the tractors is back with the precious seismo tapes, playing battleship while our back teeth are being shaken out by earthquakes—excuse the word. What a thrill! Glorious adventure!" Zaino, the communications specialist who had been out of a job almost constantly since the landing, spoke sourly. The captain was the only one who saw fit to answer.

"If you want adventure, you made a mistake exploring space. The only space adventures I've heard of are secondhand stories built on guesswork; the people who really had them weren't around to tell about it. Unless Dr. Marini discovers a set of Mercurian monsters at the last minute and they invade the ship or cut off one of the tractors, I'm afraid you'll have to do without adventures." Zaino grimaced.

"That sounds funny coming from a spaceman, Captain. I didn't really mean adventure, though; all I want is something to do besides betting whether the next quake will come in one minute or five. I haven't even had to fix a suit-radio since we touched down. How about my going out with one of the tractors on this last trip, at least?"

"It's all right with me," replied Rowson, "but Dr. Mardikian runs the professional part of this operation. I require that Spurr, Trackman, Hargedon and Aiello go as drivers, since without them even a minor mechanical problem would be more than an adventure. As I recall it, Dr. Harmon, Dr. Schlossberg, Dr. Marini and Dr. Mardikian are scheduled to go; but if any one of them is willing to let you take his or her place, I certainly don't mind."

The radioman looked around hopefully. The geologists and the biologist shook their heads negatively, firmly and unanimously; but the astronomer pondered for a moment. Zaino watched tensely.

"It may be all right," Schlossberg said at last. "What I want to get is a set of wind, gas pressure, gas temperature and gas composition measures around the route. I didn't expect to be more meteorologist than astronomer when we left Earth, and didn't have exactly the right equipment. Hargedon and Aiello helped me improvise some, and this is the first chance to use it on Darkside. If you can learn what has to be done with it before starting time, though, you are welcome to my place."

The communicator got to his feet fast enough to leave the deck in Mercury's feeble gravity.

"Lead me to it, Doc. I guess I can learn to read a homemade weathervane!"

"Is that merely bragging, or a challenge?" drawled a voice which had not previously joined the discussion. Zaino flushed a bit.

"Sorry, Luigi," he said hastily. "I didn't mean it just that way. But I still think I can run the stuff."

"Likely enough," Aiello replied. "Remember though, it wasn't made just for talking into." Schlossberg, now on his feet, cut in quickly.

"Come on, Arnie. We'll have to suit up to see the equipment; it's outside."

He shepherded the radioman to the hatch at one side of the deck and shooed him down toward the engine and air lock levels. Both were silent for some moments; but safely out of earshot of Deck Five the younger man looked up and spoke.

"You needn't push, Doc. I wasn't going to make anything of it. Luigi was right, and I asked for it." The astronomer slowed a bit in his descent.

"I wasn't really worried," he replied, "but we have several months yet before we can get away from each other, and I don't like talk that could set up grudges. Matter of fact, I'm even a little uneasy about having the girls along, though I'm no misogynist."

"Girls? They're not—"

"There goes your foot again. Even Harmon is about ten years older than you, I suppose. But they're girls to me. What's more important, they no doubt think of themselves as girls."

"Even Dr. Burkett? That is—I mean—"

"Even Dr. Burkett. Here, get into your suit. And maybe you'd better take out the mike. It'll be enough if you can listen for the next hour or two." Zaino made no answer, suspecting with some justice that anything he said would be wrong.

Each made final checks on the other's suit; then they descended one more level to the airlock. This occupied part of the same deck as the fusion plants, below the wings and reaction mass tanks but above the main engine. Its outer door was just barely big enough to admit a space-suited person. Even with the low air pressure carried by spaceships, a large door area meant large total force on jamb, hinges and locks. It opened onto a small balcony from which a ladder led to the ground. The two men paused on the balcony to look over the landscape.

This hadn't changed noticeably since the last time either had been out, though there might have been some small difference in the volcanic cones a couple of miles away to the northeast. The furrows down the sides of these, which looked as though they had been cut by water but were actually bone-dry ash slides, were always undergoing alteration as gas from below kept blowing fresh scoria fragments out of the craters.

The spines—steep, jagged fragments of rock which thrust upward from the plain beyond and to both sides of the cones—seemed dead as ever.

The level surface between the *Albireo* and the cones was more interesting. Mardikian and Schlossberg believed it to be a lava sheet dating from early in Mercury's history, when more volatile substances still existed in the surface rocks to cut down their viscosity when molten. They supposed that much—perhaps most—of the surface around the "twilight" belt had been flooded by this very liquid lava, which had cooled to a smoother surface than most Earthly lava flows.

How long it had stayed cool they didn't guess. But both men felt sure that Mercury must have periodic upheavals as heat accumulated inside it—heat coming not from radioactivity but from tidal energy. Mercury's orbit is highly eccentric. At perihelion, tidal force tries to pull it apart along the planet-to-sun line, while at aphelion the tidal force is less and the little world's own gravity tries to bring it back to a spherical shape. The real change in form is not great, but a large force working through even a small amount of distance can mean a good deal of energy.

If the energy can't leak out—and Mercury's rocks conduct heat no better than those of Earth—the temperature must rise.

Sooner or later, the men argued, deeply buried rock must fuse to magma. Its liquefaction would let the bulk of the planet give farther under tidal stress, so heat would be generated even faster. Eventually a girdle of magma would have to form far below the crust all around the twilight strip, where the tidal strain would be greatest. Sooner or later this would melt its way to the surface, giving the zone a period of intense volcanic activity and, incidentally, giving the planet a temporary atmosphere.

The idea was reasonable. It had, the astronomer admitted, been suggested long before to account for supposed vulcanism on the moon. It justified the careful examination that Schlossberg and Zaino gave the plain before they descended the ladder; for it made reasonable the occasional changes which were observed to occur in the pattern of cracks weaving over its surface.

No one was certain just how permanent the local surface was—though no one could really justify feeling safer on board the *Albireo* than outside on the lava. If anything really drastic happened, the ship would be no protection.

The sun, hanging just above the horizon slightly to the watcher's right, cast long shadows which made the cracks stand out clearly; as far as either man could see, nothing had changed recently. They descended the ladder carefully—even the best designed space suits are somewhat vulnerable—and made their way to the spot where the tractors were parked.

A sheet-metal fence a dozen feet high and four times as long provided shade, which was more than a luxury this close to the sun. The tractors were parked in this shadow, and beside and between them were piles of equipment and specimens. The apparatus Schlossberg had devised was beside the tractor at the north end of the line, just inside the shaded area.

It was still just inside the shade when they finished, four hours later. Hargedon had joined them during the final hour and helped pack the equipment in the tractor he was to drive. Zaino had had no trouble in learning to make the observations Schlossberg wanted, and the youngster was almost unbearably cocky. Schlossberg hoped, as they returned to the *Albireo*, that no one would murder the communications expert in the next twelve hours. There would be nothing to worry about after the trip started; Hargedon was quite able to keep anyone in his place without being nasty about it. If Zaino had been going with Aiello or Harmon—but he wasn't, and it was pointless to dream up trouble.

And no trouble developed all by itself.

Zaino was not only still alive but still reasonably popular when the first of the tractors set out, carrying Eileen Harmon and Eric Trackman, the *Albireo's* nuclear engineer.

It started more than an hour before the others, since the stratigrapher's drilling program, "done" or not, took extra time. The tractor hummed off to the south, since both Darkside routes required a long detour to pass the chasm to the west. Routes had been worked out from the stereo-photos taken during the orbital survey. Even Darkside had been covered fairly well with Uniquantum film under Venus light.

The Harmon-Trackman vehicle was well out of sight when Mardikian and Aiello started out on one of the Brightside routes, and a few minutes later Marini set out on the other with the space-suit technician, Mary Spurr, driving.

Both vehicles disappeared quickly into a valley to the northeast, between the ash cones and a thousand-foot spine which rose just south of them. All the tractors were in good radio contact; Zaino made sure of that before he abandoned the radio watch to Rowson, suited up and joined Hargedon at the remaining one. They climbed in, and Hargedon set it in motion.

At about the same time, the first tractor came into view again, now traveling north on the farther side of the chasm. Hargedon took this as evidence that the route thus far was unchanged, and kicked in highest speed.

The cabin was pretty cramped, even though some of the equipment had been attached outside. The men could not expect much comfort for the next week.

Hargedon was used to the trips, however. He disapproved on principle of people who complained about minor inconveniences such as having to sleep in space suits; fortunately, Zaino's interest and excitement overrode any thought he might have had about discomfort.

This lasted through the time they spent doubling the vast crack in Mercury's crust, driving on a little to the north of the ship on the other side and then turning west toward the dark hemisphere. The route was identical to that of Harmon's machine for some time, though no trace of its passage showed on the hard surface. Then Hargedon angled off toward the southwest. He had driven this run often enough to know it well even without the markers which had been set out with the seismographs. The photographic maps were also aboard. With them, even Zaino had no trouble keeping track of their progress while they remained in sunlight.

However, the sun sank as they traveled west. In two hours its lower rim would have been on the horizon, had they been able to see the horizon; as it was, more of the "sea level" lava plain was in shadow than not even near the ship, and their route now lay in semidarkness.

The light came from peaks projecting into the sunlight, from scattered skylight which was growing rapidly fainter and from the brighter celestial objects such as Earth. Even with the tractor's lights it was getting harder to spot crevasses and seismometer markers. Zaino quickly found the fun wearing off . . . though his pride made him cover this fact as best he could.

If Hargedon saw this, he said nothing. He set Zaino to picking up every other instrument, as any partner would have, making no allowance for the work the youngster was doing for Schlossberg. This might, of course, have had the purpose of keeping the radioman too busy to think about discomfort. Or it might merely have been Hargedon's idea of normal procedure.

Whatever the cause, Zaino got little chance to use the radio once they had driven into the darkness. He managed only one or two brief talks with those left at the ship.

The talks might have helped his morale, since they certainly must have given the impression that nothing was going on in the ship while at least he had something to do in the tractor. However, this state of affairs did not last. Before the vehicle was four hours out of sight of the *Albireo*, a broadcast by Camille Burkett reached them.

The mineralogist's voice contained at least as much professional enthusiasm as alarm, but everyone listening must have thought promptly of the dubious stability of Mercury's crust. The call was intended for her fellow geologists Mardikian and Harmon. But it interested Zaino at least as much.

"Joe! Eileen! There's a column of what looks like black smoke rising over Northeast Spur. It can't be a real fire, of course; I can't see its point of origin, but if it's the convection current it seems to me the source must be pretty hot. It's the closest thing to a genuine volcano I've seen since we arrived; it's certainly not another of those ash mounds. I should think you'd still be close enough to make it out, Joe. Can you see anything?"

The reply from Mardikian's tractor was inaudible to Zaino and Hargedon, but Burkett's answer made its general tenor plain.

"I hadn't thought of that. Yes, I'd say it was pretty close to the Brightside route. It wouldn't be practical for you to stop your run now to come back to see. You couldn't do much about it anyway. I could go out to have a look and then report to you. If the way back is blocked there'll be plenty of time to work out another." Hargedon and Zaino passed questioning glances at each other during the shorter pause that followed.

"I know there aren't," the voice then went on, responding to the words they could not hear, "but it's only two or three miles, I'd say. Two to the spur and not much farther to where I could see the other side. Enough of the way is in shade so I could make it in a suit easily enough. I can't see calling back either of the Darkside tractors. Their work is just as important as the rest—anyway, Eileen is probably out of range. She hasn't answered yet."

Another pause.

"That's true. Still, it would mean sacrificing that set of seismic records—no, wait. We could go out later for those. And Mel could take his own weather measures on the later trip. There's plenty of time!"

Pause, longer this time.

"You're right, of course. I just wanted to get an early look at this volcano, if it is one. We'll let the others finish their runs, and when you get back you can check the thing from the other side yourself. If it is blocking your way there's time to find an alternate route. We could be doing that from the maps in the meantime, just in case."

Zaino looked again at his companion.

"Isn't that just my luck!" he exclaimed. "I jump at the first chance to get away from being bored to death. The minute I'm safely away, the only interesting thing of the whole operation happens—back at the ship!"

"Who asked to come on this trip?"

"Oh, I'm not blaming anyone but myself. If I'd stayed back there the volcano would have popped out here somewhere, or else waited until we were gone."

"If it is a volcano. Dr. Burkett didn't seem quite sure."

"No, and I'll bet a nickel she's suiting up right now to go out and see. I hope she comes back with something while we're still near enough to hear about it."

Hargedon shrugged. "I suppose it was also just your luck that sent you on a Darkside trip? You know the radio stuff. You knew we couldn't reach as far this way with the radios. Didn't you think of that in advance?"

"I didn't think of it, any more than you would have. It was bad luck, but I'm not grousing about it. Let's get on with this job." Hargedon nodded with approval, and possibly with some surprise, and the tractor hummed on its way.

The darkness deepened around the patches of lava shown by the driving lights; the sky darkened toward a midnight hue, with stars showing ever brighter through it; and radio reception from the *Albireo* began to get spotty. Gas density at the ion layer was high enough so that recombination of molecules with their radiation-freed electrons was rapid. Only occasional streamers of ionized gas reached far over Darkside. As these thinned out, so did radio reception. Camille Burkett's next broadcast came through very poorly.

There was enough in it, however, to seize the attention of the two men in the tractor.

She was saying:"—real all right, and dangerous. It's the . . . thing I ever saw . . . kinds of lava from what looks like . . . same vent. There's high viscosity stuff building a spatter cone to end all spatter cones, and some very thin fluid from somewhere at the bottom. The flow has already blocked the valley used by the Brightside routes and is coming along it. A new return route will have to be found for the tractors that . . . was spreading fast when I saw it. I can't tell how much will come. But unless it stops there's nothing at all to keep the flow away from the ship. It isn't coming fast, but it's coming. I'd advise all tractors to turn back. Captain Rowson reminds me that only one takeoff is possible. If we leave this site, we're committed to leaving Mercury. Arnie and Ren, do you hear me?"

Zaino responded at once. "We got most of it, Doctor. Do you really think the ship is in danger?"

"I don't know. I can only say that *if* this flow continues the ship will have to leave, because this area will sooner or later be covered. I can't guess how likely . . . check further to get some sort of estimate. It's different from any Earthly lava source—maybe you heard—should try to get Eileen and Eric back, too. I can't raise them. I suppose they're well out from under the ion layer by now. Maybe you're close enough to them to catch them with diffracted waves. Try, anyway. Whether you can raise them or not you'd better start back yourself."

Hargedon cut in at this point. "What does Dr. Mardikian say about that? We still have most of the seismometers on this route to visit."

"I think Captain Rowson has the deciding word here, but if it helps your decision Dr. Mardikian has already started back. He hasn't finished his route, either. So hop back here, Ren. And Arnie, put that technical skill you haven't had to use yet to work raising Eileen and Eric."

"What I can do, I will," replied Zaino, "but you'd better tape a recall message and keep it going out on—let's see—band F."

"All right. I'll be ready to check the volcano as soon as you get back. How long?"

"Seven hours—maybe six and a half," replied Hargedon. "We have to be careful."

"Very well. Stay outside when you arrive; I'll want to go right out in the tractor to get a closer look." She cut off.

"And *that* came through clearly enough!" remarked Hargedon as he swung the tractor around. "I've been awake for fourteen hours, driving off and on for ten of them; I'm about to drive for another six; and then I'm to stand by for more."

"Would you like me to do some of the driving?" asked Zaino.

"I guess you'll have to, whether I like it or not," was the rather lukewarm reply. "I'll keep on for a while, though—until we're back in better light. You get at your radio job."

Zaino tried. Hour after hour he juggled from one band to another. Once he had Hargedon stop while he went out to attach a makeshift antenna which, he hoped, would change his output from broadcast to some sort of beam; after this he kept probing the sky with the "beam," first listening to the *Albireo*'s broadcast in an effort to find projecting wisps of ionosphere and then, whenever he thought he had one, switching on his transmitter and driving his own message at it.

Not once did he complain about lack of equipment or remark how much better he could do once he was back at the ship.

Hargedon's silence began to carry an undercurrent of approval not usual in people who spent much time with Zaino. The technician made no further reference to the suggestion of switching drivers. They came in sight of the *Albireo* and doubled the chasm with Hargedon still at the wheel, Zaino still at his radio and both of them still uncertain whether any of the calls had gotten through.

Both had to admit, even before they could see the ship, that Burkett had had a right to be impressed.

The smoke column showed starkly against the sky, blowing back over the tractor and blocking the sunlight which would otherwise have glared into the driver's eyes. Fine particles fell from it in a steady shower; looking back, the men could see tracks left by their vehicle in the deposit which had already fallen.

As they approached the ship the dark pillar grew denser and narrower, while the particles raining from it became coarser. In some places the ash was drifting into fairly deep piles, giving Hargedon some anxiety about possible concealed cracks. The last part of the trip, along the edge of the great chasm and around its end, was really dangerous; cracks running from its sides were definitely spreading. The two men reached the *Albireo* later than Hargedon had promised, and found Burkett waiting impatiently with a pile of apparatus beside her.

She didn't wait for them to get out before starting to organize.

"There isn't much here. We'll take off just enough of what you're carrying to make room for this. No—wait. I'll have to check some of your equipment; I'm going to need one of Milt Schlossberg's gadgets, I think, so leave that on. We'll take—"

"Excuse me, Doctor," cut in Hargedon. "Our suits need servicing, or at least mine will if you want me to drive you. Perhaps Arnie can help you load for a while, if you don't think it's too important for him to get at the radio—"

"Of course. Excuse me. I should have had someone out here to help me with this. You two go on in. Ren, please get back as soon as you can. I can do the work here; none of this stuff is very heavy."

Zaino hesitated as he swung out of the cab. True, there wasn't too much to be moved, and it wasn't very heavy in Mercury's gravity, and he really should be at the radio; but the thirty-nine-year-old mineralogist was a middle-aged lady by his standards, and shouldn't be allowed to carry heavy packages . . .

"Get along, Arnie!" the middle-aged lady interrupted this train of thought. "Eric and Eileen are getting farther away and harder to reach every second you dawdle!"

He got, though he couldn't help looking northeast as he went rather than where he was going.

The towering menace in that direction would have claimed anyone's attention. The pillar of sable ash was rising straighter, as though the wind were having less effect on it. An equally black cone had risen into sight beyond Northeast Spur—a cone that must have grown to some two thousand feet in roughly ten hours. It had far steeper sides than the cinder mounds near it; it couldn't be made of the same loose ash. Perhaps it consisted of half-melted particles which were fusing together as they fell—that might be what Burkett had meant by "spatter-cone." Still, if that were the case, the material fountaining from the cone's top should be lighting the plain with its incandescence rather than casting an inky shadow for its entire height.

Well, that was a problem for the geologists; Zaino climbed aboard and settled to his task.

The trouble was that he could do very little more here than he could in the tractor. He could have improvised longer-wave transmitting coils whose radiations would have diffracted a little more effectively beyond the horizon, but the receiver on the missing vehicle would not have detected them. He had more power at his disposal, but could only beam it into empty space with his better antennae. He had better equipment for locating any projecting wisps of charged gas which might reflect his waves, but he was already located under a solid roof of the stuff—the *Albireo* was technically on Brightside. Bouncing his beam from this layer still didn't give him the range he needed, as he had found both by calculation and trial.

What he really needed was a relay satellite. The target was simply too far around Mercury's sharp curve by now for anything less.

Zaino's final gesture was to set his transmission beam on the lowest frequency the tractor would pick up, aim it as close to the vehicle's direction as he could calculate from map and itinerary and set the recorded return message going. He told Rowson as much.

"Can't think of anything else?" the captain asked. "Well, neither can I, but of course it's not my field. I'd give a year's pay if I could. How long before they should be back in range?"

"About four days. A hundred hours, give or take a few. They'll be heading back anyway by that time."

"Of course. Well, keep trying."

"I am—or rather, the equipment is. I don't see what else I can do unless a really bright idea should suddenly sprout. Is there anywhere else I could be useful? I'm as likely to have ideas working as just sitting."

"We can keep you busy, all right. But how about taking a transmitter up one of those mountains? That would get your wave farther."

"Not as far as it's going already. I'm bouncing it off the ion layer, which is higher than any mountain we've seen on Mercury even if it's nowhere near as high as Earth's."

"Hmph. All right."

"I could help Ren and Dr. Burkett. I could hang on outside the tractor—"

"They've already gone. You'd better call them, though, and keep a log of what they do."

"All right." Zaino turned back to his board and with no trouble raised the tractor carrying Hargedon and the mineralogist. The latter had been trying to call the *Albireo* and had some acid comments about radio operators who slept on the job.

"There's only one of me, and I've been trying to get the Darkside team," he pointed out. "Have you found anything new about this lava flood?"

"Flow, not flood," corrected the professional automatically. "We're not in sight of it yet. We've just rounded the corner that takes us out of your sight. It's over a mile yet, and a couple of more corners, before we get to the spot where I left it. Of course, it will be closer than that by now. It was spreading at perhaps a hundred yards an hour then. That's one figure we must refine. . . . Of course, I'll try to get samples, too. I wish there were some way to get samples of the central cone. The whole thing is the queerest volcano I've ever heard of. Have you gotten Eileen started back?"

"Not as far as I can tell. As with your cone samples, there are practical difficulties," replied Zaino. "I haven't quit yet, though."

"I should think not. If some of us were paid by the idea we'd be pretty poor, but the perspiration part of genius is open to all of us."

"You mean I should charge a bonus for getting this call through?" retorted the operator.

Whatever Burkett's reply to this might have been was never learned; her attention was diverted at that point.

"We've just come in sight of the flow. It's about five hundred yards ahead. We'll get as close as seems safe, and I'll try to make sure whether it's really lava or just mud."

"Mud? Is that possible? I thought there wasn't—couldn't be—any water on this planet!"

"It is, and there probably isn't. The liquid phase of mud doesn't have to be water, even though it usually is on Earth. Here, for example, it might conceivably be sulfur."

"But if it's just mud, it wouldn't hurt the ship, would it?"

"Probably not."

"Then why all this fuss about getting the tractors back in a hurry?"

The voice which answered reminded him of another lady in his past, who had kept him after school for drawing pictures in math class.

"Because in my judgment the flow is far more likely to be lava than mud, and if I must be wrong I'd rather my error were one that left us alive. I have no time at the moment to explain the basis of my judgment. I will be reporting our activities quite steadily from now on, and would prefer that you not interrupt unless a serious emergency demands it, or you get a call from Eileen.

"We are about three hundred yards away now. The front is moving about as fast as before, which suggests that the flow is coming only along this valley. It's only three or four feet high, so viscosity is very low or density very high. Probably the former, considering where we are. It's as black as the smoke column."

"Not glowing?" cut in Zaino thoughtlessly.

"*Black*, I said. Temperature will be easier to measure when we get closer. The front is nearly straight across the valley, with just a few lobes projecting ten or twelve yards and one notch where a small spine is being surrounded. By the way, I trust you're taping all this?" Again Zaino was reminded of the afternoon after school.

"Yes, Ma'am," he replied. "On my one and only monitor tape."

"Very well. We're stopping near the middle of the valley one hundred yards from the front. I am getting out, and will walk as close as I can with a sampler and a radiometer. I assume that the radio equipment will continue to relay my suit broadcast back to you." Zaino cringed a little, certain as he was that the tractor's electronic apparatus was in perfect order.

It struck him that Dr. Burkett was being more snappish than usual. It never crossed his mind that the woman might be afraid.

"Ren, don't get any closer with the tractor unless I call. I'll get a set of temperature readings as soon as I'm close enough. Then I'll try to get a sample. Then I'll come back with that to the tractor, leave it and the radiometer and get the markers to set out."

"Couldn't I be putting out the markers while you get the sample, Doctor?"

"You could, but I'd rather you stayed at the wheel." Hargedon made no answer, and Burkett resumed her description for the record.

"I'm walking toward the front, a good deal faster than it's flowing toward me. I am now about twenty yards away, and am going to take a set of radiation-temperature measures." A brief pause. "Readings coming. Nine sixty. Nine eighty. Nine ninety—that's from the bottom edge near the spine that's being surrounded. Nine eighty-five—" The voice droned on until about two dozen readings had been taped. Then, "I'm going closer now. The sampler is just a ladle on a twelve-foot handle we improvised, so I'll have to get that close. The stuff is moving slowly; there should be no trouble. I'm in reach now. The lava is very liquid; there's no trouble getting the sampler in—or out again—it's not very dense, either. I'm heading back toward the tractor now. No, Ren, don't come to meet me."

There was a minute of silence, while Zaino pictured the space-suited figure with its awkwardly long burden, walking away from the creeping menace to the relative safety of the tractor. "It's frozen solid already; we needn't worry about spilling. The temperature is about—five eighty. Give me the markers, please."

Another pause, shorter this time. Zaino wondered how much of that could be laid to a faster walk without the ladle and how much to the lessening distance between flow and tractor. "I'm tossing the first marker close to the edge—it's landed less than a foot from the lava. They're all on a light cord at ten-foot intervals; I'm paying out the cord as I go back to the tractor. Now we'll stand by and time the arrival at each marker as well as we can."

"How close are you to the main cone?" asked Zaino.

"Not close enough to see its base, I'm afraid. Or to get a sample of it, which is worse. We—goodness, what was that?"

Zaino had just time to ask, "What was what?" when he found out.

For a moment, he thought that the *Albireo* had been flung bodily into the air. Then he decided that the great metal pillar had merely fallen over. Finally he realized that the ship was still erect, but the ground under it had just tried to leave.

Everyone in the group had become so used to the almost perpetual ground tremors that they had ceased to notice them; but this one demanded attention. Rowson, using language which suggested that his career might not have been completely free of adventure after all, flashed through the communication level on his way down to the power section. Schlossberg and Babineau followed, the medic pausing to ask Zaino if he were all right. The radioman merely nodded affirmatively; his attention was already back at his job. Burkett was speaking a good deal faster than before.

"Never mind if the sample isn't lashed tight yet—if it falls off there'll be plenty more. There isn't time! Arnie, get in touch with Dr. Mardikian and Dr. Marini. Tell them that this volcano is explosive, that all estimates of what the flow may do are off until we can make more measures, and in any case the whole situation is unpredictable. Everyone should get back as soon as possible. Remember, we decided that those big craters Eileen checked were not meteor pits. I don't know whether this thing will let go in the next hour, the next year, or at all. Maybe what's happening now will act as a safety valve—but let's get out. Ren, that flow is speeding up and getting higher, and the ash rain is getting a lot worse. Can you see to drive?"

She fell silent. Zaino, in spite of her orders, left his set long enough to leap to the nearest port for a look at the volcano.

He never regretted it.

Across the riven plain, whose cracks were now nearly hidden under the new ash, the black cone towered above the nearer elevations. It was visibly taller than it had been only a few hours before. The fountain from its top was thicker, now jetting straight up as though wind no longer meant a thing to the fiercely driven column of gas and dust. The darkness was not so complete; patches of red and yellow incandescence showed briefly in the pillar, and glowing sparks rather than black cinders rained back on the steep slopes. Far above, a ring of smoke rolled and spread about the column, forming an ever-broadening blanket of opaque cloud above a landscape which had never before been shaded from the sun. Streamers of lightning leaped between cloud and pillar, pillar and mountain, even cloud and ground. Any thunder there might have been was drowned in the howl of the escaping gas, a roar which seemed to combine every possible note from the shrillest possible whistle to a bass felt by the chest rather than heard by the ears. Rowson's language had become inaudible almost before he had disappeared down the hatch.

For long moments the radioman watched the spreading cloud, and wondered whether the *Albireo* could escape being struck by the flickering, ceaseless lightning. Far above the widening ring of cloud the smoke fountain drove, spreading slowly in the thinning atmosphere and beyond it. Zaino had had enough space experience to tell at a glance whether a smoke or dust cloud was in air or not. This wasn't, at least at the upper extremity . . .

And then, quite calmly, he turned back to his desk, aimed the antenna straight up, and called Eileen Harmon. She answered promptly.

The stratigrapher listened without interruption to his report and the order to return. She conferred briefly with her companion, replied, "We'll be back in twelve hours," and signed off. And that was that.

Zaino settled back with a sigh, and wondered whether it would be tactful to remind Rowson of his offer of a year's pay.

All four vehicles were now homeward bound; all one had to worry about was whether any of them would make it. Hargedon and Burkett were fighting their way through an ever-increasing ash rain a scant two miles away—ash which not only cut visibility but threatened to block the way with drifts too deep to negotiate. The wind, now blowing fiercely toward the volcano, blasted the gritty stuff against their front window as though it would erode through; and the lava flow, moving far faster than the gentle ooze they had never quite measured, surged—and glowed—grimly behind.

A hundred miles or more to the east, the tractors containing Mardikian, Marini and their drivers headed southwest along the alternate route their maps had suggested; but Mardikian, some three hours in the lead, reported that he could see four other smoke columns in that general direction.

Mercury seemed to be entering a new phase. The maps might well be out of date.

Harmon and Trackman were having no trouble at the moment, but they would have to pass the great chasm. This had been shooting out daughter cracks when Zaino and Hargedon passed it hours before. No one could say what it might be like now, and no one was going out to make sure.

"We can see you!" Burkett's voice came through suddenly. "Half a mile to go, and we're way ahead of the flow."

"But it's coming?" Rawson asked tensely. He had returned from the power level at Zaino's phoned report of success.

"It's coming."

"How fast? When will it get here? Do you know whether the ship can stand contact with it?"

"I don't know the speed exactly. There may be two hours, maybe five or six. The ship can't take it. Even the temperature measures I got were above the softening point of the alloys, and it's hotter and much deeper now. Anyway, if the others aren't back before the flow reaches the ship they won't get through. The tractor wheels would char away, and I doubt that the bodies would float. You certainly can't wade through the stuff in a space suit, either."

"And you think there can't be more than five or six hours before the flow arrives?"

"I'd say that was a very optimistic guess. I'll stop and get a better speed estimate if you want, but won't swear to it."

Rowson thought for a moment.

"No," he said finally, "don't bother. Get back here as soon as you can. We need the tractor and human muscles more than we need even expert guesses." He turned to the operator.

"Zaino, tell all the tractors there'll be no answer from the ship for a while, because no one will be aboard. Then suit up and come outside." He was gone.

Ten minutes later, six human beings and a tractor were assembled in the flame-lit near-darkness outside the ship. The cloud had spread to the horizon, and the sun was gone. Burkett and Hargedon had arrived, but Rowson wasted no time on congratulations.

"We have work to do. It will be easy enough to keep the lava from the ship, since there seems to be a foot or more of ash on the ground and a touch of main drive would push it into a ringwall around us; but that's not the main problem. We have to keep it from reaching the chasm anywhere south of us, since that's the way the others will be coming. If they're cut off, they're dead. It will be brute work. We'll use the tractor any way we can think of. Unfortunately it has no plow atttachment, and I can't think of anything aboard which could be turned into one. You have shovels, such as they are. The ash is light, especially here, but there's a mile and a half of dam to be built. I don't see how it can possibly be done . . . but it's going to be."

"Come on, Arnie! You're young and strong," came the voice of the mineralogist. "You should be able to lift as much of this stuff as I can. I understand you were lucky enough to get hold of Eileen—have you asked for the bonus yet?—but your work isn't done."

"It wasn't luck," Zaino retorted. Burkett, in spite of her voice, seemed much less of a schoolmistress when encased in a space suit and carrying a shovel, so he was able to talk back to her. "I was simply alert enough to make use of existing conditions, which I had to observe for myself in spite of all the scientists around. I'm charging the achievement to my regular salary. I saw—"

He stopped suddenly, both with tongue and shovel. Then, "Captain!"

"What is it?"

"The only reason we're starting this wall here is to keep well ahead of the flow so we can work as long as possible, isn't it?"

"Yes, I suppose so. I never thought of trying anywhere else. The valley would mean a much shorter dam, but if the flow isn't through it by now it would be before we could get there—oh! Wait a minute!"

"Yes, sir. You can put the main switch anywhere in a D.C. circuit. Where are the seismology stores we never had to use?"

Four minutes later the tractor set out from the *Albireo*, carrying Rowson and Zaino. Six minutes after that it stopped at the base of the ash cone which formed the north side of the valley from which the lava was coming. They parked a quarter of the way around the cone's base from the emerging flood and started to climb on foot, both carrying burdens.

Forty-seven minutes later they returned empty-handed to the vehicle, to find that it had been engulfed by the spreading liquid.

With noticeable haste they floundered through the loose ash a few yards above the base until they had outdistanced the glowing menace, descended and started back across the plain to where they knew the ship to be, though she was invisible through the falling detritus. Once they had to detour around a crack. Once they encountered one which widened toward the chasm on their right, and they knew a detour would be impossible. Leaping it seemed impossible, too, but they did it. Thirty seconds after this, forty minutes after finding the tractor destroyed, the landscape was bathed in a magnesium-white glare as the two one-and-a-half kiloton charges planted just inside the crater rim let go.

"Should we go back and see if it worked?" asked Zaino.

"What's the use? The only other charges we had were in the tractor. Thank goodness they were nuclear instead of H.E. If it didn't work we'd have more trouble to get back than we're having now."

"If it didn't work, is there any point in going back?"

"Stop quibbling and keep walking. Dr. Burkett, are you listening?"

"Yes, Captain."

"We're fresh out of tractors, but if you want to try it on foot you might start a set of flow measures on the lava. Arnie wants to know whether our landslide slid properly."

However, the two were able to tell for themselves before getting back to the *Albireo*.

The flow didn't stop all at once, of course; but with the valley feeding it blocked off by a pile of volcanic ash four hundred feet high on one side, nearly fifty on the other and more than a quarter of a mile long, its enthusiasm quickly subsided. It was thin, fluid stuff, as Burkett had noted; but as it spread it cooled, and as it cooled it thickened.

Six hours after the blast it had stopped with its nearest lobe almost a mile from the ship, less than two feet thick at the edge.

When Mardikian's tractor arrived, Burkett was happily trying to analyze samples of the flow, and less happily speculating on how long it would be before the entire area would be blown off the planet. When Marini's and Harmon's vehicles arrived, almost together, the specimens had been loaded and everything stowed for acceleration. Sixty seconds after the last person was aboard, the *Albireo* left Mercury's surface at two gravities.

The haste, it turned out, wasn't really necessary. She had been in parking orbit nearly forty-five hours before the first of the giant volcanoes reached its climax, and the one beside their former site was not the first. It was the fourth.

"And that seems to be that," said Camille Burkett rather tritely as they drifted a hundred miles above the little world's surface. "Just a belt of white-hot calderas all around the planet. Pretty, if you like symmetry."

"I like being able to see it from this distance," replied Zaino, floating weightless beside her. "By the way, how much bonus should I ask for getting that idea of putting the seismic charges to use after all?"

"I wouldn't mention it. Any one of us might have thought of that. We all knew about them."

"Anyone *might* have. Let's speculate on how long it would have been before anyone *did*."

"It's still not like the other idea, which involved your own specialty. I still don't see what made you suppose that the gas pillar from the volcano would be heavily charged enough to reflect your radio beam. How did that idea strike you?"

Zaino thought back, and smiled a little as the picture of lightning blazing around pillar, cloud and mountain rose before his eyes.

"You're not quite right," he said. "I was worried about it for a while, but it didn't actually strike me."

It fell rather flat; Camille Burkett, Ph.D., had to have it explained to her.

James Blish

James Blish (1921–75) was perhaps the most sophisticated of the literary critics grown inside the SF field. Though self-educated, he was respected as a James Joyce scholar and was a music critic as well. Of all SF writers at mid-century, Blish most worshipped the Modernists and most aspired to "high" art.

Blish moved permanently to England in the 1960s, where his writing was taken more seriously as contemporary literature than in the U.S. His major achievements in science fiction are generally regarded as the four-volume *Cities in Flight* (1970) and *A Case of Conscience* (1958), a classic theological SF novel. His short fiction, collected in *The Seedling Stars* (1957), *The Best of James Blish* (1979), and several other volumes, is also a major body of work in the modern field. He also edited the first SF anthology about the arts of the future, *New Dreams This Morning* (1966).

Perhaps his most ambitious project began with *A Case of Conscience*, about the discovery of Christian aliens without original sin, which is linked to an even larger literary construct (Blish called it *After Such Knowledge*—essentially an ongoing theological argument) involving an additional non-genre novel about Francis Bacon, *Doctor Mirabilis* (1964), and two fantasy novels about the end of the world, *Black Easter* (1968) and *The Day After Judgement* (1971).

At a time in the 1950s when science fiction as a whole had ignored the arts and artists as subjects for most of its history, Blish published this story. Blish said: "Ostensibly this is a story about the future of serious music." It is of course more broadly about art. Such writers as Brian Aldiss, Samuel R. Delany, Michael Moorcock, and Bruce Sterling carry on the intellectual tradition of Blish today.

A WORK OF ART

Instantly, he remembered dying. He remembered it, however, as if at two removes—as though he were remembering a memory, rather than an actual event; as though he himself had not really been there when he died.

Yet the memory was all from his own point of view, not that of some detached and disembodied observer which might have been his soul. He had been most conscious of the rasping, unevenly drawn movements of the air in his chest. Blurring rapidly, the doctor's face had bent over him, loomed, come closer, and then had vanished as the doctor's head passed below his cone of vision, turned sideways to listen to his lungs.

It had become rapidly darker, and then, only then, had he realized that these were to be his last minutes. He had tried dutifully to say Pauline's name, but his memory contained no record of the sound—only of the rattling breath and of the film of sootiness thickening in the air, blotting out everything for an instant.

Only an instant, and then the memory was over. The room was bright again, and the ceiling, he noticed with wonder, had turned a soft green. The doctor's head lifted again and looked down at him.

It was a different doctor. This one was a far younger man, with an ascetic face and gleaming, almost fey eyes. There was no doubt about it. One of the last conscious thoughts he had had was that of gratitude that the attending physician, there at the end, had not been the one who secretly hated him for his one-time associations with the Nazi hierarchy. The attending doctor, instead, had worn an expression amusingly proper for that of a Swiss expert called to the deathbed of an eminent man: a mixture of worry at the prospect of losing so eminent a patient, and complacency at the thought that, at the old man's age, nobody could blame this doctor if he died. At eighty-five, pneumonia is a serious matter, with or without penicillin.

"You're all right now," the new doctor said, freeing his patient's head of a whole series of little silver rods which had been clinging to it by a sort of network cap. "Rest a minute and try to be calm. Do you know your name?"

He drew a cautious breath. There seemed to be nothing at all the matter with his lungs now; indeed, he felt positively healthy. "Certainly," he said, a little nettled. "Do you know yours?"

The doctor smiled crookedly. "You're in character, it appears," he said. "My name is Barkun Kris; I am a mind sculptor. Yours?"

"Richard Strauss."

"Very good," Dr. Kris said, and turned away. Strauss, however, had already been diverted by a new singularity. *Strauss* is a word as well as a name in German; it has many meanings—an ostrich, a bouquet; von Wolzogen had had a high old time working all the possible puns into the libretto of *Feuersnot*. And it happened to be the first German word to be spoken either by himself or by Dr. Kris since that twice-removed moment of death. The language was not French or Italian, either. It was most like English, but not the English Strauss knew; nevertheless, he was having no trouble speaking it and even thinking in it.

Well, he thought, *I'll be able to conduct* The Love of Danae, *after all. It isn't every composer who can premier his own opera posthumously.* Still, there was something queer about all this—the queerest part of all being that conviction, which would not go away, that he had actually been dead for just a short time. Of course, medicine was making great strides, but . . .

"Explain all this," he said, lifting himself to one elbow. The bed was different, too, and not nearly as comfortable as the one in which he had died. As for the room, it looked more like a dynamo shed than a sickroom. Had modern medicine taken to reviving its corpses on the floor of the Siemanns-Schukert plant?

"In a moment," Dr. Kris said. He finished rolling some machine back into what Strauss impatiently supposed to be its place, and crossed to the pallet. "Now. There are many things you'll have to take for granted without attempting to understand then, Dr. Strauss. Not everything in the world today is explicable in terms of your assumptions. Please bear that in mind."

"Very well. Proceed."

"The date," Dr. Kris said, "is 2161 by your calendar—or, in other words, it is now two hundred and twelve years after your death. Naturally, you'll realize that by this time nothing remains of your body but the bones. The body you have now was volunteered for your use. Before you look into a mirror to see what it's like, remember that its physical difference from the one you were used to is all in your favor. It's in perfect health, not unpleasant for other people to look at, and its physiological age is about fifty."

A miracle? No, not in this new age, surely. It is simply a work of science. But what a science! This was Nietzsche's eternal recurrence and the immortality of the superman combined into one.

"And where is this?" the composer said.

"In Port York, part of the State of Manhattan, in the United States. You will find the country less changed in some respects than I imagine you anticipate. Other changes, of course, will seem radical to you, but it's hard for me to predict which ones will strike you that way. A certain resilience on your part will bear cultivating."

"I understand," Strauss said, sitting up. "One question, please; is it still possible for a composer to make a living in this century?"

"Indeed it is," Dr. Kris said, smiling. "As we expect you to do. It is one of the purposes for which we've—brought you back."

"I gather, then," Strauss said somewhat dryly, "that there is still a demand for my music. The critics in the old days—"

"That's not quite how it is," Dr. Kris said. "I understand some of your work is still played, but frankly I know very little about your current status. My interest is rather—"

A door opened somewhere, and another man came in. He was older and more ponderous than Kris and had a certain air of academicism, but he, too, was wearing the oddly tailored surgeon's gown and looked upon Kris' patient with the glowing eyes of an artist.

"A success, Kris?" he said. "Congratulations."

"They're not in order yet," Dr. Kris said. "The final proof is what counts. Dr. Strauss, if you feel strong enough, Dr. Seirds and I would like to ask you some questions. We'd like to make sure your memory is clear."

"Certainly. Go ahead."

"According to our records," Kris said, "you once knew a man whose initials were R. K. L.; this was while you were conducting at the Vienna *Staatsoper.*" He made the double "a" at least twice too long, as though German were a dead language he was striving to pronounce in some "classical" accent. "What was his name, and who was he?"

"That would be Kurt List—his first name was Richard, but he didn't use it. He was assistant stage manager."

The two doctors looked at each other. "Why did you offer to write a new overture to *The Woman Without a Shadow* and give the manuscript to the city of Vienna?"

"So I wouldn't have to pay the garbage removal tax on the Maria Theresa villa they had given me."

"In the backyard of your house at Garmisch-Partenkirchen there was a tombstone. What was written on it?"

Strauss frowned. That was a question he would be happy to be unable to answer. If one is to play childish jokes upon oneself, it's best not to carve them in stone and put the carving where you can't help seeing it every time you go out to tinker with the Mercedes. "It says," he replied wearily, " 'Sacred to the memory of Guntram, Minnesinger, slain in a horrible way by his father's own symphony orchestra.' "

"When was *Guntram* premiered?"

"In—let me see—1894, I believe."

"Where?"

"In Weimar."

"Who was the leading lady?"

"Pauline de Ahna."

"What happened to her afterwards?"

"I married her. Is she . . . ," Strauss began anxiously.

"No," Dr. Kris said. "I'm sorry, but we lack the data to reconstruct more or less ordinary people."

The composer sighed. He did not know whether to be worried or not. He had loved Pauline, to be sure; on the other hand, it would be pleasant to be able to live the new life without being forced to take off one's shoes every time one entered the house, so as not to scratch the polished hardwood floors. And also pleasant, perhaps, to have two o'clock in the afternoon come by without hearing Pauline's everlasting, "Richard—*jetzt komponiert!*"

"Next question," he said.

For reasons which Strauss did not understand, but was content to take for granted, he was separated from Drs. Kris and Seirds as soon as both were satisfied that the composer's memory was reliable and his health stable. His estate, he was given to understand, had long since been broken up—a sorry end for what had been one of the principal fortunes of Europe—but he was given sufficient money to set up lodgings and resume an active life. He was provided, too, with introductions which proved valuable.

It took longer than he had expected to adjust to the changes that had taken place in music alone. Music was, he quickly began to suspect, a dying art, which would soon have a status not much above that held by flower arranging back in what he thought of as his own century. Certainly it couldn't be denied that the trend toward fragmentation, already visible back in his own time, had proceeded almost to completion in 2161.

He paid no more attention to American popular tunes than he had bothered to pay in his previous life. Yet it was evident that their assembly-line production methods—all the ballad composers openly used a slide-rule-like device called a Hit Machine—now had their counterparts almost throughout serious music.

The conservatives these days, for instance, were the twelve-tone composers—always, in Strauss's opinion, dryly mechanical but never more so than now. Their gods—Berg, Schoenberg, Webern—were looked upon by the concert-going public as great masters, on the abstruse side perhaps, but as worthy of reverence as any of the Three B's.

There was one wing of the conservatives however, that had gone the twelve-tone procedure one better. These men composed what was called "stochastic music," put together by choosing each individual note by consultation with tables of random numbers. Their bible, their basic text, was a volume called *Operational Aesthetics*, which in turn derived from a discipline called information theory, and not one word of it seemed to touch upon any of the techniques and customs of composition which Strauss knew. The ideal of this group was to produce music which would be "universal"—that is, wholly devoid of any trace of the composer's individuality, wholly a musical expression of the universal Laws of Chance. The Laws of Chance seemed to have a style of their own, all right, but to Strauss it seemed the style of an idiot child being taught to hammer a flat piano, to keep him from getting into trouble.

By far the largest body of work being produced, however, fell into a category mis- leadingly called science-music. The term reflected nothing but the titles of the works, which dealt with space flight, time travel, and other subjects of a romantic or an unlikely nature. There was nothing in the least scientific about the music, which consisted of a mélange of clichés and imitations of natural sounds, in which Strauss was horrified to see his own time-distorted and diluted image.

The most popular form of science-music was a nine-minute composition called a concerto, though it bore no resemblance at all to the classical concerto form; it was instead a sort of free rhapsody after Rachmaninoff—long after. A typical one—"Song of Deep Space," it was called, by somebody named H. Val- erion Krafft—began with a loud assault on the tam-tam, after which all the strings rushed up the scale in unison, followed at a respectful distance by the harp and one clarinet in parallel 6/4's. At the top of the scale cymbals were bashed together, *forte possible,* and the whole orchestra launched itself into a major-minor wailing sort of melody; the whole orchestra, that is, except for the French horns, which were plodding back down the scale again in what was evi- dently supposed to be a countermelody. The second phrase of the theme was picked up by a solo trumpet with a suggestion of tremolo, the orchestra died back to its roots to await the next cloudburst, and at this point—as any four- year-old could have predicted—the piano entered with the second theme.

Behind the orchestra stood a group of thirty women, ready to come in with a wordless chorus intended to suggest the eeriness of Deep Space—but at this point, too, Strauss had already learned to get up and leave. After a few such experiences he could also count upon meeting in the lobby Sindi Noniss, the agent to whom Dr. Kris had introduced him and who was handling the reborn composer's output—what there was of it thus far. Sindi had come to expect these walkouts on the part of his client and patiently awaited them, standing beneath a bust of Gian-Carlo Menotti, but he liked them less and less, and lately had been greeting them by turning alternately red and white, like a totipotent barber pole.

"You shouldn't have done it," he burst out after the Krafft incident. "You can't just walk out on a new Krafft composition. The man's the president of the Interplanetary Society for Contemporary Music. How am I ever going to per- suade them that you're a contemporary if you keep snubbing them?"

"What does it matter?" Strauss said. "They don't know me by sight."

"You're wrong; they know you very well, and they're watching every move you make. You're the first major composer the mind sculptors ever tackled, and the ISCM would be glad to turn you back with a rejection slip."

"Why?"

"Oh," said Sindi, "there are lots of reasons. The sculptors are snobs; so are the ISCM boys. Each of them wanted to prove to the other that their own art is the king of them all. And then there's the competition; it would be easier to flunk you than to let you into the market. I really think you'd better go back in. I could make up some excuse—"

"No," Strauss said shortly. "I have work to do."

"But that's just the point. Richard. How are we going to get an opera produced without the ISCM? It isn't as though you wrote theremin solos, or something that didn't cost so—"

"I have work to do," he said, and left.

And he did, work which absorbed him as had no other project during the last thirty years of his former life. He had scarcely touched pen to music paper— both had been astonishingly hard to find—when he realized that nothing in his long career had provided him with touchstones by which to judge what music he should write *now*.

The old tricks came swarming back by the thousands, to be sure: the sudden, unexpected key changes at the crest of a melody, the interval stretching, the piling of divided strings, playing in the high harmonics, upon the already tottering top of a climax, the scurry and bustle as phrases were passed like lightning from one choir of the orchestra to another, the flashing runs in the brass, the chuckling in the clarinets, the snarling mixtures of colors to emphasize dramatic tension—all of them.

But none of them satisfied him now. He had been content with them for most of a lifetime and had made them do an astonishing amount of work. But now it was time to strike out afresh. Some of the tricks, indeed, actively repelled him: Where had he gotten the notion, clung to for decades, that violins screaming out in unison somewhere in the stratosphere were a sound interesting enough to be worth repeating inside a single composition, let alone in all of them?

And nobody, he reflected contentedly, ever approached such a new beginning better equipped. In addition to the past lying available in his memory, he had always had a technical armamentarium second to none; even the hostile critics had granted him that. Now that he was, in a sense, composing his first opera— his first after fifteen of them!—he had every opportunity to make it a masterpiece.

And every such intention.

There were of course, many minor distractions. One of them was that search for old-fashioned score paper, and a pen and ink with which to write on it. Very few of the modern composers, it developed, wrote their music at all. A large bloc of them used tape, patching together snippets of tone and sound snipped from other tapes, superimposing one tape on another, and varying the results by twirling an elaborate array of knobs this way or that. Almost all the composers of 3-V scores, on the other hand, wrote on the sound track itself, rapidly scribbling jagged wiggly lines which, when passed through a photocell-audio circuit, produced a noise reasonably like an orchestra playing music, overtones and all.

The last-ditch conservatives who still wrote notes on paper did so with the aid of a musical typewriter. The device, Strauss had to admit, seemed perfected at last; it had manuals and stops like an organ, but it was not much more than twice as large as a standard letter-writing typewriter and produced a neat page. But he was satisfied with his own spidery, highly legible manuscript and refused to abandon it, badly though the one pen nib he had been able to buy coarsened it. It helped to tie him to his past.

Joining the ISCM had also caused him some bad moments, even after Sindi had worked him around the political roadblocks. The Society man who examined his qualifications as a member had run through the questions with no more interest than might have been shown by a veterinarian examining his four-thousandth sick calf.

"Had anything published?"

"Yes, nine tone poems, about three hundred songs, an—"

"Not when you were alive," the examiner said, somewhat disquietingly. "I mean since the sculptors turned you out again."

"Since the sculptors—ah, I understand. Yes, a string quartet, two song cycles, a—"

"Good. Alfie, write down, 'Songs.' Play an instrument?"

"Piano."

"Hmmm." The examiner studied his fingernails. "Oh well. Do you read music? Or do you use a Scriber, or tape clips? Or a Machine?"

"I read."

"Here." The examiner sat Strauss down in front of a viewing lectern, over the lit surface of which an endless belt of translucent paper was traveling. On the paper was an immensely magnified sound track. "Whistle me the tune of that, and name the instruments it sounds like."

"I don't read that *Musiksticheln*," Strauss said frostily, "or write it, either. I use standard notation, on music paper."

"Alfie, write down, 'Reads notes only.'" He laid a sheet of grayly printed music on the lectern above the ground glass. "Whistle me that."

"That" proved to be a popular tune called "Vangs, Snifters, and Store-Credit Snooky," which had been written on a Hit Machine in 2159 by a guitar-faking politician who sang it at campaign rallies. (In some respects, Strauss reflected, the United States had indeed not changed very much.) It had become so popular that anybody could have whistled it from the title alone, whether he could read the music or not. Strauss whistled it and, to prove his bona fides, added, "It's in the key of B flat."

The examiner went over to the green-painted upright piano and hit one greasy black key. The instrument was horribly out of tune—the note was much nearer to the standard 440/cps A than it was to B flat—but the examiner said, "So it is. Alfie, write down, 'Also reads flats.' All right, son, you're a member. Nice to have you with us; not many people can read that old-style notation anymore. A lot of them think they're too good for it."

"Thank you," Strauss said.

"My feeling is, if it was good enough for the old masters, it's good enough for us. We don't have people like them with us these days, it seems to me. Except for Dr. Krafft, of course. They were *great* back in the old days—men like Shilkrit, Steiner, Tiomkin, and Pearl . . . and Wilder and Jannsen. Real goffin."

"*Doch gewiss*," Strauss said politely.

But the work went forward. He was making a little income now, from small works. People seemed to feel a special interest in a composer who had come out of the mind sculptors' laboratories, and in addition the material itself, Strauss was quite certain, had merits of its own to help sell it.

It was the opera that counted, however. That grew and grew under his pen, as fresh and new as his new life, as founded in knowledge and ripeness as his long, full memory. Finding a libretto had been troublesome at first. While it was possible that something existed that might have served among the current scripts for 3-V—though he doubted it—he found himself unable to tell the good from the bad through the fog cast over both by incomprehensibly technical production directions. Eventually, and for only the third time in his whole career, he had fallen back upon a play written in a language other than his own, and—for the first time—decided to set it in that language.

The play was Christopher Fry's *Venus Observed*, in all ways a perfect Strauss opera libretto, as he came gradually to realize. Though nominally a comedy, with a complex farcical plot, it was a verse play with considerable depth to it, and a number of characters who cried out to be brought by music into three dimensions, plus a strong undercurrent of autumnal tragedy, of leaf-fall and apple-fall—precisely the kind of contradictory dramatic mixture which von Hofmannsthal had supplied him with in *The Knight of the Rose*, in *Ariadne at Naxos*, and in *Arabella*.

Alas for von Hofmannsthal, but here was another long-dead playwright who seemed nearly as gifted, and the musical opportunities were immense. There was, for instance, the fire which ended Act II; what a gift for a composer to whom orchestration and counterpoint were as important as air and water! Or take the moment where Perpetua shoots the apple from the Duke's hand; in that one moment a single passing reference could add Rossini's marmoreal *William Tell* to the musical texture as nothing but an ironic footnote! And the Duke's great curtain speech, beginning:

> *Shall I be sorry for myself? In Mortality's name*
> *I'll be sorry for myself. Branches and boughs,*
> *Brown hills, the valleys faint with brume,*
> *A burnish on the lake. . . .*

There was a speech for a great tragic comedian in the spirit of Falstaff: the final union of laughter and tears, punctuated by the sleepy comments of Reedbeck, to whose sonorous snore (trombones, no less than five of them, *con sordini?*) the opera would gently end. . . .

What could be better? And yet he had come upon the play only by the unlikeliest series of accidents. At first he had planned to do a straight knockabout farce, in the idiom of *The Silent Woman*, just to warm himself up. Remembering that Zweig had adapted that libretto for him, in the old days, from a play by Ben Jonson, Strauss had begun to search out English plays of the period just after Jonson's, and had promptly run aground on an awful specimen in heroic couplets called *Venice Preserv'd*, by one Thomas Otway. The Fry play had directly followed the Otway in the card catalogue, and he had looked at it out of curiosity; why should a twentieth-century playwright be punning on a title from the eighteenth?

After two pages of the Fry play, the minor puzzle of the pun disappeared entirely from his concern. His luck was running again; he had an opera.

Sindi worked miracles in arranging for the performance. The date of the premiere was set even before the score was finished, reminding Strauss pleasantly of those heady days when Fuestner had been snatching the conclusion of *Elektra* off his worktable a page at a time, before the ink was even dry, to rush it to the engraver before publication deadline. The situation now, however, was even more complicated, for some of the score had to be scribed, some of it taped, some of it engraved in the old way, to meet the new techniques of performance; there were moments when Sindi seemed to be turning quite gray.

But *Venus Observed* was, as usual, forthcoming complete from Strauss's pen in plenty of time. Writing the music in first draft had been hellishly hard work, much more like being reborn than had been that confused awakening in Barkun Kris' laboratory, with its overtones of being dead instead, but Strauss found that he still retained all of his old ability to score from the draft almost effortlessly, as undisturbed by Sindi's half-audible worrying in the room with him as he was by the terrifying supersonic bangs of the rockets that bulleted invisibly over the city.

When he was finished, he had two days still to spare before the beginning of rehearsals. With those, furthermore, he would have nothing to do. The techniques of performance in this age were so completely bound up with the electronic arts as to reduce his own experience—he, the master *Kapellmeister* of them all—to the hopelessly primitive.

He did not mind. The music, as written, would speak for itself. In the meantime he found it grateful to forget the months-long preoccupation with the stage for a while. He went back to the library and browsed lazily through old poems, vaguely seeking texts for a song or two. He knew better than to bother with recent poets; they could not speak to him, and he knew it. The Americans of his own age, he thought, might give him a clue to understanding this America of 2161, and if some such poem gave birth to a song, so much the better.

The search was relaxing, and he gave himself up to enjoying it. Finally he struck a tape that he liked; a tape read in a cracked old voice that twanged of Idaho as that voice had twanged in 1910, in Strauss' own ancient youth. The poet's name was Pound; he said, on the tape:

> "... the souls of all men great
> At times pass through us,
> And we are melted into them, and are not
> Save reflexions of their souls.
> Thus I am Dante for a space and am
> One François Villon, a ballad-lord and thief,
> Or am such holy ones I may not write,
> Lest Blasphemy be writ against my name;
> This for an instant and the flame is gone.
> 'Tis as in midmost us there glows a sphere
> Translucent, molten gold, that is the 'I'
> And into this some form projects itself:
> Christus, or John, or eke the Florentine;
> And as the clear space is not if a form's
> Imposed thereon,
> So cease we from all being for the time,
> And these, the masters of the Soul, live on."

He smiled. That lesson had been written again and again from Plato onward. Yet the poem was a history of his own case, a sort of theory for the metempsychosis he had undergone, and in its formal way it was moving. It would be fitting to make a little hymn of it, in honor of his own rebirth, and of the poet's insight.

A series of solemn, breathless chords framed themselves in his inner ear, against which the words might be intoned in a high, gently bending hush at the beginning . . . and then a dramatic passage in which the great names of Dante and Villon would enter ringing like challenges to Time. . . . He wrote for a while in his notebook before he returned the spool to its shelf.

These, he thought, are good auspices.

And so the night of the premiere arrived, the audience pouring into the hall, the 3-V cameras riding on no visible supports through the air, and Sindi calculating his share of his client's earnings by a complicated game he played on his fingers, the basic law of which seemed to be that one plus one equals ten. The hall filled to the roof with people from every class, as though what was to come would be a circus rather than an opera.

There were, surprisingly, nearly fifty of the aloof and aristocratic mind sculptors, clad in formal clothes which were exaggerated black versions of their surgeons' gowns. They had bought a block of seats near the front of the auditorium, where the gigantic 3-V figures which would shortly fill the "stage" before them (the real singers would perform on a small stage in the basement) could not but seem monstrously out of proportion, but Strauss supposed that they had taken this into account and dismissed it.

There was a tide of whispering in the audience as the sculptors began to trickle in, and with it an undercurrent of excitement, the meaning of which was unknown to Strauss. He did not attempt to fathom it, however; he was coping with his own mounting tide of opening-night tension, which, despite all the years, he had never quite been able to shake.

The sourceless, gentle light in the auditorium dimmed, and Strauss mounted the podium. There was a score before him, but he doubted that he would need it. Directly before him, poking up from among the musicians, were the inevitable 3-V snouts, waiting to carry his image to the singers in the basement.

The audience was quiet now. This was the moment. His baton swept up and then decisively down, and the prelude came surging up out of the pit.

For a little while he was deeply immersed in the always tricky business of keeping the enormous orchestra together and sensitive to the flexing of the musical web beneath his hand. As his control firmed and became secure, however, the task became slightly less demanding, and he was able to pay more attention to what the whole sounded like.

There was something decidedly wrong with it. Of course there were the occasional surprises as some bit of orchestral color emerged with a different *Klang* than he had expected; that happened to every composer, even after a lifetime of experience. And there were moments when the singers, entering upon a phrase more difficult to handle than he had calculated, sounded like someone about to fall off a tightrope (although none of them actually fluffed once; they were as fine as troupe of voices as he had ever had to work with).

But these were details. It was the overall impression that was wrong. He was losing not only the excitement of the premiere—after all, that couldn't last at the same pitch all evening—but also his very interest in what was coming from the stage and the pit. He was gradually tiring, his baton arm becoming heavier; as the second act mounted to what should have been an impassioned outpouring of shining tone, he was so bored as to wish he could go back to his desk to work on that song.

Then the act was over; only one more to go. He scarcely heard the applause. The twenty minutes' rest in his dressing room was just barely enough to give him the necessary strength.

And suddenly, in the middle of the last act, he understood.

There was nothing new about the music. It was the old Strauss all over again—but weaker, more dilute than ever. Compared with the output of composers like Krafft, it doubtless sounded like a masterpiece to this audience. But he knew.

The resolutions, the determination to abandon the old clichés and mannerisms, the decision to say something new—they had all come to nothing against the force of habit. Being brought to life again meant bringing to life as well all those deeply graven reflexes of his style. He had only to pick up his pen and they overpowered him with easy automatism, no more under his control than the jerk of a finger away from a flame.

His eyes filled; his body was young, but he was an old man, an old man. Another thirty-five years of this? Never. He had said all this before, centuries before. Nearly a half century condemned to saying it all over again, in a weaker and still weaker voice, aware that even this debased century would come to recognize in him only the burnt husk of greatness?—no, never, never.

He was aware, dully, that the opera was over. The audience was screaming its joy. He knew the sound. They had screamed that way when *Day of Peace* had been premiered, but they had been cheering the man he had been, not the man that *Day of Peace* showed with cruel clarity he had become. Here the sound was even more meaningless: cheers of ignorance, and that was all.

He turned slowly. With surprise, and with a surprising sense of relief, he saw that the cheers were not, after all, for him.

They were for Dr. Barkun Kris.

Kris was standing in the middle of the bloc of mind sculptors, bowing to the audience. The sculptors nearest him were shaking his hand one after the other. More grasped at it as he made his way to the aisle and walked forward to the podium. When he mounted the rostrum and took the composer's limp hand, the cheering became delirious.

Kris lifted his arm. The cheering died instantly to an intent hush.

"Thank you," he said clearly. "Ladies and gentlemen, before we take leave of Dr. Strauss, let us again tell him what a privilege it has been for us to hear this fresh example of his mastery. I am sure no farewell could be more fitting."

The ovation lasted five minutes and would have gone another five if Kris had not cut it off.

"Dr. Strauss," he said, "in a moment, when I speak a certain formulation to you, you will realize that your name is Jerom Bosch, born in our century and with a life in it all your own. The superimposed memories which have made you assume the mask, the *persona*, of a great composer will be gone. I tell you this so that you may understand why these people here share your applause with me."

A wave of asserting sound.

"The art of mind sculpture—the creation of artificial personalities for aesthetic enjoyment—may never reach such a pinnacle again. For you should understand that as Jerom Bosch you had no talent for music at all; indeed, we searched a long time to find a man who was utterly unable to carry even the simplest tune. Yet we were able to impose upon such unpromising material not only the personality, but the genius, of a great composer. That genius belongs entirely to you—to the *persona* that thinks of itself as Richard Strauss. None of the credit goes to the man who volunteered for the sculpture. That is your triumph, and we salute you for it."

Now the ovation could no longer be contained. Strauss, with a crooked smile, watched Dr. Kris bow. This mind sculpturing was a suitably sophisticated kind of cruelty for this age, but the impulse, of course, had always existed. It was the same impulse that had made Rembrandt and Leonardo turn cadavers into art works.

It deserved a suitably sophisticated payment under the *lex talionis:* an eye for an eye, a tooth for a tooth—and a failure for a failure.

No, he need not tell Dr. Kris that the "Strauss" he had created was as empty of genius as a hollow gourd. The joke would always be on the sculptor, who was incapable of hearing the hollowness of the music now preserved on the 3-V tapes.

But for an instant a surge of revolt poured through his bloodstream. *I am I,* he thought. *I am Richard Strauss until I die, and will never be Jerom Bosch, who was utterly unable to carry even the simplest tune.* His hand, still holding the baton, came sharply up, through whether to deliver or to ward off a blow he could not tell.

He let it fall again, and instead, at last, bowed—not to the audience, but to Dr. Kris. He was sorry for nothing, as Kris turned to him to say the word that would plunge him back into oblivion, except that he would now have no chance to set that poem to music.

E. M. Forster

E. M. Forster (1879–1970) was one of the great novelists (*Howard's End* [1910]; *A Passage to India* [1924]) of the century and one of the great literary critics (*Aspects of the Novel* [1927]). Leslie A. Fiedler, in the introduction to his excellent anthology of SF, *In Dreams Awake* (1975), summarizes how the personal and aesthetic rupture between Henry James and H. G. Wells after about 1900 became metaphorically institutionalized in the Jamesian separation of literature into "high" and "low." Forster, like James, felt that Wells was a pernicious literary and cultural influence and wrote this story as an anti-Wellsian piece, in reaction to *A Modern Utopia* (1905), in 1908—though it was not collected until 1928. It stands as an eloquent criticism of the urban and technological strain that pervades science fiction by a high Modernist.

Modernism was certainly opposed to science fiction from early in the century, and more so when science fiction became in the 1920s a low-class genre. C. S. Lewis was one of the few respectable academics who could see any value in the genre. Forster, who had no use for worship of the machine, portrays his future hive-world as reducing humans to insects, fungus, cripples. And Forster's story is a dystopia, or anti-utopia, one of the crucial texts that gave the anti-utopian story the odor of "high" art and respectability in this century—and the utopia the aura of "low."

THE MACHINE STOPS

PART I
The Airship

Imagine, if you can, a small room, hexagonal in shape like the cell of a bee. It is lighted neither by window nor by lamp, yet it is filled with a soft radiance. There are no apertures for ventilation, yet the air is fresh. There are no musical instruments, and yet, at the moment that my meditation opens, this room is throbbing with melodious sounds. An armchair is in the center, by its side a reading desk—that is all the furniture. And in the armchair there sits a swaddled lump of flesh—a woman, about five feet high, with a face as white as a fungus. It is to her that the little room belongs.

An electric bell rang.

The woman touched a switch and the music was silent.

"I suppose I must see who it is," she thought, and set her chair in motion. The chair, like the music, was worked by machinery, and it rolled her to the other side of the room, where the bell still rang importunately.

"Who it is?" she called. Her voice was irritable, for she had been interrupted often since the music began. She knew several thousand people; in certain directions human intercourse had advanced enormously.

But when she listened into the receiver, her white face wrinkled into smiles, and she said:

"Very well. Let us talk, I will isolate myself. I do not expect anything important will happen for the next five minutes—for I can give you fully five minutes, Kuno. Then I must deliver my lecture on 'Music during the Australian Period.'"

She touched the isolation knob, so that no one else could speak to her. Then she touched the lighting apparatus, and the little room was plunged into darkness.

"Be quick!" she called, her irritation returning. "Be quick, Kuno; here I am in the dark wasting my time."

But it was fully fifteen seconds before the round plate that she held in her hands began to glow. A faint blue light shot across it, darkening to purple, and presently she could see the image of her son, who lived on the other side of the earth, and he could see her.

"Kuno, how slow you are."

He smiled gravely.

"I really believe you enjoy dawdling."

"I have called you before, Mother, but you were always busy or isolated. I have something particular to say."

"What is it, dearest boy? Be quick. Why could you not send it by pneumatic post?"

"Because I prefer saying such a thing. I want—"

"Well?"

"I want you to come and see me."

Vashti watched his face in the blue plate.

"But I can see you!" she exclaimed. "What more do you want?"

"I want to see you not through the Machine," said Kuno. "I want to speak to you not through the wearisome Machine."

"Oh, hush!" said his mother, vaguely shocked. "You mustn't say anything against the Machine."

"Why not?"

"One mustn't."

"You talk as if a god had made the Machine," cried the other. "I believe that you pray to it when you are unhappy. Men made it, do not forget that. Great men, but men. The Machine is much, but it is not everything. I see something like you in this plate, but I do not see you. I hear something like you through this telephone, but I do not hear you. That is why I want you to come. Come and stop with me. Pay me a visit, so that we can meet face to face, and talk about the hopes that are in my mind."

She replied that she could scarcely spare the time for a visit.

"The airship barely takes two days to fly between me and you."

"I dislike airships."

"Why?"

"I dislike seeing the horrible brown earth, and the sea, and the stars when it is dark. I get no ideas in an airship."

"I do not get them anywhere else."

"What kind of ideas can the air give you?"

He paused for an instant.

"Do you not know four big stars that form an oblong, and three stars close together in the middle of the oblong, and hanging from these stars, three other stars?"

"No, I do not. I dislike the stars. But did they give you an idea? How interesting; tell me."

"I had an idea that they were like a man."

"I do not understand."

"The four big stars are the man's shoulders and his knees. The three stars in the middle are like the belts that men wore once, and the three stars hanging are like a sword."

"A sword?"

"Men carried swords about with them, to kill animals and other men."

"It does not strike me as a very good idea, but it is certainly original. When did it come to you first?"

"In the airship—" He broke off, and she fancied that he looked sad. She could not be sure, for the Machine did not transmit *nuances* of expression. It gave only a general idea of people—an idea that was good enough for all practical purposes, Vashti thought. The imponderable bloom, declared by a discredited philosophy to be the actual essence of intercourse, was rightly ignored by the Machine, just as the imponderable bloom of the grape was ignored by the manufacturers of artificial fruit. Something "good enough" had long since been accepted by our race.

"The truth is," he continued, "that I want to see these stars again. They are curious stars. I want to see them not from the airship, but from the surface of the earth, as our ancestors did, thousands of years ago. I want to visit the surface of the earth."

She was shocked again.

"Mother, you must come, if only to explain to me what is the harm of visiting the surface of the earth."

"No harm," she replied, controlling herself. "But no advantage. The surface of the earth is only dust and mud; no life remains on it, and you would need a respirator, or the cold of the outer air would kill you. One dies immediately in the outer air."

"I know; of course I shall take all precautions."

"And besides—"

"Well?"

She considered, and chose her words with care. Her son had a queer temper, and she wished to dissuade him from the expedition.

"It is contrary to the spirit of the age," she asserted.

"Do you mean by that, contrary to the Machine?"

"In a sense, but—"

His image in the blue plate faded.

"Kuno!"

He had isolated himself.

For a moment Vashti felt lonely.

Then she generated the light, and the sight of her room, flooded with radiance and studded with electric buttons, revived her. There were buttons and switches everywhere—buttons to call for food, for music, for clothing. There was the hot-bath button, by pressure of which a basin of (imitation) marble rose out of the floor, filled to the brim with a warm deodorized liquid. There was the cold-bath button. There was the button that produced literature. And there were of course the buttons by which she communicated with her friends. The room, though it contained nothing, was in touch with all that she cared for in the world.

Vashti's next move was to turn off the isolation switch, and all the accumulations of the last three minutes burst upon her. The room was filled with the noise of bells, and speaking tubes. What was the new food like? Could she recommend it? Had she had any ideas lately? Might one tell her one's own ideas? Would she make an engagement to visit the public nurseries at an early date?—say this day month.

To most of these questions she replied with irritation—a growing quality in that accelerated age. She said that the new food was horrible. That she could not visit the public nurseries through press of engagements. That she had no ideas of her own but had just been told one—that four stars and three in the middle were like a man: she doubted there was much in it. Then she switched off her correspondents, for it was time to deliver her lecture on Australian music.

The clumsy system of public gatherings had been long since abandoned; neither Vashti nor her audience stirred from their rooms. Seated in her armchair she spoke, while they in their armchairs heard her, fairly well, and saw her, fairly well. She opened with a humorous account of music in the pre-Mongolian epoch, and went on to describe the great outburst of song that followed the Chinese conquest. Remote and primeval as were the methods of I-San-So and the Brisbane school, she yet felt (she said) that study of them might repay the musician of today: they had freshness; they had, above all, ideas.

Her lecture, which lasted ten minutes, was well received, and at its conclusion she and many of her audience listened to a lecture on the sea; there were ideas to be got from the sea; the speaker had donned a respirator and visited it lately. Then she fed, talked to many friends, had a bath, talked again, and summoned her bed.

The bed was not to her liking. It was too large, and she had a feeling for a small bed. Complaint was useless, for beds were of the same dimension all over the world, and to have had an alternative size would have involved vast alterations in the Machine. Vashti isolated herself—it was necessary, for neither day nor night existed under the ground—and reviewed all that had happened since she had summoned the bed last. Ideas? Scarcely any. Events—was Kuno's invitation an event?

By her side, on the little reading desk, was a survival from the ages of litter—one book. This was the Book of the Machine. In it were instructions against every possible contingency. If she was hot or cold or dyspeptic or at a loss for a word, she went to the book, and it told her which button to press. The Central Committee published it. In accordance with a growing habit, it was richly bound.

Sitting up in the bed, she took it reverently in her hands. She glanced round the glowing room as if someone might be watching her. Then, half ashamed, half joyful, she murmured, "O Machine! O Machine!" and raised the volume to her lips. Thrice she kissed it, thrice inclined her head, thrice she felt the delirium of acquiescence. Her ritual performed, she turned to page 1367, which gave the times of the departure of the airships from the island in the Southern Hemisphere, under whose soil she lived, to the island in the Northern Hemisphere, whereunder lived her son.

She thought, "I have not the time."

She made the room dark and slept; she awoke and made the room light; she ate and exchanged ideas with her friends, and listened to music and attended lectures; she made the room dark and slept. Above her, beneath her, and around her, the Machine hummed eternally; she did not notice the noise, for she had been born with it in her ears. The earth, carrying her, hummed as it sped through silence, turning her now to the invisible sun, now to the invisible stars. She awoke and made the room light.

"Kuno!"

"I will not talk to you," he answered, "until you come."

"Have you been on the surface of the earth since we spoke last?"

His image faded.

Again she consulted the book. She became very nervous and lay back in her chair palpitating. Think of her as without teeth or hair. Presently she directed the chair to the wall, and pressed an unfamiliar button. The wall swung apart slowly. Through the opening she saw a tunnel that curved slightly, so that its goal was not visible. Should she go to see her son, here was the beginning of the journey.

Of course, she knew all about the communication system. There was nothing mysterious in it. She would summon a car and it would fly with her down the tunnel until it reached the lift that communicated with the airship station: the system had been in use for many, many years, long before the universal establishment of the Machine. And of course she had studied the civilization that had immediately preceded her own—the civilization that had mistaken the functions of the system, and had used it for bringing people to things, instead of for bringing things to people. Those funny old days, when men went for change of air instead of changing the air in their rooms! And yet—she was frightened of the tunnel: she had not seen it since her last child was born. It curved—but not quite as she remembered; it was brilliant—but not quite as brilliant as a lecturer had suggested. Vashti was seized with the terrors of direct experience. She shrank back into the room, and the wall closed up again.

"Kuno," she said, "I cannot come to see you. I am not well."

Immediately an enormous apparatus fell onto her out of the ceiling, a thermometer was automatically inserted between her lips, a stethoscope was automatically laid upon her heart. She lay powerless. Cool pads soothed her forehead. Kuno had telegraphed to her doctor.

So the human passions still blundered up and down in the Machine. Vashti drank the medicine that the doctor projected into her mouth, and the machinery retired into the ceiling. The voice of Kuno was heard asking how she felt.

"Better." Then, with irritation: "But why do you not come to me instead?"

"Because I cannot leave this place."

"Why?"

"Because, any moment, something tremendous may happen."

"Have you been on the surface of the earth yet?"

"Not yet."

"Then what is it?"

"I will not tell you through the machine."

She resumed her life.

But she thought of Kuno as a baby, his birth, his removal to the public nurseries, her one visit to him there, his visits to her—visits which stopped when the Machine had assigned him a room on the other side of the earth. "Parents, duties of," said the book of the Machine, "cease at the moment of birth. P. 422327483." True, but there was something special about Kuno—indeed there had been something special about all her children—and, after all, she must brave the journey if he desired it. And "something tremendous might happen." What did that mean? The nonsense of a youthful man, no doubt, but she must go. Again she pressed the unfamiliar button, again the wall swung back, and she saw the tunnel that curved out of sight. Clasping the Book, she rose, tottered onto the platform, and summoned the car. Her room closed behind her: the journey to the Northern Hemisphere had begun.

Of course, it was perfectly easy. The car approached and in it she found armchairs exactly like her own. When she signaled, it stopped, and she tottered into the lift. One other passenger was in the lift, the first fellow creature she had seen face to face for months. Few traveled in these days, for, thanks to the advance of science, the earth was exactly alike all over. Rapid intercourse, from which the previous civilization had hoped so much, had ended by defeating itself. What was the good of going to Peking when it was just like Shrewsbury? Why return to Shrewsbury when it would be just like Peking? Men seldom moved their bodies; all unrest was concentrated in the soul.

The airship service was a relic from the former age. It was kept up because it was easier to keep it up than to stop it or to diminish it, but it now far exceeded the wants of the population. Vessel after vessel would rise from the vomitories of Rye or of Christchurch (I use the antique names), would sail into the crowded sky, and would draw up at the wharves of the south—empty. So nicely adjusted was the system, so independent of meteorology, that the sky, whether calm or cloudy, resembled a vast kaleidoscope whereon the same patterns periodically recurred. The ship on which Vashti sailed started now at sunset, now at dawn. But always, as it passed above Rheims, it would neighbor the ship that served between Helsingfors and the Brazils, and, every third time it surmounted the Alps, the fleet of Palermo would cross its track behind. Night and day, wind and storm, tide and earthquake impeded man no longer. He had harnessed Leviathan. All the old literature, with its praise of Nature and its fear of Nature, rang false as the prattle of a child.

Yet as Vashti saw the vast flank of the ship, stained with exposure to the outer air, her horror of direct experience returned. It was not quite like the airship in the cinematophote. For one thing it smelled—not strongly or unpleasantly, but it did smell, and with her eyes shut she should have known that a new thing was close to her. Then she had to walk to it from the lift, had to submit to glances from the other passengers. The man in front dropped his Book—no great matter, but it disquieted them all. In the rooms, if the Book was dropped, the floor raised it mechanically, but the gangway to the airship was not so prepared, and the sacred volume lay motionless. They stopped—the thing was unforeseen—and the man, instead of picking up his property, felt the muscles of his arm to see how they had failed him. Then someone actually said with direct utterance: "We shall be late"—and they trooped on board, Vashti treading on the pages as she did so.

Inside, her anxiety increased. The arrangements were old-fashioned and rough. There was even a female attendant, to whom she would have to announce her wants during the voyage. Of course, a revolving platform ran the length of the boat, but she was expected to walk from it to her cabin. Some cabins were better than others, and she did not get the best. She thought the attendant had been unfair, and spasms of rage shook her. The glass valves had closed; she could not go back. She saw, at the end of the vestibule, the lift in which she had ascended going quietly up and down, empty. Beneath those corridors of shining tiles were rooms, tier below tier, reaching far into the earth, and in each room there sat a human being, eating, or sleeping, or producing ideas. And buried deep in the hive was her own room. Vashti was afraid.

"O Machine! O Machine!" she murmured, and caressed her Book, and was comforted.

Then the sides of the vestibule seemed to melt together, as do the passages that we see in dreams; the lift vanished, the Book that had been dropped slid to the left and vanished, polished tiles rushed by like a stream of water, there was a slight jar, and the airship, issuing from its tunnel, soared above the waters of a tropical ocean.

. It was night. For a moment she saw the coast of Sumatra edged by the phosphorescence of waves, and crowned by lighthouses, still sending forth their disregarded beams. These also vanished, and only the stars distracted her. They were not motionless, but swayed to and fro above her head, thronging out of one skylight into another, as if the universe and not the airship was careening. And, as often happens on clear nights, they seemed now to be in perspective, now on a plane; now piled tier beyond tier into the infinite heavens, now concealing infinity, a roof limiting for ever the visions of men. In either case they seemed intolerable. "Are we to travel in the dark?" called the passengers angrily, and the attendant, who had been careless, generated the light and pulled down the blinds of pliable metal. When the airships had been built, the desire to look direct at things still lingered in the world. Hence the extraordinary number of skylights and windows, and the proportionate discomfort to those who were civilized and refined. Even in Vashti's cabin one star peeped through a flaw in the blind, and after a few hours' uneasy slumber, she was disturbed by an unfamiliar glow, which was the dawn.

Quick as the ship had sped westward, the earth had rolled eastward quicker still, and had dragged back Vashti and her companions toward the sun. Science could prolong the night, but only for a little, and those high hopes of neutralizing the earth's diurnal revolution had passed, together with hopes that were possibly higher. To "keep pace with the sun," or even to outstrip it, had been the aim of the civilization preceding this. Racing airplanes had been built for the purpose, capable of enormous speed, and steered by the greatest intellects of the epoch. Round the globe they went, round and round, westward, westward, round and round, amidst humanity's applause. In vain. The globe went eastward quicker still, horrible accidents occurred, and the Committee of the Machine, at the time rising into prominence, declared the pursuit illegal, unmechanical, and punishable by Homelessness.

Of Homelessness more will be said later.

Doubtless the Committee was right. Yet the attempt to "defeat the sun" aroused the last common interest that our race experienced about the heavenly bodies, or indeed about anything. It was the last time that men were compacted by thinking of a power outside the world. The sun had conquered, yet it was the end of his spiritual dominion. Dawn, midday, twilight, the zodiacal path, touched neither men's lives nor their hearts, and science retreated into the ground, to concentrate herself upon problems that she was certain of solving.

So when Vashti found her cabin invaded by a rosy finger of light, she was annoyed and tried to adjust the blind. But the blind flew up altogether, and she saw through the skylight small pink clouds, swaying against a background of blue, and as the sun crept higher, its radiance entered direct, brimming down the wall, like a golden sea. It rose and fell with the airship's motion, just as waves rise and fall, but it advanced steadily, as the tide advances. Unless she was careful, it would strike her face. A spasm of horror shook her, and she rang for the attendant. The attendant too was horrified, but she could do nothing; it was not her place to mend the blind. She could only suggest that the lady should change her cabin, which she accordingly prepared to do.

People were almost exactly alike all over the world, but the attendant of the airship, perhaps owing to her exceptional duties, had grown a little out of the common. She had often to address passengers with direct speech, and this had given her a certain roughness and originality of manner. When Vashti swerved away from the sunbeams with a cry, she behaved barbarically—she put out her hand to steady her.

"How dare you!" exclaimed the passenger. "You forget yourself!"

The woman was confused, and apologized for not having let her fall. People never touched one another. The custom had become obsolete, owing to the Machine.

"Where are we now?" asked Vashti haughtily.

"We are over Asia," said the attendant, anxious to be polite.

"Asia?"

"You must excuse my common way of speaking. I have got into the habit of calling places over which I pass by their unmechanical names."

"Oh, I remember Asia. The Mongols came from it."

"Beneath us, in the open air, stood a city that was once called Simla."

"Have you ever heard of the Mongols and of the Brisbane school?"

"No."

"Brisbane also stood in the open air."

"Those mountains to the right—let me show you them." She pushed back a metal blind. The main chain of the Himalayas was revealed. "They were once called the Roof of the World, those mountains."

"What a foolish name!"

"You must remember that, before the dawn of civilization, they seemed to be an impenetrable wall that touched the stars. It was supposed that no one but the gods could exist above their summits. How we have advanced, thanks to the Machine!"

"How we have advanced, thanks to the Machine!" said Vashti.

"How we have advanced, thanks to the Machine!" echoed the passenger who had dropped his Book the night before and who was standing in the passage.

"And that white stuff in the cracks?—what is it?"

"I have forgotten its name."

"Cover the window, please. These mountains give me no ideas."

The northern aspect of the Himalayas was in deep shadow: on the Indian slope the sun had just prevailed. The forests had been destroyed during the literature epoch for the purpose of making newspaper pulp, but the snows were awakening to their morning glory, and clouds still hung on the breasts of Kinchinjunga. In the plain were seen the ruins of cities, with diminished rivers creeping by their walls, and by the sides of these were sometimes the signs of vomitories, marking the cities of today. Over the whole prospect airships rushed, crossing and intercrossing with incredible aplomb, and rising nonchalantly when they desired to escape the perturbations of the lower atmosphere and to traverse the Roof of the World.

"We have indeed advanced, thanks to the Machine," repeated the attendant, and hid the Himalayas behind a metal blind.

The day dragged wearily forward. The passengers sat each in his cabin, avoiding one another with an almost physical repulsion and longing to be once more under the surface of the earth. There were eight or ten of them, mostly young males, sent out from the public nurseries to inhabit the rooms of those who had died in various parts of the earth. The man who had dropped his Book was on the homeward journey. He had been sent to Sumatra for the purpose of propagating the race. Vashti alone was traveling by her private will.

At midday she took a second glance at the earth. The airship was crossing another range of mountains, but she could see little, owing to clouds. Masses of black rock hovered below her and merged indistinctly into gray. Their shapes were fantastic; one of them resembled a prostrate man.

"No ideas here," murmured Vashti, and hid the Caucasus behind a metal blind.

In the evening she looked again. They were crossing a golden sea, in which lay many small islands and one peninsula.

She repeated, "No ideas here," and hid Greece behind a metal blind.

PART II
The Mending Apparatus

By a vestibule, by a lift, by a tubular railway, by a platform, by a sliding door—by reversing all the steps of her departure did Vashti arrive at her son's room, which exactly resembled her own. She might well declare that the visit was superfluous. The buttons, the knobs, the reading desk with the Book, the temperature, the atmosphere, the illumination—all were exactly the same. And if Kuno himself, flesh of her flesh, stood close beside her at last, what profit was there in that? She was too well bred to shake him by the hand.

Averting her eyes, she spoke as follows:

"Here I am. I have had the most terrible journey and greatly retarded the development of my soul. It is not worth it, Kuno; it is not worth it. My time is too precious. The sunlight almost touched me, and I have met with the rudest people. I can stop only a few minutes. Say what you want to say, and then I must return."

"I have been threatened with Homelessness," said Kuno.

She looked at him now.

"I have been threatened with Homelessness, and I could not tell you such a thing through the Machine."

Homelessness means death. The victim is exposed to the air, which kills him.

"I have been outside since I spoke to you last. The tremendous thing has happened, and they have discovered me."

"But why shouldn't you go outside?" she exclaimed. "It is perfectly legal, perfectly mechanical, to visit the surface of the earth. I have lately been to a lecture on the sea; there is no objection to that; one simply summons a respirator and gets an Egression permit. It is not the kind of thing that spiritually minded people do, and I begged you not to do it, but there is no legal objection to it."

"I did not get an Egression permit."

"Then how did you get out?"

"I found out a way of my own."

The phrase conveyed no meaning to her, and he had to repeat it.

"A way of your own?" she whispered. "But that would be wrong."

"Why?"

The question shocked her beyond measure.

"You are beginning to worship the Machine," he said coldly. "You think it irreligious of me to have found out a way of my own. It was just what the Committee thought, when they threatened me with Homelessness."

At this she grew angry. "I worship nothing!" she cried. "I am most advanced. I don't think you irreligious, for there is no such thing as religion left. All the fear and the superstition that existed once have been destroyed by the Machine. I meant only that to find out a way of your own was—Besides there is no new way out."

"So it is always supposed."

"Except through the vomitories, for which one must have an Egression permit, it is impossible to get out. The Book says so."

"Well, the Book's wrong, for I have been out on my feet."

For Kuno was possessed of a certain physical strength.

By these days it was a demerit to be muscular. Each infant was examined at birth, and all who promised undue strength were destroyed. Humanitarians may protest, but it would have been no true kindness to let an athlete live; he would never have been happy in that state of life to which the Machine had called him; he would have yearned for trees to climb, rivers to bathe in, meadows and hills against which he might measure his body. Man must be adapted to his surroundings, must he not? In the dawn of the world our weakly must be exposed on Mount Taygetus; in its twilight our strong will suffer euthanasia, that the Machine may progress, that the Machine may progress, that the Machine may progress eternally.

"You know that we have lost the sense of space. We say space is 'annihilated,' but we have annihilated not space but the sense thereof. We have lost a part of ourselves. I determined to recover it, and I began by walking up and down the platform of the railway outside my room. Up and down, until I was tired, and so did recapture the meaning of 'Near' and 'Far.' 'Near' is a place to which I can get quickly *on my feet*, not a place to which the train or the airship will take me quickly. 'Far' is a place to which I cannot get quickly on my feet; the vomitory is 'far,' though I could be there in thirty-eight seconds by summoning the train. Man is the measure. That was my first lesson. Man's feet are the measure for distance, his hands are the measure for ownership, his body is the measure for all that is lovable and desirable and strong. Then I went further: it was then that I called to you for the first time, and you would not come.

"This city, as you know, is built deep beneath the surface of the earth, with only the vomitories protruding. Having paced the platform outside my own room, I took the lift to the next platform and paced that also, and so with each in turn, until I came to the topmost, above which begins the earth. All the platforms were exactly alike, and all that I gained by visiting them was to develop my sense of space and my muscles. I think I should have been content with this—it is not a little thing—but as I walked and brooded, it occurred to me that our cities had been built in the days when men still breathed the outer air, and that there had been ventilation shafts for the workmen. I could think of nothing but these ventilation shafts. Had they been destroyed by all the food-tubes and medicine tubes and music tubes that the Machine has evolved lately? Or did traces of them remain? One thing was certain. If I came upon them anywhere, it would be in the railway tunnels of the topmost story. Everywhere else, all space was accounted for.

"I am telling my story quickly, but don't think that I was not a coward or that your answers never depressed me. It is not the proper thing, it is not mechanical, it is not decent to walk along a railway tunnel. I did not fear that I might tread upon a live rail and be killed. I feared something far more intangible—doing what was not contemplated by the Machine. Then I said to myself, 'Man is the measure,' and I went, and after many visits I found an opening.

"The tunnels, of course, were lighted. Everything is light, artificial light; darkness is the exception. So when I saw a black gap in the tiles, I knew that it was an exception, and rejoiced. I put in my arm—I could put in no more at first—and waved it round and round in ecstasy. I loosened another tile, and put in my head, and shouted into the darkness: 'I am coming, I shall do it yet,' and my voice reverberated down endless passages. I seemed to hear the spirits of those dead workmen who had returned each evening to the starlight and to their wives, and all the generations who had lived in the open air called back to me, 'You will do it yet, you are coming.'"

He paused, and, absurd as he was, his last words moved her. For Kuno had lately asked to be a father, and his request had been refused by the Committee. His was not a type that the Machine desired to hand on.

"Then a train passed. It brushed by me, but I thrust my head and arms into the hole. I had done enough for one day, so I crawled back to the platform, went down in the lift, and summoned my bed. Ah, what dreams! And again I called you, and again you refused."

She shook her head and said:

"Don't. Don't talk of these terrible things. You make me miserable. You are throwing civilization away."

"But I had got back the sense of space, and a man cannot rest then. I determined to get in at the hole and climb the shaft. And so I exercised my arms. Day after day I went through ridiculous movements, until my flesh ached, and I could hang by my hands and hold the pillow of my bed outstretched for many minutes. Then I summoned a respirator, and started.

"It was easy at first. The mortar had somehow rotted, and I soon pushed some more tiles in, and clambered after them into the darkness, and the spirits of the dead comforted me. I don't know what I mean by that. I just say what I felt. I felt, for the first time, that a protest had been lodged against corruption, and that even as the dead were comforting me, so I was comforting the unborn. I felt that humanity existed, and that it existed without clothes. How can I possibly explain this? It was naked, humanity seemed naked, and all these tubes and buttons and machineries neither came into the world with us, nor will they follow us out, nor do they matter supremely while we are here. Had I been strong, I would have torn off every garment I had, and gone out into the outer air unswaddled. But this is not for me, nor perhaps for my generation. I climbed with my respirator and my hygienic clothes and my dietetic tabloids! Better thus than not at all.

"There was a ladder, made of some primeval metal. The light from the railway fell upon its lowest rungs, and I saw that it led straight upward out of the rubble at the bottom of the shaft. Perhaps our ancestors ran up and down it a dozen times daily, in their building. As I climbed, the rough edges cut through my gloves so that my hands bled. The light helped me for a little, and then came darkness and, worse still, silence which pierced my ears like a sword. The Machine hums! Did you know that? Its hum penetrates our blood, and may even guide our thoughts. Who knows! I was getting beyond its power. Then I thought: 'This silence means that I am doing wrong.' But I heard voices in the silence, and again they strengthened me." He laughed. "I had need of them. The next moment I cracked my head against something."

She sighed.

"I had reached one of those pneumatic stoppers that defend us from the outer air. You may have noticed them on the airship. Pitch dark, my feet on the rungs of an invisible ladder, my hands cut; I cannot explain how I lived through this part, but the voices still comforted me, and I felt for fastenings. The stopper, I suppose, was about eight feet across. I passed my hand over it as far as I could reach. It was perfectly smooth. I felt it almost to the center. Not quite to the center, for my arm was too short. Then the voice said: 'Jump. It is worth it. There may be a handle in the center, and you may catch hold of it and so come to us your own way. And if there is no handle, so that you may fall and are dashed to pieces—it is still worth it: you will still come to us your own way.' So I jumped. There was a handle, and—"

He paused. Tears gathered in his mother's eyes. She knew that he was fated. If he did not die today he would die tomorrow. There was not room for such a person in the world. And with her pity disgust mingled. She was ashamed at having borne such a son, she who had always been so respectable and so full of ideas. Was he really the little boy to whom she had taught the use of his stops and buttons, and to whom she had given his first lessons in the Book? The very hair that disfigured his lip showed that he was reverting to some savage type. On atavism the Machine can have no mercy.

"There was a handle, and I did catch it. I hung tranced over the darkness and heard the hum of these workings as the last whisper in a dying dream. All the things I had cared about and all the people I had spoken to through tubes appeared infinitely little. Meanwhile the handle revolved. My weight had set something in motion and I spun slowly, and then—

"I cannot describe it. I was lying with my face to the sunshine. Blood poured from my nose and ears and I heard a tremendous roaring. The stopper, with me clinging to it, had simply been blown out of the earth, and the air that we make down here was escaping through the vent into the air above. It burst up like a fountain. I crawled back to it—for the upper air hurts—and, as it were, I took great sips from the edge. My respirator had flown goodness knows where, my clothes were torn. I just lay with my lips close to the hole, and I sipped until the bleeding stopped. You can imagine nothing so curious. This hollow in the grass—I will speak of it in a minute—the sun shining into it, not brilliantly but through marbled clouds—the peace, the nonchalance, the sense of space, and, brushing my cheek, the roaring fountain of our artificial air! Soon I spied my respirator, bobbing up and down in the current high above my head, and higher still were many airships. But no one ever looks out of airships, and in any case they could not have picked me up. There I was, stranded. The sun shone a little way down the shaft, and revealed the topmost rung of the ladder, but it was hopeless trying to reach it. I should either have been tossed up again by the escape, or else have fallen in, and died. I could only lie on the grass, sipping and sipping, and from time to time glancing around me.

"I knew that I was in Wessex, for I had taken care to go to a lecture on the subject before starting. Wessex lies above the room in which we are talking now. It was once an important state. Its kings held all the southern coast from the Andredswald to Cornwall, while the Wansdyke protected them on the north, running over the high ground. The lecturer was concerned only with the rise of Wessex, so I do not know how long it remained an international power, nor would the knowledge have assisted me. To tell the truth, I could do nothing but laugh during this part. There was I, with a pneumatic stopper by my side and a respirator bobbing over my head, imprisoned, all three of us, in a grass-grown hollow that was edged with fern."

Then he grew grave again.

"Lucky for me that it was a hollow. For the air began to fall back into it and to fill it as water fills a bowl. I could crawl about. Presently I stood. I breathed a mixture, in which the air that hurts predominated whenever I tried to climb the sides. This was not so bad. I had not lost my tabloids and remained ridiculously cheerful, and as for the Machine, I forgot about it altogether. My one aim now was to get to the top, where the ferns were, and to view whatever objects lay beyond.

"I rushed the slope. The new air was still too bitter for me and I came rolling back, after a momentary vision of something gray. The sun grew very feeble, and I remembered that he was in Scorpio—I had been to a lecture on that too. If the sun is in Scorpio and you are in Wessex, it means that you must be as quick as you can or it will get too dark. (This is the first bit of useful information I have ever got from a lecture, and I expect it will be the last.) It made me try frantically to breathe the new air, and to advance as far as I dared out of my pond. The hollow filled so slowly. At times I thought that the fountain played with less vigor. My respirator semed to dance nearer the earth; the roar was decreasing."

He broke off.

"I don't think this is interesting you. The rest will interest you even less. There are no ideas in it, and I wish that I had not troubled you to come. We are too different, Mother."

She told him to continue.

"It was evening before I climbed the bank. The sun had very nearly slipped out of the sky by this time, and I could not get a good view. You, who have just crossed the Roof of the World, will not want to hear an account of the little hills that I saw—low colorless hills. But to me they were living and the turf that covered them was a skin, under which their muscles rippled, and I felt that those hills had called with incalculable force to men in the past, and that men had loved them. Now they sleep—perhaps for ever. They commune with humanity in dreams. Happy the man, happy the woman, who awakes the hills of Wessex. For though they sleep, they will never die."

His voice rose passionately.

"Cannot you see, cannot all you lecturers see, that it is we that are dying, and that down here the only thing that really lives is the Machine? We created the Machine, to do our will, but we cannot make it do our will now. It has robbed us of the sense of space and of the sense of touch; it has blurred every human relation and narrowed down love to a carnal act, it has paralyzed our bodies and our wills, and now it compels us to worship it. The Machine develops—but not on our lines. The Machine proceeds—but not to our goal. We exist only as the blood corpuscles that course through its arteries, and if it could work without us, it would let us die. Oh, I have no remedy—or, at least, only one—to tell men again and again that I have seen the hills of Wessex as Aelfrid saw them when he overthrew the Danes.

"So the sun set. I forgot to mention that a belt of mist lay between my hill and other hills, and that it was the color of pearl."

He broke off for the second time.

"Go on," said his mother wearily.

He shook his head.

"Go on. Nothing that you say can distress me now. I am hardened."

"I had meant to tell you the rest, but I cannot: I know that I cannot: good-bye."

Vashti stood irresolute. All her nerves were tingling with his blasphemies. But she was also inquisitive.

"This is unfair," she complained. "You have called me across the world to hear your story, and hear it I will. Tell me—as briefly as possible, for this is a disastrous waste of time—tell me how you returned to civilization."

"Oh—that!" he said, starting. "You would like to hear about civilization. Certainly. Had I got to where my respirator fell down?"

"No—but I understand everything now. You put on your respirator, and managed to walk along the surface of the earth to a vomitory, and there your conduct was reported to the Central Committee."

"By no means."

He passed his hand over his forehead, as if dispelling some strong impression. Then, resuming his narrative, he warmed to it again.

"My respirator fell about sunset. I had mentioned that the fountain seemed feebler, had I not?"

"Yes."

"About sunset, it let the respirator fall. As I said, I had entirely forgotten about the Machine, and I paid no great attention at the time, being occupied with other things. I had my pool of air, into which I could dip when the outer keenness became intolerable, and which would possibly remain for days, provided that no wind sprang up to disperse it. Not until it was too late did I realize what the stoppage of the escape implied. You see—the gap in the tunnel had been mended; the Mending Apparatus; the Mending Apparatus, was after me.

"One other warning I had, but I neglected it. The sky at night was clearer than it had been in the day, and the moon, which was about half the sky behind the sun, shone into the dell at moments quite brightly. I was in my usual place—on the boundary between the two atmospheres—when I thought I saw something dark move across the bottom of the dell, and vanish into the shaft. In my folly, I ran down. I bent over and listened, and I thought I heard a faint scraping noise in the depths.

"At this—but it was too late—I took alarm. I determined to put on my respirator and to walk right out of the dell. But my respirator had gone. I knew exactly where it had fallen—between the stopper and the aperture—and I could even feel the mark that it had made in the turf. It had gone, and I realized that something evil was at work, and I had better escape to the other air, and, if I must die, die running toward the cloud that had been the color of a pearl. I never started. Out of the shaft—it is too horrible. A worm, a long white worm, had crawled out of the shaft and was gliding over the moonlit grass.

"I screamed. I did everything that I should not have done; I stamped upon the creature instead of flying from it, and it at once curled round the ankle.

Then we fought. The worm let me run all over the dell, but edged up my leg as I ran. 'Help!' I cried. (That part is too awful. It belongs to the part that you will never know.) 'Help!' I cried. (Why cannot we suffer in silence?) 'Help!' I cried. Then my feet were wound together. I fell, I was dragged away from the dear ferns and the living hills, and past the great metal stopper (I can tell you this part), and I thought it might save me again if I caught hold of the handle. It also was enwrapped, it also. Oh, the whole dell was full of the things. They were searching it in all directions; they were denuding it, and the white snouts of others peeped out of the hole, ready if needed. Everything that could be moved they brought—brushwood, bundles of fern, everything, and down we all went intertwined into hell. The last things that I saw, ere the stopper closed after us, were certain stars, and I felt that a man of my sort lived in the sky. For I did fight, I fought till the very end, and it was only my head hitting against the ladder that quieted me. I woke up in this room. The worms had vanished; I was surrounded by artificial air, artificial light, artificial peace, and my friends were calling to me down speaking-tubes to know whether I had come across any new ideas lately."

Here his story ended. Discussion of it was impossible, and Vashti turned to go.

"It will end in Homelessness," she said quietly.

"I wish it would," retorted Kuno.

"The Machine has been most merciful."

"I prefer the mercy of God."

"By that superstitious phrase, do you mean that you could live in the outer air?"

"Yes."

"Have you ever seen, round the vomitories, the bones of those who were extruded after the Great Rebellion?"

"Yes."

"They were left where they perished for our edification. A few crawled away, but they perished, too—who can doubt it? And so with the Homeless of our own day. The surface of the earth supports life no longer."

"Indeed."

"Ferns and a little grass may survive, but all higher forms have perished. Has any airship detected them?"

"No."

"Has any lecturer dealt with them?"

"No."

"Then why this obstinacy?"

"Because I have seen them," he exploded.

"Seen *what?*"

"Because I have seen her in the twilight—because she came to my help when I called—because she, too, was entangled by the worms, and, luckier than I, was killed by one of them piercing her throat."

He was mad. Vashti departed, nor, in the troubles that followed, did she ever see his face again.

PART III
The Homeless

During the years that followed Kuno's escapade, two important developments took place in the Machine. On the surface they were revolutionary, but in either case men's minds had been prepared beforehand, and they did but express tendencies that were latent already.

The first of these was the abolition of respirators.

Advanced thinkers, like Vashti, had always held it foolish to visit the surface of the earth. Airships might be necessary, but what was the good of going out for mere curiosity and crawling along for a mile or two in a terrestrial motor? The habit was vulgar and perhaps faintly improper: it was unproductive of ideas, and had no connection with the habits that really mattered. So respirators were abolished, and with them, of course, the terrestrial motors, and except for a few lecturers, who complained that they were debarred access to their subject matter, the development was accepted quietly. Those who still wanted to know what the earth was like had after all only to listen to some gramophone or to look into some cinematophote. And even the lecturers acquiesced when they found that a lecture on the sea was none the less stimulating when compiled out of other lectures that had already been delivered on the same subject. "Beware of firsthand ideas!" exclaimed one of the most advanced of them. "Firsthand ideas do not really exist. They are but the physical impressions produced by love and fear, and on this gross foundation who could erect a philosophy? Let your ideas be secondhand, and if possible tenthhand, for then they will be far removed from that disturbing element—direct observation. Do not learn anything about this subject of mine—the French Revolution. Learn instead what I think that Enicharmon thought Urizen thought Gutch thought Ho-Yung thought Chi-Bo-Sing thought Lafcadio Hearn thought Carlyle thought Mirabeau said about the French Revolution. Through the medium of these ten great minds the blood that was shed at Paris and the windows that were broken at Versailles will be clarified to an idea which you may employ most profitably in your daily lives. But be sure that the intermediates are many and varied, for in history one authority exists to counteract another. Urizen must counteract the skepticism of Ho-Young and Enicharmon, I must myself counteract the impetuosity of Gutch. You who listen to me are in a better position to judge about the French Revolution than I am. Your descendants will be even in a better position than you, for they will learn what you think. I think, and yet another intermediate will be added to the chain. And in time"—his voice rose—"there will come a generation that has got beyond facts, beyond impressions, a generation absolutely colorless, a generation

> "seraphically free
> From taint of personality,

"which will see the French Revolution not as it happened, nor as they would like it to have happened, but as it would have happened had it taken place in the days of the Machine."

Tremendous applause greeted this lecture, which did but voice a feeling already latent in the minds of men—a feeling that terrestrial facts must be ignored, and that the abolition of respirators was a positive gain. It was even suggested that airships should be abolished too. This was not done, because airships had somehow worked themselves into the Machine's system. But year by year they were used less, and mentioned less by thoughtful men.

The second great development was the reestablishment of religion.

This, too, had been voiced in the celebrated lecture. No one could mistake the reverent tone in which the peroration had concluded, and it awakened a responsive echo in the heart of each. Those who had long worshiped silently now began to talk. They described the strange feeling of peace that came over them when they handled the Book of the Machine, the pleasure that it was to repeat certain numerals out of it, however little meaning those numerals conveyed to the outward ear, the ecstasy of touching a button however unimportant, or of ringing an electric bell however superfluously.

"The Machine," they exclaimed, "feeds us and clothes us and houses us; through it we speak to one another, through it we see one another, in it we have our being. The Machine is the friend of ideas and the enemy of superstition: the Machine is omnipotent, eternal; blessed is the Machine." And before long this allocution was printed on the first page of the Book, and in subsequent editions the ritual swelled into a complicated system of praise and prayer. The word "religion" was sedulously avoided, and in theory the Machine was still the creation and the implement of man. But in practice all, save a few retrogrades, worshiped it as divine. Nor was it worshiped in unity. One believer would be chiefly impressed by the blue optic plates, through which he saw other believers; another by the Mending Apparatus, which sinful Kuno had compared to worms; another by the lifts, another by the Book. And each would pray to this or to that, and ask it to intercede for him with the Machine as a whole. Persecution— that also was present. It did not break out, for reasons that will be set forward shortly. But it was latent, and all who did not accept the minimum known as "undenominational Mechanism" lived in danger of Homelessness, which means death, as we know.

To attribute these two great developments to the Central Committee is to take a very narrow view of civilization. The Central Committee announced the developments, it is true, but they were no more the cause of them than were the kings of the imperialistic period the cause of war. Rather did they yield to some invincible pressure, which came no one knew whither, and which, when gratified, was succeeded by some new pressure equally invincible. To such a state of affairs it is convenient to give the name of progress. No one confessed the Machine was out of hand. Year by year it was served with increased efficiency and decreased intelligence. The better a man knew his own duties upon it, the less he understood the duties of his neighbor, and in all the world there was not one who understood the monster as a whole. Those master brains had perished. They had left full directions, it is true, and their successors had each of them mastered a portion of those directions. But Humanity, in its desire for comfort, had overreached itself. It had exploited the riches of nature too far. Quietly and complacently, it was sinking into decadence, and progress had come to mean the progress of the Machine.

As for Vashti, her life went peacefully forward until the final disaster. She made her room dark and slept; she awoke and made the room light. She lectured and attended lectures. She exchanged ideas with her innumerable friends and believed she was growing more spiritual. At times a friend was granted Euthanasia, and left his or her room for the homelessness that is beyond all human conception. Vashti did not much mind. After an unsuccessful lecture, she would sometimes ask for Euthanasia herself. But the death rate was not permitted to exceed the birth rate, and the Machine had hitherto refused it to her.

The troubles began quietly, long before she was conscious of them.

One day she was astonished at receiving a message from her son. They never communicated, having nothing in common, and she had only heard indirectly that he was still alive, and had been transferred from the Northern Hemisphere, where he had behaved so mischievously, to the Southern—indeed, to a room not far from her own.

"Does he want me to visit him?" she thought. "Never again, never. And I have not the time."

No, it was madness of another kind.

He refused to visualize his face upon the blue plate, and speaking out of the darkness with solemnity said:

"The Machine stops."

"What do you say?"

"The Machine is stopping, I know it; I know the signs."

She burst into a peal of laughter. He heard her and was angry, and they spoke no more.

"Can you imagine anything more absurd?" she cried to a friend. "A man who was my son believes that the Machine is stopping. It would be impious if it was not mad."

"The Machine is stopping?" her friend replied. "What does that mean? The phrase conveys nothing to me."

"Nor to me."

"He does not refer, I suppose, to the trouble there has been lately with the music?"

"Oh, no, of course not. Let us talk about music."

"Have you complained to the authorities?"

"Yes, and they say it wants mending, and referred me to the Committee of the Mending Apparatus. I complained of those curious gasping sighs that disfigure the symphonies of the Brisbane school. They sound like someone in pain. The Committee of the Mending Apparatus say that it shall be remedied shortly."

Obscurely worried, she resumed her life. For one thing, the defect in the music irritated her. For another thing, she could not forget Kuno's speech. If he had known that the music was out of repair—he could not know it, for he detested music—if he had known that it was wrong, "the Machine stops" was exactly the venomous sort of remark he would have made. Of course, he had made it at a venture, but the coincidence annoyed her, and she spoke with some petulance to the Committee of the Mending Apparatus.

They replied, as before, that the defect would be set right shortly.

"Shortly! At once!" she retorted. "Why should I be worried by imperfect music? Things are always put right at once. If you do not mend it at once, I shall complain to the Central Committee."

"No personal complaints are received by the Central Committee," the Committee of the Mending Apparatus replied.

"Through whom am I to make my complaint, then?"

"Through us."

"I complain then."

"Your complaint shall be forwarded in its turn."

"Have others complained?"

This question was unmechanical, and the Committee of the Mending Apparatus refused to answer it.

"It is too bad!" she exclaimed to another of her friends. "There never was such an unfortunate woman as myself. I can never be sure of my music now. It gets worse and worse each time I summon it."

"I too have my troubles," the friend replied. "Sometimes my ideas are interrupted by a slight jarring noise."

"What is it?"

"I do not know whether it is inside my head or inside the wall."

"Complain in either case."

"I have complained, and my complaint will be forwarded in its turn to the Central Committee."

Time passed, and they resented the defects no longer. The defects had not been remedied, but the human tissues in that latter day had become so subservient that they readily adapted themselves to every caprice of the Machine. The sigh at the crisis of the Brisbane symphony no longer irritated Vashti; she accepted it as part of the melody. The jarring noise, whether in the head or in the wall, was no longer resented by her friend. And so with the moldy artificial fruit, so with the bath water that began to stink, so with the defective rhymes that the poetry machine had taken to emitting. All were bitterly complained of at first, and then acquiesced in and forgotten. Things went from bad to worse unchallenged.

It was otherwise with the failure of the sleeping apparatus. That was a more serious stoppage. There came a day when over the whole world—in Sumatra, in Wessex, in the innumerable cities of Courland and Brazil—the beds, when summoned by their tired owners, failed to appear. It may seem a ludicrous matter, but from it we may date the collapse of humanity. The Committee responsible for the failure was assailed by complaints, whom it referred, as usual, to the Committee of the Mending Apparatus, who in its turn assured them that their complaints would be forwarded to the Central Committee. But the discontent grew, for mankind was not yet sufficiently adaptable to do without sleeping.

"Someone is meddling with the Machine—" they began.

"Someone is trying to make himself king, to reintroduce the personal element."

"Punish that man with Homelessness."

"To the rescue! Avenge the Machine! Avenge the Machine!"

"War! Kill the man!"

But the Committee of the Mending Apparatus now came forward, and allayed the panic with well-chosen words. It confessed that the Mending Apparatus was itself in need of repair.

The effect of this frank confession was admirable.

"Of course," said a famous lecturer—he of the French Revolution, who gilded each new decay with splendor—"of course we shall not press our complaints now. The Mending Apparatus has treated us so well in the past that we all sympathize with it, and will wait patiently for its recovery. In its own good time it will resume its duties. Meanwhile let us do without our beds, our tabloids, our other little wants. Such, I feel sure, would be the wish of the Machine."

Thousands of miles away his audience applauded. The Machine still linked them. Under the seas, beneath the roots of the mountains, ran the wires through which they saw and heard, the enormous eyes and ears that were their heritage, and the hum of many workings clothed their thoughts in one garment of subserviency. Only the old and sick remained ungrateful, for it was rumored that Euthanasia, too, was out of order, and that pain had reappeared among men.

It became difficult to read. A blight entered the atmosphere and dulled its luminosity. At times Vashti could scarcely see across her room. The air, too, was foul. Loud were the complaints, impotent the remedies, heroic the tone of the lecturer as he cried: "Courage! courage! What matter so long as the Machine goes on? To it the darkness and the light are one." And though things improved again after a time, the old brilliancy was never recaptured, and humanity never recovered from its entrance into twilight. There was hysterical talk of "measures," of "provisional dictatorship," and the inhabitants of Sumatra were asked to familiarize themselves with the workings of the central power station, the said power station being situated in France. But for the most part panic reigned, and men spent their strength praying to their Books, tangible proofs of the Machine's omnipotence. There were gradations of terror—at times came rumors of hope— the Mending Apparatus was almost mended—the enemies of the Machine had been got under—new "nerve centers" were evolving which would do the work even more magnificently than before. But there came a day when, without the slightest warning, without any previous hint of feebleness, the entire communication system broke down, all over the world, and the world, as they understood it, ended.

Vashti was lecturing at the time, and her earlier remarks had been punctuated with applause. As she proceeded the audience became silent, and at the conclusion there was no sound. Somewhat displeased, she called to a friend who was a specialist in sympathy. No sound: doubtless the friend was sleeping. And so with the next friend whom she tried to summon, and so with the next, until she remembered Kuno's cryptic remark, "The Machine stops."

The phrase still conveyed nothing. If Eternity was stopping it would of course be set going shortly.

For example, there were still a little light and air—the atmosphere had improved a few hours previously. There was still the Book, and while there was the Book there was security.

Then she broke down, for with the cessation of activity came an unexpected terror—silence.

She had never known silence, and the coming of it nearly killed her—it did kill many thousands of people outright. Ever since her birth she had been surrounded by the steady hum. It was to the ear what artificial air was to the lungs, and agonizing pains shot across her head. And scarcely knowing what she did, she stumbled forward and pressed the unfamiliar button, the one that opened the door of her cell.

Now the door of the cell worked on a simple hinge of its own. It was not connected with the central power station, dying far away in France. It opened, rousing immoderate hopes in Vashti, for she thought that the Machine had been mended. It opened, and she saw the dim tunnel that curved far away toward freedom. One look, and then she shrank back. For the tunnel was full of people—she was almost the last in that city to have taken alarm.

People at any time repelled her, and these were nightmares from her worst dreams. People were crawling about, people were screaming, whimpering, gasping for breath, touching each other, vanishing in the dark, and ever and anon being pushed off the platform on to the live rail. Some were fighting round the electric bells, trying to summon trains which could not be summoned. Others were yelling for Euthanasia or for respirators, or blaspheming the Machine. Others stood at the doors of their cells fearing, like herself, either to stop in them or to leave them, and behind all the uproar was silence—the silence which is the voice of the earth and of the generations who have gone.

No—it was worse than solitude. She closed the door again and sat down to wait for the end. The disintegration went on, accompanied by horrible cracks and rumbling. The valves that restrained the Medical Apparatus must have been weakened, for it ruptured and hung hideously from the ceiling. The floor heaved and fell and flung her from her chair. A tube oozed toward her serpent fashion. And at last the final horror approached—light began to ebb, and she knew that civilization's long day was closing.

She whirled round, praying to be saved from this, at any rate, kissing the Book, pressing button after button. The uproar outside was increasing, and even penetrated the wall. Slowly the brilliancy of her cell was dimmed, the reflections faded from her metal switches. Now she could not see the reading stand, now not the Book, though she held it in her hand. Light followed the flight of sound, air was following light, and the original void returned to the cavern from which it had been so long excluded. Vashti continued to whirl, like the devotees of an earlier religion, screaming, praying, striking at the buttons with bleeding hands.

It was thus that she opened her prison and escaped—escaped in the spirit: at least so it seems to me, ere my meditation closes. That she escapes in the body— I cannot perceive that. She struck, by chance, the switch that released the door, and the rush of foul air on her skin, the loud throbbing whispers in her ears, told her that she was facing the tunnel again, and that tremendous platform on which she had seen men fighting. They were not fighting now. Only the whispers remained, and the little whimpering groans. They were dying by hundreds out in the dark.

She burst into tears.

Tears answered her.

They wept for humanity, those two, not for themselves. They could not bear that this should be the end. Ere silence was completed their hearts were opened, and they knew what had been important on the earth. Man, the flower of all flesh, the noblest of all creatures visible, man who had once made god in his image, and had mirrored his strength on the constellations, beautiful naked man was dying, strangled in the garments that he had woven. Century after century had he toiled, and here was his reward. Truly the garment had seemed heavenly at first, shot with the colors of culture, sewn with the threads of self-denial. And heavenly it had been so long as it was a garment and no more, so long as man could shed it at will and live by the essence that is his soul, and the essence, equally divine, that is his body. The sin against the body—it was for that they wept in chief; the centuries of wrong against the muscles and the nerves, and those five portals by which we can alone apprehend—glozing it over with talk of evolution, until the body was white pap, the home of ideas as colorless, last sloshy stirrings of a spirit that had grasped the stars.

"Where are you?" she sobbed.

His voice in the darkness said, "Here."

"Is there any hope, Kuno?"

"None for us."

"Where are you?"

She crawled toward him over the bodies of the dead. His blood spurted over her hands.

"Quicker," he gasped, "I am dying—but we touch, we talk, not through the Machine."

He kissed her.

"We have come back to our own. We die, but we have recaptured life, as it was in Wessex, when Aelfrid overthrew the Danes. We know what they know outside, they who dwelt in the cloud that is the color of a pearl."

"But, Kuno, is it true? Are there still men on the surface of the earth? Is this—this tunnel, this poisoned darkness—really not the end?"

He replied:

"I have seen them, spoken to them, loved them. They are hiding in the mist and the ferns until our civilization stops. Today they are the Homeless—tomorrow—"

"Oh, tomorrow—some fool will start the Machine again, tomorrow."

"Never," said Kuno, "never. Humanity has learned its lesson."

As he spoke the whole city was broken like a honeycomb. An airship had sailed in through the vomitory into a ruined wharf. It crashed downward, exploding as it went, rending gallery after gallery with its wings of steel. For a moment they saw the nations of the dead, and, before they joined them, scraps of the untainted sky.

Margaret St. Clair

Margaret St. Clair (1911–96) was a prolific and popular writer who published more than 130 stories and eight SF novels from 1945 to the 1980s. Some of her stories have been collected in *Three Worlds of Futurity* (1964), *Change the Sky and Other Stories* (1974) and *The Best of Margaret St. Clair* (1985). *The Dolphins of Altair* (1967) is probably the most ambitious of the novels.

The majority of the novels were written after 1960 but nearly all of the stories in the 1950s, when she also published under the pseudonym Idris Seabright, under which she was for a time more highly regarded. (It was a common practice that allowed a writer to sell more stories to a single magazine . . . two could appear in a single issue without the feeling of overexposure. In the 1940s, Henry Kuttner's pseudonym, Lewis Padgett, was arguably more respected than his own name. In fact a few writers, including Randall Garrett and Robert Silverberg at one point in the 1950s, wrote the entire contents of magazine issues under a variety of pseudonyms.) St. Clair's short stories represent her at her best. She is two of the significant woman writers operating in science fiction at a time when it was overwhelmingly written and read by men.

"The historic task of science fiction is to develop a global consciousness," she said in an essay introducing her collection, *The Best of Margaret St. Clair,* in 1985. This affecting story is certainly an example. It is about beauty, death, and colonialism.

BRIGHTNESS FALLS FROM THE AIR

Kerr used to go into the tepidarium of the identification bureau to practice singing. The tepidarium was a big room, filled almost from wall to wall by the pool of glittering preservative, and he liked its acoustics. The bodies of the bird people would drift a little back and forth in the pellucid fluid as he sang, and he liked to look at them. If the tepidarium was a little morbid as a place to practice singing, it was (Kerr used to think) no more morbid than the rest of the world in which he was living. When he had sung for as long as he thought good for his voice—he had no teacher—he would go to one of the windows and watch the luminous trails that meant the bird people were fighting again. The trails would float down slowly against the night sky as if they were made of star dust. But after Kerr met Rhysha, he stopped all that.

Rhysha came to the bureau one evening just as he was going on duty. She had come to claim a body. The bodies of the bird people often stayed in the bureau for a considerable time. Ordinary means of transportation were forbidden to the bird people because of their extra-terrestrial origin, and it was hard for them to get to the bureau to identify their dead. Rhysha made the identifica-tion—it was her brother—paid the bureau's fee from a worn purse, and indicated on the proper form the disposal she wanted made of the body. She was quiet and controlled in her grief. Kerr had watched the televised battles of the bird people once or twice, but this was the first time he had ever seen one of them alive and face to face. He looked at her with interest and curiosity, and then with wonder and delight.

The most striking thing about Rhysha was her glowing, deep turquoise plumage. It covered her from head to heels in what appeared to be a clinging velvet cloak. The coloring was so much more intense than that of the bodies in the tepidarium that Kerr would have thought she belonged to a different species than they.

Her face, under the golden top-knot, was quite human, and so were her slender, leaf-shaped hands; but there was a fantastic, light-boned grace in her movements such as no human being ever had. Her voice was low, with a 'cello's fullness of tone. Everything about her, Kerr thought, was rare and delightful and curious. But there was a shadow in her face, as if a natural gaiety had been repressed by the overwhelming harshness of circumstance.

"Where shall I have the ashes sent?" Kerr asked as he took the form.

She plucked indecisively at her pink lower lip. "I am not sure. The manager where we are staying has told us we must leave tonight, and I do not know where we will go. Could I come back again to the bureau when the ashes are ready?"

It was against regulations, but Kerr nodded. He would keep the capsule of ashes in his locker until she came. It would be nice to see her again.

She came, weeks later, for the ashes. There had been several battles of the bird people in the interval, and the pool in the tepidarium was full. As Kerr looked at her, he wondered how long it would be before she too was dead.

He asked her new address. It was a fantastic distance away, in the worst part of the city, and after a little hesitation he told her that if she could wait until his shift was over he would be glad to walk back with her.

She looked at him doubtfully. "It is most kind of you, but—but an Earthman was kind to us once. The children used to stone him."

Kerr had never thought much about the position of the non-human races in his world. If it was unjust, if they were badly treated, he had thought it no more than a particular instance of the general cruelty and stupidity. Now anger flared up in him.

"That's all right," he said harshly. "If you don't mind waiting."

Rhysha smiled faintly. "No, I don't mind," she said.

Since there were still some hours to go on his shift, he took her into a small reception room where there was a chaise longue. "Try to sleep," he said.

A little before three he came to rouse her, and found her lying quiet but awake. They left the bureau by a side door.

The city was as quiet at this hour as it ever was. All the sign projectors, and most of the street lights, had been turned off to save power, and even the vast, disembodied voices that boomed out of the air all day long and half the night were almost silent. The darkness and quiescence of the city made it seem easy for them to talk as they went through the streets.

Kerr realised afterwards how confident he must have been of Rhysha's sympathy to have spoken to her as freely as he did. And she must have felt an equal confidence in him, for after a little while she was telling him fragments of her history and her people's past without reserve.

"After the Earthmen took our planet," she said, "we had nothing left they wanted. But we had to have food. Then we discovered that they liked to watch us fight."

"You fought before the Earthmen came?" Kerr asked.

"Yes. But not as we fight now. It was a ritual then, very formal, with much politeness and courtesy. We did not fight to get things from each other, but to find out who was brave and could give us leadership. The Earth people were impatient with our ritual—they wanted to see us hurting and being hurt. So we learned to fight as we fight now, hoping to be killed.

"There was a time, when we first left our planet and went to the other worlds where people liked to watch us, when there were many of us. But there have been many battles since then. Now there are only a few left."

At the cross street a beggar slouched up to them. Kerr gave him a coin. The man was turning away with thanks when he caught sight of Rhysha's golden top-knot. "God-damned Extey!" he said in sudden rage. "Filth! And you, a man, going around with it! Here!" He threw the coin at Kerr.

"Even the beggars!" Rhysha said. "Why is it, Kerr, you hate us so?"

"Because we have wronged you," he answered, and knew it was the truth. "Are we always so unkind, though?"

"As the beggar was? Often . . . it is worse."

"Rhysha, you've got to get away from here."

"Where?" she answered simply. "Our people have discussed it so many times! There is no planet on which there are not already billions of people from Earth. You increase so fast!

"And besides, it doesn't matter. You don't need us, there isn't any place for us. We cared about that once, but not any more. We're so tired—all of us, even the young ones like me—we're so tired of trying to live."

"You mustn't talk like that," Kerr said harshly. "I won't let you talk like that. You've got to go on. If we don't need you now, Rhysha, we will."

From the block ahead of them there came the wan glow of a municipal tele-screen. Late as the hour was, it was surrounded by a dense knot of spectators. Their eyes were fixed greedily on the combat that whirled dizzily over the screen.

Rhysha tugged gently at Kerr's sleeve. "We had better go around," she said in a whisper. Kerr realized with a pang that there would be trouble if the viewers saw a "man" and an Extey together. Obediently he turned.

They had gone a block further when Kerr (for he had been thinking) said: "My people took the wrong road, Rhysha, about two hundred years ago. That was when the council refused to accept, even in principle, any form of population control. By now we're stifling under the pressure of our own numbers, we're crushed shapeless under it. Everything has had to give way to our one basic problem, how to feed an ever-increasing number of hungry mouths. Morality has dwindled into feeding ourselves. And we have the battle sports over the telecast to keep us occupied.

"But I think—I believe—that we'll get into the right road again sometime. I've read books of history, Rhysha. This isn't the first time we've chosen the wrong road. Some day there'll be room for your people, Rhysha, if only—" he hesitated—"if only because you're so beautiful."

He looked at her earnestly. Her face was remote and bleak. An idea came to him. "Have you ever heard anyone sing, Rhysha?"

"Sing? No, I don't know the word."

"Listen, then." He fumbled over his repertory and decided, though the music was not really suited to his voice, on Tamino's song to Pamina's portrait. He sang it for her as they walked along.

Little by little Rhysha's face relaxed. "I like that," she said when the song was over. "Sing more, Kerr."

"Do you see what I was trying to tell you?" he said at last, after many songs. "If we could make songs like that, Rhysha, isn't there hope for us?"

"For you, perhaps. Not us," Rhysha answered. There was anger in her voice. "Stop it, Kerr. I do not want to be waked."

But when they parted she clasped hands with him and told him where they could meet again. "You are really our friend," she said without coquetry.

When he next met Rhysha, Kerr said: "I brought you a present. Here." He handed her a parcel. "And I've some news, too."

Rhysha opened the little package. An exclamation of pleasure broke from her lips. "Oh, lovely! What a lovely thing! Where did you get it, Kerr?"

"In a shop that sells old things, in the back." He did not tell her he had given ten days' pay for the little turquoise locket. "But the stones are lighter than I realized. I wanted something that would be the color of your plumage."

Rhysha shook her head. "No, this is the color it should be. This is right." She clasped the locket around her neck and looked down at it with pleasure. "And now, what is the news you have for me?"

"A friend of mine is a clerk in the city records. He tells me a new planet, near gamma Cassiopeiae, is being opened for colonization.

"I've filed the papers, and everything is in order. The hearing will be held on Friday. I'm going to appear on behalf of the Ngayir, your people, and ask that they be allotted space on the new world."

Rhysha turned white. He started toward her, but she waved him away. One hand was still clasping her locket, that was nearly the color of her plumage.

The hearing was held in a small auditorium in the basement of the Colonization building. Representatives of a dozen groups spoke before Kerr's turn came.

"Appearing on behalf of the Ngayir," the arbitrator read from a form in his hand, "S 3687 Kerr. And who are the Ngayir, S-Kerr? Some Indian group?"

"No, sir," Kerr said. "They are commonly known as the bird people."

"Oh, a conservationist!" The arbitrator looked at Kerr not unkindly. "I'm sorry, but your petition is quite out of order. It should never have been filed. Immigration is restricted by executive order to terrestials . . ."

Kerr dreaded telling Rhysha of his failure, but she took it with perfect calm.

"After you left I realised it was impossible," she said.

"Rhysha, I want you to promise me something. I can't tell you how sure I am that humanity is going to need your people sometime. It's true, Rhysha. I'm going to keep trying. I'm not going to give up.

"Promise me this, Rhysha: promise me that neither you nor the members of your group will take part in the battles until you hear from me again."

Rhysha smiled. "All right, Kerr."

Preserving the bodies of people who have died from a variety of diseases is not without its dangers. Kerr did not go to work that night or the next or for many nights. His dormitory chief, after listening to him shout in delirium for some hours, called a doctor, who filled out a hospital requisition slip.

He was gravely ill, and his recovery was slow. It was nearly five weeks before he was released.

He wanted above all things to find Rhysha. He went to the place where she had been living and found that she had gone, no one knew where. In the end, he went to the identification bureau and begged for his old job there. Rhysha would, he was sure, think of coming to the bureau to get in touch with him.

He was still shaky and weak when he reported for work the next night. He went into the tepidarium about nine o'clock, during a routine inspection. And there Rhysha was.

He did not know her for an instant. The lovely turquoise of her plumage had faded to a dirty drab. But the little locket he had given her was still around her neck.

He got the big jointed tongs they used for moving bodies out of the pool, and put them in position. He lifted her out very gently and put her down on the edge of the pool. He opened the locket. There was a note inside.

"Dear Kerr," he read in Rhysha's clear, handsome script, "you must forgive me for breaking my promise to you. They would not let me see you when you were sick, and we were all so hungry. Besides, you were wrong to think your people would ever need us. There is no place for us in your world.

"I wish I could have heard you sing again. I liked to hear you sing. Rhysha."

Kerr looked from the note to Rhysha's face, and back at the note. It hurt too much. He did not want to realize that she was dead.

Outside, one of the vast voices that boomed portentously down from the sky half the night long began to speak: "Don't miss the newest, fastest battle sport. View the Durga battles, the bloodiest combats ever televised. Funnier than the bird people's battles, more thrilling than an Anda war, you'll . . ."

Kerr gave a cry. He ran to the window and closed it. He could still hear the voice. But it was all that he could do.

Michael Shaara

Michael Shaara (1929–88) was one of the bright young SF writers of the early 1950s, who left the genre in 1957 after producing a number of fine short stories, and later wrote a boxing novel and the Pulitzer Prize-winning American Civil War novel, *The Killer Angels* (1974). Most of his short stories are collected in *Soldier Boy* (1982), along with an after-word reminiscing about his early days in science fiction, the excitement of selling to John W. Campbell's *Astounding*, the frustrations of dealing with genre markets. Algis Budrys remembers that Robert Sheckley, Michael Shaara and he were the hot new writers of 1952–53.

After the generally positive editorial reaction to *Soldier Boy*, Shaara completed an SF novel, *The Herald* (1981—actually published before the collection, which was delayed, but not published as a genre novel, since Shaara had won the Pulitzer and his publisher was certain that a genre label would compromise his, and their, reputation). *The Encyclopedia of Science Fiction* praises his writing for its "quick, revelatory ironies about the human condition." I recall joking with him in 1982 that this, of all his stories, was predictive and that it had already come true. It is still coming true.

2066: ELECTION DAY

Early that afternoon Professor Larkin crossed the river into Washington, a thing he always did on Election Day, and sat for a long while in the Polls. It was still called the Polls, in this year A.D. 2066, although what went on inside bore no relation at all to the elections of primitive American history. The Polls was now a single enormous building which rose out of the green fields where the ancient Pentagon had once stood. There was only one of its kind in Washington, only one Polling Place in each of the forty-eight states, but since few visited the Polls nowadays, no more were needed.

In the lobby of the building, a great hall was reserved for visitors. Here you could sit and watch the many-colored lights dancing and flickering on the huge panels above, listen to the weird but strangely soothing hum and click of the vast central machine. Professor Larkin chose a deep soft chair near the long line of booths and sat down. He sat for a long while smoking his pipe, watching the people go in and out of the booths with strained, anxious looks on their faces.

Professor Larkin was a lean, boyish-faced man in his late forties. With the pipe in his hand he looked much more serious and sedate than he normally felt, and it often bothered him that people were able to guess his profession almost instantly. He had a vague idea that it was not becoming to look like a college professor, and he often tried to change his appearance—a loud tie here, a sport coat there—but it never seemed to make any difference. He remained what he was, easily identifiable, Professor Harry L. (Lloyd) Larkin, Ph.D., Dean of the Political Science Department at a small but competent college just outside of Washington.

It was his interest in Political Science which drew him regularly to the Polls at every election. Here he could sit and feel the flow of American history in the making, and recognize, as he did now, perennial candidates for the presidency. Smiling, he watched a little old lady dressed in pink, very tiny and very fussy, flit doggedly from booth to booth. Evidently her test marks had not been very good. She was clutching her papers tightly in a black-gloved hand, and there was a look of prim irritation on her face. But *she* knew how to run this country, by George, and one of these days *she* would be President. Harry Larkin chuckled.

But it did prove one thing. The great American dream was still intact. The tests were open to all. And anyone could still grow up to be President of the United States.

Sitting back in his chair, Harry Larkin remembered his own childhood, how the great battle had started. There were examinations for everything in those days—you could not get a job streetcleaning without taking a civil-service examination—but public office needed no qualification at all. And first the psychologists, then the newspapers, had begun calling it a national disgrace. And, considering the caliber of some of the men who went into public office, it *was* a national disgrace. But then psychological testing came of age, really became an exact science, so that it was possible to test a man thoroughly—his knowledge, his potential, his personality. And from there it was a short but bitterly fought step to—SAM.

SAM. UNCLE SAM, as he had been called originally, the last and greatest of all electronic brains. Harry Larkin peered up in unabashed awe at the vast battery of lights which flickered above him. He knew that there was more to SAM than just this building, more than all the other forty-eight buildings put together, that SAM was actually an incredibly enormous network of electronic cells which had its heart in no one place, but its arms in all. It was an unbelievably complex analytical computer which judged a candidate far more harshly and thoroughly than the American public could ever have judged him. And crammed in its miles of memory banks lay almost every bit of knowledge mankind had yet discovered. It was frightening, many thought of it as a monster, but Harry Larkin was unworried.

The thirty years since the introduction of SAM had been thirty of America's happiest years. In a world torn by continual war and unrest, by dictators, puppet governments, the entire world had come to know and respect the American President for what he was: the best possible man for the job. And there was no doubt that he was the best. He had competed for the job in fair examination against the cream of the country. He had to be a truly remarkable man to come out on top.

The day was long since past when just any man could handle the presidency. A full century before men had begun dying in office, cut down in their prime by the enormous pressures of the job. And that was a hundred years ago. Now the job had become infinitely more complex, and even now President Creighton lay on his bed in the White House, recovering from a stroke, an old, old man after one term of office.

Harry Larkin shuddered to think what might have happened had America not adopted the system of "the best qualified man." All over the world this afternoon men waited for word from America, the calm and trustworthy words of the new President, for there had been no leader in America since President Creighton's stroke. His words would mean more to the people, embroiled as they were in another great crisis, than the words of their own leaders. The leaders of other countries fought for power, bought it, stole it, only rarely earned it. But the American President was known the world over for his honesty, his intelligence, his desire for peace. Had he not those qualities, "old UNCLE SAM" would never have elected him.

Eventually, the afternoon nearly over, Harry Larkin rose to leave. By this time the President was probably already elected. Tomorrow the world would return to peace. Harry Larkin paused in the door once before he left, listened to the reassuring hum from the great machine. Then he went quietly home, walking quickly and briskly toward the most enormous fate on Earth.

"My name is Reddington. You know me?"

Harry Larkin smiled uncertainly into the phone.

"Why . . . yes, I believe so. You are, if I'm not mistaken, general director of the Bureau of Elections."

"Correct," the voice went on quickly, crackling in the receiver, "and you are supposed to be an authority on Political Science, right?"

"Supposed to be?" Larkin bridled. "Well, it's distinctly possible that I—"

"All right, all right," Reddington blurted. "No time for politeness. Listen, Larkin, this is a matter of urgent national security. There will be a car at your door—probably be there when you put this phone down. I want you to get into it and hop on over here. I can't explain further. I know your devotion to the country, and if it wasn't for that I would not have called you. But don't ask questions. Just come. No time. Good-bye."

There was a click. Harry Larkin stood holding the phone for a long shocked moment, then he heard a pounding at the door. The housekeeper was out, but he waited automatically before going to answer it. He didn't like to be rushed, and he was confused. Urgent national security? Now what in blazes—

The man at the door was an Army major. He was accompanied by two young but very large sergeants. They identified Larkin, then escorted him politely but firmly down the steps into a staff car. Larkin could not help feeling abducted, and a completely characteristic rage began to rise in him. But he remembered what Reddington had said about national security and so sat back quietly with nothing more than an occasional grumble.

He was driven back into Washington. They took him downtown to a small but expensive apartment house he could neither identify nor remember, and escorted him briskly into an elevator. When they reached the suite upstairs they opened the door and let him in, but did not follow him. They turned and went quickly away.

Somewhat ruffled, Larkin stood for a long moment in the hall by the hat table, regarding a large rubber plant. There was a long sliding door before him, closed, but he could hear an argument going on behind it. He heard the word "SAM" mentioned many times, and once he heard a clear sentence: ". . . Government by machine. I will not tolerate it!" Before he had time to hear any more, the doors slid back. A small, square man with graying hair came out to meet him. He recognized the man instantly as Reddington.

"Larkin," the small man said, "glad you're here." The tension on his face showed also in his voice. "That makes all of us. Come in and sit down." He turned back into the large living room. Larkin followed.

"Sorry to be so abrupt," Reddington said, "but it was necessary. You will see. Here, let me introduce you around."

Larkin stopped in involuntary awe. He was used to the sight of important men, but not so many at one time, and never so close. There was Secretary Kell, of Agriculture; Wachsmuth, of Commerce; General Vines, Chief of Staff; and a battery of others so imposing that Larkin found his mouth hanging embarrassingly open. He closed it immediately.

Reddington introduced him. The men nodded one by one, but they were all deathly serious, their faces drawn, and there was now no conversation. Reddington waved him to a chair. Most of the others were standing, but Larkin sat.

Reddington sat directly facing him. There was a long moment of silence during which Larkin realized that he was being searchingly examined. He flushed, but sat calmly with his hands folded in his lap. After a while Reddington took a deep breath.

"Dr. Larkin," he said slowly, "what I am about to say to you will die with you. There must be no question of that. We cannot afford to have any word of this meeting, any word at all, reach anyone not in this room. This includes your immediate relatives, your friends, anyone—anyone at all. Before we continue, let me impress you with that fact. This is a matter of the gravest national security. Will you keep what is said here in confidence?"

"If the national interests—" Larkin began, then he said abruptly, "of course." Reddington smiled slightly.

"Good. I believe you. I might add that just the fact of your being here, Doctor, means that you have already passed the point of no return . . . well, no matter. There is no time. I'll get to the point."

He stopped, looking around the room. Some of the other men were standing and now began to move in closer. Larkin felt increasingly nervous, but the magnitude of the event was too great for him to feel any worry. He gazed intently at Reddington.

"The Polls close tonight at eight o'clock." Reddington glanced at his watch. "It is now six-eighteen. I must be brief. Doctor, do you remember the prime directive that we gave to SAM when he was first built?"

"I think so," said Larkin slowly.

"Good. You remember then that there was one main order. SAM was directed to elect, quote, *the best qualified man*. Unquote. Regardless of any and all circumstances, religion, race, so on. The orders were clear—the best qualified man. The phrase has become world famous. But unfortunately"—he glanced up briefly at the men surrounding him—"the order was a mistake. Just whose mistake does not matter. I think perhaps the fault lies with all of us, but—it doesn't matter. What matters is this: SAM will not elect a president."

Larkin struggled to understand. Reddington leaned forward in his chair.

"Now follow me closely. We learned this only late this afternoon. We are always aware, as you no doubt know, of the relatively few people in this country who have a chance for the presidency. We know not only because they are studying for it, but because such men as these are marked from their childhood to be outstanding. We keep close watch on them, even to assigning the Secret Service to protect them from possible harm. There are only a very few. During this last election we could not find more than fifty. All of those people took the tests this morning. None of them passed."

He paused, waiting for Larkin's reaction. Larkin made no move.

"You begin to see what I'm getting at? *There is no qualified man.*"

Larkin's eyes widened. He sat bolt upright.

"Now it hits you. If none of those people this morning passed, there is no chance at all for any of the others tonight. What is left now is simply crackpots and malcontents. They are privileged to take the tests, but it means nothing. SAM is not going to select anybody. Because sometime during the last four years the presidency passed the final limit, the ultimate end of man's capabilities, and with scientific certainty we know that there is probably no man alive who is, according to SAM's directive, qualified."

"But," Larkin interrupted, "I'm not quite sure I follow. Doesn't the phrase 'elect the best qualified man' mean that we can at least take the best we've got?"

Reddington smiled wanly and shook his head.

"No. And that was our mistake. It was quite probably a psychological block, but none of us ever considered the possibility of the job surpassing human ability. Not then, thirty years ago. And we also never seemed to remember that SAM is, after all, only a machine. He takes the words to mean exactly what they say: Elect the best, comma, *qualified*, comma, man. But do you see, if there is *no* qualified man, SAM cannot possibly elect the best. So SAM will elect no one at all. Tomorrow this country will be without a president. And the result of that, more than likely, will mean a general war."

Larkin understood. He sat frozen in his chair.

"So you see our position," Reddington went on wearily. "There's nothing we can do. Reelecting President Creighton is out of the question. His stroke was permanent, he may not last the week. And there is no possibility of tampering with SAM, to change the directive. Because, as you know, SAM is foolproof, had to be. The circuits extend through all forty-eight states. To alter the machine at all requires clearing through all forty-eight entrances. We can't do that. For one thing, we haven't time. For another, we can't risk letting the world know there is no qualified man.

"For a while this afternoon, you can understand, we were stumped. What could we do? There was only one answer, we may come back to it yet. Give the presidency itself to SAM—"

A man from across the room, whom Larkin did not recognize, broke in angrily.

"Now Reddington, I told you, that is government by machine! And I will not stand—"

"What else can you *do!*" Reddington whirled, his eyes flashing, his tension exploding now into rage. "Who else knows all the answers? Who else can compute in two seconds the tax rate for Mississippi, the parity levels for wheat, the probable odds on a military engagement? Who else but SAM! And why didn't we do it long ago, just feed the problems to *him*, SAM, and not go on killing man after man, great men, *decent* men like poor Jim Creighton, who's on his back now and dying because people like you—" He broke off suddenly and bowed his head. The room was still. No one looked at Reddington. After a moment he shook his head. His voice, when he spoke, was husky.

"Gentlemen, I'm sorry. This leads nowhere." He turned back to Larkin.

Larkin had begun to feel the pressure. But the presence of these men, of Reddington's obvious profound sincerity, reassured him. Creighton had been a great president; he had surrounded himself with some of the finest men in the country. Larkin felt a surge of hope that such men as these were available for one of the most critical hours in American history. For critical it was, and Larkin knew as clearly as anyone there what the absence of a president in the morning—no deep reassurance, no words of hope—would mean. He sat waiting for Reddington to continue.

"Well, we have a plan. It may work, it may not. We may all be shot. But this is where you come in. I hope for all our sakes you're up to it."

Larkin waited.

"The plan," Reddington went on, slowly, carefully, "is this. SAM has one defect. We can't tamper with it. But we *can* fool it. Because when the brain tests a man, it does not at the same time identify him. We do the identifying ourselves. So if a man named Joe Smith takes the personality tests and another man also named Joe Smith takes the Political Science tests, the machine has no way of telling them apart. Unless our guards supply the difference, SAM will mark up the results of both tests to one Joe Smith. We can clear the guards, no problem there. The first problem was to find the eight men to take the eight tests."

Larkin understood. He nodded.

"Exactly. Eight specialists," Reddington said. "General Vines will take the Military; Burden, Psychology; Wachsmuth, Economics; and so on. You, of course, will take the Political Science. We can only hope that each man will come out with a high enough score in his own field so that the combined scores of our mythical 'candidate' will be enough to qualify him. Do you follow me?"

Larkin nodded dazedly. "I think so. But—"

"It should work. It has to work."

"Yes," Larkin murmured, "I can see that. But who, who will actually wind up—"

"As president?" Reddington smiled very slightly and stood up.

"That was the most difficult question of all. At first we thought there was no solution. Because a president must be so many things—consider. A president blossoms instantaneously, from nonentity, into the most important job on earth. Every magazine, every newspaper in the country immediately goes to work on his background, digs out his life story, anecdotes, sayings, and so on. Even a very strong fraud would never survive it. So the first problem was believability. The new president must be absolutely believable. He must be a man of obvious character, of obvious intelligence, but more than that, his former life must fit the facts: he must have had both the time and the personality to prepare himself for the office.

"And you see immediately what all that means. Most businessmen are out. Their lives have been too social, they wouldn't have had the time. For the same reason all government and military personnel are also out, and we need hardly say that anyone from the Bureau of Elections would be immediately suspect. No. You see the problem. For a while we thought that the time was too short, the risk too great. But then the only solution, the only possible chance, finally occurred to us.

"The only believable person would be—a professor. Someone whose life has been serious but unhurried, devoted to learning but at the same time isolated. The only really believable person. And not a scientist, you understand, for a man like that would be much too overbalanced in one direction for our purpose. No, simply a professor, preferably in a field like Political Science, a man whose sole job for many years has been teaching, who can claim to have studied in his spare time, his summers—never really expected to pass the tests and all that, a humble man, you see—"

"Political Science," Larkin said.

Reddington watched him. The other men began to close in on him.

"Yes," Reddington said gently. "Now do you see? It is our only hope. Your name was suggested by several sources, you are young enough, your reputation is well known. We think that you would be believable. And now that I've seen you"—he looked around slowly—"I for one am willing to risk it. Gentlemen, what do you say?"

Larkin, speechless, sat listening in mounting shock while the men agreed solemnly, one by one. In the enormity of the moment he could not think at all. Dimly, he heard Reddington.

"I know. But, Doctor, there is no time. The Polls close at eight. It is now almost seven."

Larkin closed his eyes and rested his head on his hands. Above him, Reddington went on inevitably.

"All right. You are thinking of what happens after. Even if we pull this off and you are accepted without question, what then? Well, it will simply be the old system all over again. You will be at least no worse off than presidents before SAM. Better even, because if worse comes to worst, there is always SAM. You can feed all the bad ones to him. You will have the advice of the cabinet, of the military staff. We will help you in every way we can, some of us will sit with you on all conferences. And you know more about this than most of us, you have studied government all your life.

"But all this, what comes later, is not important. Not now. If we can get through tomorrow, the next few days, all the rest will work itself out. Eventually we can get around to altering SAM. But we must have a president in the morning. You are our only hope. You can do it. We all know you can do it. At any rate there is no other way, no time. Doctor," he reached out and laid his hand on Larkin's shoulder, "shall we go to the Polls?"

It passed, as most great moments in a man's life do, with Larkin not fully understanding what was happening to him. Later he would look back to this night and realize the enormity of the decision he had made, the doubts, the sleeplessness, the responsibility and agony toward which he moved. But in that moment he thought nothing at all. Except that it was Larkin's country, Larkin's America. And Reddington was right. There was nothing else to do. He stood up.

They went to the Polls.

At 9:30 that evening, sitting alone with Reddington back at the apartment, Larkin looked at the face of the announcer on the television screen, and heard himself pronounced President-elect of the United States.

Reddington wilted in front of the screen. For a while neither man moved. They had come home alone, just as they had gone into the Polls one by one in the hope of arousing no comment. Now they sat in silence until Reddington turned off the set. He stood up and straightened his shoulders before turning to Larkin. He stretched out his hand.

"Well, may God help us," he breathed, "we did it."

Larkin took his hand. He felt suddenly weak. He sat down again, but already he could hear the phone ringing in the outer hall. Reddington smiled.

"Only a few of my closest friends are supposed to know about that phone. But every time anything big comes up—" He shrugged. "Well," he said, still smiling, "let's see how it works."

He picked up the phone and with it an entirely different manner. He became amazingly light and cheerful, as if he was feeling nothing more than the normal political goodwill.

"Know him? Of course I know him. Had my eye on the guy for months. Really nice guy, wait'll you meet him . . . yup, college professor, Political Science, written a couple of books . . . must know a hell of a lot more than Poli Sci, though. Probably been knocking himself out in his spare time. But those teachers, you know how it is, they don't get any pay, but all the spare time in the world. . . . Married? No, not that I know of—"

Larkin noticed with wry admiration how carefully Reddington had slipped in that bit about spare time, without seeming to be making an explanation. He thought wearily to himself, I hope that I don't have to do any talking myself. I'll have to do a lot of listening before I can chance any talking.

In a few moments Reddington put down the phone and came back. He had on his hat and coat.

"Had to answer a few," he said briefly, "make it seem natural. But you better get dressed."

"Dressed? Why?"

"Have you forgotten?" Reddington smiled patiently. "You're due at the White House. The Secret Service is already tearing the town apart looking for you. We were supposed to alert them. Oh, by the saints, I hope that wasn't too bad a slip."

He pursed his mouth worriedly while Larkin, still dazed, got into his coat. It was beginning now. It had already begun. He was tired but it did not matter. That he was tired would probably never matter again. He took a deep breath. Like Reddington, he straightened his shoulders.

The Secret Service picked them up halfway across town. That they knew where he was, who he was, amazed him and worried Reddington. They went through the gates of the White House and drove up before the door. It was opened for him as he put out his hand, he stepped back in a reflex action, from the sudden blinding flares of the photographer's flashbulbs. Reddington behind him took him firmly by the arm. Larkin went with him gratefully, unable to see, unable to hear anything but the roar of the crowd from behind the gates and the shouted questions of the reporters.

Inside the great front doors it was suddenly peaceful again, very quiet and pleasantly dark. He took off his hat instinctively. Luckily he had been here before, he recognized the lovely hall and felt not awed but at home. He was introduced quickly to several people whose names made no impression on him. A woman smiled. He made an effort to smile back. Reddington took him by the arm again and led him away. There were people all around him, but they were quiet and hung back. He saw the respect on their faces. It sobered him, quickened his mind.

"The President's in the Lincoln Room," Reddington whispered. "He wants to see you. How do you feel?"

"All right."

"Listen."

"Yes."

"You'll be fine. You're doing beautifully. Keep just that look on your face."

"I'm not trying to keep it there."

"You aren't?" Reddington looked at him. "Good. Very good." He paused and looked again at Larkin. Then he smiled.

"It's done it. I thought it would but I wasn't sure. But it does it every time.

A man comes in here, no matter what he was before, no matter what he is when he goes out, but he feels it. Don't you feel it?"

"Yes. It's like—"

"What?"

"It's like . . . when you're in here . . . you're *responsible.*"

Reddington said nothing. But Larkin felt a warm pressure on his arm.

They paused at the door of the Lincoln Room. Two Secret Service men, standing by the door, opened it respectfully. They went on in, leaving the others outside.

Larkin looked across the room to the great, immortal bed. He felt suddenly very small, very tender. He crossed the soft carpet and looked down at the old man.

"Hi," the old man said. Larkin was startled, but he looked down at the broad weakly smiling face, saw the famous white hair and the still-twinkling eyes, and found himself smiling in return.

"Mr. President," Larkin said.

"I hear your name is Larkin." The old man's voice was surprisingly strong, but as he spoke now Larkin could see that the left side of his face was paralyzed. "Good name for a president. Indicates a certain sense of humor. Need a sense of humor. Reddington, how'd it go?"

"Good as can be expected, sir." He glanced briefly at Larkin. "The President knows. Wouldn't have done it without his okay. Now that I think of it, it was probably he who put the Secret Service on us."

"You're doggone right," the old man said. "They may bother the by-jingo out of you, but those boys are necessary. And also, if I hadn't let them know we knew Larkin was material—" He stopped abruptly and closed his eyes, took a deep breath. After a moment he said: "Mr. Larkin?"

"Yes, sir."

"I have one or two comments. You mind?"

"Of course not, sir."

"I couldn't solve it. I just . . . didn't have time. There were so many other things to do." He stopped and again closed his eyes. "But it will be up to you, son. The presidency . . . must be preserved. What they'll start telling you now is that there's only one way out, let SAM handle it. Reddington, too," the old man opened his eyes and gazed sadly at Reddington, "he'll tell you the same thing, but don't you believe it.

"Sure, SAM knows all the answers. Ask him a question on anything, on levels of parity tax rates, on anything. And right quick SAM will compute you out an answer. So that's what they'll try to do, they'll tell you to take it easy and let SAM do it.

"Well, all right, up to a certain point. But, Mr. Larkin, understand this. SAM is like a book. Like a book, he knows the answers. *But only those answers we've already found out.* We gave SAM those answers. A machine is not creative, neither is a book. Both are only the product of creative minds. Sure, SAM could hold the country together. But growth, man, there'd be no more growth! No new ideas, new solutions, change, progress, development! And America *must* grow, must progress—"

He stopped, exhausted. Reddington bowed his head. Larkin remained idly calm. He felt a remarkable clarity in his head.

"But, Mr. President," he said slowly, "if the office is too much for one man, then all we can do is cut down on his powers—"

"Ah," the old man said faintly, "there's the rub. Cut down on what? If I sign a tax bill, I must know enough about taxes to be certain that the bill is the right one. If I endorse a police action, I must be certain that the strategy involved is militarily sound. If I consider farm prices . . . you see, you see, what will you cut? The office is responsible for its acts. It must remain responsible. You cannot take just someone else's word for things like that, you must make your own decisions. Already we sign things we know nothing about, bills for this, bills for that, on somebody's word."

"What do you suggest?"

The old man cocked an eye toward Larkin, smiled once more with half his mouth, anciently worn, only hours from death, an old, old man with his work not done, never to be done.

"Son, come here. Take my hand. Can't lift it myself."

Larkin came forward, knelt by the side of the bed. He took the cold hand, now gaunt and almost translucent, and held it gently.

"Mr. Larkin," the President said. "God be with you, boy. Do what you can. Delegate authority. Maybe cut the term in half. But keep us human, please, keep us growing, keep us alive." His voice faltered, his eyes closed. "I'm very tired. God be with you."

Larkin laid the hand gently on the bed cover. He stood for a long moment looking down. Then he turned with Reddington and left the room.

Outside, he waited until they were past the Secret Service men and then turned to Reddington.

"Your plans for SAM. What do you think now?"

Reddington winced.

"I couldn't see any way out."

"But what about now? I have to know."

"I don't know. I really don't know. But . . . let me tell you something."

"Yes."

"Whatever I say to you from now on is only advice. You don't have to take it. Because understand this: however you came in here tonight, you're going out the president. You were elected. Not by the people maybe, not even by SAM. But you're President by the grace of God and that's enough for me. From this moment on you'll be President to everybody in the world. We've all agreed. Never think that you're only a fraud, because you aren't. You heard what the President said. You take it from here."

Larkin looked at him for a long while. Then he nodded once, briefly.

"All right," he said.

"One more thing."

"Yes?"

"I've got to say this. Tonight, this afternoon, I didn't really know what I was doing to you. I thought . . . well . . . the crisis came. But you had no time to think. That wasn't right. A man shouldn't be pushed into a thing like this without time to think. The old man just taught me something about making your own decisions. I should have let you make yours."

"It's all right."

"No, it isn't. You remember him in there. Well. That's you four years from tonight. If you live that long."

Now it was Larkin who reached out and patted Reddington on the shoulder.

"That's all right, too," he said.

Reddington said nothing. When he spoke again, Larkin realized he was moved.

"We have the greatest luck, this country," he said tightly. "At all the worst times we always seem to find all the best people."

"Well," Larkin said hurriedly, "we'd better get to work. There's a speech due in the morning. And the problem of SAM. And . . . oh, I've got to be sworn in."

He turned and went off down the hall. Reddington paused a moment before following him. He was thinking that he could be watching the last human President the United States would ever have. But—once more he straightened his shoulders.

"Yes, sir," he said softly, "Mr. President."

Charles Harness

Charles Harness (1915–   ) wrote one highly regarded SF novel in the 1950s, *Flight into Yesterday* (*The Paradox Men*, 1953). Damon Knight, in a famous review essay, said, "Harness told me in 1950 that he had spent two years writing the story, and had put into it every fictional idea that occurred to him during the time. He must have studied his model [van Vogt] with painstaking care." But Knight's point is that Harness surpasses van Vogt in SF: "All this, packed even more tightly than the original, symmetrically arranged, the loose ends tucked in, and every outrageous twist of the plot fully justified both in science and in logic." Brian W. Aldiss is also partisan to it: "This novel may be considered as the climax to the billion year spree . . . I call it Wide Screen Baroque . . . Harness's novel has a zing of its own, like whiskey and champagne, the drink of the Nepalese sultans."

After such praise, it is difficult to understand why Harness has suffered such comparative neglect, except that his career as a patent attorney allowed him only occasional time to write. His second novel, *The Ring of Ritornel*, was not published until 1968, and this third, *Wolfhead*, in 1978. Seven more novels followed between 1980 and 1991, altogether a significant body of genre work. Most of his short fiction has never been collected.

His only collection, *The Rose* (1966), was an obscure paperback original, containing the title novella and two other fine stories. Michael Moorcock, though, in an essay about "The Rose," calls it Harness's "greatest novel," and says, "although most of Harness's work is written in the magazine style of the time and at first glance appears to have only the appeal of colorful escapism, reminiscent of A. E. van Vogt or James Blish of the same period, it contains nuances and "throw away" ideas that show a serious (never earnest) mind operating at a much deeper and broader level than its contemporaries."

Moorcock goes on to say, " 'The Rose' [is] crammed with delightful notions—what some SF readers call 'ideas'—but these are essentially icing on the cake of Harness's fiction. [His] stories are what too little science fiction is—true stories of ideas, coming to grips with the big abstract problems of human existence and attempting to throw fresh, philosophical light on them."

"The Rose" was first published in a British SF magazine in 1953, at a time when not a hundred copies of such a publication were seen in the U.S., and not reprinted in America until 1966, long after the dust had settled from *Flight into Yesterday*. Except for the few new readers caught by the sixties paperbacks, the story, which deserves a place on the shelf next to the works of Cordwainer Smith, fell into obscurity. Here it is again, at last, one of the finest examples of "Grand Opera" science fiction.

THE ROSE

Her ballet slippers made a soft slapping sound, moody, mournful, as Anna van Tuyl stepped into the annex of her psychiatrical consulting room and walked toward the tall mirror.

Within seconds she would know whether she was ugly.

As she had done half a thousand times in the past two years, the young woman faced the great glass squarely, brought her arms up gracefully and rose upon her tip-toes. And there resemblance to past hours ceased. She did not proceed to an uneasy study of her face and figure. She could not. For her eyes, as though acting with a wisdom and volition of their own, had closed tightly.

Anna van Tuyl was too much the professional psychiatrist not to recognize that her subconscious mind had shrieked its warning. Eyes still shut, and breathing in great gasps, she dropped from her toes as if to turn and leap away. Then gradually she straightened. She must force herself to go through with it. She might not be able to bring herself here, in this mood of candid receptiveness, twice in one lifetime. It must be now.

She trembled in brief, silent premonition, then quietly raised her eyelids.

Sombre eyes looked out at her, a little darker than yesterday: pools ploughed around by furrows that today gouged a little deeper—the result of months of squinting up from the position into which her spinal deformity had thrust her neck and shoulders. The pale lips were pressed together just a little tighter in their defence against unpredictable pain. The cheeks seemed bloodless having been bleached finally and completely by the Unfinished Dream that haunted her sleep, wherein a nightingale fluttered about a white rose.

As if in brooding confirmation, she brought up simultaneously the pearl-translucent fingers of both hands to the upper borders of her forehead, and there pushed back the incongruous masses of newly-grey hair from two tumorous bulges—like incipient horns. As she did this she made a quarter turn, exposing to the mirror the humped grotesquerie of her back.

Then by degrees, like some netherworld Narcissus, she began to sink under the bizarre enchantment of that misshapen image. She could retain no real awareness that this creature was she. That profile, as if seen through witch-opened eyes, might have been that of some enormous toad, and this flickering metaphor paralyzed her first and only forlorn attempt at identification.

In a vague way, she realized that she had discovered what she had set out to discover. She was ugly. She was even very ugly.

The change must have been gradual, too slow to say of any one day: Yesterday I was not ugly. But even eyes that hungered for deception could no longer deny the cumulative evidence.

So slow—and yet so fast. It seemed only yesterday that had found her face down on Matthew Bell's examination table, biting savagely at a little pillow as his gnarled fingertips probed grimly at her upper thoracic vertebrae.

Well, then, she was ugly. But she'd not give in to self-pity. To hell with what she looked like! To hell with mirrors!

On sudden impulse she seized her balancing tripod with both hands, closed her eyes, and swung.

The tinkling of falling mirror glass had hardly ceased when a harsh and gravelly voice hailed her from her office. "Bravo!"

She dropped the practice tripod and whirled, aghast. "Matt!"

"Just thought it was time to come in. But if you want to bawl a little, I'll go back out and wait. No?" Without looking directly at her face or pausing for a reply, he tossed a packet on the table. "There it is. Honey, if I could write a ballet score like your *Nightingale and the Rose*, I wouldn't care if my spine was knotted in a figure eight."

"You're crazy," she muttered stonily, unwilling to admit that she was both pleased and curious. "You don't know what it means to have once been able to pirouette, to balance *en arabesque*. And anyway"—she looked at him from the corner of her eye—"how could anyone tell whether the score's good? There's no Finale as yet. It isn't finished."

"Neither is the Mona Lisa, *Kublai Khan*, or a certain symphony by Schubert."

"But this is different. A plotted ballet requires an integrated sequence of events leading up to a climax—to a Finale. I haven't figured out the ending. Did you notice I left a thirty-eight-beat hiatus just before The Nightingale dies? I still need a death song for her. She's entitled to die with a flourish." She couldn't tell him about The Dream—that she always awoke just before that death song began.

"No matter. You'll get it eventually. The story's straight out of Oscar Wilde, isn't it? As I recall, The Student needs a Red Rose as admission to the dance, but his garden contains only white roses. A foolish, if sympathetic Nightingale thrusts her heart against a thorn on a white rose stem, and the resultant ill-advised transfusion produces a Red Rose . . . and a dead Nightingale. Isn't that about all there is to it?"

"Almost. But I still need The Nightingale's death song. That's the whole point of the ballet. In a plotted ballet, every chord has to be fitted to the immediate action, blended with it, so that it supplements it, explains it, unifies it, and carries the action toward the climax. That death song will make the difference between a good score and a superior one. Don't smile. I think some of my individual scores are rather good, though of course I've never heard them except on my own piano. But without a proper climax, they'll remain unintegrated. They're all variants of some elusive dominating leitmotiv—some really marvellous theme I haven't the greatness of soul to grasp. I know it's something profound and poignant, like the *liebestod* theme in *Tristan*. It probably states a fundamental musical truth, but I don't think I'll ever find it. The Nightingale dies with her secret."

She paused, opened her lips as though to continue, and then fell moodily silent again. She wanted to go on talking, to lose herself in volubility. But now the reaction of her struggle with the mirror was setting in, and she was suddenly very tired. Had she ever wanted to cry? Now she thought only of sleep. But a furtive glance at her wristwatch told her it was barely ten o'clock.

The man's craggy eyebrows dropped in an imperceptible frown, faint, yet craftily alert. "Anna, the man who read your *Rose* score wants to talk to you about staging it for the Rose Festival—you know, the annual affair in the Via Rosa."

"I—an unknown—write a Festival ballet?" She added with dry incredulity: "The Ballet Committee is in complete agreement with your friend, of course?"

"He *is* the Committee."

"What did you say his name was?"

"I didn't."

She peered up at him suspiciously. "I can play games, too. If he's so anxious to use my music, why doesn't *he* come to see *me?*"

"He isn't that anxious."

"Oh, a big shot, eh?"

"Not exactly. It's just that he's fundamentally indifferent toward the things that fundamentally interest him. Anyway, he's got a complex about the Via Rosa—loves the district and hates to leave it, even for a few hours."

She rubbed her chin thoughtfully. "Will you believe it, I've never been there. That's the rose-walled district where the ars-gratia-artis professionals live, isn't it? Sort of a plutocratic Rive Gauche?"

The man exhaled in expansive affection. "That's the Via, all right. A six-hundred pound chunk of Carrara marble in every garret, resting most likely on the grand piano. Poppa chips furiously away with an occasional glance at his model, who is momma, posed *au naturel.*"

Anna watched his eyes grow dreamy as he continued. "Momma is a little restless, having suddenly recalled that the baby's bottle and that can of caviar should have come out of the atomic warmer at some nebulous period in the past. Daughter sits before the piano keyboard, surreptitiously switching from Czerny to a torrid little number she's going to try on the trap-drummer in Dorran's Via orchestra. Beneath the piano are the baby and mongrel pup. Despite their tender age, this thing is already in their blood. Or at least, their stomachs, for they have just finished an *hors d'oeuvre* of marble chips and now amiably share the *pièce de résistance,* a battered but rewarding tube of Van Dyke brown."

Anna listened to this with widening eyes. Finally she gave a short amazed laugh. "Matt Bell, you really love that life, don't you?"

He smiled. "In some ways the creative life is pretty carefree. I'm just a psychiatrist specializing in psychogenetics. I don't know an arpeggio from a drypoint etching, but I like to be around people that do." He bent forward earnestly. "These artists—these golden people—they're the coming force in society. And you're one of them, Anna, whether you know it or like it. You and your kind are going to inherit the earth—only you'd better hurry if you don't want Martha Jacques and her National Security scientists to get it first. So the battle lines converge in Renaissance II. Art versus Science. Who dies? Who lives?" He looked thoughtful, lonely. He might have been pursuing an introspective monologue in the solitude of his own chambers.

"This Mrs. Jacques," said Anna. "What's she like? You asked me to see her tomorrow about her husband, you know."

"Darn good looking woman. The most valuable mind in history, some say. And if she really works out something concrete from her Sciomnia equation, I guess there won't be any doubt about it. And that's what makes her potentially the most dangerous human being alive: National Security is fully aware of her value, and they'll coddle her tiniest whim—at least until she pulls something tangible out of Sciomnia. Her main whim for the past few years has been her errant husband, Mr. Ruy Jacques."

"Do you think she really loves him?"

"Just between me and you she hates his guts. So naturally she doesn't want any other woman to get him. She has him watched, of course. The Security Bureau cooperate with alacrity, because they don't want foreign agents to approach *her* through *him*. There have been ugly rumors of assassinated models . . . But I'm digressing." He cocked a quizzical eye at her. "Permit me to repeat the invitation of your unknown admirer. Like you, he's another true child of the new Renaissance. The two of you should find much in common—more than you can now guess. I'm very serious about this, Anna. Seek him out immediately—tonight—now. There aren't any mirrors in the Via."

"Please, Matt."

"Honey," he growled, "to a man my age you aren't ugly. And this man's the same. If a woman is pretty, he paints her and forgets her. But if she's some kind of an artist, he talks to her, and he can get rather endless sometimes. If it's any help to your self-assurance, he's about the homeliest creature on the face of the earth. You'll look like De Milo alongside him."

The woman laughed shortly. "I can't get mad at you, can I? Is he married?"

"Sort of." His eyes twinkled. "But don't let that concern you. He's a perfect scoundrel."

"Suppose I decide to look him up. Do I simply run up and down the Via paging all homely friends of Dr. Matthew Bell?"

"Not quite. If I were you I'd start at the entrance—where they have all those queer side-shows and one-man exhibitions. Go on past the vendress of love philters and work down the street until you find a man in a white suit with polka dots."

"How perfectly odd! And then what? How can I introduce myself to a man whose name I don't know? Oh, Matt, this is so silly, so *childish* . . ."

He shook his head in slow denial. "You aren't going to think about names when you see him. And your name won't mean a thing to him, anyway. You'll be lucky if you aren't 'hey you' by midnight. But it isn't going to matter."

"It isn't too clear why you don't offer to escort me." She studied him calculatingly. "And I think you're withholding his name because you know I wouldn't go if you revealed it."

He merely chuckled.

She lashed out: "Damn you, get me a cab."

"I've had one waiting half an hour."

CHAPTER TWO

"Tell ya what the professor's gonna do, ladies and gentlemen. He's gonna defend not just one paradox. Not just two. Not just a dozen. No, ladies and gentlemen, the professor's gonna defend *seventeen*, and all in the space of one short hour, without repeating himself, and including a brand-new one he has just thought up today: 'Music owes its meaning to its ambiguity.' Remember, folks, an axiom is just a paradox the professor's already got hold of. The cost of this dazzling display . . . don't crowd there, mister . . .'"

Anna felt a relaxing warmth flowing over her mind, washing at the encrusted strain of the past hour. She smiled and elbowed her way through the throng and on down the street, where a garishly lighted sign, bat-wing doors, and a forlorn cluster of waiting women announced the next attraction:

"FOR MEN ONLY. Daring blindfold exhibitions and variety entertainments continuously."

Inside, a loudspeaker was blaring: "Thus we have seen how to compose the ideal end-game problem in chess. And now, gentlemen, for the small consideration of an additional quarter . . ."

But Anna's attention was now occupied by a harsh cawing from across the street.

"Love philters! Works on male or female! Any age! Never fails!"

She laughed aloud. Good old Matt! He had foreseen what these glaring multifaceted nonsensical stimuli would do for her. Love philters! Just what she needed!

The vendress of love philters was of ancient vintage, perhaps seventy-five years old. Above cheeks of wrinkled leather her eyes glittered speculatively. And how weirdly she was clothed! Her bedraggled dress was a shrieking purple. And under that dress was another of the same hue, though perhaps a little faded. And under *that*, still another.

"That's why they call me Violet," cackled the old woman, catching Anna's stare. "Better come over and let me mix you one."

But Anna shook her head and passed on, eyes shining. Fifteen minutes later, as she neared the central Via area, her receptive reverie was interrupted by the outburst of music ahead.

Good! Watching the street dancers for half an hour would provide a highly pleasant climax to her escapade. Apparently there wasn't going to be any man in a polka dot suit. Matt was going to be disappointed but it certainly wasn't her fault she hadn't found him.

There was something oddly familiar about that music.

She quickened her pace, and then, as recognition came, she began to run as fast as her crouching back would permit. This was *her* music—the prelude to Act III of her ballet!

She burst through the mass of spectators lining the dance square. The music stopped. She stared out into the scattered dancers, and what she saw staggered the twisted frame of her slight body. She fought to get air through her vacuously wide mouth.

In one unearthly instant, a rift had threaded its way through the dancer-packed square, and a pasty white face, altogether spectral, had looked down that open rift into hers. A face over a body that was enveloped in a strange glowing gown of shimmering white. She thought he had also been wearing a white academic mortar board, but the swarming dancers closed in again before she could be sure.

She fought an unreasoning impulse to run.

Then, as quickly as it had come, logic reasserted itself; the shock was over. Odd costumes were no rarity on the Via. There was no cause for alarm.

She was breathing almost normally when the music died away and someone began a harsh harangue over the public address system. "Ladies and gentlemen, it is our rare good fortune to have with us tonight the genius who composed the music you have been enjoying."

A sudden burst of laughter greeted this, seeming to originate in the direction of the orchestra, and was counterpointed by an uncomplimentary blare from one of the horns.

"Your mockery is misplaced, my friends. It just so happens that this genius is not I, but another. And since she has thus far had no opportunity to join in the revelry, your inimitable friend, as The Student, will take her hand, as The Nightingale, in the final *pas de deux* from Act III. That should delight her, yes?"

The address system clicked off amid clapping and a buzz of excited voices, punctuated by occasional shouts.

She must escape! She must get away!

Anna pressed back into the crowd. There was no longer any question about finding a man in a polka dot suit. *That* creature in white certainly wasn't he. Though how could he have recognized her?

She hesitated. Perhaps he had a message from the other one, if there really was one with polka dots.

No, she'd better go. This was turning out to be more of a nightmare than a lark.

Still—

She peeked back from behind the safety of a woman's sleeve, and after a moment located the man in white.

His pasty-white face with its searching eyes was much closer. But what had happened to his *white* cap and gown? *Now*, they weren't white at all! What optical fantasy was this? She rubbed her eyes and looked again.

The cap and gown seemed to be made up of green and purple polka dots on a white background! So he was her man!

She could see him now as the couples spread out before him, exchanging words she couldn't hear, but which seemed to carry an irresistible laugh response.

Very well, she'd wait.

Now that everything was cleared up and she was safe again behind her armor of objectivity, she studied him with growing curiosity. Since that first time she had never again got a good look at him. Someone always seemed to get in the way. It was almost, she thought, as though he was working his way out toward her, taking every advantage of human cover, like a hunter closing in on wary quarry, until it was too late . . .

He stood before her.

There were harsh clanging sounds as his eyes locked with hers. Under that feral scrutiny the woman maintained her mental balance by the narrowest margin.

The Student.

The Nightingale, for love of The Student, makes a Red Rose. An odious liquid was burning in her throat, but she couldn't swallow.

Gradually she forced herself into awareness of a twisted, sardonic mouth framed between aquiline nose and jutting chin. The face, plastered as it was by white powder, had revealed no distinguishing features beyond its unusual size. Much of the brow was obscured by the many tassels dangling over the front of his travestied mortarboard cap. Perhaps the most striking thing about the man was not his face, but his body. It was evident that he had some physical deformity, to outward appearances not unlike her own. She knew intuitively that he was not a true hunchback. His chest and shoulders were excessively broad, and he seemed, like her, to carry a mass of superfluous tissue on his upper thoracic vertebrae. She surmised that the scapulae would be completely obscured.

His mouth twisted in subtle mockery. "Bell said you'd come." He bowed and held out his right hand.

"It is very difficult for me to dance," she pleaded in a low hurried voice. "I'd humiliate us both."

"I'm no better at this than you, and probably worse. But I'd never give up dancing merely because someone might think I look awkward. Come, we'll use the simplest steps."

There was something harsh and resonant in his voice that reminded her of Matt Bell. Only . . . Bell's voice had never set her stomach churning.

He held out his other hand.

Behind him the dancers had retreated to the edge of the square, leaving the centre empty, and the first beats of her music from the orchestra pavilion floated to her with ecstatic clarity.

Just the two of them, out there . . . before a thousand eyes. . . .

Subconsciously she followed the music. There was her cue—the signal for The Nightingale to fly to her fatal assignation with the white rose.

She must reach out both perspiring hands to this stranger, must blend her deformed body into his equally misshapen one. She must, because he was The Student, and she was The Nightingale.

She moved toward him silently and took his hands.

As she danced, the harsh-lit street and faces seemed gradually to vanish. Even The Student faded into the barely perceptible distance, and she gave herself up to The Unfinished Dream.

CHAPTER THREE

She dreamed that she danced alone in the moonlight, that she fluttered in solitary circles in the moonlight, fastened and appalled by the thing she must do to create a Red Rose. She dreamed that she sang a strange and magic song, a wondrous series of chords, the song she had so long sought. Pain buoyed her on excruciating wings, then flung her heavily to earth. The Red Rose was made, and she was dead.

She groaned and struggled to sit up.

Eyes glinted at her out of pasty whiteness. "That was quite a *pas*—only more *de seul* than *de deux*," said The Student.

She looked about in uneasy wonder.

They were sitting together on a marble bench before a fountain. Behind them was a curved walk bounded by a high wall covered with climbing green, dotted here and there with white.

She put her hand to her forehead. "Where are we?"

"This is White Rose Park."

"How did I get here?"

"You danced in on your own two feet through the archway yonder."

"I don't remember . . ."

"I thought perhaps you were trying to lend a bit of realism to the part. But you're early."

"What do you mean?"

"There are only white roses growing in here, and even *they* won't be in full bloom for another month. In late June they'll be a real spectacle. You mean you didn't know about this little park?"

"No. I've never ever been in the Via before. And yet . . ."

"And yet what?"

She hadn't been able to tell anyone—not even Matt Bell—what she was now going to tell this man, an utter stranger, her companion of an hour. He had to be told because, somehow, he too was caught up in the dream ballet.

She began haltingly. "Perhaps I *do* know about this place. Perhaps someone told me about it, and the information got buried in my subconscious mind until I wanted a white rose. There's really something behind my ballet that Dr. Bell didn't tell you. He couldn't, because I'm the only one who knows. The *Rose* comes from my dreams. Only, a better word is nightmares. Every night the score starts from the beginning. In The Dream, I dance. Every night, for months and months, there was a little more music, a little more dancing. I tried to get it out of my head, but I couldn't. I started writing it down, the music and the choreography."

The man's unsmiling eyes were fixed on her face in deep absorption.

Thus encouraged, she continued. "For the past several nights I have dreamed almost the complete ballet, right up to the death of The Nightingale. I suppose I identify myself so completely with The Nightingale that I subconsciously censor her song as she presses her breast against the thorn on the white rose. That's where I always awakened, or at least, always did before tonight. But I think I heard the music tonight. It's a series of chords . . . thirty-eight chords, I believe. The first nineteen were frightful, but the second nineteen were marvellous. Everything was too real to wake up. The Student, The Nightingale, the white roses."

But now the man threw back his head and laughed raucously. "You ought to see a psychiatrist!"

Anna bowed her head humbly.

"Oh, don't take it too hard," he said. "My wife's even after *me* to see a psychiatrist."

"Really?" Anna was suddenly alert. "What seems to be wrong with you? I mean, what does she object to?"

"In general, my laziness. In particular, it seems I've forgotten how to read and write." He gave her widening eyes a sidelong look. "I'm a perfect parasite, too. Haven't done any real work in months. What would *you* call it if you couldn't work until you had the final measures of the *Rose*, and you kept waiting, and nothing happened?"

"Hell."

He was glumly silent.

Anna asked, hesitantly, yet with a growing certainty. "This thing you're waiting for . . . might it have anything to do with the ballet? Or to phrase it from your point of view, do you think the completion of my ballet may help answer your problem?"

"Might. Couldn't say."

She continued quietly. "You're going to have to face it eventually, you know. Your psychiatrist is going to ask you. How will you answer?"

"I won't. I'll tell him to go to the devil."

"How can you be so sure he's a *he*?"

"Oh? Well, if he's a *she*, she might be willing to pose *al fresco* an hour or so. The model shortage is quite grave you know, with all of the little dears trying to be painters."

"But if she doesn't have a good figure?"

"Well, maybe her face has some interesting possibilities. It's a rare woman who's a total physical loss."

Anna's voice was very low. "But what if *all* of her were very ugly? What if your proposed psychiatrist were me, *Mr. Ruy Jacques?*"

His great dark eyes blinked, then his lips pursed and exploded into insane laughter. He stood up suddenly. "Come, my dear, whatever your name is, and let the blind lead the blind."

"Anna van Tuyl," she told him, smiling.

She took his arm. Together they strolled around the arc of the walk toward the entrance arch.

She was filled with a strange contentment.

Over the green-crested wall at her left, day was about to break, and from the Via came the sound of groups of die-hard revellers, breaking up and drifting away, like spectres at cock-crow. The cheerful clatter of milk bottles got mixed up in it somehow.

They paused at the archway while the man kicked at the seat of the pants of a spectre whom dawn had returned to slumber beneath the arch. The sleeper cursed and stumbled to his feet in bleary indignation.

"Excuse us, Willie," said Anna's companion, motioning for her to step through.

She did, and the creature of the night at once dropped into his former sprawl.

Anna cleared her throat. "Where now?"

"At this point I must cease to be a gentleman, *I'm* returning to the studio for some sleep, and *you* can't come. For, if your physical energy is inexhaustible, mine is not." He raised a hand as her startled mouth dropped open. "Please, dear Anna, don't insist. Some other night, perhaps."

"Why, you—"

"Tut tut." He turned a little and kicked again at the sleeping man. "I'm not an utter cad, you know. I would never abandon a weak, frail, unprotected woman in the Via."

She was too amazed now even to splutter.

Ruy Jacques reached down and pulled the drunk up against the wall of the arch, where he held him firmly. "Dr. Anna van Tuyl, may I present Willie the Cork."

The Cork grinned at her in unfocused somnolence.

"Most people call him the Cork because, that's what seals in the bottle's contents," said Jacques. "*I* call him the Cork because he's always bobbing up. He looks like a bum, but that's just because he's a good actor. He's really a Security man tailing me at my wife's request, and he'd only be too delighted for a little further conversation with you. A cheery good morning to you both!"

A milk truck wheeled around the corner. Jacques leaped for its running board, and he was gone before the psychiatrist could voice the protest boiling up in her.

A gurgling sigh at her feet drew her eyes down momentarily. The Cork was apparently bobbing once more on his own private alcoholic ocean.

Anna snorted in mingled disgust and amusement, then hailed a cab. As she slammed the door, she took one last look at Willie. Not until the cab rounded the corner and cut off his muffled snores did she realize that people usually don't snore with their eyes half-opened and looking at you, especially with eyes no longer blurred with sleep, but hard and glinting.

CHAPTER FOUR

Twelve hours later, in another cab and in a different part of the city, Anna peered absently out at the stream of traffic. Her mind was on the coming conference with Martha Jacques. Only twelve hours ago Mrs. Jacques had been just a bit of necessary case history. Twelve hours ago Anna hadn't really cared whether Mrs. Jacques followed Bell's recommendation and gave her the case. Now it was all different. She wanted the case, and she was going to get it.

Ruy Jacques—how many hours awaited her with this amazing scoundrel, this virtuoso of liberal—nay, loose—arts, who held locked within his remarkable mind the missing pieces of their joint jigsaw puzzle of The Rose?

That jeering, mocking face—what would it look like without makeup? Very ugly, she hoped. Beside his, her own face wasn't too bad.

Only—he was married, and she was en route at this moment to discuss preliminary matters with his wife, who, even if she no longer loved him, at least had prior rights to him. There were considerations of professional ethics even in thinking about him. Not that she could ever fall in love with him or any other patient. Particularly with one who had treated her so cavalierly. Willie the Cork, indeed!

As she waited in the cold silence of the great antechamber adjoining the office of Martha Jacques, Anna sensed that she was being watched. She was quite certain that by now she'd been photographed, x-rayed for hidden weapons, and her fingerprints taken from her professional card. In colossal central police files a thousand miles away, a bored clerk would be leafing through her dossier for the benefit of Colonel Grade's visigraph in the office beyond.

In a moment—

"Dr. van Tuyl to see Mrs. Jacques. Please enter door B-3," said the tinny voice of the intercom.

She followed a guard to the door, which he opened for her.

This room was smaller. At the far end a woman, a very lovely woman, whom she took to be Martha Jacques, sat peering in deep abstraction at something on the desk before her. Beside the desk, and slightly to the rear, a moustached man in plain clothes stood, reconnoitring Anna with hawklike eyes. The description fitted what Anna had heard of Colonel Grade, Chief of the National Security Bureau.

Grade stepped forward and introduced himself curtly, then presented Anna to Mrs. Jacques.

And then the psychiatrist found her eyes fastened to a sheet of paper on Mrs. Jacques' desk. And as she stared, she felt a sharp dagger of ice sinking into her spine, and she grew slowly aware of a background of brooding whispers in her mind, heart-constricting in their suggestions of mental disintegration.

For the thing drawn on the paper, in red ink, was—although warped, incomplete, and misshapen—unmistakably a rose.

"Mrs. Jacques!" cried Grade.

Martha Jacques must have divined simultaneously Anna's great interest in the paper. With an apologetic murmur she turned it face down. "Security regulations, you know. I'm really supposed to keep it locked up in the presence of visitors." Even a murmur could not hide the harsh metallic quality of her voice.

So *that* was why the famous Sciomnia formula was sometimes called the "Jacques Rosette": when traced in an everexpanding wavering red spiral in polar coordinates, it was . . . a Red Rose.

The explanation brought at once a feeling of relief and a sinister deepening of the sense of doom that had overshadowed her for months. So you, too, she thought wonderingly, seek The Rose. Your artist-husband is wretched for want of it, and now you. But do you seek the same rose? Is the rose of the scientist the true rose, and Ruy Jacques' the false? What *is* The Rose? Will I ever know?

Grade broke in. "Your brilliant reputation is deceptive, Dr. van Tuyl. From Dr. Bell's description, we had pictured you as an older woman."

"Yes," said Martha Jacques, studying her curiously. "We really had in mind an older woman, one less likely to . . . to—"

"To involve your husband emotionally?"

"Exactly," said Grade. "Mrs. Jacques must have her mind completely free from distractions. However"—he turned to the woman scientist—"it is my studied opinion that we need not anticipate difficulty from Dr. van Tuyl on that account."

Anna felt her throat and cheeks going hot as Mrs. Jacques nodded in damning agreement: "I think you're right, Colonel."

"Of course," said Grade, "*Mr.* Jacques may not accept her."

"That remains to be seen," said Martha Jacques. "He might tolerate a fellow artist." To Anna: "Dr. Bell tells us that you compose music, or something like that?"

"Something like that," nodded Anna. She wasn't worried. It was a question of waiting. This woman's murderous jealousy, though it might some day destroy her, at the moment concerned her not a whit.

Colonel Grade said: "Mrs. Jacques has probably warned you that her husband is somewhat eccentric; he may be somewhat difficult to deal with at times. On this account, the Security Bureau is prepared to triple your fee, if we find you acceptable."

Anna nodded gravely. Ruy Jacques and money, too!

"For most of your consultations you'll have to track him down," said Martha Jacques. "He'll never come to you. But considering what we're prepared to pay, this inconvenience should be immaterial."

Anna thought briefly of that fantastic creature who had singled her out of a thousand faces. "That will be satisfactory. And now, Mrs. Jacques, for my preliminary orientation, suppose you describe some of the more striking behaviorisms that you've noted in your husband."

"Certainly. Dr. Bell, I presume, has already told you that Ruy has lost the ability to read and write. Ordinarily that's indicative of advanced dementia praecox, isn't it? However, I think Mr. Jacques' case presents a more complicated picture, and my own guess is schizophrenia rather than dementia. The dominant and most frequently observed psyche is a megalomanic phase, during which he tends to harangue his listeners on various odd subjects. We've picked up some of these speeches on a hidden recorder and made a Zipf analysis of the word-frequencies."

Anna's brows creased dubiously. "A Zipf count is pretty mechanical."

"But scientific, undeniably scientific. I have made a careful study of the method, and can speak authoritatively. Back in the forties Zipf of Harvard proved that in a representative sample of English, the interval separating the repetition of the same word was inversely proportional to its frequency. He provided a mathematical formula for something previously known only qualitatively: that a too-soon repetition of the same or similar sound is distracting and grating to the cultured mind. If we must say the same thing in the next paragraph, we avoid repetition with an appropriate synonym. But not the schizophrenic. His disease disrupts his higher centres of association, and certain discriminating neural networks are no longer available for his writing and speech. He has no compunction against immediate and continuous tonal repetition."

"A rose is a rose is a rose . . ." murmured Anna.

"Eh? How did you know what this transcription was about? Oh, you were just quoting Gertrude Stein? Well, I've read about her, and she proves my point. She admitted that she wrote under autohypnosis, which we'd call a light case of schizo. But she could be normal, too. My husband never is. He goes on like this all the time. This was transcribed from one of his monologues. Just listen:

" 'Behold, Willie, through yonder window the symbol of your mistress' defeat: the rose! The rose, my dear Willie, grows not in murky air. The smoky metropolis of yester-year drove it to the country. But now, with the unsullied skyline of your atomic age, the red rose returns. How mysterious, Willie, that the rose continues to offer herself to us dull, plodding humans. We see nothing in her but a pretty flower. Her regretful thorns forever declare our inept clumsiness, and her lack of honey chides our gross sensuality. Ah, Willie, let us become as birds! For only the winged can eat the fruit of the rose and spread her pollen . . .' "

Mrs. Jacques looked up at Anna. "Did you keep count? He used the word 'rose' no less than five times, when once or twice was sufficient. He certainly had no lack of mellifluous synonyms at his disposal, such as 'red flower,' 'thorned plant,' and so on. And instead of saying 'the red rose returns' he should have said something like 'it comes back'."

"And lose the triple alliteration?" smiled Anna. "No, Mrs. Jacques, I'd re-examine that diagnosis very critically. Everyone who talks like a poet isn't necessarily insane."

A tiny bell began to jangle on a massive metal door in the right-hand wall.

"A message for me," growled Grade. "Let it wait."

"We don't mind," said Anna, "if you want to have it sent in."

"It isn't *that*. That's my private door, and I'm the only one who knows the combination. But I told them not to interrupt us, unless it dealt with this specific interview."

Anna thought of the eyes of Willie the Cork, hard and glistening. Suddenly she knew that Ruy Jacques had not been joking about the identity of the man. Was The Cork's report just now getting on her dossier? Mrs. Jacques wasn't going to like it. Suppose they turned her down. Would she dare seek out Ruy Jacques under the noses of Grade's trigger men?

"Damn that fool," muttered Grade. "I left strict orders about being disturbed. Excuse me."

He strode angrily toward the door. After a few seconds of dial manipulation, he turned the handle and pulled it inward. A hand thrust something metallic at him. Anna caught whispers. She fought down a feeling of suffocation as Grade opened the cassette and read the message.

The Security officer walked leisurely back toward them. He stroked his moustache coolly, handed the bit of paper to Martha Jacques, then clasped his hands behind his back. For a moment he looked like a glowering bronze statue. "Dr. van Tuyl, you didn't tell us that you were already acquainted with Mr. Jacques. Why?"

"You didn't ask me."

Martha Jacques said harshly: "That answer is hardly satisfactory. How long have you known Mr. Jacques? I want to get to the bottom of this."

"I met him last night for the first time in the Via Rosa. We danced. That's all. The whole thing was purest coincidence."

"You are his lover," accused Martha Jacques.

Anna colored. "You flatter me, Mrs. Jacques."

Grade coughed. "She's right. Mrs. Jacques. I see no sex-based espionage."

"Then maybe it's even subtler," said Martha Jacques. "These platonic females are still worse, because they sail under false colors. She's after Ruy, I tell you."

"I assure you," said Anna, "that your reaction comes as a complete surprise to me. Naturally, I shall withdraw from the case at once."

"But it doesn't end with that," said Grade curtly. "The national safety may depend on Mrs. Jacques' peace of mind during the coming weeks. I *must* ascertain your relation with Mr. Jacques. And I must warn you that if a compromising situation exists, the consequences will be most unpleasant." He picked up the telephone. "Grade. Get me the O.D."

Anna's palms were uncomfortably wet and sticky. She wanted to wipe them on the sides of her dress, but then decided it would be better to conceal all signs of nervousness.

Grade barked into the mouthpiece. "Hello! That you, Packard? Send me—"

Suddenly the room vibrated with the shattering impact of massive metal on metal.

The three whirled toward the sound.

A stooped, loudly dressed figure was walking away from the great and inviolate door of Colonel Grade, drinking in with sardonic amusement the stuporous faces turned to him. It was evident he had just slammed the door behind him with all his strength.

Insistent squeakings from the teleset stirred Grade into a feeble response. "Never mind . . . it's Mr. Jacques . . ."

CHAPTER FIVE

The swart ugliness of that face verged on the sublime. Anna observed for the first time the two horn-like protuberances on his forehead, which the man made no effort to conceal. His black woollen beret was cocked jauntily over one horn; the other, the visible one, bulged even more than Anna's horns, and to her fascinated eyes he appeared as some Greek satyr; Silenus with an eternal hangover, or Pan wearying of fruitless pursuit of fleeting nymphs. It was the face of a cynical post-gaol Wilde, of a Rimbaud, of a Goya turning his brush in saturnine glee from Spanish grandees to the horror-world of Ensayos.

Like a phantom voice Matthew Bell's cryptic prediction seemed to float into her ears again: ". . . much in common . . . more than you guess . . ."

There was so little time to think. Ruy Jacques must have recognized her frontal deformities even while that tasselated mortar-board of his Student costume had prevented her from seeing his. He must have identified her as a less advanced case of his own disease. Had he foreseen the turn of events here? Was he here to protect the only person on earth who might help him? That wasn't like him. He just wasn't the sensible type. She got the uneasy impression that he was here solely for his own amusement—simply to make fools of the three of them.

Grade began to sputter. "Now see here, Mr. Jacques. It's impossible to get in through that door. It's my private entrance. I changed the combination myself only this morning." The moustache bristled indignantly. "I must ask the meaning of this."

"Pray do, Colonel, pray do."

"Well, then, what is the meaning of this?"

"None, Colonel. Have you no faith in your own syllogisms? No one can open your private door but you. Q.E.D. No one did. I'm not really here. No smiles? Tsk tsk! Paragraph 6, p. 80 of the Manual of Permissible Military Humor officially recognizes the paradox."

"There's no such publication—" stormed Grade.

But Jacques brushed him aside. He seemed now to notice Anna for the first time, and bowed with exaggerated punctilio. "My profound apologies, madame. You were standing so still, so quiet, that I mistook you for a rose bush." He beamed at each in turn. "Now isn't this delightful? I feel like a literary lion. It's the first time in my life that my admirers ever met for the express purpose of discussing my work."

How could he know that we were discussing his "composition," wondered Anna. *And how did he open the door?*

"If you'd eavesdropped long enough," said Martha Jacques, "you'd have learned we weren't admiring your 'prose poem'. In fact, I think it's pure nonsense."

No, thought Anna, he couldn't have eavesdropped, because we didn't talk about his speech after Grade opened the door. There's something here—in this room—that *tells* him.

"You don't even think it's poetry?" repeated Jacques, wide-eyed. "Martha, coming from one with your scientifically developed poetical sense, this is utterly damning."

"There *are* certain well recognized approaches to the appreciation of poetry," said Martha Jacques doggedly. "You ought to have the autoscanner read you some books on the aesthetic laws of language. It's all there."

The artist blinked in great innocence. "*What's* all there?"

"Scientific rules for analyzing poetry. Take the mood of a poem. You can very easily learn whether it's gay or sombre just by comparing the proportion of low-pitched vowels—*u* and *o*, that is—to the high-pitched vowels—*a*, *e* and *i*."

"Well, what do you know about that!" He turned a wondering face to Anna. "And she's right! Come to think of it, in Milton's *L'Allegro*, most of the vowels are high-pitched, while in his *Il Penseroso*, they're mostly low-pitched. Folks, I believe we've finally found a yardstick for genuine poetry. No longer must we flounder in poetastical soup. Now let's see." He rubbed his chin in blank-faced thoughtfulness. "Do you know, for years I've considered Swinburne's lines mourning Charles Baudelaire to be the distillate of sadness. But that, of course, was before I had heard of Martha's scientific approach, and had to rely solely on my unsophisticated, untrained, uninformed feelings. How stupid I was! For the thing is crammed with high-pitched vowels, and long *e* dominates: 'thee,' 'sea,' 'weave,' 'eve,' 'heat,' 'sweet,' 'feet' . . ." He struck his brow as if in sudden comprehension. "Why, it's gay! I must set it to a snappy polka!"

"Drivel," sniffed Martha Jacques. "Science—"

"—is simply a parasitical, adjectival, and useless occupation devoted to the quantitative restatement of Art," finished the smiling Jacques. "Science is functionally sterile; it creates nothing; it says nothing new. The scientist can never be more than a humble camp-follower of the artist. There exists no scientific truism that hasn't been anticipated by creative art. The examples are endless. Uccello worked out mathematically the laws of perspective in the fifteenth century; but Kallicrates applied the same laws two thousand years before in designing the columns of the Parthenon. The Curies thought they invented the idea of 'half-life'—of a thing vanishing in proportion to its residue. The Egyptians tuned their lyre-strings to dampen according to the same formula. Napier thought he invented logarithms—entirely overlooking the fact that the Roman brass workers flared their trumpets to follow a logarithmic curve."

"You're deliberately selecting isolated examples," retorted Martha Jacques.

"Then suppose you name a few so-called scientific discoveries," replied the man. "I'll prove they were scooped by an artist, every time."

"I certainly shall. How about Boyle's gas law? I suppose you'll say Praxiteles knew all along that gas pressure runs inversely proportional to its volume at a given temperature?"

"I expected something more sophisticated. That one's too easy. Boyle's gas law, Hooke's law of springs, Galileo's law of pendulums, and a host of similar hogwash simply state that compression, kinetic energy, or whatever name you give it, is inversely proportional to its reduced dimensions, and is proportional to the amount of its displacement in the total system. Or, as the artist says, impact results from, and is proportional to, displacement of an object within its milieu. Could the final couplet of a Shakespearean sonnet enthral us if our minds hadn't been conditioned, held in check, and compressed in suspense by the preceding fourteen lines? Note how cleverly Donne's famous poem builds up to its crash line, 'It tolls for thee!' By blood, sweat, and genius, the Elizabethans lowered the entropy of their creations in precisely the same manner and with precisely the same result as when Boyle compressed his gases. And the method was long old when *they* were young. It was old when the Ming artists were painting the barest suggestions of landscapes on the disproportionate backgrounds of their vases. The Shah Jahan was aware of it when he designed the long eye-restraining reflecting pool before the Taj Mahal. The Greek tragedians knew it. Sophocles' *Oedipus* is still unparalleled in its suspensive pacing toward climax. Solomon's imported Chaldean arthitects knew the effect to be gained by spacing the Holy of Holies at a distance from the temple pylae, and the Cro-Magnard magicians with malice aforethought painted their marvellous animal scenes only in the most inaccessible crannies of their limestone caves."

Martha Jacques smiled coldly. "Drivel, drivel, drivel. But never mind. One of these days soon I'll produce evidence you'll be *forced* to admit art can't touch."

"If you're talking about Sciomnia, there's *real* nonsense for you," countered Jacques amiably. "Really, Martha, it's a frightful waste of time to reconcile biological theory with the unified field theory of Einstein, which itself merely reconciles the relativity and quantum theories, a futile gesture in the first place. Before Einstein announced *his* unified theory in 1949, the professors handled the problem very neatly. They taught the quantum theory on Mondays, Wednesdays and Fridays and the relativity theory on Tuesdays, Thursdays and Saturdays. On the Sabbath they rested in front of their television sets. What's the good of Sciomnia, anyway?"

"It's the final summation of all physical and biological knowledge," retorted Martha Jacques. "And as such, Sciomnia represents the highest possible aim of human endeavor. Man's goal in life is to understand his environment, to analyze it to the last iota—to know what he controls. The first person to understand Sciomnia may well rule not only this planet, but the whole galaxy—not that he'd want to, but he could. That person may not be me—but will certainly be a scientist, and not an irresponsible artist."

"But Martha," protested Jacques. "Where did you pick up such a weird philosophy? The highest aim of man is *not* to analyze, but to synthesize—to *create*. If you ever solve all of the nineteen sub-equations of Sciomnia, you'll be at a dead end. There'll be nothing left to analyze. As Dr. Bell the psychogeneticist says, overspecialization, be it mental, as in the human scientist, or dental, as in the sabre-tooth tiger, is just a synonym for extinction. But if we continue to create, we shall eventually discover how to transcend—"

Grade coughed, and Martha Jacques cut in tersely: "Never mind what Dr. Bell says. Ruy, have you ever seen this woman before?"

"The rose bush? Hmm." He stepped over to Anna and looked squarely down at her face. She flushed and looked away. He circled her in slow, critical appraisal, like a prospective buyer in a slave market of ancient Baghdad. "Hmm," he repeated doubtfully.

Anna breathed faster; her cheeks were the hue of beets. But she couldn't work up any sense of indignity. On the contrary, there was something illogically delicious about being visually pawed and handled by this strange leering creature.

Then she jerked visibly. What hypnotic insanity was this? This man held her life in the palm of his hand. If he acknowledged her, the vindictive creature who passed as his wife would crush her professionally. If he denied her, they'd know he was lying to save her—and the consequences might prove even less pleasant. And what difference would her ruin make to *him?* She had sensed at once his monumental selfishness. And even if that conceit, that gorgeous self-love, urged him to preserve her for her hypothetical value in finishing up the *Rose* score, she didn't see how he was going to manage it.

"Do you recognize her, Mr. Jacques," demanded Grade.

"I do," came the solemn reply.

Anna stiffened.

Martha Jacques smiled thinly. "Who is she?"

"Miss Ethel Twinkham, my old spelling teacher. How are you, Miss Twinkham? What brings you out of retirement?"

"I'm not Miss Twinkham," said Anna dryly. "My name is Anna van Tuyl. For your information, we met last night in the Via Rosa."

"Oh! Of course!" He laughed happily. "I seem to remember now, quite indistinctly. And I want to apologize, Miss Twinkham. My behavior was execrable, I suppose. Anyway, if you will just leave the bill for damages with Mrs. Jacques, her lawyer will take care of everything. You can even throw in ten per cent, for mental anguish."

Anna felt like clapping her hands in glee. The whole Security office was no match for this fiend.

"You're getting last night mixed up with the night before," snapped Martha Jacques. "You met Miss van Tuyl last night. You were with her several hours. Don't lie about it."

Again Ruy Jacques peered earnestly into Anna's face. He finally shook his head. "Last night? Well, I can't deny it. Guess you'll have to pay up, Martha. Her face *is* familiar, but I just can't remember what I did to make her mad. The bucket of paint and the slumming dowager was *last* week, wasn't it?"

Anna smiled. "You didn't injure me. We simply danced together on the square, that's all. I'm here at Mrs. Jacques' request." From the corner of her eye she watched Martha Jacques and the colonel exchange questioning glances, as if to say, "Perhaps there is really nothing between them."

But the scientist was not completely satisfied. She turned her eyes on her husband. "It's a strange coincidence that you should come just at this time. Exactly why *are* you here, if not to becloud the issue of this woman and your future psychiatrical treatment? Why don't you answer? What is the matter with you?"

For Ruy Jacques stood there, swaying like a stricken satyr, his eyes coals of pain in a face of anguished flames. He contorted backward once, as though attempting to placate furious fangs tearing at the hump on his back.

Anna leaped to catch him as he collapsed.

He lay cupped in her lap moaning voicelessly. Something in his hump, which lay against her left breast, seethed and raged like a genie locked in a bottle.

"Colonel Grade," said the psychiatrist quietly, "you will order an ambulance. I must analyze this pain syndrome at the clinic immediately."

Ruy Jacques was hers.

CHAPTER SIX

"Thanks awfully for coming, Matt," said Anna warmly.

"Glad to, honey." He looked down at the prone figure on the clinic cot. "How's our friend?"

"Still unconscious, and under general analgesic. I called you in because I want to air some ideas about this man that scare me when I think about them alone."

The psychogeneticist adjusted his spectacles with elaborate casualness. "Really? Then you think you've found what's wrong with him? Why he can't read or write?"

"Does it have to be something *wrong?*"

"What else would you call it? A . . . *gift?*"

She studied him narrowly. "I might—and you might—if he got something in return for his loss. That would depend on whether there was a net gain, wouldn't it? And don't pretend you don't know what I'm talking about. Let's get out in the open. You've known the Jacques—both of them—for years. You had me put on his case because you think he and I might find in the mind and body of the other a mutual solution to our identical aberrations. Well?"

Bell tapped imperturbably at his cigar. "As you say, the question is, whether he got enough in return—enough to compensate for his lost skills."

She gave him a baffled look. "All right, then, I'll do the talking. Ruy Jacques opened Grade's private door, when Grade alone knew the combination. And when he got in the room with us, he knew what we had been talking about. It was just as though it had all been written out for him, somehow. You'd have thought the lock combination had been pasted on the door, and that he'd looked over a transcript of our conversation."

"Only, he can't read," observed Bell.

"You mean, he can't read . . . *writing?*"

"What else is there?"

"Possibly some sort of thought residuum . . . in *things*. Perhaps some message in the metal of Grade's door, and in certain objects in the room." She watched him closely. "I see you aren't surprised. You've known this all along."

"I admit nothing. You, on the other hand, must admit that your theory of thought-reading is superficially fantastic."

"So would writing be—to a Neanderthal cave dweller. But tell me, Matt, where do our thoughts go after we think them? What is the extra-cranial fate of those feeble, intricate electric oscillations we pick up on the encephalograph? We know they can and do penetrate the skull, that they can pass through bone, like radio waves. Do they go on out into the universe forever? Or do dense substances like Grade's door eventually absorb them all? Do they set up their wispy patterns in metals, which then begin to vibrate in sympathy, like piano wires responding to a noise?"

Bell drew heavily on his cigar. "Seriously, I don't know. But I will say this: your theory is not inconsistent with certain psychogenetic predictions."

"Such as?"

"Eventual telemusical communication of all thought. The encephalograph, you know, looks oddly like a musical sound track. Oh, we can't expect to convert overnight to communication of pure thought by pure music. Naturally, crude transitional forms will intervene. But *any* type of direct idea transmission that involves the sending and receiving of rhythm and modulation as such is a cut higher than communication in a verbal medium, and may be a rudimentary step upward toward true musical communion, just as dawn man presaged true words with allusive, onomatapoeic monosyllables."

"There's your answer, then," said Anna. "Why should Ruy Jacques trouble to read, when every bit of metal around him is an open book?" She continued speculatively. "You might look at it this way. Our ancestors forgot how to swing through the trees when they learned how to walk erect. Their history is recapitulated in our very young. Almost immediately after birth, a human infant can hang by his hands, apelike. And then, after a week or so, he forgets what no human infant ever really needed to know. So now Ruy forgets how to read. A great pity. Perhaps. But if the world were peopled with Ruys, they wouldn't need to know how, for after the first few years of infancy, they'd learn to use their metal-empathic sense. They might even say, 'It's all very nice to be able to read and write and swing about in trees when you're *quite* young, but after all, one matures.'"

She pressed a button on the desk slide viewer that sat on a table by the artist's bed. "This is a radiographic slide of Ruy's cerebral hemispheres as viewed from above, probably old stuff to you. It shows that the 'horns' are not mere localized growths in the prefrontal area, but extend as slender tracts around the respective hemispheric peripheries to the visuo-sensory area of the occipital lobes, where they turn and enter the cerebral interior, there to merge in an enlarged ball-like juncture at a point over the cerebellum where the pineal 'eye' is ordinarily found."

"But the pineal is completely missing in the slide," demurred Bell.

"That's the question," countered Anna. "*Is* the pineal absent—or, are the 'horns' actually the pineal, enormously enlarged and bifurcated? I'm convinced that the latter is the fact. For reasons presently unknown to me, this heretofore small, obscure lobe has grown, bifurcated, and forced its destructive dual limbs not only through the soft cerebral tissue concerned with the ability to read, but also has gone on to skirt half the cerebral circumference to the forehead, where even the hard frontal bone of the skull has softened under its pressure." She looked at Bell closely. "I infer that it's just a question of time before I, too, forget how to read and write."

Bell's eyes drifted evasively to the immobile face of the unconscious artist. "But the number of neurons in a given mammalian brain remains constant after birth," he said. "These cells can throw out numerous dendrites and create increasingly complex neural patterns as the subject grows older, but he can't grow any more of the primary neurons."

"I know. That's the trouble. Ruy can't grow more brain, but he has." She touched her own "horns" wonderingly. "And I guess I have, too. *What*—?"

Following Bell's glance, she bent over to inspect the artist's face, and started as from a physical blow.

Eyes like anguished talons were clutching hers.

His lips moved, and a harsh whisper swirled about her ears like a desolate wind: "... The Nightingale ... in death ... greater beauty unbearable ... *but watch* ... THE ROSE!"

White-faced, Anna staggered backwards through the door.

CHAPTER SEVEN

Bell's hurried footsteps were just behind her as she burst into her office and collapsed on the consultation couch. Her eyes were shut tight, but over her labored breathing she heard the psychogeneticist sit down and leisurely light another cigar.

Finally she opened her eyes. "Even *you* found out something that time. There's no use asking me what he meant."

"Isn't there? Who will dance the part of The Student on opening night?"

"Ruy. Only, he will really do little beyond provide support to the prima ballerina, The Nightingale, that is, at the beginning and end of the ballet."

"And who plays The Nightingale?"

"Ruy hired a professional—La Tanid."

Bell blew a careless cloud of smoke toward the ceiling. "Are you sure *you* aren't going to take the part?"

"The role is strenuous in the extreme. For me, it would be a physical impossibility."

"Now."

"What do you mean—*now?*"

He looked at her sharply. "You know very well what I mean. You know it so well your whole body is quivering. Your ballet première is four weeks off—but you know and I know that Ruy has already seen it. Interesting." He tapped coolly at his cigar. "*Almost as interesting as your belief he saw you playing the part of The Nightingale.*"

Anna clenched her fists. This must be faced rationally. She inhaled deeply, and slowly let her breath out. "How can even *he* see things that haven't happened yet?"

"I don't know for sure. But I can guess, and so could you if you'd calm down a bit. We do know that the pineal is a residuum of the single eye that our very remote seagoing ancestors had in the centre of their fishy foreheads. Suppose this fossil eye, now buried deep in the normal brain, were reactivated. What would we be able to see with it? Nothing spatial, nothing dependent on light stimuli. But let us approach the problem inductively. I shut one eye. The other can fix Anna van Tuyl in a depthless visual plane. But with two eyes I can follow you stereoscopically, as you move about in space. Thus, adding an eye adds a dimension. With the pineal as a third eye I should be able to follow you through time. So Ruy's awakened pineal should permit him at least a hazy glimpse of the future."

"What a marvellous—and terrible gift."

"But not without precedent," said Bell. "I suspect that a more or less reactivated pineal lies behind every case of clairvoyance collected in the annals of para-psychology. And I can think of at least one historical instance in which the pineal has actually tried to penetrate the forehead, though evidently only in monolobate form. All Buddhist statues carry a mark on the forehead symbolic of an 'inner eye'. From what we know now, Budda's 'inner eye' was something more than symbolic."

"Granted. But a time-sensitive pineal still doesn't explain the pain in Ruy's hump. Nor the hump itself, for that matter."

"What," said Bell, "makes you think the hump is anything more than what it seems—a spinal disease characterized by a growth of laminated tissue?"

"It's not that simple, and you know it. You're familiar with 'phantom limb' cases, such as where the amputee retains an illusion of sensation or pain in the amputated hand or foot?"

He nodded.

She continued: "But you know, of course, that amputation isn't an absolute prerequisite to a 'phantom'. A child born armless may experience phantom limb sensations for years. Suppose such a child were thrust into some improbable armless society, and their psychiatrists tried to cast his sensory pattern into their own mould. How could the child explain to them the miracle of arms, hands, fingers—things of which he had occasional sensory intimations, but had never seen, and could hardly imagine? Ruy's case is analogous. He is four-limbed and presumably springs from normal stock. Hence the phantom sensations in his hump point toward a *potential* organ—a foreshadowing of the future, rather than toward memories of a limb once possessed. To use a brutish example, Ruy is like the tadpole rather than the snake. The snake had his legs briefly, during the evolutionary recapitulation of his embryo. The tadpole has yet to shed his tail and develop legs. But one might assume that each has some faint phantom sensoria of legs."

Bell appeared to consider this. "That still doesn't account for Ruy's pain. I wouldn't think the process of growing a tail would be painful for a tadpole, nor a phantom limb for Ruy—if it's inherent in his physical structure. But be that as it may, from all indications he is still going to be in considerable pain when that narcotic wears off. What are you going to do for him *then?* Section the ganglia leading to his hump?"

"Certainly not. Then he would *never* be able to grow that extra organ. Anyhow, even in normal phantom limb cases, cutting nerve tissue doesn't help. Excision of neuromas from limb stumps brings only temporary relief—and may actually aggravate a case of hyperaesthesia. No, phantom pain sensations are central rather then peripheral. However, as a temporary analgesic I shall try a two per cent solution of novocaine near the proper thoracic ganglia." She looked at her watch. "We'd better be getting back to him."

CHAPTER EIGHT

Anna withdrew the syringe needle from the man's side and rubbed the last puncture with an alcoholic swab.

"How do you feel, Ruy?" asked Bell.

The woman stooped beside the sterile linens and looked at the face of the prone man. "He doesn't," she said uneasily. "He's out cold again."

"Really?" Bell bent over beside her and reached for the man's pulse. "But it was only two per cent novocaine. Most remarkable."

"I'll order a counter-stimulant," said Anna nervously. "I don't like this."

"Oh, come, girl. Relax. Pulse and respiration normal. In fact, I think you're nearer collapse than he. This is very interesting . . ." His voice trailed off in musing surmise. "Look, Anna, there's nothing to keep both of us here. He's in no danger whatever. I've got to run along. I'm sure you can attend to him."

I know, she thought. You want me to be alone with him.

She acknowledged his suggestion with a reluctant nod of her head, and the door closed behind his chuckle.

For some moments thereafter she studied in deep abstraction the regular rise and fall of the man's chest.

So Ruy Jacques had set another medical precedent. He'd received a local anaesthetic that should have done nothing more than desensitise the deformed growth in his back for an hour or two. But here he lay, in apparent coma, just as though under a general cerebral anaesthetic.

Her frown deepened.

X-ray plates had showed his dorsal growth simply as a compacted mass of cartilaginous laminated tissue (the same as hers) penetrated here and there by neural ganglia. In deadening those ganglia she should have accomplished nothing more than local anaesthetization of that tissue mass, in the same manner that one anaesthetizes an arm or leg by deadening the appropriate spinal ganglion. But the actual result was not local, but general. It was as though one had administered a mild local to the radial nerve of the forearm to deaden pain in the hand, but had instead anaesthetized the cerebrum.

And *that*, of course, was utterly senseless, completely incredible, because anaesthesia works from the higher neural centres down, not vice versa. Deadening a certain area of the parietal lobe could kill sensation in the radial nerve and the hand, but a hypo in the radial nerve wouldn't knock out the parietal lobe of the cerebrum, because the parietal organization was neurally superior. Analogously, anaesthetizing Ruy Jacques' hump shouldn't have deadened his entire cerebrum, because certainly his cerebrum was to be presumed neurally superior to that dorsal malformation.

To be presumed . . .

But with Ruy Jacques, presumptions were—invalid.

So *that* was what Bell had wanted her to discover. Like some sinister reptile of the Mesozoic, Ruy Jacques had *two* neural organizations, one in his skull and one on his back, the latter being superior to, and in some degree controlling, the one in his skull, just as the cerebral cortex in human beings and other higher animals assists and screens the work of the less intricate cerebellum, and just as the cerebellum governs the still more primitive medulla oblongata in the lower vertebrata, such as in frogs and fishes. In anaesthetizing his bump, she had disrupted communications in his highest centres of consciousness, and in anaesthetizing the higher, dorsal centre, she had apparently simultaneously deactivated his "normal" brain.

As full realization came, she grew aware of a curious numbness in her thighs, and of faint overtones of mingled terror and awe in the giddy throbbing in her forehead. Slowly, she sank into the bedside chair.

For as this man was, so must she become. The day lay ahead when *her* pineal growths must stretch to the point of disrupting the grey matter in her occipital lobes, and destroy her ability to read. And the time must come, too, when *her* dorsal growth would inflame her whole body with its anguished writhing, as it had done his, and try with probable equal futility to burst its bonds.

And all of this must come—soon; before her ballet première, certainly. The enigmatic skein of the future would be unravelled to her evolving intellect even as it now was to Ruy Jacques'. She could find all the answers she sought . . . Dream's end . . . The Nightingale's death song . . . The Rose. And she would find them whether she wanted to or not.

She groaned uneasily.

At the sound, the man's eyelids seemed to tremble; his breathing slowed momentarily, then became faster.

She considered this in perplexity. He was unconscious, certainly; yet he made definite responses to aural stimuli. Possibly she had anaesthetized neither member of the hypothetical brain-pair, but had merely cut, temporarily, their lines of intercommunication, just as one might temporarily disorganize the brain of a laboratory animal by anaesthetizing the pons Varolii linking the two cranial hemispheres.

Of one thing she was sure: Ruy Jacques, unconscious, and temporarily mentally disintegrate, was not going to conform to the behavior long standardized for other unconscious and disintegrate mammals. Always one step beyond what she ever expected. Beyond man. Beyond genius.

She arose quietly and tiptoed the short distance to the bed.

When her lips were a few inches from the artist's right ear, she said softly: "What is your name?"

The prone figure stirred uneasily. His eyelids fluttered, but did not open. His wine-colored lips parted, then shut, then opened again. His reply was a harsh, barely intelligible whisper: "Zhak."

"What are you doing?"

"Searching . . ."

"For what?"

"A red rose."

"There are many red roses."

Again his somnolent, metallic whisper: "No, there is but one."

She suddenly realized that her own voice was becoming tense, shrill. She forced it back into a lower pitch. "Think of that rose. Can you see it?"

"Yes . . . yes!"

She cried: "*What is the rose?*"

It seemed that the narrow walls of the room would clamour forever their outraged metallic modesty, if something hadn't frightened away their pain. Ruy Jacques opened his eyes and struggled to rise on one elbow.

On his sweating forehead was a deep frown. But his eyes were apparently focused on nothing in particular, and despite his seemingly purposive motor reaction, she knew that actually her question had but thrown him deeper into his strange spell.

Swaying a little on the dubious support of his right elbow, he muttered: "*You are not the rose . . . not yet . . . not yet . . .*"

She gazed at him in shocked stupor as his eyes closed slowly and he slumped back on the sheet. For a long moment there was no sound in the room but his deep and rhythmic breathing.

CHAPTER NINE

Without turning form her glum perusal of the clinic grounds framed in her window, Anna threw the statement over her shoulder as Bell entered the office. "Your friend Jacques refuses to return for a check-up. I haven't seen him since he walked out a week ago."

"Is that fatal?"

She turned blood-shot eyes on him. "Not to Ruy."

The man's expression twinkled. "He's your patient, isn't he? It's your duty to make a house call."

"I certainly shall. I was going to call him on the visor to make an appointment."

"He doesn't have a visor. Everybody just walks in. There's something doing in his studio nearly every night. If you're bashful, I'll be glad to take you."

"No thanks. I'll go alone—early."

Bell chuckled. "I'll see you tonight."

CHAPTER TEN

Number 98 was a sad, ramshackled, four-storey, plaster-front affair, evidently thrown up during the materials shortage of the late forties.

Anna took a deep breath, ignored the unsteadiness of her knees, and climbed the half dozen steps of the front stoop.

There seemed to be no exterior bell. Perhaps it was inside. She pushed the door in and the waning evening light followed her into the hall. From somewhere came a frantic barking, which was immediately silenced.

Anna peered uneasily up the rickety stairs, then whirled as a door opened behind her.

A fuzzy canine muzzle thrust itself out of the crack in the doorway and growled cautiously. And in the same crack, farther up, a dark wrinkled face looked out at her suspiciously. "Whaddaya want?"

Anna retreated half a step. "Does he bite?"

"Who, Mozart? Nah, he couldn't dent a banana." The creature added with anile irrelevance, "Ruy gave him to me because Mozart's dog followed him to the grave."

"Then this is where Mr. Jacques lives?"

"Sure, fourth floor, but you're early." The door opened wider. "Say, haven't I seen you somewhere before?"

Recognition was simultaneous. It was that animated stack of purple dresses, the ancient vendress of love philters.

"Come in, dearie," purred the old one, "and I'll mix you up something special."

"Never mind," said Anna hurriedly. "I've got to see Mr. Jacques." She turned and ran toward the stairway.

A horrid floating cackle whipped and goaded her flight, until she stumbled out on the final landing and set up an insensate skirling on the first door she came to.

From within an irritated voice called: "Aren't you getting a little tired of that? Why don't you come in and rest your knuckles?"

"Oh." She felt faintly foolish. "It's me—Anna van Tuyl."

"Shall I take the door off its hinges, doctor?"

Anna turned the knob and stepped inside.

Ruy Jacques stood with his back to her, palette in hand, facing an easel bathed in the slanting shafts of the setting sun. He was apparently blocking in a caricature of a nude model lying, face averted, on a couch beyond the easel.

Anna felt a sharp pang of disappointment. She'd wanted him to herself a little while. Her glance flicked about the studio.

Framed canvases obscured by dust were stacked willy-nilly about the walls of the big room. Here and there were bits of statuary. Behind a nearby screen the disarray of a cot peeped out at her. Beyond the screen was a wire-phono. In the opposite wall was a door that evidently opened into the model's dressing alcove. In the opposite corner stood a battered electronic piano which she recognized as the Fourier audiosynthesizer type.

She gave an involuntary gasp as the figure of a man suddenly separated from the piano and bowed to her.

Colonel Grade.

So the lovely model with the invisible face must be—Martha Jacques.

There was no possibility of mistake, for now the model had turned her face a little, and acknowledged Anna's faltering stare with complacent mockery.

Of all evenings, why did Martha Jacques have to pick *this* one?

The artist faced the easel again. His harsh jeer floated back to the psychiatrist: "Behold the perfect female body!"

Perhaps it was the way he said this that saved her. She had a fleeting suspicion that he had recognized her disappointment, had anticipated the depths of her gathering despair, and had deliberately shaken her back into reality.

In a few words he had borne upon her the idea that his enormously complex mind contained neither love nor hate, even for his wife, and that while he found in her a physical perfection suitable for transference to canvas or marble, nevertheless he writhed in a secret torment over this very perfection, as though in essence the woman's physical beauty simply stated a lack he could not name, and might never know.

With a wary, futile motion he lay aside his brushes and palette. "Yes, Martha is perfect, physically and mentally, and knows it." He laughed brutally. "What she doesn't know, is that frozen beauty admits of no plastic play of meaning. There's nothing behind perfection, because it has no meaning but itself."

There was a clamour on the stairs. "Hah!" cried Jacques. "*More* early-comers. The word must have got around that Martha brought the liquor. School's out, Mart. Better hop into the alcove and get dressed."

Matthew Bell was among the early arrivals. His face lighted up when he saw Anna, then clouded when he picked out Grade and Martha Jacques.

Anna noticed that his mouth was twitching worriedly as he motioned to her. "What's wrong?" she asked.

"Nothing—yet. But I wouldn't have let you come if I'd known *they'd* be here. Has Martha given you any trouble?"

"No. Why should she? I'm here ostensibly to observe Ruy in my professional capacity."

"You don't believe that, and if you get careless, *she* won't either. So watch your step with Ruy while Martha's around. And even when she's not around. Too many eyes here—Security men—Grade's crew. Just don't let Ruy involve you in anything that might attract attention. So much for that. Been here long?"

"I was the first guest—except for *her* and Grade."

"Hmm. I should have escorted you. Even though you're his psychiatrist, this sort of thing sets her to thinking."

"I can't see the harm of coming alone. It isn't as though Ruy were going to try to make love to me in front of all these people."

"That's exactly what it is as though!" He shook his head and looked about him. "Believe me, I know him better than you. The man is insane . . . unpredictable."

Anna felt a tingle of anticipation . . . or was it of apprehension? "I'll be careful," she said.

"Then come on. If I can get Martha and Ruy into one of their eternal Science-versus-Art arguments, I believe they'll forget about you."

CHAPTER ELEVEN

"I repeat," said Bell, "we are watching the germination of another Renaissance. The signs are unmistakable, and should be of great interest to practicing sociologists and policemen." He turned from the little group beginning to gather about him and beamed artlessly at the passing fate of Colonel Grade.

Grade paused. "And just what are the signs of a renaissance?" he demanded.

"Mainly climatic change and enormously increased leisure, Colonel. Either alone can make a big difference, combined, the result is multiplicative rather than additive."

Anna watched Bell's eyes rove the room and join with those of Martha Jacques, as he continued: "Take temperature. In seven thousand B.C. *homo sapiens,* even in the Mediterranean area, was a shivering nomad; fifteen or twenty centuries later a climatic upheaval had turned Mesopotamia, Egypt and the Yangste valley into garden spots, and the first civilizations were born. Another warm period extending over several centuries and ending about twelve hundred A.D. launched the Italian Renaissance and the great Ottoman culture, before the temperature started falling again. Since the middle of the seventeenth century the mean temperature of New York City has been increasing at the rate of about one-tenth of a degree per year. In another century palm trees will be commonplace on Fifth Avenue." He broke off and bowed benignantly. "Hello, Mrs. Jacques. I was just mentioning that in past renaissances, mild climates and bounteous crops gave man leisure to think, and to create."

When the woman shrugged her shoulders and made a gesture as though to walk on, Bell continued hurriedly: "Yes, *those* renaissances gave us the Parthenon, *The Last Supper*, the Taj Mahal. *Then*, the *artist* was supreme. But this time it might not happen that way, because we face a simultaneous technologic and climatic optimum. Atomic energy has virtually abolished labor as such, but without the international leavening of common art that united the first Egyptian, Sumerian, Chinese and Greek cities. Without pausing to consolidate his gains, the scientist rushes on to greater things, to Sciomnia, and to a Sciomnic power source"—he exchanged a sidelong look with the woman scientist—"a machine which, we are informed, may overnight fling man toward the nearer stars. When that day comes, the artist is through . . . unless . . ."

"Unless what?" asked Martha Jacques coldly.

"Unless this Renaissance, sharpened and intensified as it has been by its double maxima of climate and science, is able to force a response comparable to that of the Aurignacean Renaissance of twenty-five thousand B.C., to wit, the flowering of the Cro-Magnon, the first of the modern men. Wouldn't it be ironic if our greatest scientist solved Sciomnia, only to come a cropper at the hands of what may prove to be one of the first primitive specimens of *homo superior*— her husband?"

Anna watched with interest as the psychogeneticist smiled engagingly at Martha Jacques' frowning face, while at the same time he looked beyond her to catch the eye of Ruy Jacques, who was plinking in apparent aimlessness at the keyboard of the Fourier piano.

Martha Jacques said curtly: "I'm afraid, Dr. Bell, that I can't get too excited about your Renaissance. When you come right down to it, local humanity, whether dominated by art or science, is nothing but a temporary surface scum on a primitive backwoods planet."

Bell nodded blandly. "To most scientists Earth is admittedly commonplace. Psychogeneticists, on the other hand, consider this planet and its people one of the wonders of the universe."

"Really?" asked Grade. "And just what have we got here that they don't have on Betelgeuse?"

"Three things," replied Bell. "One—Earth's atmosphere has enough carbon dioxide to grow the forest-spawning grounds of man's primate ancestors, thereby ensuring an unspecialized, quasi-erect, manually-activated species capable of indefinite psychophysical development. It might take the saurian life of a desert planet another billion years to evolve an equal physical and mental structure. Two—that same atmosphere had a surface pressure of 760 mm. of mercury and a mean temperature of about 25 degrees Centigrade—excellent conditions for the transmission of sound, speech, and song; and those early men took to it like a duck to water. Compare the difficulty of communication by direct touching of antennae, as the arthropodic pseudo-homindal citizens of certain airless worlds must do. Three—the solar spectrum within its very short frequency range of 760 to 390 millimicrons offers seven colors of remarkable variety and contrast, which our ancestors quickly made their own. From the beginning, they could see that they moved in multichrome beauty. Consider the ultra-sophisticate dwelling in a dying sun system—and pity him for he can see only red and a little infra red."

"If that's the only difference," snorted Grade, "I'd say you psychogeneticists were getting worked up over nothing."

Bell smiled past him at the approaching figure of Ruy Jacques. "You may be right, of course, Colonel, but I think you're missing the point. To the psycho-geneticist it appears that terrestrial environment is promoting the evolution of a most extraordinary being—a type of *homo* whose energies beyond the barest necessities are devoted to strange, unproductive activities. And to what end? We don't know—yet. But we can guess. Give a psychogeneticist Eohippus and the grassy plains, and he'd predict the modern horse. Give him archeopteryx and a dense atmosphere, and he could imagine the swan. Give him *h. sapiens* and a two-day work week, or better yet, Ruy Jacques and a no-day work week, and what will he predict?"

"The poorhouse?" asked Jacques, sorrowfully.

Bell laughed. "Not quite. An evolutionary spurt, rather. As *sapiens* turns more and more into his abstract world of the arts, music in particular, the psychoge-neticist foresees increased communication in terms of music. This might require certain cerebral realignments in *sapiens*, and perhaps the development of special membranous neural organs—which in turn might lead to completely new mental and physical abilities, and the conquest of new dimensions—just as the human tongue eventually developed from a tasting organ into a means of long distance vocal communication."

"Not even in Ruy's Science/Art diatribes," said Mrs. Jacques, "have I heard greater nonsense. If this planet is to have any future worthy of the name, you can be sure it will be through the leadership of her scientists."

"I wouldn't be too sure," countered Bell. "The artist's place in society has advanced tremendously in the past half-century. And I mean the minor artist— who is identified simply by his profession and not by any exceptional reputation. In our own time we have seen the financier forced to extend social equality to the scientist. And today the palette and musical sketch pad are gradually toppling the test tube and the cyclotron from their pedestals. In the first Renaissance the merchant and soldier inherited the ruins of church and feudal empire; in this one we peer through the crumbling walls of capitalism and nationalism and see the artist . . . or the scientist . . . ready to emerge as the cream of society. The question is, *which one?*"

"For the sake of law and order," declared Colonel Grade, "it must be the scientist, working in the defence of his country. Think of the military insecurity of an art-dominated society. If—"

Ruy Jacques broke in: "There is only one point on which I must disagree with you." He turned a disarming smile on his wife. "I really don't see how the scientist fits into the picture at all. Do you, Martha? For the artist is *already* supreme. He dominates the scientist, and if he likes, he is perfectly able to draw upon his more sensitive intuition for those various restatements of artistic principles that the sci-entists are forever trying to fob off on a decreasingly gullible public under the guise of novel scientific laws. I say that the artist is aware of those 'new' laws long before the scientist, and has the option of presenting them to the public in a pleasing art form or as a dry, abstruse equation. He may, like da Vinci, express his discovery of a beautiful curve in the form of a breathtaking spiral staircase in a *château* at Blois, or, like Dürer, he may analyze the curve mathematically and announce its logarithmic formula. In either event he anticipates Descartes, who was the first mathematician to rediscover the logarithmic spiral.''

The woman laughed grimly. "All right. *You're* an artist. Just what scientific law have *you* discovered?''

"I have discovered," answered the artist with calm pride, "what will go down in history as 'Jacques' Law of Stellar Radiation'.''

Anna and Bell exchanged glances. The older man's look of relief said plainly: "The battle is joined; they'll forget you.''

Martha Jacques peered at the artist suspiciously. Anna could see that the woman was genuinely curious but caught between her desire to crush, to damn any such amateurish "discovery" and her fear that she was being led into a trap. Anna herself, after studying the exaggerated innocence of the man's wide, unblinking eyes knew immediately that he was subtly enticing the woman out on the rotten limb of her own dry perfection.

In near-hypnosis Anna watched the man draw a sheet of paper from his pocket. She marvelled at the superb blend of diffidence and braggadocio with which he unfolded it and handed it to the woman scientist.

"Since I can't write, I had one of the fellows write it down for me, but I think he got it right," he explained. "As you see, it boils down to seven prime equations.''

Anna watched a puzzled frown steal over the woman's brow. "But each of these equations expands into hundreds more, especially the seventh, which is the longest of them all." The frown deepened. "Very interesting. Already I see hints of the Russell diagram . . .''

The man started. "What! H. N. Russell, who classified stars into spectral classes? You mean he scooped me?''

"Only if your work is accurate, which I doubt.''

The artist stammered: "But—''

"And here," she continued in crisp condemnation, "is nothing more than a restatement of the law of light-pencil wavering, which explains why stars twinkle and planets don't, and which has been known for two hundred years.''

Ruy Jacques' face lengthened lugubriously.

The woman smiled grimly and pointed. "These parameters are just a poor approximation of the Bethe law of nuclear fission in stars—old since the thirties.''

The man stared at the scathing finger. "Old . . . ?''

"I fear so. But still not bad for an amateur. If you kept at this sort of thing all your life, you might eventually develop something novel. But this is a mere hodge-podge, a rehash of material any real scientist learned in his teens.''

"But Martha," pleaded the artist, "surely it isn't *all* old?''

"I can't say with certainty, of course," returned the woman with malice-edged pleasure, "until I examine every sub-equation. I can only say that, fundamentally, scientists long ago anticipated the artist, represented by the great Ruy Jacques. In the aggregate, your amazing Law of Stellar Radiation has been known for two hundred years or more.''

Even as the man stood there, as though momentarily stunned by the enormity of his defeat, Anna began to pity his wife.

The artist shrugged his shoulders wistfully. "Science versus Art. So the artist has given his all, and lost. Jacques' Law must sing its swan song, then be forever forgotten." He lifted a resigned face toward the scientist. "Would you, my dear, administer the *coup de grâce* by setting up the proper co-ordinates in the Fourier audiosynthesizer?"

Anna wanted to lift a warning hand, cry out to the man that he was going too far, that the humiliation he was preparing for his wife was unnecessary, unjust, and would but thicken the wall of hatred that cemented their antipodal souls together.

But it was too late. Martha Jacques was already walking toward the Fourier piano, and within seconds had set up the polar-defined data and had flipped the toggle switch. The psychiatrist found her mind and tongue to be literally paralyzed by the swift movement of this unwitting drama, which was now toppling over the brink of its tragicomic climax.

A deep silence fell over the room.

Anna caught an impression of avid faces, most of whom—Jacques' most intimate friends—would understand the nature of his little playlet and would rub salt into the abraded wound he was delivering his wife.

Then in the space of three seconds, it was over.

The Fourier piano had synthesized the seven equations, six short, one long, into their tonal equivalents, and it was over.

Dorran, the orchestra leader, broke the uneasy stillness that followed. "I say, Ruy old chap," he blurted, "just what is the difference in 'Jacques' Law of Stellar Radiation' and 'Twinkle, twinkle, little star'?"

Anna, in mingled amusement and sympathy, watched the face of Martha Jacques slowly turn crimson.

The artist replied in amazement. "Why, now that you mention it, there does seem to be a little resemblance."

"It's a dead ringer!" cried a voice.

" 'Twinkle, twinkle' is an old continental folk tune," volunteered another. "I once traced it from Haydn's 'Surprise Symphony' back to the fourteenth century."

"Oh, but that's quite impossible," protested Jacques. "Martha has just stated that science discovered it first, only two hundred years ago."

The woman's voice dripped *aqua regia*. "You planned this deliberately, just to humiliate me in front of these . . . these clowns."

"Martha, I assure you . . . !"

"I'm warning you for the last time, Ruy. If you ever again humiliate me, I'll probably kill you!"

Jacques backed away in mock alarm until he was swallowed up in a swirl of laughter.

The group broke up, leaving the two women alone. Suddenly aware of Martha Jacques' bitter scrutiny. Anna flushed and turned toward her.

Martha Jacques said: "Why can't you make him come to his senses? I'm paying you enough."

Anna gave her a slow wry smile. "Then I'll need your help. And you aren't helping when you deprecate his sense of values—odd though they may seem to you."

"But Art is really so *foolish!* Science—"

Anna laughed shortly. "You see? Do you wonder he avoids you?"

"What would *you* do?"

"*I?*" Anna swallowed dryly.

Martha Jacques was watching her with narrowed eyes. "Yes, you. *If you wanted him?*"

Anna hesitated, breathing uneasily. Then gradually her eyes widened, became dreamy and full, like moons rising over the edge of some unknown, exotic land. Her lips opened with a nerveless fatalism. She didn't care what she said:

"I'd forget that I want, above all things, to be beautiful. I would think only of him. I'd wonder what he's thinking, and I'd forsake my mental integrity and try to think as he thinks. I'd learn to see through his eyes, and to hear through his ears. I'd sing over his successes, and hold my tongue when he failed. When he's moody and depressed, I wouldn't probe or insist that-I-could-help-you-if-you'd-only-let-me. Then—"

Martha Jacques snorted. "In short, you'd be nothing but a selfless shadow, devoid of personality or any mind or individuality of your own. That might be all right for one of your type. But for a scientist, the very thought is ridiculous!"

The psychiatrist lifted her shoulders delicately. "I agree. It *is* ridiculous. What *sane* woman at the peak of her profession would suddenly toss up her career to merge—you'd say 'submerge'—her identity, her very existence, with that of an utterly alien male mentality?"

"What woman, indeed?"

Anna mused to herself, and did not answer. Finally she said: "And yet, that's the price; take it or leave it, they say. What's a girl to do?"

"Stick up for her rights!" declared Martha Jacques spiritedly.

"All hail to unrewarding perseverance!" Ruy Jacques was back, swaying slightly. He pointed his half-filled glass toward the ceiling and shouted: "Friends! A toast! Let us drink to the two charter members of the Knights of the Crimson Grail." He bowed in saturnine mockery to his glowering wife. "To Martha! May she soon solve the Jacques Rosette and blast humanity into the heavens!"

Simultaneously he drank and held up a hand to silence the sudden spate of jeers and laughter. Then, turning toward the now apprehensive psychiatrist, he essayed a second bow of such sweeping grandiosity that his glass was upset. As he straightened, however, he calmly traded glasses with her. "To my old school-teacher, Dr. van Tuyl. A nightingale whose secret ambition is to become as beautiful as a red red red rose. May Allah grant her prayers." He blinked at her beatifically in a sudden silence. "What was that comment, doctor?"

"I said you were a drunken idiot," replied Anna. "But let it pass." She was panting, her head whirling. She raised her voice to the growing cluster of faces. "Ladies and gentlemen, I offer you the third seeker of the grail! A truly great artist. Ruy Jacques, a child of the coming epoch, whose sole aim is not aimlessness, as he would like you to think, but a certain marvellous rose. Her curling petals shall be of subtle texture, yet firm withal, and brilliant red. It is this rose that he must find, to save his mind and body, and to put a soul in him."

"She's right!" cried the artist in dark glee. "To Ruy Jacques, then! Join in, everybody. The party's on Martha!"

He downed his glass, then turned a suddenly grave face to his audience. "But it's really such a pity in Anna's case, isn't it? Because her cure is so simple."

The psychiatrist listened; her head was throbbing dizzily.

"As any *competent* psychiatrist could tell her," continued the artist mercilessly, "she has identified herself with the nightingale in her ballet. The nightingale isn't much to look at. On top it's a dirty brown; at bottom, you might say it's a drab grey. But ah! The soul of this plain little bird! Look into my soul, she pleads. Hold me in your strong arms, look into my soul, and think me as lovely as a red rose."

Even before he put his wineglass down on the table, Anna knew what was coming. She didn't need to watch the stiffening cheeks and flaring nostrils of Martha Jacques, nor the sudden flash of fear in Bell's eyes, to know what was going to happen next.

He held out his arms to her, his swart satyr-face nearly impassive save for its eternal suggestion of sardonic mockery.

"You're right," she whispered, half to him, half to some other part of her, listening, watching. "I *do* want you to hold me in your arms and think me beautiful. But you can't, because you don't love me. It won't work. Not yet. Here, I'll prove it.

As from miles and centuries away, she heard Grade's horrified gurgle.

But her trance held. She entered the embrace of Ruy Jacques, and held her face up to his as much as her spine would permit, and closed her eyes.

He kissed her quickly on the forehead and released her. "There! Cured!"

She stood back and surveyed him thoughtfully. "I wanted you to see for yourself, that nothing can be beautiful to you—at least not until you learn to regard someone else as highly as you do Ruy Jacques."

Bell had drawn close. His face was wet, grey. He whispered: "Are you two insane? Couldn't you save this sort of thing for a less crowded occasion?"

But Anna was rolling rudderless in a fatalistic calm. "I had to show him something. Here. Now. He might never have tried it if he hadn't had an audience. Can you take me home now?"

"Worst thing possible," replied Bell agitatedly. "That'd just confirm Martha's suspicions." He looked around nervously. "She's gone. Don't know whether that's good or bad. But Grade's watching us. Ruy, if you've got the faintest intimations of decency, you'll wander over to that group of ladies and kiss a few of them. May throw Martha off the scent. Anna, you stay here. Keep talking. Try to toss it off as an amusing incident." He gave a short strained laugh. "Otherwise you're going to wind up as the First Martyr in the Cause of Art."

"I beg your pardon, Dr. van Tuyl."

It was Grade. His voice was brutally cold, and the syllables were clipped from his lips with a spine-tingling finality.

"Yes, Colonel?" said Anna nervously.

"The Security Bureau would like to ask you a few questions."

"Yes?"

Grade turned and stared icily at Bell. "It is preferred that the interrogation be conducted in private. It should not take long. If the lady would kindly step into the model's dressing room, my assistant will take over from there."

"Dr. van Tuyl was just leaving," said Bell huskily. "Did you have a coat, Anna?"

With a smooth unobtrusive motion Grade unsnapped the guard on his hip holster. "If Dr. van Tuyl leaves the dressing room within ten minutes, alone, she may depart from the studio in any manner she pleases."

Anna watched her friend's face become even paler. He wet his lips, then whispered, "I think you'd better go, Anna. Be careful."

CHAPTER TWELVE

The room was small and nearly bare. Its sole furnishings were an ancient calendar, a clothes tree, a few stacks of dusty books, a table (bare save for a roll of canvas patching tape) and three chairs.

In one of the chairs, across the table, sat Martha Jacques.

She seemed almost to smile at Anna; but the amused curl of her beautiful lips was totally belied by her eyes, which pulsed hate with the paralyzing force of physical blows.

In the other chair sat Willie the Cork, almost unrecognizable in his groomed neatness.

The psychiatrist brought her hand to her throat as though to restore her voice, and at the movement, she saw from the corner of her eye that Willie, in a lightning motion, had simultaneously thrust his hand into his coat pocket, invisible below the table. She slowly understood that he held a gun on her.

The man was the first to speak, and his voice was so crisp and incisive that she doubted her first intuitive recognition. "Obviously, I shall kill you if you attempt any unwise action. So please sit down, Dr. van Tuyl. Let us put our cards on the table."

It was too incredible, too unreal, to arouse any immediate sense of fear. In numb amazement she pulled out the chair and sat down.

"As you may have suspected for some time," continued the man curtly, "I am a Security agent."

Anna found her voice. "I know only that I am being forcibly detained. What do you want?"

"Information, doctor. What government do you represent?"

"None."

The man fairly purred. "Don't you realize, doctor, that as soon as you cease to answer responsively, I shall kill you?"

Anna van Tuyl looked from the man to the woman. She thought of circling hawks, and felt the intimations of terror. What could she have done to attract such wrathful attention? She didn't know. But then, *they* couldn't be sure about *her*, either. This man didn't want to kill her until he found out more. And by that time surely he'd see that it was all a mistake.

She said: "Either I am a psychiatrist attending a special case, or I am not. I am in no position to prove the positive. Yet, by syllogistic law, you must accept it as a possibility until you prove the negative. Therefore, until you have given me an opportunity to explain or disprove any evidence to the contrary, you can never be certain in your own mind that I am other than what I claim to be."

The man smiled, almost genially. "Well put, doctor. I hope they've been paying you what you are worth." He bent forward suddenly. "Why are you trying to make Ruy Jacques fall in love with you?"

She stared back with widening eyes. "What did you say?"

"Why are you trying to make Ruy Jacques fall in love with you?"

She could meet his eyes squarely enough, but her voice was now very faint: "I didn't understand you at first. You said . . . that I'm trying to make him fall in love with me." She pondered this for a long wondering moment, as though the idea were utterly new. "And I guess . . . it's true."

The man looked blank, then smiled with sudden appreciation. "You *are* clever. Certainly, you're the first to try *that* line. Though I don't know what you expect to gain with your false candour."

"False? Didn't you mean it yourself? No, I see you didn't. But Mrs. Jacques does. And she hates me for it. But I'm just part of the bigger hate she keeps for *him*. Even her Sciomnia equation is just part of that hate. She isn't working on a biophysical weapon just because she's a patriot, but more to spite him, to show him that her science is superior to—"

Martha Jacques' hand lashed viciously across the little table and struck Anna in the mouth.

The man merely murmured: "Please control yourself a bit longer, Mrs. Jacques. Interruptions from outside would be most inconvenient at this point." His humorless eyes returned to Anna. "One evening a week ago, when Mr. Jacques was under your care at the clinic, you left stylus and paper with him."

Anna nodded. "I wanted him to attempt automatic writing."

"What is 'automatic writing'?"

"Simply writing done while the conscious mind is absorbed in a completely extraneous activity, such as music. Mr. Jacques was to focus his attention on certain music composed by me while holding stylus and paper in his lap. If his recent inability to read and write was caused by some psychic block, it was quite possible that his subconscious mind might bypass the block, and he would write—just as one 'doodles' unconsciously when talking over the visor."

He thrust a sheet of paper at her. "Can you identify this?"

What was he driving at? She examined the sheet hesitantly. "It's just a blank sheet from my private monogrammed stationery. Where did you get it?"

"From the pad you left with Mr. Jacques."

"So?"

"We also found another sheet from the same pad under Mr. Jacques' bed. It had some interesting writing on it."

"But Mr. Jacques personally reported nil results."

"He was probably right."

"But you said he wrote something?" she insisted; momentarily her personal danger faded before her professional interest.

"I didn't say *he* wrote anything."

"Wasn't it written with that same stylus?"

"It was. But I don't think he wrote it. It wasn't in his handwriting."

"That's often the case in automatic writing. The script is modified according to the personality of the dissociated subconscious unit. The alteration is sometimes so great as to be unrecognizable as the handwriting of the subject."

He peered at her keenly. "This script was perfectly recognizable, Dr. van Tuyl. I'm afraid you've made a grave blunder. Now, shall I tell you in *whose* handwriting?"

She listened to her own whisper: "Mine?"

"Yes."

"What does it say?"

"You know very well."

"But I don't." Her underclothing was sticking to her body with a damp clammy feeling. "At least you ought to give me a chance to explain it. May I see it?"

He regarded her thoughtfully for a moment, then reached into his pocket sheaf. "Here's an electrostat. The paper, texture, ink, everything, is a perfect copy of your original."

She studied the sheet with a puzzled frown. There were a few lines of scribblings in purple. But it *wasn't* in her handwriting. In fact, it wasn't even hand-writing—just a mass of illegible scrawls!

Anna felt a thrill of fear. She stammered: "What are you trying to do?"

"You don't deny you wrote it?"

"Of course I deny it." She could no longer control the quaver in her voice. Her lips were leaden masses, her tongue a stone slab. "It's—unrecognizable . . ."

The Cork floated with sinister patience. "In the upper left hand corner is your monogram: 'A. vT.', the same as on the first sheet. You will admit that, at least?"

For the first time, Anna really examined the presumed trio of initials enclosed in the familiar ellipse. The ellipse was there. But the print within it was—gibberish. She seized again at the first sheet—the blank one. The feel of the paper, even the smell, stamped it as genuine. It had been hers. But the monogram! "Oh no!" she whispered.

Her panic-stricken eyes flailed about the room. The calendar . . . same picture of the same cow . . . *but the rest* . . . ! A stack of books in the corner . . . titled in gold leaf . . . gathering dust for months . . . the label on the roll of patching tape on the table . . . even the watch on her wrist.

Gibberish. She could no longer read. She had forgotten how. Her ironic gods had chosen this critical moment to blind her with their brilliant bounty.

Then take it! And play for time!

She wet trembling lips. "I'm unable to read. My reading glasses are in my bag, outside." She returned the script. "If *you'd* read it, I might recognize the contents."

The man said: "I thought you might try this, just to get my eyes off you. If you don't mind, I'll quote from memory:

" '—what a queer climax for The Dream! Yet, inevitable. Art versus Science decrees that one of us must destroy the Sciomniac weapon; but that could wait until we become more numerous. So, what I do is for him alone, and his future depends on appreciating it. Thus, Science bows to Art, but even Art isn't all. The Student must know the one greater thing when he sees The Nightingale dead, for only then will he recognize . . . ' "

He paused.

"Is that all?" asked Anna.

"That's all."

"Nothing about a . . . rose?"

"No. What is 'rose' a code word for?"

Death? mused Anna. Was the rose a cryptolalic synonym for the grave? She closed her eyes and shivered. Were those really *her* thoughts, impressed into the mind and wrist of Ruy Jacques from some grandstand seat at her own ballet three weeks hence? But after all, why was it so impossible? Coleridge claimed *Kublai Khan* had been dictated to him through automatic writing. And that English mystic, William Blake, freely acknowledged being the frequent amanuensis for an unseen personality. And there were numerous other cases. So, from some unseen time and place, the mind of Anna van Tuyl had been attuned to that of Ruy Jacques, and his mind had momentarily forgotten that both of them could no longer write, and had recorded a strange reverie.

It was then that she noticed the—whispers.

No—not whispers—not exactly. More like rippling vibrations, mingling, rising, falling. Her heart beats quickened when she realized that their eerie pattern was soundless. It was as though something in her mind was suddenly vibrating *en rapport* with a subetheric world. Messages were beating at her for which she had no tongue or ear; they were beyond sound—beyond knowledge, and they swarmed dizzily around her from all directions. From the ring she wore. From the bronze buttons of her jacket. From the vertical steam piping in the corner. From the metal reflector of the ceiling light.

And the strongest and most meaningful of all showered steadily from the invisible weapon. The Cork grasped in his coat pocket. Just as surely as though she had seen it done, she knew that the weapon had killed in the past. And not just once. She found herself attempting to unravel those thought residues of death—once—twice—three times . . . beyond which they faded away into steady, indecipherable time-muted violence.

And now that gun began to scream: "Kill! Kill! Kill!"

She passed her palm over her forehead. Her whole face was cold and wet. She swallowed noisily.

CHAPTER THIRTEEN

Ruy Jacques sat before the metal illuminator near his easel, apparently absorbed in the profound contemplation of his goatish features, and oblivious to the mounting gaiety about him. In reality he was almost completely lost in a soundless, sardonic glee over the triangular death-struggle that was nearing its climax beyond the inner wall of his studio, and which was magnified in his remarkable mind to an incredible degree by the paraboloid mirror of the illuminator.

Bell's low urgent voice began hacking at him again. "Her blood will be on your head. All you need to do is to go in there. Your wife wouldn't permit any shooting with you around."

The artist twitched his misshapen shoulders irritably. "*Maybe.* But why should I risk my skin for a silly little nightingale?"

"Can it be that your growth beyond *sapiens* has served simply to sharpen your objectivity, to accentuate your inherent egregious want to identity with even the best of your fellow creatures? Is the indifference that has driven Martha nearly insane in a bare decade now too ingrained to respond to the first known female of your own unique breed?" Bell sighed heavily. "You don't have to answer. The very senselessness of her impending murder amuses you. Your nightingale is about to be impaled on her thorn—for nothing—as always. Your sole regret at the moment is that you can't twit her with the assurance that you will study her corpse diligently to find there the rose you seek."

"Such unfeeling heartlessness," said Jacques in regretful agreement, "is only to be expected in one of Martha's blunderings. I mean The Cork, of course. Doesn't he realize that Anna hasn't finished the score of her ballet? Evidently has no musical sense at all. I'll bet he was even turned down for the policemen's charity quarter. You're right, as usual, doc. We must punish such philistinism." He tugged at his chin, then rose from the folding stool.

"What are you going to do?" demanded the other sharply.

The artist weaved toward the phono cabinet. "Play a certain selection from Tchaikovsky's *Sixth.* If Anna's half the girl you think, she and Peter Ilyitch will soon have Mart eating out of their hands."

Bell watching him in anxious, yet half-trusting frustration as the other selected a spool from his library of electronic recordings and inserted it into the playback sprocket. In mounting mystification, he saw Jacques turn up the volume control as far as it would go.

CHAPTER FOURTEEN

Murder, a one-act play directed by Mrs. Jacques, thought Anna. With sound effects by Mr. Jacques. But the facts didn't fit. It was unthinkable that Ruy would do anything to accommodate his wife. If anything, he would try to thwart Martha. But what was his purpose in starting off in the finale of the first movement of the *Sixth?* Was there some message there that he was trying to get across to her?

There was. She had it. She was going to live. If—

"In a moment," she told The Cork in a tight voice, "you are going to snap off the safety catch of your pistol, revise slightly your estimated line of fire, and squeeze the trigger. Ordinarily you could accomplish all three acts in almost instantaneous sequence. At the present moment, if I tried to turn the table over on you, you could put a bullet in my head before I could get well started. But in another sixty seconds you will no longer have that advantage, because your motor nervous system will be laboring under the superimposed pattern of the extraordinary Second Movement of the symphony that we now hear from the studio."

The Cork started to smile, then he frowned faintly. "What do you mean?"

"All motor acts are carried out in simple rhythmic patterns. We walk in the two-four time of the march. We waltz, use a pickaxe, and manually grasp or replace objects in three-four rhythm."

"This nonsense is purely a play for time," interjected Martha Jacques. "Kill her."

"It is a fact," continued Anna hurriedly. (Would that Second Movement never begin?) "A decade ago, when there were still a few factories using hand-assembly methods, the workmen speeded their work by breaking down the task into these same elemental rhythms, aided by appropriate music." (There! It was beginning! The immortal genius of that suicidal Russian was reaching across a century to save her!) "It so happens that the music you are hearing *now* is the Second Movement that I mentioned, and it's neither two-four nor three-four but *five-four*, an oriental rhythm that gives difficulty even to skilled occidental musicians and dancers. Subconsciously you are going to try to break it down into the only rhythms to which your motor nervous system is attuned. But you can't. Nor can *any* occidental, even a professional dancer, unless he has had special training"— her voice wobbled slightly—"in Delcrozian eurhythmics."

She crashed into the table.

Even though she had known that this must happen, her success was so complete, so overwhelming, that it momentarily appalled her.

Martha Jacques and The Cork had moved with anxious, rapid jerks, like puppets in a nightmare. But their rhythm was all wrong. With their ingrained four-time motor responses strangely modulated by a five-time pattern, the result was inevitably the arithmetical composite of the two: a neural beat, which could activate muscle tissue only when the two rhythms were in phase.

The Cork had hardly begun his frantic, spasmodic squeeze of the trigger when the careening table knocked him backward to the floor, stunned, beside Martha Jacques. It required but an instant for Anna to scurry around and extract the pistol from his numbed fist.

Then she pointed the trembling gun in the general direction of the carnage she had wrought and fought an urge to collapse against the wall.

She waited for the room to stop spinning, for the white, glass-eyed face of Martha Jacques to come into focus against the fuzzy background of the cheap paint-daubed rug. And then the eyes of the woman scientists flickered and closed.

With a wary glance at the weapon muzzle, The Cork gingerly pulled a leg from beneath the table edge: "You have the gun," he said softly. "You can't object if I assist Mrs. Jacques?"

"I *do* object," said Anna faintly. "She's merely unconscious . . . feels nothing. I want her to stay that way for a few minutes. If you approach her or make any unnecessary noise, I will probably kill you. So—both of you must stay here until Grade investigates. I know you have a pair of handcuffs. I'll give you ten seconds to lock yourself to that steam pipe in the corner—hands *behind* you, please."

She retrieved the roll of adhesive patching tape from the floor and fixed several strips across the agent's lips, following with a few swift loops around the ankles to prevent him stamping his feet.

A moment later, her face a damp mask, she closed the door leisurely behind her and stood there, breathing deeply and searching the room for Grade.

He was standing by the studio entrance, staring at her fixedly. When she favored him with a glassy smile, he simply shrugged his shoulders and began walking slowly toward her.

In growing panic her eyes darted about the room. Bell and Ruy Jacques were leaning over the phono, apparently deeply absorbed in the racing clangor of the music. She saw Bell nod a covert signal in her direction, but without looking directly at her. She tried not to seem hurried as she strolled over to join them. She knew that Grade was now walking toward them and was but a few steps away when Bell lifted his head and smiled.

"Everything all right?" said the psychogeneticist loudly.

She replied clearly: "Fine. Mrs. Jacques and a Security man just wanted to ask some questions." She drew in closer. Her lips framed a question to Bell: "Can Grade hear?"

Bell's lips formed a soft, nervous guttural: "No. He's moving off toward the dressing room door. If what I suspect happened behind that door is true, you have about ten seconds to get out of here. And then you've got to hide." He turned abruptly to the artist. "Ruy, you've got to take her down into the Via. Right now—*immediately*. Watch your opportunity and lose her when no one is looking. It shouldn't be too hard in that mob."

Jacques shook his head doubtfully. "Martha isn't going to like this. You know how strict she is on etiquette. I think there's a very firm statement in Emily Post that the host should never, never, *never* walk out on his guests before locking up the liquor and silverware. Oh, well, if you insist."

CHAPTER FIFTEEN

"Tell ya what the professor's gonna do, ladies and gentlemen. He's gonna defend not just one paradox. Not just two. But seventeen! In the space of one short hour, and without repeating himself, and including one he just thought up five minutes ago: 'Security is dangerous.' "

Ruy frowned, then whispered to Anna: "That was for us. He means Security men are circulating. Let's move on. Next door. They won't look for a woman there."

Already he was pulling her away toward the chess parlor. They both ducked under the For Men Only sign (which she could no longer read), pushed through the bat-wing doors, and walked unobtrusively down between the wall and a row of players. One man looked up briefly out of the corner of his eyes as they passed.

The woman paused uneasily. She had sensed the nervousness of the barker even before Ruy, and now still fainter impressions were beginning to ripple over the straining surface of her mind. They were coming from that chess player: from the coins in his pocket; from the lead weights of his chess pieces; and especially from the weapon concealed somewhere on him. The resonant histories of the chess pieces and coins she ignored. They held the encephalographic residua of too many minds. The invisible gun was clearer. There was something abrupt and violent, alternating with a more subtle, restrained rhythm. She put her hand to her throat as she considered one interpretation: *Kill—but wait.* Obviously, he'd dare not fire with Ruy so close.

"Rather warm here, too," murmured the artist. "Out we go."

As they stepped out into the street again, she looked behind her and saw that the man's chair was empty.

She held the artist's hand and pushed and jabbed after him, deeper into the revelling sea of humanity.

She ought to be thinking of ways to hide, of ways to use her new sensory gift. But another, more imperative train of thought continually clamored at her, until finally she yielded to a gloomy brooding.

Well, it was true. She wanted to be loved, and she wanted Ruy to love her. And he knew it. Every bit of metal on her shrieked her need for his love.

But—was she ready to love him? No! How could she love a man who lived only to paint that mysterious unpaintable scene of the nightingale's death, and who loved only himself? He was fascinating, but what sensible woman would wreck her career for such unilateral fascination? Perhaps Martha Jacques was right, after all.

"So you got him, after all!"

Anna whirled toward the crazy crackle, nearly jerking her hand from Ruy's grasp.

The vendress of love-philters stood leaning against the front centre pole of her tent, grinning toothily at Anna.

While the young woman stared dazedly at her, Jacques spoke up crisply: "Any strange men been around, Violet?"

"Why, Ruy," she replied archly, "I think you're jealous. What kind of men?"

"Not the kind that haul you off to the alcoholic ward on Saturday nights. Not city dicks. Security men—quiet—seem slow, but really fast—see everybody—everything."

"Oh, *them.* Three went down the street two minutes ahead of you."

He rubbed his chin. "That's not so good. They'll start at that end of the Via and work up toward us until they meet the patrol behind us."

"Like grains of wheat between the millstones," cackled the crone. "*I knew* you'd turn to crime, sooner or later, Ruy. You were the only tenant I had who paid the rent regular."

"Mart's lawyer did that."

"Just the same, it looked mighty suspicious. You want to try the alley behind the tent?"

"Where does it lead?"

"Cuts back into the Via, at White Rose Park."

Anna started. "White rose?"

"We were there that first night," said Jacques. "You remember it—big rose-walled cul-de-sac. Fountain. Pretty, but not for us, not now. Has only one entrance. We'll have to try something else."

The psychiatrist said hesitantly: "No, wait."

For some moments she had been struck by the sinister contrast in this second descent into the Via and the irresponsible gaiety of that first night. The street, the booths, the laughter seemed the same, but really weren't. It was like a familiar musical score, subtly altered by some demoniac hand, raised into some harsh and fatalistic minor key. It was like the second movement of Tchaikovsky's *Romeo and Juliet:* all the bright promises of the first movement were here, but repetition had transfigured them into frightful premonitions.

She shivered. That second movement, that echo of destiny, was sweeping through her in ever faster tempo, as though impatient to consummate its assignation with her. Come safety, come death, she must yield to the pattern of repetition.

Her voice had a dream-like quality: "Take me again to the White Rose Park."

"What! Talk sense! Out here in the open you may have a chance."

"But I *must* go there. Please, Ruy. I think it's something about a white rose. Don't look at me as though I were crazy. Of course I'm crazy. If you don't want to take me, I'll go alone. But I'm going."

His hard eyes studied her in speculative silence, then he looked away. As the stillness grew, his face mirrored his deepening introspection. "At that, the possibilities are intriguing. Martha's stooges are sure to look in on you. But will they be able to see you? Is the hand that wields the pistol equally skilled with the brush and palette? Unlikely. Art and Science again. Pointillist school versus police school. A good one on Martha—if it works. Anna's dress is green. Complement of green is purple. Violet's dress should do it."

"My dress?" cried the old woman. "What are you up to, Ruy?"

"Nothing. Luscious. I just want you to take off one of your dresses. The outer one will do."

"Sir!" Violet began to sputter in barely audible gasps.

Anna had watched all this in vague detachment, accepting it as one of the man's daily insanities. She had no idea what he wanted with a dirty old purple dress, but she thought she knew how she could get it for him, while simultaneously introducing another repetitive theme into this second movement of her hypothetical symphony.

She said: "He's willing to make you a fair trade, Violet."

The sputtering stopped. The old woman eyed them both suspiciously. "Meaning what?"

"He'll drink one of your love potions."

The leathery lips parted in amazement. "*I'm* agreeable, if *he* is, but I know he isn't. Why, that scamp doesn't love any creature in the whole world, except maybe himself."

"And yet he's ready to make a pledge to his beloved," said Anna.

The artist squirmed. "I like you, Anna, but I won't be trapped. Anyway, it's all nonsense. What's a glass of acidified water between friends?"

"The pledge isn't to me, Ruy. It's to a Red Rose." He peered at her curiously. "Oh? Well, if it will please you . . . All right, Violet, but off with that dress before you pour up."

Why, wondered Anna, do I keep thinking his declaration of love to a red rose is my death sentence? It's moving too fast. Who, what—is The Red Rose? The Nightingale dies in making the white rose red. So *she*—or I—can't be The Red Rose. Anyway, The Nightingale is ugly, and The Rose is beautiful. And why must The Student have a Red Rose? How will it admit him to his mysterious dance?

"Ah, Madame De Medici is back." Jacques took the glass and purple bundle the old woman put on the table. "What are the proper words?" he asked Anna.

"Whatever you want to say."

His eyes, suddenly grave, looked into hers. He said quietly: "If ever The Red Rose presents herself to me, I shall love her forever."

Anna trembled as he upended the glass.

CHAPTER SIXTEEN

A little later they slipped into the Park of the White Roses. The buds were just beginning to open, and thousands of white floreate eyes blinked at them in the harsh artificial light. As before, the enclosure was empty, and silent, save for the chattering splashing of its single fountain.

Anna abandoned a disconnected attempt to analyze the urge that had brought her here a second time. It's all too fatalistic, she thought, too involved. If I've entrapped myself, I can't feel bitter about it. "Just think," she murmured aloud, "in less than ten minutes it will all be over, one way or the other."

"Really? But where's my red rose?"

How could she even *consider* loving this jeering beast? She said coldly: "I think you'd better go. It may be rather messy in here soon." She thought of how her body would look, sprawling, misshapen, uglier than ever. She couldn't let him see her that way.

"Oh, we've plenty of time. No red rose, eh? Hmm. It seems to me, Anna, that you're composing yourself for death prematurely. There really is that little matter of the rose to be taken care of first, you know. As The Student, I must insist on my rights."

What made him be this way? "Ruy, please . . ." Her voice was trembling, and she was suddenly very near to tears.

"There, dear, don't apologize. Even the best of us are thoughtless at times. Though I must admit, I never expected such lack of consideration, such poor manners, in *you*. But then, at heart, you aren't really an artist. You've no appreciation of form." He began to untie the bundled purple dress, and his voice took on the argumentative dogmatism of a platform lecturer. "The perfection of form, of technique, is the highest achievement possible to the artist. When he subordinates form to subject matter, he degenerates eventually into a boot-lick, a scientist, or, worst of all, a Man with a Message. Here, catch!" He tossed the gaudy garment at Anna, who accepted it in rebellious wonder.

Critically, the artist eyed the nauseating contrast of the purple and green dresses, glanced momentarily toward the semi-circle of white-budded wall beyond, and then continued: "There's nothing like a school-within-a-school to squeeze dry the dregs of form. And whatever their faults, the pointillists of the impressionist movement could depict color with magnificent depth of chroma. Their palettes held only the spectral colors, and they never mixed them. Do you know why the Seines of Seurat are so brilliant and luminous? It's because the water is made of dots of pure green, blue, red and yellow, alternating with white in the proper proportion." He motioned with his hand, and she followed as he walked slowly on around the semi-circular gravel path. "What a pity Martha isn't here to observe our little experiment in tricolor stimulus. Yes, the scientific psychologists finally gave arithmetical vent to what the pointillists knew long before them—that a mass of points of any three spectral colors—or of one color and its complementary color—can be made to give any imaginable hue simply by varying their relative proportion."

Anna thought back to that first night of the street dancers. So *that* was why his green and purple polka dot academic gown had first seemed white!

At his gesture, she stopped and stood with her humped back barely touching the mass of scented buds. The arched entrance was a scant hundred yards to her right. Out in the Via an ominous silence seemed to be gathering. The Security men were probably roping off the area, certain of their quarry. In a minute or two, perhaps sooner, they would be at the archway, guns drawn.

She inhaled deeply and wet her lips.

The man smiled. "You hope I know what I'm doing, don't you? So do I."

"I think I understand your theory," said Anna, "but I don't think it has much chance of working."

"Tush, child." He studied the vigorous play of the fountain speculatively. "The pigment should never harangue the artist. You're forgetting that there isn't really such a color as white. The pointillists knew how to simulate white with alternating dots of primary colors long before the scientists learned to spin the same colors on a disc. And those old masters could even make white from just two colors: a primary and its complementary color. Your green dress is our primary; Violet's purple dress is its complementary. Funny, mix 'em as pigments into a homogeneous mass, and you get brown. But daub 'em on the canvas side by side, stand back the right distance, and they blend into white. All you have to do is hold Vi's dress at arm's length, at your side, with a strip of rosebuds and green leaves looking out between, and you'll have that white rose you came here in search of."

She demurred: "But the angle of visual interruption won't be small enough to blend the colors into white, even if the police don't come any nearer than the archway. The eye sees two objects as one only when the visual angle between the two is less than sixty seconds of arc."

"That old canard doesn't apply too strictly to colors. The artist relies more on the suggestibility of the mind rather than on the mechanical limitations of the retina. Admittedly, if our lean-jawed friends stared in your direction for more than a fraction of a second, they'd see you not as a whitish blur, but as a woman in green holding out a mass of something purple. But they aren't going to give your section of the park more than a passing glance." He pointed past the fountain toward the opposite horn of the semi-circular path. "I'm going to stand over *there*, and the instant someone sticks his head in through the archway, I'm going to start walking. Now, as every artist knows, normal people in western cultures absorb pictures from left to right, because they're laevo-dextro readers. So our agent's first glance will be toward you, and then his attention will be momentarily distracted by the fountain in the centre. And before he can get back to you, I'll start walking, and his eyes will have to come on to me. His attentive transition, of course, must be sweeping and imperative, yet so smooth, so subtle, that he will suspect no control. Something like Alexander's painting, *Lady on a Couch*, where the converging stripes of the lady's robe carry the eye forcibly from the lower left margin to her face at the upper right."

Anna glanced nervously toward the garden entrance, then whispered entreatingly, "Then you'd better go. You've got to be beyond the fountain when they look in."

He sniffed. "All right, I know when I'm not wanted. That's the gratitude I get for making you into a rose."

"I don't care a tinker's damn for a *white* rose. Scat!"

He laughed, then turned and started on around the path.

As Anna followed the graceful stride of his long legs, her face began to writhe in alternate bitterness and admiration. She groaned softly. "You—*fiend!* You gorgeous, egotistical, insufferable, unattainable *FIEND!* You aren't elated because you're saving my life; *I* am just a blotch of pigment in your latest masterpiece. *I hate you!*"

He was past the fountain now, and nearing the position he had earlier indicated.

She could see that he was looking toward the archway. She was afraid to look there.

Now he must stop and wait for his audience.

Only he didn't. His steps actually hastened.

That meant . . .

The woman trembled, closed her eyes, and froze into a paralytic stupor through which the crunch of the man's sandals filtered as from a great distance, muffled, mocking.

And then, from the direction of the archway, came the quiet scraping of more footsteps.

In the next split second she would know life or death.

But even now, even as she was sounding the iciest depths of her terror, her lips were moving with the clear insight of imminent death. "No, I don't hate you. I love you, Ruy. I have loved you from the first."

At that instant a blue-hot ball of pain began crawling slowly up within her body, along her spine, and then outward between her shoulder blades, into her spinal hump. The intensity of that pain forced her slowly to her knees and pulled her head back in an invitation to scream.

But no sound came from her convulsing throat.

It was unendurable, and she was fainting.

The sound of footsteps died away down the Via. At least Ruy's ruse had worked.

And as the mounting anguish spread over her back, she understood that all sound had vanished with those retreating footsteps, forever, because she could no longer hear, nor use, her vocal chords. She had forgotten how, but she didn't care.

For her hump had split open, and something had flopped clumsily out of it, and she was drifting gently outward into blackness.

CHAPTER SEVENTEEN

The glum face of Ruy Jacques peered out through the studio window into the night-awakening Via.

Before I met you, he brooded, loneliness was a magic, ecstatic blade drawn across my heart strings; it healed the severed strands with every beat, and I had all that I wanted save what I had to have—the Red Rose. My search for that Rose alone matters! I must believe this. I must not swerve, even for the memory of you, Anna, the first of my own kind I have ever met. I must not wonder if they killed you, nor even care. They must have killed you . . . It's been three weeks.

Now I can seek The Rose again. Onward into loneliness.

He sensed the nearness of familiar metal behind him. "Hello, Martha," he said, without turning. "Just get here?"

"Yes. How's the party going?" Her voice seemed carefully expressionless.

"Fair. You'll know more when you get the liquor bill."

"Your ballet opens tonight, doesn't it?" Still that studied tonelessness.

"You know damn well it doesn't." His voice held no rancour. "La Tanid took your bribe and left for Mexico. It's just as well. I can't abide a prima ballerina who'd rather eat than dance." He frowned slightly. Every bit of metal on the woman was singing in secret elation. She was thinking of a great triumph—something far beyond her petty victory in wrecking his opening night. His searching mind caught hints of something intricate, but integrated, completed—and deadly. Nineteen equations. The Jacques Rosette. Sciomnia.

"So you've finished your toy," he murmured. "You've got what you wanted, and you think you've destroyed what I wanted."

Her reply was harsh, suspicious. "How did you know, when not even Grade is sure? Yes, my weapon is finished. I can hold in one hand a thing that can obliterate your whole Via in an instant. A city, even a continent would take but a little longer. Science versus Art! Bah! This concrete embodiment of biophysics is the answer to your puerile Renaissance—your precious feather-bed world of music and painting! You and your kind are helpless when I and my kind choose to act. In the final analysis Science means *force*—the ability to control the minds and bodies of men."

The shimmering surface of his mind was now catching the faintest wisps of strange, extraneous impressions, vague and disturbing, and which did not seem to originate from metal within the room. In fact, he could not be sure they originated from metal at all.

He turned to face her. "How can Science control all men when it can't even control individuals—Anna van Tuyl, for example?"

She shrugged her shoulders. "You're only partly right. They failed to find her, but her escape was pure accident. In any event, she no longer represents any danger to me or to the political group that I control. Security has actually dropped her from their shoot-on-sight docket."

He cocked his head slightly and seemed to listen. "*You* haven't, I gather."

"You flatter her. She was never more than a pawn in our little game of Science versus Art. Now that she's off the board, and I've announced checkmate against you, I can't see that she matters."

"So Science announces checkmate? Isn't that a bit premature? Suppose Anna shows up again, with or without the conclusion of her ballet score? Suppose we find another prima? What's to keep us from holding *The Nightingale and the Rose* tonight, as scheduled?"

"Nothing," replied Martha Jacques coolly. "Nothing at all, except that Anna van Tuyl has probably joined your former prima at the South Pole by this time, and anyway, a new ballerina couldn't learn the score in the space of two hours, even if you found one. If this wishful thinking comforts you, why, pile it on!"

Very slowly Jacques put his wine glass on the nearby table. He washed his mind clear with a shake of his satyrish head, and strained every sense into receptivity. Something was being etched against that slurred background of laughter and clinking glassware. Then he sensed—or heard—something that brought tiny beads of sweat to his forehead and made him tremble.

"What's the matter with you?" demanded the woman.

As quickly as it had come, the chill was gone.

Without replying, he strode quickly into the centre of the studio.

"Fellow revellers!" he cried. "Let us prepare to double, nay, *re*-double our merriment!" With sardonic satisfaction he watched the troubled silence spread away from him, faster and faster, like ripples around a plague spot.

When the stillness was complete, he lowered his head, stretched out his hand as if in horrible warning, and spoke in the tense spectral whisper of Poe's Roderick Usher:

"Madmen! I tell you that she now stands without the door!"

Heads turned; eyes bulged toward the entrance.

There, the door knob was turning slowly.

The door swung in, and left a cloaked figure framed in the doorway.

The artist started. He had been certain that this must be Anna.

It *must* be Anna, yet it could not be. The once frail, cruelly bent body now stood superbly erect beneath the shelter of the cloak. There was no hint of spinal deformity in this woman, and there were no marring lines of pain about her faintly smiling mouth and eyes, which were fixed on his. In one graceful motion her hands reached up beneath the cloak and set it back on her shoulders. Then, after an almost instantaneous *demi-plie*, she floated twice, like some fragile flower dancing in a summer breeze, and stood before him *sur les pointes*, with her cape billowing and fluttering behind her in mute encore.

Jacques looked down into eyes that were dark fires. But her continued silence was beginning to disturb and irritate him. He responded to it almost by reflex, refusing to admit to himself his sudden enormous happiness: "A woman without a tongue! By the gods! Her sting is drawn!" He shook her by the shoulders, roughly, as though to punish this fault in her that had drawn the familiar acid to his mouth.

Her arms moved up, cross-fashioned, and her hands covered his. She smiled, and a harp-arpeggio seemed to wing across his mind, and the tones rearranged themselves into words, like images on water suddenly smooth:

"Hello again, darling. Thanks for being glad to see me."

Something in him collapsed. His arms dropped and he turned his head away. "It's no good, Anna. Why'd you come back? Everything's falling apart. Even our ballet. Martha bought out our prima."

Again that lilting cascade of tones in his brain: "I know, dear, but it doesn't matter. I'll sub beautifully for La Tanid. I know the part perfectly. And I know The Nightingale's death song, too."

"Hah!" he laughed harshly, annoyed at his exhibition of discouragement and her ready sympathy. He stretched his right leg into a mocking *pointe tendue*. "Marvellous! You have the exact amount of drab clumsiness that we need in a Nightingale. And as for the death song, why of course you and you alone know how that ugly little bird feels when"—his eyes were fixed on her mouth in sudden, startled suspicion, and he finished the rest of the sentence inattentively, with no real awareness of its meaning—"when she dies on the thorn."

As he waited, the melody formed, vanished, and reformed and resolved into the strangest thing he had ever known: "What you are thinking is true. My lips do not move. I cannot talk. I've forgotten how, just as we both forgot how to read and write. But even the plainest nightingale can sing, and make the white rose red."

This was Anna transfigured. Three weeks ago he had turned his back and left a diffident disciple to an uncertain fate. Confronting him now was this dark angel bearing on her face the luminous stamp of death. In some manner that he might never learn, the gods had touched her heart and body, and she had borne them straightway to him.

He stood, musing in alternate wonder and scorn. The old urge to jeer at her suddenly rose in his gorge. His lips contorted, then gradually relaxed, as an indescribable elation began to grow within him.

He could thwart Martha yet!

He leaped to the table and shouted: "Your attention, friends! In case you didn't get all this, we've found a ballerina! The curtain rises tonight on our première performance, as scheduled!"

Over the clapping and cheering, Dorran, the orchestra conductor, shouted: "Did I understand that Dr. van Tuyl has finished The Nightingale's death song? We'll have to omit that tonight, won't we? No chance to rehearse . . ."

Jacques looked down at Anna for a moment. His eyes were very thoughtful when he replied: "She says it won't be omitted. What I mean is, keep that thirty-eight rest sequence in the death scene. Yes, do that, and we shall see . . . what we shall see . . ."

"Thirty-eight rests as presently scored, then?"

"Yes. All right, boys and girls. Let's be on our way. Anna and I will follow shortly."

CHAPTER EIGHTEEN

Now it was a mild evening in late June, in the time of the full blooming of the roses, and the Via floated in a heady, irresistible tide of attar. It got into the tongues of the children and lifted their laughter and shouts an octave. It stained the palettes of the artists along the sidewalks, so that, despite the bluish glare of the artificial lights, they could paint only in delicate crimsons, pinks, yellows and whites. The petalled current swirled through the side-shows and eternally new exhibits and gave them a veneer of perfection; it eddied through the canvas flap of the vendress of love philters and erased twenty years from her face. It brushed a scented message across the responsive mouths of innumerable pairs of lovers, blinding them to the appreciative gaze of those who stopped to watch them.

And the lovely dead petals kept fluttering through the introspective mind of Ruy Jacques, clutching and whispering. He brushed their skittering dance aside and considered the situation with growing apprehension. In her recurrent Dreams he thought, Anna had always awakened just as the Nightingale began her death song. But now she knew the death song. So she knew the Dream's end. Well, it must not be so bad, or she wouldn't have returned. Nothing was going to happen, not really. He shot the question at her: There was no danger any more, was there? Surely the ballet would be a superb success? She'd be enrolled with the immortals.

Her reply was grave, yet it seemed to amuse her. It gave him a little trouble; there were no words for its exact meaning. It was something like "Immortality begins with death."

He glanced at her face uneasily. "Are you looking for trouble?"

"Everything will go smoothly."

After all, he thought, she believes she has looked into the future and has seen what will happen.

"The Nightingale will not fail The Student," she added with a queer smile. "You'll get your Red Rose."

"You can be plainer than that," he muttered. "Secrets . . . secrets . . . why all this you're-too-young-to-know business?"

But she laughed in his mind, and the enchantment of that laughter took his breath away. Finally he said: "I admit I don't know what you're talking about. But if you're about to get involved in anything on my account, forget it. I won't have it."

"Each does the thing that makes him happy. The Student will never be happy until he finds The Rose that will admit him to his Dance. The Nightingale will never be happy until The Student holds her in his arms and thinks her as lovely as a Red Rose. I think we may both get what we want."

He growled: "You haven't the faintest idea what you're talking about."

"Yes I have, especially right now. For ten years I've urged people not to inhibit their healthy inclinations. At the moment I don't have any inhibitions at all. It's a wonderful feeling. I've never been so happy, I think. For the first and last time in my life, I'm going to kiss you."

Her hand tugged at his sleeve. As he looked down into that enchanted face, he knew that this night was hers, that she was privileged in all things, and that whatever she willed must yield to her.

They had stopped at the temporarily-erected stage-door. She rose *sur les pointes*, took his face in her palms, and like a hummingbird drinking her first nectar, kissed him on the mouth.

A moment later she led him into the dressing-room corridor.

He stifled a confused impulse to wipe the back of his hand across his lips. "Well . . . well, just remember to take it easy. Don't try to be spectacular. The artificial wings won't take it. Canvas stretched on duralite and piano wire calls for adagio. A fast pirouette, and they're ripped off. Besides, you're out of practice. Control your enthusiasm in Act I or you'll collapse in Act II. Now, run on to your dressing room. Cue in five minutes!"

There is a faint, yet distinct anatomical difference in the foot of the man and that of the woman, which keeps him earthbound, while permitting her, after long and arduous training, to soar *sur les pointes*. Owing to the great and varied beauty of the arabesques open to the ballerina poised on her extended toes, the male danseur at one time existed solely as a shadowy *porteur*, and was needed only to supply unobtrusive support and assistance in the exquisite *enchainements* of the ballerina. Iron muscles in leg and torso are vital in the danseur, who must help maintain the illusion that his whirling partner is made of fairy gossamer, seeking to wing skyward from his restraining arms.

All this flashed through the incredulous mind of Ruy Jacques as he whirled in a double *fouetté* and followed from the corner of his eye the grey figure of Anna van Tuyl, as, wings and arms aflutter, she pirouetted in the second *enchainement* of Act I, away from him and toward the *maître de ballet*.

It was all well enough to give the illusion of flying, of alighting apparently weightless, in his arms—that was what the audience loved. But that it could ever *really* happen—*that* was simply impossible. Stage wings—things of grey canvas and duralite frames—couldn't subtract a hundred pounds from one hundred and twenty.

And yet . . . it had seemed to him that she had actually flown.

He tried to pierce her mind—to extract the truth from the bits of metal about her. In a gust of fury he dug at the metal outline of those remarkable wings.

In the space of seconds his forehead was drenched in cold sweat, and his hands were trembling. Only the fall of the curtain on the first act saved him as he stumbled through his exit *entrechat*.

What had Matt Bell said? "To communicate in his new language of music, one may expect our man of the future to develop specialized membranous organs, which, of course, like the tongue, will have dual functional uses, possibly leading to the conquest of time as the tongue has conquered space."

Those wings were not wire and metal, but flesh and blood.

He was so absorbed in his ratiocination that he failed to become aware of an acutely unpleasant metal radiation behind him until it was almost upon him. It was an intricate conglomeration of matter, mostly metal, resting perhaps a dozen feet behind his back, showering the lethal presence of his wife.

He turned with nonchalant grace to face the first tangible spawn of the Sciomnia formula.

It was simply a black metal box with a few dials and buttons. The scientist held it lightly in her lap as she sat at the side of the table.

His eyes passed slowly from it to her face, and he knew that in a matter of minutes Anna van Tuyl—and all Via Rosa beyond her—would be soot floating in the night wind.

Martha Jacques' face was sublime with hate. "Sit down," she said quietly.

He felt the blood leaving his cheeks. Yet he grinned with a fair show of geniality as he dropped into the chair. "Certainly. I've got to kill time somehow until the end of Act I."

She pressed a button on the box surface.

His volition vanished. His muscles were locked, immobile. He could not breathe.

Just as he was convinced that she planned to suffocate him, her finger made another swift motion toward the box, and he sucked in a great gulp of air. His eyes could move a little, but his larnyx was still paralyzed.

Then the moments began to pass, endlessly, it seemed to him.

The table at which they sat was on the right wing of the stage. The woman sat facing into the stage, while his back was to it. She followed the preparations of the troupe for Act II with moody, silent eyes, he with straining ears and metal-empathic sense.

Only when he heard the curtain sweeping across the street-stage to open the second act did the woman speak.

"She *is* beautiful. And so graceful with those piano-wire wings, just as if they were part of her. I don't wonder she's the first woman who ever really interested you. Not that you really *love* her. You'll never love anyone."

From the depths of his paralysis he studied the etched bitterness of the face across the table. His lips were parched, and his throat a desert.

She thrust a sheet of paper at him, and her lip curled. "Are you still looking for that rose? Search no further, my ignorant friend. There it is—Sciomnia, complete, with its nineteen sub-equations."

The lines of unreadable symbols dug like nineteen relentless harpoons ever deeper into his twisting, racing mind.

The woman's face grimaced in fleeting despair. "Your own wife solves Sciomnia and you condescend to keep her company until you go on again at the end of Act III. I wish I had a sense of humor. All I knew was to paralyze your spinal column. Oh, don't worry. It's purely temporary. I just didn't want you to warn her. And I know what torture it is for you not to be able to talk." She bent over and turned a knurled knob on the side of the black steel box. "There, at least you can whisper. You'll be completely free after the weapon fires."

His lips moved in a rapid slur. "Let us bargain, Martha. Don't kill her. I swear never to see her again."

She laughed, almost gaily.

He pressed on. "But you have all you really want. Total fame, total power, total knowledge, the body perfect. What can her death and the destruction of the Via give you?"

"Everything."

"Martha, for the sake of all humanity to come, don't do this thing! I know something about Anna van Tuyl that perhaps even Bell doesn't—something she has concealed very adroitly. That girl is the most precious creature on earth!"

"It's precisely because of that opinion—which I do not necessarily share— that I shall include her in my general destruction of the Via." Her mouth slashed at him: "Oh, but it's wonderful to see you squirm. For the first time in your miserable thirty years of life you really want something. You've got to crawl down from that ivory tower of indifference and actually plead with me, whom you've never even taken the trouble to despise. You and your damned art. Let's see it save her now!"

The man closed his eyes and breathed deeply. In one rapid, complex surmise, he visualized an *enchainement* of postures, a *pas de deux* to be played with his wife as an unwitting partner. Like a skilled chess player, he had analyzed various variations of her probable responses to his gambit, and he had every expectation of a successful climax. And therein lay his hesitation, for success meant his own death.

Yes, he could not eradicate the idea from his mind. Even at this moment he believed himself intrigued more by the novel, if macabre, possibilities inherent in the theme rather than its superficial altruism. While seeming to lead Martha through an artistic approach to the murder of Anna and the Via, he could, in a startling, off key climax, force her to kill him instead. It amused him enormously to think that afterward, she would try to reduce the little comedy to charts and graph paper in an effort to discover how she had been hypnotized.

It was the first time in his life that he had courted physical injury. The emotional sequence was new, a little heady. He could do it; he need only be careful about his timing.

After hurling her challenge at him, the woman had again turned morose eyes downstage, and was apparently absorbed in a grudging admiration of the second act. But that couldn't last long. The curtain on Act II would be her signal.

And there it was, followed by a muffled roar of applause. He must stall her through most of Act III, and then . . .

He said quickly: "We still have a couple of minutes before the last act begins, where The Nightingale dies on the thorn. There's no hurry. You ought to take time to do this thing properly. Even the best assassinations are not purely a matter of science. I'll wager you never read De Quincey's little essay on murder as a fine art. No? You see, you're a neophyte, and could do with a few tips from an old hand. You must keep in mind your objects: to destroy both the Via and Anna. But mere killing won't be enough. You've got to make *me* suffer too. Suppose you shoot Anna when she comes on at the beginning of Act III. Only fair. The difficulty is that Anna and the others will never know what hit them. You don't give them the opportunity to bow to you as their conqueror."

He regarded her animatedly. "You see, can't you, my dear, that some extraordinarily difficult problems in composition are involved?"

She glared at him, and seemed about to speak.

He continued hastily: "Not that I'm trying to dissuade you. You have the basic concept, and despite your lack of experience, I don't think you'll find the problem of technique insuperable. Your prelude was rather well done: freezing me *in situ*, as it were, to state your theme simply and without adornment, followed immediately by variations of dynamic and suggestive portent. The finale is already implicit; yet it is kept at a disciplined arm's length while the necessary structure is formed to support it and develop its stern message."

She listened intently to him, and her eyes were narrow. The expression on her face said: "Talk all you like. This time, you won't win."

Somewhere beyond the flimsy building-board stage wing he heard Dorran's musicians tuning up for Act III.

His dark features seemed to grow even more earnest, but his voice contained a perceptible burble. "So you've blocked in the introduction and the climax. A beginning and an end. The *real* problem comes now: how much, and what kind—of a middle? Most beginning murderesses would simply give up in frustrated bafflement. A few would shoot the moment Anna floats into the white rose garden. In my opinion, however, considering the wealth of material inherent in your composition, such abbreviation would be inexcusably primitive and garish—if not actually vulgar."

Martha Jacques blinked, as though trying to break through some indescribable spell that was being woven about her. Then she laughed shortly. "Go on. I wouldn't miss this for anything. Just when *should* I destroy the Via?"

The artist sighed. "You see? Your only concern is the *result*. You completely ignore the *manner* of its accomplishment. Really, Mart, I should think you'd show more insight into your first attempt at serious art. Now please don't misunderstand me, dear. I have the warmest regard for your spontaneity and enthusiasm: to be sure, they're quite indispensable when dealing with hackneyed themes, but headlong eagerness is not a substitute for method, or for art. We must search out and exploit subsidiary themes, intertwine them in subtle counterpoint with the major motifs. The most obvious minor theme is the ballet itself. That ballet is the loveliest thing I've ever seen or heard. Nevertheless, *you* can give it a power, a dimension, that even Anna wouldn't suspect possible, simply by blending it contrapuntally into your own work. It's all a matter of firing at the proper instant." He smiled engagingly. "I see that you're beginning to appreciate the potentialities of such unwitting collaboration."

The woman studied him through heavy-lidded eyes. She said slowly: "You *are* a great artist—and a loathesome beast."

He smiled still more amiably. "Kindly restrict your appraisals to your fields of competence. You haven't, as yet, sufficient background to evaluate me as an artist. But let us return to your composition. Thematically, it's rather pleasing. The form, pacing, and orchestration are irreproachable. It is adequate. And its very adequacy condemns it. One detects a certain amount of diffident imitation and over-attention to technique common to artists working in a new medium. The overcautious sparks of genius aren't setting us aflame. The artist isn't getting enough of his own personality into the work. And the remedy is as simple as the diagnosis: the artist must penetrate his work, wrap it around him, give it the distilled, unique essence of his heart and mind, so that it will blaze up and reveal his soul even through the veil of unidiomatic technique."

He listened a moment to the music outside. "As Anna wrote her musical score, a hiatus of thirty-eight rests precedes the moment The Nightingale drops dying from the thorn. At the start of that silence, you could start to run off your nineteen sub-equations in your little tin box, audio-Fourier style. You might even route the equations into the loudspeaker system, if our gadget is capable of remote control."

For a long time she appraised him calculatingly. "I finally think I understand you. You hoped to unnerve me with your savage, over-accentuated satire, and make me change my mind. So you aren't a beast, and even though I see through you, you're even a greater artist than I at first imagined."

He watched as the woman made a number of adjustments on the control panel of the black box. When she looked up again, her lips were drawn into hard purple ridges.

She said: "But it would be too great a pity to let such art go to waste, especially when supplied by the author of 'Twinkle, twinkle, little star'. And you will indulge an amateur musician's vanity if I play *my* first Fourier composition *fortissimo*."

He answered her smile with a fleeting one of his own. "An artist should never apologize for self-admiration. But watch your cueing. Anna should be clasping the white rose thorn to her breast in thirty seconds, and that will be your signal to fill in the first half of the thirty-eight rest hiatus. Can you see her?"

The woman did not answer, but he knew that her eyes were following the ballet on the invisible stage and Dorran's baton, beyond, with fevered intensity.

The music glided to a halt.

"Now!" hissed Jacques.

She flicked a switch on the box.

They listened, frozen, as the multi-throated public address system blared into life up and down the two miles of the Via Rosa.

The sound of Sciomnia was chill, metallic, like the cruel crackle of ice heard suddenly in the intimate warmth of an enchanted garden, and it seemed to chatter derisively, well aware of the magic that it shattered.

As it clattered and skirled up its harsh tonal staircase, it seemed to shriek: "Fools! Leave this childish nonsense and follow me! I am Science! I AM ALL!"

And, Ruy Jacques, watching the face of the prophetess of the God of Knowledge, was for the first time in his life aware of the possibility of utter defeat.

As he stared in mounting horror, her eyes rolled slightly upward, as though buoyed by some irresistible inner flame, which the pale translucent cheeks let through.

But as suddenly as they had come, the nineteen chords were over, and then, as though to accentuate the finality of that mocking manifesto, a ghastly aural afterimage of silence began building up around his world.

For a near eternity it seemed to him that he and this woman were alone in the world, that, like some wicked witch, she had, through her cacophonic creation, immutably frozen the thousands of invisible watchers beyond the thin walls of the stage wings.

It was a strange, yet simple thing that broke the appalling silence and restored sanity, confidence, and the will to resist to the man: from somewhere far away, a child whimpered.

Breathing as deeply as his near paralysis would permit, the artist murmured: "Now, Martha, in a moment I think you will hear why I suggested your Fourier broadcast. I fear Science has been had once mo—"

He never finished, and her eyes, which were crystallising into question marks, never fired their barbs.

A towering tidal wave of tone was engulfing the Via, apparently of no human source and from no human instrument.

Even he, who had suspected in some small degree what was coming, now found his paralysis once more complete. Like the woman scientist opposite him, he could only sit in motionless awe, with eyes glazing, jaw dropping, and tongue cleaving to the roof of his mouth.

He knew that the heart strings of Anna van Tuyl were one with this mighty sea of song, and that it took its ecstatic timbre from the reverberating volutes of that godlike mind.

And as the magnificent chords poured out in exquisite consonantal sequence, now with a sudden reedy delicacy, now with the radiant gladness of cymbals, he knew that his plan must succeed.

For, chord for chord, tone for tone, and measure for measure, The Nightingale was repeating in her death song the nineteen chords of Martha Jacques' Sciomnia equations.

Only now those chords were transfigured, as though some Parnassian composer were compassionately correcting and magically transmuting the work of a dull pupil.

The melody spiralled heavenward on wings. It demanded no allegiance; it hurled no pronunciamento. It held a message, but one almost too glorious to be grasped. It was steeped in boundless aspiration, but it was at peace with man and his universe. It sparkled humility, and in its abnegation there was grandeur. Its very incompleteness served to hint at its boundlessness.

And then it, too, was over. The death song was done.

Yes, thought Ruy Jacques, it is the Sciomnia, rewritten, recast, and breathed through the blazing soul of a goddess. And when Martha realizes this, when she sees how I tricked her into broadcasting her trifling, inconsequential effort, she is going to fire her weapon—at *me.*

He watched the woman's face go livid, her mouth work in speechless hate.

"You *knew!*" she screamed. "You did it to humiliate me!"

Jacques began to laugh. It was a nearly silent laughter, rhythmic with mounting ridicule, pitiless in its mockery.

"Stop that!"

But his abdomen was convulsing in rigid helplessness, and tears began to stream down his cheeks.

"I warned you once before!" yelled the woman. Her hand darted toward the black box and turned its long axis toward the man.

Like a period punctuating the rambling, aimless sentence of his life, a ball of blue light burst from a cylindrical hole in the side of the box.

His laughter stopped suddenly. He looked from the box to the woman with growing amazement. He could bend his neck. His paralysis was gone.

She stared back, equally startled. She gasped: "Something went wrong! *You should be dead!*"

The artist didn't linger to argue.

In his mind was the increasingly urgent call of Anna van Tuyl.

CHAPTER TWENTY

Dorran waved back the awed mass of spectators as Jacques knelt and transferred the faerie body from Bell's arms into his own.

"I'll carry you to your dressing room," he whispered. "I might have known you'd over-exert yourself."

Her eyes opened in the general direction of his face; in his mind came the tinkling of bells: "No . . . don't move me."

He looked up at Bell. "I think she's hurt! Take a look here!" He ran his hands over the seething surface of the wing folded along her side and breast: It was fevered fire.

"I can do nothing," replied the latter in a low voice. "She will tell you that I can do nothing."

"Anna!" cried Jacques. "What's wrong? What happened?"

Her musical reply formed in his mind. "Happened? Sciomnia was quite a thorn. Too much energy for one mind to disperse. Need two . . . three. Three could dematerialize weapon itself. Use wave formula of matter. Tell the others."

"*Others?* What are you talking about?" His thoughts whirled incoherently.

"Others like us. Coming soon. Bakine, dancing in streets of Leningrad. In Mexico City . . . the poetess Orteza. Many . . . this generation. *The Golden People.* Matt Bell guessed. Look!"

An image took fleeting form in his mind. First it was music, and then it was pure thought, and then it was a crisp strange air in his throat and the twang of something marvellous in his mouth. Then it was gone. "What was that?" he gasped.

"The Zhak symposium, seated at wine one April evening in the year 2437. Probability world. May . . . not occur. Did you recognize yourself?"

"Twenty-four thirty-seven?" His mind was fumbling.

"Yes. Couldn't you differentiate your individual mental contour from the whole? I thought you might. The group was still somewhat immature in the twenty-hundreds. By the fourteenth millennium . . ."

His head reeled under the impact of something titanic.

". . . your associated mental mass . . . creating a star of the M spectral class . . . galaxy now two-thirds terrestrialized . . ."

In his arms her wings stirred uneasily; all unconsciously he stroked the hot membranous surface and rubbed the marvellous bony framework with his fingers. "But Anna," he stammered, "I do not understand how this can be."

Her mind murmured in his. "Listen carefully, Ruy. Your pain . . . when your wings tried to open and couldn't . . . you needed certain psychoglandular stimulus. When you learn how to"—here a phrase he could not translate—"afterwards, they open . . ."

"When I learn—*what?*" he demanded. "What did you say I had to know, to open my wings?"

"One thing. The one thing . . . must have . . . to see the Rose."

"Rose—rose—*rose!*" he cried in near exasperation. "All right, then, my dutiful Nightingale, how long must I wait for you to make this remarkable Red Rose? I ask you, where is it?"

"Please . . . not just yet . . . in your arms just a little longer . . . while we finish ballet. Forget yourself, Ruy. Unless . . . leave prison . . . own heart . . . never find The Rose. Wings never unfold . . . remain a mortal. Science . . . isn't all. Art isn't . . . one thing greater . . . Ruy! I can't prolong . . ."

He looked up wildly at Bell.

The psychogeneticist turned his eyes away heavily. "Don't you understand? She has been dying ever since she absorbed that Sciomniac blast."

A faint murmur reached the artist's mind. "So you couldn't learn . . . poor Ruy . . . poor Nightingale . . ."

As he stared stuporously, her dun-colored wings began to shudder like leaves in an October wind.

From the depths of his shock he watched the fluttering of the wings give way to a sudden convulsive straining of her legs and thighs. It surged upward through her blanching body, through her abdomen and chest, pushing her blood before it and out into her wings, which now appeared more purple than grey.

To the old woman standing at his side, Bell observed quietly: "Even *homo superior* has his death struggle . . ."

The vendress of love philters nodded with anile sadness. "And she knew the answer . . . lost . . . lost . . ."

And still the blood came, making the wing membranes thick and taut.

"Anna!" shrieked Ruy Jacques. "You *can't* die. I won't let you! I love you! *I love you!*"

He had no expectation that she could still sense the images in his mind, nor even that she was still alive.

But suddenly, like stars shining their brief brilliance through a rift in storm clouds, her lips parted in a gay smile. Her eyes opened and seemed to bathe him in an intimate flow of light. It was during this momentary illumination, just before the lips solidified into their final enigmatic mask, that he thought he heard, as from a great distance, the opening measures of Weber's *Invitation to the Dance.*

At this moment the conviction formed in his numbed understanding that her loveliness was now supernal, that greater beauty could not be conceived or endured.

But even as he gazed in stricken wonder, the blood-gorged wings curled slowly up and out, enfolding the ivory breast and shoulders in blinding scarlet, like the petals of some magnificent rose.

Frank Belknap Long

Frank Belknap Long (1903–92) as a young man was the closest friend and associate of H. P. Lovecraft. Long was a poet and fiction writer who became adept at the new SF genre in the 1920s and continued to publish widely for decades. His first book (of poetry) appeared in 1924, and he remained actively writing through the 1980s.

Weird science fiction, which borders on the supernatural, was characteristic of the Lovecraft "Circle" that included Long, Donald and Howard Wandrei, Clark Ashton Smith, Robert E. Howard, Robert Bloch, Fritz Leiber, and others, and centered around the pulp magazine *Weird Tales* in the 1920s and '30s. Lovecraft was a rationalist, but the affect of the fiction was fear and wonder.

Long's reputation in later years, after the 1960s, was dominated by the impact of his early horror fiction, and he suffered as well as benefitted from the adulation of the followers of Lovecraft, who cared little for his non-Lovecraftian writings. He wrote a number of women's gothic romances under his wife's name when he found it difficult to sell his own books.

His early stories are clearly influenced by Lovecraft, and of them the most famous is this one, which decades later would be one of the models for Stephen King's "The Mist." It is a paradigm of the alien creatures from another dimension story in genre science fiction.

THE HOUNDS OF TINDALOS

1

I'm glad you came," said Chalmers. He was sitting by the window and his face was very pale. Two tall candles guttered at his elbow and cast a sickly amber light over his long nose and slightly receding chin. Chalmers would have nothing modern about his apartment. He had the soul of a mediaeval ascetic, and he preferred illuminated manuscripts to automobiles, and leering stone gargoyles to radios and adding-machines.

As I crossed the room to the settee he had cleared for me I glanced at his desk and was surprised to discover that he had been studying the mathematical formulae of a celebrated contemporary physicist, and that he had covered many sheets of thin yellow paper with curious geometric designs.

"Einstein and John Dee are strange bedfellows," I said as my gaze wandered from his mathematical charts to the sixty or seventy quaint books that comprised his strange little library. Plotinus and Emanuel Moscopulus, St. Thomas Aquinas and Frenicle de Bessy stood elbow to elbow in the somber ebony bookcase, and chairs, table and desk were littered with pamphlets about mediaeval sorcery and witchcraft and black magic, and all of the valiant glamorous things that the modern world has repudiated.

Chalmers smiled engagingly, and passed me a Russian cigarette on a curiously carved tray. "We are just discovering now," he said, "that the old alchemists and sorcerers were two-thirds *right*, and that your modern biologist and materialist is nine-tenths *wrong*."

"You have always scoffed at modern science," I said, a little impatiently.

"Only at scientific dogmatism," he replied. "I have always been a rebel, a champion of originality and lost causes; that is why I have chosen to repudiate the conclusions of contemporary biologists."

"And Einstein?" I asked.

"A priest of transcendental mathematics!" he murmured reverently. "A profound mystic and explorer of the great *suspected*."

"Then you do not entirely despise science."

"Of course not," he affirmed. "I merely distrust the scientific positivism of the past fifty years, the positivism of Haeckel and Darwin and of Mr. Bertrand Russell. I believe that biology has failed pitifully to explain the mystery of man's origin and destiny."

"Give them time," I retorted.

Chalmers' eyes glowed. "My friend," he murmured, "your pun is sublime. Give them *time*. That is precisely what I would do. But your modern biologist scoffs at time. He has the key but he refuses to use it. What do we know of time, really? Einstein believes that it is relative, that it can be interpreted in terms of space, of *curved* space. But must we stop there? When mathematics fails us can we not advance by—insight?"

"You are treading on dangerous ground," I replied. "That is a pitfall that your true investigator avoids. That is why modern science has advanced so slowly. It accepts nothing that it cannot demonstrate. But you—"

"I would take hashish, opium, all manner of drugs. I would emulate the sages of the East. And then perhaps I would apprehend—"

"What?"

"The fourth dimension."

"Theosophical rubbish!"

"Perhaps. But I believe that drugs expand human consciousness. William James agreed with me. And I have discovered a new one."

"A new drug?"

"It was used centuries ago by Chinese alchemists, but it is virtually unknown in the West. Its occult properties are amazing. With its aid and the aid of my mathematical knowledge I believe that I can *go back through time*."

"I do not understand."

"Time is merely our imperfect perception of a new dimension of space. Time and motion are both illusions. Everything that has existed from the beginning of the world *exists now*. Events that occurred centuries ago on this planet continue to exist in another dimension of space. Events that will occur centuries from now *exist already*. We cannot perceive their existence because we cannot enter the dimension of space that contains them. Human beings as we know them are merely fractions, infinitesimally small fractions of one enormous whole. Every human being is linked with *all* the life that has preceded him on this planet. All of his ancestors are parts of him. Only time separates him from his forebears, and time is an illusion and does not exist."

"I think I understand," I murmured.

"It will be sufficient for my purpose if you can form a vague idea of what I wish to achieve. I wish to strip from my eyes the veils of illusion that time has thrown over them, and see the *beginning and the end.*"

"And you think this new drug will help you?"

"I am sure that it will. And I want you to help me. I intend to take the drug immediately. I cannot wait. I must *see.*" His eyes glittered strangely. "I am going back, back through time."

He rose and strode to the mantel. When he faced me again he was holding a small square box in the palm of his hand. "I have here five pellets of the drug Liao. It was used by the Chinese philosopher Lao Tze, and while under its influence he visioned Tao. Tao is the most mysterious force in the world; it surrounds and pervades all things; it contains the visible universe and everything that we call reality. He who apprehends the mysteries of Tao sees clearly all that was and will be."

"Rubbish!" I retorted.

"Tao resembles a great animal, recumbent, motionless, containing in its enormous body all the worlds of our universe, the past, the present and the future. We see portions of this great monster through a slit, which we call time. With the aid of this drug I shall enlarge the slit. I shall behold the great figure of life, the great recumbent beast in its entirety."

"And what do you wish me to do?"

"Watch, my friend. Watch and take notes. And if I go back too far you must recall me to reality. You can recall me by shaking me violently. If I appear to be suffering acute physical pain you must recall me at once."

"Chalmers," I said, "I wish you wouldn't make this experiment. You are taking dreadful risks. I don't believe that there is any fourth dimension and I emphatically do not believe in Tao. And I don't approve of your experimenting with unknown drugs."

"I know the properties of this drug," he replied. "I know precisely how it affects the human animal and I know its dangers. The risk does not reside in the drug itself. My only fear is that I may become lost in time. You see, I shall assist the drug. Before I swallow this pellet I shall give my undivided attention to the geometric and algebraic symbols that I have traced on this paper." He raised the mathematical chart that rested on his knee. "I shall prepare my mind for an excursion into time. I shall approach the fourth dimension with my conscious mind before I take the drug which will enable me to exercise occult powers of perception. Before I enter the dream world of the Eastern mystics I shall acquire all of the mathematical help that modern science can offer. This mathematical knowledge, this conscious approach to an actual apprehension of the fourth dimension of time, will supplement the work of the drug. The drug will open up stupendous new vistas—the mathematical preparation will enable me to grasp them intellectually. I have often grasped the fourth dimension in dreams, emotionally, intuitively, but I have never been able to recall, in waking life, the occult splendors that were momentarily revealed to me.

"But with your aid, I believe that I can recall them. You will take down everything that I say while I am under the influence of the drug. No matter how strange or incoherent my speech may become you will omit nothing. When I awake I may be able to supply the key to whatever is mysterious or incredible. I am not sure that I shall succeed, but if I *do* succeed"—his eyes were strangely luminous—"*time will exist for me no longer!*"

He sat down abruptly. "I shall make the experiment at once. Please stand over there by the window and watch. Have you a fountain pen?"

I nodded gloomily and removed a pale green Waterman from my upper vest pocket.

"And a pad, Frank?"

I groaned and produced a memorandum book. "I emphatically disapprove of this experiment," I muttered. "You're taking a frightful risk."

"Don't be an asinine old woman!" he admonished. "Nothing that you can say will induce me to stop now. I entreat you to remain silent while I study these charts."

He raised the charts and studied them intently. I watched the clock on the mantel as it ticked out the seconds, and a curious dread clutched at my heart so that I choked.

Suddenly the clock stopped ticking, and exactly at that moment Chalmers swallowed the drug.

I rose quickly and moved toward him, but his eyes implored me not to interfere. "The clock has stopped," he murmured. "The forces that control it approve of my experiment. *Time* stopped, and I swallowed the drug. I pray God that I shall not lose my way."

He closed his eyes and leaned back on the sofa. All of the blood had left his face and he was breathing heavily. It was clear that the drug was acting with extraordinary rapidity.

"It is beginning to get dark," he murmured. "Write that. It is beginning to get dark and the familiar objects in the room are fading out. I can discern them vaguely through my eyelids, but they are fading swiftly."

I shook my pen to make the ink come and wrote rapidly in shorthand as he continued to dictate.

"I am leaving the room. The walls are vanishing and I can no longer see any of the familiar objects. Your face, though, is still visible to me. I hope that you are writing. I think that I am about to make a great leap—a leap through space. Or perhaps it is through time that I shall make the leap. I cannot tell. Everything is dark, indistinct."

He sat for a while silent, with his head sunk upon his breast. Then suddenly he stiffened and his eyelids fluttered open. "God in heaven!" he cried. "I *see!*"

He was straining forward in his chair, staring at the opposite wall. But I knew that he was looking beyond the wall and that the objects in the room no longer existed for him. "Chalmers," I cried, "Chalmers, shall I wake you?"

"Do not!" he shrieked. "I see *everything*. All of the billions of lives that preceded me on this planet are before me at this moment. I see men of all ages, all races, all colors. They are fighting, killing, building, dancing, singing. They are sitting about rude fires on lonely gray deserts, and flying through the air in monoplanes. They are riding the seas in bark canoes and enormous steamships; they are painting bison and mammoths on the walls of dismal caves and covering huge canvases with queer futuristic designs. I watch the migrations from Atlantis. I watch the migrations from Lemuria. I see the elder races—a strange horde of black dwarfs overwhelming Asia, and the Neandertalers with lowered heads and bent knees ranging obscenely across Europe. I watch the Achaeans streaming into the Greek islands, and the crude beginnings of Hellenic culture. I am in Athens and Pericles is young. I am standing on the soil of Italy. I assist in the rape of the Sabines; I march with the Imperial Legions. I tremble with awe and wonder as the enormous standards go by and the ground shakes with the tread of the victorious *bastati*. A thousand naked slaves grovel before me as I pass in a litter of gold and ivory drawn by night-black oxen from Thebes, and the flower-girls scream *'Ave Caesar'* as I nod and smile. I am myself a slave on a Moorish galley. I watch the erection of a great cathedral. Stone by stone it rises, and through months and years I stand and watch each stone as it falls into place. I am burned on a cross head downward in the thyme-scented gardens of Nero, and I watch with amusement and scorn the torturers at work in the chambers of the Inquisition.

"I walk in the holiest sanctuaries; I enter the temples of Venus. I kneel in adoration before the Magna Mater, and I throw coins on the bare knees of the sacred courtesans who sit with veiled faces in the groves of Babylon. I creep into an Elizabethan theater and with the stinking rabble about me I applaud *The Merchant of Venice*. I walk with Dante through the narrow streets of Florence. I meet the young Beatrice, and the hem of her garment brushes my sandals as I stare enraptured. I am a priest of Isis, and my magic astounds the nations. Simon Magus kneels before me, imploring my assistance, and Pharaoh trembles when I approach. In India I talk with the Masters and run screaming from their presence, for their revelations are as salt on wounds that bleed.

"I perceive everything *simultaneously*. I perceive everything from all sides; I am a part of all the teeming billions about me. I exist in all men and all men exist in me. I perceive the whole of human history in a single instant, the past and the present.

"By simply *straining* I can see farther and farther back. Now I am going back through strange curves and angles. Angles and curves multiply about me. I perceive great segments of time through *curves*. There is *curved time*, and *angular time*. The beings that exist in angular time cannot enter curved time. It is very strange.

"I am going back and back. Man has disappeared from the earth. Gigantic reptiles crouch beneath enormous palms and swim through the loathly black waters of dismal lakes. Now the reptiles have disappeared. No animals remain upon the land, but beneath the waters, plainly visible to me, dark forms move slowly over the rotting vegetation.

"The forms are becoming simpler and simpler. Now they are single cells. All about me there are angles—strange angles that have no counterparts on the earth. I am desperately afraid.

"There is an abyss of being which man has never fathomed."

I stared. Chalmers had risen to his feet and he was gesticulating helplessly with his arms. "I am passing through unearthly angles; I am approaching—oh, the burning horror of it."

"Chalmers!" I cried. "Do you wish me to interfere?"

He brought his right hand quickly before his face, as though to shut out a vision unspeakable. "Not yet!" he cried; "I will go on. I will see—what—lies—beyond—"

A cold sweat streamed from his forehead and his shoulders jerked spasmodically. "Beyond life there are"—his face grew ashen with terror—"*things* that I cannot distinguish. They move slowly through angles. They have no bodies, and they move slowly through outrageous angles."

It was then that I became aware of the odor in the room. It was a pungent, indescribable odor, so nauseous that I could scarcely endure it. I stepped quickly to the window and threw it open. When I returned to Chalmers and looked into his eyes I nearly fainted.

"I think they have scented me!" he shrieked. "They are slowly turning toward me."

He was trembling horribly. For a moment he clawed at the air with his hands. Then his legs gave way beneath him and he fell forward on his face, slobbering and moaning.

I watched him in silence as he dragged himself across the floor. He was no longer a man. His teeth were bared and saliva dripped from the corners of his mouth.

"Chalmers," I cried. "Chalmers, stop it! Stop it, do you hear?"

As if in reply to my appeal he commenced to utter hoarse convulsive sounds which resembled nothing so much as the barking of a dog, and began a sort of hideous writhing in a circle about the room. I bent and seized him by the shoulders. Violently, desperately, I shook him. He turned his head and snapped at my wrist. I was sick with horror, but I dared not release him for fear that he would destroy himself in a paroxysm of rage.

"Chalmers," I muttered, "you must stop that. There is nothing in this room that can harm you. Do you understand?"

I continued to shake and admonish him, and gradually the madness died out of his face. Shivering convulsively, he crumpled into a grotesque heap on the Chinese rug.

I carried him to the sofa and deposited him upon it. His features were twisted in pain, and I knew that he was still struggling dumbly to escape from abominable memories.

"Whisky," he muttered. "You'll find a flask in the cabinet by the window—upper left-hand drawer."

When I handed him the flask his fingers tightened about it until the knuckles showed blue. "They nearly got me," he gasped. He drained the stimulant in immoderate gulps, and gradually the color crept back into his face.

"That drug was the very devil!" I murmured.

"It wasn't the drug," he moaned.

His eyes no longer glared insanely, but he still wore the look of a lost soul.

"They scented me in time," he moaned. "I went too far."

"What were *they* like?" I said, to humor him.

He leaned forward and gripped my arm. He was shivering horribly. "No words in our language can describe them!" He spoke in a hoarse whisper. "They are symbolized vaguely in the myth of the Fall, and in an obscene form which is occasionally found engraved on ancient tablets. The Greeks had a name for them, which veiled their essential foulness. The tree, the snake and the apple—these are the vague symbols of a most awful mystery."

His voice had risen to a scream. "Frank, Frank, a terrible and unspeakable *deed* was done in the beginning. Before time, the *deed*, and from the deed—"

He had risen and was hysterically pacing the room. "The seeds of the deed move through angles in dim recesses of time. They are hungry and athirst!"

"Chalmers," I pleaded to quiet him. "We are living in the third decade of the Twentieth Century."

"They are lean and athirst!" he shrieked. "*The Hounds of Tindalos!*"

"Chalmers, shall I phone for a physician?"

"A physician cannot help me now. They are horrors of the soul, and yet"—

he hid his face in his hands and groaned—"they are real, Frank. I saw them for a ghastly moment. For a moment I stood on the *other side.* I stood on the pale gray shores beyond time and space. In an awful light that was not light, in a silence that shrieked, I saw *them.*

"All the evil in the universe was concentrated in their lean, hungry bodies. Or had they bodies? I saw them only for a moment; I cannot be certain. *But I heard them breathe.* Indescribably for a moment I felt their breath upon my face. They turned toward me and I fled screaming. In a single moment I fled screaming through time. I fled down quintillions of years.

"But they scented me. Men awake in them cosmic hungers. We have escaped, momentarily, from the foulness that rings them round. They thirst for that in us which is clean, which emerged from the deed without stain. There is a part of us which did not partake in the deed, and that they hate. But do not imagine that they are literally, prosaically evil. They are beyond good and evil as we know it. They are that which in the beginning fell away from cleanliness. Through the deed they became bodies of death, receptacles of all foulness. But they are not evil in *our* sense because in the spheres through which they move there is no thought, no morals, no right or wrong as we understand it. There is merely the pure and the foul. The foul expresses itself through angles; the pure through curves. Man, the pure part of him, is descended from a curve. Do not laugh. I mean that literally."

I rose and searched for my hat. "I'm dreadfully sorry for you, Chalmers," I said, as I walked toward the door. "But I don't intend to stay and listen to such gibberish. I'll send my physician to see you. He's an elderly, kindly chap and he won't be offended if you tell him to go to the devil. But I hope you'll respect his advice. A week's rest in a good sanitarium should benefit you immeasurably."

I heard him laughing as I descended the stairs, but his laughter was so utterly mirthless that it moved me to tears.

2

When Chalmers phoned the following morning my first impulse was to hang up the receiver immediately. His request was so unusual and his voice was so wildly hysterical that I feared any further association with him would result in the impairment of my own sanity. But I could not doubt the genuineness of his misery, and when he broke down completely and I heard him sobbing over the wire I decided to comply with his request.

"Very well," I said. "I will come over immediately and bring the plaster."

En route to Chalmers' home I stopped at a hardware store and purchased twenty pounds of plaster of Paris. When I entered my friend's room he was crouching by the window watching the opposite wall out of eyes that were feverish with fright. When he saw me he rose and seized the parcel containing the plaster with an avidity that amazed and horrified me. He had extruded all of the furniture and the room presented a desolate appearance.

"It is just conceivable that we can thwart them!" he exclaimed, "But we must work rapidly. Frank, there is a stepladder in the hall. Bring it here immediately. And then fetch a pail of water."

"What for?" I murmured.

He turned sharply and there was a flush on his face. "To mix the plaster, you fool!" he cried. "To mix the plaster that will save our bodies and souls from a contamination unmentionable. To mix the plaster that will save the world from—Frank, *they must be kept out!*"

"Who?" I murmured.

"The Hounds of Tindalos!" he muttered. "They can only reach us through angles. We must eliminate all angles from this room. I shall plaster up all of the corners, all of the crevices. We must make this room resemble the interior of a sphere."

I knew that it would have been useless to argue with him. I fetched the stepladder, Chalmers mixed the plaster, and for three hours we labored. We filled in the four corners of the wall and the intersections of the floor and wall and the wall and ceiling, and we rounded the sharp angles of the window-seat.

"I shall remain in this room until they return in time," he affirmed when our task was completed. "When they discover that the scent leads through curves they will return. They will return ravenous and snarling and unsatisfied to the foulness that was in the beginning, before time, beyond space."

He nodded graciously and lit a cigarette. "It was good of you to help," he said.

"Will you not see a physician, Chalmers?" I pleaded.

"Perhaps—tomorrow," he murmured. "But now I must watch and wait."

"Wait for what?" I urged.

Chalmers smiled wanly. "I know that you think me insane," he said. "You have a shrewd but prosaic mind, and you cannot conceive of an entity that does not depend for its existence on force and matter. But did it ever occur to you, my friend, that force and matter are merely the barriers to perception imposed by time and space? When one knows, as I do, that time and space are identical and that they are both deceptive because they are merely imperfect manifestations of a higher reality, one no longer seeks in the visible world for an explanation of the mystery and terror of being."

I rose and walked toward the door.

"Forgive me," he cried. "I did not mean to offend you. You have a superlative intellect, but I—I have a *superhuman* one. It is only natural that I should be aware of your limitations."

"Phone if you need me," I said, and descended the stairs two steps at a time. "I'll send my physician over at once," I muttered, to myself. "He's a hopeless maniac, and heaven knows what will happen if someone doesn't take charge of him immediately."

3

The following is a condensation of two announcements which appeared in the Partridgeville Gazette *for July 3, 1928:*

Earthquake Shakes Financial District

At 2 o'clock this morning an earth tremor of unusual severity broke several plate-glass windows in Central Square and completely disorganized the electric and street railway systems. The tremor was felt in the outlying districts and the steeple of the First Baptist

Church on Angell Hill (designed by Christopher Wren in 1717) was entirely demolished. Firemen are now attempting to put out a blaze which threatens to destroy the Partridge-ville Glue Works. An investigation is promised by the mayor and an immediate attempt will be made to fix responsibility for this disastrous occurrence.

OCCULT WRITER MURDERED BY UNKNOWN GUEST

Horrible Crime in Central Square

Mystery Surrounds Death of Halpin Chalmers

At 9 A.M. today the body of Halpin Chalmers, author and journalist, was found in an empty room above the jewelry store of Smithwick and Isaacs, 24 Central Square. The coroner's investigation revealed that the room had been rented furnished to Mr. Chalmers on May 1, and that he had himself disposed of the furniture a fortnight ago. Chalmers was the author of several recondite books on occult themes, and a member of the Bibliographic Guild. He formerly resided in Brooklyn, New York.

At 7 A.M. Mr. L. E. Hancock, who occupies the apartment opposite Chalmers' room in the Smithwick and Isaacs establishment, smelt a peculiar odor when he opened his door to take in his cat and the morning edition of the *Partridgeville Gazette*. The odor he describes as extremely acrid and nauseous, and he affirms that it was so strong in the vicinity of Chalmers' room that he was obliged to hold his nose when he approached that section of the hall.

He was about to return to his own apartment when it occurred to him that Chalmers might have accidentally forgotten to turn off the gas in his kitchenette. Becoming considerably alarmed at the thought, he decided to investigate, and when repeated tappings on Chalmers' door brought no response he notified the superintendent. The latter opened the door by means of a pass key, and the two men quickly made their way into Chalmers' room. The room was utterly destitute of furniture, and Hancock asserts that when he first glanced at the floor his heart went cold within him, and that the superintendent, without saying a word, walked to the open window and stared at the building opposite for fully five minutes.

Chalmers lay stretched upon his back in the center of the room. He was starkly nude, and his chest and arms were covered with a peculiar bluish pus or ichor. His head lay grotesquely upon his chest. It had been completely severed from his body, and the features were twisted and torn and horribly mangled. Nowhere was there a trace of blood.

The room presented a most astonishing appearance. The intersections of the walls, ceiling and floor had been thickly smeared with plaster of Paris, but at intervals fragments had cracked and fallen off, and someone had grouped these upon the floor about the murdered man so as to form a perfect triangle.

Beside the body were several sheets of charred yellow paper. These bore fantastic geometric designs and symbols and several hastily scrawled sentences. The sentences were almost illegible and so absurd in content that they furnished no possible clue to the perpetrator of the crime. "I am waiting and watching," Chalmers wrote. "I sit by the window and watch walls and ceiling. I do not believe they can reach me, but I must beware of the Doels. Perhaps *they* can help them break through. The satyrs will help, and they can advance through the scarlet circles. The Greeks knew a way of preventing that. It is a great pity that we have forgotten so much."

On another sheet of paper, the most badly charred of the seven or eight fragments found by Detective Sergeant Douglas (of the Partridgeville Reserve), was scrawled the following:

"Good God, the plaster is falling! A terrific shock has loosened the plaster and it is falling. An earthquake perhaps! I never could have anticipated this. It is growing dark in the room. I must phone Frank. But can he get here in time? I will try. I will recite the Einstein formula. I will—God, they are breaking through! They are breaking through! Smoke is pouring from the corners of the wall. Their tongues—ahhhhh—"

In the opinion of Detective Sergeant Douglas, Chalmers was poisoned by some obscure chemical. He has sent specimens of the strange blue slime found on Chalmers' body to the Partridgeville Chemical Laboratories; and he expects the report will shed new light on one of the most mysterious crimes of recent years. That Chalmers entertained a guest on the evening preceding the earthquake is certain, for his neighbor distinctly heard a low murmur of conversation in the former's room as he passed it on his way to the stairs. Suspicion points strongly to this unknown visitor and the police are diligently endeavoring to discover his identity.

4

Report of James Morton, chemist and bacteriologist:

My dear Mr. Douglas:

The fluid sent to me for analysis is the most peculiar that I have ever examined. It resembles living protoplasm, but it lacks the peculiar substances known as enzymes. Enzymes catalyze the chemical reactions occurring in living cells, and when the cell dies they cause it to disintegrate by hydrolyzation. Without enzymes protoplasm should possess enduring vitality, i.e., immortality. Enzymes are the negative components, so to speak, of unicellular organism, which is the basis of all life. That living matter can exist without enzymes biologists emphatically deny. And yet the substance that you have sent me is alive and it lacks these "indispensable" bodies. Good God, sir, do you realize what astounding new vistas this opens up?

5

Excerpt from The Secret Watchers *by the late Halpin Chalmers:*

What if, parallel to the life we know, there is another life that does not die, which lacks the elements that destroy *our* life? Perhaps in another dimension there is a *different* force from that which generates our life. Perhaps this force emits energy, or something similar to energy, which passes from the unknown dimension where *it* is and creates a new form of cell life in our dimension. No one knows that such new cell life does exist in our dimension. Ah, but I have seen *its* manifestations. I have *talked* with them. In my room at night I have talked with the Doels. And in dreams I have seen their maker. I have stood on the dim shore beyond time and matter and seen *it*. It moves through strange curves and outrageous angles. Some day I shall travel in time and meet *it* face to face.

Adam Wiśniewski-Snerg
Translated by Tomasz Mirkowicz

Adam Snerg (1937–95) lived in Warsaw, Poland. He published his first story in 1968 and his first novel, *Robot* in 1973. *Robot* takes place inside a bomb shelter below a large city torn out of the Earth by an alien spaceship and carried through space to an unknown destination as a scientists' sample collected for later study. It is an ambitious investigation into the nature of time, evolution, free will, and the theory of relativity. Polish SF fans voted in the best Polish SF book published since World War Two, quite an honor in Stanislaw Lem's native country.

He published three later novels that were fantastic but not science fiction, and then in 1990 published an original and highly controversial non-fiction work presenting his own theory of the space-time continuum. At the time of his death by his own hand in August, 1995, he had been working on another non-fiction book, a more accessible version of his theory.

"The Angel of Violence" is one of his six uncollected short stories and the first of his works to be translated into English, in a translation commissioned for this book.

THE ANGEL OF VIOLENCE

On the thirteenth floor of the Cybernetics Institute Lucy interrupted the guide's patter to tell her that several of the tourists were missing. They had lagged behind the group and probably lost their way in the maze of corridors and rooms of the vast building, the chief attraction of the tour around the recently excavated ancient city. The guide did not seem in the least put out. Instead of worrying about her missing charges or explaining the exhibits on display to the remaining tourists, she continued to praise the sound and light show her agency organized every night in the ruins of a nearby nuclear power plant.

Lucy got lost on the sixteenth floor. She had lingered a moment too long by the main computer, staring dumbly at the old cabinets housing the giant electronic brain. The guide had said that it makers, medieval craftsmen once known as "programmers," were assured a permanent place in the annals of history. And yet "the moving beauty of this priceless treasure"—the guide's exact words—did not move Lucy in the least. She decided to ask the woman for some pointers on appreciating ancient artifacts. But when she went out into the corridor, it was empty.

She couldn't hear the other tourists and had no idea which way they had gone. She started looking for them, wandering in and out of ancient labs filled with primitive, twenty-first-century equipment.

Time had not been kind to the priceless exhibits. Their plastic parts were full of holes made by second-generation borers, and their metal parts, the paint removed long ago by colonies of industrious, once unknown microorganisms, were corroded and covered with rust peeling away in large flakes.

The group was nowhere in sight. After another fifteen minutes Lucy gave up her search and, feeling oppressed by the somber atmosphere of the ancient building, decided to forgo the rest of the tour. She resolved to take the elevator to the ground floor and find her way to the antique bus waiting in front of the Institute.

She had her first misadventure in the elevator: it stopped between floors. Lucy pressed the alarm button. After a brief silence a male voice spoke to her from a speaker set above the buttons.

"Do you want to be the queen?" it asked.

"Do I want to be *what?*"

"The king's wife, the first lady of the realm."

"The king's wife?"

"Yes."

"You must be joking!"

"No, I'm not. You can become the queen."

"How?"

"No problem. It so happens we are looking for the right candidate. The former queen had to go. The tourists are already downstairs, waiting for you."

"Where?"

"Press the sixth floor button. Then go to room 628."

The unusual offer had taken her by surprise, but Lucy quickly guessed what it was all about: some kind of show put on by the tourist agency in the ruins of the freshly excavated city. It sounded intriguing. She liked surprises. Why shouldn't she play a part in some medieval drama? She had heard of picturesque castles built on the forbidden peaks of nuclear power plants by tyrants armed with tridents who forced their subjects to watch television. Maybe she wasn't confusing different historical periods, but she was overjoyed at the prospect of participating in the show, the more so since she'd be viewing everything from the queen's throne.

Although she pressed the right button, the elevator passed the sixth floor and continued to descend; it passed the ground floor and finally stopped on the sixth underground level. Lucy hadn't even known there were any underground levels in the building.

She walked down a wide, clean corridor until she reached room 628. She opened the door and walked in.

The first things she saw were the bare legs of a woman standing behind a metal screen suspended from the ceiling.

"Excuse me," Lucy said, "I was told some kind of show is being staged here."

The woman hidden by the screen gave a jump and moved a little closer. But the screen, hanging in front of an open doorway leading to the next room, continued to cover her, so all Lucy saw were the woman's legs.

"Do you know where the tourists are waiting?"

The legs were very shapely. But when they walked out from behind the screen and with one bare foot kicked the door shut, Lucy stopped admiring their proportions. She could hardly believe her eyes.

The legs weren't attached to a body! Lucy screamed with horror and ran into the next room. Inside, she saw many more pairs of moving legs. Although no people were present, the whole room was filled with animated motion.

A sign on the wall said: "PROSTHETIC WORKS—LOWER LIMBS." A slowly moving conveyor belt passed along a row of machines. Each machine was operated by a pair of synthetic hands steered efficiently by invisible plastic tendons. Imitating human hands to perfection, they were assembling artificial legs. At the end of the assembly line the legs jumped off the conveyor belt. The last machine joined them into matching pairs and sent them off to an obstacle course. After completing it, the legs marched obediently to the next section, where a mechanical fitter equipped them with arms.

Each hasp joining the legs together, its ends inserted into their thighs, had the shape of an inverted U. The fitter attached the arms to the top of the hasp. A dozen of such limbomats were already working on the assembly line or molding parts from which the limbs were made; others were repairing defective machines or building new ones.

Lucy noticed one limbomat standing by a high-tension console and suddenly felt the muscles of her legs and arms tense as if she were a weightlifter readying to set a world record. When she caught sight of the video cameras and antennas attached to the walls, she began to understand what had happened.

She knew that the twenty-first century scientists who had abandoned the building during an earthquake had left all the machinery running, supplied with energy from a local source. The room she was in was an old workshop that had originally produced prototypes of artificial limbs for the handicapped. Cut off for centuries from the rest of the world, the Institute's main computer had carried on production, resourcefully modifying and improving the artificial limbs. It was a case of perfect symbiosis: the computer created more and more advanced limbomats, steering their artificial nervous systems by remote control, while they—replacing the human technicians—maintained and expanded his electronic brain.

When Lucy had walked into the view of the computer's video cameras, she had immediately caught its attention. After years of controlling artificial limbs the computer wanted to test its power over real ones. A live human being was just what it needed.

Lucy wanted to flee, but as soon as the computer registered her presence, her muscles turned rigid as if numbed by electric shock. For several minutes her whole body jerked convulsively, until finally, after a violent battle over its control between two command centers—her own brain and the electronic brain of the computer—her body began to carry out the machine's orders.

Propelled by regular impulses, she passed the conveyor belt and came to a large door which opened by itself, revealing an unusual sight.

All the tourists who had strayed from the group were standing in the middle of an enormous chamber. They smiled at the terrified girl. After her initial shock she smiled back at them. She wondered whether the computer had really forced her to walk in here; maybe she had just imagined it. Anyway, now she was back among people she knew; she was so relieved, she could have hugged them.

She took a few steps in their direction, then once again looked at them, and froze.

The very moment she had sighed with relief, happy her misadventures were over, one of the men raised the heavy ax he was holding and with one blow split in two the skull of the tourist standing next to him. As the man toppled to the floor, a stiff cable with a sharp hook at the end shot out from the side of the chamber. It embedded itself in the body and began pulling it toward the wall, to a pile of similarly massacred corpses, leaving an ugly red stain on the shiny marble floor.

Lucy screamed with horror, but her scream was cut short by a painful constriction of her throat. The strange power was again taking control of her body. Plastic limbs ripped off her clothes. She stumbled toward the exit. She would have fallen, but her leg muscles held her up, artificially tensed by the computer's will.

Naked, her back toward the silent group, she waited for a deadly blow. The brutal murder she had witnessed kept replaying itself in her mind. She was overcome by a sense of unreality, just like a few minutes ago, when she walked into the workshop and saw the moving legs.

Instead of an ax blow, she felt the touch of another of the limbed monsters. It was pulling over her head a long dress richly decorated with golden lace. Although her heart was pounding with fear, outwardly she seemed as calm as if she were getting ready for a party. She could move her head freely. All of a sudden she realized there was something odd about the tourists and, in spite of her fear, looked at them more closely.

They were all smiling and standing as still as statues, not saying a word. And they were all dressed in costumes from early antiquity and armed with equally ancient weapons: axes, tridents, swords, spears, even clubs studded with iron nails.

A minute later another incident made her blood curdle. As she watched, a woman lifted her spear and threw it with incredible strength. It pierced the chest of a young man, its tip coming out his back. When he fell the woman walked over to him, surefooted, and pulled her weapon out of his bloodied chest. The dying man continued to smile even when the hook embedded itself in his side and started dragging him off toward the wall.

What happened over the next twenty minutes in the huge silent chamber was as mysterious as the computer's method of controlling the nervous systems of living organisms. Tensing the tourists' muscles, it forced them to participate in what seemed like a cross between an exotic ritual dance and the drill of ancient recruits.

During this macabre extravaganza the hook pulled away two more corpses. The limbomats left the chamber, closing the door behind them. Before leaving, they attached something heavy to Lucy's back. Forced by a series of impulses, she began walking toward the group of tourists. Suddenly she was made to stop and turn around. Looking at the wall, she saw a large white computer set in a deep recess.

Then she saw a second computer, a black one, set in a recess in the opposite wall.

Just as she began to grasp what was happening, a thin wisp of smoke shot out from the black computer. There was a crackle of short-circuiting cables and the overhead lights went out. The stench of burning insulation filled the air. Both computer screens were still alight in the dark, and so was every other square of the marble floor: it became clear to the terror-stricken tourists that they were standing on a huge chessboard and were the unwilling participants in a game of chess played by two computers.

A limbomat with a burning torch in one hand rushed into the chamber. Two others opened a fuse box and began repairing the damage. The tourists remained in their spots on the chessboard. One of the pieces, a man dressed in white, made a move. The white computer clearly didn't need the overhead lights and, having summoned the repair crew, continued the game.

Each side of the huge chessboard measured eight yards. In the light of the torch the white squares became somewhat dimmer but remained visible. The insulation must have caught fire when the cable was overloaded by the sudden surge in electricity needed by one of the players to solve an exceptionally difficult problem. Now Lucy knew why the limbomats had dressed some tourists in white and some in black costumes. She noted that she herself was wearing a white dress and was standing outside the chessboard, though near its edge, on the side of the black computer. At first this seemed a good sign: she was beyond the battlefield and hadn't yet participated in the game that obviously had been going on for some time.

Did this mean that she was in no danger?

There were twenty people on the chessboard. The corpses of twelve more, eliminated from the game, were piled by the wall. The tourists wore hats and helmets in the shapes of the pieces they represented in the game. Miserable, they twisted their necks looking around. So far they had been convinced that they'd either be killed by a sudden blow or have to deal one themselves at a random moment picked by the main computer; now they realized their fate depended on the situation on the chessboard. If the two computers involved in the game decided on a draw or if one checkmated the other, this would save the lives of the remaining tourists; otherwise only the two kings were certain to survive.

The white computer had foreseen many of the moves a long time ago. That's why, when Lucy entered the elevator, it invited her to be the queen. As soon as she thought of this, the man in front of her walked off the chessboard, while she, obeying the impulses in her legs, quickly took his place.

The man, a white pawn, had reached the eighth line and so could be replaced by any figure of the white computer's choice. The pawn's promotion, when Lucy took his place, seemed as innocent as a change of guards.

As soon as she stepped on the chessboard, she lifted her hands to the mysterious weight on her back; with one hand she detached a crossbow and a quiver of bolts and with the other a golden crown, which she placed on her head. The crossbow's string was drawn. Lucy notched a bolt and aimed it at the black king.

In response to the white computer's "check" the black player shielded his king with a knight. Lucy turned to the middle of the chessboard. A sudden impulse made her release the bolt. She heard the twang of the bowstring but, having quickly closed her eyes, did not see the bolt hit its target. She opened them at the sound of a deadweight dropping to the floor. A black bishop's helmet rolled toward her feet. The bolt had pierced the heart of the felled figure. Lucy recognized the woman who had earlier thrown her spear at the young man. After the shot, Lucy's muscles forced her to leave her square. She walked, surefooted, to the spot where her victim had stood.

The black computer wasted no time in responding to its opponent's move: one of its pawns decapitated with his sword a white knight. The role of knight was played by an old boxing coach armed with a trident; the pawn was his pupil, a young, superbly built heavyweight. The blow was delivered with such force that the old man's weapon flew out of his hand and with a loud *clunk!* hit the white computer.

Several crooked lines appeared on its screen; the image wavered and split. As this was happening, Lucy was forced to walk to a new spot. The next moment the screen returned to normal and Lucy felt her legs tense again; she marched back to her former position.

She knew she was the white queen. At an earlier stage of the game the white player had lost or, more likely, sacrificed this piece to improve his overall position. Now, after the foreseen promotion of the pawn and the exchange of several pieces, neither player had a visible lead or more pieces than his opponent—a situation typical of most games played by champions. Even if she had known chess well enough to tell whether the white computer had a positional advantage, she would have been unable to do so at this macabre moment when, in the glow of the burning torch, the hook pulled two more bodies toward the wall.

A red light began blinking on top of the black computer, and it pointed its video camera's snout at Lucy. The white computer rewound a few feet of its videotape and played the last segment to show the accident it had suffered. It even made Lucy stomp her foot, but the black computer—as if refusing to accept the white player's arguments—repeated its angry signals.

It was clear that the black chess player, citing the accepted rules, was protesting his opponent's decision to take back the move he had made with his queen, while the white player was trying to explain he had been temporarily indisposed.

A limbomat controlled by the judge—the main computer—rushed up to the white computer and, brandishing a heavy hammer, forced the machine to obey the rules. Lucy received a command to return to the spot in question. She did so. Walking to it, she saw a man who, when they were sightseeing the city, had always lagged behind, lost in thought, until finally one of the other tourists, as a joke, had discreetly pinned to his back a scrap of paper with the words: TOUR'S END. Lucy had talked with this man, a composer, the day before and had enjoyed their conversation.

Now he marched past her, a black rook-shaped helmet on his head, and stopped three squares away, ready to defend the black queen, played by Lucy's friend.

The black queen had not yet removed her weapon from her back. She was waiting for the white computer's move. Lucy could see her imploring gaze. She herself felt she was going to faint, but she rested her crossbow against the floor and began turning its handle to draw the bowstring. Her heart was pounding; she realized the white computer had decided on an exchange of queens in order to force the black rook—by making it kill Lucy—to move to a less advantageous spot.

She felt as if she were shooting at her own mirror image when her bolt hit the other queen in the belly.

She didn't look at the composer's face when the hook started to pull away her friend's body. She didn't want to see the smile the machine forced him to wear. Wishing to shorten her own agony, she stretched her neck toward the black rook's descending ax. It dropped past her head and chopped off her arm and then rose once more, glinting in the light of the torch—and fell again.

She heard waves beating softly against the shore and, instead of pain in her arm, felt a gentle breeze caress her naked skin. Only the golden crown was still exerting pressure on her temples, so she lifted her hand to push it back. She could move her limbs freely. When she opened her eyes, she was sure she was dreaming.

First she saw the sky. There were a few small clouds, but otherwise it was clear blue, stretching to the horizon. When she raised herself a little, she saw the sea. She was lying under a red umbrella, dressed in a swimming suit. The sparse clouds were hanging low over the beach. The gentle breeze rippled the water. A number of people were sunbathing on the sand.

For a moment she stared into the distance, and then she noticed cables running from her forehead to the plastic box standing by her bag. Suddenly she regained her awareness of time and place. She took the heavy ring off her head, wound the cable around it, and placed it on the blanket. She knew now who she was and where she was. Although this wasn't the first cassette she had seen, she still had trouble believing that what had happened to her a moment ago was just a nightmarish illusion. The magnetic dream produced by the local videofate company had seemed incredibly real.

She walked out from under the umbrella into the sun. She was still thinking of what she'd been through when she heard her husband's voice:

"Why don't we go swimming before lunch?"

"Where were you?"

"Talking to the engineer of this beach. In exchange for the Martian's ear I gave him, he told me about the secret report he just received. The news is really alarming."

"What's happening?"

"The seventh squadron of shuffling dishes is swimming our way. They are expected to invade this shore tomorrow." He laughed. "The locals are preparing nets, clubs, impregnating agents, and glow paints for painting their tentacles. Maybe here, in Borneo, where everybody's already got a flying saucer, an attack by tentacled sea monsters is exactly what is needed to alleviate the boredom. And it should create a boom in the souvenir trade. How did you like *The Angel of Violence?*"

"What?"

He bent over the machine, took out the cassette, and showed her the colorful label with the words THE ANGEL OF VIOLENCE printed across the drawing of a white computer.

"It was a nightmare!" she cried. "How could you get me something so awful?"

"You wanted to see a horror videofate."

"You should have warned me what it was about!"

"That wouldn't have done you any good. The moment you turn on the machine you lose all consciousness of your real past. It becomes replaced by a fictitious one, created to fit the plot on tape."

"Do all horror videofates end with the viewer's simulated death?"

"Yes, with no exception. If the viewing is interrupted, he or she dies in a sudden accident. Time flies with incredible speed in a videofate; in one day you go through a whole life."

A child left alone under the next umbrella suddenly began crying and jumping around on one foot. From the radio tack stuck to the heel of its other foot emerged an announcer's voice:

"We have just received news from Singapore concerning the anthropoid apes living in a nature preserve on one of the islands off the coast of Borneo. The leader of the gorillas, who have reached a very high level of intelligence, called a press conference and proudly announced that scientists from his pack will soon construct their first atom bomb. The gorillas, of course, do not intend to use this medieval weapon against the chimpanzees inhabiting the neighboring preserve, although the gorilla leader did say its detonation would be a definite solution to their differences. He also said the gorillas feel their security among all of the island's inhabitants."

Lucy pulled the talking tack out of the child's foot, still thinking of the videofate. She could not get used to the sudden change of environment, the more so since she was now twenty years older than in the film.

"Where is that island?" she asked her husband.

"There." He pointed toward the horizon.

For several minutes they stared in silence.

"Time for lunch," Lucy's husband finally said. "I want to go for a last swim before we leave the beach. You coming?"

The water was clear and warm. On the way back to their spot on the sand they passed a group of people playing volleyball. Suddenly Lucy screamed and covered her face with her hands. A move made by one of the players who jumped to hit the ball had terrified her. The strangers stopped playing and stood there, waiting.

They smiled at her, but this was no help; she felt she was back on the chessboard and a deadly blow would split her skull any moment.

"Why did these machines force people to kill their friends?" she asked her husband when they reached their blanket.

"You mean in *The Angel of Violence?*"

"Yes."

"Simple. They were programmed by two chess players and were checking the merits of their respective game plans."

"On people?"

He looked at her serious face. "Is that what's bothering you? Look, it was just a story, some improbable rubbish made up by the scriptwriters of horror videofates."

"Wait. . . . Didn't multimillion medieval armies murder each other freely? they weren't made-up criminals, were they?"

He laughed loudly. "Of course not! You silly thing, you really don't know? Soldiers killed willingly and died gladly. And they weren't criminals because in those days all bad people locked away in prisons. Just think! If things were otherwise, if good people did not kill of their own free will, then in order to explain the mechanism of war we'd have to accept as fact a version of history very much like the plot of *The Angel of Violence*. And because the idea of two invisible players hunched over the chessboard of the world is too fanciful to contemplate, we would be forced to assume that medieval kings had at their disposal fantastic machines allowing them to control remotely the muscles of millions and that they used these machines to make peace loving people kill each other."

"But it does sound fantastic, doesn't it? Bad people locked away in prisons, and good people—" She didn't finish. As she spoke the beach became dissected by long black shadows cast by standing tourists. It seemed as if a blindingly brilliant sun had torn asunder the darkness of night. The glow of the most nightmarish dawn imaginable illuminated the sky behind Lucy's back.

In the blink of an eye the whole shore was drenched with heat. A crimson flash, ten times brighter than the sun, scorched the lush vegetation, engulfing it in flames and reducing to ash; human bodies were transformed into pillars of fire.

A fraction of a second earlier Lucy had turned toward the source of light. The cloud of an atomic explosion, gigantic in size, mushroomed over the island of the apes. Its top reached high into the atmosphere. She knew that in a few seconds the coast would be hit by a thundering shock wave and everything, including her, would be swept off the surface of the earth.

But she wasn't there to see this.

She discovered that she was lying inside a glass cubicle. Her naked body was submerged in a transparent liquid. In the sudden silence a pleasant female voice spoke into her ear:

"We apologize for interrupting your videofate. Is your number nine hundred forty billion five million seventy-one?"

On a small console at the end of the glass container she saw the silver number 940,005,000,071.

"Yes," she said.

"How old are you?"

The age indicator had golden numerals. "Nineteen."

"Then everything's in order," the pleasant voice said. "After waiting your turn for a hundred and twenty years you have obtained the right to twenty-four hours of authentic life. Your place will be free in an hour's time; that's why we had to wake you. Get ready! In fifteen minutes an express elevator will take your cabin two and a half miles up, to the roof of Europe. You will see the real sun, water, and trees. Once again we apologize for turning off your videofate. Enjoy yourself!"

All around, behind the glass walls of their cubicles, narrow as coffins, rested the sleeping forms of human beings. Only Lucy lay with her eyes open. For a dozen minutes or so she stared at the millions of naked bodies arranged symmetrically in lighted glass rows, converging in infinity.

The indicators on the console were behind a pane of glass. Lucy broke it with her elbow. She closed her eyes and yanked out all the cables, but when she opened her eyes and saw the world around her unchanged, she placed her wrist on the broken glass—to turn the picture off forever.

Algis Budrys

Algis Budrys (1931–   ) is the author of a number of SF novels including the highly re-garded *Rogue Moon* (1960) and *Michelmas* (1977), the latest of which is *Hard Landing* (1993). Some of his short fiction, predominantly from the 1950s, is collected in *The Un-expected Dimension* (1960), *Budrys's Inferno* (1963), and *Blood and Burning* (1978).

James Blish in a laudatory essay on Budrys in his famous critical work, *More Issues at Hand* (1970), says, "His gifts go far beyond craftsmanship into that instinctual realm where dwell the genuine ear for the melos and the polyphony of the English language, and the fundamental insight into the human heart." Gene Wolfe, in *Science Fiction Writ-ers*, says "Every age and every genre produce a few writers too good for them . . . Budrys is one of these. He is, in the best sense, too serious a writer for science fiction." And like Blish, Budrys is one of the best critics of science fiction, probably the best in the generation after Blish, Damon Knight, and Theodore Sturgeon, from the mid-'60s to the mid-'80s. A collection of his reviews and essays from *Galaxy* in the 1960s is *Benchmarks: Galaxy Bookshelf* (1985). Presently he is publishing and editing his own magazine of SF, *Tomorrow.*

Most SF writers sooner or later address the theme of human evolution and many at-tempt to portray what a superior human might be like. Budrys imagines he might be like Gus.

NOBODY BOTHERS GUS

Two years earlier, Gus Kusevic had been driving slowly down the narrow back road into Boonesboro.

It was good country for slow driving, particularly in the late spring. There was nobody else on the road. The woods were just blooming into a deep, rich green as yet unburned by summer, and the afternoons were still cool and fresh. And, just before he reached the Boonesboro town line, he saw the locked and weath-ered cottage standing for sale on its quarter-acre lot.

He had pulled his roadcar up to a gentle stop, swung sideways in his seat, and looked at it.

It needed paint; the siding had gone from white to gray, and the trim was faded. There were shingles missing here and there from the roof, leaving squares of darkness on the sun-bleached rows of cedar, and inevitably, some of the win-dowpanes had cracked. But the frame hadn't slouched out of square, and the roof hadn't sagged. The chimney stood up straight.

He looked at the straggled clumps and windrowed hay that were all that re-mained of the shrubbery and the lawn. His broad, homely face bunched itself into a quiet smile along its well-worn seams. His hands itched for the feel of a spade.

He got out of the roadcar, walked across the road and up to the cottage door, and copied down the name of the real estate dealer listed on the card tacked to the door frame.

Now it was almost two years later, early in April, and Gus was top-dressing his lawn.

Earlier in the day he'd set up a screen beside the pile of topsoil behind his house, shoveled the soil through the screen, mixed it with broken peat moss, and carted it out to the lawn, where he left it in small piles. Now he was carefully raking it out over the young grass in a thin layer that covered only the roots, and let the blades peep through. He intended to be finished by the time the second half of the Giants-Kodiaks doubleheader came on. He particularly wanted to see it because Halsey was pitching for the Kodiaks, and he had something of an avuncular interest in Halsey.

He worked without waste motion or excess expenditure of energy. Once or twice he stopped and had a beer in the shade of the rose arbor he'd put up around the front door. Nevertheless, the sun was hot; by early afternoon, he had his shirt off.

Just before he would have been finished, a battered flivver settled down in front of the house. It parked with a flurry of its rotors, and a gangling man in a worn serge suit, with thin hair plastered across his tight scalp, climbed out and looked at Gus uncertainly.

Gus had glanced up briefly while the flivver was on its silent way down. He'd made out the barely-legible "Falmouth County Clerk's Office" lettered over the faded paint on its door, shrugged, and gone on with what he was doing.

Gus was a big man. His shoulders were heavy and broad; his chest was deep, grizzled with thick, iron-gray hair. His stomach had gotten a little heavier with the years, but the muscles were still there under the layer of flesh. His upper arms were thicker than a good many thighs, and his forearms were enormous.

His face was seamed by a network of folds and creases. His flat cheeks were marked out by two deep furrows that ran from the sides of his bent nose, merged with the creases bracketing his wide lips, and converged toward the blunt point of his jaw. His pale blue eyes twinkled above high cheekbones which were covered with wrinkles. His close-cropped hair was as white as cotton.

Only repeated and annoying exposure would give his body a tan, but his face was permanently browned. The pink of his body sunburn was broken in several places by white scar tissue. The thin line of a knife cut emerged from the tops of his pants and faded out across the right side of his stomach. The other significant area of scarring lay across the uneven knuckles of his heavy-fingered hands.

The clerk looked at the mailbox to make sure of the name, checking it against an envelope he was holding in one hand. He stopped and looked at Gus again, mysteriously nervous.

Gus abruptly realized that he probably didn't present a reassuring appearance. With all the screening and raking he'd been doing, there'd been a lot of dust in the air. Mixed with perspiration, it was all over his face, chest, arms, and back. Gus knew he didn't look very gentle even at his cleanest and best-dressed. At the moment, he couldn't blame the clerk for being skittish.

He tried to smile disarmingly.

The clerk ran his tongue over his lips, cleared his throat with a slight cough, and jerked his head toward the mail box. "Is that right? You Mr. Kusevic?"

Gus nodded. "That's right. What can I do for you?"

The clerk held up the envelope. "Got a notice here from the County Council," he muttered, but he was obviously much more taken up by his effort to equate Gus with the rose arbor, the neatly edged and carefully tended flower beds, the hedges, the flagstoned walk, the small goldfish pond under the willow tree, the white-painted cottage with its window boxes and bright shutters, and the curtains showing inside the sparkling windows.

Gus waited until the man was through with his obvious thoughts, but something deep inside him sighed quietly. He had gone through this moment of bewilderment with so many other people that he was quite accustomed to it, but that is not the same thing as being oblivious.

"Well, come on inside," he said after a decent interval. "It's pretty hot out here, and I've got some beer in the cooler."

The clerk hesitated again. "Well, all I've got to do it deliver this notice—" he said, still looking around. "Got the place fixed up real nice, don't you?"

Gus smiled. "It's my home. A man likes to live in a nice place. In a hurry?"

The clerk seemed to be troubled by something in what Gus had said. Then he looked up suddenly, obviously just realizing he'd been asked a direct question. "Huh?"

"You're not in any hurry, are you? Come on in; have a beer. Nobody's expected to be a ball of fire on a spring afternoon."

The clerk grinned uneasily. "No . . . nope, guess not." He brightened. "O.K.! Don't mind if I do."

Gus ushered him into the house, grinning with pleasure. Nobody's seen the inside of the place since he'd fixed it up; the clerk was the first visitor he'd had since moving in. There weren't even any delivery men; Boonesboro was so small you had to drive in for your own shopping. There wasn't any mail carrier service, of course—not that Gus ever received any mail.

He showed the clerk into the living room. "Have a seat. I'll be right back." He went quickly out to the kitchen, took some beer out of the cooler, loaded a tray with glasses, a bowl of chips and pretzels, and the beer, and carried it out.

The clerk was up, looking around the library that covered two of the living room walls.

Looking at his expression, Gus realized with genuine regret that the man wasn't the kind to doubt whether an obvious clod like Kusevic had read any of this stuff. A man like that could still be talked to, once the original misconceptions were knocked down. No, the clerk was too plainly mystified that a grown man would fool with books. Particularly a man like Gus; now, one of these kids that messed with college politics, that was something else. But a grown man oughtn't to act like that.

Gus saw it had been a mistake to expect anything of the clerk. He should have known better, whether he was hungry for company or not. He'd *always* been hungry for company, and it was time he realized, once and for all, that he just plain wasn't going to find any.

He set the tray down on the table, uncapped a beer quickly, and handed it to the man.

"Thanks," the clerk mumbled. He took a swallow, sighed loudly, and wiped his mouth with the back of his hand. He looked around the room again. "Cost you a lot to have all this put in?"

Gus shrugged. "Did most of it myself. Built the shelves and furniture; stuff like that. Some of the paintings I had to buy, and the books and records."

The clerk grunted. He seemed to be considerably ill at ease, probably because of the notice he'd brought, whatever it was. Gus found himself wondering what it could possibly be, but, now that he'd made the mistake of giving the man a beer, he had to wait politely until it was finished before he could ask.

He went over to the TV set. "Baseball fan?" he asked the clerk.

"Sure!"

"Giants-Kodiaks ought to be on." He switched the set on and pulled up a hassock, sitting on it so as not to get one of the chairs dirty. The clerk wandered over and stood looking at the screen, taking slow swallows of his beer.

The second game had started, and Halsey's familiar figure appeared on the screen as the set warmed up. The lithe young lefthander was throwing with his usual boneless motion, apparently not working hard at all, but the ball was whipping past the batters with a sizzle that the home plate microphone was picking up clearly.

Gus nodded toward Halsey. "He's quite a pitcher, isn't he?"

The clerk shrugged. "Guess so. Walker's their best man, though."

Gus sighed as he realized he'd forgotten himself again. The clerk wouldn't pay much attention to Halsey, naturally.

But he was getting a little irritated at the man, with his typical preconceptions of what was proper and what wasn't, of who had a right to grow roses and who didn't.

"Offhand," Gus said to the clerk, "could you tell me what Halsey's record was, last year?"

The clerk shrugged. "Couldn't tell you. Wasn't bad—I remember that much. 13-7, something like that."

Gus nodded to himself. "Uh-huh. How'd Walker do?"

"Walker! Why, man, Walker just won something like twenty-five games, that's all. And three no-hitters. How'd Walker do? Huh!"

Gus shook his head. "Walker's a good pitcher, all right—but he didn't pitch any no-hitters. And he only won eighteen games."

The clerk wrinkled his forehead. He opened his mouth to argue and then stopped. He looked like a sure-thing better who'd just realized that his memory had played him a trick.

"Say—I think you're right! Huh! Now what the Sam Hill made me think Walker was the guy? And you know something—I've been talking about him all winter, and nobody once called me wrong?" The clerk scratched his head. "Now, *somebody* pitched them games! Who the dickens was it?" He scowled in concentration.

Gus silently watched Halsey strike out his third batter in a row, and his face wrinkled into a slow smile. Halsey was still young; just hitting his stride. He threw himself into the game with all the energy and enjoyment a man felt when he realized he was at his peak, and that, out there on the mound in the sun, he was as good as any man who ever had gone before him in this profession.

Gus wondered how soon Halsey would see the trap he'd set for himself.

Because it wasn't a contest. Not for Halsey. For Christy Mathewson, it had been a contest. For Lefty Grove and Dizzy Dean, for Bob Feller and Slats Gould, it had been a contest. But for Halsey it was just a complicated form of solitaire that always came out right.

Pretty soon, Halsey'd realize that you can't handicap yourself at solitaire. If you knew where all the cards are; if you knew that unless you deliberately cheated against yourself, you couldn't help but win—what good was it? One of these days, Halsey'd realize there wasn't a game on Earth he couldn't beat; whether it was a physical contest, organized and formally recognized as a game, or whether it was the billion-triggered pinball machine called Society.

What then, Halsey? What then? And if you find out, please, in the name of whatever kind of brotherhood we share, let me know.

The clerk grunted. "Well, it don't matter, I guess. I can always look it up in the record book at home."

Yes, you can, Gus commented silently. But you won't notice what it says, and, if you do, you'll forget it and never realize you've forgotten.

The clerk finished his beer, set it down on the tray, and was free to remember what he'd come here for. He looked around the room again, as though the memory were a cue of some kind.

"Lots of books," he commented.

Gus nodded, watching Halsey walk out to the pitcher's mound again.

"Uh . . . you read 'em all?"

Gus shook his head.

"How about that one by the Miller fellow? I hear that's a pretty good one."

So. The clerk had a certain narrow interest in certain aspects of certain kinds of literature.

"I suppose it is," Gus answered truthfully. "I read the first three pages, once." And, having done so, he'd known how the rest of it was going to go, who would do what when, and he'd lost interest. The library had been a mistake, just one of a dozen similar experiments. If he'd wanted an academic familiarity with human literature, he could just as easily have picked it up by browsing through bookstores, rather than buying the books and doing substantially the same thing at home. He couldn't hope to extract any emotional empathies, no matter what he did.

Face it, though; rows of even useless books were better than bare wall. The trappings of culture were a bulwark of sorts, even though it was a learned culture and not a *felt* one, and meant no more to him than the culture of the Incas. Try as he might, he could never be an Inca. Nor even a Maya or an Aztec, or any kind of kin, except by the most tenuous of extensions.

But he had no culture of his own. There was the thing; the emptiness that nevertheless ached; the rootlessness, the complete absence of a place to stand and say: "This is my own."

Halsey struck out the first batter in the inning with three pitches. Then he put a slow floater precisely where the next man could get the best part of his bat on it, and did not even look up as the ball screamed out of the park. He struck out the next two men with a total of eight pitches.

Gus shook his head slowly. That was the first symptom; when you didn't bother to be subtle about your handicapping any more.

The clerk held out the envelope. "Here," he said brusquely, having finally shilly-shallied his resolution up to the point of doing it despite his obvious nervousness at Gus' probable reaction.

Gus opened the envelope and read the notice. Then, just as the clerk had been doing, he looked around the room. A dark expression must have flickered over his face, because the clerk became even more hesitant. "I . . . I want you to know I regret this. I guess all of us do."

Gus nodded hastily. "Sure, sure." He stood up and looked out the front window. He smiled crookedly, looking at the top-dressing spread carefully over the painstakingly rolled lawn, which was slowly taking form on the plot where he had plowed last year and picked out pebbles, seeded and watered, shoveled top-soil, laid out flower beds . . . ah, there was no use going into that now. The whole plot, cottage and all, was condemned, and that was that.

"They're . . . they're turnin' the road into a twelve-lane freight highway," the clerk explained.

Gus nodded absently.

The clerk moved closer and dropped his voice. "Look—I was told to tell you this. Not in writin'." He sidled even closer, and actually looked around before he spoke. He laid his hand confidentially on Gus' bare forearm.

"Any price you ask for," he muttered, "is gonna be O.K., as long as you don't get too greedy. The county isn't paying this bill. Not even the state, if you get what I mean."

Gus got what he meant. Twelve-lane highways aren't built by anything but national governments.

He got more than that. National governments don't work this way unless there's a good reason.

"Highway between Hollister and Farnham?" he asked.

The clerk paled. "Don't know for sure," he muttered.

Gus smiled thinly. Let the clerk wonder how he'd guessed. It couldn't be much of a secret, anyway—not after the grade was laid out and the purpose became self-evident. Besides, the clerk wouldn't wonder very long.

A streak of complete perversity shot through Gus. He recognized its source in his anger at losing the cottage, but there was no reason why he shouldn't allow himself to cut loose.

"What's your name?" he asked the clerk abruptly.

"Uh . . . Harry Danvers."

"Well, Harry, suppose I told you I could stop that highway, if I wanted to? Suppose I told you that no bulldozer could get near this place without breaking down, that no shovel could dig this ground, that sticks of dynamite just plain wouldn't explode if they tried to blast? Suppose I told you that if they put in the highway, it would turn soft as ice cream if I wanted it to, and run away like a river?"

"Huh?"

"Hand me your pen."

Danvers reached out mechanically and handed it to him. Gus put it between his palms and rolled it into a ball. He dropped it and caught it as it bounced up sharply from the soft, thick rug. He pulled it out between his fingers, and it returned to its cylindrical shape. He unscrewed the cap, flattened it out into a sheet between two fingers, scribbled on it, rolled it back into a cap, and, using his fingernail to draw out the ink which was now part of it, permanently inscribed Danvers' name just below the surface of the metal. Then he screwed the cap on again and handed the pen back to the country clerk. "Souvenir," he said.

The clerk looked down at it.

"Well?" Gus asked. "Aren't you curious about how I did it and what I am?"

The clerk shook his head. "Good trick. I guess you magician fellows must spend a lot of time practicing, huh? Can't say I could see myself spendin' that much working time on a hobby."

Gus nodded. "That's a good, sound, practical point of view," he said. Particularly when all of us automatically put out a field that damps curiosity, he thought. What point of view *could* you have?

He looked over the clerk's shoulder at the lawn, and one side of his mouth twisted sadly.

Only God can make a tree, he thought, looking at the shrubs and flower beds. Should we all, then, look for our challenge in landscape gardening? Should we become the gardeners of the rich humans in the expensive houses, driving up in our old, rusty trucks, oiling our lawnmowers, kneeling on the humans' lawns with our clipping shears, coming to the kitchen door to ask for a drink of water on a hot summer day?

The highway. Yes, he could stop the highway. Or make it go around him. There was no way of stopping the curiosity damper, no more than there was a way of willing his heart to stop, but it could be stepped up. He could force his mind to labor near overload, and no one would ever even *see* the cottage, the lawn, the rose arbor, or the battered old man, drinking his beer. Or rather, seeing them, would pay them absolutely no attention.

But the first time he went into town, or when he died, the field would be off, and then what? The curiosity, then investigation, then, perhaps a fragment of theory here or there to be fitted to another somewhere else. And then what? Pogrom?

He shook his head. The humans couldn't win, and would lose monstrously. *That* was why he couldn't leave the humans a clue. He had no taste for slaughtering sheep, and he doubted if his fellows did.

His fellows. Gus stretched his mouth. The only one he could be sure of was Halsey. There had to be others, but there was no way of finding them. They provoked no reaction from the humans; they left no trail to follow. It was only if they showed themselves, like Halsey, that they could be seen. There was, unfortunately, no private telepathic party line among them.

He wondered if Halsey hoped someone would notice him and get in touch. He wondered if Halsey even suspected there were others like himself. He wondered if anyone had noticed *him*, when Gus Kusevic's name had been in the papers occasionally.

It's the dawn of my race, he thought. The first generation—or is it, and does it matter—and I wonder where the females are.

He turned back to the clerk. "I want what I paid for the place," he said. "No more."

The clerk's eyes widened slightly, then relaxed, and he shrugged. "Suit yourself. But if it was me, I'd soak the government good."

Yes, Gus thought, you doubtless would. But I don't want to, because you simply don't take candy from babies.

So the superman packed his bags and got out of the human's way. Gus choked a silent laugh. The damping field. The damping-field. The thrice-cursed, ever-benevolent, foolproof, autonomic, protective damping field.

Evolution had, unfortunately, not yet realized that there was such a thing as human society. It produced a being with a certain modification from the human stock, thereby arriving at practical psi. In order to protect this feeble new species, whose members were so terribly sparse, it gave them the perfect camouflage.

Result: When young Augustin Kusevic was enrolled in school, it was discovered that he had no birth certificate. No hospital recalled his birth. As a matter of brutal fact, his human parents sometimes forgot his existence for days at a time.

Result: When young Gussie Kusevic tried to enter high school, it was discovered that he had never entered grammar school. No matter that he could quote teachers' names, textbooks, or classroom numbers. No matter if he could produce report cards. They were misfiled, and the anguished interviews forgotten. No one doubted his existence—people remembered the fact of his being, and the fact of his having acted and being acted upon. But only as though they had read it in some infinitely boring book.

He had no friends, no girl, no past, no present, no love. He had no place to stand. Had there been such things as ghosts, he would have found his fellowship there.

By the time of his adolescence, he had discovered an absolute lack of involvement with the human race. He studied it, because it was the salient feature of his environment. He did not live with it. It said nothing to him that was of personal value; its motivations, morals, manners and morale did not find responsive reactions in him. And his, of course, made absolutely no impression on it.

The life of the peasant of ancient Babylon is of interest to only a few historical anthropologists, none of whom actually want to *be* Babylonian peasants.

Having solved the human social equation from his dispassionate viewpoint, and caring no more than the naturalist who finds that deer are extremely fond of green aspen leaves, he plunged into physical release. He discovered the thrill of picking fights and winning them; of *making* somebody pay attention to him by smashing his nose.

He might have become a permanent fixture on the Manhattan docks, if another longshoreman hadn't slashed him with a carton knife. The cultural demand on him had been plain. He'd had to kill the man.

That had been the end of unregulated personal combat. He discovered, not to his horror but to his disgust, that he could get away with murder. No investigation had been made; no search was attempted.

So that had been the end of that, but it had led him to the only possible evasion of the trap to which he had been born. Intellectual competition being meaningless, organized sports became the only answer. Simultaneously regulating his efforts and annotating them under a mound of journalistic record-keeping, they furnished the first official continuity his life had ever known. People still forgot his accomplishments, but when they turned to the records, his name was undeniably there. A dossier can be misfiled. School records can disappear. But something more than a damping field was required to shunt aside the mountain of news copy and statistics that drags, ball-like, at the ankle of even the mediocre athlete.

It seemed to Gus—and he thought of it a great deal—that this chain of progression was inevitable for any male of his kind. When, three years ago, he had discovered Halsey, his hypothesis was bolstered. But what good was Halsey to another male? To hold mutual consolation sessions with? He had no intention of ever contacting the man.

The clerk cleared his throat. Gus jerked his head around to look at him, startled. He'd forgotten him.

"Well, guess I'll be going. Remember, you've only got two months."

Gus gestured noncommittally. The man had delivered his message. Why didn't he acknowledge he'd served his purpose, and go?

Gus smiled ruefully. What purpose did *homo nondescriptus* serve, and where was he going? Halsey was already walking downhill along the well-marked trail. *Were* there others? If so, then they were in another rut, somewhere, and not even the tops of their heads showed. He and his kind could recognize each other only by an elaborate process of elimination; they had to watch for the people no one noticed.

He opened the door for the clerk, saw the road, and found his thoughts back with the highway.

The highway would run from Hollister, which was a railroad junction, to the Air Force Base at Farnham, where his calculations in sociomathematics had long ago predicted the first starship would be constructed and launched. The trucks would rumble up the highway, feeding the open maw with men and material.

He cleaned his lips. Up there in space, somewhere; somewhere outside the Solar System, was another race. The imprint of their visits here was plain. The humans would encounter them, and again he could predict the result; the humans would win.

Gus Kusevic could not go along to investigate the challenges that he doubted lay among the stars. Even with scrapbooks full of notices and clippings, he had barely made his career penetrate the public consciousness. Halsey, who had exuberantly broken every baseball record in the books, was known as a "pretty fair country pitcher."

What credentials could he present with his application to the Air Force? Who would remember them the next day if he had any? What would become of the records of his inoculations, his physical check-ups, his training courses? Who would remember to reserve a bunk for him, or stow supplies for him, or add his consumption to the total when the time came to allow for oxygen?

Stow away? Nothing easier. But, again; who would die so he could live within the tight lattice of shipboard economy? Which sheep would he slaughter, and to what useful purpose, in the last analysis?

"Well, so long," the clerk said.

"Good-bye," Gus said.

The clerk walked down the flagstones and out to his flivver.

I think, Gus said to himself, it would have been much better for us if Evolution had been a little less protective and a little more thoughtful. An occasional pogrom wouldn't have done us any harm. A ghetto at least keeps the courtship problem solved.

Our seed has been split on the ground.

Suddenly, Gus ran forward, pushed by something he didn't care to name. He looked up through the flivver's open door, and the clerk looked down apprehensively.

"Danvers, you're a sports fan," Gus said hastily, realizing his voice was too urgent; that he was startling the clerk with his intensity.

"That's right," the clerk answered, pushing himself nervously back along the seat.

"Who's heavyweight champion of the world?"

"Mike Frazier. Why?"

"Who'd he beat for the title? Who used to be champion?"

The clerk pursed his lips. "Huh! It's been years—gee, I don't know. I don't remember. I could look it up, I guess."

Gus exhaled slowly. He half-turned and looked back toward the cottage, the lawn, the flower beds, the walk, the arbor, and the fish pond under the willow tree. "Never mind," he said, and walked back into the house while the clerk wobbled his flivver into the air.

The TV set was blaring with sound. He checked the status of the game.

It had gone quickly. Halsey had pitched a one-hitter so far, and the Giants' pitcher had done almost as well. The score was tied at 1–1, the Giants were at bat, and it was the last out in the ninth inning. The camera boomed in on Halsey's face.

Halsey looked at the batter with complete disinterest in his eyes, wound up, and threw the home-run ball.

Dino Buzzati

Dino Buzzati (1906–72) was one of the important Italian writers to emerge after the second world war. His principal modes were the absurd and the fantastic. He first came to international attention with his contemporary novel *The Tartar Steppe* (1945). His only SF novel, *Larger Than Life* (1960), a big computer story (a mainframe computer is programmed with the personality of a woman), is undistinguished. Critics agree, however, that his major work was in his short stories.

"The effectiveness of a fantastic story will depend on its being told in the most simple and practical terms . . . fantasy should be as close as possible to journalism," Buzzati said. He wrote a number of SF stories but has never been published or recognized as a writer of the genre in English. A collection of his fantasy and SF is, it seems to me, overdue. This story is a small, graceful piece on a classic SF idea.

THE TIME MACHINE

The first great installation to slow down time was built near Grosseto, in Mariscano. In fact, the inventor, the famous Aldo Cristofari, was a native of Grosseto. This Cristofari, a professor at the University of Pisa, had been interested in the problem for at least twenty years and had conducted marvelous experiments in his laboratory, especially on the germination of legumes. In the academic world, however, he was thought a visionary. Until, under the aegis of his supporter, the financier Alfredo Lopez, the society for the construction of Diacosia was created. From then on Aldo Cristofari was regarded as a genius, a benefactor to humanity.

His invention consisted of a special electrostatic field called "Field C," within which natural phenomena required an abnormally longer period of time to complete their life cycles. In the first decisive experiments, this delay did not exceed five or six units per thousand; in practice, that is to say, it was almost unnoticeable. Yet once Cristofari had discovered the principle, he made very rapid progress. With the installation at Mariscano the rate of retardation was increased to nearly half. This meant that an organism with an average life span of ten years could be inserted in Field C and reach an age of twenty years.

The installation was built in a hilly zone, and it was not effective beyond a range of 800 meters. In a circle with a diameter of one and a half kilometers, animals and plants would grow and age half as quickly as those on the rest of the earth. Man could now hope to live for two centuries. And so—from the Greek for two hundred—the name Diacosia was chosen.

The zone was practically uninhabited. The few peasants who lived there were given the choice of staying or relocating elsewhere with a sizeable settlement.

They preferred to clear out. The area was entirely enclosed within an insurmountable fence. There was only one entrance, and it was carefully guarded. In a short time there rose immense skyscrapers, a gigantic nursing home (for terminally ill patients who desired to prolong the little life they had left), movie houses, and theaters, all amid a forest of villas. And in the middle, at a height of forty meters, stood a circular antenna similar to those used for radar; this constituted the center of Field C. The power plant was completely underground.

Once the installation was finished, the entire world was informed that within three months the city would open its doors. To gain admission, and above all to reside there, cost an enormous sum. All the same, thousands of people from every corner of the globe were tempted. The subscriptions quickly exhausted the available housing. But then the fear began, and the flow of applicants was slower than anticipated.

What was there to fear? First of all, anyone who had settled in the city for any appreciable length of time could not leave without injury. Imagine an organism accustomed to the new, slower pace of physical existence. Suddenly transplant it from Field C to an area where life moves twice as fast; the function of every organ would have to accelerate immediately. And if it is easy for a runner to slow down, it is not so easy for someone moving slowly to bolt into a mad dash. The violent disequilibrium could have harmful or simply fatal consequences.

As a result, anyone who was born in the city was strictly forbidden to leave it. It was only logical to expect that an organism created in that slower speed could not be shifted to an environment that ran, we might say, in double time without risking destruction. In anticipation of this problem, special booths for acceleration and retardation were to be constructed on the perimeter of Field C so that anyone who left or entered it might gradually acclimate himself to the new pace and avoid the trauma of an abrupt change (they were similar to decompression chambers for deep-sea divers). But these booths were delicate devices, still in the planning stage. They would not be in service for many years.

In short, the citizens of Diacosia would live much longer than other men and women, but in exile. They were forced to give up their country, old friends, travel. They could no longer have a variety of lovers and acquaintances. It was as if they had been sentenced to life imprisonment, although they enjoyed every imaginable luxury and convenience.

But there was more. The danger posed by an escape could also be caused by any damage to the installation. It is true that there were two generators in the power plant, and that if one stopped, the other began to operate automatically. But what if both malfunctioned? What if there was a blackout? What if a cyclone or lightning struck the antenna? What if there was a war, or some outrage?

Diacosia was inaugurated at a celebration for its first group of citizens, who numbered 11,365. For the most part, they were people over fifty. Cristofari, who did not intend to settle in the city, was absent. He was represented by one Stoermer, a Swiss who was the director of the installation. There was a simple ceremony.

At the foot of the transmitting antenna that rose in the public garden, precisely at noon, Stoermer announced that from that moment on in Diacosia men and women would age exactly one-half as slowly as before. The antenna emitted a very soft hum, which was, moreover, pleasing to the ear. In the beginning, no one noticed the altered conditions. Only toward evening did some people feel a kind of lethargy, as if they were being held back. Very soon they started to talk, walk, chew with their usual composure. The tension of life subsided. Everything required greater effort.

About one month later, in *Technical Monthly*, a magazine based in Buffalo, the Nobel laureate Edwin Mediner published an article that proved to be the death knell for Diacosia. Mediner maintained that Cristofari's installation carried a grave threat. Time—we here present a synthesis of his argument in plain words—tends to rush headlong, and if it does not encounter the resistance of any matter, it will assume a progressively accelerated pace, with a tendency to increase to infinity. Thus any retardation of the flow of time requires immense effort, while it is nothing at all to augment its speed—just as in a river it is difficult to go against the current, but easy to follow it. From this observation Mediner formulated the following law: If one wishes to slow down natural phenomena, the necessary energy is directly proportional to the square of the retardation to be obtained; if one wishes to speed them up, on the other hand, the acceleration is directly proportional to the cube of the necessary energy. For example, ten units of energy are enough to achieve an acceleration of one thousand units; but the same ten units of energy applied to achieve the opposite purpose hardly produce a retardation of three units. In the first case, in fact, the human intervention operates in the same direction as time, which expects as much, so to speak. Mediner argued that Field C was such that it could operate in both directions; and an error in maintenance or a breakdown of some minor mechanism was sufficient to reverse the effect of the emission. In this case, instead of extending life to twice its average length, the machine would devour it precipitously. In the space of a few minutes, the citizens of Diacosia would age decades. And there followed the mathematical proof.

After Edwin Mediner's revelation, a wave of panic swept through the city of longevity. A few people, overlooking the risk of abruptly reentering an "accelerated environment," took flight. But Cristofari's assurances about the efficiency of the installation and the very fact that nothing had happened placated the anxieties. Life in Diacosia continued its monotonous succession of identical, placid, colorless days. Pleasures were weak and insipid, the throbbing delirium of love lacked the overpowering force it once had, news, voices, even the music that came from the outside world were now unpleasant because of their great speed. In a word, life was less interesting, despite the constant distractions. And yet this boredom was slight when compared to the thought that tomorrow, when one by one their contemporaries would pass away, the citizens of Diacosia would still be young and strong; and then their contemporaries' children would gradually die off, but the Diacosians would be full of vigor; and even their contemporaries' grandchildren and great-grandchildren would leave the world, and they who were still alive, with decades of good years ahead of them, would read the obituary notices. This was the thought that dominated the community, that calmed restless spirits, that resolved jealousies and quarrels; this was why they were not agonized as before by the passage of time and the future presented itself as a vast landscape and when confronted by disappointment men and women told themselves: Why worry about it? I'll think about it tomorrow, there isn't any hurry.

After two years, the population had climbed to 52,000, and already the first generation of Diacosians had been born. They would reach full maturity at forty. After ten years, more than 120,000 creatures swarmed over that square kilometer, and slowly, much more slowly than in other cities where time galloped, the skyline rose to dizzying heights. Diacosia had now become the greatest wonder of the world. Caravans of tourists lined the periphery, observing through the gates those people who were so different, who moved with the slowness of MS victims succumbing to paralysis.

The phenomenon lasted twenty years. And a few seconds were enough to destroy it. How did the tragedy occur? Was it caused by a man's will? Or was it chance? Perhaps one of the technicians, anguished by love or illness, wanted to abbreviate his torment and set the catastrophe in motion. Or was he maddened simply from exasperation with that empty, egocentric life, concerned only with self-preservation? And so he purposely reversed the effect of the machine, freeing the vandal forces of time.

It was May 17th, a warm, sunny day. In the fields, along the fence that ran around the perimeter, hundreds of curious observers were stationed, their eyes riveted to people just like them, whose life passed twice as slowly. From within the city came the thin, harmonious voice of the antenna. It had a bell-like resonance. The present writer was there that day and he observed a group of four children playing with a ball. "How old are you?" I asked the oldest one. "Last month I was twenty," she answered politely, but with exaggerated slowness. And their way of running was strange: all soft, viscous movements, like a film shot in slow motion. Even the ball had less bounce for them.

Beyond the fence were the lawns and paths of a garden; the barrier surrounding the buildings began at about fifty meters. A breeze moved the leaves in the trees, yet languidly, it seemed, as if they were leaden. Suddenly, about three in the afternoon, the remote hum of antenna grew more intense and rose like a siren, an unbearable piercing whistle. I will never forget what happened. Even today, at a distance of years, I awake in the dead of night with a start, confronting that horrible vision.

Before my eyes the four children stretched monstrously. I saw them grow, fatten, become adults. Beards sprouted from male chins. Transformed this way and half naked, their childhood clothes having split under the pressure of the lightning growth, they were seized with terror. They opened their mouths to speak, but what came out was a strange noise I had never heard before. In the vortex of unleashed time, the syllables all ran together, like a record played at a higher, mad speed. That gurgling quickly turned into a wheeze, then a desperate shout.

The four children looked around for help, saw us and rushed toward the railing. But life burned inside them; at the railing, a matter of seven or eight seconds, four old people arrived, with white hair and beards, flaccid and bony. One managed to seize the fence with his skeletal hands. He collapsed at once, together with his companions. They were dead. And the decrepit bodies of those poor children immediately gave off a foul odor. They were decomposing, flesh fell away, bones appeared, even the bones—before my very eyes—dissolved into a whitish dust.

Only then did the fatal scream of the machine subside and finally fall silent. Mediner's prophecy came true. For reasons that will forever remain unknown, the time machine had reversed its operation, and a few seconds were enough to swallow three or four centuries of life.

Now a gloomy, sepulchral silence has frozen the city. The shadow of abject old age has fallen over the skyscrapers, which had just been resplendent with glory and hope. The walls are wrinkled; ominous lines and creases have appeared, oozing black liquids amid a fringe of rotting spider webs. And there is dust everywhere. Dust, stillness, silence. Of the two hundred thousand wealthy, fortunate people who had wanted to live for centuries there remained nothing but white dust, collecting here and there, as on millennial tombs.

Philip José Farmer

Philip José Farmer (1918–   ) is a powerful and energetic writer of fantasy and SF who has published over fifty novels and hundreds of short stories. His most famous novels and stories are the Riverworld series, beginning with *To Your Scattered Bodies Go* (1971), which feature such historical personages as Richard Francis Burton, Mark Twain, and Jack London as central characters. He entered the genre with a powerful short story, "The Lovers" (1952), a mixture of alien biology and sex that earned him a not-undeserved reputation as a taboo-breaker and a somewhat shocking writer, if not downright disgusting. He has written most often about psychology, sex, and race, often all three at once.

Leslie A. Fiedler called him the best living science fiction writer. *The Encyclopedia of Science Fiction* says, "Farmer is governed by an instinct for extremity. Of all science fiction writers of the first or second rank, he is perhaps the most threateningly impish, and the most anarchic."

Farmer was so underpaid and underappreciated for so long in his career that when Kurt Vonnegut wrote of a fictional hack SF writer Kilgore Trout, who was psychologically and philosophically profound while writing of absurd things, Farmer identified with Trout and ultimately obtained Vonnegut's permission to write an SF novel under that name— even though Vonnegut had really been thinking of himself.

Farmer's chief mode is a startling confrontation with psychological states and symbols made literal and manifest. This story certainly does that. It is Freudian science fiction.

MOTHER

I

"Look, Mother. The clock is running backward."

Eddie Fetts pointed to the hands on the pilot room dial.

Dr. Paula Fetts said, "The crash must have reversed it."

"How could it do that?"

"I can't tell you. I don't know everything, Son."

"Oh!"

"Well, don't look at me so disappointedly. I'm a pathologist, not an electronician."

"Don't be so cross, Mother. I can't stand it. Not now."

He walked out of the pilot room. Anxiously, she followed him. The burial of the crew and her fellow scientists had been very trying for him. Spilled blood had always made him dizzy and sick; he could scarcely control his hands enough to help her sack the scattered bones and entrails.

He had wanted to put the corpses in the nuclear furnace, but she had forbidden that. The Geigers amidships were ticking loudly, warning that there was invisible death in the stern.

The meteor that struck the moment the ship came out of Translation into normal space had probably wrecked the engine room. So she had understood from the incoherent high-pitched phrases of a colleague before he fled to the pilot room. She had hurried to find Eddie. She feared his cabin door would still be locked, as he had been making a tape of the aria "Heavy Hangs the Albatross" from Gianelli's *Ancient Mariner*.

Fortunately, the emergency system had automatically thrown out the locking circuits. Entering, she had called out his name in fear he'd been hurt. He was lying half unconscious on the floor, but it was not the accident that had thrown him there. The reason lay in the corner, released from his lax hand; a quart free-fall Thermos, rubber-nippled. From Eddie's open mouth charged a breath of rye that not even Nodor pills had been able to conceal.

Sharply she had commanded him to get up and onto the bed. Her voice, the first he had ever heard, pierced through the phalanx of Old Red Star. He struggled up, and she, though smaller, had thrown every ounce of her weight into getting him up and onto the bed.

There she had lain down with him and strapped them both in. She understood that the lifeboat had been wrecked also, and that it was up to the captain to bring the yacht down safely to the surface of this charted but unexplored planet, Baudelaire. Everybody else had gone to sit behind the captain, strapped in crash-chairs, unable to help except with their silent backing.

Moral support had not been enough. The ship had come in on a shallow slant. Too fast. The wounded motors had not been able to hold her up. The prow had taken the brunt of the punishment. So had those seated in the nose.

Dr. Fetts had held her son's head on her bosom and prayed out loud to her God. Eddie had snored and muttered. Then there was a sound like the clashing of the gates of doom—a tremendous bong as if the ship were a clapper in a gargantuan bell tolling the most frightening message human ears may hear—a blinding blast of light—and darkness and silence.

A few moments later Eddie began crying out in a childish voice, "Don't leave me to die, Mother! Come back! Come back!"

Mother was unconscious by his side, but he did not know that. He wept for a while, then he lapsed back into his rye-fogged stupor—if he had ever been out of it—and slept. Again, darkness and silence.

It was the second day since the crash, if "day" could describe that twilight state on Baudelaire. Dr. Fetts followed her son wherever he went. She knew he was very sensitive and easily upset. All his life she had known it and had tried to get between him and anything that would cause trouble. She had succeeded, she thought, fairly well until three months ago when Eddie had eloped.

The girl was Polina Fameux, the ash-blond long-legged actress whose tridi image, taped, had been shipped to frontier stars where a small acting talent meant little and a large and shapely bosom much. Since Eddie was a well-known Metro tenor, the marriage made a big splash whose ripples ran around the civilized Galaxy.

Dr. Fetts had felt very bad about the elopement, but she had, she hoped, hidden her grief very well beneath a smiling mask. She didn't regret having to give him up; after all, he was a full-grown man, no longer her little boy. But, really, aside from the seasons at the Met and his tours, he had not been parted from her since he was eight.

That was when she went on a honeymoon with her second husband. And then she and Eddie had not been separated long, for Eddie had gotten very sick, and she'd had to hurry back and take care of him, as he had insisted she was the only one who could make him well.

Moreover, you couldn't count his days at the opera as a total loss, for he vised her every noon and they had a long talk—no matter how high the vise bills ran.

The ripples caused by her son's marriage were scarcely a week old before they were followed by even bigger ones. They bore the news of the separation of Eddie and his wife. A fortnight later, Polina applied for divorce on grounds of incompatibility. Eddie was handed the papers in his mother's apartment. He had come back to her the day he and Polina had agreed they "couldn't make a go of it," or, as he phrased it to his mother, "couldn't get together."

Dr. Fetts was, of course, very curious about the reason for their parting, but, as she explained to her friends, she "respected" his silence. What she didn't say was that she had told herself the time would come when he would tell her all.

Eddie's "nervous breakdown" started shortly afterward. He had been very irritable, moody, and depressed, but he got worse the day a so-called friend told Eddie that whenever Polina heard his name mentioned, she laughed loud and long. The friend added that Polina had promised to tell some day the true story of their brief merger.

That night his mother had to call in a doctor.

In the days that followed, she thought of giving up her position as research pathologist at De Kruif and taking all her time to help him "get back on his feet." It was a sign of the struggle going on in her mind that she had not been able to decide within a week's time. Ordinarily given to swift consideration and resolution of a problem, she could not agree to surrender her beloved quest into tissue regeneration.

Just as she was on the verge of doing what was for her the incredible and the shameful, tossing a coin, she had been vised by her superior. He told her she had been chosen to go with a group of biologists on a research cruise to ten preselected planetary systems.

Joyfully, she had thrown away the papers that would turn Eddie over to a sanatorium. And, since he was quite famous, she had used her influence to get the government to allow him to go along. Ostensibly, he was to make a survey of the development of opera on planets colonized by Terrans. That the yacht was not visiting any colonized globes seemed to have been missed by the bureaus concerned. But it was not the first time in the history of a government that its left hand knew not what its right was doing.

Actually, he was to be "rebuilt" by his mother, who thought herself much more capable of curing him than any of the prevalent A, F, J, R, S, K, or H therapies. True, some of her friends reported amazing results with some of the symbol-chasing techniques. On the other hand, two of her close companions had tried them all and had gotten no benefits from any of them. She was his mother; she could do more for him than any of those "alphabatties"; he was flesh of her flesh, blood of her blood. Besides, he wasn't so sick. He just got awfully blue sometimes and made theatrical but insincere threats of suicide or else just sat and stared into space. But she could handle him.

II

So now it was that she followed him from the backward-running clock to his room. And saw him step inside, look for a second, and then turn to her with a twisted face.

"Neddie is ruined, Mother. Absolutely ruined."

She glanced at the piano. It had torn from the wall-racks at the moment of impact and smashed itself against the opposite wall. To Eddie it wasn't just a piano; it was Neddie. He had a pet name for everything he contacted for more than a brief time. It was as if he hopped from one appellation to the next, like an ancient sailor who felt lost unless he was close to the familiar and designated points of the shoreline. Otherwise, Eddie seemed to be drifting helplessly in a chaotic ocean, one that was anonymous and amorphous.

Or, analogy more typical of him, he was like the nightclubber who feels submerged, drowning, unless he hops from table to table, going from one well-known group of faces to the next, avoiding the featureless and unnamed dummies at the strangers' tables.

He did not cry over Neddie. She wished he would. He had been so apathetic during the voyage. Nothing, not even the unparalleled splendor of the naked stars nor the inexpressible alienness of strange planets, had seemed to lift him very long. If he would only weep or laugh loudly or display some sign that he was reacting violently to what was happening. She would even have welcomed his striking her in anger or calling her "bad" names.

But no, not even during the gathering of the mangled corpses, when he looked for a while as if he were going to vomit, would he give way to his body's demand for expression. She understood that if he were to throw up, he would be much better for it, would have gotten rid of much of the psychic disturbance along with the physical.

He would not. He had kept on raking flesh and bones into the large plastic bags and kept a fixed look of resentment and sullenness.

She hoped now that the loss of his piano would bring tears and shaking shoulders. Then she could take him in her arms and give him sympathy. He would be her little boy again, afraid of the dark, afraid of the dog killed by a car, seeking her arms for the sure safety, the sure love.

"Never mind, Baby," she said. "When we're rescued, we'll get you a new one."

"When—!"

He lifted his eyebrows and sat down on the bed's edge.

"What do we do now?"

She became very brisk and efficient.

"The ultrad automatically started working the moment the meteor struck. If it's survived the crash, it's still sending SOS's. If not, then there's nothing we can do about it. Neither of us knows how to repair it.

"However, it's possible that in the last five years since this planet was located, other expeditions may have landed here. Not from Earth but from some of the colonies. Or from nonhuman globes. Who knows? It's worth taking a chance. Let's see."

A single glance was enough to wreck their hopes. The ultrad had been twisted and broken until it was no longer recognizable as the machine that sent swifter-than-light waves through the no-ether.

Dr. Fetts said with false cheeriness, "Well, that's that! So what? It makes things too easy. Let's go into the storeroom and see what we can see."

Eddie shrugged and followed her. There she insisted that each take a panrad. If they had to separate for any reason, they could always communicate and also, using the DF's—the built-in direction finders—locate each other. Having used them before, they knew the instruments' capabilities and how essential they were on scouting or camping trips.

The panrads were lightweight cylinders about two feet high and eight inches in diameter. Crampacked, they held the mechanisms of two dozen different utilities. Their batteries lasted a year without recharging, they were practically indestructible and worked under almost any conditions.

Keeping away from the side of the ship that had the huge hole in it, they took the panrads outside. The long wave bands were searched by Eddie while his mother moved the dial that ranged up and down the shortwaves. Neither really expected to hear anything, but to search was better than doing nothing.

Finding the modulated wave-frequencies empty of any significant noises, he switched to the continuous waves. He was startled by a dot-dashing.

"Hey, Mom! Something in the 1000 kilocycles! Unmodulated!"

"Naturally, Son," she said with some exasperation in the midst of her elation. "What would you expect from a radio-telegraphic signal?"

She found the band on her own cylinder. He looked blankly at her. "I know nothing about radio, but that's not Morse."

"What? You must be mistaken!"

"I—I don't think so."

"Is it or isn't it? Good God, Son, can't you be certain of *anything!*"

She turned the amplifier up. As both of them had learned Galacto-Morse through sleeplearn techniques, she checked him at once.

"You're right. What do you make of it?"

His quick ear sorted out the pulses.

"No simple dot and dash. Four different time-lengths."

He listened some more.

"They've got a certain rhythm, all right. I can make out definite groupings. Ah! That's the sixth time I've caught that particular one. And there's another. And another."

Dr. Fetts shook her ash-blond head. She could make out nothing but a series of zzt-zzt-zzt's.

Eddie glanced at the DF needle.

"Coming from NE by E. Should we try to locate?"

"Naturally," she replied. "But we'd better eat first. We don't know how far away it is, or what we'll find there. While I fix a hot meal, you get our field trip stuff ready."

"O.K.," he said with more enthusiasm than he had shown for a long time.

When he came back he ate everything in the large dish his mother had prepared on the unwrecked galley stove.

"You always did make the best stew," he said.

"Thank you. I'm glad you're eating again, Son. I am surprised. I thought you'd be sick about all this."

He waved vaguely but energetically.

"The challenge of the unknown. I have a sort of feeling this is going to turn out much better than we thought. Much better."

She came close and sniffed his breath. It was clean, innocent even of stew. That meant he'd taken Nodor, which probably meant he'd been sampling some hidden rye. Otherwise, how explain his reckless disregard of the possible dangers? It wasn't like him.

She said nothing, for she knew that if he tried to hide a bottle in his clothes or field sack while they were tracking down the radio signals, she would soon find it. And take it away. He wouldn't even protest, merely let her lift it from his limp hand while his lips swelled with resentment.

III

They set out. Both wore knapsacks and carried the panrads. He carried a gun over his shoulder, and she had snapped onto her sack her small black bag of medical and lab supplies.

High noon of late autumn was topped by a weak red sun that barely managed to make itself seen through the eternal double layer of clouds. Its companion, an even smaller blob of lilac, was setting on the northwestern horizon. They walked in a sort of bright twilight, the best that Baudelaire ever achieved. Yet, despite the lack of light, the air was warm. It was a phenomenon common to certain planets behind the Horsehead Nebula, one being investigated but as yet unexplained.

The country was hilly, with many deep ravines. Here and there were prominences high enough and steep-sided enough to be called embryo mountains. Considering the roughness of the land however, there was a surprising amount of vegetation. Pale green, red, and yellow bushes, vines, and little trees clung to every bit of ground, horizontal or vertical. All had comparatively broad leaves that turned with the sun to catch the light.

From time to time, as the two Terrans strode noisily through the forest, small multicolored insect-like and mammal-like creatures scuttled from hiding place to hiding place. Eddie decided to carry his gun in the crook of his arm. Then, after they were forced to scramble up and down ravines and hills and fight their way through thickets that became unexpectedly tangled, he put it back over his shoulder, where it hung from a strap.

Despite their exertions, they did not tire quickly. They weighed about twenty pounds less than they would have on Earth and, though the air was thinner, it was richer in oxygen.

Dr. Fetts kept up with Eddie. Thirty years the senior of the twenty-three-year-old, she passed even at close inspection for his older sister. Longevity pills took care of that. However, he treated her with all the courtesy and chivalry that one gave one's mother and helped her up the steep inclines, even though the climbs did not appreciably cause her deep chest to demand more air.

They paused once by a creek bank to get their bearings.

"The signals have stopped," he said.

"Obviously," she replied.

At that moment the radar-detector built into the panrad began to ping. Both of them automatically looked upward.

"There's no ship in the air."

"It can't be coming from either of those hills," she pointed out. "There's nothing but a boulder on top of each one. Tremendous rocks."

"Nevertheless, it's coming from there, I think. Oh! Oh! Did you see what I saw? Looked like a tall stalk of some kind being pulled down behind that big rock."

She peered through the dim light. "I think you were imagining things, Son. I saw nothing."

Then, even as the pinging kept up, the zzting started again. But after a burst of noise, both stopped.

"Let's go up and see what we shall see," she said.

"Something screwy," he commented. She did not answer.

They forded the creek and began the ascent. Halfway up, they stopped to sniff in puzzlement at a gust of some heavy odor coming downwind.

"Smells like a cageful of monkeys," he said.

"In heat," she added. If his was the keener ear, hers was the sharper nose.

They went on up. The RD began sounding its tiny hysterical gonging. Nonplused, Eddie stopped. The DF indicated the radar pulses were not coming from the top of the hill they were climbing, as formerly, but from the other hill across the valley. Abruptly, the panrad fell silent.

"What do we do now?"

"Finish what we started. This hill. Then we go to the other one."

He shrugged and then hastened after her tall slim body in its long-legged coveralls. She was hot on the scent, literally, and nothing could stop her. Just before she reached the bungalow-sized boulder topping the hill, he caught up with her. She had stopped to gaze intently at the DF needle, which swung wildly before it stopped at neutral. The monkey-cage odor was very strong.

"Do you suppose it could be some sort of radio-generating mineral?" she asked, disappointedly.

"No. Those groupings were semantic. And that smell . . ."

"Then what—?"

He didn't know whether to feel pleased or not that she had so obviously and suddenly thrust the burden of responsibility and action on him. Both pride and a curious shrinking affected him. But he did feel exhilarated. Almost, he thought, he felt as if he were on the verge of discovering what he had been looking for for a long time. What the object of his search had been, he could not say. But he was excited and not very much afraid.

He unslung his weapon, a two-barreled combination shotgun and rifle. The panrad was still quiet.

"Maybe the boulder is camouflage for a spy outfit," he said. He sounded silly, even to himself.

Behind him, his mother gasped and screamed. He whirled and raised his gun, but there was nothing to shoot. She was pointing at the hilltop across the valley, shaking, and saying something incoherent.

He could make out a long slim antenna seemingly projecting from the monstrous boulder crouched there. At the same time, two thoughts struggled for first place in his mind: one, that it was more than a coincidence that both hills had almost identical stone structures on their brows, and, two, that the antenna must have been recently stuck out, for he was sure he had not seen it the last time he looked.

He never got to tell her his conclusions, for something thin and flexible and irresistible seized him from behind. Lifted into the air, he was borne backward. He dropped the gun and tried to grab the bands or tentacles around him and tear them off with his bare hands. No use.

He caught one last glimpse of his mother running off down the hillside. Then a curtain snapped down, and he was in total darkness.

IV

Eddie sensed himself, still suspended, twirled around. He could not know for sure, of course, but he thought he was facing in exactly the opposite direction. Simultaneously, the tentacles binding his legs and arms were released. Only his waist was still gripped. It was pressed so tightly that he cried out with pain.

Then, boot-toes bumping on some resilient substance, he was carried forward. Halted, facing he knew not what horrible monster, he was suddenly assailed— not by a sharp beak or tooth or knife or some other cutting or mangling instrument—but by a dense cloud of that same monkey perfume.

In other circumstances, he might have vomited. Now his stomach was not given the time to consider whether it should clean house or not. The tentacle lifted him higher and thrust him against something soft and yielding—something fleshlike and womanly—almost breastlike in texture and smoothness and warmth and in its hint of gentle curving.

He put his hands and feet out to brace himself, for he thought for a moment he was going to sink in and be covered up—enfolded—ingested. The idea of a gargantuan amoeba-thing hiding within a hollow rock—or a rocklike shell— made him writhe and yell and shove at the protoplasmic substance.

But nothing of the kind happened. He was not plunged into a smothering and slimy jelly that would strip him of his skin and then his flesh and then dissolve his bones. He was merely shoved repeatedly against the soft swelling. Each time, he pushed or kicked or struck at it. After a dozen of these seemingly purposeless acts, he was held away, as if whatever was doing it was puzzled by his behavior.

He had quit screaming. The only sounds were his harsh breathing and the zzts and pings from the panrad. Even as he became aware of them, the zzts changed tempo and settled into a recognizable pattern of bursts—three units that crackled out again and again.

"Who are you? Who are you?"

Of course, it could just as easily had been, "What are you?" or "What the hell!" or "Nov smoz ka pop?"

Or nothing—semantically speaking.

But he didn't think the latter. And when he was gently lowered to the floor, and the tentacle went off to only-God-knew-where in the dark, he was sure that the creature was communicating—or trying to—with him.

It was this thought that kept him from screaming and running around in the lightless and fetid chamber, brainlessly seeking an outlet. He mastered his panic and snapped open a little shutter in the panrad's side and thrust in his right-hand index finger. There he poised it above the key and in a moment, when the thing paused in transmitting, he sent back, as best he could, the pulses he had received. It was not necessary for him to turn on the light and spin the dial that would put him on the 1000 kc band. The instrument would automatically key that frequency in with the one he had just received.

The oddest part of the whole procedure was that his whole body was trembling almost uncontrollably—one part excepted. That was his index finger, his one unit that seemed to him to have a definite function in this otherwise meaningless situation. It was the section of him that was helping him to survive—the only part that knew how—at that moment. Even his brain seemed to have no connection with his finger. That digit was himself, and the rest just happened to be linked to it.

When he paused, the transmitter began again. This time the units were unrecognizable. There was a certain rhythm to them, but he could not know what they meant. Meanwhile, the RD was pinging. Something somewhere in the dark hole had a beam held tightly on him.

He pressed a button on the panrad's top, and the built-in flashlight illuminated the area just in front of him. He saw a wall of reddish-gray rubbery substance. On the wall was a roughly circular, light gray swelling about four feet in diameter. Around it, giving it a Medusa appearance, were coiled twelve very long, very thin tentacles.

Though he was afraid that if he turned his back to them the tentacles would seize him once more, his curiosity forced him to wheel about and examine his surroundings with the bright beam. He was in an egg-shaped chamber about thirty feet long, twelve wide, and eight to ten high in the middle. It was formed of a reddish-gray material, smooth except for irregular intervals of blue or red pipes. Veins and arteries?

A door-sized portion of the wall had a vertical slit running down it. Tentacles fringed it. He guessed it was a sort of iris and that it had opened to drag him inside. Starfish-shaped groupings of tentacles were scattered on the walls or hung from the ceiling. On the wall opposite the iris was a long and flexible stalk with a cartilaginous ruff around its free end. When Eddie moved, it moved, its blind point following him as a radar antenna tracks the thing it is locating. That was what it was. And unless he was wrong, the stalk was also a C.W. transmitter-receiver.

He shot the light round. When it reached the end farthest from him, he gasped. Ten creatures were huddled together facing him! About the size of half-grown pigs, they looked like nothing so much as unshelled snails; they were eyeless, and the stalk growing from the forehead of each was a tiny duplicate of that on the wall. They didn't look dangerous. Their open mouths were little and toothless, and their rate of locomotion must be slow, for they moved like snails, on a large pedestal of flesh—a foot-muscle.

Nevertheless, if he were to fall asleep they could overcome him by force of numbers, and those mouths might drip an acid to digest him, or they might carry a concealed poisonous sting.

His speculations were interrupted violently. He was seized, lifted, and passed on to another group of tentacles. He was carried beyond the antenna-stalk and toward the snail-beings. Just before he reached them, he was halted, facing the wall. An iris, hitherto invisible, opened. His light shone into it, but he could see nothing but convolutions of flesh.

His panrad gave off a new pattern of dit-dot-deet-dats. The iris widened until it was large enough to admit his body, if he were shoved in head first. Or feet first. It didn't matter. The convolutions straightened out and became a tunnel. Or a throat. From thousands of little pits emerged thousands of tiny, razor sharp teeth. They flashed out and sank back in, and before they had disappeared thousands of other wicked little spears darted out and past the receding fangs.

Meat-grinder.

Beyond the murderous array, at the end of the throat, was a huge pouch of

water. Steam came from it, and with it an odor like that of his mother's stew.
Dark bits, presumably meat, and pieces of vegetables floated on the seething
surface.

Then the iris closed, and he was turned around to face the slugs. Gently, but
unmistakably, a tentacle spanked his buttocks. And the panrad zzzted a warning.

Eddie was not stupid. He knew now that the ten creatures were not dangerous
unless he molested them. In which case he had just seen where he would go if
he did not behave.

Again he was lifted and carried along the wall until he was shoved against the
light gray spot. The monkey-cage odor, which had died out, became strong again.
Eddie identified its source with a very small hole which appeared in the wall.

When he did not respond—he had no idea yet how he was supposed to act—
the tentacles dropped him so unexpectedly that he fell on his back. Unhurt by
the yielding flesh, he rose.

What was the next step? Exploration of his resources. Itemization: The panrad. A sleeping-bag, which he wouldn't need as long as the present too-warm
temperature kept up. A bottle of Old Red Star capsules. A free-fall Thermos
with attached nipple. A box of A-2-Z rations. A Foldstove. Cartridges for his
double-barrel, now lying outside the creature's boulderish shell. A roll of toilet
paper. Toothbrush. Paste. Soap. Towel. Pills: Nodor, hormone, vitamin, longevity, reflex, and sleeping. And a thread-thin wire, a hundred feet long when un-
coiled, that held prisoner in its molecular structure a hundred symphonies, eighty
operas, a thousand different types of musical pieces, and two thousand great
books ranging from Sophocles and Dostoyevsky to the latest bestseller. It could
be played inside the panrad.

He inserted it, pushed a button, and spoke, "Eddie Fetts's recording of Puc-
cini's 'Che gelida manina,' please."

And while he listened approvingly to his own magnificent voice, he zipped
open a can he had found in the bottom of the sack. His mother had put into
it the stew left over from their last meal in the ship.

Not knowing what was happening, yet for some reason sure he was for the
present safe, he munched meat and vegetables with a contented jaw. Transition
from abhorrence to appetite sometimes came easily for Eddie.

He cleaned out the can and finished with some crackers and a chocolate bar.
Rationing was out. As long as the food lasted, he would eat well. Then, if nothing
turned up, he would . . . But then, he reassured himself as he licked his fingers,
his mother, who was free, would find some way to get him out of his trouble.

She always had.

V

The panrad, silent for a while, began signaling. Eddie spotlighted the antenna
and saw it was pointing at the snail-beings, which he had, in accordance with
his custom, dubbed familiarly. Sluggos he called them.

The Sluggos crept toward the wall and stopped close to it. Their mouths,
placed on the tops of their heads, gaped like so many hungry young birds. The
iris opened, and two lips formed into a spout. Out of it streamed steaming-hot

water and chunks of meat and vegetables. Stew! Stew that fell exactly into each waiting mouth.

That was how Eddie learned the second phrase of Mother Polyphema's language. The first message had been, "What are you?" This was, "Come and get it!"

He experimented. He tapped out a repetition of what he'd last heard. As one, the Sluggos—except the one then being fed—turned to him and crept a few feet before halting, puzzled.

Inasmuch as Eddie was broadcasting, the Sluggos must have had some sort of built-in DF. Otherwise they wouldn't have been able to distinguish between his pulses and their Mother's.

Immediately after, a tentacle smote Eddie across the shoulders and knocked him down. The panrad zzzted its third intelligible message: "Don't ever do that!"

And then a fourth, to which the ten young obeyed by wheeling and resuming their former positions.

"This way, children."

Yes, they were the offspring, living, eating, sleeping, playing, and learning to communicate in the womb of their mother—the Mother. They were the mobile brood of this vast immobile entity that had scooped up Eddie as a frog scoops up a fly. This Mother. She who had once been just such a Sluggo until she had grown hog-sized and had been pushed out of her Mother's womb. And who, rolled into a tight ball, had free-wheeled down her natal hill, straightened out at the bottom, inched her way up the next hill, rolled down, and so on. Until she found the empty shell of an adult who had died. Or, if she wanted to be a first class citizen in her society and not a prestigeless *occupée*, she found the bare top of a tall hill—or any eminence that commanded a big sweep of territory—and there squatted.

And there she put out many thread-thin tendrils into the soil and into the cracks in the rocks, tendrils that drew sustenance from the fat of her body and grew and extended downward and ramified into other tendrils. Deep underground the rootlets worked their instinctive chemistry; searched for and found the water, the calcium, the iron, the copper, the nitrogen, the carbons, fondled earthworms and grubs and larvae, teasing them for the secrets of their fats and proteins; broke down the wanted substance into shadowy colloidal particles; sucked them up the thready pipes of the tendrils and back to the pale and slimming body crouching on a flat space atop a ridge, a hill, a peak.

There, using the blueprints stored in the molecules of the cerebellum, her body took the building blocks of elements and fashioned them into a very thin shell of the most available material, a shield large enough so she could expand to fit it while her natural enemies—the keen and hungry predators that prowled twilighted Baudelaire—nosed and clawed it in vain.

Then, her evergrowing bulk cramped, she would resorb the hard covering. And if no sharp tooth found her during that process of a few days, she would cast another and a larger. And so on through a dozen or more.

Until she had become the monstrous and much reformed body of an adult and virgin female. Outside would be the stuff that so much resembled a boulder, that was, actually, rock: either granite, diorite, marble, basalt, or maybe just plain limestone. Or sometimes iron, glass, or cellulose.

Within was the centrally located brain, probably as large as a man's. Surrounding it, the tons of organs: the nervous system, the mighty heart, or hearts, the four stomachs, the microwave and longwave generators, the kidneys, bowels, tracheae, scent and taste organs, the perfume factory which made odors to attract animals and birds close enough to be seized, and the huge womb. And the antennae—the small one inside for teaching and scanning the young, and a long and powerful stalk on the outside, projecting from the shelltop, retractable if danger came.

The next step was from virgin to Mother, lower-case to upper-case as designated in her pulse-language by a longer pause before a word. Not until she was deflowered could she take a high place in her society. Immodest, unblushing, she herself made the advances, the proposals, and the surrender.

After which, she ate her mate.

The clock in the panrad told Eddie he was in his thirtieth day of imprisonment when he found out that little bit of information. He was shocked, not because it offended his ethics, but because he himself had been intended to be the mate. And the dinner.

His finger tapped, "Tell me, Mother, what you mean."

He had not wondered before how a species that lacked males could reproduce. Now he found that, to the Mothers, all creatures except themselves were male. Mothers were immobile and female. Mobiles were male. Eddie had been mobile. He was, therefore, a male.

He had approached this particular Mother during the mating season, that is, midway through raising a litter of young. She had scanned him as he came along the creekbanks at the valley bottom. When he was at the foot of the hill, she had detected his odor. It was new to her. The closest she could come to it in her memorybanks was that of a beast similar to him. From her description, he guessed it to be an ape. So she had released from her repertoire its rut stench. When he seemingly fell into the trap, she had caught him.

He was supposed to attack the conception-spot, that light gray swelling on the wall. After he had ripped and torn it enough to begin the mysterious workings of pregnancy, he would have been popped into her stomach-iris.

Fortunately, he had lacked the sharp beak, the fang, the claw. And she had received her own signals back from the panrad.

Eddie did not understand why it was necessary to use a mobile for mating. A Mother was intelligent enough to pick up a sharp stone and mangle the spot herself.

He was given to understand that conception would not start unless it was accompanied by a certain titillation of the nerves—a frenzy and its satisfaction. Why this emotional state was needed, Mother did not know.

Eddie tried to explain about such things as genes and chromosomes and why they had to be present in highly developed species.

Mother did not understand.

Eddie wondered if the number of slashes and rips in the spot corresponded to the number of young. Or if there were a large number of potentialities in the heredity-ribbons spread out under the conception-skin. And if the haphazard irritation and consequent stimulation of the genes paralleled the chance combining of genes in human male-female mating. Thus resulting in offspring with traits that were combinations of their parents.

Or did the inevitable devouring of the mobile after the act indicate more than an emotional and nutritional reflex? Did it hint that the mobile caught up scattered gene-nodes, like hard seeds, along with the torn skin, in its claws and tusks, that these genes survived the boiling in the stew-stomach, and were later passed out in the feces? Where animals and birds picked them up in beak, tooth, or foot, and then, seized by other Mothers in this oblique rape, transmitted the heredity-carrying agents to the conception-spots while attacking them, the nodules being scraped off and implanted in the skin and blood of the swelling even as others were harvested? Later, the mobiles were eaten, digested, and ejected in the obscure but ingenious and never-ending cycle? Thus ensuring the continual, if haphazard, recombining of genes, chances for variations in offspring, opportunities for mutations, and so on?

Mother pulsed that she was nonplused.

Eddie gave up. He'd never know. After all, did it matter?

He decided not, and rose from his prone position to request water. She pursed up her iris and spouted a tepid quartful into his Thermos. He dropped in a pill, swished it around till it dissolved, and drank a reasonable facsimile of Old Red Star. He preferred the harsh and powerful rye, though he could have afforded the smoothest. Quick results were what he wanted. Taste didn't matter, as he disliked all liquor tastes. Thus he drank what the Skid Row bums drank and shuddered even as they did, renaming it Old Rotten Tar and cursing the fate that had brought them so low they had to gag such stuff down.

The rye glowed in his belly and spread quickly through his limbs and up to his head, chilled only by the increasing scarcity of the capsules. When he ran out—then what? It was at times like this that he most missed his mother.

Thinking about her brought a few large tears. He snuffled and drank some more and when the biggest of the Sluggos nudged him for a back-scratching, he gave it instead a shot of Old Red Star. A slug for Sluggo. Idly, he wondered what effect a taste for rye would have on the future of the race when these virgins became Mothers.

At that moment he was shaken by what seemed a lifesaving idea. These creatures could suck up the required elements from the earth and with them duplicate quite complex molecular structures. Provided, of course, they had a sample of the desired substance to brood over in some cryptic organ.

Well, what easier to do than give her one of the cherished capsules? One could become any number. Those, plus the abundance of water pumped up through hollow underground tendrils from the nearby creek, would give enough to make a master-distiller green!

He smacked his lips and was about to key her his request when what she was transmitting penetrated his mind.

Rather cattily, she remarked that her neighbor across the valley was putting on airs because she, too, held prisoner a communicating mobile.

VI

The Mothers had a society as hierarchical as table-protocol in Washington or peck-order in a barnyard. Prestige was what counted, and prestige was determined by the broadcasting power, the height of the eminence on which the Mother sat, which governed the extent of her radar-territory, and the abundance and novelty and wittiness of her gossip. The creature that had snapped Eddie up was a queen. She had precedence over thirty-odd of her kind; they all had to let her broadcast first, and none dared start pulsing until she quit. Then, the next in order began, and so on down the line. Any of them could be interrupted at any time by Number One, and if any of the lower echelon had something interesting to transmit, she could break in on the one then speaking and get permission from the queen to tell her tale.

Eddie knew this, but he could not listen in directly to the hilltop-gabble. The thick pseudo-granite shell barred him from that and made him dependent upon her womb-stalk for relayed information.

Now and then Mother opened the door and allowed her young to crawl out. There they practiced beaming and broadcasting at the Sluggos of the Mother across the valley. Occasionally that Mother deigned herself to pulse the young, and Eddie's keeper reciprocated to her offspring.

Turnabout.

The first time the children had inched through the exit-iris, Eddie had tried, Ulysses-like, to pass himself off as one of them and crawl out in the midst of the flock. Eyeless, but no Polyphemus, Mother had picked him out with her tentacles and hauled him back in.

It was following that incident that he had named her Polyphema.

He knew she had increased her own already powerful prestige tremendously by possession of that unique thing—a transmitting mobile. So much had her importance grown that the Mothers on the fringes of her area passed on the news to others. Before he had learned her language, the entire continent was hooked up. Polyphema had become a veritable gossip columnist; tens of thousands of hillcrouchers listened in eagerly to her accounts of her dealings with the walking paradox: a semantic male.

That had been fine. Then, very recently, the Mother across the valley had captured a similar creature. And in one bound she had become Number Two in the area and would, at the slightest weakness on Polyphema's part, wrest the top position away.

Eddie became wildly excited at the news. He had often daydreamed about his mother and wondered what she was doing. Curiously enough, he ended many of his fantasies with lip-mutterings, reproaching her almost audibly for having left him and for making no try to rescue him. When he became aware of his attitude, he was ashamed. Nevertheless, the sense of desertion colored his thoughts.

Now that he knew she was alive and had been caught, probably while trying to get him out, he rose from the lethargy that had lately been making him doze the clock around. He asked Polyphema if she would open the entrance so he could talk directly with the other captive. She said yes. Eager to listen in on a conversation between two mobiles, she was very cooperative. There would be a mountain of gossip in what they would have to say. The only thing that dented her joy was that the other Mother would also have access.

Then, remembering she was still Number One and would broadcast the details first, she trembled so with pride and ecstasy that Eddie felt the floor shaking.

Iris open, he walked through it and looked across the valley. The hillsides were still green, red, and yellow, as the plants on Baudelaire did not lose their leaves during winter. But a few white patches showed that winter had begun. Eddie shivered from the bite of cold air on his naked skin. Long ago he had taken off his clothes. The womb-warmth had made garments too uncomfortable; moreover, Eddie, being human, had had to get rid of waste products. And Polyphema, being a Mother, had had periodically to flush out the dirt with warm water from one of her stomachs. Every time the tracheae-vents exploded streams that swept the undesirable elements out through her door-iris, Eddie had become soaked. When he abandoned dress, his clothes had gone floating out. Only by sitting on his pack did he keep it from a like fate.

Afterward, he and the Sluggos had been dried off by warm air pumped through the same vents and originating from the mighty battery of lungs. Eddie was comfortable enough—he'd always liked showers—but the loss of his garments had been one more thing that kept him from escaping. He would soon freeze to death outside unless he found the yacht quickly. And he wasn't sure he remembered the path back.

So now, when he stepped outside, he retreated a pace or two and let the warm air from Polyphema flow like a cloak from his shoulders.

Then he peered across the half-mile that separated him from his mother, but he could not see her. The twilight state and the dark of the unlit interior of her captor hid her.

He tapped in Morse, "Switch to the talkie, same frequency." Paula Fetts did so. She began asking him frantically if he were all right.

He replied he was fine.

"Have you missed me terribly, Son?"

"Oh, very much."

Even as he said this he wondered vaguely why his voice sounded so hollow. Despair at never again being able to see her, probably.

"I've almost gone crazy, Eddie. When you were caught I ran away as fast as I could. I had no idea what horrible monster it was that was attacking us. And then, halfway down the hill, I fell and broke my leg . . ."

"Oh, no, Mother!"

"Yes. But I managed to crawl back to the ship. And there, after I'd set it myself, I gave myself B.K. shots. Only, my system didn't react like it's supposed to. There are people that way, you know, and the healing took twice as long.

"But when I was able to walk, I got a gun and a box of dynamite. I was going to blow up what I thought was a kind of rock-fortress, an outpost for some kind of extee. I'd no idea of the true nature of these beasts. First, though, I decided to reconnoiter. I was going to spy on the boulder from across the valley. But I was trapped by this thing.

"Listen, Son. Before I'm cut off, let me tell you not to give up hope. I'll be out of here before long and over to rescue you."

"How?"

"If you remember, my lab kit holds a number of carcinogens for field work. Well, you know that sometimes a Mother's conception-spot when it is torn up during mating, instead of begetting young, goes into cancer—the opposite of pregnancy. I've injected a carcinogen into the spot and a beautiful carcinoma has developed. She'll be dead in a few days."

"Mom! You'll be buried in that rotting mass!"

"No. This creature has told me that when one of her species dies, a reflex opens the labia. That's to permit their young—if any—to escape. Listen, I'll—"

A tentacle coiled about him and pulled him back through the iris, which shut.

When he switched back to C.W., he heard, "Why didn't you communicate? What were you doing? Tell me! Tell me!"

Eddie told her. There was a silence that could only be interpreted as aston-ishment. After Mother had recovered her wits, she said, "From now on, you will talk to the other male through me."

Obviously, she envied and hated his ability to change wave-bands and, per-haps, had a struggle to accept the idea.

"Please," he persisted, not knowing how dangerous were the waters he was wading in, "please let me talk to my mother di—"

For the first time, he heard her stutter.

"Wha-wha-what? Your Mo-Mo-Mother?"

"Yes. Of course."

The floor heaved violently beneath his feet. He cried out and braced himself to keep from falling and then flashed on the light. The walls were pulsating like shaken jelly, and the vascular columns had turned from red and blue to gray. The entrance-iris sagged open, like a lax mouth, and the air cooled. He could feel the drop in temperature in her flesh with the soles of his feet.

It was some time before he caught on.

Polyphema was in a state of shock.

What might have happened had she stayed in it, he never knew. She might have died and thus forced him out into the winter before his mother could escape. If so, and he couldn't find the ship, he would die. Huddled in the warmest corner of the egg-shaped chamber, Eddie contemplated that idea and shivered to a degree for which the outside air couldn't account.

VII

However, Polyphema had her own method of recovery. It consisted of spewing out the contents of her stew-stomach, which had doubtless become filled with poisons draining out of her system from the blow. Her ejection of the stuff was the physical manifestation of the psychical catharsis. So furious was the flood that her foster son was almost swept out in the hot tide, but she, reacting instinctively, had coiled tentacles about him and the Sluggos. Then she followed the first upchucking by emptying her other three water-pouches, the second hot and the third lukewarm and the fourth, just filled, cold.

Eddie yelped as the icy water doused him.

Polyphema's irises closed again. The floor and walls gradually quit quaking; the temperature rose; and her veins and arteries regained their red and blue. She was well again. Or so she seemed.

But when, after waiting twenty-four hours, he cautiously approached the sub-ject, he found she not only would not talk about it, she refused to acknowledge the existence of the other mobile.

Eddie, giving up hope of conversation, thought for quite a while. The only conclusion he could come to, and he was sure he'd grasped enough of her psy-chology to make it valid, was that the concept of a mobile female was utterly unacceptable.

Her world was split into two: mobile and her kind, the immobile. Mobile meant food and mating. Mobile meant—male. The Mothers were—female.

How the mobiles reproduced had probably never entered the hillcrouchers' minds. Their science and philosophy were on the instinctive body-level. Whether they had some notion of spontaneous generation or amoeba-like fission being responsible for the continued population of mobiles, or they'd just taken for granted they "growed," like Topsy, Eddie never found out. To them, they were female and the rest of the protoplasmic cosmos was male.

That was that. Any other idea was more than foul and obscene and blasphemous. It was—unthinkable.

Polyphema had received a deep trauma from his words. And though she seemed to have recovered, somewhere in those tons of unimaginably complicated flesh a bruise was buried. Like a hidden flower, dark purple, it bloomed, and the shadow it cast was one that cut off a certain memory, a certain tract, from the light of consciousness. That bruise-stained shadow covered that time and event which the Mother, for reasons unfathomable to the human being, found necessary to mark KEEP OFF.

Thus, though Eddie did not word it, he understood in the cells of his body, he felt and knew, as if his bones were prophesying and his brain did not hear, what came to pass.

Sixty-six hours later by the panrad clock, Polyphema's entrance-lips opened. Her tentacles darted out. They came back in, carrying his helpless and struggling mother.

Eddie, roused out of a doze, horrified, paralyzed, saw her toss her lab kit at him and heard an inarticulate cry from her. And saw her plunged, headforemost, into the stomach-iris.

Polyphema had taken the one sure way of burying the evidence.

Eddie lay face down, nose mashed against the warm and faintly throbbing flesh of the floor. Now and then his hands clutched spasmodically as if he were reaching for something that someone kept putting just within his reach and then moving away.

How long he was there he didn't know, for he never again looked at the clock.

Finally, in the darkness, he sat up and giggled inanely, "Mother always did make good stew."

That set him off. He leaned back on his hands and threw his head back and howled like a wolf under a full moon.

Polyphema, of course, was dead-deaf, but she could radar his posture, and her keen nostrils deduced from his body-scent that he was in terrible fear and anguish.

A tentacle glided out and gently enfolded him.

"What is the matter?" zzted the panrad.

He stuck his finger in the keyhole.

"I have lost my mother!"

"?"

"She's gone away, and she'll never come back."

"I don't understand. *Here I am.*"

Eddie quit weeping and cocked his head as if he were listening to some inner voice. He snuffled a few times and wiped away the tears, slowly disengaged the tentacle, patted it, walked over to his pack in a corner, and took out the bottle of Old Red Star capsules. One he popped into the Thermos; the other he gave to her with the request she duplicate it, if possible. Then he stretched out on his side, propped on one elbow like a Roman in his sensualities, sucked the rye through the nipple, and listened to a medley of Beethoven, Mussorgsky, Verdi, Strauss, Porter, Feinstein, and Waxworth.

So the time—if there were such a thing there—flowed around Eddie. When he was tired of music or plays or books, he listened in on the area hookup. Hungry, he rose and walked—or often just crawled—to the stew-iris. Cans of rations lay in his pack; he had planned to eat those until he was sure that— what was it he was forbidden to eat? Poison? Something had been devoured by Polyphema and the Sluggos. But sometime during the music-rye orgy, he had forgotten. He now ate quite hungrily and with thought for nothing but the satisfaction of his wants.

Sometimes the door-iris opened, and Billy Greengrocer hopped in. Billy looked like a cross between a cricket and a kangaroo. He was the size of a collie, and he bore in a marsupialian pouch vegetables and fruit and nuts. These he extracted with shiny green, chitinous claws and gave to Mother in return for meals of stew. Happy symbiote, he chirruped merrily while his many-faceted eyes, revolving independently of each other, looked one at the Sluggos and the other at Eddie.

Eddie, on impulse, abandoned the 1000 kc band and roved the frequencies until he found that both Polyphema and Billy were emitting a 108 wave. That, apparently, was their natural signal. When Billy had his groceries to deliver, he broadcast. Polyphema, in turn, when she needed them, sent back to him. There was nothing intelligent on Billy's part; it was just his instinct to transmit. And the Mother was, aside from the "semantic" frequency, limited to that one band. But it worked out fine.

VIII

Everything was fine. What more could a man want? Free food, unlimited liquor, soft bed, air-conditioning, shower-baths, music, intellectual works (on the tape), interesting conversation (much of it was about him), privacy, and security.

If he had not already named her, he would have called her Mother Gratis.

Nor were creature comforts all. She had given him the answers to all his questions, all . . .

Except one.

That was never expressed vocally by him. Indeed, he would have been incapable of doing so. He was probably unaware that he had such a question.

But Polyphema voiced it one day when she asked him to do her a favor.

Eddie reacted as if outraged.

"One does not—! One does not—!"

He choked, and then he thought, How ridiculous! She is not—

And looked puzzled, and said, "But she is."

He rose and opened the lab kit. While he was looking for a scalpel, he came across the carcinogens. He threw them through the half-opened labia far out and down the hillside.

Then he turned and, scalpel in hand, leaped at the light gray swelling on the wall. And stopped, staring at it, while the instrument fell from his hand. And picked it up and stabbed feebly and did not even scratch the skin. And again let it drop.

"What is it? What is it?" crackled the panrad hanging from his wrist.

Suddenly, a heavy cloud of human odor—mansweat—was puffed in his face from a nearby vent.

"????"

And he stood, bent in a half-crouch, seemingly paralyzed. Until tentacles seized him in fury and dragged him toward the stomach-iris, yawning man-sized.

Eddie screamed and writhed and plunged his finger in the panrad and tapped, "All right! All right!"

And once back before the spot, he lunged with a sudden and wild joy; he slashed savagely; he yelled. "Take that! And that, P . . ." and the rest was lost in a mindless shout.

He did not stop cutting, and he might have gone on and on until he had quite excised the spot had not Polyphema interfered by dragging him toward her stomach-iris again. For ten seconds he hung there, helpless and sobbing with a mixture of fear and glory.

Polyphema's reflexes had almost overcome her brain. Fortunately, a cold spark of reason lit up a corner of the vast, dark, and hot chapel of her frenzy.

The convolutions leading to the steaming, meat-laden pouch closed and the foldings of flesh rearranged themselves. Eddie was suddenly hosed with warm water from what he called the "sanitation" stomach. The iris closed. He was put down. The scalpel was put back in the bag.

For a long time Mother seemed to be shaken by the thought of what she might have done to Eddie. She did not trust herself to transmit until her nerves were settled. When they were, she did not refer to his narrow escape. Nor did he.

He was happy. He felt as if a spring, tight-coiled against his bowels since he and his wife had parted, was now, for some reason, released. The dull vague pain of loss and discontent, the slight fever and cramp in his entrails, and the apathy that sometimes afflicted him, were gone. He felt fine.

Meanwhile, something akin to deep affection had been lighted, like a tiny candle under the drafty and overtowering roof of a cathedral. Mother's shell housed more than Eddie; it now curved over an emotion new to her kind. This was evident by the next event that filled him with terror.

For the wounds in the spot healed and the swelling increased into a large bag. Then the bag burst and ten mouse-sized Sluggos struck the floor. The impact had the same effect as a doctor spanking a newborn baby's bottom; they drew in their first breath with shock and pain; their uncontrolled and feeble pulses filled the ether with shapeless SOS's.

When Eddie was not talking with Polyphema or listening in or drinking or sleeping or eating or bathing or running off the tape, he played with the Sluggos. He was, in a sense, their father. Indeed, as they grew to hog-size, it was hard for their female parent to distinguish him from her young. As he seldom walked any more, and was often to be found on hands and knees in their midst, she could not scan him too well. Moreover, something in the heavywet air or in the diet had caused every hair on his body to drop off. He grew very fat. Generally speaking, he was one with the pale, soft, round, and bald offspring. A family likeness.

There was one difference. When the time came for the virgins to be expelled, Eddie crept to one end, whimpering, and stayed there until he was sure Mother was not going to thrust him out into the cold, dark, and hungry world.

The final crisis over, he came back to the center of the floor. The panic in his breast had died out, but his nerves were still quivering. He filled his Thermos and then listened for a while to his own tenor singing the "Sea Things" aria from his favorite opera, Gianelli's *Ancient Mariner*. Suddenly, he burst out and accompanied himself, finding himself thrilled as never before by the concluding words.

> *And from my neck so free*
> *The Albatross fell off, and sank*
> *Like lead into the sea.*

Afterward, voice silent but heart singing, he switched off the wire and cut in on Polyphema's broadcast.

Mother was having trouble. She could not precisely describe to the continent-wide hookup this new and almost inexpressible emotion she felt about the mobile. It was a concept her language was not prepared for. Nor was she helped any by the gallons of Old Red Star in her bloodstream.

Eddie sucked at the plastic nipple and nodded sympathetically and drowsily at her search for words. Presently, the Thermos rolled out of his hand.

He slept on his side, curled in a ball, knees on his chest and arms crossed, neck bent forward. Like the pilot room chronometer whose hands reversed after the crash, the clock of his body was ticking backward, ticking backward . . .

In the darkness, in the moistness, safe and warm, well fed, much loved.

Rudyard Kipling

Rudyard Kipling (1865–1936) is one of the major literary figures influencing the flowering of science fiction in the twentieth century. Kipling wrote two great SF stories, "With the Night Mail" and this one, a sequel set in the same imagined future. With them he became one of the progenitors of the genre. H. G. Wells was the great imaginative force behind Scientific Romance from 1895 to at least the 1920s, but Rudyard Kipling was the most popular English language writer of his day, and it was not Wellsian but Kiplingesque storytelling and attitudes—and politics—that dominated American science fiction in the 1940s and '50s. While Robert A. Heinlein certainly borrowed techniques liberally from the fiction of H. G. Wells, the effect of his classic stories is markedly Kiplingesque. Poul Anderson and Gordon R. Dickson, to name only two others among many, also acknowledge a debt to Kipling.

Even though he wrote very little actual science fiction, fantastic elements abound in Kipling's fiction. The recent (1992) publication of a volume of *The Science Fiction of Rudyard Kipling*, laden with encomiums from such diverse SF writers as Jerry Pournelle, Gene Wolfe, and John Brunner, only confirms his enduring appeal and influence.

In his introduction to that volume John Brunner points out that Kipling uses the historic present tense, in his day an unusual usage in English, which became part of the arsenal of SF writers. He also points out, in his introduction to "As Easy as ABC," the crucial fact that Kipling was, politically, the ancestor of what we today call Libertarians. Brunner quotes Kipling's 1923 speech at St. Andrews to this effect: "At any price I can pay, let me own myself. And the price is worth paying if you keep what you have bought."

"As Easy as ABC" is if anything a companion piece to Forster's "The Machine Stops," a criticism of the Wellsian urban utopia, but with an attitude that leads toward, not away from, genre science fiction.

AS EASY AS ABC

The ABC, that semi-elected, semi-nominated body of a few score persons, controls the Planet. Transportation is Civilization, our motto runs. Theoretically we do what we please, so long as we do not interfere with the traffic and all it implies. Practically, the ABC confirms or annuals all international arrangements, and, to judge from its last report, finds our tolerant, humorous, lazy little Planet only too ready to shift the whole burden of public administration on its shoulders.

"With the Night Mail," *Actions and Reactions*

Isn't it almost time that our Planet took some interest in the proceedings of the Aerial Board of Control? One knows that easy communications nowadays, and lack of privacy in the past, have killed all curiosity among mankind, but as the Board's Official Reporter I am bound to tell my tale.

At 9:30 A.M., 26 August, A.D. 2065, the Board, sitting in London, was informed by De Forest that the District of Northern Illinois had riotously cut itself out of all systems and would remain disconnected till the Board should take over and administer it direct.

Every Northern Illinois freight and passenger tower was, he reported, out of action; all District main, local, and guiding lights had been extinguished; all General Communications were dumb, and through traffic had been diverted. No reason had been given, but he gathered unofficially from the Mayor of Chicago that the District complained of "crowd-making and invasion of privacy."

As a matter of fact, it is of no importance whether Northern Illinois stay in or out of planetary circuit; as a matter of policy, any complaint of invasion of privacy needs immediate investigation, lest worse follow.

By 9:45 A.M. De Forest, Dragomiroff (Russia), Takahira (Japan), and Pirolo (Italy) were empowered to visit Illinois and "to take such steps as might be necessary for the resumption of traffic and *all that that implies.*" By 10 A.M. the Hall was empty, and the four Members and I were aboard what Pirolo insisted on calling "my leetle godchild"—that is to say, the new *Victor Pirolo.* Our Planet prefers to know Victor Pirolo as a gentle, grey-haired enthusiast who spends his time near Foggia, inventing or creating new breeds of Spanish-Italian olive-trees; but there is another side to his nature—the manufacture of quaint inventions, of which the *Victor Pirolo* is, perhaps, not the least surprising. She and a few score sister-craft of the same type embody his latest ideas. But she is not comfortable. An ABC boat does not take the air with the level-keeled lift of a liner, but shoots up rocket-fashion like the "aeroplane" of our ancestors, and makes her height at top-speed from the first. That is why I found myself sitting suddenly on the large lap of Eustace Arnott, who commands the ABC Fleet. One knows vaguely that there is such a thing as a Fleet somewhere on the planet, and that, theoretically, it exists for the purposes of what used to be known as "war." Only a week before, while visiting a glacier sanatorium behind Gothaven, I had seen some squadrons making false auroras far to the north while they maneuvered round the Pole; but, naturally, it had never occurred to me that the things could be used in earnest.

Said Arnott to De Forest as I staggered to a seat on the chart-room divan: "We're tremendously grateful to 'em in Illinois. We've never had a chance of exercising all the Fleet together. I've turned in a General Call, and I expect we'll have at least two hundred keels aloft this evening."

"Well aloft?" De Forest asked.

"Of course, sir. Out of sight till they're called for."

Arnott laughed as he lolled over the transparent chart-table where the map of the summer-blue Atlantic slid along, degree by degree, in exact answer to our progress. Our dial already showed 320 m.p.h. and we were two thousand feet above the uppermost traffic lines.

"Now, where is this Illinois District of yours?" said Dragomiroff. "One travels so much, one sees so little. Oh, I remember! It is in North America."

De Forest, whose business it is to know the out districts, told us that it lay at the foot of Lake Michigan, on a road to nowhere in particular, was about half an hour's run from end to end, and, except in one corner, as flat as the sea. Like most flat countries nowadays, it was heavily guarded against invasion of privacy by forced timber—fifty-foot spruce and tamarack, grown in five years. The population was close on two millions, largely migratory between Florida and California, with a backbone of small farms (they call a thousand acres a farm in Illinois) whose owners come into Chicago for amusements and society during the winter. They were, he said, noticeably kind, quiet folk, but a little exacting, as all flat countries must be, in their notions of privacy. There had, for instance, been no printed news-sheet in Illinois for twenty-seven years. Chicago argued that engines for printed news sooner or later developed into engines for invasion of privacy, which in turn might bring the old terror of Crowds and blackmail back to the Planet. So news-sheets were not.

"And that's Illinois," De Forest concluded. "You see, in the Old Days, she was in the forefront of what they used to call 'progress,' and Chicago—"

"Chicago?" said Takahira. "That's the little place where there is Salati's Statue of the Negro in Flames? A fine bit of old work."

"When did you see it?" asked De Forest quickly. "They only unveil it once a year."

"I know. At Thanksgiving. It was then," said Takahira, with a shudder. "And they sang MacDonough's Song, too."

"Whew!" De Forest whistled. "I did not know that! I wish you'd told me before. MacDonough's Song may have had its uses when it was composed, but it was an infernal legacy for any man to leave behind."

"It's protective instinct, my dear fellows," said Pirolo, rolling a cigarette. "The Planet, she has had her dose of popular government. She suffers from inherited agoraphobia. She has no—ah—use for crowds."

Dragomiroff leaned forward to give him a light. "Certainly," said the white-bearded Russian, "the Planet has taken all precautions against crowds for the past hundred years. What is our total population today? Six hundred million, we hope; five hundred, we think; but—but if next year's census shows more than four hundred and fifty, I myself will eat all the extra little babies. We have cut the birth-rate out—right out! For a long time we have said to Almighty God, 'Thank You, Sir, but we do not much like Your game of life, so we will not play.'"

"Anyhow," said Arnott defiantly, "men live a century apiece on the average now."

"Oh, that is quite well! I am rich—you are rich—we are all rich and happy because we are so few and we live so long. Only I think Almighty God He will remember what the Planet was like in the time of Crowds and the Plague. Perhaps He will send us nerves. Eh, Pirolo?"

The Italian blinked into space. "Perhaps," he said, "He has sent them already. Anyhow, you cannot argue with the Planet. She does not forget the Old Days, and—what can you do?"

"For sure we can't remake the world." De Forest glanced at the map flowing smoothly across the table from west to east. "We ought to be over our ground by nine tonight. There won't be much sleep afterwards."

On which hint we dispersed, and I slept till Takahira waked me for dinner. Our ancestors thought nine hours' sleep ample for their little lives. We, living thirty years longer, feel ourselves defrauded with less than eleven out of the twenty-four.

By ten o'clock we were over Lake Michigan. The west shore was lightless, except for a dull ground-glare at Chicago, and a single traffic-directing light— its leading beam pointing north—at Waukegan on our starboard bow. None of the Lake villages gave any sign of life; and inland, westward, so far as we could see, blackness lay unbroken on the level earth. We swooped down and skimmed low across the dark, throwing calls county by county. Now and again we picked up the faint glimmer of a house-light, or heard the rasp and rend of a cultivator being played across the fields, but Northern Illinois as a whole was one inky, apparently uninhabited, waste of high, forced woods. Only our illuminated map, with its little pointer switching from county to county, as we wheeled and twisted, gave us any idea of our position. Our calls, urgent, pleading, coaxing or commanding, through the General Communicator brought no answer. Illinois strictly maintained her own privacy in the timber which she grew for that purpose.

"Oh, this is absurd!" said De Forest. "We're like an owl trying to work a wheat-field. Is this Bureau Creek? Let's land, Arnott, and get hold of some one."

We brushed over a belt of forced woodland—fifteen-year-old maple sixty feet high—grounded on a private meadow-dock, none too big, where we moored to our own grapnels, and hurried out through the warm dark night towards a light in a verandah. As we neared the garden gate I could have sworn we had stepped knee-deep in quicksand, for we could scarcely drag our feet against the prickling currents that clogged them. After five paces we stopped, wiping our foreheads, as hopelessly stuck on dry smooth turf as so many cows in a bog.

"Pest!" cried Pirolo angrily. "We are ground-circuited. And it is my own system of ground-circuits too! I know the pull."

"Good evening," said a girl's voice from the verandah. "Oh, I'm sorry! We've locked up. Wait a minute."

We heard the click of a switch, and almost fell forward as the currents round our knees were withdrawn.

The girl laughed, and laid aside her knitting. An old-fashioned Controller stood at her elbow, which she reversed from time to time, and we could hear the snort and clank of the obedient cultivator half a mile away, behind the guardian woods.

"Come in and sit down," she said. "I'm only playing a plough. Dad's gone to Chicago to—Ah! Then it was *your* call I heard just now!"

She had caught sight of Arnott's Board uniform, leaped to the switch, and turned it full on.

We were checked, gasping, waist-deep in current this time, three yards from the verandah.

"We only want to know what's the matter with Illinois," said De Forest placidly.

"Then hadn't you better go to Chicago and find out?" she answered. "There's nothing wrong here. We own ourselves."

"How can we go anywhere if you won't loose us?" De Forest went on, while Arnott scowled. Admirals of Fleets are still quite human when their dignity is touched.

"Stop a minute—you don't know how funny you look!" She put her hands on her hips and laughed mercilessly.

"Don't worry about that," said Arnott, and whistled. A voice answered from the *Victor Pirolo* in the meadow.

"Only a single-fuse ground-circuit!" Arnott called. "Sort it out gently, please."

We heard the ping of a breaking lamp; a fuse blew out somewhere in the verandah roof, frightening a nest full of birds. The ground-circuit was open. We stooped and rubbed our tingling ankles.

"How rude—how very rude of you!" the maiden cried.

"Sorry, but we haven't time to look funny," said Arnott. "We've got to go to Chicago; and if I were you, young lady, I'd go into the cellars for the next two hours, and take mother with me."

Off he strode, with us at his heels, muttering indignantly, till the humour of the thing struck and doubled him up with laughter at the foot of the gangway ladder.

"The Board hasn't shown what you might call a fat spark on this occasion," said De Forest, wiping his eyes. "I hope I didn't look as big a fool as you did, Arnott! Hullo! What on earth is that? Dad coming home from Chicago?"

There was a rattle and a rush, and a five-plough cultivator, blades in air like so many teeth, trundled itself at us round the edge of the timber, fuming and sparking furiously.

"Jump!" said Arnott, as we bundled ourselves through the none-too-wide door. "Never mind about shutting it. Up!"

The *Victor Pirolo* lifted like a bubble, and the vicious machine shot just underneath us, clawing high as it passed.

"There's a nice little spit-kitten for you!" said Arnott, dusting his knees. "We ask her a civil question. First she circuits us and then she plays a cultivator at us!"

"And then we fly," said Dragomiroff. "If I were forty years more young, I would go back and kiss her. Ho! Ho!"

"I," said Pirolo, "would smack her! My pet ship has been chased by a dirty plough; a—how do you say?—agricultural implement."

"Oh, that is Illinois all over," said De Forest. "They don't content themselves with talking about privacy. They arrange to have it. And now, where's your alleged fleet, Arnott? We must assert ourselves against this wench."

Arnott pointed to the black heavens.

"Waiting on—up there," said he. "Shall I give them the whole installation, sir?"

"Oh, I don't think the young lady is quite worth that," said De Forest. "Get over Chicago, and perhaps we'll see something."

In a few minutes we were hanging at two thousand feet over an oblong block of incandescence in the centre of the little town.

"That looks like the old City Hall. Yes, there's Salati's Statue in front of it," said Takahira. "But what on earth are they doing to the place? I thought they used it for a market nowadays! Drop a little, please."

We could hear the sputter and crackle of road-surfacing machines—the cheap Western type which fuse stone and rubbish into lava-like ribbed glass for their rough country roads. Three or four surfacers worked on each side of a square of ruins. The brick and stone wreckage crumbled, slid forward, and presently spread out into white-hot pools of sticky slag, which the levelling-rods smoothed more or less flat. Already a third of the big block had been so treated, and was cooling to dull red before our astonished eyes.

"It is the Old Market," said De Forest. "Well, there's nothing to prevent Illinois from making a road through a market. It doesn't interfere with traffic, that I can see."

"Hsh!" said Arnott, gripping me by the shoulder. "Listen! They're singing. Why on the earth are they singing?"

We dropped again till we could see the black fringe of people at the edge of that glowing square.

At first they only roared against the roar of the surfacers and levellers. Then the words came up clearly—the words of the Forbidden Song that all men knew, and none let pass their lips—poor Pat MacDonough's Song, made in the days of the Crowds and the Plague—every silly word of it loaded to sparking-point with the Planet's inherited memories of horror, panic, fear, and cruelty. And Chicago—innocent, contented little Chicago—was singing it aloud to the infernal tune that carried riot, pestilence and lunacy round our Planet a few generations ago!

> *Once there was The People—Terror gave it birth;*
> *Once there was The People, and it made a hell of earth!*

(Then the stamp and pause):

> *Earth arose and crushed it. Listen, oh, ye slain!*
> *Once there was The People—it shall never be again!*

The levellers thrust in savagely against the ruins as the song renewed itself again, again and again, louder than the crash of the melting walls.

De Forest frowned.

"I don't like that," he said. "They've broken back to the Old Days! They'll be killing somebody soon. I think we'd better divert 'em, Arnott."

"Ay, ay, sir." Arnott's hand went to his cap, and we heard the hull of the *Victor Pirolo* ring to the command: "Lamps! Both watches stand by! Lamps! Lamps! Lamps!"

"Keep still!" Takahira whispered to me. "Blinkers, please, quartermaster."

"It's all right—all right!" said Pirolo from behind, and to my horror slipped over my head some sort of rubber helmet that locked with a snap. I could feel thick colloid bosses before my eyes, but I stood in absolute darkness.

"To save the sight," he explained, and pushed me on to the chart-room divan. "You will see in a minute."

As he spoke I became aware of a thin thread of almost intolerable light, let down from heaven at an immense distance—one vertical hairsbreadth of frozen lightning.

"Those are our flanking ships," said Arnott at my elbow. "That one is over Galena. Look south—that other one's over Keithburg. Vincennes is behind us, and north yonder is Winthrop Woods. The Fleet's in position, sir"—this to De Forest. "As soon as you give the word."

"Ah no! No!" cried Dragomiroff at my side. I could feel the old man tremble. "I do not know all that you can do, but be kind! I ask you to be a little kind to them below! This is horrible—horrible!"

> *When a Woman kills a Chicken,*
> *Dynasties and Empires sicken,*

Takahira quoted. "It is too late to be gentle now."

"Then take off my helmet! Take off my helmet!" Dragomiroff began hysterically.

Pirolo must have put his arm round him.

"Hush," he said, "I am here. It is all right, Ivan, my dear fellow."

"I'll just send our little girl in Bureau County a warning," said Arnott. "She don't deserve it, but we'll allow her a minute or two to take mamma to the cellar."

In the utter hush that followed the growling spark after Arnott had linked up his Service Communicator with the invisible Fleet, we heard MacDonough's Song from the city beneath us grow fainter as we rose to position. Then I clapped my hand before my mask lenses for it was as though the floor of Heaven had been riddled and all the inconceivable blaze of suns in the making was poured through the manholes.

"You needn't count," said Arnott. I had had no thought of such a thing. "There are two hundred and fifty keels up there, five miles apart. Full power, please, for another twelve seconds."

The firmament, as far as eye could reach, stood on pillars of white fire. One fell on the glowing square at Chicago, and turned it black.

"Oh! Oh! Oh! Can men be allowed to do such things?" Dragomiroff cried, and fell across our knees.

"Glass of water, please," said Takahira to a helmeted shape that leaped forward. "He is a little faint."

The lights switched off, and the darkness stunned like an avalanche. We could hear Dragomiroff's teeth on the glass edge.

Pirolo was comforting him.

"All right, allra-ight," he repeated. "Come and lie down. Come below and take off your mask. I give you my word, old friend, it is all right. They are my siege-lights. Little Victor Pirolo's leetle lights. You know *me!* I do not hurt people."

"Pardon!" Dragomiroff moaned. "I have never seen Death. I have never seen the Board take action. Shall we go down and burn them alive, or is that already done?"

"Oh, hush," said Pirolo, and I think he rocked him in his arms.

"Do we repeat, sir?" Arnott asked De Forest.

"Give 'em a minute's break," De Forest replied. "They may need it."

We waited a minute, and then MacDonough's Song, broken but defiant, rose from undefeated Chicago.

"They seem fond of that tune," said De Forest. "I should let 'em have it, Arnott."

"Very good, sir," said Arnott, and felt his way to the Communicator keys.

No lights broke forth, but the hollow of the skies made herself the mouth for one note that touched the raw fibre of the brain. Men hear such sounds in delirium, advancing like tides from horizons beyond the ruled foreshores of space.

"That's our pitch-pipe," said Arnott. "We may be a bit ragged. I've never conducted two hundred and fifty performers before." He pulled out the couplers, and struck a full chord on the Service Communicators.

The beams of light leaped down again, and danced, solemnly and awfully, a stilt-dance, sweeping thirty or forty miles left and right at each stiff-legged kick, while the darkness delivered itself—there is no scale to measure against that utterance—of the tune to which they kept time. Certain notes—one learnt to expect them with terror—cut through one's marrow, but, after three minutes, thought and emotion passed in indescribable agony.

We saw, we heard, but I think we were in some sort swooning. The two hundred and fifty beams shifted, re-formed, straddled and split, narrowed, widened, rippled in ribbons, broke into a thousand white-hot parallel lines, melted and revolved in interwoven rings like old-fashioned engine-turning, flung up to the zenith, made as if to descend and renew the torment, halted at the last instant, twizzled insanely round the horizon, and vanished, to bring back for the hundredth time darkness more shattering than their instantly renewed light over all Illinois. Then the tune and lights ceased together, and we heard one single devastating wail that shook all the horizon as a rubbed wet finger shakes the rim of a bowl.

"Ah, that is my new siren," said Pirolo. "You can break an iceberg in half, if you find the proper pitch. They will whistle by squadrons now. It is the wind through pierced shutters in the bows."

I had collapsed beside Dragomiroff, broken and snivelling feebly, because I had been delivered before my time to all the terrors of Judgement Day, and the Archangels of the Resurrection were hailing me naked across the Universe to the sound of the music of the spheres.

Then I saw De Forest smacking Arnott's helmet with his open hand. The wailing died down in a long shriek as a black shadow swooped past us, and returned to her place above the lower clouds.

"I hate to interrupt a specialist when he's enjoying himself," said De Forest. "But, as a matter of fact, all Illinois has been asking us to stop for these last fifteen seconds."

"What a pity." Arnott slipped off his mask. "I wanted you to hear us really hum. Our lower C can lift street-paving."

"It is Hell—Hell!" cried Dragomiroff, and sobbed aloud.

Arnott looked away as he answered:

"It's a few thousand volts ahead of the old shoot-'em-and-sink-'em game, but I should scarcely call it *that*. What shall I tell the Fleet, sir?"

"Tell 'em we're very pleased and impressed. I don't think they need wait on any longer. There isn't a spark left down there." De Forest pointed. "They'll be deaf and blind."

"Oh, I think not, sir. The demonstration lasted less than ten minutes."

"Marvellous!" Takahira sighed. "I should have said it was half a night. Now, shall we go down and pick up the pieces?"

"But first a small drink," said Pirolo. "The Board must not arrive weeping at its own works."

"I am an old fool—an old fool!" Dragomiroff began piteously. "I did not know what would happen. It is all new to me. We reason with them in Little Russia."

Chicago North landing-tower was unlighted, and Arnott worked his ship into the clips by her own lights. As soon as these broke out we heard groanings of horror and appeal from many people below.

"All right," shouted Arnott into the darkness. "We aren't beginning again!" We descended by the stairs, to find ourselves knee-deep in a grovelling crowd, some crying that they were blind, others beseeching us not to make anymore noises, but the greater part writhing face downward, their hands or their caps before their eyes.

It was Pirolo who came to our rescue. He climbed the side of a surfacing-machine, and there, gesticulating as though they could see, made oration to those afflicted people of Illinois.

"You stchewpids!" he began. "There is nothing to fuss for. Of course, your eyes will smart and be red tomorrow. You will look as if you and your wives had drunk too much, but in a little while you will see again as well as before. I tell you this, and I—I am Pirolo. Victor Pirolo!"

The crowd with one accord shuddered, for many legends attach to Victor Pirolo of Foggia, deep in the secrets of God.

"Pirolo?" An unsteady voice lifted itself. "Then tell us was there anything except light in those lights of yours just now?"

The question was repeated from every corner of the darkness.

Pirolo laughed.

"No!" he thundered. (Why have small men such large voices?) "I give you my word and the Board's word that there was nothing except light—just light! You stchewpids! Your birth rate is too low already as it is. Some day I must invent something to send it up, but send it down—never!"

"Is that true?—We thought—somebody said—"

One could feel the tension relax all round.

"You *too* big fools," Pirolo cried. "You could have sent us a call and we would have told you."

"Send you a call!" a deep voice shouted. "I wish you had been at our end of the wire."

"I'm glad I wasn't," said De Forest. "It was bad enough from behind the lamps. Never mind! It's over now. Is there any one here I can talk business with? I'm De Forest—for the Board."

"You might begin with me, for one—I'm Mayor," the bass voice replied.

A big man rose unsteadily from the street, and staggered towards us where we sat on the broad turf-edging, in front of the garden fences.

"I ought to be the first on my feet. Am I?" said he.

"Yes," said De Forest, and steadied him as he dropped down beside us.

"Hello, Andy. Is that you?" a voice called.

"Excuse me," said the Mayor; "that sounds like my Chief of Police, Bluthner!"

"Bluthner it is; and here's Mulligan and Keefe—on their feet."

"Bring 'em up please, Blut. We're supposed to be the Four in charge of this hamlet. What we says, goes. And, De Forest, what do you say?"

"Nothing—yet," De Forest answered, as we made room for the panting, reeling men. "You've cut out of system. Well?"

"Tell the steward to send down drinks, please," Arnott whispered to an orderly at his side.

"Good!" said the Mayor, smacking his dry lips. "Now I suppose we can take it, De Forest, that henceforward the Board will administer us direct?"

"Not if the Board can avoid it," De Forest laughed. "The ABC is responsible for the planetary traffic only."

"*And all that that implies.*" The big Four who ran Chicago chanted their Magna Charta like children at school.

"Well, get on," said De Forest wearily. "What is your silly trouble anyway?"

"Too much dam' Democracy," said the Mayor, laying his hand on De Forest's knee.

"So? I thought Illinois had had her dose of that."

"She has. That's why. Blut, what did you do with our prisoners last night?"

"Locked 'em in the water-tower to prevent the women killing 'em," the Chief of Police replied. "I'm too blind to move just yet, but—"

"Arnott, send some of your people, please, and fetch 'em along," said De Forest.

"They're triple-circuited," the Mayor called. "You'll have to blow out three fuses." He turned to De Forest, his large outline just visible in the paling darkness. "I hate to throw any more work on the Board. I'm an administrator myself, but we've had a little fuss with our Serviles. What? In a big city there's bound to be a few men and women who can't live without listening to themselves, and who prefer drinking out of pipes they don't own both ends of. They inhabit flats and hotels all the year round. They say it saves 'em trouble. Anyway, it gives 'em more time to make trouble for their neighbours. We call 'em Serviles locally. And they are apt to be tuberculous."

"Just so!" said the man called Mulligan. "Transportation is Civilization. Democracy is Disease. I've proved it by the blood-test, every time."

"Mulligan's our Health Officer, and a one-idea man," said the Mayor, laughing. "But it's true that most Serviles haven't much control. They *will* talk; and when people take to talking as a business, anything may arrive—mayn't it, De Forest?"

"Anything—except the facts of the case," said De Forest, laughing.

"I'll give you those in a minute," said the Mayor. "Our Serviles got to talking—first in their houses and then on the streets, telling men and women how to manage their own affairs. (You can't teach a Servile not to finger his neighbour's soul.) That's invasion of privacy, of course, but in Chicago we'll suffer anything sooner than make crowds. Nobody took much notice, and so I let 'em alone. My fault! I was warned there would be trouble, but there hasn't been a crowd or murder in Illinois for nineteen years."

"Twenty-two," said his Chief of Police.

"Likely. Anyway, we'd forgot such things. So, from talking in the houses and on the streets, our Serviles go to calling a meeting at the Old Market yonder." He nodded across the square where the wrecked buildings heaved up grey in the dawn-glimmer behind the square-cased statue of The Negro in Flames. "There's nothing to prevent any one calling meetings except that it's against human nature to stand in a crowd, besides being bad for the health. I ought to have known by the way our men and women attended that first meeting that trouble was brewing. There were as many as a thousand in the market-place, touching each other. Touching! Then the Serviles turned in all tongue-switches and talked, and we—"

"What did they talk about?" said Takahira.

"First, how badly things were managed in the city. That pleased us Four—we were on the platform—because we hoped to catch one or two good men for City work. You know how rare executive capacity is. Even if we didn't it's—it's refreshing to find any one interested enough in our job to damn our eyes. You don't know what it means to work, year in, year out, without a spark of difference with a living soul."

"Oh, don't we!" said De Forest. "There are times on the Board when we'd give our positions if any one would kick us out and take hold of things themselves."

"But they won't," said the Mayor ruefully. "I assure you, sir, we Four have done things in Chicago, in the hope of rousing people, that would have discredited Nero. But what do they say? 'Very good, Andy. Have it your own way. Anything's better than a crowd. I'll go back to my land.' You *can't* do anything with folk who can go where they please, and don't want anything on God's earth except their own way. There isn't a kick or a kicker left on the Planet."

"Then I suppose that little shed yonder fell down by itself?" said De Forest. We could see the bare and still smoking ruins, and hear the slag-pools crackle as they hardened and set.

"Oh, that's only amusement. Tell you later. As I was saying, our Serviles held the meeting, and pretty soon we had to ground-circuit the platform to save 'em from being killed. And that didn't make our people any more pacific."

"How d'you mean?" I ventured to ask.

"If you've ever been ground-circuited," said the Mayor, "you'll know it don't improve any man's temper to be held up straining against nothing. No, sir! Eight or nine hundred folk kept pawing and buzzing like flies in treacle for two hours, while a pack of perfectly safe Serviles invades their mental and spiritual privacy, may be amusing to watch, but they are not pleasant to handle afterwards."

Pirolo chuckled.

"Our folk own themselves. They were of opinion things were going too far and too fiery. I warned the Serviles; but they're born house-dwellers. Unless a fact hits 'em on the head, they cannot see it. Would you believe me, they went on to talk of what they called 'popular government'? They did! They wanted us to go back to the old Voodoo-business of voting with papers and wooden boxes, and word-drunk people and printed formulas, and news-sheets! They said they practised it among themselves about what they'd have to eat in their flats and hotels. Yes, sir! They stood up behind Bluthner's doubled ground-circuits, and they said that, in this present year of grace, *to* self-owning men and women, *on* that very spot! Then they finished"—he lowered his voice cautiously—"by talking about 'The People.' And then Bluthner he had to sit up all night in charge of the circuits because he couldn't trust his men to keep 'em shut."

"It was trying 'em too high," the Chief of Police broke in. "But we couldn't hold the crowd ground-circuited for ever. I gathered in all the Serviles on charge of crowd-making, and put 'em in the water-tower, and then I let things cut loose. I had to! The District lit like a sparked gas-tank!"

"The news was out over seven degrees of country," the Mayor continued; "and when once it's a question of invasion of privacy, goodbye to right and reason in Illinois! They began turning out traffic-lights and locking up landing-towers on Thursday night. Friday, they stopped all traffic and asked for the Board to take over. Then they wanted to clean Chicago off the side of the Lake and rebuild elsewhere—just for a souvenir of 'The People' that the Serviles talked about. I suggested that they should slag the Old Market where the meeting was held, while I turned in a call to you all on the Board. That kept 'em quiet till you came along. And—and now *you* can take hold of the situation."

"Any chance of their quieting down?" De Forest asked.

"You can try," said the Mayor.

De Forest raised his voice in the face of the reviving crowd that had edged in towards us. Day was come.

"Don't you think this business can be arranged?" he began. But there was a roar of angry voices:

"We've finished with Crowds! We aren't going back to the Old Days! Take us over! Take the Serviles away! Administer direct or we'll kill 'em! Down with The People!"

An attempt was made to begin MacDonough's Song. It got no further than the first line, for the *Victor Pirolo* sent down a warning drone on one stopped horn. A wrecked side-wall of the Old Market tottered and fell inwards on the slag-pools. None spoke or moved till the last of the dust had settled down again, turning the steel case of Salati's Statue ashy grey.

"You see you'll just *have* to take us over," the Mayor whispered.

De Forest shrugged his shoulders.

"You talk as if executive capacity could be snatched out of the air like so much horse-power. Can't you manage yourselves on any terms?" he said.

"We can, if you say so. It will only cost those few lives to begin with."

The Mayor pointed across the square, where Arnott's men guided a stumbling group of ten or twelve men and women to the lake front and halted them under the Statue.

"Now I think," said Takahira under his breath, "there will be trouble."

The mass in front of us growled like beasts.

At that moment the sun rose clear, and revealed the blinking assembly to itself. As soon as it realized that it was a crowd we saw the shiver of horror and mutual repulsion shoot across it precisely as the steely flaws shot across the lake outside. Nothing was said, and, being half blind, of course it moved slowly. Yet in less than fifteen minutes most of that vast multitude—three thousand at the lowest count—melted away like frost on south eaves. The remnant stretched themselves on the grass, where a crowd feels and looks less like a crowd.

"These mean business," the Mayor whispered to Takahira. "There are a good-ish few women there who've borne children. I don't like it."

The morning draught off the lake stirred the trees round us with promise of a hot day; the sun reflected itself dazzlingly on the canister-shaped covering of Salati's Statue; cocks crew in the gardens, and we could hear gate-latches clicking in the distance as people stumblingly resought their homes.

"I'm afraid there won't be any morning deliveries," said De Forest. "We rather upset things in the country last night."

"That makes no odds," the Mayor returned. "We're all provisioned for six months. We take no chances."

Nor, when you come to think of it, does any one else. It must be three-quarters of a generation since any house or city faced a food shortage. Yet is there house or city on the Planet today that has not half a year's provisions laid in? We are like the shipwrecked seamen in the old books, who, having once nearly starved to death, ever afterwards hide away bits of food and biscuit. Truly we trust no Crowds, nor system based on Crowds!

De Forest waited till the last footstep had died away. Meantime the prisoners at the base of the Statue shuffled, posed, and fidgeted, with the shamelessness of quite little children. None of them were more than six feet high, and many of them were as grey-haired as the ravaged, harassed heads of old pictures. They huddled together in actual touch, while the crowd, spaced at large intervals, looked at them with congested eyes.

Suddenly a man among them began to talk. The Mayor had not in the least exaggerated. It appeared that our Planet lay sunk in slavery beneath the heel of the Aerial Board of Control. The orator urged us to arise in our might, burst our prison doors and break our fetters (all his metaphors, by the way, were of the most medieval). Next he demanded that every matter of daily life, including most of the physical functions, should be submitted for decision at any time of the week, month, or year to, I gathered, anybody who happened to be passing by or residing within a certain radius, and that everybody should forthwith abandon his concerns to settle the matter, first by crowd-making, next by talking to the crowds made, and lastly by describing crosses on pieces of paper, which rubbish should later be counted with certain mystic ceremonies and oaths. Out of this amazing play, he assured us, would automatically arise a higher, nobler, and kinder world, based—he demonstrated this with the awful lucidity of the insane—based on the sanctity of the Crowd and the villainy of the single person. In conclusion, he called loudly upon God to testify to his personal merits and integrity. When the flow ceased, I turned bewildered to Takahira, who was nodding solemnly.

"Quite correct," said he. "It is all in the old books. He has left nothing out, not even the war-talk."

"But I don't see how this stuff can upset a child, much less a district," I replied.

"Ah, you are too young," said Dragomiroff. "For another thing, you are not a mamma. Please look at the mammas."

Ten or fifteen women who remained had separated themselves from the silent men, and were drawing in towards the prisoners. It reminded one of the stealthy encircling, before the rush in at the quarry, of wolves round musk-oxen in the North. The prisoners saw, and drew together more closely. The Mayor covered his face with his hands for an instant. De Forest, bareheaded, stepped forward between the prisoners and the slowly, stiffly moving line.

"That's all very interesting," he said to the dry-lipped orator. "But the point seems to be that you've been making crowds and invading privacy."

A woman stepped forward, and would have spoken, but there was a quick assenting murmur from the men, who realized that De Forest was trying to pull the situation down to ground-line.

"Yes! Yes!" they cried. "We cut out because they made crowds and invaded privacy! Stick to that! Keep on that switch! Lift the Serviles out of this! The Board's in charge! Hsh!"

"Yes, the Board's in charge," said De Forest. "I'll take formal evidence of crowd-making if you like, but the Members of the Board can testify to it. Will that do?"

The women had closed in another pace, with hands that clenched and unclenched at their sides.

"Good! Good enough!" the men cried. "We're content. Only take them away quickly."

"Come along up!" said De Forest to the captives. "Breakfast is quite ready."

It appeared, however, that they did not wish to go. They intended to remain in Chicago and make crowds. They pointed out that De Forest's proposal was gross invasion of privacy.

"My dear fellow," said Pirolo to the most voluble of the leaders, "you hurry, or your crowd that can't be wrong will kill you!"

"But that would be murder," answered the believer in crowds; and there was a roar of laughter from all sides that seemed to show the crisis had broken.

A woman stepped forward from the line of women, laughing, I protest, as merrily as any of the company. One hand, of course, shaded her eyes, the other was at her throat.

"Oh, they needn't be afraid of being killed!" she called.

"Not in the least," said De Forest. "But don't you think that, now the Board's in charge, you might go home while we get these people away?"

"I shall be home long before that. It—it has been rather a trying day."

She stood up to her full height, dwarfing even De Forest's six-foot-eight, and smiled, with eyes closed against the fierce light.

"Yes, rather," said De Forest. "I'm afraid you feel the glare a little. We'll have the ship down."

He motioned to the *Pirolo* to drop between us and the sun, and at the same time to loop-circuit the prisoners, who were a trifle unsteady. We saw them stiffen to the current where they stood. The woman's voice went on, sweet and deep and unshaken:

"I don't suppose you men realize how much this—this sort of thing means to a woman. I've borne three. We women don't want our children given to Crowds. It must be an inherited instinct. Crowds make trouble. They bring back the Old Days. Hate, fear, blackmail, publicity, 'The People'—*That! That! That!"* She pointed to the Statue, and the crowd growled once more.

"Yes, if they are allowed to go on," said De Forest. "But this little affair—"

"It means so much to us women that this—this little affair should never happen again. Of course, never's a big word, but one feels so strongly that it is important to stop crowds at the very beginning. Those creatures"—she pointed with her left hand at the prisoners swaying like seaweed in a tideway as the circuit pulled them—"those people have friends and wives and children in the city and elsewhere. One doesn't want anything done to *them*, you know. It's terrible to force a human being out of fifty or sixty years of good life. I'm only forty myself. I know. But, at the same time, one feels that an example should be made, because no price is too heavy to pay if—if these people and *all that they imply* can be put an end to. Do you quite understand, or would you be kind enough to tell your men to take the casing off the Statue? It's worth looking at."

"I understand perfectly. But I don't think anybody here wants to see the Statue on an empty stomach. Excuse me one moment." De Forest called up to the ship, "A flying loop ready on the port side, if you please." Then to the woman he said with some crispness, "You might leave us a little discretion in the matter."

"Oh, of course. Thank you for being so patient. I know my arguments are silly, but—" She half turned away and went on in a changed voice, "Perhaps this will help you to decide."

She threw out her right arm with a knife in it. Before the blade could be returned to her throat or her bosom it was twitched from her grip, sparked as it flew out of the shadow of the ship above, and fell flashing in the sunshine at the foot of the Statue fifty yards away. The outflung arm was arrested, rigid as a bar for an instant, till the releasing circuit permitted her to bring it slowly to her side. The other women shrank back silent among the men.

Pirolo rubbed his hands, and Takahira nodded.

"That was clever of you, De Forest," said he.

"What a glorious pose!" Dragomiroff murmured, for the frightened woman was on the edge of tears.

"Why did you stop me? I would have done it!" she cried.

"I have no doubt you would," said De Forest. "But we can't waste a life like yours on these people. I hope the arrest didn't sprain your wrist; it's so hard to regulate a flying loop. But I think you are quite right about those persons' women and children. We'll take them all away with us if you promise not to do anything stupid to yourself."

"I promise—I promise." She controlled herself with an effort. "But it is so important to us women. We know what it means; and I thought if you saw I was in earnest—"

"I saw you were, and you've gained your point. I shall take all your Serviles away with me at once. The Mayor will make lists of their friends and families in the city and the district, and he'll ship them after us this afternoon."

"Sure," said the Mayor, rising to his feet. "Keefe, if you can see, hadn't you better finish levelling off the Old Market? It don't look sightly the way it is now, and we shan't use it for crowds anymore."

."I think you had better wipe out that Statue as well, Mr Mayor," said De Forest. "I don't question its merits as a work of art, but I believe it's a shade morbid."

"Certainly, sir. Oh, Keefe! Slag the Negro before you go on to fuse the Market. I'll get to the Communicators and tell the District that the Board is in charge. Are you making any special appointments, sir?"

"None. We haven't men to waste on these backwoods. Carry on as before, but under the Board. Arnott, run your Serviles aboard, please. Ground ship and pass them through the bilge-doors. We'll wait till we've finished with this work of art."

The prisoners trailed past him, talking fluently, but unable to gesticulate in the drag of the current. Then the surfacers rolled up, two on each side of the Statue. With one accord the spectators looked elsewhere, but there was no need. Keefe turned on full power, and the thing simply melted within its case. All I saw was a surge of white-hot metal pouring over the plinth, a glimpse of Salati's inscription, "To the Eternal Memory of the Justice of the People," ere the stone base itself cracked and powdered into finest lime. The crowd cheered.

"Thank you," said De Forest; "but we want our breakfasts, and I expect you do too. Goodbye, Mr Mayor! Delighted to see you at any time, but I hope I shan't have to, officially, for the next thirty years. Goodbye, madam. Yes. We're all given to nerves nowadays. I suffer from them myself. Goodbye, gentlemen all! You're under the tyrannous heel of the Board from this moment, but if ever you feel like breaking your fetters you've only to let us know. This is no treat to us. Good luck!"

We embarked amid shouts, and did not check our lift till they had dwindled into whispers. Then De Forest flung himself on the chartroom divan and mopped his forehead.

"I don't mind men," he panted, "but women are the devil!"

"Still the devil," said Pirolo cheerfully. "That one would have suicided."

"I know it. That was why I signalled for the flying loop to be clapped on her. I owe you an apology for that, Arnott. I hadn't time to catch your eye, and you were busy with our caitiffs. By the way, who actually answered my signal? It was a smart piece of work."

"Ilroy," said Arnott; "but he overloaded the wave. It may be pretty gallery-work to knock a knife out of a lady's hand, but didn't you notice how she rubbed 'em? He scorched her fingers. Slovenly, I call it."

"Far be it from me to interfere with Fleet discipline, but don't be too hard on the boy. If that woman had killed herself they would have killed every Servile and everything related to a Servile throughout the district by nightfall."

"That was what she was playing for," Takahira said. "And with our Fleet gone we could have done nothing to hold them."

"I may be ass enough to walk into a ground-circuit," said Arnott, "but I don't dismiss my Fleet till I'm reasonably sure that trouble is over. They're in position still, and I intend to keep 'em there till the Serviles are shipped out of the district. That last little crowd meant murder, my friends."

"Nerves! All nerves!" said Pirolo. "You cannot argue with agoraphobia."

"And it is not as if they had seen much dead—or *is* it?" said Takahira.

"In all my ninety years I have never seen death." Dragomiroff spoke as one who would excuse himself. "Perhaps that was why—last night—"

Then it came out as we sat over breakfast, that, with the exception of Arnott and Pirolo, none of us had ever seen a corpse, or knew in what manner the spirit passes.

"We're a nice lot to flap about governing the Planet," De Forest laughed. "I confess, now it's all over, that my main fear was I mightn't be able to pull it off without losing a life."

"I thought of that too," said Arnott; "but there's no death reported, and I've enquired everywhere. What are we supposed to do with our passengers? I've fed 'em."

"We're between two switches," De Forest drawled. "If we drop them in any place that isn't under the Board, the natives will make their presence an excuse for cutting out, same as Illinois did, and forcing the Board to take over. If we drop them in any place under the Board's control they'll be killed as soon as our backs are turned."

"If you say so," said Pirolo thoughtfully, "I can guarantee that they will become extinct in process of time, quite happily. What is their birth-rate now?"

"Go down and ask 'em," said De Forest.

"I think they might become nervous and tear me to bits," the philosopher of Foggia replied.

"Not really? Well?"

"Open the bilge-doors," said Takahira with a downward jerk of the thumb.

"Scarcely—after all the trouble we've taken to save 'em," said De Forest.

"Try London," Arnott suggested. "You could turn Satan himself loose there, and they'd only ask him to dinner."

"Good man! You've given me an idea. Vincent! Oh, Vincent!" He threw the General Communicator open so that we could all hear, and in a few minutes the chartroom filled with the rich, fruity voice of Leopold Vincent, who has purveyed all London her choicest amusements for the last thirty years. We answered with expectant grins, as though we were actually in the stalls of, say, the Combination on a first night.

"We've picked up something in your line," De Forest began.

"That's good, dear man. If it's old enough. There's nothing to beat the old things for business purposes. Have you seen *London, Chatham, and Dover* at Earl's Court? No? I thought I missed you there. Im-mense! I've had the real steam locomotive engines built from the old designs and the iron rails cast specially by hand. Cloth cushions in the carriages, too! Im-mense! And paper railway tickets. And Polly Milton."

"Polly Milton back again!" said Arnott rapturously. "Book me two stalls for tomorrow night. What's she singing now, bless her?"

"The old songs. Nothing comes up to the old touch. Listen to this, dear men." Vincent carolled with flourishes:

> *Oh, cruel lamps of London,*
> *If tears your light could drown,*
> *Your victims' eyes would weep them,*
> *Oh, lights of London Town!*

"Then they weep."

"You see?" Pirolo waved his hands at us. "The old world always weeped when it saw crowds together. It did not know why, but it weeped. We know why, but we do not weep, except when we pay to be made to by fat, wicked old Vincent."

"Old, yourself!" Vincent laughed. "I'm a public benefactor, I keep the world soft and united."

"And I'm De Forest of the Board," said De Forest acidly, "trying to get a little business done. As I was saying, I've picked up a few people in Chicago."

"I cut out. Chicago is—"

"Do listen! They're perfectly unique."

"Do they build houses of baked mudblocks while you wait—eh? That's an old contact."

"They're an untouched primitive community, with all the old ideas."

"Sewing-machines and maypole-dances? Cooking on coal-gas stoves, lighting pipes with matches, and driving horses? Gerolstein tried that last year. An absolute blow-out!"

De Forest plugged him wrathfully, and poured out the story of our doings for the last twenty-four hours on the top-note.

"And they do it *all* in public," he concluded. "You can't stop 'em. The more public, the better they are pleased. They'll talk for hours—like you! Now you can come in again!"

"Do you really mean they know how to vote?" said Vincent. "Can they act it?"

"Act? It's their life to 'em! And you never saw such faces! Scarred like volcanoes. Envy, hatred, and malice in plain sight. Wonderfully flexible voices. They weep, too."

"Aloud? In public?"

"I guarantee. Not a spark of shame or reticence in the entire installation. It's the chance of your career."

"D'you say you've brought their voting props along—those papers and ballot-box things?"

"No, confound you! I'm not a luggage-lifter. Apply direct to the Mayor of Chicago. He'll forward you everything. Well?"

"Wait a minute. Did Chicago want to kill 'em? That 'ud look well on the Communicators."

"Yes! They were only rescued with difficulty from a howling mob—if you know what that is."

"But I don't," answered the Great Vincent simply.

"Well then, they'll tell you themselves. They can make speeches hours long."

"How many are there?"

"By the time we ship 'em all over they'll be perhaps a hundred, counting children. An old world in miniature. Can't you see it?"

"M-yes; but I've got to pay for it if it's a blow-out, dear man."

"They can sing the old war songs in the streets. They can get word-drunk, and make crowds, and invade privacy in the genuine old-fashioned way; and they'll do the voting trick as often as you ask 'em a question."

"Too good!" said Vincent.

"You unbelieving Jew! I've got a dozen head aboard here. I'll put you through direct. Sample 'em yourself."

He lifted the switch and we listened. Our passengers on the lower deck at once, but not less than five at a time, explained themselves to Vincent. They had been taken from the bosom of their families, stripped of their possessions, given food without finger-bowls, and cast into captivity in a noisome dungeon.

"But look here," said Arnott aghast; "they're saying what isn't true. My lower deck isn't noisome, and I saw to the finger-bowls myself."

"My people talk like that sometimes in Little Russia," said Dragomiroff. "We reason with them. We never kill. No!"

"But it's not true," Arnott insisted. "What can you do with people who don't tell facts? They're mad!"

"Hsh!" said Pirolo, his hand to his ear. "It is such a little time since all the Planet told lies."

We heard Vincent silkily sympathetic. Would they, he asked, repeat their assertions in public—before a vast public? only let Vincent give them a chance, and the Planet, they vowed, should ring with their wrongs. Their aim in life— two women and a man explained it together—was to reform the world. Oddly enough, this also had been Vincent's life-dream. He offered them an arena in which to explain, and by their living example to raise the Planet to loftier levels. He was eloquent on the moral uplift of a simple, old-world life presented in its entirety to a deboshed civilization.

Could they—would they—for three months certain, devote themselves under his auspices, as missionaries, to the elevation of mankind at a place called Earl's Court, which he said, with some truth, was one of the intellectual centres of the Planet? They thanked him, and demanded (we could hear his chuckle of delight) time to discuss and to vote on the matter. The vote, solemnly managed by counting heads—one head, one vote—was favourable. His offer, therefore, was accepted, and they moved a vote of thanks to him in two speeches—one by what they called the "proposer" and the other by the "seconder."

Vincent threw over to us, his voice shaking with gratitude:

"I've got 'em! Did you hear those speeches? That's Nature, dear men. Art can't teach *that*. And they voted as easily as lying. I've never had a troupe of natural liars before. Bless you, dear men! Remember, you're on my free lists for ever, anywhere—all of you. Oh, Gerolstein will be sick—sick!"

"Then you think they'll do?" said De Forest.

"Do? The Little Village'll go crazy! I'll knock up a series of old-world plays for 'em. Their voices will make you laugh and cry. My God, dear men, where *do* you suppose they picked up all their misery from, on this sweet earth? I'll have a pageant of the world's beginnings, and Mosenthal shall do the music. I'll—"

"Go and knock up a village for 'em by tonight. We'll meet you at No. 15 West Landing Tower," said De Forest. "Remember the rest will be coming along tomorrow."

"Let 'em all come!" said Vincent. "You don't know how hard it is nowadays even for me, to find something that really gets under the public's damned iridium-plated hide. But I've got it at last. Goodbye!"

"Well," said De Forest when we had finished laughing, "if any one understood corruption in London I might have played off Vincent against Gerolstein, and sold my captives at enormous prices. As it is, I shall have to be their legal adviser tonight when the contracts are signed. And they won't exactly press any commission on me, either."

"Meantime," said Takahira, "we cannot, of course, confine members of Leopold Vincent's last-engaged company. Chairs for the ladies, please, Arnott."

"Then I go to bed," said De Forest. "I can't face any more women!" And he vanished.

When our passengers were released and given another meal (finger-bowls came first this time) they told us what they thought of us and the Board; and, like Vincent, we all marvelled how they had contrived to extract and secrete so much bitter poison and unrest out of the good life God gives us. They raged, they stormed, they palpitated, flushed and exhausted their poor, torn nerves, panted themselves into silence, and renewed the senseless, shameless attacks.

"But can't you understand," said Pirolo pathetically to a shrieking woman, "that if we'd left you in Chicago you'd have been killed?"

"No, we shouldn't. You were bound to save us from being murdered."

"Then we should have had to kill a lot of other people."

"That doesn't matter. We were preaching the Truth. You can't stop us. We shall go on preaching in London; and *then* you'll see!"

"You can see now," said Pirolo, and opened a lower shutter.

We were closing on the Little Village, with her three million people spread out at ease inside her ring of girdling Main-Traffic lights—those eight fixed beams at Chatham, Tonbridge, Redhill, Dorking, Woking, St Albans, Chipping Ongar, and Southend.

Leopold Vincent's new company looked, with small pale faces, at the silence, the size, and the separated houses.

Then some began to weep aloud, shamelessly—always without shame.

Michael Swanwick

Michael Swanwick (1950–   ) distinguished himself with a group of notable short stories in the early and mid-'80s. He has written both science fiction and fantasy, and, after reaching the height of his powers as a SF novelist in *Stations of the Tide* (1991), has turned increasingly toward fantasy in his two most recent novels, *The Iron Dragon's Daughter* (1993) and *Jack Faust* (1997).

"My father was an engineer . . . but I was lured away from engineering by science, and then lured away from science by literature," he says. *Science Fiction Writers* calls him "an author who produces thoughtful, speculative work in a complex, literary style without a strong, action-oriented plot." His early short fiction is collected in *Gravity's Angels* (1991).

Swanwick is also the author of two influential critical essays, one on science fiction, "User's Guide to the Postmoderns" (1985), and one on fantasy, "In The Tradition . . ." (1994). He remains one of the most significant genre writers of the '90s. "Ginungagap" was his first published story. It appeared in a special SF issue of the distinguished literary magazine *Triquarterly*. The title refers to the primordial chaos out of which the universe was born in Norse mythology.

GINUNGAGAP

Abigail checked out of Mother of Mercy and rode the translator web to Toledo Cylinder in Juno Industrial Park. Stars bloomed, dwindled, disappeared five times. It was a long trek, halfway around the sun.

Toledo was one of the older commercial cylinders, now given over almost entirely to bureaucrats, paper pushers, and free-lance professionals. It was not Abigail's favorite place to visit, but she needed work and 3M had already bought out of her contract.

The job broker had dyed his chest hairs blond and his leg hairs red. They clashed wildly with his green *cache-sexe* and turquoise jewelry. His fingers played on a keyout, bringing up an endless flow of career trivia. "Cute trick you played," he said.

Abigail flexed her new arm negligently. It was a good job, but pinker than the rest of her. And weak, of course, but exercise would correct that. "Thanks," she said. She laid the arm underneath one breast and compared the colors. It matched the nipple perfectly. Definitely too pink. "Work outlook any good?"

"Naw," the broker said. A hummingbird flew past his ear, a nearly undetectable parting of the air. "I see here that you applied for the Proxima colony."

"They were full up," Abigail said. "No openings for a gravity bum, hey?"

"I didn't say that," the broker grumbled. "I'll find—Hello! What's this?" Abigail craned her neck, couldn't get a clear look at the screen. "There's a tag on your employment record."

"What's that mean?"

"Let me read." A honeysuckle flower fell on Abigail's hair and she brushed it off impatiently. The broker had an open-air office, framed by hedges and roofed over with a trellis. Sometimes Abigail found the older Belt cylinders a little too lavish for her taste.

"Mmp." The broker looked up. "Bell-Sandia wants to hire you. Indefinite term one-shot contract." He swung the keyout around so she could see. "*Very* nice terms, but that's normal for a high risk contract."

"High risk? From B-S, the Friendly Communications People? What kind of risk?"

The broker scrolled up new material. "There." He tapped the screen with a finger. "The language is involved, but what it boils down to is they're looking for a test passenger for a device they've got that uses black holes for interstellar travel."

"Couldn't work," Abigail said. "The tidal forces—"

"Spare me. Presumably they've found a way around that problem. The question is, are you interested or not?"

Abigail stared up through the trellis at a stream meandering across the curved land overhead. Children were wading in it. She counted to a hundred very slowly, trying to look as if she needed to think it over.

Abigail strapped herself into the translation harness and nodded to the technician outside the chamber. The tech touched her console and a light stasis field immobilized Abigail and the air about her while the chamber wall irised open. In a fluid bit of technological sleight of hand, the translator rechanneled her inertia and gifted her with a velocity almost, but not quite, that of the speed of light.

Stars bloomed about her and the sun dwindled. She breathed in deeply and— was in the receiver device. Relativity had cheated her of all but a fraction of the transit time. She shrugged out of harness and frog-kicked her way to the lip station's tug dock.

The tug pilot grinned at her as she entered, then turned his attention to his controls. He was young and wore streaks of brown makeup across his chest and thighs—only slightly darker than his skin. His mesh vest was almost in bad taste, but he wore it well and looked roguish rather than overdressed. Abigail found herself wishing she had more than a *cache-sexe* and nail polish on—some jewelry or makeup, perhaps. She felt drab in comparison.

The star-field wraparound held two inserts routed in by synchronous cameras. Alphanumerics flickered beneath them. One showed her immediate destination, the Bell-Sandia base *Arthur C. Clarke*. It consisted of five wheels, each set inside the other and rotating at slightly differing speeds. The base was done up in red-and-orange supergraphics. Considering its distance from the Belt factories, it was respectably sized.

Abigail latched herself into the passenger seat as the engines cut in. The second insert—

Ginungagap, the only known black hole in the sun's gravity field, was discovered in 2023, a small voice murmured. *Its presence explained the long-puzzling variations in the orbits of the outer planets. The* Arthur C. Clarke *was . . .*

"Is this necessary?" Abigail asked.

"Absolutely," the pilot said. "We abandoned the tourist program a year or so ago, but somehow the rules never caught up. They're very strict about the regs here." He winked at Abigail's dismayed expression. "Hold tight a minute while—" His voice faded as he tinkered with the controls.

. . . established forty years later and communications with the Proxima colony began shortly thereafter. Ginungagap . . .

The voice cut off. She grinned thanks. "Abigail Vanderhoek."

"Cheyney," the pilot said. "You're the gravity bum, right?"

"Yeah."

"I used to be a vacuum bum myself. But I got tired of it, and grabbed the first semipermanent contract that came along."

"I kind of went the other way."

"Probably what I should have done," Cheyney said amiably. "Still, it's a rough road. I picked up three scars along the way." He pointed them out: a thick slash across his abdomen, a red splotch beside one nipple, and a white crescent half obscured by his scalp. "I could've had them cleaned up, but the way I figure, life is just a process of picking up scars and experience. So I kept 'em."

If she had thought he was trying to impress her, Abigail would have slapped him down. But it was clearly just part of an ongoing self-dramatization, possibly justified, probably not. Abigail suspected that, tour trips to Earth excepted, the *Clarke* was as far down a gravity well as Cheyney had ever been. Still he did have an irresponsible, boyish appeal. "Take me past the net?" she asked.

Cheyney looped the tug around the communications net trailing the *Clarke*. Kilometers of steel lace passed beneath them. He pointed out a small dish antenna on the edge and a cluster of antennae on the back. "The loner on the edge transmits into Ginungagap," he said. "The others relay information to and from Mother."

"Mother?"

"That's the traditional name for the *Arthur C. Clarke*." He swung the tug about with a careless sweep of one arm, and launched into a long and scurrilous story about the origin of the nickname. Abigail laughed, and Cheyney pointed a finger. "There's Ginungagap."

Abigail peered intently. "Where? I don't see a thing." She glanced at the second wraparound insert, which displayed a magnified view of the black hole. It wasn't at all impressive: a red smear against black nothingness. In the starfield it was all but invisible.

"Disappointing, hey? But still dangerous. Even this far out, there's a lot of ionization from the accretion disk."

"Is that why there's a lip station?"

"Yeah. Particle concentration varies, but if the translator was right at the *Clarke*, we'd probably lose about a third of the passengers."

Cheyney dropped Abigail off at Mother's crew lock and looped the tug off and away. Abigail wondered where to go, what to do now.

"You're the gravity bum we're dumping down Ginungagap." The short, solid man was upon her before she saw him. His eyes were intense. His *cache-sexe* was a conservative orange. "I liked the stunt with the arm. It takes a lot of guts to do something like that." He pumped her arm. "I'm Paul Girard. Head of external security. In charge of your training. You play verbal Ping-Pong?"

"Why do you ask?" she countered automatically.

"Don't you know?"

"Should I?"

"Do you mean now or later?"

"Will the answer be different later?"

A smile creased Paul's solid face. "You'll do." He took her arm, led her along a sloping corridor. "There isn't much prep time. The dry run is scheduled in two weeks. Things will move pretty quickly after that. You want to start your training now?"

"Do I have a choice?" Abigail asked, amused.

Paul came to a dead stop. "Listen," he said. "Rule number one: don't play games with *me*. You understand? Because I always win. Not sometimes, not usually—always."

Abigail yanked her arm free. "You maneuvered me into that," she said angrily.

"Consider it part of your training." He stared directly into her eyes. "No matter how many gravity wells you've climbed down, you're still the product of a near-space culture—protected, trusting, willing to take things at face value. This is a dangerous attitude, and I want you to realize it. I want you to learn to look behind the mask of events. I want you to grow up. And you will."

Don't be so sure. A small smile quirked Paul's face as if he could read her thoughts. Aloud, Abigail said, "That sounds a little excessive for a trip to Proxima."

"Lesson number two," Paul said: "don't make easy assumptions. You're not going to Proxima." He led her outward-down the ramp to the next wheel, pausing briefly at the juncture to acclimatize to the slower rate of revolution. "You're going to visit spiders." He gestured. "The crew room is this way."

The crew room was vast and cavernous, twilight gloomy. Keyouts were set up along winding paths that wandered aimlessly through the work space. Puddles of light fell on each board and operator. Dark-loving foliage was set between the keyouts.

"This is the heart of the beast," Paul said. "The green keyouts handle all Proxima communications—pretty routine by now. But the blue . . ." His eyes glinting oddly, he pointed. Over the keyouts hung silvery screens with harsh, grainy images floating on their surfaces, black-and-white blobs that Abigail could not resolve into recognizable forms.

"Those," Paul said, "are the spiders. We're talking to them in real-time. Response delay is almost all due to machine translation."

In a sudden shift of perception, the blobs became arachnid forms. That mass of black fluttering across the screen was a spider leg and *that* was its thorax. Abigail felt an immediate, primal aversion, and then it was swept away by an all-encompassing wonder.

"Aliens?" she breathed.

"Aliens."

They actually looked no more like spiders than humans looked like apes. The eight legs had an extra joint each, and the mandible configuration was all wrong. But to an untrained eye they would do.

"But this is—How long have you—? Why in God's name are you keeping this a secret?" An indefinable joy arose in Abigail. This opened a universe of possibilities, as if after a lifetime of being confined in a box someone had removed the lid.

"Industrial security," Paul said. "The gadget that'll send you through Ginungagap to *their* black hole is a spider invention. We're trading optical data for it, but the law won't protect our rights until we've demonstrated its use. We don't want the other corporations cutting in." He nodded toward the nearest black-and-white screen. "As you can see, they're weak on optics."

"I'd love to talk . . ." Abigail's voice trailed off as she realized how little-girl hopeful she sounded.

"I'll arrange an introduction."

There was a rustling to Abigail's side. She turned and saw a large black tomcat with white boots and belly emerge from the bushes. "This is the esteemed head of Alien Communications," Paul said sourly.

Abigail started to laugh, then choked in embarrassment as she realized that he was not speaking of the cat. "Julio Dominguez, section chief for translation," Paul said. "Abigail Vanderhoek, gravity specialist."

The wizened old man smiled professorially. "I assume our resident gadfly has explained how the communications net works, has he not?"

"Well—" Abigail began.

Dominguez clucked his tongue. He wore a yellow *cache-sexe* and matching bow tie, just a little too garish for a man his age. "Quite simple, actually. Escape velocity from a black hole is greater than the speed of light. Therefore, within Ginungagap the speed of light is no longer the limit to the speed of communications."

He paused just long enough for Abigail to look baffled. "Which is just a stuffy way of saying that when we aim a stream of electrons into the boundary of the stationary limit, they emerge elsewhere—out of another black hole. And if we aim them *just so*"—his voice rose whimsically—"they'll emerge from the black hole of our choosing. The physics is simple. The finesse is in aiming the electrons."

The cat stalked up to Abigail, pushed its forehead against her leg, and mewed insistently. She bent over and picked it up. "But nothing can emerge from a black hole," she objected.

Dominguez chuckled. "Ah, but anything can fall in, hey? A positron can fall in. But a positron falling into Ginungagap in positive time is only an electron falling out in negative time. Which means that a positron falling into a black hole in negative time is actually an electron falling out in positive time—exactly the effect we want. Think of Ginungagap as being the physical manifestation of an equivalence sign in mathematics."

"Oh," Abigail said, feeling very firmly put in her place. White moths flittered along the path. The cat watched, fascinated, while she stroked its head.

"At any rate, the electrons do emerge, and once the data are in, the theory has to follow along meekly."

"Tell me about the spiders," Abigail said before he could continue. The moths were darting up, sideward, down, a chance ballet in three dimensions.

"The *aliens*," Dominguez said, frowning at Paul, "are still a mystery to us. We exchange facts, descriptions, recipes for tools, but the important questions do not lend themselves to our clumsy mathematical codes. Do they know of love? Do they appreciate beauty? Do they believe in God, hey?"

"Do they want to eat us?" Paul threw in.

"Don't be ridiculous," Dominguez snapped. "Of course they don't."

The moths parted when they came to Abigail. Two went to either side; one flew over her shoulder. The cat batted at it with one paw. "The cat's name is Garble," Paul said. "The kids in Bio cloned him up."

Dominguez opened his mouth, closed it again.

Abigail scratched Garble under the chin. He arched his neck and purred all but noiselessly. "With your permission," Paul said. He stepped over to a keyout and waved its operator aside.

"Technically you're supposed to speak a convenience language, but if you keep it simple and non-idiomatic, there shouldn't be any difficulty." He touched the keyout. "Ritual greetings, spider." There was a blank pause. Then the spider moved, a hairy leg flickering across the screen.

"Hello, human."

"Introductions: Abigail Vanderhoek. She is our representative. She will ride the spinner." Another pause. More leg waving.

"Hello, Abigail Vanderhoek. Transition of vacuum garble resting garble commercial benefits garble still point in space."

"Tricky translation," Paul said. He signed to Abigail to take over.

Abigail hesitated, then said, "Will you come to visit us? The way we will visit you?"

"No, you see—" Dominguez began, but Paul waved him to silence.

"No, Abigail Vanderhoek. We are sulfur-based life."

"I do not understand."

"You can garble black hole through garble spinner because you are carbon-based life. Carbon forms chains easily but sulfur combines in lattices or rosettes. Our garble simple form garble. Sometimes sulfur forms short chains."

"We'll explain later," Paul said. "Go on, you're doing fine."

Abigail hesitated again. What do you say to a spider, anyway? Finally, she asked, "Do you want to eat us?"

"Oh, Christ, get her off that thing," Dominguez said, reaching for the keyout.

Paul blocked his arm. "No," he said. "I want to hear this."

Several of the spider legs wove intricate patterns. "The question is false. Sulfur-based life derives no benefit from eating carbon-based life."

"You see," Dominguez said.

"But if it were possible," Abigail persisted. "If you *could* eat us and derive benefit. Would you?"

"Yes, Abigail Vanderhoek. With great pleasure."

Dominguez pushed her aside. "We're terribly sorry," he said to the alien. "This is a horrible, horrible misunderstanding. You!" he shouted to the operator. "Get back on and clear this mess up."

Paul was grinning wickedly. "Come," he said to Abigail. "We've accomplished enough here for one day."

As they started to walk away, Garble twisted in Abigail's arms and leaped free. He hit the floor on all fours and disappeared into the greenery. "Would they really eat us?" Abigail asked. Then amended it to, "Does that mean they're hostile?"

Paul shrugged. "Maybe they thought we'd be insulted if they *didn't* offer to eat us." He led her to her quarters. "Tomorrow we start training for real. In the meantime, you might make up a list of all the ways the spiders could hurt us if we set up transportation and they *are* hostile. Then another list of all the reasons we shouldn't trust them." He paused. "I've done it myself. You'll find that the lists get rather extensive."

Abigail's quarters weren't flashy, but they fit her well. A full star field was routed to the walls, floor, and ceiling, only partially obscured by a trellis inner frame that supported fox-grape vines. Somebody had done research into her tastes.

"Hi." The cheery greeting startled her. She whirled, saw that her hammock was occupied.

Cheyney sat up, swung his legs over the edge of the hammock, causing it to rock lightly. "Come on in." He touched an invisible control and the star field blue-shifted down to a deep, erotic purple.

"Just what do you think you're doing here?" Abigail asked.

"I had a few hours free," Cheyney said, "so I thought I'd drop by and seduce you."

"Well, Cheyney, I appreciate your honesty," Abigail said. "So I won't say no."

"Thank you."

"I'll say maybe some other time. Now get lost. I'm tired."

"Okay." Cheyney hopped down, walked jauntily to the door. He paused. "You said, 'Later,' right?"

"I said *maybe* later."

"Later. Gotcha." He winked and was gone.

Abigail threw herself into the hammock, red-shifted the star field until the universe was a sparse smattering of dying embers.

Annoying creature! There was no hope for anything more than the most superficial of relationships with him. She closed her eyes, smiled. Fortunately, she wasn't currently in the market for a serious relationship.

She slept.

She was falling . . .

Abigail had landed the ship an easy walk from 3M's robot laboratory. The lab's geodesic dome echoed white clouds to the north, where Nix Olympus peeked over the horizon. Otherwise all—land, sky, rocks—was standard issue Martian orange. She had clambered to the ground and shrugged on the supply backpack.

Resupplying 3M-RL stations was a gut contract, easy but dull. So perhaps she was less cautious than usual going down the steep, rock-strewn hillside, or perhaps the rock would have turned under her no matter how carefully she placed her feet. Her ankle twisted and she lurched sideways, but the backpack had shifted her center of gravity too much for her to be able to recover.

Arms windmilling, she fell.

The rock slide carried her downhill in a panicky flurry of dust and motion, tearing her flesh and splintering her bones. But before she could feel pain, her suit shot her full of a nerve synthetic, translating sensation into colors—reds, russets, and browns, with staccato yellow spikes when a rock smashed into her ribs. So that she fell in a whirling rainbow of glorious light.

She came to rest in a burst of orange. The rocks were settling about her. A spume of dust drifted away, out toward the distant red horizon. A large, jagged slab of stone slid by, gently shearing off her backpack. Tools, supplies, airpacks flew up and softly rained down.

A spanner as long as her arm slammed down inches from Abigail's helmet. She flinched, and suddenly events became real. She kicked her legs and sand and dust fountained up. Drawing her feet under her body—the one ankle bright gold—she started to stand.

And was jerked to the ground by a sudden tug on one arm. Even as she turned her head, she became aware of a deep purple sensation in her left hand. It was pinioned to a rock not quite large enough to stake a claim to. There was no color in the fingers.

"Cute," she muttered. She tugged at the arm, pushed at the rock. Nothing budged.

Abigail nudged the radio switch with her chin. "Grounder to Lip Station," she said. She hesitated, feeling foolish, then said, "Mayday. Repeat, Mayday. Could you guys send a rescue party down for me?"

There was no reply. With a sick green feeling in the pit of her stomach, Abigail reached a gloved hand around the back of her helmet. She touched something jagged, a sensation of mottled rust, the broken remains of her radio.

"I think I'm in trouble." She said it aloud and listened to the sound of it. Flat, unemotional—probably true. But nothing to get panicky about.

She took quick stock of what she had to work with. One intact suit and helmet. One spanner. A worldful of rocks, many close at hand. Enough air for— she checked the helmet readout—almost an hour. Assuming the lip station ran its checks on schedule and was fast on the uptake, she had almost half the air she needed.

Most of the backpack's contents were scattered too far away to reach. One rectangular gaspack, however, had landed nearby. She reached for it but could not touch it, squinted but could not read the label on its nozzle. It was almost certainly liquid gas—either nitrogen or oxygen—for the robot lab. There was a slim chance it was the spare airpack. If it was, she might live to be res-cued.

Abigail studied the landscape carefully, but there was nothing more. "Okay, then, it's an airpack." She reached as far as her tethered arm would allow. The gaspack remained a tantalizing centimeter out of reach.

For an instant she was stymied. Then, feeling like an idiot, she grabbed the spanner. She hooked it over the gaspack. Felt the gaspack move grudgingly. Slowly nudged it toward herself.

By the time Abigail could drop the spanner and draw in the gaspack, her good arm was blue with fatigue. Sweat running down her face, she juggled the gaspack to read its nozzle markings.

It was liquid oxygen—useless. She could hook it to her suit and feed in the contents, but the first breath would freeze her lungs. She released the gaspack and lay back, staring vacantly at the sky.

Up there was civilization: tens of thousands of human stations strung together by webs of communication and transportation. Messages flowed endlessly on laser cables. Translators borrowed and lent momentum, moving streams of trav-elers and cargo at almost (but not quite) the speed of light. A starship was being readied to carry a third load of colonists to Proxima. Up there, free from gravity's relentless clutch, people lived in luxury and ease. Here, however . . .

"I'm going to die." She said it softly and was filled with wondering awe. Because it was true. She was going to die.

Death was a black wall. It lay before her, extending to infinity in all directions, smooth and featureless and mysterious. She could almost reach out an arm and touch it. Soon she would come up against it and, if anything lay beyond, pass through. Soon, very soon, she would *know*.

She touched the seal to her helmet. It felt gray—smooth and inviting. Her fingers moved absently, tracing the seal about her neck. With sudden horror, Abigail realized that she was thinking about undoing it, releasing her air, throw-ing away the little time she had left. . . .

She shuddered. With sudden resolve, she reached out and unsealed the shoul-der seam of her captive arm.

The seal clamped down, automatically cutting off air loss. The flesh of her damaged arm was exposed to the raw Martian atmosphere. Abigail took up the gaspack and cradled it in the pit of her good arm. Awkwardly, she opened the nozzle with the spanner.

She sprayed the exposed arm with liquid oxygen for over a minute before she was certain it had frozen solid. Then she dropped the gaspack, picked up the spanner, and swung.

Her arm shattered into a thousand fragments.

She stood up.

Abigail awoke, tense and sweaty. She blue-shifted the walls up to normal light, and sat up. After a few minutes of clearing her head, she set the walls to cycle from red to blue in a rhythm matching her normal pulse. Eventually the womb-cycle lulled her back to sleep.

"Not even close," Paul said. He ran the tape backward, froze it on a still shot of the spider twisting two legs about each other. "That's the morpheme for 'extreme disgust,' remember. It's easy to pick out, and the language kids say that any statement with this gesture should be reversed in meaning. Irony, see? So when the spider says that the strong should protect the weak, it means—"

"How long have we been doing this?"

"Practically forever," Paul said cheerfully. "You want to call it a day?"

"Only if it won't hurt my standing."

"Hah! Very good." He switched off the keyout. "Nicely thought out. You're absolutely right; it would have. However, as reward for realizing this, you can take off early *without* it being noted on your record."

"Thank you," Abigail said sourly.

Like most large installations, the *Clarke* had a dozen or so smaller structures tagging along after it in minimum maintenance orbits. When Abigail discovered that these included a small wheel gymnasium, she had taken to putting in an hour's exercise after each training shift. Today she put in two.

The first hour she spent shadowboxing and practicing *savate* in heavy-gee to work up a sweat. The second hour she spent in the axis room, performing free-fall gymnastics. After the first workout, it made her feel light and nimble and good about her body.

She returned from the wheel gym sweaty and cheerful to find Cheyney in her hammock again. "Cheyney," she said, "this is not the first time I've had to kick you out of there. Or even the third, for that matter."

Cheyney held his palms up in mock protest. "Hey, no," he said. "Nothing like that today. I just came by to watch the raft debate with you."

Abigail felt pleasantly weary, decidedly uncerebral. "Paul said something about it, but . . ."

"Turn it on, then. You don't want to miss it." Cheyney touched her wall, and a cluster of images sprang to life at the far end of the room.

"Just what is a raft debate anyway?" Abigail asked, giving in gracefully. She hoisted herself onto the hammock, sat beside him. They rocked gently for a moment.

"There's this raft, see? It's adrift and powerless and there's only enough oxygen on board to keep one person alive until rescue. Only there are three on board—two humans and a spider."

"Do spiders breathe oxygen?"

"It doesn't matter. This is a hypothetical situation." Two thirds of the image area were taken up by Dominguez and Paul, quietly waiting for the debate to begin. The remainder showed a flat spider image.

"Okay, what then?"

"They argue over who gets to survive. Dominguez argues that he should, since he's human and human culture is superior to spider culture. The spider argues for itself and its culture." He put an arm around her waist. "You smell nice."

"Thank you." She ignored the arm. "What does Paul argue?"

"He's the devil's advocate. He argues that no one deserves to live and they should dump the oxygen."

"Paul would enjoy that role," Abigail said. Then, "What's the point to this debate?"

"It's an entertainment. There isn't supposed to be a point."

Abigail doubted it was that simple. The debate could reveal a good deal about the spiders and how they thought, once the language types were done with it. Conversely, the spiders would doubtless be studying the human responses. *This could be interesting,* she thought. Cheyney was stroking her side now, lightly but with great authority. She postponed reaction, not sure whether she liked it or not.

Louise Chang, a vaguely high-placed administrator, blossomed in the center of the image cluster. "Welcome," she said, and explained the rules of the debate. "The winner will be decided by acclaim," she said, "with half the vote being human and half alien. Please remember not to base your vote on racial chauvinism, but on the strengths of the arguments and how well they are presented." Cheyney's hand brushed casually across her nipples; they stiffened. The hand lingered. "The debate will begin with the gentleman representing the aliens presenting his thesis."

The image flickered as the spider waved several legs. "Thank you, Ms. Chairman. I argue that I should survive. My culture is superior because of our technological advancement. Three examples. Humans have used translation travel only briefly, yet we have used it for sixteens of garble. Our black hole technology is superior. And our garble has garble for the duration of our society."

"Thank you. The gentleman representing humanity?"

"Thank you, Ms. Chairman." Dominguez adjusted an armlet. Cheyney leaned back and let Abigail rest against him. Her head fit comfortably against his shoulder. "My argument is that technology is neither the sole nor the most important measure of a culture. By these standards dolphins would be considered brute animals. The aesthetic considerations—the arts, theology, and the tradition of philosophy—are of greater import. As I shall endeavor to prove."

"He's chosen the wrong tactic," Cheyney whispered in Abigail's ear. "That must have come across as pure garble to the spiders."

"Thank you. Mr. Girard?"

Paul's image expanded. He theatrically swigged from a small flask and hoisted it high in the air. "Alcohol! There's the greatest achievement of the human race!" Abigail snorted. Cheyney laughed out loud. "But I hold that neither Mr. Dominguez nor the distinguished spider deserves to live, because of the disregard both cultures have for sentient life." Abigail looked at Cheyney, who shrugged. "As I shall endeavor to prove." His image dwindled.

Chang said, "The arguments will now proceed, beginning with the distinguished alien."

The spider and then Dominguez ran through their arguments, and to Abigail they seemed markedly lackluster. She didn't give them her full attention, because Cheyney's hands were moving most interestingly across unexpected parts of her body. He might not be too bright, but he was certainly good at some things. She nuzzled her face into his neck, gave him a small peck, returned her attention to the debate.

Paul blossomed again. He juggled something in his palm, held his hand open to reveal three ball bearings. "When I was a kid I used to short out the school module and sneak up to the axis room to play marbles." Abigail smiled, remembering similar stunts she had played. "For the sake of those of us who are spiders, I'll explain that marbles is a game played in free-fall for the purpose of developing coordination and spatial perception. You make a six-armed star of marbles in the center..."

One of the bearings fell from his hand, bounced noisily, and disappeared as it rolled out of camera range. "Well, obviously it can't be played here. But the point is that when you shoot the marble just right, it hits the end of one arm and its kinetic energy is transferred from marble to marble along that arm. So that the shooter stops and the marble at the far end of the arm flies away." Cheyney was stroking her absently now, engrossed in the argument.

"Now, we plan to send a courier into Ginungagap and out the spiders' black hole. At least, that's what we say we're going to do.

"But what exits from a black hole is not necessarily the same as what went into its partner hole. We throw an electron into Ginungagap and another one pops out elsewhere. It's identical. It's a direct causal relationship. But it's like the marbles—they're identical to each other and have the same kinetic force. It's simply not the same electron."

Cheyney's hand was still, motionless. Abigail prodded him gently, touching his inner thigh. "Anyone who's interested can see the equations. Now, when we send messages, this doesn't matter. The message is important, not the medium. However, when we send a human being in . . . what emerges from the other hole will be cell for cell, gene for gene, atom for atom identical. *But it will not be the same person.*" He paused a beat, smiled.

"I submit, then, that this is murder. And further, that by conspiring to commit murder, both the spider and human races display absolute disregard for intelligent life. In short, no one on the raft deserves to live. And I rest my case."

"Mr. Girard!" Dominguez objected, even before his image was restored to full size. "The simplest mathematical proof is an identity: that A equals A. Are you trying to deny this?"

Paul held up the two ball bearings he had left. "These marbles are identical too. But they are not the same marble."

"We know the phenomenon you speak of," the spider said. "It is as if garble the black hole bulges out simultaneously. There is no violation of continuity. The two entities are the same. There is no death."

Abigail pulled Cheyney down, so that they were both lying on their sides, still able to watch the images. "So long as you happen to be the second marble and not the first," Paul said. Abigail tentatively licked Cheyney's ear.

"He's right," Cheyney murmured.

"No he's not," Abigail retorted. She bit his earlobe.

"You mean that?"

"Of course I mean that. He's confusing semantics with reality." She engrossed herself in a study of the back of his neck.

"Okay."

Abigail suddenly sensed that she was missing something. "Why do you ask?" She struggled into a sitting position. Cheyney followed.

"No particular reason." Cheyney's hands began touching her again. But Abigail was sure something had been slipped past her.

They caressed each other lightly while the debate dragged to an end. Not paying much attention, Abigail voted for Dominguez, and Cheyney voted for Paul. As a result of a nearly undivided spider vote, the spider won. "I told you Dominguez was taking the wrong approach," Cheyney said. He hopped off the hammock. "Look, I've got to see somebody about something. I'll be right back."

"You're not leaving *now?*" Abigail protested, dumbfounded. The door irised shut.

Angry and hurt, she leaped down, determined to follow him. She couldn't remember ever feeling so insulted.

Cheyney didn't try to be evasive; it apparently did not occur to him that she might follow. Abigail stalked him down a corridor, up an in-ramp, and to a door that irised open for him. She recognized that door.

Thoughtfully she squatted on her heels behind an untrimmed boxwood and waited. A minute later, Garble wandered by, saw her, and demanded attention. "Scat!" she hissed. He butted his head against her knee. "Then be quiet, at least." She scooped him up. His expression was smug.

The door irised open and Cheyney exited, whistling. Abigail waited until he was gone, stood, went to the door, and entered. Fish darted between long fronds under a transparent floor. It was an austere room, almost featureless. Abigail looked, but did not see a hammock.

"So Cheyney's working for you now," she said coldly. Paul looked up from a corner keyout.

"As a matter of fact, I've just signed him to permanent contract in the crew room. He's bright enough. A bit green. Ought to do well."

"Then you admit that you put him up to grilling me about your puerile argument in the debate?" Garble struggled in her arms. She juggled him into a more comfortable position. "And that you staged the argument for my benefit in the first place?"

"Ah," Paul said. "I knew the training was going somewhere. You've become very wary in an extremely short time."

"Don't evade the question."

"I needed your honest reaction," Paul said. "Not the answer you would have given me, knowing your chances of crossing Ginungagap rode on it."

Garble made an angry noise. "You tell him, Garble!" she said. "That goes double for me." She stepped out the door. "You lost the debate," she snapped.

Long after the door had irised shut, she could feel Paul's amused smile burning into her back.

Two days after she returned to kick Cheyney out of her hammock for the final time, Abigail was called to the crew room. "Dry run," Paul said. "Attendance is mandatory." And cut off.

The crew room was crowded with technicians, triple the number of keyouts. Small knots of them clustered before the screens, watching. Paul waved her to him.

"There," he motioned to one screen. "That's Clotho—the platform we built for the transmission device. It's a hundred kilometers off. I wanted more, but

Dominguez overruled me. The device that'll unravel you and dump you down Ginungagap is that doohickey in the center." He tapped a keyout and the platform zoomed up to fill the screen. It was covered by a clear, transparent bubble. Inside, a space-suited figure was placing something into a machine that looked like nothing so much as a giant armor-clad clamshell. Abigail looked, blinked, looked again.

"That's Garble," she said indignantly.

"Complain to Dominguez. I wanted a baboon."

The clamshell device closed. The space-suited tech left in his tug, and alphanumerics flickered, indicating the device was in operation. As they watched, the spider-designed machinery immobilized Garble, transformed his molecules into one long continuous polymer chain, and spun it out an invisible opening at near light speed. The water in his body was separated out, piped away, and preserved. The electrolyte balances were recorded and simultaneously transmitted in a parallel stream of electrons. It would reach the spider receiver along with the lead end of the cat-polymer, to be used in the reconstruction.

Thirty seconds passed. Now Garble was only partially in Clotho. The polymer chain, invisible and incredibly long, was passing into Ginungagap. On the far side the spiders were beginning to knit it up.

If all was going well . . .

Ninety-two seconds after they flashed on, the alphanumerics stopped twinkling on the screen. Garble was gone from Clotho. The clamshell opened and the remote cameras showed it to be empty. A cheer arose.

Somebody boosted Dominguez atop a keyout. Intercom cameras swiveled to follow. He wavered fractionally, said "My friends," and launched into a speech. Abigail didn't listen.

Paul's hand fell on her shoulder. It was the first time he had touched her since their initial meeting. "He's only a scientist," he said. "He had no idea how close you are to that cat."

"Look, I *asked* to go. I knew the risks. But Garble's just an animal; he wasn't given the choice."

Paul groped for words. "In a way, this is what your training has been about—the reason you're going across instead of someone like Dominguez. He projects his own reactions onto other people. If—"

Then, seeing that she wasn't listening, he said, "Anyway, you'll have a cat to play with in a few hours. They're only keeping him long enough to test out the life support systems."

There was a festive air to the second gathering. The spiders reported that Garble had translated flawlessly. A brief visual display showed him stalking about Clotho's sister platform, irritable but apparently unharmed.

"There," somebody said. The screen indicated that the receiver net had taken in the running end of the cat's polymer chain. They waited a minute and a half and the operation was over.

It was like a conjuring trick: the clamshell closed on emptiness. Water was piped in. Then it opened and Garble floated over its center, quietly licking one paw.

Abigail smiled at the homeliness of it. "Welcome back, Garble," she said quietly. "I'll get the guys in Bio to brew up some cream for you."

Paul's eyes flicked in her direction. They lingered for no time at all, long enough to file away another datum for future use, and then his attention was elsewhere. She waited until his back was turned and stuck out her tongue at him.

The tub docked with Clotho and a technician floated in. She removed her helmet self-consciously, aware of her audience. One hand extended, she bobbed toward the cat, calling softly.

"Get that jerk on the line," Paul snapped. "I want her helmet back on. That's sloppy. That's real—"

And in that instant Garble sprang.

Garble was a black-and-white streak that flashed past the astonished tech, through the air lock, and into the open tug. The cat pounced on the pilot panel. Its forelegs hit the controls. The hatch slammed shut, and the tug's motors burst into life.

Crew room techs grabbed wildly at their keyouts. The tech on Clotho frantically tried to fit her helmet back on. And the tug took off, blasting away half the protective dome and all the platform's air.

The screens showed a dozen different scenes, lenses shifting from close to distant and back. "Cheyney," Paul said quietly. Dominguez was frozen, looking bewildered. "Take it out."

"It's coming right at us!" somebody shouted.

Cheyney's fingers flicked: rap-tap-rap.

A bright nuclear flower blossomed.

There was silence, dead and complete, in the crew room. *I'm missing something,* Abigail thought. *We just blew up 5 percent of our tug fleet to kill a cat.*

"*Pull* that transmitter!" Paul strode through the crew room, scattering orders. "Nothing goes out! You, you, and you"—he yanked techs away from their keyouts—"*off* those things. I want the whole goddamned net shut *down.*"

"Paul . . . ," an operator said.

"Keep on receiving." He didn't bother to look. "Whatever they want to send. Dump it all in storage and don't merge any of it with our data until we've gone over it."

Alone and useless in the center of the room, Dominguez stuttered, "What—what happened?"

"You blind idiot!" Paul turned on him viciously. "Your precious aliens have just made their first hostile move. The cat that came back was nothing like the one we sent. They made changes. They retransmitted it with instructions wet-wired into its brain."

"But why would they want to steal a tug?"

"*We don't know!*" Paul roared. "Get that through your head. We don't know their motives and we don't know how they think. But we would have known a lot more about their intentions than we wanted if I hadn't rigged that tug with an abort device."

"You didn't—" Dominguez began. He thought better of the statement.

"—have the authority to rig that device," Paul finished for him. "That's right. I didn't." His voice was heavy with sarcasm.

Dominguez seemed to shrivel. He stared bleakly, blankly, about him, then turned and left, slightly hunched over. Thoroughly discredited in front of the people who worked for him.

That was cold, Abigail thought. She marveled at Paul's cruelty. Not for an instant did she believe that the anger in his voice was real, that he was capable of losing control.

Which meant that in the midst of confusion and stress, Paul had found time to make a swift play for more power. To Abigail's newly suspicious eye, it looked like a successful one, too.

For five days Paul held the net shut by sheer willpower and force of personality. Information came in but did not go out. Bell-Sandia administration was not behind him; too much time and money had been sunk into Clotho to abandon the project. But Paul had the support of the tech crew, and he knew how to use it.

"Nothing as big as Bell-Sandia runs on popularity," Paul explained. "But I've got enough sympathy from above, and enough hesitation and official cowardice to keep this place shut down long enough to get a message across."

The incoming information flow fluctuated wildly, shifting from subject to subject. Data sequences were dropped halfway through and incomplete. Nonsense came in. The spiders were shifting through strategies in search of the key that would reopen the net.

"When they start repeating themselves," Paul said, "we can assume they understand the threat."

"But we *wouldn't* shut the net down permanently," Abigail pointed out.

Paul shrugged. "So it's a bluff."

They were sharing an after-shift drink in a fifth-level bar. Small red lizards scuttled about the rock wall behind the bartender. "And if your bluff doesn't work?" Abigail asked. "If it's all for nothing—what then?"

Paul's shoulders sagged, a minute shifting of tensions. "Then we trust in the goodwill of the spiders," he said. "We let them call the shots. And they will treat us benevolently or not, depending. In either case," his voice became dark, "I'll have played a lot of games and manipulated a lot of people for no reason at all." He took her hand. "If that happens, I'd like to apologize." His grip was tight, his knuckles pale.

That night Abigail dreamed she was falling.

Light rainbowed all about her, in a violent splintering of bone and tearing of flesh. She flung out an arm and it bounced on something warm and yielding.

"Abigail."

She twisted and tumbled and something smashed into her ribs. Bright spikes of yellow darted up.

"Abigail!" Someone was shaking her, speaking loudly into her face. The rocks and sky went gray, were overlaid by unresolved images. Her eyelids struggled apart, fell together, opened.

"Oh," she said.

Paul rocked back on his heels. Fish darted about in the water beneath him. "There now," he said. Blue-green lights shifted gently underwater, moving in long, slow arcs. "Dream over?"

Abigail shivered, clutched his arm, let go of it almost immediately. She nodded.

"Good. Tell me about it."

"I—" Abigail began. "Are you asking me as a human being or in your official capacity?"

"I don't make that distinction."

She stretched out a leg and scratched her big toe, to gain time to think. She really didn't have any appropriate thoughts. "Okay," she said, and told him the entire dream.

Paul listened intently, rubbed a thumb across his chin thoughtfully when she was done. "We hired you on the basis of that incident, you know," he said. "Coolness under stress. Weak body image. There were a lot of gravity bums to choose from. But I figured you were just a hair tougher, a little bit grittier."

"What are you trying to tell me? That I'm replaceable?"

Paul shrugged. "Everybody's replaceable. I just wanted to be sure you knew that you could back out if you want. It wouldn't wreck our project."

"I don't want to back out." Abigail chose her words carefully, spoke them slowly, to avoid giving vent to the anger she felt building up inside. "Look, I've been on the gravity circuit for ten years. I've been everywhere in the system there is to go. Did you know that there are less than two thousand people alive who've set foot on Mercury *and* Pluto? We've got a little club; we get together once a year." Seaweed shifted about her; reflections of the floor lights formed nebulous swimming shapes on the walls. "I've spent my entire life going around and around and around the sun, and never really getting anywhere. I want to travel, and there's nowhere left for me to go. So you offer me a way out and then ask if I want to back down. Like hell I do!"

"Why don't you believe that going through Ginungagap is death?" Paul asked quietly. She looked into his eyes, saw cool calculations going on behind them. It frightened her, almost. He was measuring her, passing judgment, warping events into long logical chains that did not take human factors into account. He was an alien presence.

"It's—common sense, is all. I'll be the same when I exit as when I go in. There'll be no difference, not an atom's worth, not a scintilla."

"The *substance* will be different. Every atom will be different. Not a single electron in your body will be the same one you have now."

"Well, how does that differ so much from normal life?" Abigail demanded. "All our bodies are in constant flux. Molecules come and go. Bit by bit, we're replaced. Does that make us different people from moment to moment? 'All that is body is as coursing vapors,' right?"

Paul's eyes narrowed. "Marcus Aurelius. Your quotation isn't complete, though. It goes on: 'All that is of the soul is dreams and vapors.'"

"What's that supposed to mean?"

"It means that the quotation doesn't say what you claimed it did. If you care to read it literally, it argues the opposite of what you're saying."

"Still, you can't have it both ways. Either the me that comes out of the spider black hole is the same as the one who went in, or I'm not the same person as I was an instant ago."

"I'd argue differently," Paul said. "But no matter. Let's go back to sleep."

He held out a hand, but Abigail felt no inclination to accept it. "Does this mean I've passed your test?"

Paul closed his eyes, stretched a little. "You're still reasonably afraid of dying, and you don't believe that you will," he said. "Yeah. You pass."

"Thanks a heap," Abigail said. They slept, not touching, for the rest of the night.

Three days later Abigail woke up, and Paul was gone. She touched the wall and spoke his name. A recording appeared. "Dominguez has been called up to Administration," it said. Paul appeared slightly distracted; he had not looked directly into the recorder and his image avoided Abigail's eyes. "I'm going to re-open the net before he returns. It's best we beat him to the punch." The recording clicked off.

Abigail routed an intercom call through to the crew room. A small chime notified him of her call, and he waved a hand in combined greeting and direction to remain silent. He was hunched over a keyout. The screen above it came to life.

"Ritual greetings, spider," he said.

"Hello, human. We wish to pursue our previous inquiry: the meaning of the term 'art' which was used by the human Dominguez six-sixteenths of the way through his major presentation."

"This is a difficult question. To understand a definition of art, you must first know the philosophy of aesthetics. This is a comprehensive field of knowledge comparable to the study of perception. In many ways it is related."

"What is the trade value of this field of knowledge?"

Dominguez appeared, looking upset. He opened his mouth, and Paul touched a finger to his own lips, nodding his head toward the screen.

"Significant. Our society considers art and science as being of roughly equal value."

"We will consider what to offer in exchange."

"Good. We also have a question for you. Please wait while we select the phrasing." He cut the translation lines, turned to Dominguez. "Looks like your raft gambit paid off. Though I'm surprised they bit at that particular piece of bait."

Dominguez looked weary. "Did they mention the incident with the cat?"

"No, nor the communications blackout."

The old man sighed. "I always felt close to the aliens," he said. "Now they seem—cold, inhuman." He attempted a chuckle. "That was almost a pun, wasn't it?"

"In a human, we'd call it a professional attitude. Don't let it spoil your accomplishment," Paul said. "This could be as big as optics." He opened the communications line again. "Our question is now phrased." Abigail noted he had not told Dominguez of her presence.

"Please go ahead."

"Why did you alter our test animal?"

Much leg waving. "We improved the ratios garble centers of perception garble wetware garble making the animal twelve-sixteenths as intelligent as a human. We thought you would be pleased."

"We were not. Why did the test animal behave in a hostile manner toward us?"

The spider's legs jerked quickly and it disappeared from the screen. Like an echo, the machine said, "Please wait."

Abigail watched Dominguez throw Paul a puzzled look. In the background, a man with a leather sack looped over one shoulder was walking slowly along the twisty access path. His hand dipped into the sack, came out, sprinkled fireflies among the greenery. Dipped in, came out again. Even in the midst of crisis the trivia of day-to-day existence went on.

The spider reappeared, accompanied by two of its own kind. Their legs interlaced and retreated rapidly, a visual pantomime of an excited conversation. Finally one of their number addressed the screen.

"We have discussed the matter."

"So I see."

"It is our conclusion that the experience of translation through Ginungagap had a negative effect on the test animal. This was not anticipated. It is new knowledge. We know little of the psychology of carbon-based life."

"You're saying the test animal was driven mad?"

"Key word did not translate. We assume understanding. Steps must be taken to prevent a recurrence of this damage. Can you do this?"

Paul said nothing.

"Is this the reason why communications were interrupted?"

No reply.

"There is a cultural gap. Can you clarify?"

"Thank you for your cooperation," Paul said, and switched the screen off. "You can set your people to work," he told Dominguez. "No reason why they should answer the last few questions, though."

"Were they telling the truth?" Dominguez asked wonderingly.

"Probably not. But at least now they'll think twice before trying to jerk us around again." He winked at Abigail, and she switched off the intercom.

They re-ran the test using a baboon shipped out from the Belt Zoological Gardens. Abigail watched it arrive from the lip station, crated and snarling.

"They're a lot stronger than we are," Paul said. "Very agile. If the spiders want to try any more tricks, we couldn't offer them better bait."

The test went smooth as silk. The baboon was shot through Ginungagap, held by the spiders for several hours, and returned. Exhaustive testing showed no tampering with the animal.

Abigail asked how accurate the tests were. Paul hooked his hands behind his back. "We're returning the baboon to the Belt. We wouldn't do that if we had any doubts. But—" He raised an eyebrow, asking Abigail to finish the thought.

"But if they're really hostile, they won't underestimate us twice. They'll wait for a human to tamper with."

Paul nodded.

The night before Abigail's send-off they made love. It was a frenzied and desperate act, performed wordlessly and without tenderness. Afterward they lay together, Abigail idly playing with Paul's curls.

"Gail . . ." His head was hidden in her shoulder; she couldn't see his face. His voice was muffled.

"Mmmm?"

"Don't go."

She wanted to cry. Because as soon as he said it, she knew it was another test, the final one. And she also knew that Paul wanted her to fail it. That he honestly believed transversing Ginungagap would kill her, and that the woman who emerged from the spiders' black hole would not be herself.

His eyes were shut; she could tell by the creases in his forehead. He knew what her answer was. There was no way he could avoid knowing.

Abigail sensed that this was as close to a declaration of emotion as Paul was capable of. She felt how he despised himself for using his real emotions as yet another test, and how he could not even pretend to himself that there were circumstances under which he would *not* so test her. *This must be how it feels to think as he does*, she thought. *To constantly scrabble after every last implication, like eternally picking at a scab.*

"Oh, Paul," she said.

He wrenched about, turning his back to her. "Sometimes I wish"—his hands rose in front of his face like claws; they moved toward his eyes, closed into fists—"that for just ten goddamned minutes I could turn my mind off." His voice was bitter.

Abigail huddled against him, looped a hand over his side and onto his chest. "Hush," she said.

The tug backed away from Clotho, dwindling until it was one of a ring of bright sparks pacing the platform. Mother was a point source lost in the star field. Abigail shivered, pulled off her arm bands and shoved them into a storage sack. She reached for her *cache-sexe*, hesitated.

The hell with it, she thought. *It's nothing they haven't seen before.* She shucked it off, stood naked. Gooseflesh rose on the backs of her legs. She swam to the transmittal device, feeling awkward under the distant watching eyes.

Abigail groped into the clamshell. "Go," she said.

The metal closed about her seamlessly, encasing her in darkness. She floated in a lotus position, bobbing slightly.

A light, gripping field touched her, stilling her motion. On cue, hypnotic commands took hold in her brain. Her breathing became shallow; her heart slowed. She felt her body ease into stasis. The final command took hold.

Abigail weighed 50 keys. Even though the water in her body would not be transmitted, the polymer chain she was to be transformed into would be 275 kilometers long. It would take 15 minutes and 17 seconds to unravel at light speed, negligibly longer at translation speed. She would still be sitting in Clotho when the spiders began knitting her up.

It was possible that Garble had gone mad from a relatively swift transit. Paul doubted it, but he wasn't taking any chances. To protect Abigail's sanity, the meds had wet-wired a travel fantasy into her brain. It would blind her to external reality while she traveled.

She was an eagle. Great feathered wings extended out from her shoulders. Clotho was gone, leaving her alone in space. Her skin was red and leathery, her breasts hard and unyielding. Feathers covered her thighs, giving way at the knees to talons.

She moved her wings, bouncing lightly against the thin solar wind swirling down into Ginungagap. The vacuum felt like absolute freedom. She screamed a predator's exultant shrill. Nothing enclosed her; she was free of restrictions forever.

Below her lay Ginungagap, the primal chasm, an invisible challenge marked by a red smudge of glowing gases. It was inchoate madness, a gibbering, impersonal force that wanted to draw her in, to crush her in its embrace. Its hunger was fierce and insatiable.

Abigail held her place briefly, effortlessly. Then she folded her wings and dove.

A rain of X rays stung through her, the scattering of Ginungagap's accretion disk. They were molten iron passing through a ghost. Shrieking defiance, she attacked, scattering sparks in her wake.

Ginungagap grew, swelled until it swallowed up her vision. It was purest black, unseeable, unknowable, a thing of madness. It was Enemy.

A distant objective part of her knew that she was still in Clotho, the polymer chain being unraveled from her body, accelerated by a translator, passing through two black holes, and simultaneously being knit up by the spiders. It didn't matter.

She plunged into Ginungagap as effortlessly as if it were the film of a soap bubble.

In—

—And out.

It was like being reversed in a mirror, or watching an entertainment run backward. She was instantly flying out the way she came. The sky was a mottled mass of violet light.

The stars before her brightened from violet to blue. She craned her neck, looked back at Ginungagap, saw its disk-shaped nothingness recede, and screamed in frustration because it had escaped her. She spread her wings to slow her flight and—

—was sitting in a dark place. Her hand reached out, touched metal, recognized the inside of a clamshell device.

A hairline crack of light looped over her, widened. The clamshell opened.

Oceans of color bathed her face. Abigail straightened, and the act of doing so lifted her up gently. She stared through the transparent bubble at a phosphorescent foreverness of light.

My God, she thought. *The stars.*

The stars were thicker, more numerous than she was used to seeing them—large and bright and glittery rich. She was probably someplace significant, in a star cluster or the center of the galaxy; she couldn't guess. She felt irrationally happy to simply *be;* she took a deep breath, then laughed.

"Abigail Vanderhoek."

She turned to face the voice, and found that it came from a machine. Spiders crouched beside it, legs moving silently. Outside, in the hard vacuum, were more spiders.

"We regret any pain this may cause," the machine said.

Then the spiders rushed forward. She had no time to react. Sharp mandibles loomed before her, then dipped to her neck. Impossibly swift, they sliced through her throat, severed her spine. A sudden jerk and her head was separated from her body.

It happened in an instant. She felt brief pain, and the dissociation of actually *seeing* her decapitated body just beginning to react. And then she died.

A spark. A light. *I'm alive,* she thought. Consciousness returned like an ancient cathode tube warming up. Abigail stretched slowly, bobbing gently in the air, collecting her thoughts. She was in the sister-Clotho again—not in pain, her head and neck firmly on her shoulders. There were spiders in the platform, and a few floating outside.

"Abigail Vanderhoek," the machine said. "We are ready to begin negotiations."

Abigail said nothing.

After a moment, the machine said, "Are you damaged? Are your thoughts impaired?" A pause, then, "Was your mind not protected during transit?"

"Is that you waving the legs there? Outside the platform?"

"Yes. It is important that you talk with the other humans. You must convey our questions. They will not communicate with us."

"I have a few questions of my own," Abigail said. "I won't cooperate until you answer them."

"We will answer any questions provided you neither garble nor garble."

"What do you take me for?" Abigail asked. "Of course I won't."

Long hours later she spoke to Paul and Dominguez. At her request the spiders had withdrawn, leaving her alone. Dominguez looked drawn and haggard. "I swear we had no idea the spiders would attack you," Dominguez said. "We saw it on the screens. I was certain you'd been killed. . . ." His voice trailed off.

"Well, I'm alive, no thanks to you guys. Just what *is* this crap about an explosive substance in my bones, anyway?"

"An explosive—I swear we know nothing of anything of the kind."

"A close relative to plastique," Paul said. "I had a small editing device attached to Clotho's translator. It altered roughly half the bone marrow in your sternum, pelvis, and femurs in transmission. I'd hoped the spiders wouldn't pick up on it so quickly."

"You actually did," Abigail marveled. "The spiders weren't lying; they decapitated me in self-defense. What the holy hell did you think you were *doing?*"

"Just a precaution," Paul said. "We wet-wired you to trigger the stuff on command. That way, we could have taken out the spider installation if they'd tried something funny."

"Um," Dominguez said, "this *is* being recorded. What I'd like to know, Ms. Vanderhoek, is how you escaped being destroyed."

"I didn't," Abigail said. "The spiders killed me. Fortunately, they anticipated the situation, and recorded the transmission. It was easy for them to recreate me—after they edited out the plastique."

Dominguez gave her an odd look. "You don't—feel anything particular about this?"

"Like what?"

"Well—" He turned to Paul helplessly.

"Like the real Abigail Vanderhoek died and you're simply a very realistic copy," Paul said.

"Look, we've been through this garbage before," Abigail began angrily.

Paul smiled formally at Dominguez. It was hard to adjust to seeing the two in flat black-and-white. "She doesn't believe a word of it."

"If you guys can pull yourselves up out of your navels for a minute," Abigail said, "I've got a line on something the spiders have that you want. They claim they've sent probes through their black hole."

"Probes?" Paul stiffened. Abigail could sense the thoughts coursing through his skull, of defenses and military applications.

"Carbon-hydrogen chain probes. Organic probes. Self-constructing transmitters. They've got a carbon-based secondary technology."

"Nonsense," Dominguez said. "How could they convert back to coherent matter without a receiver?"

Abigail shrugged. "They claim to have found a loophole."

"How does it work?" Paul snapped.

"They wouldn't say. They seemed to think you'd pay well for it."

"That's very true," Paul said slowly. "Oh, yes."

The conference took almost as long as her session with the spiders had. Abigail was bone weary when Dominguez finally said, "That ties up the official minutes. We now stop recording." A line tracked across the screen, was gone. "If you want to speak to anyone off the record, now's your chance. Perhaps there is someone close to you . . ."

"Close? No." Abigail almost laughed. "I'll speak to Paul alone, though."

A spider floated by outside Clotho II. It was a golden, crablike being, its body slightly opalescent. It skittered along unseen threads strung between the open platforms of the spider star-city. "I'm listening," Paul said.

"You turned me into a *bomb*, you freak."

"So?"

"I could have been killed."

"Am I supposed to care?"

"You damn well ought to, considering the liberties you've taken with my fair white body."

"Let's get one thing understood," Paul said. "The woman I slept with, the woman I cared for, is dead. I have no feelings toward or obligations to you whatsoever."

"Paul," Abigail said. "*I'm not dead.* Believe me, I'd know if I were."

"How could I possibly trust what you think or feel? It could all be attitudes the spiders wet-wired into you. We know they have the technology."

"How do you know that *your* attitudes aren't wet-wired in? For that matter, how do you know anything is real? I mean, these are the most sophomoric philosophic ideas there are. But I'm the same woman I was a few hours ago. My memories, opinions, feelings—they're all the same as they were. There's absolutely no difference between me and the woman you slept with on the *Clarke*."

"I know." Paul's eyes were cold. "That's the horror of it." He snapped off the screen.

Abigail found herself staring at the lifeless machinery. *God, that hurt*, she thought. *It shouldn't, but it hurt.* She went to her quarters.

The spiders had done a respectable job of preparing for her. There were no green plants, but otherwise the room was the same as the one she'd had on the *Clarke*. They'd even been able to spin the platform, giving her an adequate down-orientation. She sat in her hammock, determined to think pleasanter thoughts. About the offer the spiders had made, for example. The one she hadn't told Paul and Dominguez about.

Banned by their chemistry from using black holes to travel, the spiders needed a representative to see to their interests among the stars. They had offered her the job.

Or perhaps the plural would be more appropriate—they had offered her the jobs. Because there were too many places to go for one woman to handle them all. They needed a dozen—in time, perhaps, a hundred—Abigail Vanderhoeks.

In exchange for licensing rights to her personality, the right to make as many duplicates of her as were needed, they were willing to give her the rights to the self-reconstructing black hole platforms.

It would make her a rich woman—a hundred rich women—back in human space. And it would open the universe. She hadn't committed herself yet, but there was no way she was going to turn down the offer. The chance to see a thousand stars? No, she would not pass it by.

When she got old, too, they could create another Abigail from their recording, burn her new memories into it, and destroy her old body.

I'm going to see the stars, she thought. *I'm going to live forever.* She couldn't understand why she didn't feel elated, wondered at the sudden rush of melancholy that ran through her like the precursor of tears.

Garble jumped into her lap, offered his belly to be scratched. The spiders had recorded him, too. They had been glad to restore him to his unaltered state when she made the request. She stroked his stomach and buried her face in his fur.

"Pretty little cat," she told him. "I thought you were dead."

Mildred Clingerman

Mildred Clingerman (1918–) wrote only a dozen or so SF and fantasy stories, but her works were a memorable feature of *The Magazine of Fantasy & Science Fiction* in the 1950s, and often reprinted. Her only book, *A Cupful of Space* (1961), collects all the stories. She was one of a notable group of women writers, including Judith Merril, Margaret St. Clair, and Shirley Jackson, who helped give *F & SF* a special aspect in that decade and beyond. I would describe that flavor, with the benefit of four decades of hindsight, as a *Twilight Zone* flavor.

In addition to genre science fiction and horror, *F & SF* published stories focused on an ordinary character (and this was unusual because genre science fiction had developed into a literature of extraordinary characters, usually exclusively men), often a woman, experiencing something extraordinary, something fantastic. The emotional point was often sentimental, as well as ironic.

This is the kind of plot Rod Serling appropriated, marketed, and made his own brand name, making television history in the process. Clingerman—along with Richard Matheson, Charles Beaumont and a few other men from *Fantasy & Science Fiction* who generally get almost all the credit—was one of the true originals.

This story, published in 1952, was her first. The central character is, to say the least, unusual in science fiction. She seems to have stepped out of a mid-century tale in *The Saturday Evening Post* into an SF story, and then to belong there.

MINISTER WITHOUT PORTFOLIO

Mrs. Chriswell's little roadster came to a shuddering halt. Here was the perfect spot. Only one sagging wire fence to step over and not a cow in sight. Mrs. Chriswell was terrified of cows, and if the truth were told, only a little less afraid of her daughter-in-law, Clara. It was all Clara's idea that her mother-in-law should now be lurking in meadows peering at birds. Clara had been delighted with the birdwatching idea, but frankly, Mrs. Chriswell was bored with birds. They *flew* so much. And as for their colours, it was useless for her to speculate. Mrs. Chriswell was one of those rare women who are quite, quite colour-blind.

"But, Clara," Mrs. Chriswell had pleaded, "what's the point if I can't tell what colour they are?"

"Well, but, darling," Clara had said crisply, "how much cleverer if you get to know them just from the distinctive markings!"

Mrs. Chriswell, sighing a little as she recalled the firm look of Clara's chin, manoeuvred herself and her burdens over the sagging wire fence. She successfully juggled the binoculars, the heavy bird book, and her purse, and thought how ghastly it was at sixty to be considered so useless that she must be provided with harmless occupations to keep her out of the way.

Since Mr. Chriswell's death she had moved in with her son and his wife to face a life of enforced idleness. The servants resented her presence in the kitchen, so cooking was out. Clara and the snooty nursemaid would brook no interference with the nursery routine, so Mrs. Chriswell had virtually nothing to do. Even her crocheted doilies disappeared magically soon after their presentation to Clara and the modern furniture.

Mrs. Chriswell shifted the heavy bird book and considered rebelling. The sun was hot and her load was heavy. As she toiled on across the field she thought she saw the glint of sun on water. She would sit and crochet in the shade nearby and remove the big straw cartwheel hat Clara termed "just the thing."

Arrived at the trees, Mrs. Chriswell dropped her burdens and flung the hat willy-nilly. Ugly, ridiculous thing. She glanced around for the water she thought she'd seen, but there was no sign of it. She leaned back against a tree trunk and sighed blissfully. A little breeze had sprung up and was cooling the damp tendrils on her forehead. She opened her big purse and scrambled through the muddle of contents for her crochet hook and the ball of thread attached to a half-finished doily. In her search she came across the snapshots of her granddaughters—in colour, they were, but unfortunately Mrs. Chriswell saw them only in various shades of grey. The breeze was getting stronger now, very pleasant, but the dratted old cartwheel monstrosity was rolling merrily down the slight grade to the tangle of berry bushes a few yards away. Well, it would catch on the brambles. But it didn't. The wind flirted it right around the bushes, and the hat disappeared.

"Fiddle!" Mrs. Chriswell dared not face Clara without the hat. Still hanging on to the bulky purse, she got up to give chase. Rounding the tangle of bushes, she ran smack into a tall young man in uniform.

"Oh!" Mrs. Chriswell said. "Have you seen my hat?"

The young man smiled and pointed on down the hill. Mrs. Chriswell was surprised to see her hat being passed from hand to hand among three other tall young men in uniform. They were laughing at it, and she didn't much blame them. They were standing beside a low, silvery aircraft of some unusual design. Mrs. Chriswell studied it a moment, but, really, she knew nothing about such things. . . . The sun glinted off it, and she realized this was what she had thought was water. The young man beside her touched her arm. She turned towards him and saw that he had put a rather lovely little metal hat on his head. He offered her one with grave courtesy. Mrs. Chriswell smiled up at him and nodded. The young man fitted the hat carefully, adjusting various little ornamental knobs on the top of it.

"Now we can talk," he said. "Do you hear well?"

"My dear boy," Mrs. Chriswell said, "of course I do. I'm not so old as all that." She found a smooth stone and sat down to chat. This was much nicer than birdwatching, or even crochet.

The tall young man grinned and signalled excitedly to his companions. They too put on little metal hats and came bounding up the hill. Still laughing, they deposited the cartwheel in Mrs. Chriswell's lap. She patted the stone by way of invitation, and the youngest looking one of the four dropped down beside her.

"What is your name, Mother?" he asked.

"Ida Chriswell," she said. "What's yours?"

"My name is Jord," the boy said.

Mrs. Chriswell patted his hand. "That's a nice, unusual name." The boy grabbed Mrs. Chriswell's hand and rubbed it against the smoothness of his cheek.

"You are like my Mother's Mother," the boy explained, "whom I have not seen in too long." The other young men laughed, and the boy looked abashed and stealthily wiped with his hands at a tear that slid down his nose.

Mrs. Chriswell frowned warningly at the laughter and handed him her clean pocket handkerchief, scented with lavender. Jord turned it over and over in his hands, and then tentatively sniffed at it.

"It's all right," Mrs. Chriswell said. "Use it. I have another." But Jord only breathed more deeply of the faint perfume in its folds.

"This is only the thinnest thread of melody," he said, "but, Mother Ida, it is very like one note from the Harmony Hills of home!" He passed the handkerchief all around the circle, and the young men sniffed at it and smiled.

Mrs. Chriswell tried to remember if she had ever read of the Harmony Hills, but Mr. Chriswell had always told her she was lamentably weak in geography, and she supposed that this was one of her blank spots, like where on earth was Timbuktu? Or the Hellandgone people were always talking about? But it was rude not to make some comment. Wars shifted people about such a lot, and these boys must be homesick and weary of being strangers, longing to talk of home. She was proud of herself for realizing that they were strangers. But there was something. . . . Hard to say, really. The way they had bounded up the hill? Mountain people, perhaps, to whom hills were mere springboards to heights beyond.

"Tell me about your hills," she said.

"Wait," Jord said. "I will show you." He glanced at his leader as if for approval. The young man who had fitted her hat nodded. Jord drew a fingernail across the breast of his uniform. Mrs. Chriswell was surprised to see a pocket opening where no pocket had been before. Really, the Air Force did amazing things with its uniforms, though, frankly, Mrs. Chriswell thought the cut of these a bit extreme.

Carefully, Jord was lifting out a packet of gossamer material. He gently pressed the centre of the packet and it blossomed out into voluminous clouds of feather-weight threads, held loosely together in a wave like a giant spider web. To Mrs. Chriswell's eyes the mesh of threads was the colour of fog, and almost as insubstantial.

"Do not be afraid," Jord said softly, stepping closer to her. "Bend your head, close your eyes, and you shall hear the lovely Harmony Hills of home."

There was one quick-drawn breath of almost-fear, but before she shut her eyes Mrs. Chriswell saw the love in Jord's, and in that moment she knew how rarely she had seen this look, anywhere . . . anytime. If Jord had asked it of her, it was all right. She closed her eyes and bowed her head, and in that attitude of prayer she felt a soft weightlessness descend upon her. It was as if twilight had come down to drape itself on her shoulders. And then the music began. Behind the darkness of her eyes it rose in majesty and power, in colours she had never seen, never guessed. It blossomed like flowers—giant forests of them. Their scents were intoxicating and filled her with joy. She could not tell if the blending perfumes made the music, or if the music itself created the flowers and the perfumes that poured forth from them. She did not care. She wanted only to go on forever listening to all this colour. It seemed odd to be listening to colour, perhaps, but after all, she told herself, it would seem just as odd to me to *see* it.

She sat blinking at the circle of young men. The music was finished. Jord was putting away the gossamer threads in the secret pocket, and laughing aloud at her astonishment.

"Did you like it, Mother Ida?" He dropped down beside her again and patted her wrinkled face, still pink with excitement.

"Oh, Jord," she said, "how lovely . . . Tell me . . ."

But the leader was calling them all to order. "I'm sorry, Mother Ida, we must hurry about our business. Will you answer some questions? It is very important."

"Of course," Mrs. Chriswell said. She was still feeling a bit dazed. "If I can . . . If it's like the quizzes on the TV, though, I'm not very good at it."

The young man shook his head. "We," he said, "have been instructed to investigate and report on the true conditions of this . . . of the world." He pointed at the aircraft glittering in the sunlight. "We have travelled all around in that slow machine, and our observations have been accurate. . . ." He hesitated, drew a deep breath and continued. ". . . and perhaps we shall be forced to give an unfavourable report, but this depends a great deal on the outcome of our talk with you. We are glad you stumbled upon us. We were about to set out on a foray to secure some individual for questioning. It is our last task." He smiled. "And Jord, here, will not be sorry. He is sick for home and loved ones." He sighed, and all the other young men echoed the sigh.

"Every night," Mrs. Chriswell said, "I pray for peace on earth. I cannot bear to think of boys like you fighting and dying, and the folks at home waiting and waiting . . ." She glanced all around at their listening faces. "And I'll tell you something else," she said, "I find I can't really hate anybody, even the enemy." Around the circle the young men nodded at each other. "Now ask me your questions." She fumbled in her purse for her crochet work and found it.

Beside her Jord exclaimed with pleasure at the sight of the half-finished doily. Mrs. Chriswell warmed to him even more.

The tall young man began his grave questioning. They were very simple questions, and Mrs. Chriswell answered them without hesitation. Did she believe in God? Did she believe in the dignity of man? Did she truly abhor war? Did she believe that man was capable of love for his neighbour? The questions went on and on, and Mrs. Chriswell crocheted while she gave her answers.

At last, when the young man had quite run out of questions, and Mrs. Chriswell had finished the doily, Jord broke the sun-lazy silence that had fallen upon them.

"May I have it, Mother?" He pointed to the doily. Mrs. Chriswell bestowed it upon him with great pleasure, and Jord, like a very small boy, stuffed it greedily into another secret pocket. He pointed at her stuffed purse.

"May I look, Mother?"

Mrs. Chriswell indulgently passed him her purse. He opened it and poured the litter of contents on the ground between them. The snapshots of Mrs. Chriswell's grandchildren stared up at him. Jord smiled at the pretty little-girl faces. He groped in the chest pocket and drew out snapshots of his own. "These," he told Mrs. Chriswell proudly, "are my little sisters. Are they not like these little girls of yours? Let us exchange, because soon I will be at home with them, and there will be no need for pictures. I would like to have yours."

Mrs. Chriswell would have given Jord the entire contents of the purse if he had asked for them. She took the snapshots he offered and looked with pleasure at the sweet-faced children. Jord still stirred at the pile of possessions from Mrs. Chriswell's purse. By the time she was ready to leave he had talked her out of three illustrated recipes torn from magazines, some swatches of material, and two pieces of peppermint candy.

The young man who was the leader helped her to remove the pretty little hat when Mrs. Chriswell indicated he should. She would have liked to keep it, but she didn't believe Clara would approve. She clapped the straw monstrosity on her head, kissed Jord's cheek, waved goodbye to the rest, and groped her way around the berry bushes. She had to grope because her eyes were tear-filled. They had saluted her so grandly as she left.

Clara's usually sedate household was in an uproar when Mrs. Chriswell returned. All the radios in the house were blaring. Even Clara sat huddled over the one in the library. Mrs. Chriswell heard a boy in the street crying "EXTRA! EXTRA!" and the upstairs maid almost knocked her down getting out the front door to buy one. Mrs. Chriswell, sleepy and somewhat sunburned, supposed it was something about the awful war.

She was just turning up the stairs to her room when the snooty nursemaid came rushing down to disappear kitchenwards with another newspaper in her hand. Good, the children were alone. She'd stop in to see them. Suddenly she heard the raised voices from the back of the house. The cook was yelling at somebody. "I tell you, I saw it! I took out some garbage and there it was, right over me!" Mrs. Chriswell lingered at the foot of the stairway puzzled by all the confusion. The housemaid came rushing in with the extra edition. Mrs. Chriswell quietly reached out and took it. "Thank you, Nadine," she said. The nursemaid was still staring at her as she climbed the stairs.

Edna and Evelyn were sitting on the nursery floor, a candy box between them, and shrieking at each other when their grandmother opened the door. They were cramming chocolates into their mouths between shrieks. Their faces and pinafores were smeared with the candy. Edna suddenly yanked Evelyn's hair, hard. "Pig!" she shouted. "You got three more than I did!"

"Children! Children! Not fighting?" Mrs. Chriswell was delighted. Here was something she could cope with. She led them firmly to the bathroom and washed their faces. "Change your frocks," she said, "and I'll tell you my adventure."

There were only hissing accusals and whispered countercharges behind her as she turned her back on the children to scan the newspaper. The headlines leapt up at her.

Mysterious broadcast interrupts programmes on all wave lengths
Unknown woman saves world, say men from space
One sane human found on earth
Cooking, needlework, home, religious interests sway space judges

Every column of the paper was crowded with the same unintelligible nonsense. Mrs. Chriswell folded it neatly, deposited it on the table, and turned to tie her granddaughters' sashes and tell her adventure.

"... And then he gave me some lovely photographs. In colour, he said ... Good little girls, just like Edna and Evelyn. Would you like to see them?"

Edna made a rude noise with her mouth pursed. Evelyn's face grew saintlike in retaliation. "Yes, show us," she said.

Mrs. Chriswell passed them the snapshots, and the children drew close together for the moment before Evelyn dropped the pictures as if they were blazing. She stared hard at her grandmother while Edna made a gagging noise.

"Green!" Edna gurgled. "Gaaa . . . green skins!"

"Grandmother!" Evelyn was tearful. "Those children are frog-coloured!"

Mrs. Chriswell bent over to pick up the pictures. "Now, now, children," she murmured absently. "We don't worry about the colour of people's skins. Red . . . yellow . . . black . . . we're all God's children. Asia or Africa, makes no difference . . ." But before she could finish her thought, the nursemaid loomed disapprovingly in the doorway. Mrs. Chriswell hurried out to her own room, while some tiny worry nagged at her mind. "Red, yellow, black, white," she murmured over and over, "and brown . . . but green . . . ?" Geography had always been her weak point. Green . . . Now where on earth . . . ?

William Tenn

William Tenn is the pseudonym of Philip Klass (1920–   ), most of whose major SF work was published in the 1950s. He is legendary in the SF field as a wit and a satirist—and for his writing block, which has prevented him from finishing nearly any fiction from the early 1960s to the mid-'90s. His one novel, *Of Men and Monsters* (1968), was published along with five volumes of his short fiction containing most of his earlier work in that year, but he has had no books since.

In an essay introducing his first collection, *Of All Possible Worlds* (1955), he offered an eloquent defense of the genre and revealed a "passionate belief in science fiction as a means of literary expression that has particular validity and significance in this age." He recently retired from a long and distinguished career as a teacher of writing at Pennsylvania State University, where he was the mentor of, among others, David Morrell. *The Encyclopedia of Science Fiction* calls Tenn "one of the genre's very few genuinely comic, genuinely incisive writers of short fiction."

Dictionary of Literary Biography (volume 8) singles out "Time in Advance" as "one of Tenn's most thoughtful satires . . . its protagonist is one of Tenn's best-developed characters." It is a complex moral and psychological investigation. What if it were possible to serve your punishment before committing your crime? It seems to me one of the best stories from one of the best writers in the history of genre science fiction.

TIME IN ADVANCE

Twenty minutes after the convict ship landed at the New York Spaceport, reporters were allowed aboard. They came boiling up the main corridor, pushing against the heavily armed guards who were conducting them, the feature-story men and by-line columnists in the lead, the TV people with their portable but still-heavy equipment cursing along behind.

As they went, they passed little groups of spacemen in the black-and-red uniform of the Interstellar Prison Service walking rapidly in the opposite direction, on their way to enjoy five days of planetside leave before the ship roared away once more with a new cargo of convicts.

The impatient journalists barely glanced at these drab personalities who were spending their lives in a continuous shuttle from one end of the Galaxy to the other. After all, the life and adventures of an IPS man had been done thousands of times, done to death. The big story lay ahead.

In the very belly of the ship, the guards slid apart two enormous sliding doors—and quickly stepped aside to avoid being trampled. The reporters almost flung themselves against the iron bars that ran from floor to ceiling and completely shut off the great prison chamber. Their eager, darting stares were met with at most a few curious glances from the men in coarse gray suits who lay or sat in the tiers of bunks that rose in row after sternly functional row all the way down the cargo hold. Each man clutched—and some caressed—small package neatly wrapped in plain brown paper.

The chief guard ambled up on the other side of the bars, picking the morning's breakfast out of his front teeth. "Hi, boys," he said. "Who're you looking for—as if I didn't know?"

One of the older, more famous columnists held the palm of his hand up warningly. "Look, Anderson: no games. The ship's been almost a half-hour late in landing and we were stalled for fifteen minutes at the gangplank. Now where the hell are they?"

Anderson watched the TV crews shoulder a place for themselves and their equipment right up to the barrier. He tugged a last bit of food out of one of his molars.

"Ghouls," he muttered. "A bunch of grave-happy, funeral-hungry ghouls." Then he hefted his club experimentally a couple of times and clattered it back and forth against the bars. "Crandall!" he bellowed. "Henck! Front and center!"

The cry was picked up by the guards strolling about, steadily, measuredly, club-twirlingly, inside the prison pen. "Crandall! Henck! Front and center!" It went ricocheting authoritatively up and down the tremendous curved walls. "Crandall! Henck! Front and center!"

Nicholas Crandall sat up cross-legged in his bunk on the fifth tier and grimaced. He had been dozing and now he rubbed a hand across his eyes to erase the sleep. There were three parallel scars across the back of his hand, old and brown and straight scars such as an animal's claws might rake out. There was also a curious zigzag scar just above his eyes that had a more reddish novelty. And there was a tiny, perfectly round hole in the middle of his left ear which, after coming fully awake, he scratched in annoyance.

"Reception committee," he grumbled. "Might have known. Same old goddam Earth as ever."

He flipped over on his stomach and reached down to pat the face of the little man snoring on the bunk immediately under him. "Otto," he called. "Blotto Otto—up and at 'em! They want us."

Henck immediately sat up in the same cross-legged fashion, even before his eyes had opened. His right hand went to his throat where there was a little network of zigzag scars of the same color and size as the one Crandall had on his forehead. The hand was missing an index and forefinger.

"Henck here, sir," he said thickly, then shook his head and stared up at Crandall. "Oh—Nick. What's up?"

"We've arrived, Blotto Otto," the taller man said from the bunk above. "We're on Earth and they're getting our discharges ready. In about half an hour, you'll be able to wrap that tongue of yours around as much brandy, beer, vodka and rotgut whiskey as you can pay for. No more prison-brew, no more raisin-jack from a tin can under the bed, Blotto Otto."

Henck grunted and flopped down on his back again. "In half an hour, but not now, so why did you have to go and wake me up? What do you take me for, some dewy, post-crime, petty-larceny kid, sweating out my discharge with my eyes open and my gut wriggling? Hey, Nick, I was dreaming of a new way to get Elsa, a brand-new, really ugly way."

"The screws are in an uproar," Crandall told him, still in a low, patient voice. "Hear them? They want us, you and me."

Henck sat up again, listened a moment, and nodded. "Why is it," he asked, "that only space-screws have voices like that?"

"It's a requirement of the service," Crandall assured him. "You've got to be at least a minimum height, have a minimum education and with a minimum nasty voice of just the right ear-splitting quality before you can get to be a space-screw. Otherwise, no matter how vicious a personality you have, you are just plain out of luck and have to stay behind on Earth and go on getting your kicks by running down slowpoke 'copters driven by old ladies."

A guard stopped below, banged angrily at one of the metal posts that supported their tier of bunks. "Crandall! Henck! You're still convicts, don't you forget that! If you don't front-and-center in a double-time hurry, I'll climb up there and work you over once more for old-time's sake!"

"Yes, *sir!* Coming, *sir!*" they said in immediate, mumbling unison and began climbing down from bunk to bunk, each still clutching the brown-paper package that contained the clothes they had once worn as free men and would shortly be allowed to wear again.

"Listen, Otto." Crandall leaned down as they climbed and brought his lips close to the little man's ear in the rapid-fire, extremely low-pitched prison whisper. "They're taking us to meet the television and news boys. We're going to be asked a lot of questions. One thing you want to be sure to keep your lip buttoned about—"

"Television and news? Why us? What do they want with us?"

"Because we're celebrities, knockhead! We've seen it through for the big rap and come out on the other side. How many men do you think have made it? But *listen*, will you? If they ask you who it is you're after, you just shut up and smile. You don't answer that question. Got that? You don't tell them whose murder you were sentenced for, no matter what they say. They can't make you. That's the law."

Henck paused a moment, one and a half bunks from the floor. "But, Nick, *Elsa* knows! I told her that day, just before I turned myself in. She knows I wouldn't take a murder rap for anyone but her!"

"She knows, she knows, of *course* she knows!" Crandall swore briefly and almost inaudibly. "But she can't *prove* it, you goddam human blotter! Once you say so in public, though, she's entitled to arm herself and shoot you down on sight—pleading self-defense. And till you say so, she can't; she's still your poor wife whom you've promised to love, honor and cherish. As far as the world is concerned—"

The guard reached up with his club and jolted them both angrily across the back. They dropped to the floor and cringed as he snarled over them: "Did I say you could have a talk-party? *Did I?* If we have any time left before you get your discharge, I'm taking you cuties into the guard-room for one last big going-over. Now pick them up and put them down!"

They scuttled in front of him obediently, like a pair of chickens before a snapping collie. At the barred gate near the end of the prison hold, he saluted and said: "Pre-criminals Nicholas Crandall and Otto Henck, sir."

Chief Guard Anderson wiped the salute back at him carelessly. "These gentlemen want to ask you fellas a couple of questions. Won't hurt you to answer. That's all, O'Brien."

His voice was very jovial. He was wearing a big, gentle, half-moon smile. As the subordinate guard saluted and moved away, Crandall let his mind regurgitate memories of Anderson all through this month-long trip from Proxima Centaurus.

Anderson nodding thoughtfully as that poor Minelli—Steve Minelli, hadn't that been his name?—was made to run through a gauntlet of club-swinging guards for going to the toilet without permission. Anderson chuckling just a moment before he'd kicked a gray-headed convict in the groin for talking on the chow-line. Anderson—

Well, the guy had guts, anyway, knowing that his ship carried two pre-criminals who had served out a murder sentence. But he probably also knew that they wouldn't waste the murder on him, however viciously he acted. A man doesn't volunteer for a hitch in hell just so he can knock off one of the devils.

"Do we have to answer these questions, sir?" Crandall asked cautiously, tentatively.

The chief guard's smile lost the tiniest bit of its curvature. "I said it wouldn't hurt you, didn't I? But other things might. They *still* might, Crandall. I'd like to do these gentlemen from the press a favor, so you be nice and cooperative, eh?" He gestured with his chin, ever so slightly, in the direction of the guard-room and hefted his club a bit.

"Yes, sir," Crandall said, while Henck nodded violently. "We'll be cooperative, sir."

Dammit, he thought, *if only I didn't have such a use for that murder! Let's keep remembering Stephanson, boy, no one but Stephanson! Not Anderson, not O'Brien, not anybody else: the name under discussion is Frederick Stoddard Stephanson!*

While the television men on the other side of the bars were fussing their equipment into position, the two convicts answered the preliminary, inevitable questions of the feature writers:

"How does it feel to be back?"

"Fine, just fine."

"What's the first thing you're going to do when you get your discharge?"

"Eat a good meal." (From Crandall.)

"Get roaring drunk." (From Henck.)

"Careful you don't wind up right behind bars again as a post-criminal." (From one of the feature writers.) A good-natured laugh in which all of them, the newsmen, Chief Guard Anderson, and Crandall and Henck, participated.

"How were you treated while you were prisoners?"

"Oh, pretty good." (From both of them, concurrent with a thoughtful glance at Anderson's club.)

"Either of you care to tell us who you're going to murder?"

(Silence.)

"Either of you changed your mind and decided not to commit the murder?"

(Crandall looked thoughtfully up, while Henck looked thoughtfully down.) Another general laugh, a bit more uneasy this time, Crandall and Henck not participating.

"All right, we're set. Look this way, please," the television announcer broke in. "And smile, men—let's have a really *big* smile."

Crandall and Henck dutifully emitted big smiles, which made three smiles, for Anderson had moved into the cheerful little group.

The two cameras shot out of the grasp of their technicians, one hovering over them, one moving restlessly before their faces, both controlled, at a distance, by the little box of switches in the cameramen's hands. A red bulb in the nose of one of the cameras lit up.

"Here we are, ladies and gentlemen of the television audience," the announcer exuded in a lavish voice. "We are on board the convict ship *Jean Valjean*, which has just landed at the New York Spaceport. We are here to meet two men— two of the rare men who have managed to serve all of a voluntary sentence for murder and thus are legally entitled to commit one murder apiece.

"In just a few moments, they will be discharged after having served out seven full years on the convict planets—and they will be free to kill any man or woman in the Solar System with absolutely no fear of any kind of retribution. Take a good look at them, ladies and gentlemen of the television audience—it might be you they are after!"

After this cheering thought, the announcer let a moment or two elapse while the cameras let their lenses stare at the two men in prison gray. Then he stepped into range himself and addressed the smaller man.

"What is your name, sir?" he asked.

"Pre-criminal Otto Henck, 525514," Blotto Otto responded automatically, though not able to repress a bit of a start at the *sir*.

"How does it feel to be back?"

"Fine, just fine."

"What's the first thing you're going to do when you get your discharge?"

Henck hesitated, then said, "Eat a good meal," after a shy look at Crandall.

"How were you treated while you were a prisoner?"

"Oh, pretty good. As good as you could expect."

"As good as a criminal could expect, eh? Although you're not really a criminal yet, are you? You're a pre-criminal."

Henck smiled as if this were the first time he was hearing the term. "That's right, sir. I'm a pre-criminal."

"Want to tell the audience who the person is you're going to become a criminal for?"

Henck looked reproachfully at the announcer, who chuckled throatily—and alone.

"Or if you've changed your mind about him or her?" There was a pause. Then the announcer said a little nervously: "You've served seven years on danger-filled, alien planets, preparing them for human colonization. That's the maximum sentence the law allows, isn't it?"

"That's right, sir. With the pre-criminal discount for serving the sentence in advance, seven years is the most you can get for murder."

"Bet you're glad we're not back in the days of capital punishment, eh? That would make the whole thing impractical, wouldn't it? Now, Mr. Henck—or pre-criminal Henck, I guess I should still call you—suppose you tell the ladies and gentlemen of our television audience: What was the most horrifying experience you had while you were serving your sentence?"

"Well," Otto Henck considered carefully. "About the worst of the lot, I guess, was the time on Antares VIII, the second prison camp I was in, when the big wasps started to spawn. They got a wasp on Antares VIII, see, that's about a hundred times the size of—"

"Is that how you lost two fingers on your right hand?"

Henck brought his hand up and studied it for a moment. "No. The forefinger—I lost the forefinger on Rigel XII. We were building the first prison camp on the planet and I dug up a funny kind of red rock that had all sorts of little bumps on it. I poked it, kind of—you know, just to see how hard it was or something—and the tip of my finger disappeared. *Pow*—just like that. Later on, the whole finger got infected and the medics had to cut it off.

"It turned out I was lucky, though; some of the men—the convicts, I mean—ran into bigger rocks than the one I found. Those guys lost arms, legs—one guy even got swallowed whole. They weren't really rocks, see. They were alive—they were alive and hungry! Rigel XII was lousy with them. The middle finger—I lost the middle finger in a dumb kind of accident on board ship while we were being moved to—"

The announcer nodded intelligently, cleared his throat and said: "But those wasps, those giant wasps on Antares VIII—they were the worst?"

Blotto Otto blinked at him for a moment before he found the conversation again.

"Oh. They sure were! They were used to laying their eggs in a kind of monkey they have on Antares VIII, see? It was real rough on the monkey, but that's how the baby wasps got their food while they were growing up. Well, we get out there and it turns out that the wasps can't see any difference between those Antares monkeys and human beings. First thing you know, guys start collapsing all over the place and when they're taken to the dispensary for an X-ray, the medics see that they're completely crammed—"

"Thank you very much, Mr. Henck, but Herkimer's Wasp has already been seen by and described to our audience at least three times in the past on the Interstellar Travelogue, which is carried by this network, as you ladies and gentlemen no doubt remember, on Wednesday evening from seven to seven-thirty P.M. terrestrial standard time. And now, Mr. Crandall, let me ask you, sir: How does it feel to be back?"

Crandall stepped up and was put through almost exactly the same verbal paces as his fellow prisoner.

There was one major difference. The announcer asked him if he expected to find Earth much changed. Crandall started to shrug, then abruptly relaxed and grinned. He was careful to make the grin an extremely wide one, exposing a maximum of tooth and a minimum of mirth.

"There's one big change I can see already," he said. "The way those cameras float around and are controlled from a little switch-box in the cameraman's hand. That gimmick wasn't around the day I left. Whoever invented it must have been pretty clever."

"Oh, yes?" The announcer glanced briefly backward. "You mean the Stephanson Remote Control Switch? It was invented by Frederick Stoddard Stephanson about five years ago—Was it five years, Don?"

"Six years," said the cameraman. "Went on the market five years ago."

"It was *invented* six years ago," the announcer translated. "It went on the market *five* years ago."

Crandall nodded. "Well, this Frederick Stoddard Stephanson must be a clever man, a very clever man." And he grinned again into the cameras. *Look at my teeth,* he thought to himself. *I know you're watching, Freddy. Look at my teeth and shiver.*

The announcer seemed a bit disconcerted. "Yes," he said. "Exactly. Now, Mr. Crandall, what would you describe as the most horrifying experience in your entire . . ."

After the TV men had rolled up their equipment and departed, the two precriminals were subjected to a final barrage of questions from the feature writers and columnists in search of odd shreds of color.

"What about the women in your life?" "What books, what hobbies, what amusements filled your time?" "Did you find out that there are no atheists on convict planets?" "If you had the whole thing to do over again—"

As he answered, drably, courteously, Nicholas Crandall was thinking about Frederick Stoddard Stephanson seated in front of his luxurious wall-size television set.

Would Stephanson have clicked it off by now? Would he be sitting there, staring at the blank screen, pondering the plans of the man who had outlived odds estimated at ten thousand to one and returned after seven full, unbelievable years in the prison camps of four insane planets?

Would Stephanson be examining his blaster with sucked-in lips—the blaster that he might use only in an open-and-shut situation of self-defense? Otherwise, he would incur the full post-criminal sentence for murder, which, without the fifty per cent discount for punishment voluntarily undergone in advance of the crime, was as much as fourteen years in the many-pronged hell from which Crandall had just returned?

Or would Stephanson be sitting, slumped in an expensive bubblechair, glumly watching a still-active screen, frightened out of his wits but still unable to tear himself away from the well-organized program the network had no doubt built around the return of two—count 'em: *two!*—homicidal pre-criminals?

At the moment, in all probability, the screen was showing an interview with some Earthside official of the Interstellar Prison Service, an expansive public relations character who had learned to talk in sociology.

"Tell me, Mr. Public Relations," the announcer would ask (a different announcer, more serious, more intellectual), "how often do pre-criminals serve out a sentence for murder and return?"

"According to statistics—" a rustle of papers at this point and a penetrating glance downward—"according to statistics, we may expect a man who has served a full sentence for murder, with the 50 per cent pre-criminal discount, to return only once in 11.7 years on the average."

"You would say, then, wouldn't you, Mr. Public Relations, that the return of two such men on the same day is a rather unusual situation?"

"*Highly* unusual or you television fellas wouldn't be in such a fuss over it." A thick chuckle here, which the announcer dutifully echoes.

"And what, Mr. Public Relations, happens to the others who don't return?"

A large, well-fed hand gestures urbanely. "They get killed. Or they give up. Those are the only two alternatives. Seven years is a long time to spend on those convict planets. The work schedule isn't for sissies and neither are the life-forms they encounter—the big man-eating ones as well as the small virus-sized types.

"That's why prison guards get such high salaries and such long leaves. In a sense, you know, we haven't really abolished capital punishment; we've substituted a socially useful form of Russian Roulette for it. Any man who commits or pre-commits one of a group of particularly reprehensible crimes is sent off to a planet where his services will benefit humanity and where he's forced to take his chances on coming back in one piece, if at all. The more serious the crime, the longer the sentence and, therefore, the more remote the chances."

"I see. Now, Mr. Public Relations, you say they either get killed or they give up. Would you explain to the audience, if you please, just how they give up and what happens if they do?"

Here a sitting back in the chair, a locking of pudgy fingers over paunch. "You see, any pre-criminal may apply to his warden for immediate abrogation of sentence. It's just a matter of filling out the necessary forms. He's pulled off work detail right then and there and is sent home on the very next ship out of the place. The catch is this: Every bit of time he's served up to that point is canceled—he gets nothing for it.

"If he commits an actual crime after being freed, he has to serve the full sentence. If he wants to be committed as a pre-criminal again, he has to start serving the sentence, with the discount, from the beginning. Three out of every four pre-criminals apply for abrogation of sentence in their very first year. You get a bellyful fast in those places."

"I guess you certainly do," agrees the announcer. "What about the discount, Mr. Public Relations? Aren't there people who feel that's offering the pre-criminal too much inducement?"

The barest grimace of anger flows across the sleek face, to be succeeded by a warm, contemptuous smile. "Those are people, I'm afraid, who, however well-intentioned, are not well versed in the facts of modern criminology and penology. We don't want to discourage pre-criminals; we want to *encourage* them to turn themselves in.

"Remember what I said about three out of four applying for abrogation of sentence in their very first year? Now these are individuals who were sensible enough to try to get a discount on their sentence. Are they likely to be foolish enough to risk twice as much when they have found out conclusively they can't stand a bare twelve months of it? Not to mention what they have discovered about the value of human life, the necessity for social cooperation and the general desirability of civilized processes on those worlds where simple survival is practically a matter of a sweepstakes ticket.

"The man who doesn't apply for abrogation of sentence? Well, he has that much more time to let the desire to commit the crime go cold—and that much greater likelihood of getting killed with nothing to show for it. Therefore, so few pre-criminals in *any* of the categories return to tell the tale and do the deed that the social profit is absolutely enormous! Let me give you a few figures.

"Using the Lazarus Scale, it has been estimated that the decline in premeditated homicides alone, since the institution of the pre-criminal discount, has been forty-one per cent on Earth, thirty-three and a third per cent on Venus, twenty-seven per cent—"

Cold comfort, chillingly cold comfort, that would be to Stephanson, Nicholas Crandall reflected pleasurably, those forty-one per cents and thirty-three and a third per cents. Crandall's was the balancing statistic: the man who wanted to murder, and for good and sufficient cause, one Frederick Stoddard Stephanson. He was a leftover fraction on a page of reductions and cancellations—he had returned, astonishingly, unbelievably, after seven years to collect the merchandise for which he had paid in advance.

He and Henck. Two ridiculously long long-shots. Henck's wife Elsa—was she, too, sitting in a kind of bird-hypnotized-by-a-snake fashion before her television set, hoping dimly and desperately that some comment of the Interstellar Prison Service official would show her how to evade her fate, how to get out from under the ridiculously rare disaster that was about to happen to her?

Well, Elsa was Blotto Otto's affair. Let him enjoy it in his own way; he'd paid enough for the privilege. But Stephanson was Crandall's.

Oh, let the arrogant bean-pole sweat, he prayed. *Let me take my time and let him sweat!*

The newsman kept squeezing them for story angles until a loudspeaker in the overhead suddenly cleared its diaphragm and announced:

"Prisoners, prepare for discharge! You will proceed to the ship warden's office in groups of ten, as your name is called. Convict ship discipline will be maintained throughout. Arthur, Augluk, Crandall, Ferrara, Fu-Yen, Garfinkel, Gomez, Graham, Henck—"

A half hour later, they were walking down the main corridor of the ship in their civilian clothes. They showed their discharges to the guard at the gangplank, smiled still cringingly back at Anderson, who called from a porthole, "Hey, fellas, come back soon!" and trotted down the incline to the surface of a planet they had not seen for seven agonizing and horror-crowded years.

There were a few reporters and photographers still waiting for them, and one TV crew which had been left behind to let the world see how they looked at the moment of freedom.

Questions, more questions to answer, which they could afford to be brusque about, although brusqueness to any but fellow prisoners still came hard.

Fortunately, the newsmen got interested in another pre-criminal who was with them. Fu-Yen had completed the discounted sentence of two years for aggravated assault and battery. He had also lost both arms and one leg to a corrosive moss on Procyon III just before the end of his term and came limping down the gangplank on one real and one artificial leg, unable to grasp the hand-rails.

As he was being asked, with a good deal of interest, just how he intended to commit simple assault and battery, let alone the serious kind, with his present limited resources, Crandall nudged Henck and they climbed quickly into one of the many hovering gyrocabs. They told the driver to take them to a bar—any quiet bar—in the city.

Blotto Otto almost went to pieces under the impact of actual free choice. "I can't do it," he whispered. "Nick, there's just too damn much to drink!"

Crandall settled it by ordering for him. "Two double scotches," he told the waitress. "Nothing else."

When the scotch came, Blotto Otto stared at it with the kind of affectionate and wistful astonishment a man might show toward an adolescent son whom he saw last as a babe in arms. He put out a gingerly, trembling hand.

"Here's death to our enemies," Crandall said, and tossed his down. He watched Otto sip slowly and carefully, tasting each individual drop.

"You'd better take it easy," he warned. "Elsa might have no more trouble from you than bringing flowers every visiting day to the alcoholic ward."

"No fear," Blotto Otto growled into his empty glass. "I was weaned on this stuff. And, anyway, it's the last drink I have until I dump her. That's the way I've been figuring it, Nick: one drink to celebrate, then Elsa. I didn't go through those seven years to mess myself up at the payoff."

He set the glass down. "Seven years in one steaming hell after another. And before that, twelve years with Elsa. Twelve years with her pulling every dirty trick in the book on me, laughing in my face, telling me she was my wife and had me legally where she wanted me, that I was gonna support her the way she wanted to be supported and I was gonna like it. And if I dared to get off my knees and stand on my hind legs, *pow*, she found a way to get me arrested.

"The weeks I spent in the cooler, in the workhouse, until Elsa would tell the judge maybe I'd learned my lesson, she was willing to give me one more chance! And me begging for a divorce on my knees—hell, on my belly!—no children, she's able-bodied, she's young, and her laughing in my face. When she wanted me in the cooler, see, then she's crying in front of the judge; but when we're alone, she's always laughing her head off to see me squirm.

"I supported her, Nick. Honest, I gave her almost every cent I made, but that wasn't enough. She liked to see me squirm; she *told* me she did. Well, who's squirming now?" He grunted deep in his throat. "Marriage—it's for chumps!"

Crandall looked out of the open window he was sitting against, down through the dizzy, busy levels of Metropolitan New York.

"Maybe it is," he said thoughtfully. "I wouldn't know. My marriage was good while it lasted, five years of it. Then, all of a sudden, it wasn't good any more, just so much rancid butter."

"At least she gave you a divorce," said Henck. "She didn't take you."

"Oh, Polly wasn't the kind of girl to take anyone. A little mixed up, but maybe no more than I was. Pretty Polly, I called her; Big Nick, she called me. The starlight faded and so did I, I guess. I was still knocking myself out then trying to make a go out of the wholesale electronics business with Irv. Anyone could tell I wasn't cut out to be a millionaire. Maybe that was it. Anyway, Polly wanted out and I gave it to her. We parted friends. I wonder, every once in a while, what she's—"

There was a slight splashy noise, like a seal's flipper making a gesture in the water. Crandall's eyes came back to the table a moment after the green, melon-like ball had hit it. And, at the same instant, Henck's hand had swept the ball up and hurled it through the window. The long, green threads streamed out of the ball, but by then it was falling down the side of the enormous building and the threads found no living flesh to take root in.

From the corner of his eye, Crandall had seen a man bolt out of the bar. By the way people kept looking back and forth fearfully from their table to the open doorway, he deduced that the man had thrown it. Evidently Stephanson had thought it worthwhile to have Crandall followed and neutralized.

Blotto Otto saw no point in preening over his reflexes. The two of them had learned to move fast a long time ago—over a lot of dead bodies. "A Venusian dandelion bomb," he observed. "Well, at least the guy doesn't want to kill you, Nick. He just wants to cripple you."

"That would be Stephanson's style," Crandall agreed, as they paid their check and walked past the faces which were just now beginning to turn white. "He'd never do it himself. He'd hire a bully-boy. And he'd do the hiring through an intermediary just in case the bully-boy ever got caught and blabbed. But that still wouldn't be safe enough: he wouldn't want to risk a post-criminal murder charge.

"A dose of Venusian dandelion, he'd figure, and he wouldn't have to worry about me for the rest of my life. He might even come to visit me in the home for incurables—like the way he sent me a card every Christmas of my sentence. Always the same message: 'Still mad? Love, Freddy.'"

"Quite a guy, this Stephanson," Blotto Otto said, peering around the entrance carefully before stepping out of the bar and onto the fifteenth level walkway.

"Yeah, quite a guy. He's got the world by the tail and every once in a while, just for fun, he twists the tail. I learned how he operated when we were room-mates way back in college, but do you think that did me any good? I ran into him just when that wholesale electronics business with Irv was really falling apart, about two years after I broke up with Polly.

"I was feeling blue and I wanted to talk to someone, so I told him all about how my partner was a penny-watcher and I was a big dreamer, and how between us we were turning a possible nice small business into a definite big bankruptcy. And then I got onto this remote-control switch I'd been fooling around with and how I wished I had time to develop it."

Blotto Otto kept glancing around uneasily, not from dread of another assassin, but out of the unexpected sensation of doing so much walking of his own free will. Several passersby turned around to have another stare at their out-of-fashion knee-length tunics.

"So there I was," Crandall went on. "I was a fool, I know, but take my word, Otto, you have no idea how persuasive and friendly a guy like Freddy Stephanson can be. He tells me he has this house in the country he isn't using right now and there's a complete electronics lab in the basement. It's all mine, if I want it, as long as I want it, starting next week; all I have to worry about is feeding myself. And he doesn't want any rent or anything—it's for old time's sake and because he wants to see me do something really big in the world.

"How smart could I be with a con-artist like that? It wasn't till two years later that I realized he must have had the electronics lab installed the same week I was asking Irv to buy me out of the business for a couple of hundred credits. After all, what would Stephanson, the owner of a brokerage firm, be doing with an electronics lab of his own? But who figures such things when an old room-mate's so warm and friendly and interested in you?"

Otto sighed. "So he comes up to see you every few weeks. And then, about a month after you've got it all finished and working, he locks you out of the place and moves all your papers and stuff to another joint. And he tells you he'll have it patented long before you can get it all down on paper again, and anyhow it was his place—he can always claim he was subsidizing you. Then he laughs in your face, just like Elsa. Huh, Nick?"

Crandall bit his lip as he realized how thoroughly Otto Henck must have memorized the material. How many times had they gone over each other's planned revenge and the situations which had motivated it? How many times had they told and retold the same bitter stories to each other, elicited the same responses from each other, the same questions, the same agreements and even the very same disagreements?

Suddenly, he wanted to get away from the little man and enjoy the luxury of loneliness. He saw the sparkling roof of a hotel two levels down.

"Think I'll move into that. Ought to be thinking about a place to sleep to-night."

Otto nodded at his mood rather than at his statement. "Sure. I know just how you feel. But that's pretty plush, Nick: The Capricorn-Ritz. At least twelve credits a day."

"So what? I can live high for a week, if I want to. And with my background, I can always pick up a fast job as soon as I get low. I want something plush for tonight, Blotto Otto."

"Okay, okay. You got my address, huh, Nick? I'll be at my cousin's place."

"I have it, all right. Luck with Elsa, Otto."

"Thanks, Luck with Freddy. Uh—so long." The little man turned abruptly and entered a main street elevator. When the doors slid shut, Crandall found that he was feeling very uncomfortable. Henck had meant more to him than his own brother. Well, after all, he'd been with Henck day and night for a long time now. And he hadn't seen Dan for—how long was it?—almost nine years.

He reflected on how little he was attached to the world, if you excluded the rather negative desire of removing Stephanson from it. One thing he should get soon was a girl—almost any girl.

But, come to think of it, there was something he needed even more.

He walked swiftly to the nearest drugstore. It was a large one, part of a chain. And there, featured prominently in the window, was exactly what he wanted.

At the cigar counter, he said to the clerk: "It's pretty cheap. Do they work all right?"

The clerk drew himself up. "Before we put an item on sale, sir, it is tested thoroughly. We are the largest retail outlet in the Solar System—*that's* why it's so cheap."

"All right. Give me the medium-sized one. And two boxes of cartridges."

With the blaster in his possession, he felt much more secure. He had a good deal of confidence—based on years of escaping creatures with hair-trigger nervous systems—in his ability to duck and wriggle and jump to one side. But it would be nice to be able to fight back. And how did he know how soon Stephanson would try again?

He registered under a false name, a ruse he thought of at the last moment. That it wasn't worth much, as ruses went, he found out when the bellhop, after being tipped, said: "Thank you, Mr. Crandall. I hope you get your victim, sir."

So he was a celebrity. Probably everyone in the world knew exactly what he looked like. All of which might make it a bit more difficult to get at Stephanson.

While he was taking a bath, he asked the television set to check through Information's file on the man. Stephanson had been rich and moderately important seven years ago; with the Stephanson Switch—how do you like that, the *Stephanson* Switch!—he must be even richer now and much more important.

He was. The television set informed Crandall that in the last calendar month, there were sixteen news items relating to Frederick Stoddard Stephanson. Crandall considered, then asked for the most recent.

That was datelined today. "Frederick Stephanson, the president of the Stephanson Investment Trust and Stephanson Electronics Corporation, left early this morning for his hunting lodge in Central Tibet. He expects to remain there for at least—"

"That's enough!" Crandall called through the bathroom door.

Stephanson was scared! The arrogant bean-pole was frightened silly! That was something; in fact, it was a large part of the return on those seven years. Let him seethe in his own sweat for a while, until he found the actual killing, when it did come at last, almost welcome.

Crandall asked the set for the fresh news and was immediately treated to a bulletin about himself and how he had registered at the Capricorn-Ritz under the name of Alexander Smathers. "But neither is the correct name, ladies and gentlemen," the playback rolled out unctuously. "Neither Nicholas Crandall nor Alexander Smathers is the right name for this man. There is only one name for that man—and that name is death! Yes, the grim reaper has taken up residence at the Ritz-Capricorn Hotel tonight, and only he knows which one of us will not see another sunrise. That man, that grim reaper, that deputy of death, is the only one among us who knows—"

"Shut up!" Crandall yelled, exasperated. He had almost forgotten the kind of punishment a free man was forced to endure.

The private phone circuit on the television screen lit up. He dried himself, hurried into clothes and asked, "Who's calling?"

"Mrs. Nicholas Crandall," said the operator's voice.

He stared at the blank screen for a moment, absolutely thunderstruck. Polly! Where in the world had she come from? And how did she know where he was? No, the last part was easy—he was a celebrity.

"Put her on," he said at last.

Polly's face filled the screen. Crandall studied her quizzically. She'd aged a bit, but possibly it wasn't obvious at anything but this magnification.

As if she realized it herself, Polly adjusted the controls of her set and her face dwindled to life-size, the rest of her body as well as her surroundings coming into the picture. She was evidently in the living room of her home; it looked like a low-to-middle-income-range furnished apartment. But she looked good— awfully good. There were such warm memories . . .

"Hi, Polly. What's this all about? You're the last person I expected to call me."

"Hello, Nick." She lifted her hand to her mouth and stared over its knuckles for some time at him. Then: "Nick. Please. Please don't play games with me."

He dropped into a chair. "Huh?"

She began to cry. "Oh, Nick! *Don't!* Don't be that cruel! I know why you served that sentence—those seven years. The moment I heard your name to-day, I knew why you did it. But, Nick, it was only one man—just one man, Nick!"

"Just one man *what?*"

"It was just that one man I was unfaithful with. And I thought he loved me, Nick. I wouldn't have divorced you if I'd known what he was really like. But you know, Nick, don't you? You know how much he made me suffer. I've been punished enough. Don't kill me, Nick! Please don't kill me!"

"Listen, Polly," he began, completely confused. "Polly girl, for heaven's sake—"

"Nick!" she gulped hysterically. "Nick, it was over eleven years ago—ten, at least. Don't kill me for that, please, Nick, Nick, truly, I wasn't unfaithful to you for more than a year, two years at the most. Truly, Nick! And, Nick, it was only that one affair—the others didn't count. They were just, just casual things. They didn't matter at all, Nick! But don't kill me! Don't kill me!" She held both hands to her face and began rocking back and forth, moaning uncontrollably.

Crandall stared at her for a moment and moistened his lips. Then he said, "Whew!" and turned the set off. He leaned back in his chair. Again he said, "Whew!" and this time it hissed through his teeth.

Polly! Polly had been unfaithful during their marriage. For a year—no, two years! And—what had she said?—the others, the *others* had just been casual things!

The woman he had loved, the woman he suspected he had always loved, the woman he had given up with infinite regret and a deep sense of guilt when she had come to him and said that the business had taken the best part of him away from her, but that since it wasn't fair to ask him to give up something that obviously meant so much to him—

Pretty Polly. Polly girl. He'd never thought of another woman in all their time together. And if anyone, anyone at all, had ever suggested—had so much as *hinted*—he'd have used a monkey wrench on the meddler's face. He'd given her the divorce only because she'd asked for it, but he'd hoped that when the business got on its feet and Irv's bookkeeping end covered a wider stretch of it, they might get back together again. Then, of course, business grew worse, Irv's wife got sick and he put even less time in at the office and—

"I feel," he said to himself numbly, "as if I've just found out for certain that there is no Santa Claus. Not Polly, not all those good years! One affair! And the others were just casual things!"

The telephone circuit went off again. "Who is it?" he snarled.

"Mr. Edward Ballaskia."

"What's he want?" Not *Polly, not Pretty Polly!*

An extremely fat man came on the screen. He looked to right and left cautiously. "I must ask you, Mr. Crandall, if you are positive that this line isn't tapped."

"What the hell do you want?" Crandall found himself wishing that the fat man were here in person. He'd love to sail into sombody right now.

Mr. Edward Ballaskia shook his head disapprovingly, his jowls jiggling slowly behind the rest of his face. "Well, then, sir, if you won't give me your assurances, I am forced to take a chance. I am calling, Mr. Crandall, to ask you to forgive your enemies, to turn the other cheek. I am asking you to remember faith, hope and charity—and that the greatest of these is charity. In other words, sir, open your heart to him or her you intended to kill, understand the weaknesses which caused them to give offenses—and forgive them."

"Why should I?" Crandall demanded.

"Because it is to your profit to do so, sir. Not merely morally profitable—although let us not overlook the life of the spirit—but financially profitable. *Financially* profitable Mr. Crandall."

"Would you kindly tell me what you are talking about?"

The fat man leaned forward and smiled confidentially. "If you can forgive the person who caused you to go off and suffer seven long, seven *miserable* years of acute discomfort Mr. Crandall, I am prepared to make you a most attractive offer. You are entitled to commit one murder. I desire to have one murder committed. I am very wealthy. You, I judge—and please take no umbrage, sir—are very poor.

"I can make you comfortable for the rest of your life, extremely comfortable, Mr. Crandall, if only you will put aside your thoughts, your unworthy thoughts, of anger and personal vengeance. I have a business competitor, you see, who has been—"

Crandall turned him off. "Go serve your own seven years," he venomously told the blank screen. Then, suddenly, it was funny. He lay back in the chair and laughed his head off.

That butter-faced old slob! Quoting religious texts at him!

But the call had served a purpose. Somehow it put the scene with Polly in the perspective of ridicule. To think of the woman sitting in her frowsy little apartment, trembling over her dingy affairs of more than ten years ago! To think she was afraid he had bled and battled for seven years because of that!

He thought about it for a moment, then shrugged. "Well, anyway, I bet it did her good."

And now he was hungry.

He thought of having a meal sent up, just to avoid a possible rendezvous with another of Stephanson's ball-throwers but decided against it. If Stephanson was really hunting him seriously, it would not be much of a job to have something put into the food he was sent. He'd be much safer eating in a restaurant chosen at random.

Besides, a few bright lights, a little gaiety, would be really welcome. This was his first night of freedom—and he had to wash that Polly taste out of his mouth.

He checked the corridor carefully before going out. There was nothing, but the action reminded him of a tiny planet near Vega where you made exactly the same precautionary gesture every time you emerged from one of the tunnels formed by the long, parallel lines of moist, carboniferous ferns.

Because if you didn't—well, there was an enormous leech like mollusc that might be waiting there, a creature which could flip chunks of shell with prodigious force. The shell merely stunned its prey, but stunned it long enough for the leech to get in close.

And that leech could empty a man in ten minutes flat.

Once he'd been hit by a fragment of shell, and while he'd been lying there, Henck—Good old Blotto Otto! Crandall smiled. Was it possible that the two of them would look back on those hideous adventures, one day, with actual nostalgia, the kind of beery, pleasant memories that soldiers develop after even the ugliest of wars? Well, and if they did, they hadn't gone through them for the sake of fat cats like Mr. Edward Ballaskia and his sanctified dreams of evil.

Nor, when you came right down to it, for dismal little frightened trollops like Polly.

Frederick Stoddard Stephanson. Frederick Stoddard—

Somebody put an arm on his shoulder and he came to, realizing that he was halfway through the lobby.

"Nick," said a rather familiar voice.

Crandall squinted at the face at the end of the arm. That slight, pointed beard—he didn't know anyone with a beard like that, but the eyes looked so terribly familiar. . . .

"Nick," said the man with the beard. "I couldn't do it."

Those eyes—of course, it was his younger brother!

"Dan!" he shouted.

"It's me all right. Here." Something clattered to the floor. Crandall looked down and saw a blaster lying on the rug, a larger and much more expensive blaster than the one he was carrying. *Why was Dan toting a blaster? Who was after Dan?*

With the thought, there came half-understanding. And there was fear—fear of the words that might come pouring out of the mouth of a brother whom he had not seen for all these years . . .

"I could have killed you from the moment you walked into the lobby," Dan was saying. "You weren't out of the sights for a second. But I want you to know, Nick, that the post-criminal sentence wasn't the reason I froze on the firing button."

"No?" Crandall asked in a breath that was exhaled slowly through a retroactive lifetime.

"I just couldn't stand adding any more guilt about you. Ever since that business with Polly—"

"With Polly. Yes, of course, with Polly." Something seemed to hang like a weight from the point of his jaw; it pulled his head down and his mouth open. "With Polly. That business with Polly."

Dan punched his fist into an open palm twice. "I knew you'd come looking for me sooner or later. I almost went crazy waiting—and I did go nearly crazy with guilt. But I never figured you'd do it this way, Nick. Seven years to wait for you to come back!"

"That's why you never wrote to me, Dan?"

"What did I have to say? What *is* there to say? I thought I loved her, but I found out what I meant to her as soon as she was divorced. I guess I always wanted what was yours because you were my older brother, Nick. That's the only excuse I can offer and I know exactly what it's worth. Because I know what you and Polly had together, what I broke up as a kind of big practical joke. But one thing, Nick: I won't kill you and I won't defend myself. I'm too tired. I'm too guilty. You know where to find me. Anytime, Nick."

He turned and strode rapidly through the lobby, the metal spangles that were this year's high masculine fashion glittering on his calves. He didn't look back, even when he was walking past the other side of the clear plastic that enclosed the lobby.

Crandall watched him go, then said "Hm" to himself in a lonely kind of way. He reached down, retrieved the other blaster and went out to find a restaurant.

As he sat, poking around in the spiced Venusian food that wasn't one-tenth as good as he had remembered it, he kept thinking about Polly and Dan. The incidents—he could remember incidents galore, now that he had a couple of pegs on which to hang them. To think he'd never suspected—but who could suspect Polly, who could suspect Dan?

He pulled the prison discharge out of his pocket and studied it. *Having duly served a maximum penal sentence of seven years, discounted from fourteen years, Nicholas Crandall is herewith discharged in a pre-criminal status—*

—to murder his ex-wife, Polly Crandall?

—to murder his younger brother, Daniel Crandall?

Ridiculous!

But they hadn't found it so ridiculous. Both of them, so blissfully secure in their guilt, so egotistically certain that they and they alone were the objects of a hatred intense enough to endure the worst that the Galaxy had to offer in order to attain vengeance—why, they had both been so positive that their normal and already demonstrated cunning had deserted them and they had completely misread the warmth in his eyes! Either one could have switched confessions in mid-explanation. If they had only not been so preoccupied with self and had noted his astonishment in time, either or both of them could still be deceiving him!

Out of the corner of his eye, he saw that a woman was standing near his table. She had been reading his discharge over his shoulder. He leaned back and took her in while she stood and smiled at him.

She was fantastically beautiful. That is, she had everything a woman needs for great beauty—figure, facial structure, complexion, carriage, eyes, hair, all these to perfection—but she had those other final touches that, as in all kinds of art, make the difference between a merely great work and an all-time masterpiece. Those final touches included such things as sufficient wealth to create the ultimate setting in coiffure and gown, as well as the single Saturnian *paeaea* stone glowing in priceless black splendor between her breasts. Those final touches included the substantial feminine intelligence that beat in her steady eyes; and the somewhat overbred, overindulged, overspoiled quality mixed in with it was the very last piquant fillip of a positively brilliant composition in the human medium.

"May I sit with you, Mr. Crandall?" she asked in a voice of which no more could be said than that it fitted the rest of her.

Rather amused, but more exhilarated than amused, he slid over on the restaurant couch. She sat down like an empress taking her throne before the eyes of a hundred tributary kings.

Crandall knew, within approximate limits, who she was and what she wanted. She was either a reigning post-debutante from the highest social circles in the System, or a theatrical star newly arrived and still in a state of nova.

And he, as a just-discharged convict, with the power of life and death in his hands, represented a taste she had not yet been able to indulge but was determined to enjoy.

Well, in a sense it wasn't flattering, but a woman like this could only fall to the lot of an ordinary man in very exceptional circumstances; he might as well take advantage of his status. He would satisfy her whim, while she, on his first night of freedom—

"That's your discharge, isn't it?" she asked and looked at it again. There was a moistness about her upper lip as she studied it—what a strange, sense-weary patina for one so splendidly young!

"Tell me, Mr. Crandall," she asked at last, turning to him with the wet pinpoints on her lip more brilliant than ever. "You've served a pre-criminal sentence for murder. It is true, is it not, that the punishment for murder and the most brutal, degraded rape imaginable are exactly the same?"

After a long silence, Crandall called for his check and walked out of the restaurant.

He had subsided enough when he reached the hotel to stroll with care around the transparent lobby housing. No one who looked like a Stephanson trigger man was in sight, although Stephanson was a cautious gambler. One attempt having failed, he'd be unlikely to try another for some time.

But that girl! And Edward Ballaskia!

There was a message in his box. Someone had called, leaving only a number to be called back.

Now what? he wondered as he went back up to his room. Stephanson making overtures? Or some unhappy mother wanting him to murder her incurable child?

He gave the number to the set and sat down to watch the screen with a good deal of curiosity.

It flickered—a face took shape on it. Crandall barely restrained a cry of delight. He did have a friend in this city from pre-convict days. Good old dependable, plodding, realistic Irv. His old partner.

And then, just as he was about to shout an enthusiastic greeting, he locked it inside his mouth. Too many things had happened today. And there was something about the expression on Irv's face . . .

"Listen, Nick," Irv said heavily at last. "I just want to ask you one question."

"What's that, Irv?" Crandall kept himself rock-steady.

"How long have you known? When did you find out?"

Crandall ran through several possible answers in his mind, finally selecting one. "A long time now, Irv. I just wasn't in a position to do anything about it."

Irv nodded. "That's what I thought. Well, listen, I'm not going to plead with you. I know that after seven years of what you've gone through, pleading isn't going to do me any good. But, believe me or not, I didn't start dipping into the till very much until my wife got sick. My personal funds were exhausted. I couldn't borrow any more, and you were too busy with your own domestic troubles to be bothered. Then, when business started to get better, I wanted to prevent a sudden large discrepancy on the books.

"So I continued milking the business, not for hospital expenses any more and not to deceive you, Nick—really!—but just so you wouldn't find out how much I'd taken from it before. When you came to me and said you were completely discouraged and wanted out—well, there I'll admit I was a louse. I should have told you. But after all, we hadn't been doing too well as partners and I saw a chance to get the whole business in my name and on its feet, so I—I—"

"So you bought me out for three hundred and twenty credits," Crandall finished for him. "How much is the firm worth now, Irv?"

The other man averted his eyes. "Close to a million. But listen, Nick, business has been terrific this past year in the wholesale line. I didn't cheat you out of all that! Listen, Nick—"

Crandall blew a snort of grim amusement through his nostrils. "What is it, Irv?"

Irv drew out a clean tissue and wiped his forehead. "Nick," he said, leaning forward and trying hard to smile winningly. "Listen to me, Nick! You forget about it, you stop hunting me down, and I've got a proposition for you. I need a man with your technical know-how in top management. I'll give you a twenty per cent interest in the business, Nick—no, make it twenty-five per cent. Look, I'll go as high as thirty per cent—thirty-*five* per cent—"

"Do you think that would make up for those seven years?"

Irv waved trembling, conciliatory hands. "No, of course not, Nick. Nothing would. But listen, Nick. I'll make it forty-five per—"

Crandall shut him off. He sat for a while, then got up and walked around the room. He stopped and examined his blasters, the one he'd purchased earlier and the one he'd gotten from Dan. He took out his prison discharge and read it through carefully. Then he shoved it back into the tunic pocket.

He notified the switchboard that he wanted a long-distance Earthside call put through.

"Yes, sir. But there's a gentleman to see you, sir. A Mr. Otto Henck."

"Send him up. And put the call in on my screen as soon as it goes through, please, Miss."

A few moments later, Blotto Otto entered his room. He was drunk, but carried it, as he always did, remarkably well.

"What do you think, Nick? What the hell do you—"

"Sh-h-h," Crandall warned him. "My call's coming in."

The Tibetan operator said, "Go ahead, New York," and Frederick Stoddard Stephanson appeared on the screen. The man had aged more than any of the others Crandall had seen tonight. Although you never could tell with Stephanson: he always looked older when he was working out a complex deal.

Stephanson didn't say anything; he merely pursed his lips at Crandall and waited. Behind him and around him was a TV Spectacular's idea of a hunting lodge.

"All right, Freddy," Crandall said. "What I have to say won't take long. You might as well call off your dogs and stop taking chances trying to kill and/or injure me. As of this moment, I don't even have a grudge against you."

"You don't even have a grudge—" Stephanson regained his rigid self-control. "Why not?"

"Because—oh, because a lot of things. Because killing you just wouldn't be seven hellish years of satisfaction, now that I'm face to face with it. And because you didn't do any more to me than practically everybody else has done—from the cradle, for all I know. Because I've decided I'm a natural born sucker: that's just the way I'm constructed. All you did was take your kind of advantage of my kind of construction."

Stephanson leaned forward, peered intently, then relaxed and crossed his arms. "You're actually telling the truth!"

"Of course I'm telling the truth! You see these?" He held up the two blasters. "I'm getting rid of these tonight. From now on, I'll be unarmed. I don't want to have the least thing to do with weighing human life in the balance."

The other man ran an index nail under a thumb nail thoughtfully a couple of times. "I'll tell you what," he said. "If you mean what you say—and I think you do—maybe we can work out something. An arrangement, say, to pay you a bit—We'll see."

"When you don't have to?" Crandall was astonished. "But why didn't you make me an offer before this?"

"Because I don't like to be forced to do anything. Up to now, I was fighting force with more force."

Crandall considered the point. "I don't get it. But maybe that's the way you're constructed. Well, we'll see, as you said."

When he rose to face Henck, the little man was still shaking his head slowly, dazedly, intent only on his own problem. "What do you think, Nick? Elsa went on a sightseeing jaunt to the Moon last month. The line to her oxygen helmet got clogged, see, and she died of suffocation before they could do anything about it. Isn't that a *hell* of thing, Nick? One month before I finish my sentence—she couldn't wait one lousy little month! I bet she died laughing at me!"

Crandall put his arm around him. "Let's go out for a walk, Blotto Otto. We both need the exercise."

Funny how the capacity for murder affected people, he thought. There was Polly's way—and Dan's. There was old Irv bargaining frantically but still shrewdly for his life. Mr. Edward Ballaskia—and that girl in the restaurant. And there was Freddy Stephanson, the only intended victim—and the only one who wouldn't beg.

He wouldn't beg, but he might be willing to hand out largesse. Could Crandall accept what amounted to charity from Stephanson? He shrugged. Who knew what he or anyone else could or could not do?

"What do we do now, Nick?" Blotto Otto was demanding petulantly once they got outside the hotel. "That's what I want to know—what do we do?"

"Well, I'm going to do this," Crandall told him, taking a blaster in each hand. "Just this." He threw the gleaming weapons, right hand, left hand, at the transparent window walls that ran around the luxurious lobby of the Ritz-Capricorn. They struck *thunk* and then *thunk* again. The windows crashed down in long, pointed daggers. The people in the lobby swung around with their mouths open.

A policeman ran up, his badge jingling against his metallic uniform. He seized Crandall.

"I saw you! I saw you do that! You'll get thirty days for it!"

"Hm," said Crandall. "Thirty days?" He pulled his prison discharge out of his pocket and handed it to the policeman. "I tell you what we'll do, officer—Just punch the proper number of holes in this document or tear off what seems to you a proportionately sized coupon. Either or both. Handle it any way you like."

Lino Aldani

Translated by L. K. Conrad

Lino Aldani (1926–   ) is an Italian writer who is principally known for his science fiction. He is the author of a pioneering study on science fiction, *La fantascienza* (1962), the first of its kind to appear in Italy.

He began publishing SF stories in the magazine *Oltre il Cielo* in 1960, under the pseudonym of N. L. Janda. In 1963 he founded and edited, with Massimo Lo Jacono and Giulio Raiola, the magazine *Futuro*, featuring exclusively science fiction written by Italian authors. In 1964 he published his first collection, *Quarta dimensione*, and continued to sell stories to various magazines and anthologies, developing an individual style mixing traditional SF tropes and striking extrapolations with literate prose and a distinctive feel for realism. For this reason, his fiction can often be compared to that of better known Italian literary fantasists writing outside the SF genre. His situation, writing in the land of Italo Calvino and Dino Buzzati, has been analogous to the situation of, say, John Wyndham or Brian W. Aldiss publishing science fiction in the land of Aldous Huxley and George Orwell. Literary fashion seems to dictate that it matters more how and where you publish it, what class signals it gives off, than what it actually is.

Lino Aldani lived in Rome until 1968, when he decided to return to his native town. He had a variety of occupations, ranging from office worker to bartender, and later taught philosophy and mathematics in high school. He also served as mayor of his native town.

Aldani has never been a prolific writer, and only in 1977 published his first novel, *Quando le radici*. Two years later it was followed by the novella *Eclissi 2000* (included in a collection with the same title). In 1985 he published *Nel segno della luna bianca*, written in collaboration with Daniela Piegai, a skilled and enjoyable fantasy novel where his distinctive voice displays new overtones. A new collection of his short fiction appeared in 1987, *Parabole per domani*. His story "Quo Vadis Francisco?" was included in *The Penguin World Omnibus of Science Fiction* (1986), edited by Brian W. Aldiss and Sam J. Lundwall. He later developed it into his most recent novel, *La croce di ghiaccio*, published in 1989. His works have been translated worldwide and are well known in France, Germany, Russia, Japan, Spain, The Netherlands, and nearly all of Eastern Europe. He is surely the Italian SF genre writer who is best known abroad.

GOOD NIGHT, SOPHIE

Grey and blue overalls were running along the street. Grey and blue, no other colors. There were no stores, no agencies, there wasn't a single soda-fountain, or a window full of toys, or even a perfume store. Once in a while, on the fronts covered with soot, incrusted with rubbish and moss, the revolving door of a shop opened. Inside was dreamland: Oneirofilm, happiness within everybody's reach, to fit everybody's pocketbook; inside was Sophie Barlow, nude, for anyone who wanted to buy her.

There were seven of them and they were closing in from all sides. He swung violently, hitting one of them in the jaw, which sent him tumbling down the green marble staircase. Another, tall and brawny, appeared below, brandishing a bludgeon. He dodged the blow by hunching quickly, then grabbed the slave by the waist, hurling him against a column of the temple. Then, while he was trying to corner a third one, a vise of iron seized his neck. He tried to free himself, but another slave tackled his legs, and still another immobilized his left arm.

He was dragged away bodily. From the depths of the enormous cavern came the rhythmical notes of the sitars and tablas, an enervating, obsessive music, full of long quavers.

They tied him naked in front of the altar. Then the slaves fled into the galleries that opened like eye-sockets of skulls in the walls of the cavern. The air was filled with the smell of resin, a strong odor of musk and nard, and aphrodisiac atmosphere emitted by the burning torches, tripods and braziers.

When the dancing virgins appeared, the music stopped for a moment, then took up again, more intensely, accompanied by a distant choir of feminine voices.

It was an orgiastic, inebriating dance. The virgins passed by him one by one, they grazed his stomach, face and chest with their light veils and the long, soft feathers of their headdresses. Diadems and necklaces flashed in the half-light.

At the end the veils fell, slowly, one at a time. He saw the swelling of their breasts, almost felt the softness of all those limbs that were moving in front of him in a tangle of unsated desire.

Then, the long, freezing sound of a gong interrupted the dance. The music ceased. The dancers, like guilt-ridden phantoms, disappeared in the depths of the cave, and in the profound silence the priestess appeared, exceedingly beautiful, wrapped in a leopard cape. She had small bare pink feet, and between her hands clasped a long bluish knife. Her eyes, black, deep, constantly shifting, seemed to search his soul.

How long did the intolerable wait last? The knife cut his bonds with devastating slowness, her great black eyes, moist and desirous, continued to stare at him, while a jumble of words, whispering, murmuring, came to his ears in a persuasive, enticing rhythm.

She dragged him to the foot of the altar. The leopard cape slid to earth, she stretched out languidly and drew him to herself with a gesture at once sweet and imperious.

In the cavern, a conch shell of sounds and shadows, the world came and went in an ebb and flow of sighs.

Bradley turned off the machine and removed the plastic helmet. He came out of the booth, his hands and forehead damp with sweat, his breathing heavy, his pulse accelerated.

Twenty technicians, the director and the principal actress rushed to the supervisor, impatiently surrounding him. Bradley's eyes moved around, looking for an armchair.

"I want a glass of water," he said.

He stretched out gingerly on an air cushion with a long, sloping back, drying the beads of perspiration, and breathing deeply. A technician made his way through the group and handed Bradley a glass, which he emptied in one gulp.

"Well? What do you think of it?" the director asked anxiously.

Bradley waved impatiently, then shook his head.

"We're not there yet, Gustafson."

Sophie Barlow lowered her eyes. Bradley touched her hand.

"It has nothing to do with you, Sophie. You were terrific. I . . . only a great actress could have created that last embrace. But the Oneirofilm itself is artificial, unharmonious, unbalanced . . ."

"What's wrong with it?" the director asked.

"Gustafson! I said the film is *unharmonious*, don't you understand?"

"I heard you. You say it's 'unharmonious,' unbalanced. Okay, the music is Indian, four hundred years old, and the costumes are from central Africa. But the consumer isn't going to notice such subtleties, what interests him is—"

"Gustafson! The customer is always right, never forget that. Anyway, this has nothing to do with music or costumes. The problem is something else: this Oneirofilm would rattle even a bull's nerves!"

Gustafson frowned.

"Give me the script," said Bradley, "and call the aesthetic technician."

He rifled back and forth through the pages, muttering unintelligibly, as if to reconnect the ideas.

"All right," he said at last, closing the bundle of pages suddenly. "The film starts with a long canoe trip, the protagonist is alone in a hostile, strange world, there's a struggle with the river's crocodiles, and the canoe capsizes. Then we have a trek through the jungle, rather tiring, a hand-to-hand fight with the natives. The protagonist is shut up in a hut, but during the night the chieftain's daughter Aloa comes in, and provides him with directions to the temple. Then there's the embrace with Aloa in the moonlight. Speaking of which, where's Moa Mohagry?"

The technician and the director moved apart, and Moa Mohagry, a very tall Somalian woman with sculpturesque curves, stepped forward.

"You were great, Moa, but we're going to have to do the scene over again."

"Again?" Moa exclaimed. "I could do the scene over a hundred times, but I doubt it would get any better. I really gave it all I had, Bradley . . ."

"That's exactly what Gustafson's mistake was. In this Oneirofilm the major scene is the last one, when the priestess seduces the protagonist. All the other scenes are going to have to be toned down—they sould serve as atmosphere and preparation. You can't make an Oneirofilm composed of nothing but major scenes."

He turned to the aesthetic technician.

"What's the sensitivity index in the median sampling?"

"In Aloa's scene?"

"Yes, in Aloa's scene."

"84.5."

"And in the scene of the last embrace?"

"Just under 97."

Bradley shook his head.

"Theoretically it would be okay, but in practice it's all wrong. This morning I screened the scenes in the first part, one at a time. They're perfect. But the film doesn't end on the riverbank when Aloa gives herself to the protagonist. There are other, rather tiring episodes: the ones I just screened, then another trek through the jungle, and the fight with the slaves in the temple. By the time the consumer gets to this point in the film, he's exhausted, his sensory receptivity is down to a minimum. The virgins' erotic dance only partly solves the problem. I saw the film in two takes, and so I was able to appreciate the last embrace with Sophie in all its stylistic perfection. But, please, let's not mix up absolute index with relative index. The crucial thing is relative index. I'm positive that if we distributed the film the way it's put together now, the total receptivity index would fall by at least forty points, in spite of Sophie's performance."

"Bradley!" the director implored. "Now you're exaggerating."

"I'm not exaggerating," the supervisor insisted in a polemical tone. "I repeat, the last scene is a masterpiece, but the consumer gets there tired and already satisfied, in such a condition that even the most luscious fruit would taste insipid to him. Gustafson, you can't expect Sophie to accomplish miracles. The human nervous system has limits and laws."

"Then what should we do?"

"Listen to me, Gustafson. I was a director for twenty-five years, and for six years I've been a supervisor. I think I've had enough experience to give you some advice. If you leave this Oneirofilm the way it is, I won't pass it. I can't. Beyond not pleasing the public, I would risk undermining the career of an actress like Sophie Barlow. Pay attention to me, dilute all the scenes except the last, cut the embrace with Aloa, reduce it to a mere scuffle."

Moa Mohagry started angrily. Bradley took her wrist and forced her to sit on the arm of his chair.

"Listen to me, Moa. Don't think that I want to take away the right moment for you to make a big hit. You have talent, I know it. The riverbank episode shows true zeal and temperament, there's an innocent primitive passion there that would not fail to fascinate the consumer. You were fantastic, Moa. But I can't ruin a film that's cost millions, you understand, don't you? I'm going to suggest to the production committee a couple of films that will star you, Moa. There are millions and millions of consumers who go mad for Oneirofilms in a primitive setting. You'll make a big hit, too, I promise you. But not right now, it's not the right moment . . ."

Bradley got up. He felt faint, his legs weak and tired.

"Please, Gustafson. Also tone down the slaves' fight episode. Too much movement, too much violence. The waste of energy is enormous . . ."

He went tottering off, surrounded by technicians.

"Where's Sophie?" he asked as he got to the back of the room.

Sophie Barlow smiled at him.

"Come in my office," he said. "I have to talk to you."

"All right, I'm not saying anything new, they're old words, stale, you must have heard them a hundred times at school and during your training course. But it would benefit you to give them some thought."

Bradley was walking back and fourth in the room, slowly, his fingers laced together behind his back. Sophie Barlow was slouched in an armchair. From time to time she stretched out a leg and stared at the toe of her shoe.

Bradley stopped for a moment in front of her.

"What's the matter with you, Sophie? Are you having a crisis?"

The woman made a nervous, awkward gesture. "Having a crisis? Me?"

"Yes. That's why I called you into the office. You know, I don't want to read you the riot act. I simply want to remind you of the fundamental precepts of our system. I'm not young any more, Sophie. There are things I can spot right off, at the first sign. Sophie! you're running after a chimera!"

Sophie Barlow squinted and then opened her eyes wide as a cat's.

"A chimera? What's a chimera, Bradley?"

"I told you, I can spot some things right off. You're having a crisis, Sophie. I wouldn't be surprised if it had something to do with the propaganda that those pigs at the Anti-Dream League put out by the truckload to undermine our social order."

Sophie seemed not to pick up the insinuation. She said:

"Was Moa's performance really that good?"

Bradley passed a hand behind his neck. "Absolutely. Mohagry will make it big, I'm convinced of it . . ."

"Better than mine?"

Bradley snorted. "That's a meaningless question."

"I made myself clear. I want to know which of us you liked better, me or Moa."

"And I repeat, your question is idiotic, lacks common sense, and just goes to confirm my suspicion—in fact, my conviction—that you're going through a crisis. You'll get over it, Sophie. All actresses go through this phase sooner or later. It seems to be a necessary stage . . ."

"I would like to know just one thing, Bradley. Something that's never said in the schools, something nobody ever talks about. *Before.* What was there before? Was everybody really unhappy?"

Bradley took up pacing around the armchair.

"Before, there was chaos."

"Bradley! I want to know if they were really unhappy."

The man stretched out his arms disconsolately.

"I don't know, Sophie. I didn't exist at the time, I wasn't born yet. One thing is sure: if the system has asserted itself, it means that objective conditions have allowed it to do so. I would like you to be aware of one very simple fact: technology has permitted the realization of all our desires, even the most secret ones. Technology, progress, the perfection of instruments and the exact knowledge of our own minds, of our own egos . . . all of that is real, tangible. Hence even our dreams are real. Sophie, don't forget that only in very rare cases is the Oneirofilm an instrument of comfort or compensation. Almost always it is an end in itself, and when just now I had you, I enjoyed your body, your words, and your odors amid a play of exotic emotions."

"Yes, but it's always artificial . . ."

"Okay, but I wasn't aware of it. And then, even the meaning of words evolves. You use the word *artificial* in the pejorative sense it had two centuries ago. But not today, today an artificial product is no longer a surrogate, Sophie. A fluorescent lamp, correctly adjusted, gives better light than the sun. This is true of the Oneirofilm as well."

Sophie Barlow looked at her fingernails.

"When did it begin, Bradley?"

"What?"

"The system."

"Eighty-five years it's been now, as you should know."

"I do, but I mean the *dreams.* When did men begin to prefer them to reality?"

Bradley squeezed his nose, as if to collect his thoughts.

"Cinematography began to develop at the beginning of the twentieth century.

At first it was a question of two-dimensional images moving on a white screen. Then, sound, the panoramic screen, color photography were introduced. The consumers gathered by the hundreds in special projection halls to watch and listen, but they never *felt* the film, at most they experienced a latent participation through an effort of fantasy. Obviously the film was a surrogate, a real and proper artifice for titillating the erotic and adventurous taste of the public. However, movie-making then represented a very powerful instrument of psycho-social transformation. Women of that period felt the need of imitating actresses in their gestures, vocal inflections, dress. This was no less true of men. Life was lived according to the movies. First the economy was conditioned by it: the enormous demand for consumer goods—clothes, cars, comfortable housing—was of course due to real exigencies of nature, but also and above all to the ruthless, indefatigable advertising that harassed and seduced the consumer every minute of the day. Even then, men longed for the dream, were obsessed by it, day and night, but they were far from achieving it."

"They were unhappy, right?"

"I repeat, I don't know. I'm only trying to illustrate for you the stages of the process. Toward the middle of the twentieth century the standard woman, the standard situation was already in existence. It's true that there were directors and producers in those days that tried to produce cultural films, ideological movies, to communicate ideas and elevate the masses. But the phenomenon lasted only a short time. In 1956 scientists discovered the pleasure centers in the brain, and through experimentation revealed that electric stimulation of a certain part of the cortex produces an intense, voluptuous reaction in the subject. It was twenty years before the benefits of this discovery were made available to the public. The projection of the first three-dimensional movie with partial spectator participation signalled the death of the intellectual film. Now the public could experience odors and emotions; they could already partly identify with what was happening on the screen. The entire economy underwent an unprecedented transformation. The human race was starved for pleasure, luxury and power, and only asked to be satisfied at the cost of a few pennies."

"And the Oneirofilm?"

"The Oneirofilm came out, fully perfected, only a few years later. There's no reality that surpasses dreams, and the public became convinced of this very quickly. When participation is total, any competition from nature is ridiculous, any rebellion useless. If the product is perfect, the consumer is happy and the society is stable. That's the system, Sophie. And certainly your temporary crises are not likely to change it, not even the melodramatic chatter of the Naturists, unscrupulous people who go around collecting funds for the triumph of an idea that is unbalanced to start with, but for their own personal profit. If you want a good laugh—last week Herman Wolfried, one of the leaders of the Anti-Dream League, appeared in the offices of the Norfolk Company. And do you want to know why? He wanted a private Oneirofilm, five famous actresses in a mind-blowing orgy. Norfolk has accepted the commission and Wolfried is paying for it through the nose, so much the worse for him."

Sophie Barlow jumped up.

"You're lying, Bradley! You're lying on purpose, shamelessly."

"I have proof, Sophie. The Anti-Dream League is an organization out to dupe simpletons, incurable hypochondriacs and passéists. Perhaps there is some remnant of religious sentiment behind it, but at the center of it is only greed."

Sophie was on the verge of tears. Bradley moved toward her solicitously and put his hands on her shoulders in a tender, protective gesture.

"Don't think about it any more, Sophie."

He guided her over to the desk, opened the safe, and got out a small, flat, rectangular box.

"Here," said Bradley.

"What is it?"

"A present."

"For me?"

"Yes, actually it was to give you this that I called you into the office. You've made twenty Oneirofilms for our production company, an inspiring goal, as it were. The firm is honoring you with a small recognition of your worth . . ."

Sophie started to unwrap the present.

"Leave it," Bradley said. "You can open it at home. Run along now, I have a lot to do."

There was a line of helitaxis just outside the building. Sophie got into the first one, took a magazine from the side pocket of the vehicle, lit a cigarette and, flattered, contemplated her own face on the front cover. The helitaxi rose softly, steering for the center of the city.

Her lips were half-open in an attitude of offering, the color, the contrast between light and shadow, the expression ambiguous . . . Each detail seemed knowingly graded.

Sophie looked at herself as if in a mirror. At one time the job of acting had presented various negative aspects. When she made a love scene, there was a flesh and blood "partner," and she had to embrace him, tolerate the physical contact, kisses, words breathed straight into her face. The camera photographed the scene which the spectators then later saw on the screen. Now it was different. There was "Adam," the mannequin packed with electronic devices having two minute cameras conveniently placed in his eyes. "Adam" was a wonder of receptivity: if the actress caressed him, the receptivity valve registered the sensation of the caress and fixed it, together with the visual image, on the reel of Oneirofilm. Thus the consumer who would later use that reel would perceive the caress in all its sensory fidelity. The spectator was no longer passive but the protagonist.

Naturally, there were Oneirofilms for men and Oneirofilms for women. And they were not interchangeable: if a male consumer, plagued by morbid curiosity, inserted in his reception helmet a reel meant for female consumption, he would get an atrocious headache, and also risk short-circuiting the delicate wiring of the apparatus.

Sophie told the pilot to stop. The helitaxi had gone barely a dozen blocks, but Sophie decided to proceed on foot.

Grey and blue overalls were running along the street. Grey and blue, no other colors. There were no stores, no agencies, there wasn't a single soda-fountain, or a window full of toys, or even a perfume store. Once in a while, on the fronts covered with soot, incrusted with rubbish and moss, the revolving door of a shop opened. Inside, on the smooth glass counters, there was the *dream*, happiness for everybody, for all pocketbooks, and it was Sophie herself, nude, for anybody who wanted to have her.

They marched on. And Sophie Barlow marched along with them, an army of hallucinated people, people who worked three hours a day, prey to the spasms that the silence of their own shells yearned for: a room, an Amplex and a helmet. And reel after reel of Oneirofilms, millions of dreams of love, power and fame.

In the middle of the square, on a large platform draped in green, the fat man was gesticulating emphatically.

"Citizens!"

His voice raised itself as loud and clear as a dream speech, when the dreamer has the whole world singing hosannas at his feet.

"Citizens! An ancient philosopher once said that virtue is a habit. I am not here to ask the impossible of you. I would be a fool if I expected to renounce it immediately and completely. For years we have been slaves and succubuses, prisoners in the labyrinth of dreams, for years we have been groping in the dense darkness of uncommunicativeness and isolation. Citizens, I invite you to be free. Freedom is virtue, and virtue is a habit. We have cheated nature too long, we must rush to make amends, before we arrive at a total and definite death of the soul . . ."

How many times had she listened to speeches like that? The propaganda of the Anti-Dream League was sickening, it had always produced in her a profound sense of irritation. Lately, however, she had surprised and bewildered herself. Perhaps because she was an actress, when the orators in the squares spoke of sin, perdition, when they incited the crowds of consumers to abandon the "dream," she took the accusation as if it had been personally aimed at her; she felt a responsibility for the whole system. Perhaps behind the orators' emphatic tone there actually was some truth. Perhaps they hadn't told her everything at school. Maybe Bradley was wrong.

On the platform the fat man ranted and raved, pounding his fist on the wood of the lectern, red in the face, congested. Not a soul was listening to him.

When the veiled girl came out of a small side door, there were some in the crowd who stopped for a second. From the loudspeakers issued the sound of ancient oriental music. The girl began to take off her veils, dancing. She was pretty, very young, and made syncopated, light, eurhythmic gestures.

"An amateur," Sophie said to herself. "A would-be actress . . ."

When she was standing naked in the center of the platform, even the few men who had stopped to wait moved on. One or two of them laughed, and shook their heads, disappointed.

The Anti-Dream League girls stopped the passers-by, they approached the men, thrusting out their breasts in an absurd, pathetic offer.

Sophie lengthened her stride. But someone stopped her, grabbing her arm. It was a tall, dark young man, who stared at her with steady black eyes.

"What do you want?"

"To make you a proposition."

"Speak up."

"Come with me, tonight."

Sophie burst out laughing.

"With you! What for? What would I get out of it?"

The young man smiled faintly, patiently, a smile tinged with security and superiority. Clearly he was accustomed to this sort of refusal.

"Nothing," he admitted unperturbed. "But our duty is to—"

"Cut it out. We'd spend the night insulting each other, in a pitiful attempt to achieve 'natural harmony' . . . Dear boy, your friend up there on the platform is spewing forth a pile of nonsense."

"It's not nonsense," the young man retorted. "Virtue is a habit. I could—"

"No, you couldn't. You couldn't because you don't want me, and you don't want me because I'm real, true, living, human, because I would be a surrogate, a substitute for a reel of Oneirofilm which you could buy for a few pennies. And you? What could you offer me? Silly presumptuous young ass!"

"Wait! Listen to me, I beg of you—"

"Goodbye," Sophie cut him short. And continued her walk.

The words she aimed at the young man had been too harsh. It had been a uselessly hostile reaction; she might have rejected his proposition neither more nor less vehemently than the other passers-by did, with some grace, or better, with a self-sufficient smile. In the last analysis, what right did she have to insult him, perhaps to hurt his feelings? He was acting in good faith. But what about the leaders? Bradley had assured her a number of times that the directors of the Anti-Dream League were a band of swine. What if Bradley had been lying to her all along?

The suspicion had now been plaguing her for several weeks. All those speeches in the squares, the manifestos on the walks, the propagandistic pamphlets, the public proposition to experiment in natural relations with the League's activists . . . Was it possible that the whole thing was a lie? Perhaps there was some truth in what the orators and lecturers maintained, maybe the world was rotten to the core, and only a few enlightened men had eyes to see the horror and to assess such decadence.

Man as an island: they had all been reduced to this. On one side the producing class, a class that kept power and to which she herself belonged in her capacity of actress; on the other, the prostrate, blind army of consumers, men and women avid for solitude and darkness, silkworms coiled up in the silken filaments of their own dreams, pale bloodless larvae poisoned by inaction.

Sophie had been born in the glass. So had everybody else, for that matter. She did not know her mother. Millions of women, once a month, went to the Bank of Life; millions of men achieved orgasm by means of the Dream and donated semen to the Bank, which sorted it carefully and used it according to rigorous criteria. Marriage was an archaic institution. Sophie had been the child of a dream, of an unknown, anonymous man who in a dream had possessed an actress. Every man over forty could be her father, every woman between the age of forty and eighty her mother.

When she was younger, this thought had disturbed her greatly, then bit by bit she had got used to it. But lately all the doubts and anxieties of her adolescence had reared up again, vultures that patiently circled above, waiting for one of her moments of weakness. Who was that young man who had stopped her on the street? A champion of superior humanity, or a fool?

Certainly, if he had said to her, "I recognize you, Sophie Barlow. I recognize you in spite of your standard suit and your dark glasses." Or if he had said, "You're my favorite star, you're the obsession of all my days . . ." Or even if he'd said, "I want to get to know you, whoever you are, just as you really are . . ."

Instead, that lout had talked about duty. He had asked her to spend the night with him, but only to pay obeisance to the presumptuous new morality: Virtue is a habit. A habit, a routine of natural relations. Love one another, ladies and gentlemen, come together in self-denial! Each of your acts of love will contribute to the defeat and destruction of an unjust system. Unite yourselves, come together in reality, the sublime joy of the senses will not delay in manifesting itself! An exultation of sounds and lights will fill your souls, will glorify your bodies! And our children will once again be formed in the warmth of the womb, not in the cold glass of a test tube.—Wasn't this what the fat man on the platform had been preaching?

She went into a crowded store and made her way over to the sales counter, where hundreds and hundreds of Oneirofilms were neatly displayed, packed in elegant plastic boxes. She loved to read the descriptions printed on the covers, to listen to the conversations that the shoppers sometimes had with each other, or the zealous advice that the salesmen whispered in the ears of undecided customers.

She read a few titles.

Singapore: Eurasian singer (Milena Chung Lin) flees with the Spectator. Adventure in the underworld of this eastern port. Period, mid twentieth century. Night of love on a sampan.

The Battle: In the role of a heroic officer, the Spectator infiltrates an enemy encampment and sabotages its munitions dump. A last battle, bloody, victorious.

Ecstasy: The private jet of a Persian princess (masterful performance by Sophie Barlow) crashes in the Grand Canyon. Princess and Pilot (the Spectator) spend the night in a cave.

Descriptions in greater detail were to be found inside the boxes. There was no danger that an exact knowledge of the contents on the part of the consumer would lower its desirability index. Mental projection inside the Amplex was accompanied by catatonic stupor in which the memory of each independent episode never connected with the next to form a whole. One could not know, experiencing the first episode, what would happen in the second and following episodes. Even if plot descriptions were learned by heart, even if one saw the same film twenty times, the conscious ego, the everyday ego was sacrificed to the urges provoked by the reel: one ceased to be oneself in order to assume the personality, the mannerisms, the voice, the impulses suggested by the film.

A salesman sidled up to her solicitously.

"May I help you to choose a gift?"

Sophie suddenly noticed that among the mob of buyers there were no other women. This was the men's department. She moved off toward the opposite counter, mingling with women of all ages, lingering before the enormous photographs of the most popular actors.

Outer Space Belongs to Us: Commander of a spaceship (Alex Morrison) falls in love with the lady doctor on board (the Spectator), the rocket changes course to discharge the crew on one of Jupiter's moons, and the Commander heads off with his lover. Trans-galactic crossing.

Tortuga: Period, mid seventeenth century. Gallant pirate (Manuel Alvarez) abducts noblewoman (the Spectator). Jealousy and duels. Love and sea voyages under a fiery sky.

"What's it like?" asked a tall girl, her buxom body suffocating in a pair of overalls too small for her.

"Fascinating," her companion asserted. "I bought four more copies of it right away."

The other girl looked skeptical. She stretched her neck over the counter, stood on the tips of her toes to read the descriptions on the farthestmost boxes. She said something in a low voice, and her companion answered in a whisper. Sophie moved off. She spent a few minutes in the "classics" section, giving a fleeting glance to the back of the shop where men and women crowded together to buy the so-called "convenience" Oneirofilms.

When she had been younger, at school, they had told her that in former times men considered taboo anything that had to do with sex. It was highly improper to write or talk about the many aspects of love life. No woman would ever have described her desires and her sexual fantasies to a stranger. There were pornographic publications and photographs, many of which were illegal. People who bought them did it on the sly and always with a feeling of guilt or embarrassment, even when they had been passed by the Censor. But with the advent of the "system" the primitive custom of sexual modesty had become obsolete. Modesty existed, if at all, in some kinds of dreams, in "convenience" films made for the over-fifty set, where the consumer seduced or raped a teary, red-faced, trembling young girl. But in real life it had disappeared, or at least verbal modesty had. Without a shadow of embarrassment or discomfort, anybody could ask for an erotic film, the same as any other film about war or adventure.

But what about real and proper modesty? Among the many who crowded round the counters to buy the luxury in a box, who would have had the courage to disrobe in the middle of the mob? Only those activists of the Anti-Dream League, who were completely unselfconscious when they propositioned people, but perhaps not quite so unselfconscious when faced with performing what they themselves considered a weighty duty. The truth was, for nearly a century men and women had lived in a state of almost complete chastity. Solitude, the measured penumbra inside the narrow walls of their habitations, the armchairs with built-in Amplex: humanity had no desire for anything else. Faced with the greater attractions of dreams, the ambition to own a comfortable house, elegant clothes, a helicar, and other amenities had simply gone by the boards. Why beat one's brains out collecting real objects when, with an Oneirofilm that cost but a few pennies, one could live like a nabob for an hour, near stupendous women, admired, respected, served hand and foot?

Eight billion human beings vegetated inside squalid beehives, isolated in mean little holes, nourished by vitamin concentrates and soybean meal. And they felt no desire to consume anything real. After the bottom fell out of the market, the industries producing consumer goods had been abandoned all at once by financiers, who transferred their funds to companies producing Oneirofilms, the only merchandise for which there was any real demand.

She looked up toward the shining chart, and was disgusted at herself. The numbers spoke clearly. The sales chart was most eloquent. Her own Oneirofilms were the ones most in demand, more than everybody else's put together.

Sophie left the store. She walked homeward, her head bent, her step slow and listless. She didn't know how to judge that crowd of men who moved all around her, without recognizing her. Were they her slaves, or was she theirs?

The videophone rang: a streak of light in an abyss of black velvet, a peal from lofty cathedral spires in a sleepy, gray dawn.

Sophie stretched out a hand toward the pulsator-button.

A red snake zig-zagged onto the screen, lingered, seemed to explode; finally it resolved itself into Bradley's image.

"What do you want?" Sophie whined, her voice slurred with sleep. "For God's sake, what time is it?"

"It's noon. Wake up, my girl. You have to go to San Francisco."

"To San Francisco? What for? Are you out of your mind?"

"We have a co-production contract with Norfolk, Sophie. It was set for next Monday, but time presses. They need you now."

"But I'm still in bed, I'm deathly tired. I'll leave tomorrow, Bradley."

"Get dressed," the supervisor barked. "A Norfolk jet will be waiting for you at the West airport. Don't waste time."

Sophie was fuming. This extra work wasn't scheduled. What she wanted to do was spend the rest of the day in bed, resting.

She struggled out from under the covers, her eyes still shut, and sluggishly, halfheartedly undressed in the bathroom. The metallic jet of the cold shower made her shiver. She dried herself, dressed hurriedly, and left the house on the run.

She knew the methods of those types at Norfolk. They were worse than Bradley, real nitpickers. Always ready to find fault even with the scenes that had come off well.

In eight minutes, the helitaxi deposited her at the entrance to the airport. She entered by the door that led to the runway for private aircraft, and looked round for the Norfolk jet.

The pilot emerged from an outbuilding and walked over to meet her with a bouncy step.

"Sophie Barlow?"

He was tall, with light blond hair and a bronze complexion, a face that looked as if it had been baked in an oven.

"I'm Mirko Glikorich, from the Norfolk Company."

Sophie said nothing. The pilot did not think her worth a glance, and spoke staring at an indefinite point somewhere out in the airfield, two cold, aggressive eyes of a fine gray color like anthracite. He took Sophie's suitcase and marched off toward the main runway, where the Norfolk jet was being prepared for takeoff. Sophie had a hard time keeping up with him.

"Hey!" she exclaimed, balking like a thoroughbred. "I'm not a runner. Couldn't you walk a little slower?"

The pilot kept moving, without so much as turning around.

"We're late," he said curtly. "We have to be in San Francisco in three hours."

She was breathless by the time they reached the aircraft.

"Do you mind if I sit in front with you?" asked Sophie.

The pilot shrugged his shoulders. He helped her up, settled himself into the cockpit, and waited for the signal from the control tower.

Sophie looked around, full of curiosity, a bit intimidated by all the dials and switches on the instrument panel. The pilot whistled softly, impatient. Sophie groped around in the pocket of her seat and pulled out a dozen magazines. They were all at least several weeks old, some from the year before, dog-eared. Her face was on the cover of each of them. There was also an Oneirofilm catalogue folded open to the page that listed the films starring Sophie.

"Are these your things?"

The pilot didn't answer, but looked stiffly ahead. The takeoff had been gentle as a feather, and Sophie hadn't felt it at all. She glanced out the window and barely stifled an "Oh!" of surprise. A sea of houses extended itself beneath them; like a downy eyelid, the gray shell of the countryside opened up before them.

"Are these yours?" Sophie insisted.

The pilot turned his head slightly, an imperceptible movement, a lightning glance. Then he stiffened again.

"Yes," he said through his teeth.

She tried to hide the intimate gratification that always pervaded her when she met one of her ardent fans.

"What did you say your name was?"

"Glikorich," the pilot growled. "Mirko Glikorich."

"That's a Russian name, isn't it?"

"Yugoslav."

She watched him for a while. His lips were narrow and taut, his profile straight and sharp . . . Mirko looked as if he had been chiseled in rock, mute, motionless. Sophie grew impatient.

"Can I ask you a question?"

"Speak."

"Before—at the airport. You came to meet me and asked me if I was Sophie Barlow. Why? You know me, don't you? These magazines and the catalogue. I'll bet you're a fan of mine. Why did you pretend not to recognize me?"

"I didn't pretend. It's different, seeing you in person. In the end I recognized you because I knew you were supposed to turn up at that entrance at the airport. But in the middle of the crowd, no; you could have passed me without my noticing."

Sophie lit a cigarette. Maybe the pilot was right: in the crowd nobody would notice her, even without her dark glasses. She felt a kind of dull anger toward the man beside her. But she kept making an effort to talk to him. Mirko proved to be dense as a jungle, impenetrable, diffident.

"Why don't you turn on the automatic pilot?" Sophie asked. "I'm bored, Mirko. Say something to me."

The pilot remained impassive. He blinked once or twice, and stuck out his chin.

Sophie caught his arm. "Mirko! Pay attention to me! Turn on the automatic pilot and have a cigarette with me."

"I prefer to leave it on manual."

Sophie lit another cigarette, then another, using the butt of the second. She leafed through a magazine, worrying the pages in a fit of uncontrollable nervousness. She started to sing to herself, tapping her foot against the rubber lining of the cockpit. She snorted, fidgeting, and finally pretended to feel nauseated.

Mirko felt around inside the pocket of his flying suit and handed her a tablet.

Sophie was furious.

"Idiot!" she cried. "I won't stay here a moment longer. I'm going back in the cabin."

The little living room behind the cockpit was attractive. There was a couch, a stowable berth, a little table and a bar.

She poured herself a drink, a tall glass of brandy, which she gulped down at once. She poured herself another immediately, and the edges of objects began to vibrate in a bluish, inviting fog. She lowered herself to the couch, thinking of Mirko, a consumer like all the rest, an imbecile. She couldn't wait to get to San Francisco, make the film, and fly back to New York.

Now she sipped the brandy with less gusto. As she set the glass on the table, she began to feel groggy.

Suddenly, the arm of the couch was shoved against her, and an abyss seemed to open beneath, as when an elevator begins to move. She watched the glass start to slide along the tabletop, spill on the rug . . . Then, a pain in her shoulder, her forehead knocked against something . . . Fog. Red and blue globes. Roaring of motors gone wild.

"Mirko!" she cried, raising herself. The door to the cockpit seemed bolted shut. She squeezed the hostile handle and, lurching, tried to pull the door open. An emptiness inside her chest, a moment of balance, then the absurd feeling of weightlessness. She saw Mirko's back, his hands tense on the throttle, the clouds racing towards them like dream vapors.

Now Mirko was talking. In fact, he was shouting, but she wasn't aware of it. She pressed herself against the back of her seat, clenched her teeth and braced herself for the crash.

The aircraft plummeted like a corkscrew.

When she opened her eyes next, she saw a white cloud in the middle of the sky. A vulture circled far up. She was lying stretched out on her back, and something moist and fresh was pressed against her brow. She raised an arm, touched her face, temples, and removed the handkerchief soaked with water. Then she rolled over on her side.

Mirko was on his feet, over by the wrecked fuselage. Behind him, a cyclopean wall of red rock rose over the landscape.

"What happened?" she asked weakly.

The pilot stretched out his arms. "I don't know," he said, shaking his head. "I can't understand it. All of a sudden the controls weren't responding, the craft lost altitude, and then we were in a tailspin. I managed to regain control by a miracle, but it was too late. Look at the skid we took before we banged up against this rock!"

Sophie pulled herself up, rubbing her bruised shoulder.

"Do you have any idea where we are?"

Mirko lowered his eyes.

"This is the Grand Canyon," he said. "We're in one of the side chasms. This is one of the most inaccessible areas, but the Bright Angel Trail shouldn't be too far away . . ."

Sophie's eyes widened. "The Grand Canyon?"

For a moment she was speechless. Then she burst out laughing.

"The Grand Canyon!" she repeated. "That's very funny! In fact it's unbelievable."

"What's unbelievable?"

"Don't play dumb, Mirko. The engine failure, the forced landing, here, right in the middle of the Grand Canyon . . . Just like the film I made last year, *Ecstasy*. You do remember it, don't you?"

Suddenly a suspicion crossed her mind.

"Tell me something," she said, frowning. "You didn't by any chance do it on purpose, did you? I mean, there are an awful lot of coincidences here. You're a real pilot, and I may not be a Persian princess but on the other hand I am Sophie Barlow. You wanted to get marooned out here with me, didn't you? You planned it to happen just like the film."

Mirko puffed up indignantly. He turned his back on her and went over to the aircraft. Shifting aside the twisted pieces of fuselage, he managed to crawl into the cabin. He tossed out a pile of equipment, two blankets, two back-packs, a plastic canteen, a tin of synthetic food, a flashlight. He emerged from the wreck with the bottle of brandy in one hand and a heavy piece of equipment in the other.

"Let's go," he said. "Carry as much of this as you can."

"Go where?"

"Surely you don't want to rot out here among the rocks. We have to get to the main canyon. Phantom Ranch must be more than fifty miles east of here, but there's always some stupid sentimental tourist who will come west to take a picture of the pretty view."

"Did you try radioing?"

"The radio's broken. Get a move on. Take what you need and let's get out of here."

He moved fast, his stride long and springy. He had tucked the brandy bottle into his hip pocket, and he marched along stooping slightly under the burden of his pack, in which he had placed a battery and the heavy electronic device.

Sophie stumbled along behind him, carrying the food and water containers.

Half an hour later, they came to a halt. Sophie was out of breath, her eyes were pleading. Mirko stared straight ahead. It was clear that the woman was a hindrance to him, the classical ball and chain which he could not get rid of.

"Walk slower, Mirko."

The man looked at the sky, which was filling up with menacing clouds.

"Let's go," he said. "In a couple of hours it's going to be pitch black."

When they reached the main canyon, they could hardly see anything. Mirko pointed up at a place in the rocky wall, red and brown as a piece of burning paper.

"The cave," he said reverently.

"The cave," Sophie repeated. "Just like in the film. Everything is just like in the film, Mirko."

He helped her up the cliff, and lowered his pack to the floor of the black hole that opened into the rock.

She watched him as he clambered down the sandstone and granite crags, rooting out the dried-up shrubs, making big bundles of them and dragging them up to the cave entrance. "It'll be cold in a while," he said. "We'll have to start a fire."

He lit the flashlight and inspected the cave. It was about fifteen yards deep, and bent at right angles in the middle. He set the bundle of kindling right in the elbow of the cave, and lit the fire with savage delight.

They ate in silence, in the dark and glowing cave, under an enormous fluttering bat's wing.

"I opened your pack," Sophie said. "While you were down gathering kindling. I saw what you have inside there. An Amplex! What did you need to bring that along for?"

"It's worth 120 coupons," Mirko said. "For an actress like you, that's a pittance. But it takes me three months to earn that much, you see?"

He picked up the metal box and the reel case.

"Well?" Sophie asked, curious. "What are you up to now?"

"I'm going to the rear of the cave. I have a right to my privacy, don't I?"

"Yes, but what do you need the Amplex for? What are you up to, Mirko?"

The man snorted. When Sophie grabbed the reel case, he didn't put up a fight. Passive, he let the woman go through his reels at her leisure, let her read the descriptions printed on the plastic boxes.

"But these are all my films, Mirko! My heavens, you have every single one of them! *Blue Skies, Seduction, Adventure in Ceylon.* There's even a matrix, the matrix for *Ecstasy.* Is that your favorite Oneirofilm, Mirko?"

Mirko lowered his eyes without answering. Sophie closed the reel box. A matrix was a luxury relatively few people could permit themselves. The ordinary Oneirofilm, once viewed, was useless, because the Amplex demagnetized the tape as it ran through. But a matrix lasted forever, it was practically indestructible. For that reason, it cost a small fortune.

"When did you buy it?" Sophie asked.

The man shrugged, annoyed. "Oh, quit it," he snapped. "You're too curious. What do you want me to say? Your films sell millions of copies to millions and millions of consumers. I'm just one of them. I bought a matrix of *Ecstasy*. So what? What's so strange about that? There was something about it that I liked. I—"

"Go on," Sophie urged, squeezing his arm.

"A day doesn't pass that I don't watch it," the pilot said tartly. "So now why don't you leave me alone, go to sleep, because in a little while it will be daylight and we have to cover quite a few miles. I'm going to the back of the cave."

"With the Amplex?"

"Yes, for God's sake. What's it to you? I want to enjoy my film in peace."

Sophie gulped. A sudden feeling of frustration passed through her, as if all desire to live had left her. This is impossible, she thought. This can't be happening to me. What do I want, anyway, from this man who has a thousand reasons not to care a hoot about me?

She felt a desire to hurt him, to heap abuse on his head, to slap his face. But the image of Mirko embracing her broke through her inhibitions and spread through her mind.

"I'm here," she was surprised to hear herself say in a seductive tone.

Mirko wheeled round.

"What did you say?"

"I said, I'm here, Mirko. Tonight you don't need that reel."

"I don't need it?"

"No. You can have me, just like in the dream. Even better than in the dream . . ."

Mirko started to snicker. "It's not the same thing," he said. "And don't be ridiculous with this Anti-Dream League propaganda of yours. Who are you trying to kid, anyway?"

"I'll say it again: Mirko, you can have *me*."

"And I still say it's not the same thing."

"Mirko!" the woman pleaded, beside herself. "You need me, every day you run through that matrix, and you dream, dream, you keep on dreaming of this cave, the firelight, my kisses, this body of mine which I've just offered you. This is exactly like the film, you stupid fool. What are you waiting for? I can do everything that's in that film, even more, and it will be for real . . ."

For a moment Mirko wavered, then he shook his head. He turned and moved off toward the back of the cave.

"Mirko!" she cried, exasperated. "I am Sophie Barlow! Sophie Barlow, don't you understand?"

She pulled down the zipper of her overalls. Her shoulders shrugged out of the cloth shell, and she quickly pulled off the suit and threw it on the ground.

"Look at me!" she shouted. And as he turned around, she uncovered her breasts.

The fire burned brightly, red and green tongues lapping upward, emitting a penetrating odor of the primeval jungle. She watched the man's hands clench into fists, his lips trembling, as if in a long, wearisome struggle.

Mirko hesitated a moment longer, then threw the matrix in the fire and ran toward her.

First the blue light came and then the red. Then blue again. When the reel came to an end, the set turned off automatically.

Sophie lifted off the Amplex helmet. Her temples were perspiring, her heart pounding in spasms. All her extremities were trembling, particularly her hands. She couldn't keep them still. Never in her life had she lived a "dream" with such intensity, an Oneirofilm that forced her to be herself. She must thank Bradley right way.

She rang him up on the videophone. But faced with the image of the super-visor, the words stuck in her throat; she stammered, truly moved. Finally she started to cry.

Bradley waited patiently.

"A little present, Sophie. Just a trinket. When an actress reaches the peak of her career she deserves far greater rewards. And you will have them, Sophie. You will have all the recognition that's due you. Because the system is perfect. There's no going back."

"Yes, Bradley. I—"

"It will go away, Sophie. It happens to all actresses sooner or later. The last obstacle to overcome is always vanity. Even you felt that a man ought to prefer you to a dream. You fell into the most dangerous of all heresies, but we caught it in time and rushed to correct it. With a little gift. That matrix will help you to get over this crisis."

"Yes, Bradley. Please thank everybody for me, the machinist, the technicians, the director, everybody who was involved in making this Oneirofilm. Above all, thank the actor who played the pilot."

"He's a new fellow. A real live wire, no?"

"Well, thank him for me. I had some beautiful moments. And thank you too, Bradley. I can imagine how much time and money this film cost you. It's perfect. I'll keep it in the slot of honor in my Oneirofilm collection."

"Nonsense, Sophie. You belong to the ruling class. You can allow yourself a personal Oneirofilm from time to time. We have always helped each other out, haven't we?—But there's one thing I want you to bear in mind."

"What's that, Bradley?"

"That matrix. That's more than a gift. It's meant to be a warning."

"Okay, Bradley. I get your point."

"Don't forget it. Nothing is better than dreaming. And only in dreams can you deceive yourself to the contrary. I'm sure that after five or six viewings you will get the point and toss that matrix in the wastebasket."

She nodded, in tears.

"I'll see you tomorrow at nine in the screening room."

"Yes, Bradley, tomorrow at nine in the screening room. Good night, Bradley."

"Good night, Sophie."

James Morrow

James Morrow (1947–   ) is one of the leading literary satirists today, who chooses to work in the science fiction and fantasy mode. He is particularly notable for his willingness to take on large intellectual and metaphysical challenges, and for his accomplished prose style. He has often, and with some justice, been compared to Kurt Vonnegut, Jr. He is a moralist and an allegorist. He has never been comfortable with the conventions and literary habits of the SF field, and occasionally breaks them, sometimes to good effect. *The Encyclopedia of Science Fiction* says Morrow "has great difficulty giving credence to the artifices of fiction. This may be the price paid for passion and clarity of mind; and it may be a price worth paying." His major novels include *Only Begotten Daughter* (1990), in which God's daughter is born in New Jersey in the closing years of this century. *Towing Jehovah* (1994), in which God is dead and his corpse, about the size of a small city, is found floating in the Atlantic Ocean and must be towed to the Antarctic to be preserved; and its sequel, *Blameless in Abaddon* (1996), in which the corpse is sold.

"Veritas" is a satirical utopia. Kathryn Cramer, in "Sincerity and Doom," her long essay on Morrow and science fiction, says, "Beyond defrocking utopia, the story hits you in the face with the uncomfortable relationship between Art (particularly fiction) and the Lie." She also suggests that this story may be in opposition to Orson Scott Card's popular Ender series of SF novels, which aspire to a utopia in which everyone tells the truth. Morrow address the question: Will the truth set you free?

VERITAS

Pigs have wings. . . .
Rats chase cats. . . .
Snow is hot. . . .
Even now the old lies ring through the charred interior of my skull. I cannot speak them. I shall never be able to speak them—not without being dropped from here to hell in a bucket of pain. But they still inhabit me, just as they did on that momentous day when the city began to fall.
Grass is purple. . . .
Two and two make five. . . .
I awoke aggressively that morning, tearing the blankets away as if they were all that stood between myself and total alertness. Yawning vigorously, I charged into the shower, where warm water poured forth the instant the sensors detected me. I'd been with Overt Intelligence for over five years, and this was the first time I'd drawn an assignment that might be termed a plum. Spread your nostrils, Orville. Sniff her out. Sherry Urquist: some name! It sounded more like a mixed

drink than like what she allegedly was, a purveyor of falsehoods, an enemy of the city, a member of the Dissemblage. The day could not begin soon enough.

The Dissemblage was like a deity. Not much tangible evidence, but people still had faith in it. Veritas, they reasoned, must harbor its normal share of those who believe the status quo is ipso facto wrong. Paradise will have its dissidents. The real question was not, Do subversives live in our city? The real question was, How do they tell lies without going mad?

My in-shower cablevision receiver winked on. Grimacing under the studio lights, our Assistant Secretary of Imperialism discussed Veritas's growing involvement in the Lethean civil war. "So far, over four thousand of our soldiers have died," the interviewer noted. "A senseless loss," the secretary conceded. "Our policy is impossible to justify on logical grounds, which is why we've started invoking national security and other shibboleths."

Have no illusions. The Sherry Urquist assignment did not fall into my lap because somebody at Overt Intelligence liked me. It was simply this: I am a roué. If any agent had a prayer of planting this particular Dissembler, that agent was me. It's the eyebrows that do it, great bushy extrusions suggesting a predatory mammal of unusual prowess, though I must admit they draw copious support from my straight nose and full, pillowlike lips. Am I handsome as a god? Metaphorically speaking, yes.

The picture tube had fogged over, so I activated the wiper. On the screen, a seedy-looking terrier scratched its fleas. "We seriously hope you'll consider By-product Brand Dog Food," said the voice-over. "Yes, we do tie up an enormous amount of protein that might conceivably be used in relieving worldwide starvation. However, if you'll consider the supposed benefits of dogs, we believe you may wish to patronize us."

On the surface, Ms. Urquist looked innocent enough. The dossier pegged her a writer, a former newspaper reporter with several popular self-help books under her belt. She had some other commodities under her belt, too, mainly fat, unless the accompanying OIA photos exaggerated. The case against her consisted primarily of rumor. Last week a neighbor, or possibly a sanitation engineer—the dossier contradicted itself on this point—had gone through her garbage. The yield was largely what you'd expect from someone in Ms. Urquist's profession: vodka bottles, outdated caffeine tablets, computer disk boxes, an early draft of her last bestseller, *How to Find a Certain Amount of Inner Peace Some of the Time If You Are Lucky.* Then came the kicker. The figurative smoking gun. The nonliteral forbidden fruit. At the bottom of the heap, the report asserted, lay "a torn and crumpled page" from what was "almost certainly a work of fiction."

Two hundred and thirty-nine words of it, to be precise. A story, a yarn, a legend. Something made up.

ART IS A LIE, the electric posters in Washington Park reminded us. Truth was beauty, but it simply didn't work the other way around.

I left the shower, which instantly shut itself down, and padded naked into my bedroom. Clothes per se were deceitful, of course, but this was the middle of winter, so I threw on some underwear and a gray suit with the lapels cut off— no integrity in freezing to death. My apartment was peeled to a core of rectitude. Most of my friends had curtains, wall hangings, and rugs, but not I. Why take chances with one's own sanity?

The odor of stale urine hit me as I rushed down the hall toward the lobby. How unfortunate that some people translated the ban on sexually segregated restrooms—PRIVACY IS A LIE, the posters reminded us—into a general fear of toilets. Hadn't they heard of public health? Public health was guileless.

Wrapped in dew, my Plymouth Adequate glistened on the far side of Probity Street. In the old days, I'd heard, you never knew for sure that your car would be unmolested, or even there, when you left it overnight. Twenty-eight degrees Fahrenheit, yet the thing started smoothly. I took off, zooming past the wonderfully functional cinderblocks that constituted city hall and heading toward the shopping district. My interview with Sherry Urquist was scheduled for ten, so I still had time to buy a gift for my nephew's brainburn party, which would happen around two-thirty that afternoon, right after he recovered. "Yes, I did take quite a few bribes during the Wheatstone Tariff affair," a thin-voiced senatorial candidate squeaked from out of my radio, "but you have to understand. . . ." His voice faded, pushed aside by the pressure of my thoughts. Today my nephew would learn to hate a lie. Today we would rescue him from deceit's boundless sea, tossing out our lifelines and hauling him aboard the ark called Veritas. So to speak.

Money grows on trees. . . .

Horses have six legs. . . .

And suddenly you're a citizen.

What could life have been like before the cure? How did the mind tolerate a world where politicians misled, advertisers overstated, women wore makeup, and people professed love for each other at the nonliteral drop of a hat? I shivered. Did the Dissemblers know what they were playing with? How I relished the thought of advancing their doom, how badly I wanted Sherry Urquist's bulky ass hanging figuratively over the mantel of my fireplace.

I was armed for the fight. Two days earlier, the clever doctors down at the agency's Medical Division had done a bit of minor surgery, and now one of my seminal vesicles contained not only its usual cargo but also a microscopic radio transmitter. My imagination showed it to me, poised in the duct like the Greek infantry waiting for the wooden horse to arrive inside Troy.

What will they think of next?

The problem was the itch. Not a literal itch—the transmitter was one thousandth the size of a pinhead. My discomfort was philosophical. Did the beeper lie or didn't it, that was the question. It purported to be only itself, a thing, a microtransmitter, and yet some variation of duplicity seemed afoot here.

I didn't like it.

MOLLY'S RATHER EXPENSIVE TOY STORE, the sign said. Expensive: that was okay. Christmas came every year, but a kid got cured only once.

"My, aren't *you* a pretty fellow?" a female citizen sang out as I strode through the door. Marionettes dangled from the ceiling like victims of a mass lynching. Stuffed animals stampeded gently toward me from all directions.

"Your body is desirable enough," I said, casting a candid eye up and down the sales clerk. A tattered wool sweater molded itself around her emphatic breasts. Grimy white slacks encased her tight thighs. "But that nose," I added forlornly. A demanding business, citizenship.

"What brings you here?" She had one of those rare brands in which every digit is the same. 9999W, her forehead said. "You playboys are never responsible enough for parenthood."

"A fair assessment. You have kids?"

"I'm not married."

"It figures. My nephew's getting burned today."

"And you're waiting till the last minute to buy him a gift?"

"Right."

"Electric trains are popular. We sold eleven sets last week. Two were returned as defective."

She led me to a raised platform overrun by a kind of Veritas in miniature and kicked up the juice on the power-pack. A streamlined locomotive whisked a string of gleaming coaches past a factory belching an impressive facsimile of smoke.

"I wonder—is this thing a lie?" I opened the throttle, and the locomotive nearly jumped the track.

"What do you mean?"

"It claims to be a train. But it's not."

"It claims to be a *model* of a train, which it is."

I eased the locomotive into the station. "Is your price as good as anybody else's?"

"You can get the same thing for six dollars less at Marquand's."

"Don't have the time. Can you gift-wrap it?"

"Not skillfully."

"Anything will do. I'm in a hurry."

The downtown traffic was light, the lull before lunch hour, so I arrived early at Sherry Urquist's Washington Park apartment, a crumbling glass-and-steel ziggurat surmounted by a billboard that said, ASSUMING THAT GOD EXISTS, JESUS MAY HAVE BEEN HIS SON. I rode the elevator to the twentieth floor, exiting into a foyer where a handsome display of old military recruitment posters covered the fissured plaster. It was nice when somebody took the trouble to decorate a place. One could never use paint, of course. Paint was a lie. But with a little imagination. . . .

I rang the bell. Nothing. Had I gotten the time wrong? CHANNEL YOUR VIOLENT IMPULSES IN A SALUTARY DIRECTION, the nearest poster said. BECOME A MARINE.

The door swung open, and there stood our presumed subversive, a figurative cloud of confusion hovering about her heavy face, darkening her soft-boiled eyes and pulpy lips, features somewhat more attractive than the agency's photos suggested. "Did I wake you?" I asked. Her thermal pajamas barely managed to hold their contents in check, and I gave her an honest ogle. "I'm two minutes early."

"You woke me," she said. Frankness. A truth-teller, then? No, if there was one thing a Dissembler could do, it was deceive.

"Sorry," I said. I remembered the old documentary films of the oil paintings being burned. Rubens, that was the kind of sensual plumpness Sherry had going for her. Good old Peter Paul Rubens. Sneaking the Greek army inside Troy might be more entertaining than I'd thought.

She frowned, stretching her forehead brand into El Greco numerals. No one down at headquarters doubted its authenticity. Ditto her cerebroscan, voicegram, fingerprints. . . .

A citizen, and yet she had written fiction.

Maybe.

"Who are you?" Her voice was wet and deep.

"Orville Prawn," I said. A permanent truth. "I work for *Tolerable Distortions*." A more transient one; the agency had arranged for the magazine to hire me—

payroll, medical plan, pension fund, the works—for the next forty-eight hours. "Our interview. . . ." I took out a pad and pencil.

Her pained expression seemed like the real thing. "Oh, damn, I'm *sorry*." She snapped her fingers. "It's on my calendar, but I've been up against a dozen deadlines, and I—"

"Forgot?"

"Yeah." She patted my forearm and guided me into her sparsely appointed living room. "Excuse me. These pajamas are probably driving you crazy."

"Not the pajamas per se."

She disappeared, returning shortly in a dingy yellow blouse and a red skirt circumscribed by a cracked and blistered leather belt.

The interview went well, which is to say she never asked whether I worked for Overt Intelligence, whereupon the whole show would have abruptly ended. She did not wish to discuss her old books, only her current project, a popular explanation of psychoanalytic theory to be called *From Misery to Unhappiness*. My shame was like a fever, threading my body with sharp, chilled wires. A toy train was not a lie, that clerk believed. Then maybe my little transmitter wasn't one either. . . .

And maybe wishes were horses.

And maybe pigs had wings.

There was also this: Sherry Urquist was charming me. No doubt about it. A manufacturer of bestsellers is naturally stuffed with vapid thoughts and ready-made opinions, right? But instead I found myself sitting next to a first-rate mind (oh, the premier eroticism of intellect intersecting Rubens), one that could be severe with Freud for his lapses of integrity while still grasping his essential genius.

"You seem to love your work, Ms. Urquist."

"Writing is my life."

"Tell me, honestly—do you ever get any ideas for . . . fiction?"

"Fiction?"

"Short stories. Novels."

"That would be suicidal, wouldn't it?"

A blind alley, but I expected as much.

The diciest moment occurred when Sherry asked in which issue the interview would be published, and I replied that I didn't know. True enough, I told myself. Since the thing would never see print at all, it was accurate to profess ignorance of the corresponding date. Still, there came a sudden, mercifully brief surge of unease, the tides of an ancient nausea. . . .

"All this sexual tension," I said, returning the pad and pencil to my suit jacket. "Alone with a sensually plump woman in her apartment, and your face is appealing too, now that I see the logic of it. You probably even have a bedroom. I can hardly stand it."

"Sensually plump, Mr. Prawn? I'm fat."

"Eye of the beholder."

"You'd have to go through a lot of beholders in my case."

"I find you very attractive." I did.

She raised her eyebrows, corrugating her brand. "It's only fair to give warning—you try anything funny, I'll knock you flat."

I cupped her left breast, full employment for any hand, and asked, "Is this funny?"

"On one level, your action offends me deeply." She brushed my knee. "I find it presumptuous, adolescent, and symptomatic of the worst kind of male arrogance." If faking her candor, she was certainly doing a good job. "On another level . . . well, you *are* quite handsome."

"An Adonis analogue."

We kissed. She went for my belt buckle. Reaching under her blouse, I sent her bra on a well-deserved sabbatical.

"Any sexually-transmittable diseases?" she asked.

"None." I stroked her dry, stringy hair. The Trojan horse was poised to change history. "You?"

"No," she said.

The truth? I couldn't know.

To bed, then. Time to plant her and, concomitantly, the transmitter. Nice work if you can get it. I slowed myself down with irrelevant thoughts—dogs can talk, rain is red—and left her a satisfied woman.

Full of Greeks.

I had promised Gloria that I wouldn't just come to the party, I would attend the burn as well. Normally both parents were present, but Dixon's tropological scum-bucket of a father couldn't be bothered. It will only take an hour, Gloria had told me. I'd rather not, I replied. He's your nephew, for Christ's sake, she pointed out. All right, I said.

Burn hospitals were in practically every neighborhood, but Gloria insisted on the best, Veteran's Shock Institute. Taking Dixon's badly wrapped gift from the back seat, I started toward the building, a smoke-stained pile of bricks overlooking the Thomas More Bridge. I paused. Business first. In theory the transmitter was part of Sherry now, forever fixed to her uterine wall. Snug as a bug in a . . . I went back to my Adequate and slid the sensorchart out of the dash. Yes, there she was, my fine Dissembler, a flashing red dot floating near Washington Park. I wished for greater detail, so I could know exactly when she was in her kitchen, her bathroom, her bedroom. Peeping Tom goes high tech. No matter. The thing worked. We could stalk her from here to Satan's backyard. As it were.

Inside the hospital, the day's collection of burn patients was everywhere, hugging dads, clinging tearfully to moms' skirts. I'd never understood this child-worship nonsense our culture wallows in, but, even so, the whole thing started getting to me. Every eight-year-old had to do it, of course, and the disease was certainly worse than the cure. Still. . . .

I punished myself by biting my inner cheeks. Sympathy was fine, but sentimentality was wasteful. If I wanted to pity somebody, I should go up to Ward Six. Cystic fibrosis. Cancer. Am I going to die, Mommy?

Yes, dear.

Soon?

Yes, dear.

Will I see you in heaven?

Nobody knows.

I went to the front desk, where I learned that Dixon had been admitted half an hour earlier. "Room one-forty-five," said the nurse, a rotund man with a warty face. "The party will be in one-seventeen."

My nephew was already in the glass cubicle, dressed in a green smock and bound to the chair via leather thongs, one electrode strapped to his left arm, another to his right leg. Black wires trailed from the copper terminals like threads spun by a carnivorous spider. He welcomed me with a brave smile, and I held up his gift, hefting it to show that it had substance, it wasn't clothes. A nice enough kid—what I knew of him. Cute freckles, a wide, apple face. I remembered that for somebody his age, Dixon understood a great deal of symbolic logic.

A young, willowy, female nurse entered the cubicle and began snugging the helmet over his cranium. I gave Dixon a thumbs-up signal. (Soon it will be over, kid. Pigs have wings, rats chase cats, all of it.)

"Thanks for coming." Drifting out of her chair, Gloria took my arm. She was an attractive woman—same genes as me—but today she looked lousy: the anticipation, the fear. Sweat collected in her forehead brand. I had stopped proposing incest years ago. Not her game. "You're his favorite uncle, you know."

Uncle Orville. God help me. I was actually present when Gloria's marriage collapsed. The three of us were sitting in a Reconstituted Burgers when suddenly she said, I sometimes worry that you're having an affair—are you? And Tom said, yes, he was. And Gloria said, you fucker. And Tom said, right. And Gloria asked how many. And Tom said lots. And Gloria asked why. Did he do it to strengthen the marriage? And Tom said no, he just liked to screw other women.

Clipboard in hand, a small, homely doctor with MERRICK affixed to his tunic waddled into the room. "Good afternoon, folks," he said, his cheer a precarious mix of the genuine and the forced. "Bitter cold day out, huh? How are we doing here?"

"Do you care?" my sister asked.

"Hard to say." Dr. Merrick fanned me with his clipboard. "Friend of the family?"

"My brother," Gloria explained.

"He has halitosis. Glad there are two of you." Merrick smiled at the boy in the cubicle. "With just one, the kid'll sometimes go into clinical depression on us." He pressed the clipboard toward Gloria. "Informed consent, right?"

"They told me all the possibilities." She studied the clipboard. "Cardiac—"

"Cardiac arrest, cerebral hemorrhage, respiratory failure, kidney damage," Merrick recited.

"When was the last time anything like that happened?"

"They killed a little girl down at Mount Sinai on Tuesday. A freak thing, but now and then we really screw up."

After patting Dixon on his straw-colored bangs, the nurse left the cubicle and told Dr. Merrick that she was going to get some coffee.

"Be back in ten minutes," he ordered.

"Oh, but of course." Such sarcasm from one so young. "We mustn't have a *doctor* cleaning up, not when we can get some underpaid nurse to do it."

Gloria scrawled her signature.

The nurse edged out of the room.

Dr. Merrick went to the control panel.

And then it began. This bar mitzvah of the human conscience, this electroconvulsive rite of passage. A hallowed tradition. An unvarying text. Today I am a man. . . . We believe in one Lord, Jesus Christ. . . . I pledge allegiance to the flag. . . . Why is this night different from all other nights. . . . Dogs can talk. . . . Pigs have wings. To tell you the truth, I was not really thinking about Dixon's cure just then. My mind was abloom with Sherry Urquist.

Merrick pushed a button, and PIGS HAVE WINGS appeared before my nephew on a lucite tachistoscope screen. "Can you hear me, lad?" the doctor called into the microphone.

Dixon opened his mouth, and a feeble "Yes" dribbled out of the loudspeaker.

"You see those words?" Merrick asked. The lurid red characters hovered in the air like lethargic butterflies.

"Y-yes."

"When I give the order, read them aloud. Okay?"

"Is it going to hurt?" my nephew quavered.

"It's going to hurt a lot. Will you read the words when I say so?"

"I'm scared. Do I have to?"

"You have to." Merrick rested a pudgy finger on the switch. "Now!"

"P-pigs have wings." The volts ripped through Dixon. He yelped and burst into tears. "But they don't," he moaned. "Pigs don't. . . ."

My own burn flooded back. The pain. The anger.

"You're right, lad—they don't." Merrick gave the voltage regulator a subtle twist, and Gloria flinched. "You did reasonably well, boy," the doctor continued. "We're not yet disappointed in you." He handed the mike to Gloria.

"Oh, yes, Dixon," she said. "Keep up the awfully good work."

"It's not fair." Sweat speckled Dixon's forehead. "I want to go home."

As Gloria surrendered the mike, TWO AND TWO MAKE FIVE materialized. "Now, lad! Read it!"

"T-t-two and two make . . . f-five." Lightning struck. The boy shuddered, howled. Blood rolled over his lower lip. During my own burn, I had practically bitten my tongue off. "I don't want this any more," he wailed.

"It's not a choice, lad."

"Two and two make *four*." Tears threaded Dixon's freckles together. "Please stop hurting me."

"Four. Right. Smart lad." Merrick cranked up the voltage. "Ready, Dixon? Here it comes."

HORSES HAVE SIX LEGS.

"Why do I have to do this? *Why?*"

"Everybody does it. All your friends."

"H-h-horses have . . . have . . . They have *four* legs, Dr. Merrick."

"Read the words, Dixon!"

"I hate you! I hate all of you!"

"Dixon!"

He raced through it. Zap. Two hundred volts. The boy began to cough and retch, and a string of white mucus shot from his mouth like a lizard's tongue. Nothing followed: burn patients fasted for sixteen hours prior to therapy.

"Too much!" cried Gloria. "Isn't that too much?"

"The goal is five hundred," said Merrick. "It's all been worked out. You want the treatment to take, don't you?"

"Mommy! Where's my Mommy?"

Gloria tore the mike away. "Right here, dear!"

"Mommy, make them stop!"

"I can't, dear. You must try to be brave."

The fourth lie appeared. Merrick upped the voltage. "Read it, lad!"

"No!"

"Read it!"

"Uncle Orville! I want Uncle Orville!"

My throat constricted, my stomach went sour. Uncle: such a strange sound. I really was one, wasn't I? "You're doing pretty swell, Dixon," I said, taking the mike. "I think you'll like your present."

"Uncle Orville, I want to go home!"

"I got you a fine toy."

"What is it?"

"Here's a hint. It has—"

"Dixon!" Merrick grabbed the mike. "Dixon, if you don't do this, you'll never get well. They'll take you away from your mother." A threat, but wholly accurate. "Understand? They'll take you away."

Dixon balled his face into a mass of wrinkles. "Grass!" he screamed, spitting blood. "Is!" he persisted. "Purple!" He jerked like a gaffed flounder, spasm after spasm. A broad urine stain blossomed on his crotch, and despite the obligatory enema a brown fluid dripped from the hem of his smock.

"Excellent!" Merrick increased the punishment to four hundred volts. "Your cure's in sight, lad!"

"No! Please! Please! Enough!" Sweat encased Dixon's face. Foam leaked from his mouth.

"You're almost halfway there!"

"Please!"

The war continued, five more pain-tipped rockets shooting through Dixon's nerves and veins, detonating inside his mind. He asserted that rats chase cats. He lied about money, saying that it grew on trees. Worms taste like honey, he said. Snow is hot. Rain is red.

He fainted just as the final lie arrived. Even before Gloria could scream, Merrick was inside the cubicle, checking the boy's heartbeat. A begrudging admiration seeped through me. The doctor had a job, and he did it.

A single dose of smelling salts brought Dixon around.

Guiding the boy's face toward the screen, Merrick turned to me. "Ready with the switch?"

"Huh? You want me—" Ridiculous.

"Let's just get it over with. Hit the switch when I tell you."

"I'd rather not." But already my finger rested on the damn thing. Doctor's orders.

"Read, Dixon," muttered Merrick.

"I c-can't."

"One more, Dixon. Just one more and you'll be a citizen."

Blood and spittle mingled on Dixon's chin. "You all hate me! Mommy hates me!"

"I love you as much as myself," said Gloria, leaning over my shoulder. "You're going to have a wonderful party. Almost certainly."

"Really?"

"Highly likely."

"Presumably wonderful," I said. The switch burned my finger. "I love you too."

"Dogs can talk," said Dixon.

And it truly was a wonderful party. All four of Dixon's grandparents showed up, along with his teacher and twelve of his friends, half of whom had been cured in recent months, one on the previous day. Dixon marched around Room

117 displaying the evidence of his burn like war medals. The brand, of course—performed under local anesthesia immediately after his cure—plus copies of his initial cerebroscan, voicegram, and fingerprint set.

Brand, scan, gram, prints: Sherry Urquist's had all been in perfect order. She had definitely been burned. And yet there was fiction in her garbage.

The gift-opening ceremony contained one bleak moment. Pulling the train from its wrapping, Dixon blanched, garroted by panic, and Gloria had to rush him into the bathroom, where he spent several minutes throwing up. I felt like a fool. To a boy who's just been through a brainburn, an electric train has gruesome connotations.

"Thanks for coming," said Gloria. She meant it.

"I *do* like my present," Dixon averred. "A freight train would have been nicer," he added. A citizen now.

I apologized for leaving early. A big case, I explained. Very hot, very political.

"Good-bye, Uncle Orville."

Uncle. Great stuff.

I spent the rest of the day tracking my adorable Dissembler, never letting her get more than a mile from me or closer than two blocks. What agonizing hopes that dot on the map inspired, what rampant expectations. With each flash my longing intensified. Oh, Sherry, Sherry, you pulsing red angel, you stroboscope of my desire. No mere adolescent infatuation this. I dared to speak its name. "Neurotic obsession," I gushed, kissing the dot as it crossed Aquinas Avenue. "Mixed with bald romantic fantasy and lust," I added. The radio shouted at me: a hot-blooded evangelist no less enraptured than I. "Does faith tempt you, my friends? Fear not! Look into your metaphoric hearts, and you will discover how subconscious human needs project themselves onto putative revelations!"

For someone facing a wide variety of deadlines, my quarry didn't push herself particularly hard. Sherry spent the hour from four to five at the Museum of Secondary Fossil Finds. From five to six she did the Imprisoned Animals Garden. From six to seven she treated herself to dinner at Danny's Digestibles, after which she went down to the waterfront.

I cruised along Third Street, twenty yards from the Pathogen River. This was the city's frankest district, a gray mass of warehouses and abandoned stores jammed together like dead cells waiting to be sloughed off. Sherry walked slowly, aimlessly, as if . . . could it be? Yes, damn, as if arm-in-arm with another person, as if meshing her movements with those of a second, intertwined body. Probably she had met the guy at Danny's, a conceited pile of muscles named Guido or something, and now they were having a cozy stroll along the Pathogen. I pressed the dot, as if to draw Sherry away. What if she spent the night in another apartment? That would pretty much cinch it. I wondered how their passion would register. I pictured the dot going wild, love's red fibrillation.

After pausing for several seconds on the bank, the dot suddenly began prancing across the river. Odd. I fixed on the map. The Saint Joan Tunnel was half a mile away, the Thomas More Bridge even farther. I doubted that she was swimming—not in this weather, and not in the Pathogen, where the diseases of the future were born. Flying, then? The dot moved too slowly to signify an airplane. A hot-air balloon? Probably she was in a boat. Sherry and Guido, off on a romantic cruise.

I hung a left on Beach Street and sped down to the docks. Moonlight coated the Pathogen, settling into the waves, figuratively bronzing a lone, swiftly moving tugboat. I checked the map. The dot placed Sherry at least ten yards from the tug, in the exact middle of the river and heading for the opposite shore. I studied her presumed location. Nothing. Submerged, then? I knew she hadn't committed suicide; the dot's progress was too resolute. Was she in scuba gear?

I abandoned the car and attempted to find where she had entered the water, a quest that took me down concrete steps to a pier hemmed by pylons smeared with gull dung. Jagged odors shot from the dead and rotting river; water lapped over the landing with a harsh sucking sound, as if a pride of invisible lions was drinking here. My gaze settled on a metal grate, barred like the ribcage of some promethean robot. It seemed slightly askew. . . . Oh, great, Orville, let's go traipsing through the sewers, with rats nipping at our heels and slugs the size of bagels falling on our shoulders. Terrific idea.

The grate yielded readily to my reluctant hands. Had she truly gone down there? Should I follow? A demented notion, but duty called, using its shrillest voice, and, besides, this was Sherry Urquist, this was irrational need. I secured a flashlight from the car and proceeded down the ladder. It was like entering a lung. Steamy, warm. The flashlight blazed through the blackness. A weapon, I decided. Look out, all you rats and slugs. Make way. Here comes Orville Prawn, the fastest flashlight in Veritas.

I moved through a multilayered maze of soggy holes and dripping catacombs. So many ways to descend: ladders, sloping tunnels, crooked little stairways—I used them all, soon moving beyond the riverbed into other territories, places not on the OIA map.

All around me Veritas's guts were spread: its concrete intestines, gushing lead veins, buzzing nerves of steel and gutta-percha. Much to my surprise, the city even had its parasites—shacks of corrugated tin leaned against the wet brick walls, sucking secretly on the power cables and water mains. This would not do. No, to live below Veritas like this, appropriating its juices, was little more than piracy. Overt Intelligence would hear of it.

My astonishment deepened as I advanced. I could understand a few hobos setting up a shantytown down here, but how might I explain these odd chunks of civilization? These blazing streetlamps, these freshly painted picket fences, these tidy grids of rose bushes, these fountains with their stone dolphins spewing water? Paint, flowers, sculpture: so many lies in one place! Peel back the streets of any city and do you find its warped reflection, its doppelgänger mirrored in distorting glass? Or did Veritas alone harbor such anarchy, this tumor spreading beneath her unsuspecting flesh?

A sleek white cat shot out of the rose bushes and disappeared down an open manhole. At first I thought that its pursuer was a dog, but no. Wrong shape. And that tail.

The shudder began in my lower spine and expanded.

A rat.

A rat the size of an armadillo.

Chasing a cat.

I moved on. Vegetable gardens now. Two bright yellow privies. Cottages defaced with gardenia plots and strings of clematis scurrying up trellises. A building that looked suspiciously like a chapel. A park of some kind, with flagstone paths and a duck pond. Ruddy puffs of vapor bumped against the treetops.

Rain is red. . . .

I entered the park.

A pig glided over my head like a miniature dirigible, wheeling across the sky on cherub wings. At first I assumed it was a machine, but its squeal was disconcertingly organic.

"You!"

A low, liquid voice. I dropped my gaze.

Sherry shared the bench with an enormous dog, some grotesque variation on the malamute, his chin snugged into her lap. "You!" she said again, erecting the word like a barrier, a spiked vocable stopping my approach. The dog lifted his head and growled.

"Correct," I said, stock still.

"You followed me?"

"I cannot tell a lie." I examined the nearest tree. No fruit, of course, only worms and paper money.

"Dirty spy."

"Half true. I am not dirty."

She wore a buttercup dress, decorated with lace. Her thick braid lay on her shoulder like a loaf of challah. Her eyes had become cartoons of themselves, starkly outlined and richly shaded. "If you try to return"—she patted the malamute—"Max will eat you alive."

"You bet your sweet ass," said the dog.

She massaged Max's head, as if searching for the trigger that would release his attack. "I expected better of you, Mr. Prawn."

We were in a contest. Who could act the more betrayed, the more disgusted? "I'd always assumed the Dissemblage was just a group." Spit dripped off my words. "I didn't know it was . . . all this."

"Two cities," muttered Sherry, launching her index finger upward. "Truth above, dignity below." The finger descended. Her nails, I noticed, were a fluorescent green.

"Her father built it," explained the dog.

"His life's work," added Sherry.

"Are there many of you?" I asked.

"I'm the first to reach adulthood," said Sherry.

"The prototype liar?"

Her sneer evolved into a grin. "Others are hatching."

"How can you betray your city like this?" I drilled her with my stare. "Veritas, who nurtured you, suckled you?"

"Shall I kill him now?" asked the dog.

Sherry chucked Max under the chin, told him to be patient. "Veritas did not suckle me." Her gesture encompassed the entire park and, by extension, the whole of Veritas's twisted double. "*This* was my cradle—my nursery." She took a lipstick from her purse. "It's not hard to make a lie. The money trees are props. The rats and pigs trace to avant-garde microbiology."

"All I needed were vocal cords," said the dog.

She began touching up her lips. "Thanks to my father, I reached my eighth birthday knowing that pigs had wings, that snow was hot, that two and two equaled five, that worms tasted like honey . . . all of it. So when my burn came—"

"You were incurable," I said. "You walked away from the hospital ready to swindle and cheat and—"

"Write fiction. Four novels so far. Maybe you'd like to read them. You might be a bureaucratic drudge, but I'm fond of you, Orville."

"How do I know you're telling the truth?"

"You don't. And when my cadre takes over and the burn ends—it won't be hard, we'll lie our way to the top—when that happens, you won't know when *anybody's* telling the truth."

"Right," said the dog, leaping off the bench.

"Truth is beauty," I said.

Sherry winced. "My father did not mind telling the truth." Here she became an actress, that consummate species of liar, dragging out her lines. "But he hated his inability to do otherwise. Honesty without choice, he said, is slavery with a smile."

A glorious adolescent girl rode through the park astride a six-legged horse, her skin dark despite her troglodytic upbringing, her eyes alive with deceit. The *gift* of deceit, as Sherry would have it. I wondered whether Dixon was playing with his electric train just then. Probably not. Past his bedtime. I kept envisioning his cerebrum, brocaded with necessary scars.

Sherry patted the spot where the dog had been, and I sat down cautiously. "Care for one?" she asked, plucking a worm off a money tree.

"No."

"Go ahead. Try it."

"Well. . . ."

"Open your mouth and close your eyes."

The creature wriggled on my tongue, and I bit down. Pure honey. Sweet, smooth, but I did not enjoy it.

Truth above, dignity below. My index finger throbbed, prickly with that irrevocable little tug of the switch in Room 145. Five hundred volts was a lot, but what was the alternative? To restore the age of thievery and fraud?

History has it I joined Sherry's city that very night. A lie, but what do you expect—all the books are written by Dissemblers. True, sometime before dawn I did push my car into the river, the better to elude Overt Intelligence. But fully a week went by before I told Sherry about her internal transmitter. She was furious. She vowed to have the thing cut out. Go ahead, I told her, do it—but don't expect my blessing. That's another thing the historians got wrong. They say I paid for the surgery.

Call me a traitor. Call me a coward. Call me love's captive. I have called myself all these things. But—really—I did not join Sherry's city that night. That night I merely sat on a park bench staring into her exotically adorned eyes, fixing on her bright lips, holding her fluorescent fingertips.

"I want to believe whatever you tell me," I said.

"Then you'll need to have faith in me," she said.

"It's raining," noted the dog, and then he launched into a talking-dog joke.

"My cottage is over there." Sherry replaced her lipstick in her purse. She tossed her wondrous braid over her shoulder.

We rose and started across the park, hand in hand, lost in the sweet uncertainty of the moment, oblivious to the chattering dog and the lashing wind and bright red rain dancing on the purple grass.

A. E. van Vogt

A. E. van Vogt (1912–   ) is one of the giants of the Golden Age of science fiction, specifically, the flowering of modern science fiction in John W. Campbell, Jr.'s magazine, *Astounding*, between 1939 and 1949. A Canadian writer, he moved to the U.S. after World War II and spent the 1950s deeply involved in his friend L. Ron Hubbard's Dianetics (later Scientology). He is one of the most influential SF writers of that period, in some ways the dominant SF writer of the 1940s. His novel, *Slan* (1946, appearing first as a serial in *Astounding* in 1940) metaphorically represented the previously unarticulated attitude in the SF field that SF readers and writers were somehow the next stage in human evolution. "Fans are Slans" became a motto of 1940s science fiction, and van Vogt was a hero of the evolution and his influence on the next generation of SF writers, including Philip José Farmer, Philip K. Dick, and Charles Harness, was profound. *The World of Null-A* (1948) was the first work of modern science fiction to be published by a respectable hardcover house and it was a worldwide success. His fiction is filled with powerful imagery and strange ideas, often presented in dreamlike sequence, not a rational flow. His critical reputation was demolished in the U.S. in the the 1950s by Damon Knight's essay, "Cosmic Jerrybuilder: A. E. van Vogt." But van Vogt's popularity did not decrease for decades. In the 1980s Leslie A. Fiedler (in his essay "The Criticism of Science Fiction," 1983) put it succinctly: "Any bright high school sophomore can identify all the things that are wrong about van Vogt. . . . But the challenge to criticism which pretends to do justice to science fiction is to say what is right about him: to identify his mythopoeic power, his ability to evoke primordial images, his gift for redeeming the marvelous in a world in which technology has preempted the province of magic and God is dead."

This story is one of his most memorable. Ray Bradbury's later stories of the desert planet Mars, with its hidden survivals of a once-great technological civilization, are strikingly similar in atmosphere. This is van Vogt's "Martian chronicle." In this case it is easy to understand van Vogt's appeal.

ENCHANTED VILLAGE

Explorers of a new frontier" they had been called before they left for Mars.

For a while, after the ship crashed into a Martian desert, killing all on board except—miraculously—this one man, Bill Jenner spat the words occasionally into the constant, sand-laden wind. He despised himself for the pride he had felt when he first heard them.

His fury faded with each mile that he walked, and his black grief for his friends became a gray ache. Slowly he realized that he had made a ruinous misjudgment.

He had underestimated the speed at which the rocketship had been traveling.

He'd guessed that he would have to walk three hundred miles to reach the shallow, polar sea he and the others had observed as they glided in from outer space. Actually, the ship must have flashed an immensely greater distance before it hurtled down out of control.

The days stretched behind him, seemingly as numberless as the hot, red, alien sand that scorched through his tattered clothes. A huge scarecrow of a man, he kept moving across the endless, arid waste—he would not give up.

By the time he came to the mountain, his food had long been gone. Of his four water bags, only one remained, and that was so close to being empty that he merely wet his cracked lips and swollen tongue whenever his thirst became unbearable.

Jenner climbed high before he realized that it was not just another dune that had barred his way. He paused, and as he gazed up at the mountain that towered above him, he cringed a little. For an instant he felt the hopelessness of this mad race he was making to nowhere—but he reached the top. He saw that below him was a depression surrounded by hills as high as, or higher than, the one on which he stood. Nestled in the valley they made was a village.

He could see trees and the marble floor of a courtyard. A score of buildings was clustered around what seemed to be a central square. They were mostly low-constructed, but there were four towers pointing gracefully into the sky. They shone in the sunlight with a marble luster.

Faintly, there came to Jenner's ears a thin, high-pitched whistling sound. It rose, fell, faded completely, then came up again clearly and unpleasantly. Even as Jenner ran toward it, the noise grated on his ears, eerie and unnatural.

He kept slipping on smooth rock, and bruised himself when he fell. He rolled halfway down into the valley. The buildings remained new and bright when seen from nearby. Their walls flashed with reflections. On every side was vegetation—reddish-green shrubbery, yellow-green trees laden with purple and red fruit.

With ravenous intent, Jenner headed for the nearest fruit tree. Close up, the tree looked dry and brittle. The large red fruit he tore from the lowest branch, however, was plump and juicy.

As he lifted it to his mouth, he remembered that he had been warned during his training period to taste nothing on Mars until it had been chemically examined. But that was meaningless advice to a man whose only chemical equipment was in his own body.

Nevertheless, the possibility of danger made him cautious. He took his first bite gingerly. It was bitter to his tongue, and he spat it out hastily. Some of the juice which remained in his mouth seared his gums. He felt the fire on it, and he reeled from nausea. His muscles began to jerk, and he lay down on the marble to keep himself from falling. After what seemed like hours to Jenner, the awful trembling finally went out of his body and he could see again. He looked up despisingly at the tree.

The pain finally left him, and slowly he relaxed. A soft breeze rustled the dry leaves. Nearby trees took up that gentle clamor, and it struck Jenner that the wind here in the valley was only a whisper of what it had been on the flat desert beyond the mountain.

There was no other sound now. Jenner abruptly remembered the high-pitched, ever-changing whistle he had heard. He lay very still, listening intently, but there was only the rustling of the leaves. The noisy shrilling had stopped. He wondered if it had been an alarm, to warn the villagers of his approach.

Anxiously he climbed to his feet and fumbled for his gun. A sense of disaster shocked through him. It wasn't there. His mind was a blank, and then he vaguely recalled that he had first missed the weapon more than a week before. He looked around him uneasily, but there was not a sign of creature life. He braced himself. He couldn't leave, as there was nowhere to go. If necessary, he would fight to the death to remain in the village.

Carefully Jenner took a sip from his water bag, moistening his cracked lips and his swollen tongue. Then he replaced the cap and started through a double line of trees toward the nearest building. He made a wide circle to observe it from several vantage points. On one side a low, broad archway opened into the interior. Through it, he could dimly make out the polished gleam of a marble floor.

Jenner explored the buildings from the outside, always keeping a respectful distance between him and any of the entrances. He saw no sign of animal life. He reached the far side of the marble platform on which the village was built, and turned back decisively. It was time to explore interiors.

He chose one of the four tower buildings. As he came within a dozen feet of it, he saw that he would have to stoop low to get inside.

Momentarily, the implications of that stopped him. These buildings had been constructed for a life form that must be very different from human beings.

He went forward again, bent down, and entered reluctantly, every muscle tensed.

He found himself in a room without furniture. However, there were several low marble fences projecting from one marble wall. They formed what looked like a group of four wide, low stalls. Each stall had an open trough carved out of the floor.

The second chamber was fitted with four inclined planes of marble, each of which slanted up to a dais. Altogether there were four rooms on the lower floor. From one of them a circular ramp mounted up, apparently to a tower room.

Jenner didn't investigate the upstairs. The earlier fear that he would find alien life was yielding to the deadly conviction that he wouldn't. No life meant no food or chance of getting any. In frantic haste he hurried from building to building, peering into the silent rooms, pausing now and then to shout hoarsely.

Finally there was no doubt. He was alone in a deserted village on a lifeless planet, without food, without water—except for the pitiful supply in his bag—and without hope.

He was in the fourth and smallest room of one of the tower buildings when he realized that he had come to the end of his search. The room had a single stall jutting out from one wall. Jenner lay down wearily in it. He must have fallen asleep instantly.

When he awoke he became aware of two things, one right after the other. The first realization occurred before he opened his eyes—the whistling sound was back; high and shrill, it wavered at the threshold of audibility.

The other was that a fine spray of liquid was being directed down at him from the ceiling. It had an odor, of which technician Jenner took a single whiff. Quickly he scrambled out of the room, coughing, tears in his eyes, his face already burning from chemical reaction.

He snatched his handkerchief and hastily wiped the exposed parts of his body and face.

He reached the outside and there paused, striving to understand what had happened.

The village seemed unchanged.

Leaves trembled in a gentle breeze. The sun was poised on a mountain peak. Jenner guessed from its position that it was morning again and that he had slept at least a dozen hours. The glaring white light suffused the valley. Half hidden by trees and shrubbery, the buildings flashed and shimmered.

He seemed to be in an oasis in a vast desert. It was an oasis, all right, Jenner reflected grimly, but not for a human being. For him, with its poisonous fruit, it was more like a tantalizing mirage.

He went back inside the building and cautiously peered into the room where he had slept. The spray of gas had stopped, not a bit of odor lingered, and the air was fresh and clean.

He edged over the threshold, half inclined to make a test. He had a picture in his mind of a long-dead Martian creature lazing on the floor in the stall while a soothing chemical sprayed down on its body. The fact that the chemical was deadly to human beings merely emphasized how alien to man was the life that had spawned on Mars. But there seemed little doubt of the reason for the gas. The creature was accustomed to taking a morning shower.

Inside the "bathroom," Jenner eased himself feet first into the stall. As his hips came level with the stall entrance, the solid ceiling sprayed a jet of yellowish gas straight down upon his legs. Hastily Jenner pulled himself clear of the stall. The gas stopped as suddenly as it had started.

He tried it again, to make sure it was merely an automatic process. It turned on, then shut off.

Jenner's thirst-puffed lips parted with excitement. He thought, "If there can be one automatic process, there may be others."

Breathing heavily, he raced into the outer room. Carefully he shoved his legs into one of the two stalls. The moment his hips were in, a steaming gruel filled the trough beside the wall.

He stared at the greasy-looking stuff with a horrified fascination—food—and drink. He remembered the poison fruit and felt repelled, but he forced himself to bend down and put his finger into the hot, wet substance. He brought it up, dripping, to his mouth.

It tasted flat and pulpy, like boiled wood fiber. It trickled viscously into his throat. His eyes began to water and his lips drew back convulsively. He realized he was going to be sick, and ran for the outer door—but didn't quite make it.

When he finally got outside, he felt limp and unutterably listless. In that depressed state of mind, he grew aware again of the shrill sound.

He felt amazed that he could have ignored its rasping even for a few minutes. Sharply he glanced about, trying to determine its source, but it seemed to have none. Whenever he approached a point where it appeared to be loudest, then it would fade or shift, perhaps to the far side of the village.

He tried to imagine what an alien culture would want with a mind-shattering noise—although, of course, it would not necessarily have been unpleasant to them.

He stopped and snapped his fingers as a wild but nevertheless plausible notion entered his mind. Could this be music?

He toyed with the idea, trying to visualize the village as it had been long ago. Here a music-loving people had possibly gone about their daily tasks to the accompaniment of what was to them beautiful strains of melody.

The hideous whistling went on and on, waxing and waning. Jenner tried to put buildings between himself and the sound. He sought refuge in various rooms, hoping that at least one would be soundproof. None were. The whistle followed him wherever he went.

He retreated into the desert, and had to climb halfway up one of the slopes before the noise was low enough not to disturb him. Finally, breathless but immeasurably relieved, he sank down on the sand and thought blankly:

What now?

The scene that spread before him had in it qualities of both heaven and hell. It was all too familiar now—the red sands, the stony dunes, the small, alien village promising so much and fulfilling so little.

Jenner looked down at it with his feverish eyes and ran his parched tongue over his cracked, dry lips. He knew that he was a dead man unless he could alter the automatic food-making machines that must be hidden somewhere in the walls and under the floors of the buildings.

In ancient days, a remnant of Martian civilization had survived here in this village. The inhabitants had died off, but the village lived on, keeping itself clean of sand, able to provide refuge for any Martian who might come along. But there were no Martians. There was only Bill Jenner, pilot of the first rocketship ever to land on Mars.

He had to make the village turn out food and drink that he could take. Without tools, except his hands, with scarcely any knowledge of chemistry, he must force it to change its habits.

Tensely he hefted his water bag. He took another sip and fought the same grim fight to prevent himself from guzzling it down to the last drop. And, when he had won the battle once more, he stood up and started down the slope.

He could last, he estimated, not more than three days. In that time he must conquer the village.

He was already among the trees when it suddenly struck him that the "music" had stopped. Relieved, he bent over a small shrub, took a good firm hold of it— and pulled.

It came up easily, and there was a slab of marble attached to it. Jenner stared at it, noting with surprise that he had been mistaken in thinking the stalk came up through a hole in the marble. It was merely stuck to the surface. Then he noticed something else—the shrub had no roots. Almost instinctively, Jenner looked down at the spot from which he had torn the slab of marble along with the plant. There was sand there.

He dropped the shrub, slipped to his knees, and plunged his fingers into the sand. Loose sand trickled through them. He reached deep, using all his strength to force his arm and hand down; sand—nothing but sand.

He stood up and frantically tore up another shrub. It also came up easily, bringing with it a slab of marble. It had no roots, and where it had been was sand.

With a kind of mindless disbelief, Jenner rushed over to a fruit tree and shoved at it. There was a momentary resistance, and then the marble on which it stood split and lifted slowly into the air. The tree fell over with a swish and a crackle as its dry branches and leaves broke and crumbled into a thousand pieces. Underneath where it had been was sand.

Sand everywhere. A city built on sand. Mars, planet of sand. That was not completely true, of course. Seasonal vegetation had been observed near the polar ice caps. All but the hardiest of it died with the coming of summer. It had been intended that the rocketship land near one of those shallow, tideless seas.

By coming down out of control, the ship had wrecked more than itself. It had wrecked the chances for life of the only survivor of the voyage.

Jenner came slowly out of his daze. He had a thought then. He picked up one of the shrubs he had already torn loose, braced his foot against the marble to which it was attached, and tugged, gently at first, then with increasing strength.

It came loose finally, but there was no doubt that the two were part of a whole. The shrub was growing out of the marble.

Marble? Jenner knelt beside one of the holes from which he had torn a slab, and bent over an adjoining section. It was quite porous—calciferous rock, most likely, but not true marble at all. As he reached toward it, intending to break off a piece, it changed color. Astounded, Jenner drew back. Around the break, the stone was turning a bright orange-yellow. He studied it uncertainly, then tentatively he touched it.

It was as if he had dipped his fingers into searing acid. There was a sharp, biting, burning pain. With a gasp, Jenner jerked his hand clear.

The continuing anguish made him feel faint. He swayed and moaned, clutching the bruised members to his body. When the agony finally faded and he could look at the injury, he saw that the skin had peeled and that blood blisters had formed already. Grimly Jenner looked down at the break in the stone. The edges remained bright orange-yellow.

The village was alert, ready to defend itself from further attacks.

Suddenly weary, he crawled into the shade of a tree. There was only one possible conclusion to draw from what had happened, and it almost defied common sense. This lonely village was alive.

As he lay there, Jenner tried to imagine a great mass of living substance growing into the shape of buildings, adjusting itself to suit another life form, accepting the role of servant in the widest meaning of the term.

If it would serve one race, why not another? If it could adjust to Martians, why not to human beings?

There would be difficulties, of course. He guessed wearily that essential elements would not be available. The oxygen for water could come from the air ...thousands of compounds could be made from sand.... Though it meant death if he failed to find a solution, he fell asleep even as he started to think about what they might be.

When he awoke it was quite dark.

Jenner climbed heavily to his feet. There was a drag to his muscles that alarmed him. He wet his mouth from his water bag and staggered toward the entrance of the nearest building. Except for the scraping of his shoes on the "marble," the silence was intense.

He stopped short, listened, and looked. The wind had died away. He couldn't see the mountains that rimmed the valley, but the buildings were still dimly visible, black shadows in a shadow world.

For the first time, it seemed to him that, in spite of his new hope, it might be better if he died. Even if he survived, what had he to look forward to? Only too well he recalled how hard it had been to rouse interest in the trip and to raise the large amount of money required. He remembered the colossal problems that had had to be solved in building the ship, and some of the men who had solved them were buried somewhere in the Martian desert.

It might be twenty years before another ship from Earth would try to reach the only other planet in the Solar System that had shown signs of being able to support life.

During those uncountable days and nights, those years, he would be here alone. That was the most he could hope for—if he lived. As he fumbled his way to a dais in one of the rooms, Jenner considered another problem: How did one let a living village know that it must alter its processes? In a way, it must already have grasped that it had a new tenant. How could he make it realize he needed food in a different chemical combination than that which it had served in the past; that he liked music, but on a different scale system; and that he could use a shower each morning—of water, not of poison gas?

He dozed fitfully, like a man who is sick rather than sleepy. Twice he wakened, his lips on fire, his eyes burning, his body bathed in perspiration. Several times he was startled into consciousness by the sound of his own harsh voice crying out in anger and fear at the night.

He guessed, then, that he was dying.

He spent the long hours of darkness tossing, turning, twisting, befuddled by waves of heat. As the light of morning came, he was vaguely surprised to realize that he was still alive. Restlessly he climbed off the dais and went to the door.

A bitingly cold wind blew, but it felt good to his hot face. He wondered if there were enough pneumococci in his blood for him to catch pneumonia. He decided not.

In a few moments he was shivering. He retreated back into the house, and for the first time noticed that, despite the doorless doorway, the wind did not come into the building at all. The rooms were cold but not draughty.

That started an association: Where had his terrible body heat come from? He teetered over to the dais where he spent the night. Within seconds he was sweltering in a temperature of about one hundred and thirty.

He climbed off the dais, shaken by his own stupidity. He estimated that he had sweated at least two quarts of moisture out of his dried-up body on that furnace of a bed.

This village was not for human beings. Here even the beds were heated for creatures who needed temperatures far beyond the heat comfortable for men.

Jenner spent most of the day in the shade of a large tree. He felt exhausted, and only occasionally did he even remember that he had a problem. When the whistling started, it bothered him at first, but he was too tired to move away from it. There were long periods when he hardly heard it, so dulled were his senses.

Late in the afternoon he remembered the shrubs and the trees he had torn up the day before and wondered what had happened to them. He wet his swollen tongue with the last few drops of water in his bag, climbed lackadaisically to his feet, and went to look for the dried-up remains.

There weren't any. He couldn't even find the holes where he had torn them out. The living village had absorbed the dead tissue into itself and had repaired the breaks in its "body."

That galvanized Jenner. He began to think again . . . about mutations, genetic readjustments, life forms adapting to new environments. There'd been lectures on that before the ship left Earth, rather generalized talks designed to acquaint the explorers with the problems men might face on an alien planet. The important principle was quite simple: adjust or die.

The village had to adjust to him. He doubted if he could seriously damage it, but he could try. His own need to survive must be placed on as sharp and hostile a basis as that.

Frantically Jenner began to search his pockets. Before leaving the rocket he had loaded himself with odds and ends of small equipment. A jackknife, a folding metal cup, a printed radio, a tiny superbattery that could be charged by spinning an attached wheel—and for which he had brought along, among other things, a powerful electric fire lighter.

Jenner plugged the lighter into the battery and deliberately scraped the red-hot end along the surface of the "marble." The reaction was swift. The substance turned an angry purple this time. When an entire section of the floor had changed color, Jenner headed for the nearest stall trough, entering far enough to activate it.

There was a noticeable delay. When the food finally flowed into the trough, it was clear that the living village had realized the reason for what he had done. The food was a pale, creamy color, where earlier it had been a murky gray.

Jenner put his finger into it but withdrew it with a yell and wiped his finger. It continued to sting for several moments. The vital question was: Had it deliberately offered him food that would damage him, or was it trying to appease him without knowing what he could eat?

He decided to give it another chance, and entered the adjoining stall. The gritty stuff that flooded up this time was yellower. It didn't burn his finger, but Jenner took one taste and spat it out. He had the feeling that he had been offered a soup made of a greasy mixture of clay and gasoline.

He was thirsty now with a need heightened by the unpleasant taste in his mouth. Desperately he rushed outside and tore open the water bag, seeking the wetness inside. In his fumbling eagerness, he spilled a few precious drops onto the courtyard. Down he went on his face and licked them up.

Half a minute later, he was still licking, and there was still water.

The fact penetrated suddenly. He raised himself and gazed wonderingly at the droplets of water that sparkled on the smooth stone. As he watched, another one squeezed up from the apparently solid surface and shimmered in the light of the sinking sun.

He bent, and with the tip of his tongue sponged up each visible drop. For a long time he lay with his mouth pressed to the "marble," sucking up the tiny bits of water that the village doled out to him.

The glowing white sun disappeared behind a hill. Night fell, like the dropping of a black screen. The air turned cold, then icy. He shivered as the wind keened through his ragged clothes. But what finally stopped him was the collapse of the surface from which he had been drinking.

Jenner lifted himself in surprise, and in the darkness gingerly felt over the stone. It had genuinely crumbled. Evidently the substance had yielded up its available water and had disintegrated in the process. Jenner estimated that he had drunk altogether an ounce of water.

It was a convincing demonstration of the willingness of the village to please him, but there was another, less satisfying, implication. If the village had to destroy a part of itself every time it gave him a drink, then clearly the supply was not unlimited.

Jenner hurried inside the nearest building, climbed onto a dais—and climbed off again hastily, as the heat blazed up at him. He waited, to give the Intelligence a chance to realize he wanted a change, then lay down once more. The heat was as great as ever.

He gave that up because he was too tired to persist and too sleepy to think of a method that might let the village know he needed a different bedroom temperature. He slept on the floor with an uneasy conviction that it could *not* sustain him for long. He woke up many times during the night and thought, "Not enough water. No matter how hard it tries—" Then he would sleep again, only to wake once more, tense and unhappy.

Nevertheless, morning found him briefly alert; and all his steely determination was back—that iron will power that had brought him at least five hundred miles across an unknown desert.

He headed for the nearest trough. This time, after he had activated it, there was a pause of more than a minute; and then about a thimbleful of water made a wet splotch at the bottom.

Jenner licked it dry, then waited hopefully for more. When none came he reflected gloomily that somewhere in the village an entire group of cells had broken down and released their water for him.

Then and there he decided that it was up to the human being, who could move around, to find a new source of water for the village, which could not move.

In the interim, of course, the village would have to keep him alive, until he had investigated the possibilities. That meant, above everything else, he must have some food to sustain him while he looked around.

He began to search his pockets. Toward the end of his food supply, he had carried scraps and pieces wrapped in small bits of cloth. Crumbs had broken off into the pocket, and he had searched for them often during those long days in the desert. Now, by actually ripping the seams, he discovered tiny particles of meat and bread, little bits of grease and other unidentifiable substances.

Carefully he leaned over the adjoining stall and placed the scrapings in the trough there. The village would not be able to offer him more than a reasonable facsimile. If the spilling of a few drops on the courtyard could make it aware of his need for water, then a similar offering might give it the clue it needed as to the chemical nature of the food he could eat.

Jenner waited, then entered the second stall and activated it. About a pint of thick, creamy substance trickled into the bottom of the trough. The smallness of the quantity seemed evidence that perhaps it contained water.

He tasted it. It had a sharp, musty flavor and a stale odor. It was almost as dry as flour—but his stomach did not reject it.

Jenner ate slowly, acutely aware that at such moments as this the village had him at its mercy. He could never be sure that one of the food ingredients was not a slow-acting poison.

When he had finished the meal he went to a food trough in another building. He refused to eat the food that came up, but activated still another trough. This time he received a few drops of water.

He had come purposefully to one of the tower buildings. Now he started up the ramp that led to the upper floor. He paused only briefly in the room he came to, as he had already discovered that they seemed to be additional bedrooms. The familiar dais was there in a group of three.

What interested him was that the circular ramp continued to wind on upward. First to another, smaller room that seemed to have no particular reason for being. Then it wound on up to the top of the tower, some seventy feet above the ground. It was high enough for him to see beyond the rim of all the surrounding hilltops. He had thought it might be, but he had been too weak to make the climb before. Now he looked out to every horizon. Almost immediately the hope that had brought him up faded.

The view was immeasurably desolate. As far as he could see was an arid waste, and every horizon was hidden in a mist of wind-blown sand.

Jenner gazed with a sense of despair. If there were a Martian sea out there somewhere, it was beyond his reach.

Abruptly he clenched his hands in anger against his fate, which seemed inevitable now. At the very worst, he had hoped he would find himself in a mountainous region. Seas and mountains were generally the two main sources of water. He should have known, of course, that there were very few mountains on Mars. It would have been a wild coincidence if he had actually run into a mountain range.

His fury faded because he lacked the strength to sustain any emotion. Numbly he went down the ramp.

His vague plan to help the village ended as swiftly and finally as that.

The days drifted by, but as to how many he had no idea. Each time he went to eat, a smaller amount of water was doled out to him. Jenner kept telling himself that each meal would have to be his last. It was unreasonable for him to expect the village to destroy itself when his fate was certain now.

What was worse, it became increasingly clear that the food was not good for him. He had misled the village as to his needs by giving it stale, perhaps even tainted, samples, and prolonged the agony for himself. At times after he had eaten, Jenner felt dizzy for hours. All too frequently his head ached and his body shivered with fever.

The village was doing what it could. The rest was up to him, and he couldn't even adjust to an approximation of Earth food.

For two days he was too sick to drag himself to one of the troughs. Hour after hour he lay on the floor. Some time during the second night the pain in his body grew so terrible that he finally made up his mind.

"If I can get to a dais," he told himself, "the heat alone will kill me; and in absorbing my body, the village will get back some of its lost water."

He spent at least an hour crawling laboriously up the ramp of the nearest dais, and when he finally made it, he lay as one already dead. His last waking thought was: "Beloved friends, I'm coming."

The hallucination was so complete that momentarily he seemed to be back in the control room of the rocketship, and all around him were his former companions.

With a sigh of relief Jenner sank into a dreamless sleep.

He woke to the sound of a violin. It was a sad-sweet music that told of the rise and fall of a race long dead.

Jenner listened for a while and then, with abrupt excitement, realized the truth. This was a substitute for the whistling—the village had adjusted its music to him!

Other sensory phenomena stole in upon him. The dais felt comfortably warm, not hot at all. He had a feeling of wonderful physical well-being.

Eagerly he scrambled down the ramp to the nearest food stall. As he crawled forward, his nose close to the floor, the trough filled with a steamy mixture. The odor was so rich and pleasant that he plunged his face into it and slopped it up greedily. It had the flavor of thick, meaty soup and was warm and soothing to his lips and mouth. When he had eaten it all, for the first time he did not need a drink of water.

"I've won!" thought Jenner. "The village has found a way!"

After a while he remembered something and crawled to the bathroom. Cautiously, watching the ceiling, he eased himself backward into the shower stall. The yellowish spray came down, cool and delightful.

Ecstatically Jenner wriggled his four-foot-tail and lifted his long snout to let the thin streams of liquid wash away the food impurities that clung to his sharp teeth.

Then he waddled out to bask in the sun and listen to the timeless music.

Wolfgang Jeschke

Wolfgang Jeschke (1936–   ) is one of the central figures in contemporary German science fiction. He began to write science fiction in 1959, but became more involved by becoming an editor in 1969. He has edited more than 100 SF anthologies since 1970, bringing much of the best science fiction in the world into print in German in the last three decades. Since 1972 he has been the editor of the largest and most successful SF publishing line on the continent, for Heyne Verlag. Most especially, he has been a crucial force in upholding literary standards in German science fiction and for maintaining links with the SF movement in other cultures. He is a commanding presence in international science fiction.

Although he has only published two novels, both have appeared in English: *The Last Day of Creation* (1981; 1984 U.S.) and *Midas* (1987; 1990 UK). He has written a number of stories, of which this one, the centerpiece of his collection, *Der Zeiter*, may be his best. Franz Rottensteiner, in *Science Fiction Writers*, calls it "a virtuoso performance, so complex and well constructed that it can stand beside the best time travel stories, a tour-de-force that turns artifice into high art." Two forces play a complex and perhaps deadly game of domination in the past and future. It is an interesting comparison to John Crowley's "Great Work of Time," and contrast to Connie Willis's "Fire Watch."

THE KING AND THE DOLLMAKER

Stay where you are, Collins! Every move now could mean a fracture."

"Yes, Your Majesty," said Collins, and stayed where he was.

"Keep your eyes upon us!" commanded the king.

"Yes, Your Majesty," said Collins, and kept his eyes on His Majesty.

Time was slipping by. There was a deadly silence in the hall. The king was perched nervously on the edge of his throne and stared anxiously at the flickering mirror on the wall. Every time a patrol officer stepped out of the mirror, the king gave a start and leveled his gun at the man. Collins could see that the barrel trembled and that beads of sweat had formed on His Majesty's brow. The intervals grew shorter, and the guards could hardly avoid stumbling over one another. The patrol now had the room under constant control. The mirror twitched every time a man was discharged from or reabsorbed into its field. One guard stepped out into the room, looked attentively about him, and returned with a backward step into the mirror. But there was nothing special to observe. The room was empty. The walls still showed the light spots where the valuable paintings had once hung. Generations of sovereigns who had once peered morosely, critically, or solemnly from the walls upon the most recent offspring of their lineage now peered morosely, critically, or solemnly into some dark corner of the palace cellar which they had never seen during their lifetime. Even the nails had been taken out of the walls, the tapestries removed, the curtains, the furniture, everything. There was only the throne, His Majesty, the patrol's time mirror, which occasionally disgorged and reswallowed a guard, and a man standing at the triply barred and shielded window—Collins, His Majesty's Minister of Personal Security and Futurology.

The throne room was hermetically sealed, doors and windows safeguarded by energy screens. Not an insect, not even a dust particle, could have penetrated the shield, not to mention a minibattleship or a remote-controlled needle grenade.

"Tell us how long this is to continue, Collins. We cannot bear it much longer!" The king gave his minister a beseeching look. He was trembling.

Collins tossed back his cape, unclasped the purse on his belt, and drew from it a temporal strip. He held it at arm's length, as he was a bit farsighted, and examined it scrupulously. He was calm and composed; only the corners of his mouth curled ever so slightly in scorn. He had seen through more ticklish situations than this. "By Your Majesty's leave," he said, "Your Majesty's alarm is really groundless. The patrol knows that it will all turn out for the best. We have twenty-seven more minutes, during which Your Majesty is constantly supervised, before the arrival of this impenetrable ten-second time seal. From the very second that we regain access to the mirror from the timeline, this room will once again be under control."

Collins's finger ran down the temporal strip, tracing the dots indicating the guards' positions, and compared them with the date and time printed continuously along the margin. He had even jotted down the guards' names on the strip. They were his best men. One could not do more. With the exception of one short interruption, the dots lay so close to one another that they formed a solid line. Collins looked at his watch. Everything was running according to schedule.

"What is the latest report?" demanded the king. His voice was horse, fear gripped his throat.

"Nothing precise, I'm afraid, in spite of all our efforts. Your Majesty is aware of the fact that WHITE has undertaken transformations which reach far into the future. The seals are fluid, and the impenetrable time block is constantly shifting position. Our investigations are valid for but a few hours, then the temporal strips are worth no more than the paper they are printed on. Yesterday we could still supervise four days into the future; at present, this period is reduced to a scant two hours, and the block continues to grow toward us. But according to our calculations it will soon come to a standstill, so that we will eventually have thirty minutes left to supervise. But all this can of course change, should WHITE undertake a fracture."

"That's just it. That is the problem," whimpered the king. "Do something! How can you loiter about idly when I am in danger?"

"Your Majesty is not in danger," sighed Collins. "That is practically the only thing about which we are certain. After the critical moment is past, Your Majesty will be sitting upon the throne just as Your Majesty does now. Of course . . ."

"Of course what?"

"Now, Your Majesty, we have discussed it often enough. By Your Majesty's leave, should we really bring this up again now, when the moment is nearing?"

The king slouched in his seat and chewed his fingernails.

"Are you certain that I am the one who will be sitting here after the critical moment?" he asked suspiciously.

"But, Your Majesty, who else?"

"Yes, who else," muttered the king, and looked at Collins.

The minister inspected his temporal strip. The stream of dots discontinued, reappeared, only eventually to disappear altogether. Here was the seal, there the block began. What took place at these inaccessible points? Why had WHITE placed them there? Was this some kind of a trap or ruse? He had spent a great deal of time on the problem, had assigned his best men to it, but he had found no solution in spite of the innumerable facts that had been compiled. He was tired. A holiday would do him good. He looked around him at the dreary room, examined its bare walls. Got to get out of here, he thought. Choose any other time. How about dinosaur hunting in the Mesozoic era? He had grown out of that age. And he detested hunting expeditions. Too loud, too much excitement, too much drinking, and for the last few decades terribly overcrowded. They went and killed off the beasts in less than no time with their laser guns. And what if they did? Ugly creatures they were anyway. A minimal fracture. A couple of bone-collecting scientists of some later age would probably be astonished that the animals had disappeared so quickly. They would certainly find an explanation, that was what they were scientists for. The Tertiary period—yes, that would be better. It had been nice and warm then in this region. A couple of weeks of Tertiary. The patrol had a holiday center there. Plenty of rest, excellent food, saber-toothed-tiger steaks. Once, though, he had chosen a year when he himself had been there. Not that it made much difference to him if he was constantly crossing his own path—that had happened to him before, one got used to it. One had a few drinks with oneself, talked about old times, complimented oneself on how good one had still looked then and how on the other hand one had hardly aged at all since; one bored oneself to tears, felt a certain envy appear which could grow to hatred when one saw the bad habits that one had already had then and had long since wanted to get rid of but still had years later. Youth and experience stood face to face, and in between were all those years that one circled about and avoided mentioning but still could not ignore. Everyone knew that this could bring on disastrous time fractures if one were not careful, irreparable damage, intervention by the Committee, at best deportation to an ice age or to one of the first three millennia, at worst eradication from the timeline, condemnation to nonexistence, unless amnesty were granted by means of a special dispensation from the Supreme Council on the Future.

"You just stand about and say nothing!" The king's voice snapped him out of thoughts. "We asked you a question."

"I beg Your Majesty's pardon."

"What exactly is going to happen?" demanded the king peevishly. "Explain it again, step by step."

"Certainly, Your Majesty. Our guards are in control of all of the timeline which is accessible to us and are closely observing the particular area around the palace. There is absolutely no action. That is, as Your Majesty already knows, apart from the doll. . . ."

"Nonsense! Always this damned doll! How often do I have to hear that ridiculous story? What am I paying you for? Always repeating the same foolishness!"

"A small mechanical figure appears," continued Collins, unmoved, "a sort of miniature robot, with which Your Majesty deigns to play."

"Rubbish! How often must I repeat it? What on earth would I be doing with a doll? Have you ever seen me play with dolls? This is utterly absurd!"

"But by Your Majesty's leave, according to the reports of the guards, Your Majesty seems to be quite taken with this small mechanical object."

"But that is just what I don't understand! What am I to do with a doll? Am I a child? Once and for all, enough of this doll! It is beginning to get on my nerves."

The minister shrugged his shoulders and looked at his watch. "I am reporting nothing but the facts when I say that Your Majesty takes pleasure in playing with this figure, actually lays his weapon aside and gives the impression of being relieved of a burden and in extreme good humor, not to say . . ."

"Not to say what?"

"Not to say, well—like a new man."

The king leaned back with a sigh, then shook his head in annoyance and slid nervously forward again to the edge of the throne. "Doll, doll, what the devil does this doll mean?" he brooded. Then, turning and launching into Collins, "For weeks now we have heard nothing from you but reports about dolls and other such nonsense. Collins, you have failed. As Minister for the Personal Security of Our Person you have failed miserably. That can cost you your head; you are well aware of that?"

"By Your Majesty's leave, we have done everything within our means to get hold of the producer of this doll and to find and destroy the doll itself. The research has cost hundreds of years of work by our best specialists in ancient history, time manipulation, and causal coordination. Let me assure Your Majesty without exaggeration that we have done everything, absolutely everything within our power."

"You had orders to cause a fracture in order to avoid this dreadful moment, and what did you do? Nothing! You had orders to find this man in the seventeenth century and to have him disposed of, and was this corrective measure taken? No! And you babble on about your specialists and their hundreds of years of work! It does not interest us in the slightest. Did you hear? Not in the slightest! You have failed!" The king trembled with anger; his fingers tightened around the handle of his weapon. It was aimed at Collins.

"I—I most humbly beg Your Majesty's forgiveness, but as I said, we have done everything within our power."

"Did you have the doll destroyed? Yes or no! If you did, why does it keep reappearing?"

"We did destroy it—at least we destroyed one doll, but an infinite number of such dolls could exist."

"Don't talk nonsense! This simple craftsman can't have made an infinite number of dolls."

"Of course not, Your Majesty, but perhaps two or three of this type."

"And why haven't they been destroyed? Because you failed!"

"As Your Majesty already knows, and as I have allowed myself to emphasize repeatedly, this is in all probability—and in my own humble opinion—not at all where the basic problem lies. This question of the doll is certainly peculiar, but it is clearly just as unimportant as is the craftsman in the seventeenth century. We are dealing with an intervention by WHITE in which this man in the distant past plays either no part or a very subordinate one, in which his function is to lure us onto the wrong track. Your Majesty knows that I have never considered this a very promising lead. How much of a chance could a man in the pretechnical age have had? I personally am convinced that at that time man did not even have electrical energy; they were still experimenting with frogs' legs."

"One can build mechanical automats, Collins, which if they are preserved in museums or private collections can survive several thousand years. But we have other grounds to find this man dangerous. You should have had him eliminated. You had explicit instructions to do so."

"WHITE prevented it," answered Collins with a shrug of his shoulders.

"WHITE, WHITE, WHITE! Let WHITE be damned!"

They were silent. Time was slipping by.

The guards came and went. They now registered every second.

"How long is this to continue, Collins?"

"Exactly eleven minutes and thirty seconds, Your Majesty," answered the minister. He now held his watch in the palm of his hand. After this period the time mirror would blank out and be impenetrable to the patrol for a span of ten seconds.

"What is the purpose of this seal, Collins? Can you explain why WHITE had the seal placed here? What is hidden behind it? Something is happening behind it, but what?"

The king's voice trembled. The tension in the room grew.

"We don't know, Your Majesty," said the minister. "Perhaps it is just a ruse— we will know soon. But Your Majesty need have no fears, there will be no change."

"That is what your guards say. They are dolts," said the king. He coughed and gasped for breath and tugged at the collar of his black cape as if it was too tight. The handkerchief with which he wiped his brow was soaked with perspiration.

"Have you given all the orders? Is everything sealed off?"

"Exactly as Your Majesty commanded. The entire palace has been thoroughly inspected several times, the throne room especially carefully of course. There is not a single square inch that hasn't been meticulously checked. All dolls, toys, and similar objects which we were able to seize in the vicinity of this time-space point have been destroyed. The palace is locked and bolted inside and out. Nothing can penetrate this room unnoticed. Any particle, even a speck of dust, would immediately disintegrate in the energy fields. The doll must either come through the mirror or materialize in a manner unknown us; it is not in the palace now, unless it has taken on a form of energy of which we have no knowledge."

The king looked about suspiciously, as if he could discover some clue that had escaped the attention of the minister's guards, but his weapon found no target. The room was bare, there were only His Majesty upon the throne, the minister, the mirror, and the stream of guards who formed the observation chain.

"I cannot bear to see these faces any longer, Collins."

"Your Majesty has given explicit orders . . ."

"Yes, yes, I know. Are these men absolutely reliable?"

"Absolutely."

"What do you know about this dollmaker?"

"It is an odd story, Your Majesty. A relatively large part of his life seems to contain important historical facts which WHITE does not wish to have changed. As Your Majesty knows, he appears in the year 1623 in a small city in what was then Europe—now our Operations Base 7—buys a house and apparently earns a living as a simple craftsman, makes few demands on others, mingles little with the townspeople but is respected by all. On August 17, 1629, the period suddenly becomes inaccessible, closed off by a seal which severely handicaps our operations. This seal extends as far as February 2, 1655, covering almost three decades. Nevertheless, we set several of our best specialists to the task of living through the time behind the seal. Your Majesty can hardly conceive of what this meant for those men. But in spite of all our efforts the venture failed; the men were never heard of again. We could find them in neither the fifth nor the sixth decade of that century. Times then were particularly hard, wars were raging, and morale was very low. In short, by the time we could operate again we discovered that our craftsman was dead. We questioned people who knew him. Naturally we cannot examine the validity of the information they gave us, as there are no written records, but this is what we were told: One night he went into a fit of raving madness, and from that moment on he was like a different person. Formerly he had been a respected man whose advice was sought by all, but after this attack he let himself go, fell into the habit of swearing, jabbered incoherently, neglected his work, took to drink, picked quarrels, and proved himself to be generally arrogant and overbearing. For instance, he demanded that his neighbors address him as His Majesty, for which the fellows soundly thrashed him. He had apparently gone mad. He went from bad to worse, living on alms and on what he could occasionally beg or steal. One day he was found hanging by a rope in a barn, where he had apparently been for several weeks. He himself had put an end to his miserable existence. He must have been hastily buried somewhere, for we could not find his grave. We were told that this is commonly done to victims of suicide. We can fix the date of his death with relative certainly to the autumn of the year 1650. As Your Majesty can see, it is all in all nothing remarkable, perhaps not a daily occurrence in those centuries, but by no means an unusual one."

"But this doll, Collins. What about the doll?"

"We succeeded in destroying one doll. Our men blasted it and it exploded. We were not able to reconstruct it completely, but the parts that we were able to gather up in our haste in the dark give evidence of an extremely simple spring-driven mechanism, such as one finds in the clocks and music boxes of that time. There doesn't seem to be anything special about the doll either."

"Did you find anything in the following centuries?"

"We have inspected innumerable mechanical toys, only sporadically, to be sure, from the mid-twentieth century on, as there are such vast quantities of them, but we never came across anything unusual. Occasionally we found in literature evidences of more highly developed mechanisms such as we were searching for, but all our attempts to test the validity of these allusions failed. The mechanical doll was a well-loved fiction at that time, a sort of fairy-tale figure, the forerunner of the robot, I surmise. But the technical basis necessary to develop it is lacking."

"Nothing! Absolutely nothing!"

The minister shrugged his shoulders regretfully.

"How many minutes, Collins?"

"Five, Your Majesty."

"It is enough to drive one mad! Can't a stop be put to this running about?"

"I am sorry, Your Majesty, but it is Your Majesty's own command that the room be under constant supervision. This supervision cannot be countermanded without causing delicate fractures which might have dire consequences for Your Majesty's safety."

The minister kept his eye on his watch and compared the time with the temporal strips in his hand. In four minutes and thirty seconds the stream of dots indicating the guards' positions would cease for a brief period.

"Collins, have you absolutely no idea what is going to happen in the next four minutes?"

"I am afraid we know nothing for certain, Your Majesty, but . . ."

"But what?"

"But, by Your Majesty's leave, I have my suspicions."

"It is your damned duty to give thought to the situation and to express your thoughts. So go on and express them!"

"Let us assume that Your Majesty himself, on the basis of experience which Your Majesty will have gained in the future and on the basis of further development of time-travel technique, makes certain points and periods of the time-line which seem important to Your Majesty inaccessible by means of this seal."

"We see. Collins, why did you not mention such an important aspect earlier? That is a very plausible possibility; one can hardly consider it seriously enough." The king smiled in relief. He clung to this thought as to a straw. The idea that he himself could be WHITE clearly flattered him. He snapped his fingers energetically and feverishly concentrated upon the thought. Then his face clouded over again.

"But we would at least have transmitted some kind of explanatory message to ourselves in order to make this horrid situation more bearable."

"Perhaps that is impossible for reasons of security," interjected Collins.

The king shook his head. "But this doll. Where does this confounded doll fit into the picture?"

"Perhaps it is supposed to bring Your Majesty some important piece of information."

"And the dollmaker? No, no, it doesn't fit in."

"Perhaps he has nothing to do with the whole affair, perhaps he is just a secondary figure; but, on the other hand, perhaps he is the source of information."

"Perhaps, perhaps! Is that all you have to say? What do you think you are here for—to reel off vague suspicions? We can do that ourselves. You are responsible for our security. Is that clear? Such nonsense! A primitive tinsmith from twelve thousand years ago has information for us, the ruler of four planet systems and all their moons—how ridiculous! Just empty speculation and foolish twaddle!"

The king was provoked. The barrel of his weapon roamed back and forth, and Collins tried to keep out of firing range.

"Then it was a blind alley, by Your Majesty's leave, which our best forces have wasted centuries in exploring."

The king stamped his foot. "Time doesn't interest us! We want information. We want absolute security for our person, even if your people need thousands of years to guarantee it. If you go down blind alleys, it's your problem, Collins, not ours! You are a miserable failure! We are holding you responsible for the consequences. You understand what that means."

"At Your Majesty's command."

"Our command was: bring information and more information about the present sphere of time and everything connected with it; and you dare to enter this room with your suspicions! You can go to the devil with your crazy notions! We want facts and nothing but facts."

"Very well, Your Majesty, but don't forget the seal on Operations Base 7, an intervention by WHITE which made our work extremely difficult and thwarted our action in the decisive years."

"That may very well be. Perhaps there was at that moment a historical event of great importance. As you said, there was a war at the time. Perhaps our intervention would have endangered a politician or scientist of top-ranking future valence, or the great-grandfather of a politician or scientist, or heaven knows who. But that is all irrelevant. What is going to happen here and now in a few seconds? That is the only thing that matters."

Time was slipping by.

The guards came and went, came and went, dots on the temporal strip.

The king leaned back, breathing heavily. He was as white as chalk and dripped with sweat.

"Thirty more seconds, Your Majesty."

"Collins!" The king's eyes were fixed upon him beseechingly; they were filled with tears. "Collins! Keep your eyes on me! Do you hear? Don't lose sight of me for a single moment! Take note of everything, everything!"

He was leaning far forward, and his eyes swept panic-stricken across the room. He began to see dolls everywhere. They crept out from beneath his throne, came out of the walls, slipped down from the ceiling on threads. Everywhere he saw dangling limbs, expressionless plastic faces, beady glass eyes that glared maliciously at him, tiny fists that brandished daggers as big as needles or aimed minute laser pistols at him.

The king trembled and gnawed incessantly at his lower lip. Fear had complete mastery over him now. It was suffocating him. He felt as if he must either crawl off into a hole somewhere or else scream and shoot about him in blind rage.

The minister gave him a worried look.

"I can't bear this any longer, Collins!" shrieked His Majesty. "Don't just stand idly about—do something!"

His shrill voice burst into thousands of tiny splinter-sharp fragments.

Collins followed the second hand of his watch as it ticked nearer and nearer to the critical moment.

"Now."

The mirror went blank.

The minister looked carefully about the room, then fixed his gaze upon the king. The king suddenly leaned back, crossed his legs, and put aside his pistol so that both hands were free to straighten out the clothing of a small plain doll which he was holding.

The minister blinked and shook his head to dispel the optical illusion, but the doll was still there. It hadn't been there before and now it was there. He tried without success to cope with this new situation. The brain refused to accept what the eyes clearly saw. His Majesty was sitting comfortably on the throne, smoothing out the dress of this small mechanical figure, and smiling delightedly.

"Come, Collins, why are you staring so aghast at us? Have you never seen a doll before? A pretty little toy, don't you think? A dollmaker's masterpiece."

The ten seconds were over. The mirror glowed once again and the first guard stepped out into the room.

"Hello, how are you? Have a nice trip?" the king asked him in good humor.

"He-hello," stammered the bewildered man, and fled back into the mirror.

"Good morning," the king greeted the next guard who appeared.

"G-good morning, Your Majesty," he managed to stutter, and stumbled over his feet in his haste to find the mirror and disappear into it.

"This is quite an amazing doll, Collins. Go ahead and take a closer look at it."

The minister approached hesitantly.

"Would Your Majesty deign . . . an explanation . . . the rapid transformation . . . I mean, I beg Your Majesty's pardon, but I find it incomprehensible that all of a sudden Your Majesty is . . ."

". . . Like a new man, you wanted to say?"

"Yes, Your Majesty."

"You will get your explanation soon enough, in a half hour or so, when this spying finally stops." He pointed to the mirror.

"But, Your Majesty, time is running out. Your Majesty's only chance is to explain the whole situation to me immediately, so that we can undertake a fracture and take all other necessary measures, so that all may still turn out for the best. I beseech Your Majesty, this is possible for only a few minutes longer."

The king let out a peal of laughter.

"What for, Collins? Everything *is* turning out for the best. Why are you so nervous? Fetch a chair and sit down! Aren't there any chairs here?"

"But certainly Your Majesty will explain . . ."

"All in good time, Collins, all in good time. Not now. Let us first take a look at this doll. It seems to be an old piece, doesn't it, perhaps thousands of years old, but still in quite good shape. I believe it even can dance. It has probably made a long trip, we should say a very long trip, but it is still fully intact. Hard to believe what can fit into this little head, if one only knows how to go about filling it properly!" He held the small metal head of the doll between thumb and forefinger and smiled pensively.

"But, Your Majesty, I don't understand. What does this all mean?"

"Be patient, Collins, be patient. You will find out. There are just twenty minutes left. In the meantime, let us watch the review of your troops. Then we will tell you a story, a very ordinary story, but we think it will interest you nevertheless. We would wager on it."

"I am breathless with anticipation, Your Majesty."

Meanwhile, the king continued to greet with a gracious wave of the hand the guards who appeared and disappeared, as if he were holding an audience. The men gave the minister a questioning look, which he answered with a regretful shrug of his shoulders and a resigned sigh. His Majesty continued to play with the doll and seemed to be in unusually high spirits, as if all this was great fun.

Now it was Collins's turn to become nervous. He found that he had torn the temporal strip in his hand to shreds. The king said to his minister, as if he too had noticed this, "That doesn't matter, Collins. We don't need it anymore. In a quarter of an hour the stream of dots will stop anyway."

"Well, that's that, Collins. Your guards can't penetrate the mirror anymore."

The mirror was not blank. It continued to flicker, but no one stepped out from it. The minister stared in astonishment first at the instrument, then at His Majesty.

"Surprises you, doesn't it?" laughed the king.

"Indeed it does," admitted Collins. "But how is it possible?"

"Let us not anticipate."

"As Your Majesty wishes. But it has always been my task to anticipate."

"You are right. Very well, then let us begin." The king settled comfortably into his throne and cleared his throat. "Collins, you are a clever man."

"Your Majesty honors me."

"But you have made several mistakes."

"I beg Your Majesty's pardon, but what mistakes?"

"First of all, you shouldn't have taken your eyes off the mirror for one single instant, for then you would have noticed that it wasn't blank for the entire ten seconds. Not that there was anything you could have done, but you might have gained some information which would have led you to make certain further considerations. And at times you were damned close to having the answer. You almost beat us in our little game."

"Perhaps, Your Majesty. It is not clear to me—what could I have done?"

"You should have thought out the problem more carefully. Fortunately for us, you didn't. You could for instance have given more consideration to the meaning of this seal and the intervention of WHITE."

"I considered the seal a protection of important timeline intersections, where a fracture could have devastating consequences."

"All of which is true, Collins. And WHITE has to intervene, because sometimes time fissures spread underneath the seals, as a result of imprudent operations, and make repairs necessary, in order to guarantee the safety of the future, our universe, and thereby the very existence of WHITE itself."

"I understand, but why didn't WHITE seal off the entire timeline and cut off all operations of the patrol?"

"A good question. Why not? Think hard, Collins. You have a good head on your shoulders."

"Of course. Your Majesty is right. That would mean cutting off all time travel, which would in turn mean no invention of time travel, as there could be no experiments, and then the existence of WHITE would be impossible."

"Very good! Therefore, WHITE interferes only when its existence is at stake."

"But what about my mistakes, Your Majesty?"

"Without this future power, which we call WHITE, the course of our planet would speedily deteriorate into a state of hopeless confusion. WHITE was actually your opponent, Collins, but you were always looking for an opponent elsewhere. And you didn't know where to look."

"At times I suspected it, but I thought it more probable that certain political-interest groups in the empire, perhaps operating from a base in the future, were giving us trouble. But Your Majesty spoke of several mistakes."

"That is all part of the story which we are about to tell you. You must pay especially close attention to it for reasons which will also be made clear. But we want to anticipate a bit. You were hunting down this dollmaker—"

"Indeed."

"—And at times you made life difficult for him."

"As Your Majesty commanded."

"Hmm," smiled the king.

"Although without much success, I must admit, because WHITE intervened with a seal."

"Why didn't you study the past history of this person more closely, at the very time and place in which it occurred?"

"We didn't think it necessary. We already knew something of the man, though it was second- and third-hand information. The question didn't seem to be worth going into more thoroughly. It was my opinion that we had already spent too much time on him. What we had found out about him didn't seem to be helpful enough. . . ."

"Then you know that this man was born in 1594, first learned the blacksmith's trade, then became apprenticed to a watchmaker, and afterward traveled about for five years as a journeyman. During this time war broke out and he was captured by recruiting officers and forced to serve in the army; he spent the next two years with a band of men who had joined Tilly's troops. . . ."

"Yes, Your Majesty, and settled down in the town which is now our Operations Base 7; he acquired money somehow, bought himself a cottage, set up a workshop, and devoted himself entirely to his hobby of making watches and mechanical toys. He became a respected citizen of the town but refused all public offices which were offered to him; he escaped the snares of all the spinsters in the neighborhood, having decided upon a bachelor life in order to have his evenings free to pore over blueprints and tinker with mechanical instruments. He engaged a housekeeper who cooked and cleaned the house but was not allowed into the workshop. The watchmaker became more and more withdrawn, hardly leaving his house. Finally he became mentally deranged and in 1650 hung himself. As Your Majesty can see, we know quite a bit about him, but nothing which appears noteworthy to me."

"Nothing noteworthy. You are quite right, Collins. But do you also know that this man was killed in action, near Heidelberg in the year 1621? Tilly's crowd murdered and plundered its way through the countryside. He was killed either by farmers or by one of his fellow cutthroats, who probably fought with him over his booty or some woman."

"I beg Your Majesty's pardon."

"You heard correctly, Collins. The man whom you supposedly investigated so carefully was no longer alive at the time Operations Base 7 was established."

"That would have been an inexcusable error. But how does Your Majesty know this?"

"More about that later. And your third error was that you failed to have photographs taken of this man in order to examine him more closely. You would perhaps have had quite a surprise. But you and your people had eyes only for the mechanical toys. Fortunately."

There was a crafty smile on the king's face.

"I considered his appearance fully irrelevant in this case, especially as I could never rid myself of the feeling that we were on the wrong track and had wasted much too much time on the man."

"So you yourself have never seen this Weisslinger."

"No, Your Majesty. Why should I have seen him?"

The king shook his head in disapproval. Collins felt more and more uncertain.

"What a pity. Weisslinger is an extremely interesting man. You should have become acquainted with him; you would certainly have learned a great deal from him. He had much to tell, for he had been through much in his life. Perhaps you would have noticed that he wore an ingenious mask, though it was no more ingenious than masks could be in that age. You know us well, Collins, and you have a good head on your shoulders."

"I am beginning to doubt that seriously, Your Majesty."

"Now, now, Collins. It is never too late. Perhaps you will yet meet him."

"How is that possible, Your Majesty? I don't understand. . . ."

"Patience, patience! Wait until you have heard our story. Then you will have to admit that you let yourself be checkmated too easily."

"By Your Majesty's leave, I am burning with eagerness to hear the story, for I see more and more clearly that I accomplished my task much more poorly than I had originally thought."

"Indeed you did, Collins. You played miserably and recklessly."

"I most humbly beg Your Majesty's pardon."

"On the other hand, you were pitted against no mean opponent. But everything in its turn. BLACK had the victory as good as in its pocket—the situation was grim. Then it was WHITE's turn, WHITE would have to be damned tricky. . . . But where shall we begin? Ah yes, on the day when . . . Now pay strict attention! One evening . . ."

It was evening. The night watchman had just sung out the eleventh hour and had gone down the street, when a carriage drawn by two magnificent horses rounded the corner, rumbled over the cobblestones of the market square, and pulled up in front of the Red Ox Inn, directly across from the house of the dollmaker Weisslinger. The dollmaker went to his window and opened the shutters a tiny crack. He peered out in order to inspect the travelers who were arriving so late at night. He saw two men alight from the vehicle and converse with the proprietor of the Red Ox, who had come out to greet the distinguished guests and escort them into the house. The strangers apparently did not intend to enter and partake of his board and lodging, as they involved him in a conversation on the doorstep. They had a number of questions and seemed to be looking for someone in the town, for the innkeeper nodded his head several times and pointed to Weisslinger's house across the street. The strangers' eyes followed the innkeeper's finger; they carefully surveyed the market square and the neighborhood. Then they took leave of the innkeeper, pressing a gold coin into his hand, and strode toward Weisslinger's house.

"Aha," said the dollmaker knowingly to himself, and cautiously closed the shutters. "The time has come."

He quickly cleared away his mechanical instruments, drew forth several large drawings, and spread them out upon table and workbench. Then he sat down and waited. As he heard the knock on his door he hesitated, then went to the window and spoke quietly out into the darkness: "Who is there?"

"We beg your forgiveness, Master, for disturbing you at this late hour. The roads are bad and we have made very slow progress. On our travels we heard of a famous watchmaker in this area by the name of Weisslinger. Are you this man?"

"I am Weisslinger, but you honor me, I am certainly not famous. Come in."

Their thick accents indicated that they were foreigners. Weisslinger unbolted the door.

"Please forgive us for disturbing you. But we have little time and must speak with you."

"Come in, gentlemen. You aren't disturbing me at all, I was still up and working. Please excuse the disorderly room. I seldom clean it up and my housekeeper isn't allowed to come in here, she is too careless and always breaks something. Please take a seat. What brings you to this town?"

"We heard of your fame as a maker of highly ingenious dolls."

"That is not my main occupation. By trade I am actually a smith, and I have learned the watchmaker's arts as well. It is true that I have spent much of my—well—spare time making small mechanical toys such as music boxes and dancing dolls—although, I must admit, with little success, due to my insufficient craftsmanship. Please forgive me, gentlemen, I am neglecting my duties as host. But I never expect visitors and have nothing in the house to offer you. I can recommend the Red Ox across the road. You will certainly be pleased with the service there. I often have my meals there myself. The food is good and the wine cellar even better."

"That is not necessary. We have already had our evening meal."

Weisslinger took a closer look at the strangers. Their clothing was simple but elegant: black capes of fine material, close-fitting, well-cut trousers, and low boots fashioned of supple leather. They were examining the room which served both as living room and workshop. They seemed to be particularly interested in his machines, tools, and measuring instruments, which hung on the wall or lay on the workbench; it was not difficult to read from the disappointment on their faces that they had expected more.

"Would you be so kind as to demonstrate one of your models for us?" asked one of the men, trying without success to hide his discontent.

"Of course," answered Weisslinger. He carefully put away his drawings and cleared the workbench, then placed upon it one of his carved music boxes. He wound it up and let it play, then wound up a second and a third music box; the tinny tones of their simple melodies made an odd jingle-jangle. He then took up a small dancing doll with movable limbs, wound it up, and placed it on the bench with the music boxes. The springs whirred, and the doll made stiff, jerky pirouettes on the tabletop.

The gentlemen did not seem to take great interest in the demonstration; they continued to look about the room, glanced at each other and shrugged their shoulders, but pretended to be extremely interested whenever Weisslinger gave them a questioning look. Then one gentleman's eyes fell upon a grandfather clock which was standing in a corner of the room. It was an extraordinary piece with painted face, beautiful case carved out of valuable dark wood, decorated porcelain weights suspended from delicate chains, and a finely chased pendulum on which the astronomic tables and the allegorical figures of the horoscope were engraved.

"Is this clock also a work of yours?"

"Yes, sir. Does it please you?"

"It is a beautiful piece, but it doesn't keep accurate time."

"This is a curious point. You may find it hard to believe, but the clock is not supposed to keep accurate time."

"How can that be?"

"It is a long story, which I am afraid would bore you."

"Not at all!"

"Very well, if you really want to hear it. Please be seated. One day a man came to see me, a Polish count who had spent a good part of his life in Seville and Zaragoza. He was returning to his home in Poland; on his travels he had heard of me and sought me out. He inspected my clocks and toys, my tools and measuring instruments as well, and seemed to know quite a bit about the craft, as I could judge from his questions. But he denied having any extensive knowledge about such things. In any case, he was apparently satisfied with what he saw and commissioned me to build a clock for him. Nothing simpler, I thought to myself, but I was soon to change my mind. In fact, this man showed me very detailed drawings according to which the clock was to be constructed; these he had bought for a high price from a Jew in Seville. At first everything seemed simple, but I soon ran into difficulties. The more closely I investigated the drawings, the more complicated the works appeared, and I began to doubt seriously that this instrument which I was to build would function at all. The drawings were accompanied by instructions written in Arabic. The count, who could not read Arabic, had had the text translated into Spanish; this he had translated into his mother tongue and had scrawled along the margins of the old parchment documents. We spent several days trying to translate this text into German, but neither of us was capable of making enough sense out of these descriptions so that they might serve me as instructions, which they were obviously intended to be. They were more confusing than the drawings themselves, especially as they were worded in a figurative language which spoke of flowers, fragrant perfumes, and unknown spices, of strange oceans and distant lands, angels and demons, when there should have been nothing but metals and weights, screws and springs, coils and tractive forces, balances and swings of the pendulum. I was utterly bewildered and wanted to refuse the commission, but the count promised me a princely sum for my efforts, even if they should fail. In addition, he placed at my disposal a considerable percentage of this sum in cash, with which I was to procure the necessary materials and tools. I still hesitated, then he raised the sum, imploring me to at least try it. Finally I gave in and set to work. It took me weeks in these troubled times to gather the materials, as only the best would do. I had the face of the clock drawn up according to specifications; it was to be divided into sixteen hours, as if it were to measure some foreign time. I canvassed the countryside to find a cabinetmaker who could build and ornament the case according to the instructions; then we both traveled about selecting and buying the different types of wood out of which he was to construct the case—all of this in wartime, when we never knew at night if we were to see the sun the next morning. But God, all praise be His, held His shielding hand over me and my work, and in spite of all the difficulties the clock eventually took its present form, as it stands before you. It cost me three years' work. When it was finally finished, the clock actually ran, which was the last thing I expected. But the way it ran! According to the drawings, the clock was to have five hands, each of which was to trace its circle with varying speed and direction. The clock could tell the most improbable intervals and constellations of the heavenly bodies, but not the hours of the day. This must have been the invention of some insane infidel who wanted to measure the ages his damned soul would have to spend in Purgatory. It is the unchristian work of the devil which measures the eternity of Hell. Every chime of the evening bell sends its hands spinning in a different direction. . . . But I see that my story bores you, gentlemen. Please pardon my prattling on so. I don't have visitors often."

"Who gave you this commission?" inquired one of the strangers.

"A Polish count, as I already mentioned. I never did know his name. He came back once to see me, when the clock was almost finished. He spent hours studying the drawings, measured the positions of the hands, listened to the ticking of the works, made notes in a small book, sighed and shook his head, seemed at times to be discontented with the clock, then again pleasantly surprised, then once again dissatisfied; his eyes followed the pendulum as it swung back and forth, his ears noticed every change in rhythm of the buzzing and whirring mechanism, which sometimes ticked as slowly as drops of water falling from the ceiling of a cave, then again as rapidly as the hoofbeats of a herd of galloping horses— but the man never uttered a word. When I questioned him he cut me off with a wave of the hand, put his finger to his lips, and listened with such concentration to the ticking and whirring of the clock that—I hope you will pardon this severe judgment—I slowly began to question his sanity. As he departed he left me a sack of gold coins. I thanked him profusely, for this was a much greater sum than he had promised me. He smiled and promised to return soon to pick up the clock, but I never saw him again. Heaven knows why he didn't come back; perhaps he was not satisfied with my work, perhaps he had been expecting too much. Who knows? He never spoke a word of praise, which I must admit I would have been glad to hear after all the effort I put into the making of the clock; after all, I did my very best to carry out the order to his satisfaction. But perhaps he perished in that terrible war, God save his poor straying soul. These are frightful times. But you know as well as I, gentlemen, what it is to live in these times. God be merciful to us and let there at last be peace. Please blame it on my advancing age if I have gone prattling on again."

"Do you still have the drawings?"

"No, the Pole took them with him when he left this workshop for the last time. The clock was finished, I didn't need the drawings anymore. And I didn't want to keep them any longer, as they were quite valuable."

"So you know nothing more of the background or the whereabouts of your client?" inquired the strangers.

"I'm afraid not; otherwise I would have tried to find him myself. The clock has been standing in that corner now for two years. It takes up too much space in my workshop, but I can neither sell it nor give it away, much less take it apart or destroy it, because it doesn't belong to me. I am beginning to develop a passionate dislike for it; I usually cover it with a cloth and let it run down, but the silence that then fills the room is even more unbearable than the crazy ticking, so I wind it up again. But I removed three of the hands and replaced the face with a normal one; it was the only way I could bear the situation. . . ."

"Tell us if that isn't a good story, Collins!"

"It certainly is, Your Majesty. But I know it all too well. I fell for it from beginning to end."

"Why didn't you follow up that business about the clock?"

"I held this insane instrument to be the product of a sick mind, not worth our time and attention."

"We assure you, you would have had a surprise. You and your people have been standing a whisker away from the secret of the time seal. If you had only held out a little longer . . . but we expect Weisslinger would have had something to say about that."

"Your Majesty, I am an idiot."

"Dear Collins!" laughed the king. "We judged you right! You have no use for metaphysics and unsound logic, for secrets and mysterious strangers. By the way, that Polish count was an invention of ours, but he was rather good, wasn't he?"

"Yes, indeed, Your Majesty."

"And something else, Collins. Do you know that the pendulum clock was not invented before 1657 by Huygens and was patented in the same year in the States General?"

"My God." Collins was embarrassed.

"Your idiots have missed the anachronism—but not Weiss, who thereupon traced down the dollmaker and let him have some part to assemble a machine, in order to move the time seals."

"I am deeply ashamed, Your Majesty."

"Very good. Now let us continue. We haven't finished yet."

"I am curious to hear how these events untangle themselves."

"Perhaps you will be disappointed. Don't set your hopes too high. It is all very simple. Now, these two gentlemen, who had come to see Weisslinger so late at night and had listened with more and more evident boredom to his story, finally purchased one of the mechanical dolls and two other toys, paid the dollmaker well, and took their leave politely but without concealing their disappointment, exhaustion, and ill humor. After refreshing themselves at the Red Ox, they traveled on, although it was well past midnight. Weisslinger watched the coach as it rounded the corner and rumbled out of the city. He closed the shutters again and rubbed his hands with delight, as if he had just made an excellent bargain. Then he blew out the light and went to bed.

"Do you still have the doll, Collins?"

"Of course, Your Majesty, but if I may say so, it is of little value to us. We have examined it carefully. By means of a simple spring mechanism the figure rotates about a fixed point."

"Collins, you are judging things only by their source of power and mobility potential. In a way you are right; the doll isn't worth much, but it is a nice toy, one that would make many a little girl happy, even nowadays. And it is all handmade, every screw is hand-threaded."

"It is no doubt interesting, Your Majesty, but by far not as interesting as the doll Your Majesty is holding now."

"There you are right, Collins. Technique has a way of improving on the product."

"Is this doll also one of Weisslinger's creations?"

The king gave no answer, but leaning down from his throne he carefully set the doll on the floor. It took a few cautious steps to test the smoothness of the surface, then made two or three elaborate pirouettes, sprang nimbly into the air, turned a somersault, landed lightly on its feet, and ended its performance with a courteous bow. The minister applauded in admiration; the king was sunk deep in thought, but suddenly he turned to Collins.

"Where did we leave off?"

"The dollmaker, Your Majesty."

"Oh yes, we remember. Now then, listen carefully!"

It was evening. The night watchman had just sung out the eleventh hour and had gone down the street, when a carriage drawn by two magnificent horses rounded the corner, rumbled over the cobblestones of the market square, and pulled up in front of the Red Ox Inn, directly across from the house of the dollmaker Weisslinger. The dollmaker went to his window and opened the shutters a tiny crack. He peered out in order to inspect the travelers who were arriving so late at night. The innkeeper came to the door to greet the distinguished guests and escort them into the house. Much to his astonishment, nobody descended from the carriage. The coachman made no move to climb down from his box. Upon being questioned by the innkeeper, he explained by means of gestures that he was mute. The innkeeper looked about him uncertainly, then turned with a shrug of the shoulders and went back into the house, closing the door behind him. But Weisslinger remained at his post and continued to gaze in fascination at the carriage. The carriage curtains were closed, but as his eyes became more and more accustomed to the darkness, he noticed that someone had pulled one of the curtains aside and was examining his house with great interest. Time passed by, and neither observer gave up his station. At last the stranger in the carriage lit a cigarette.

"Bungler," muttered Weisslinger contemptuously, and closed the shutters. He did not bother to look again as the carriage rumbled out of the city an hour later. He was already sound asleep.

"What do you think of this version, Collins?"

"Inexcusable, Your Majesty. A cigarette in the seventeenth century! Such a mistake should never have been made by a patrolman. I give up."

"Not so fast, not so fast, Collins! Let us think. Where did we leave off?"

"The dollmaker, Your Majesty, had that evening . . ."

"Oh yes, we remember. Now pay attention!"

It was evening. The night watchman had just sung out the eleventh hour and had gone down the street, when a carriage drawn by two magnificent horses rounded the corner, rumbled over the cobblestones of the market square, and pulled up in front of the Red Ox Inn, directly across from the house of the dollmaker Weisslinger. The dollmaker went to his window and opened the shutters a tiny crack. He peered out in order to inspect the travelers who were arriving so late at night. He saw two men alight from the vehicle and converse with the innkeeper, who had come out to greet the distinguished guests and escort them into the house. The two strangers apparently did not intend to enter and partake of his board and lodging, as they involved him in a conversation on the doorstep. They had a number of questions and seemed to be looking for someone in the town, for the innkeeper nodded his head and pointed repeatedly to Weisslinger's house across the street. The strangers' eyes followed the innkeeper's finger; they carefully surveyed the market square and the neighborhood. Then they took leave of the innkeeper, pressing a gold coin into his hand, and strode toward Weisslinger's house.

At this very moment the dollmaker wound up one of his dolls and set it on the windowsill. The doll hopped nimbly to the ground and began to run. One of the men noticed it and called out to the other. They searched the square, trying to pierce the darkness with their eyes. Suddenly one of them took a leap and threw himself at the running figure, but it escaped him. The second man drew a small pistol and, aiming it, sent a spitting stream of fire whizzing toward the doll. But the tiny doll zigzagged agilely across the square and disappeared unscathed.

The long blue tongues of flame that came whipping out of the weapon licked up over the housetops, leaving glowing streaks behind them. Flashes of ghostly light lit up the market place, and the spitting, hissing, and roaring resounded so that the nearby streets fairly rattled with the echoes.

Weisslinger watched all the commotion in front of his house with amusement. In fact, he had to laugh so hard that his ribs ached.

"You miserable farmers!" he roared. "You louts! Idiots! You heroes of the laser pistols! Just take a look at that! Isn't this a marvelous joke?"

The disturbance outside had developed into a regular street fight. Fearful cries were heard as the people in the houses on the market square were awakened by the uproar. Shutters were thrown open on all sides and slammed shut again in

panic as the shooting grew wilder. The townsmen suspected bold thieves or even
enemy troops of causing the tumult, but in the general excitement and by the
dim light they could not make out the target of the shooting.

In the meantime, something very odd had happened. Out of the carriage,
which was built for four and could hold six at the very most, had swarmed fifteen
or twenty shadow forms, which set about madly chasing the doll. Their chase
gave off a fireworks display of constantly flickering pale streaks of flame, and in
their robes they fluttered about the square and the fountain like an eerie swarm
of giant moths. This frightful sight caused the inhabitants of the town who had
been disturbed by the commotion to bar their doors and windows and to hide
their valuables hastily in every niche and cranny they could find.

Master Weisslinger, however, remained at his window and watched the scuffle
with growing amusement. He even goaded on the scufflers, but his laughing,
jeering cries were drowned in the general uproar. At last one of the armed figures
succeeded in hitting the fleeing doll. It exploded with a dull boom and the parts
of its mechanism were scattered in the street. The dark-clad, shadowy forms
feverishly searched for these fragments. They threw themselves upon the pavement, lights flared up and died out again, and the men crawled about in the
street until they had convinced themselves that not a single screw or spring had
escaped them. They were like a pack of hounds fighting over a few bones thrown
into their midst.

At last every inch of pavement had been inspected and the men began to
climb back into the carriage. There was a great rush and pushing; the carriage
swayed on its wheels until at last all twenty men had managed to squeeze into
it. It had taken four men to hold the horses, which had been frightened by the
shooting and would not stop rearing and kicking. Held no longer, they set off at
a gallop, and sparks flew from the wheels as the carriage, skidding and rocking,
sped around the corner and out of the town.

As soon as the air had cleared and all was quiet outside, a few stout-hearted
citizens dared to peek out of their doors and windows to see if body and soul
were still in danger. Some courageously left their houses—carrying weapons—
and after taking a rapid look about the square began to strut about fearlessly.
Loud debates were carried on about the nocturnal raid, who the bold raiders
could have been, whom the attack was intended for, what damage had been
done, and what kind of an odd burning smell was still in the air. It turned out
that nobody had suffered any harm, and nobody's property or possessions had
been damaged or stolen. For the time being, no other conclusion could be
reached than that at least one hundred heavily armed men had caused the tumult. They had appeared out of nowhere and disappeared again like lightning
into thin air, because the appearance and intervention of so many valiant citizens
had put dread fear into their hearts.

The night watchman reported that he had intended to throw himself resolutely before the galloping horses, but then thought better of it and decided to
avoid meaningless sacrifice—not to mention the town's loss of his valuable services. Therefore, he had moved out of the path of the madly careening beasts
and had contented himself with a loud and distinct "Stop!" which the coachman, however, who brutally whipped the horses and looked like the Old Nick
himself, had insolently disregarded.

The discussions were carried on by torchlight long into the night and were
not given up until the dawn appeared and the innkeeper was too tired to con-

tinue filling beermugs and carrying them across the square to sell to those thirsty citizens who stood about the fountain celebrating their victory.

After several days and many all-night debates in the inns, the townsmen came to the agreement, after having consulted the priest, who had shown a great interest in the speculations, that it must have been a devilish apparition which had come to haunt the town. Some surmised that it was an evil omen, others went so far as to interpret it as a warning to the innkeeper of the Red Ox, who had developed the bad habit of filling his mugs less and less full, and whose beer and wine tasted more and more watered down. The rumor spread about town and came in time to the innkeeper's hearing. The evil omen before his very house gave him grounds for reflection, and soon it could be noticed, to the satisfaction of all, that he had taken his lesson to heart and no longer gave his customers any reason to complain in this respect, at least for a time.

The dollmaker meanwhile had nothing to report about the nocturnal incident. He claimed to have slept so soundly that he hadn't heard the uproar at all, although it had taken place directly outside his window. The innkeeper, who wanted to hush the nasty rumors which were damaging his business, declared that the strangers had actually wanted to talk to Weisslinger. The dollmaker laughed and replied that the innkeeper was just looking for someone else to put the blame on and that he himself had and would have nothing to do with any of these brawlers, be it the Devil Himself. After all, the rowdies had given the innkeeper and not himself the first honors of a visit, which everybody well knew and which the innkeeper had already admitted. Everybody laughed along with Weisslinger, because he knew how to use his cleverness and wit to drive his opponent into a corner. The innkeeper said no more about the matter from that time on.

"What do you say to this version, Collins?"

"Bad work, Your Majesty. Very bad work."

"Like a whole herd of bulls in a china shop. Why this large-scale action? You sent a whole regiment in there! You were lucky that the people of this period are rather superstitious. Imagine that taking place in the twentieth or twenty-first century. Interventions of such dimensions could easily start a war, if you have bad luck. Did it at least help you?"

"Not much, Your Majesty. The doll was much more complex than the ones we had bought from Weisslinger, one could say unbelievably complex by the technical standards of that time, which of course increased our suspicion. But on the other hand, there was nothing mysterious about its mechanism. We couldn't completely reconstruct it from the pieces we had collected, but there was no indication of any electronic instruments—it was certainly a purely mechanical construction. But it seems to me now almost as if the dollmaker wanted to play a trick on us, and we promptly fell for it. He probably already knew that we came from a different age. But by Your Majesty's leave, how can such an idea occur to a man in the seventeenth century?"

The king laughed.

"Don't underestimate the human imagination! The concept that man can travel in time is much older than you think."

"That may be so. We'd have to look into it," said the minister.

"Now look at that! A simple seventeenth-century mechanic has played a trick on our Collins. Shall we give you an early pension?"

"I most humbly beg Your Majesty's forgiveness. We wanted to eliminate this fracture, but it was not possible."

The minister stared at the floor in shame.

The doll now tried to walk on its hands. It succeeded on the first try.

The king smirked.

"It didn't work? Well, well. Think of that! It didn't work!"

"No, Your Majesty. It was our last chance to intervene successfully, WHITE had made everything else impossible. The seal started suddenly to move. We even had to leave important instruments at Operations Base 7. . . ."

"Time mirrors too?"

"Time mirrors too. We had to evacuate the station in a great hurry. The seal grew with threatening speed in our direction, as members of the patrol reported."

"Hmm. Does that surprise you? That could have caused a nasty fracture. Imagine the results if in this wild shooting someone had been seriously wounded or even killed. It would have put our entire history in a complete muddle. WHITE was forced to intervene, or else your people would have made more irreparable blunders."

"I beg Your Majesty's pardon, but it was an extremely important matter. For the first time one of these mysterious dolls appeared, time was pressing, and I had strictest orders. . . ."

"But you are in charge of security and must certainly be aware of the consequences of intervening along the timeline. That's what you had special training for."

Collins stared contritely at the toes of his shoes.

"Your Majesty is right. It was careless of me."

"Now then, don't make such a face about it. Nothing really serious happened," laughed the king.

"Your Majesty deigns to laugh?"

"Yes, we were just imagining the twenty men squeezing into the coach. We assume that you had an instrument installed in the coach."

"Yes, Your Majesty, one of the time mirrors from Operations Base 7."

The conversation ceased, and both men silently watched the doll. It was dancing now on its hands, now on its feet. One somersault followed another.

"Where were we?"

"The dollmaker, Your Majesty, had on that evening . . ."

"Oh yes, we remember. Now, listen carefully!"

It was evening. The night watchman had just sung out the eleventh hour and had gone down the street, when a carriage drawn by two magnificent horses rounded the corner, rumbled over the cobblestones of the market square, and pulled up in front of the Red Ox Inn, directly across from the house of the dollmaker Weisslinger. The dollmaker went to his window and opened the shutters a tiny crack. He peered out in order to inspect the travelers who were arriving so late at night. The innkeeper had come out to greet the distinguished guests and escort them into the house. To his astonishment, no one got out of the carriage. The coachman made no preparation to climb down from his box. In answer to a question from the innkeeper, he indicated by gestures that he did not understand the language. But the innkeeper did not give up so easily. In sign language he asked again if the coachman was hungry or thirsty. After a moment's hesitation the coachman nodded, pulled the brake, knotted the reins, and climbed down from the box. The innkeeper wanted to lead him into the house, but the coachman preferred first to walk up and down a bit to stretch his legs, then to see to the horses and take another look at the carriage. He then took off his dark cape and shook it out, as if to leave the dust of long journeys on bad roads behind him, hung it about his shoulders with the pale lining to the outside, and at last was ready to follow the innkeeper into the house. Master Weisslinger, at first alarmed and then pleased, had watched the whole scene with breathless interest. The coachman had not taken a deep breath inside the inn before Weisslinger was hard at work. He did something rather odd. Using special tools, he opened the enormous grandfather clock, removed the hands, loosened and pried off the face, replaced some of the works with other pieces, and tightened wires and made new connections. He then put in a new face, fastened on five hands and set them according to the new face, measured the angles they formed, reset them, measured again, wound up the clock, tightened a screw here and loosened one there, listened carefully to the irregular ticking of the clock, checked the movement of the hands, and made new adjustments until a high chirping could be heard above the ticking. Weisslinger cautiously touched some of the wire connections, and they were warm and began to glow—the wires were live then; he had tapped the timeline. The air began to crackle, and sparks flitted along the wires and bathed the room in an eerie light. The chirping had now become so loud that it drowned out the ticking of the works. Weisslinger put down his tools, wiped the sweat from his forehead, and leaned back with a sigh of relief.

"I've done it," he said. "At least it looks like it."

Then he blew out the light and went to the window again. He had to wait over an hour before the stranger finally left the inn. The latter seemed to have refreshed himself liberally, for he swayed slightly as he walked and the innkeeper escorted him to the door.

"Hallooooo there!" he called out, and waved in the direction of Weisslinger's house.

The dollmaker shook his head and said, "Just you wait!"

The innkeeper was helping the coachman to store away the horses' feedbags and to climb up onto the box again.

"Hallooo!" called the stranger again. Receiving no reply, he grunted and gave his whip a jerk, but so clumsily that it nearly hit the innkeeper. The carriage started up and rumbled at a leisurely pace out of the town, although it was well past midnight.

Weisslinger watched it disappear. Then he took a small, delicate doll out of its hiding place, took one last careful look at it, and wound it up. The doll woke up and stretched its legs. He held its little smooth head between thumb and forefinger and murmured, "You can do it. You will penetrate thousands of years and will bring me a sign. I know it now."

He put the doll on the windowsill. The little creature cautiously examined the market square.

"Run!" said the dollmaker, and gave the figure a push. With one spring the doll was on the street, whisked over the square like a shadow, and was gone. Weisslinger closed and barred the shutters and retired to bed.

"What do you think of this version, Collins?"

"I hadn't heard that one before, Your Majesty."

"We believe that, Collins, but you will get to know it well."

"How is that, Your Majesty?"

"Just wait. We are not finished yet. We are going to have to act it out together in order to round off the story."

"Your Majesty said 'together'?"

"Yes, Collins, you heard quite rightly. We are going to have to act it out together, the two of us."

"How am I to understand this?"

"It is very simple, and you will understand it clearly, as clearly as we are sitting here."

"Does Your Majesty permit me to ask a question?"

"Naturally."

"Was this doll that Weisslinger sent off that evening the same one with which Your Majesty is now playing?"

"The very same one, Collins. A few thousand years old and still fully intact. Go ahead and take a good look at it."

As if it had understood the conversation, the doll hopped upon the minister's arm, held on to his shoulder, and looked him in the eye.

"By Your Majesty's leave, it is really a marvel."

"Yes, isn't it! But where had we left off, Collins?"

"The dollmaker, Your Majesty, had on that evening . . ."

"Oh yes, now we remember. Now listen carefully!"

It was evening. The night watchman had just sung out the eleventh hour and had gone down the street, when a carriage drawn by two magnificent horses rounded the corner, rumbled over the cobblestones of the market square, and pulled up in front of the Red Ox Inn, directly across from the house of the dollmaker Weisslinger. The dollmaker went to his window and opened the shutters a tiny crack. He peered out in order to inspect the travelers who were arriving so late at night. The innkeeper had come out to greet the distinguished guests and escort them into the house. To his astonishment, no one got out of the carriage. The coachman made no move to climb down from his box, and, in answer to a question from the innkeeper, explained by means of gestures that he did not understand the language. The innkeeper looked uncertainly about him for a while, then shrugging his shoulders returned into the house and closed the door. But Weisslinger continued to stare in fascination at the carriage. The curtains of the carriage windows were drawn, but now that his eyes had become accustomed to the darkness he could see that the interior of the coach was illuminated by a pale and flickering light. Weisslinger gave a small sigh of relief, but for a while absolutely nothing happened. The coachman sat motionless and lost in thought upon his box; the reins were tied up and the brakes drawn. The horses snorted, chafed against the shaft of the carriage, and shook their harnesses. Time slipped by. At last the man climbed down, walked up and down to stretch his legs, saw to the horses, then took off his dark cape and shook it out, as if to leave the dust of long journeys on bad roads behind him, and hung it about his shoulders with the pale lining to the outside. He stepped up to the carriage and opened the door a crack. A small figure hopped out, flitted like a shadow across the square directly to the dollmaker's house, with a single spring bound to the windowsill, raised its little metallic face to Weisslinger, and made a courteous bow.

The master closed the window and unbolted the door. He cautiously peered about the market square, listened to hear if anyone might be passing by at so late an hour or if the night watchman might be approaching on his rounds, but there was no one in sight. Muffled noises drifted across from the Red Ox, where a few townsmen were drinking beer and whiling away the time with politics and card games. For the rest, all was quiet. The fountain in the market square splashed, and the horses snorted and pawed the paving stones. There was not a soul in sight. The stillness of the night lay peacefully over the town. The war was far away.

Weisslinger gave the coachman a sign.

The coachman immediately ripped open the carriage door, leaned far in and hauled out a long and obviously heavy bundle, got it with difficulty onto his shoulder, and staggered over to the dollmaker's house. The dollmaker hurried to help him carry the burden.

"Who are you, stranger?" asked the master in a whisper.

"WHITE," answered the man just as quietly. "Thank you for helping me carry him. He is damned heavy."

The bundle was a body. They carried it into the house and laid it carefully on the bed.

"Is he dead?" asked Weisslinger anxiously.

"No, he's only unconscious. He'll wake up soon."

The stranger breathed heavily.

"Damned heavy, that—uh . . . I beg your pardon . . . that fellow. Got me worked up into a good sweat. I'm getting old."

"Did everything go off all right?" Weisslinger wanted to know.

"You can see that it did."

"How did it go?"

"More about that later."

The stranger did not want to waste time. Weisslinger turned to the person on the bed and took a good look at his face.

"He has gotten fat," he laughed. Then he began to transform himself. He took off his wig, removed the clipped gray beard, and with a few clever strokes completely transformed his face, so that he looked like the mirror image of the unconscious man on the bed.

"Finished?" asked the coachman.

"Just one more minute," said Weisslinger. He rolled up the plans which hung on the walls and lay on the table, ripped them up, and threw the scraps into the fire. Then he took a hammer from the workbench and approached the grandfather clock.

"But—" interrupted the stranger, and added hesitantly, "Excuse my meddling, but shouldn't he have a chance?"

"How big were my chances?" replied Weisslinger, and gave the stranger a searching look. He swung the heavy hammer and let it smash into the clock. Glass flew, the valuable case splintered. With the second blow there was a crunching of metal, the pendulum began to clatter, and the hands whirred with increasing speed. The third blow brought the works to a standstill. He took another swing but did not finish it.

"You are right. It is a pity to destroy the clock. It cost me hours of work. With luck and skill it could be repaired. We'll leave him the tools. He can sell them, if he can find somebody to buy them. The materials alone that went into that clock are worth a pretty penny. But if he sells it all he'll be sorry. In any case, he'll get less for it than it is worth. If he can get it back into salable condition at all."

"If," said the stranger.

"I am ready," said Weisslinger.

"Take my cape." And the coachman removed his cape from his shoulders. The dollmaker drew it about himself.

"Not like that—the pale side to the inside."

Weisslinger turned it inside out. The other side was dark.

"Come quickly! He is waking up," urged the coachman.

The figure on the bed rolled over and groaned. Weisslinger took one last look around the room which had been his home for years and in which he had spent many an anxious hour between hope and desperation, many a night, half awake, half dreaming, pondering over and developing fantastic projects. Bent over his workbench, working all night through, summer and winter, he had drawn up plans, with primitive tools had turned and filed and fashioned mechanisms the precision of which his colleagues could not begin to copy. All the while he was on the lookout, constantly stepping to the window and peering out in fear, whenever strangers came to the town and stopped at the Red Ox Inn, that they were already on his trail and wanted to kidnap him or kill him or at least destroy his work.

Weisslinger turned away. He motioned to the doll, which sprang onto his shoulder, and followed the stranger, who was already impatiently waiting at the carriage and holding open the door.

"I'll climb up on the box next to you. I am curious to hear how it all went."

"All right," said the coachman, and helped him up to his perch. The carriage started up, and rumbled at a leisurely pace over the market square and out of the town.

"Now listen carefully," said the coachman. "You must put yourself into the situation and play the exact part which I am now going to describe to you. Pay very close attention, every detail is of the utmost importance."

The stranger then proceeded to give Weisslinger specific instructions on how he was to behave, what he had to say, what gestures he should make. The dollmaker had many questions, and to all of them the coachman had exact answers. He concluded all the descriptions and explanations as the carriage drew up to a dark, secluded farm, which lay deep in a vast forest through which the carriage had been driving for over an hour along narrow and overgrown tracks. They stopped. The moon had risen high in the sky and poured its cold light over the collapsing roofs of barn and sheds, over the muddy barnyard whose deep ruts were filled with water that glittered in the light, over the gardens that had run to seed, in which the weeds had grown high above the crooked fences. Everything looked dirty and dilapidated.

"Is this Operations Base 7?" asked Weisslinger.

"Yes," answered the coachman.

"It is a pigsty."

"That is the best camouflage for it. If anyone wanders into this deserted area, he should not have the impression that there is anything here worth stealing. We are fairly certain that nobody has been snuffling around here. But of course now it doesn't make any difference anymore."

The coachman took the bridle and reins off the horses, let them loose, and chased them out of the farmyard with cries and cracks of the whip.

"It's a pity. They were beautiful beasts," said Weisslinger.

"They'll find another master. First they should enjoy their freedom for a while."

They ransacked the house and sheds, destroyed all the instruments, and set fire to the farmstead. The dry wood of the old building burned like tinder; the flame shot up and in no time had reached the rooftree. The thatched roofs of the sheds blazed like torches in the night and scattered a shower of dark red sparks into the forest.

"A devilishly dangerous business we're doing," commented Weisslinger.

"But it's fun," laughed the coachman, and threw more fuel onto the fire. The heat was tremendous, and the two men withdrew into the carriage. The built-in mirror flickered and quivered in a milky light. The dollmaker smiled.

"Ready?" asked the stranger.

"Ready," said Weisslinger, and picked up the doll. Then they stepped, one after the other, through the mirror.

They had just disappeared when the rooftree of the farmhouse fell in with a great crash and a splash of sparks. The farmyard was strewn with burning shingles and splinters of wood. The fire now blazed several hundred feet into the sky and gave an eerie light far into the night. A few minutes later, a violent explosion demolished the carriage.

"What do you think of this version of the story, Collins?"

"It too is completely new to me, Your Majesty. Not only that, it is inexplicable. But still, the picture seems complete. All the pieces of the puzzle fit together. There seem to be a few pieces still missing however. Am I right, Your Majesty?"

"Quite right, Collins. But those pieces will turn up. Just have a little patience. We haven't finished the story yet."

"So WHITE intervened . . ."

The king smirked.

"We couldn't do anything about that."

"Not anymore, Collins. Not anymore."

"Right, Your Majesty, not anymore. I have to admit defeat."

"Nothing doing, Collins! There will be no giving up now. The story isn't complete. You have to keep playing. We insist on it, even if we have to order you to play. Don't disappoint us. Maybe you can make one more important move."

"I wouldn't know where to . . ."

"We have to fit all the pieces of the puzzle together to get the complete picture. Something is missing."

"Yes—for instance, why this substitution and with whom? . . . and what information did this Weisslinger receive from WHITE? That is, if—and I am not so sure of this—the coachman is in fact WHITE. What did Weisslinger find out from this stranger?"

"He was told the very same story that you just heard. But the dollmaker also heard the end of the story, which you will find out in a moment too. Then you will understand the substitution."

"I already have an idea, Your Majesty. Please carry on with the story."

"Patience, Collins. We have time, plenty of time. Limitless time is at our disposal. You will hear everything."

"I am very eager to hear it all, Your Majesty."

"Very well then. This part of the story is quite different. It takes place much earlier than all the rest that we have already told you."

The king reflected a moment before continuing.

In the meantime, the doll had begun to include double flips in its dance and whirled across the room.

"As you perhaps know, Collins, we once had a brother."

"Your Majesty has strictly forbidden any mention or even knowledge of this fact. I believe he met with a fatal accident many years ago while making some rash experiment in physics."

"That is quite right. He was killed in a time-travel experiment. How that came about, you are now about to hear. Once upon a time . . ."

Once upon a time there was a king, who was very rich and whose power extended over four solar systems and all celestial bodies within a radius of twenty light-years. This king had two sons who were very close to each other in age. When the sons were still children there lived in the palace an eccentric old man, of whom nobody at the court took any real notice. He was a mathematician and physicist and it was his responsibility to look after the electronic systems and computer center of the palace. His entire life was devoted solely to his profession, and he never participated in the social life of the court. His wife had died at an early age and since then he had lived like a recluse, eating and sleeping amid his scientific apparatus and computers and seeing and being seen by nobody for weeks on end, unless he was needed to repair a defective stereo tele-wall or one of the transmitters. He had been born on one of the most godforsaken planets of the kingdom, on which his ancestors, of ancient colonial settler stock, had settled. They had adapted themselves to the climate of the planet and could even exist out of doors in the open air. We believe his father was even a farmer.

He was sent to school, proved to be very bright, studied electronic sciences, and made quite a name for himself in his field. One day his young wife was killed in a transfer ship accident. He must have taken that very hard. He gave up physics and lived like a hermit. His resources were soon exhausted and he suffered bitter want. So he started writing stories, fairy tales full of profound and hidden meaning. He was very gifted at this but good fortune evaded him. His colleagues laughed at him because they did not understand his stories, and many people said that his great misfortune had driven him out of his senses. He was soon forgotten—no one read his works—and he led a wretched and lonely existence in a poor hut outside the city. One day the king heard of his tragic fate and commanded him to come to the palace. After much hesitation he finally accepted a position at the court. He was kept busy with occasional repairs and with the supervision of the automatic central control station and the computer installations, an occupation which did not demand much time or effort. He continued to write his fairy tales and to be derided for doing so. No one took him very seriously. But that did not seem to bother him very much. He only smiled enigmatically whenever he was asked to tell one of his stories, and his listeners turned away shaking their heads. And so he came to be known at the court as an eccentric old man whose thoughts were bewildering and whose logic was peculiar, but he seemed to be harmless, so people left him alone. Only the two princes were genuinely fond of him and considered him to be their good friend. He in turn loved them dearly, but not because he expected to gain anything by it—he had never thought of such a thing. He loved them because they were his most patient listeners and would listen for hours on end and still beg for more, delighted with his stories and never tired of hearing them. He would tell of the past and the future, of distant unknown kingdoms and their strange inhabitants; he could describe in detail the cities, the streets and squares, the palaces and markets, he could give such a clear picture of the clothing and language and the customs and habits of their inhabitants, that it seemed as if he had been to all these marvelous places and had seen them all with his own eyes. And yet he seldom left the windowless rooms of the royal computer control station, passing his days amid computers and field generators, matter transmitters and receiving sets.

Although the princes did not always understand everything he told them, it was always exciting. They liked him because he could tell fascinating stories without constantly putting in flattering phrases or wagging a moralizing finger, as the others always did.

More and more often they found the old man in his laboratory bent over technical drawings or bustling about complicated instruments. He seemed to have rediscovered his profession, but he always rolled up his drawings or wiped his hands and had time for them when they came to see him. Sometimes they watched him at work. The computers were at work day and night, figuring out integral equations which he fed into them. He fitted together tiny parts and wired electrical connections, ordered raw materials and new parts which often had to be sent in from great distances. The princes enjoyed the tingling feeling when he opened one of the small packages which had traveled through half the galaxy and now lay on his workbench, and tiny glittering instruments appeared which specialists in another part of the inhabited universe several thousand light-years away had carefully put together and packed.

One day the two boys noticed that their friend had aged visibly. He had always been in excellent health but was now suddenly declining rapidly. From one week to the next, from one day to the next, he seemed to age several years. His hair turned gray, his face became wrinkled, his eyes grew tired and red-rimmed. He became forgetful and absentminded and often had difficulty remembering the events and conversations of the previous day. His mind and body disintegrated with terrifying rapidity.

It wasn't until much later that the two boys found out the reason for this startling transformation. The old man had developed an instrument by means of which he could travel in time, and he had been spending months and years at other points on the timeline. In order not to awaken any suspicion, he always returned to the point in time from which he had departed, so that nobody noticed that he was gone and started unpleasant investigations. He had succeeded masterfully in avoiding this. No one had had the slightest notion of his excursions.

And so the years passed. The princes grew into young men and had to study a great deal, but whenever they had time they went to see their friend. One day they found him ill. His hair had turned snow-white and his cheeks were hollow and sunken. He knew that he would not live much longer but he seemed happy, as if he could look back with satisfaction on a fulfilled life. He motioned the two princes to his bedside and in a faint voice initiated them into his secret. He had used his last ounce of strength to destroy his wonderful machine, for some unknown reason, but he left behind drawings, plans, and descriptions, which would enable someone with a clever mind to reconstruct the instrument.

A few days later he died and his body was blasted after a short ceremony which few people attended. Nobody missed him at court; only the two young princes mourned their old friend.

Then they went through his legacy, rummaged through the drawers, drained all the information from the data banks, and set about puzzling out the complicated plans and drawings. The remains of the instrument were painstakingly examined and classified. The princes applied themselves with the greatest zeal to the problem, but it proved to be extraordinarily difficult. The old man's descriptions were as strange and paradoxical as his stories had been. But now the fact that they had so carefully listened to his tales proved to be a great advantage, for they had little trouble in fathoming his odd and apparently illogical way of thinking. Still, the work progressed very slowly, although they spent days and months in the laboratory of the computer control station, brooding over sketches. The king gave them complete freedom to pursue their own interests, in order that their abilities might develop more fully, and no one else paid any attention to how they spent their time.

Soon the princes quarreled, because each one had developed his own theory as to how the problem was best to be approached. Nevertheless, they managed to cooperate to such an extent that one day the mirror of the instrument began to flicker, as the descriptions indicated that it should. But what a disappointment! Its surface proved to be impenetrable. Something was missing.

Despondency seized them. Could it be that their friend had really just played a trick on them, fooled them as he had so often done with his stories? He was entirely capable of having done just that, although in this case much spoke against it. However, after more intensive study of the plans they found that the person who wished to step through the mirror had to take with him a particular instrument which would allow him to penetrate the energy field behind the mirror. This energy field would then transport him along the timeline until the poles of the instrument were reversed, at which point the person would be ejected from the energy field onto a given point on the timeline. Here he would materialize and move with normal speed in time. This mechanism had the form of an attractive brooch the size of a ten Solar piece and consisted of tiny silver leaves and innumerable microscopic crystals in which very fine copper wires were fixed; these were interconnected according to an extremely intricate circuit diagram. The reconstruction of this diagram turned out to be the knottiest problem of all.

The elder of the two princes, who was especially talented in handling tiny mechanical parts, succeeded one day in assembling this extremely complex mechanism. His brother watched as he disappeared and reappeared, only to slip off and return again through the mirror, but he could report little more than that behind the mirror he was swept away by an indefinable current, had a slight feeling of giddiness, and after a few moments was ejected from the instrument again. One could see nothing. The space behind the mirror was immersed in an impermeable milky WHITE, which surrounded one like a heavy fog through which one couldn't see one's hand before one's face. It was impossible to land in another time or even take a peek into another period; one was always thrown out of the field at the same point at which one had entered. The puzzle was still to be solved. Much later the prince discovered that this part of the timeline had been sealed off and that the seal had made travel there impossible. The inventor himself had placed this seal and many others along the timeline, in order to protect its network from careless, unintentional, or even malicious interference.

As soon as the seal was behind them, the brooch functioned perfectly, and the brothers traveled up and down and back and forth along the timeline. They got into extremely confusing situations, since they had absolutely no experience and did not know how to handle the brooch properly. They could set themselves in motion in the machine's time field but had no influence over the time and place at which they were ejected again. Fortunately, this always occurred after a very few minutes. They cautiously increased the field energy and found that they could manage stretches of a day or two, but they still could neither predict nor influence the point at which they were forced out of the field. One of the two disappeared once for six days, and his brother had trouble concealing his absence at court, but the great similarity in their appearance came to his aid.

Then came—this was all many, many years ago—the problem of the succession to the throne, which the king wanted to have settled before his death. He wanted his kingdom to remain undivided, and, according to the ancient right of the firstborn, granted the older son the crown. The second son was to be so well provided for that he could devote himself for the rest of his life to his interests, be they of an artistic or a scientific nature.

Now misfortune had it that the younger son was filled with ambition to rule the kingdom, whereas the designated heir apparent was much more inclined to the sciences than to power. It was he who had contributed the most to the construction of the instrument.

Ill-will and dissension grew and estranged the two brothers, who had once been inseparable. The heir apparent would have preferred to give up his claim to the throne in order to put an end to the wretched and disgraceful quarrel, but the king stubbornly clung to his decision, to conform to tradition and to satisfy the strong conservative elements in the kingdom. He wanted to avoid outbreaks of violence, which would only have shaken the country and awakened the avidity of greedy and jealous neighbors.

The younger brother felt slighted and sank deeper and deeper into malevolent envy. Evil courtiers encouraged him, giving him dubious advice and finally bringing him to the conclusion that he in some way or other had to have his brother eliminated. He succeeded magnificently in doing so, in a cunning manner of which no one would have thought him capable. He used the time-travel machine. The older brother could not rest until he had figured out how to materialize in times where there was no mirror and how to place and remove the seals. As he once again stepped through the mirror, his brother crept up and turned the energy of the time field up to full strength. He himself was horrified as some of the mechanisms suddenly broke down, wired connections burned out, and finally the mirror exploded. The field collapsed and the older brother, who had been carried by the ultra-high-powered transporter to some remote part of the timeline, was thrown out and landed in that distant age. What age it was nobody knew, least of all he himself, but it had to be in the past, since that was the direction in which he had set out to travel.

The court was in an uproar as the terrible accident was discovered. It was feared that the frightful event could have political consequences. Now everyone found out what the two princes had been up to for years and they cursed the dangerous games and fateful legacy of the crazy old physicist—and waited. The days turned into weeks, the weeks lengthened into months, finally an entire year had passed, but there was no sign or trace of the heir to the throne. The king ordered court mourning, for no one could imagine how or where the young man could reappear. Except his brother, of course, who from then on had an exceedingly bad conscience and lived in the constant fear that the victim of his malicious deed could reappear someday and call him to account. He could sleep only when the room was brightly lighted, awoke bathed in sweat out of a sleep troubled by uneasy dreams, started convulsively at every unaccustomed sound, grew more and more nervous and impatient, was convinced he was being pursued, treated his inferiors unjustly, and trusted no one.

·   ·   ·

"Didn't you have that impression, Collins?"

"Indeed, Your Majesty."

"As the old king died and the younger son acceded to the throne, he could not rest until he had rebuilt the time instrument, to ensure himself against all eventualities. He built up a police corps, which had to travel about in time, searching for suspicious signs along the timeline. The guards had to follow up and report on every trace which could possibly be construed as endangering His Majesty. Their supreme duty was to guarantee the security of the king under all conditions and at all times. Carelessness on the part of the patrol caused innumerable fractures, especially in the first period, and an army of scientists and mechanics was required to repair them. No great damage was done to past history, thanks to the seals, which the patrol came across in many places and which they called WHITE because the area behind the mirror within the sealed time spaces was white and permitted neither takeoff nor landing. But it was no future power which had made these points inaccessible; it was the old man, who in his wise foresight—or perhaps I should say in his better judgment—had placed the seals there. He had accomplished an enormous amount of work, both in the future and in the past; that must have cost him decades, by the way. But back to the patrol. They put in much time and effort learning ancient languages, they studied the customs of bygone civilizations, practiced using primitive weapons and instruments, learned how to handle animals, sleep in the open atmosphere and tolerate vermin and poisoned air, and accustomed their stomachs to barbaric foods, but their success was only moderate. They hunted phantoms and waylaid mechanical dolls. That is the funniest part of the whole story. They hunted a doll which they could not catch and in fact never even saw until it was too late. But why are we telling this to you? You know this part best, don't you, Collins? After all, you directed the operation."

"Quite right, Your Majesty."

"But we must tell you the rest of the story too—it is the ugliest and most distressing part. Let us tell you the fate of the prince whose bitter lot it was to be banned to a distant and obscure century, and how he fared there."

The prince had stepped through the mirror and had directed his path toward the past, in order to examine the seal which had given him trouble at the beginning of his experiments. He let himself be carried through the glimmering darkness by a slight current, then noticed suddenly that his speed was accelerating rapidly. He felt himself being whirled about, as if he were being drawn into a vortex, and nearly lost consciousness. All at once the motion ceased, the field ejected him, and it was light.

Until then he had had no idea how one could materialize without a mirror, what field energy was necessary to accomplish this, and what precautionary measures had to be taken. Now he learned it through personal experience. He materialized at about fifteen feet in the air and fell heavily to the ground. There was a stabbing pain in his right hip and he rolled over onto his face. At the same time, he realized that his hair was singed and his clothing had caught fire. He wallowed in the damp soil and smothered the flames. Exhausted, filthy, and tormented by pains, he lay immobile and tried to overcome the shock. He had to fight back tears, but after a few minutes he was able to pull himself together and attempt to sort out what had happened to him. He had not the slightest notion in which era he was stranded. His first impression was that he must be in an extremely remote area of the past, for there was still agriculture, as he could clearly see by the furrows in the ground, with which he had so painfully become acquainted. Cautiously he looked about him. He lay in the middle of an open field. There was no human settlement in the vicinity. The area was hilly, with a few isolated clumps of trees here and there. A row of scraggly bushes lined a brook which meandered down a wide valley. The countryside seemed ugly and unkempt. There was wild undergrowth everywhere, the plants were neither symmetrical nor genetically refined, and the trees appeared to be authentic and natural. Someone must have recently watered the land absurdly heavily, as the ground was damp and there were great puddles in the overgrown fields and meadows. The sky was so hazy that he could hardly tell where the sun was, but he figured that it must be near midday.

In all his misfortune he had still had the good luck not to materialize amid a thickly populated area. The pressure wave that he must have caused would certainly have torn to pieces the lungs of all living beings within a radius of a hundred yards. And if he had materialized within a solid body, the effect would have been like that of a medium-sized atom bomb, and there would have been nothing left of him. He looked about for a hiding place. He was as clearly visible to air reconnaissance here in the middle of the field as if he were lying on a silver platter. He could not stay here. His clothing, strange and in addition singed, his sudden appearance literally out of the nowhere, and his ignorance of the native language would all make him a suspicious character, and if he were picked up he would certainly be in for severe cross-examination. But nobody would believe him if he told the truth. He searched the sky but there was, fortunately, no helicopter in the area. The best thing would be to seek cover in a wood and wait there until dark. Then he would keep a lookout for lights and try to find a house or small village where he could perhaps get native clothing, food, and a minimum of equipment. After that he would see.

He got up. At once a sharp pang ran through his right hip. He must have injured himself in the unexpected fall. I hope nothing is broken, he thought, that would be a catastrophe. He limped across the fields to the nearest clump of trees, making slow and painful progress. He cursed the meteorologists who had watered the area too heavily. They must not have gotten far in developing their climate regulators. The damp earth clung in heavy clods to his soles and he often had to retrieve his shoes from the sodden field, where they stuck in the mud. He was very inadequately equipped and too lightly clothed, but it could have been worse—he could have landed in an icy winter. The trees that he was heading for stood on the far side of the narrow brook. He would have to wade the brook; jumping over it was out of the question. Every step was torture to him. As he finally reached the bank he suddenly stopped short. In the bed of the stream, washed by the shallow water, lay the mutilated corpses of two men. They were only half clothed, obviously plundered, and must have lain there for many days, for the bodies were bloated and deformed and gave off a nauseating smell. Both of them had ghastly wounds on the head and throat. They had been barbarously murdered and thrown into the brook. He had never seen anything so abhorrent before, and turned away revolted. Was this a crime? That was all he needed! There was nothing worse than getting involved in such business. He must leave the area as quickly as possible. He walked on faster, following the stream down the valley. Three hundred yards farther he came upon a caved-in bridge of rotting wood, over which a narrow road had crossed the stream. He could see that it had been destroyed by force. Here he found a third body, this time of a woman. It lay near an overturned vehicle which had been plundered

and destroyed. Apparently the culprits had intended to steal the belongings of
the woman, for baskets and crates that had been broken open lay trampled in
the fields on either side of the road and in the stream; articles of clothing and
pieces of cloth, shoes of various sizes, and objects whose function he could not
make out were strewn about. The vehicle appeared to have been a sort of supply
wagon. The woman must have defended herself to the very last, for even in
death she still clutched some of her belongings. She had apparently been shot
through the head with a large-caliber weapon; the shot had ripped away part of
her skull. He turned away, nauseated, and gathered up a few pieces of cloth,
with which he covered the body. Then he collected everything that could be of
use to him. He found an odd piece of clothing whose two tubelike appendages
were apparently intended to encase legs, and a jacket of heavy material, torn and
wet but still quite serviceable. He tried on this and that until he had outfitted
himself like a native. He had more trouble with footwear but finally found two
different foot containers made of animal skin which did not fit too badly. He
overcame his disgust at wearing the skin of a dead being next to his skin and
put them on.

He had reached his first goal, and although he did not fancy himself a looter
of corpses, at least he was not so conspicuous in his new clothing. He was aware
of the danger of his undertaking, for if he was found near the scene of the crime,
he would not have to worry much about his future. As far as he could see, a
man's life was not worth much here, and short work was made of it. He had to
be on his guard, but fortunately there was not a human being in sight. The
region must be very thinly populated and seemed to be completely inaccessible
by any means of transport—otherwise, the dead would have been found long
ago.

He took a closer look at the destroyed vehicle. It was made entirely of genuine
wood held together by bolts and strips and rings of iron, and had the most
primitive steering system imaginable. It had no means of propulsion but seemed
to have been pulled by some mechanism or even animals, which had been detached and removed from the wagon. This disconcerted him greatly. This sort
of vehicle had not been in existence for many thousand years. In which age had
he landed? He searched his mind for historical dates. How long had there been
automobiles? Their development lay just before the discovery of atomic energy
and electronics. That was the end of the second and the beginning of the third
millennium. All the horror stories and gruesome reports of those barbaric centuries which he had heard as a child now came to mind again. Had he landed
in the twentieth century or even earlier? The transport field couldn't have carried
him that far; its energy was too low. Unless . . . That couldn't be! Just keep calm,
he told himself. No hasty conclusions. First think it all over. It was surely possible
that in an electronic civilization there were people who delighted in imitating
the ancients and even had vehicles drawn by animals. Still, the dead woman
hadn't looked as if she had been traveling about on a pleasure outing. He examined the articles of clothing—no synthetics, all were made of organic substances. All observations led to the same conclusion. He must be in a
pretechnical age. If that were the case, his position was hopeless. Without great
sources of electrical energy, without electronics, precision instruments, and high-
quality raw materials, he could not help himself out of the situation. He could
only wait until help came from the future. They would search for him; his
brother would do everything in his power to find him and get him out. But how
would he find him, if he had no idea where he was? Keep calm, he repeated to

himself. There are several possibilities. He would have to find a way to send information into the future, so that they would take notice of him. He could for instance paint cryptic paintings or write enigmatic books whose anachronisms and precognition would be striking and could be interpreted as a message. But was he a painter or a writer? Would his works survive thousands of years of changing intellectual tendencies, wars and barbarianism, fire and anarchy, vandalism and the condemnation of purist sects—would they even survive him? And if so, would they be understood at the right moment as a message from him? Would anyone consider them worthy of keeping in a library or museum? Would they even be discovered among the thousands of testimonies of the art of clairvoyance and astrology, alchemy and obscure speculative philosophy, black and white magic, science fiction and fairy tales of the distant past? And after all, did his brother—the terrible suspicion which he had been constantly pushing out of his mind took clear form—did his brother have any interest at all in finding him again?

No useless speculations, he warned himself. He would find out. There was plenty of time. Perhaps he could build mechanisms which if well protected could survive several civilizations, ticking like time bombs through the ages, and at a given point attract attention to themselves and to him. If time travel were possible, then they would certainly look into his case again, whether they received a message or not. The important point was for him to establish contact, then perhaps they would find a way to him. He had to be on the alert not to overlook any signs or signals. If they really wanted to help him out of this mess, there would be no problem. It was just better for him to be a bit wary, because if it were in their interest to leave him here, then it would be up to him to make the decisive move. He must be very careful not to cause any contradictions or anachronisms; no camouflage was perfect. But this meant that he would have to know the age perfectly, would have to study it thoroughly and adapt himself completely as a contemporary, no matter how difficult this might be. He would have to gain a firm footing in this involuntary exile, and circumstances dictated that he must do so immediately. At first he was concerned only with pure survival: food, weapons, money, a relatively safe place to live, and information. All the rest he would take care of later. He was perhaps inferior to the natives in physical resistance and hardiness, but his scientific and technical knowledge would stand him in good stead. He just had to make the best use he could of the primitive resources.

He left the scene of horror behind him and scrambled over the remains of the bridge across the stream, turned off from the road, and sought a relatively dry place among the trees and bushes where he would be hidden from the eyes of any natives who might come along. It was warm and he spread out the captured clothing to dry, then examined his injured leg. The injury was painful but there was apparently no break, only a bone bruise. A few hours of rest would do him good. He let himself down upon the ground and had a more leisurely look at his surroundings. The native plants which grew on all sides of him were indescribably ugly. Birds twittered in the branches above him, but he did not have the impression that they were the diverting artificial mechanisms that he was accustomed to, for they behaved in a shy and strange manner. They must be organic beings, but he had to admit that they sang just as nicely as the artificial ones he knew. Every place he set his eyes on was swarming with life. On the ground, in the grass, on the leaves, in the bark of the trees, everywhere tiny animals were creeping and crawling, chirping and rustling. He was somewhat nauseated by so much organic life. He had been brought up in the sterile world of the plastic region, into which every few weeks a stray animal found its way, an odd insect like a fly or moth, which—if it had in some inexplicable manner penetrated the energy screen without being burned—was immediately traced by infrared searchers and chased out of the airspace or killed. I will have to get used to it, he thought. Overcoming his aversion, he let one of the quick, black, six-footed animals run across the back of his hand. It did not hurt and the animal seemed not to be poisonous.

He looked at the sky. It was empty; there were no condensation trails of departing or landing transfer ships to be seen, no observation platforms on invisible gravitation anchors, no programmed control floater in the complex network of directive beams of a ground station for surface inspection, no reflex of an energy halo which surrounded the planet and protected it from extraterrestrial attacks. The sun broke through the thin cloud layer and scattered the clouds. Its warmth and beams of energy pierced the atmosphere and gave the skin a prickling sensation.

He listened. Something had been irritating him all this time, and now he knew what it was. The environment was so quiet. Although there were birds twittering and leaves rustling, it was so unbelievably quiet that he could hear his own pulse. His ears were accustomed to a great jumble of constant sounds caused by the innumerable transport craft, the control and service mechanisms, and other useful apparatus in the palace which he had never really noticed before, as he had heard them all since birth. Now this stillness seemed like a constant dull sound to him, one that lies just under the threshold of hearing and is perceived rather than heard. The sun dried his clothing and lay with calming warmth on his face, and afternoon dozed peacefully over the countryside. The prince felt that he was tired and before he knew it he was fast asleep.

When he awoke, night had come and he saw the stars. He had never seen the inhabited universe with such clarity from the surface of the earth. With his bare eyes he could recognize two of the solar systems which belonged to his father's kingdom. Nonsense, he told himself, in this era not all of that space was settled. It gave him an odd feeling to see that the remote suns formed almost the same constellations that he knew. He shivered. In the distance he heard a strange noise. It sounded like the rumbling of thunder, and flashes of lightning blazed on the horizon, but the sky was completely clear. It looked like a bombardment with explosive chemical weapons. Could it be . . . ? Of course! That was the explanation for the signs of destruction and the bodies that he had found. It was wartime! What he saw on the horizon was the reflection of discharged explosive weapons. There must be a battle raging there. The sky grew red, probably from great fires.

That was all he had needed, to land in the middle of a period of war. Still, he thought, there might be advantages to this situation. In the general confusion it would be easier for him to mingle with the natives, to get money and weapons somehow, and to settle down somewhere. At times like this no one was going to ask many questions about his identity and background. That simplified many matters, but at the same time his situation was much more dangerous, as he might easily land between the two fronts. If he was found he might be put to the sword. He would have to trust to his good fortune.

He got up. His hip ached but he could walk. He dressed himself, tied his possessions together in a bundle, and headed off in the direction of the shooting. There must be a larger settlement there. He would cautiously approach and at first remain withdrawn but observe and gather information. After that he would decide on the further steps to be taken.

Walking across the fields and meadows turned out to be harder than he had thought. The footwork of animal skin was stiff and rubbed him so that his feet were soon in great pain. After an hour he was completely exhausted and had to rest. In addition, hunger began to gnaw at his insides. He pulled himself together and set out again, making a great detour around a forest that frightened him because he did not know how wild plants and animals reacted at night. He plodded through swamps, waded streams, and made very slow progress, because he had to stop more and more often to rest.

Emerging from a large wooded area, he heard loud cries and explosions and saw the glare of a fire. There was a farmstead in front of him. A barn was blazing in flames. He heard more explosions, laughter and piercing screams, and saw figures running and falling to the ground. He limped faster, thinking that he could perhaps help, but as he came closer he saw that even with the best intentions there was nothing he could do. He was witness to an atrocity of war. Hidden behind a hedge, he watched the actions of these people at first with astonishment and then with growing horror. They had built up a great fire, onto which they threw household utensils and furniture. The rain of sparks had set the thatched roof of the barn on fire, and the fire threatened to spread to the other buildings, but this did not seem to disturb anyone. In the flickering firelight he was presented with a grotesque and macabre scene. Several men, who were strangely clothed and who wore on their heads gigantic headgear onto which they had fixed bushes of some fluffy material, staggered about with some sort of container in their hands, from which they occasionally drank. They all appeared to be under the influence of a drug, as they could hardly stay on their feet, vomited, slipped, fell down, and tried in vain to regain their footing. Some of them lay motionless on the ground, either dead or sleeping where they had fallen. They had killed a large animal, lopped off its head, ripped out its intestines, driven a spit in barbaric manner from the hind quarters through to the neck, and hung it over the fire. Others were occupied with forcing open boxes and barrels and rummaging through their contents, over which they fought in the wildest manner, striking one another with fists and weapons and screaming curses at one another. Yet others had captured several women and girls. They formed a ring about them and, roaring with laughter, ripped their clothes from their bodies. Then they threw the poor creatures to the ground and mounted them so brutally that his breath caught in his throat. The women, also partly under the influence of the drug which they had been forced to drink, half numbed from blows on the head, weakly let themselves be mishandled and whimpered with fear, pain, and terror, while the rest of the men followed the doings of their companions and egged them on with loud cries until it was their turn. Horrified and trembling with loathing, the prince felt a great powerless rage surge up in him. If he had only had his laser gun at hand he would have blasted that rabble into the dirt until the water exploded out of their miserable skins. He shook with anger and realized with alarm that he was tending toward more aggression than he had ever thought himself capable of feeling. Had this world already drawn him into its ways, was he beginning to act like a wild man? In what frightful age had he landed?

He fled into the forest and squatted all night long under a tree, his teeth chattering, shivering with cold and horror, watching the glare of the fire and hearing the loathsome cries of the wild men in the distance.

The temperature sank lower and lower. That must be due to the missing energy halo; at night the surface of the earth gave off unhampered into space all the warmth which it had stored up during the day, causing these variations in temperature. He looked into the starlit sky. Even the distant suns looked cold and uninviting; they were still wild and uncolonized systems.

He crouched tightly, in order to gather his own body heat, but his legs grew stiff and he had to stand up and walk up and down. He was grateful to see the gray of dawn and then the sun slowly rising, and the temperature of the atmosphere soon began also to rise to a tolerable warmth. In the course of the morning the disorderly band of debauched soldiers who had afflicted the whole region with their looting and murdering finally moved on, but not until they had set fire to all that was left of the farm. They took a number of animals with them, on the backs of which they had fixed seats. Some of the men had climbed onto these seats and let themselves be carried by the patient beasts. An ingenious arrangement of cords and chains fixed about the mouth of the animal enabled the rider seated on its back to direct the organic vehicle. The prince found it most astonishing that the big strong animals submitted to such treatment.

When the band had disappeared, the prince dared to come out from his hiding place and examine the scene of devastation once again. Perhaps someone had been left behind who needed help, but basically it was hunger that drove him forward. Perhaps he could capture something edible, perhaps he could even find more information on this age, some papers or a calendar.

A gruesome sight met his eye. The charred corpses of men and women who had been shot or beaten to death lay strewn about among the smashed and smoldering remains of buildings and household goods. The women and girls had been massacred in the most grisly manner and left lying in their own blood. They were hardly distinguishable from the ravaged ground onto which they had been thrown and trampled.

The buildings of the farmstead had long since fallen in, and the flames had destroyed what remained of them. Broken vessels and smashed furniture lay in the flattened grass and in food which had been trampled into the dirt. Driven by hunger, he searched about and finally found two or three pieces of some vegetable substance which had been roasted in the fire and which seemed edible. With aversion he bit into one. It was almost tasteless but after much chewing the saliva rendered it rather sweet. He choked it down, and every bite seemed tastier than the last. Searching for something to drink, he came across the dregs of a sour, spicy liquid in the drinking vessels. He smelled it. This must be the drug. Perhaps it is alcohol, he thought, but was not quite certain. He continued the search and found a hole in the ground that was lined with stones and equipped with an instrument by means of which a container could be let down and drawn up again. He tried it out and drew up a bucket of water. Examining it carefully, he found it to be rather clean and drank in great greedy gulps. I am already a regular wild man, he told himself. I drink water out of the ground, which must be teeming with pathogenic agents, and eat dirty food in the company of corpses and surrounded by the stench of half-burnt animals and people. I may already have poisoned myself, but what can I do. I have the alternative of either dying of hunger and thirst or of being killed by the poisons and bacteria of this barbaric food. The problem was purely academic. He had no choice but to take the risk.

He examined the clothing of the corpses, which were stiff with indescribable filth, and discovered two letters in the pocket of a dead soldier. He couldn't read the handwriting, but the numbers were Arabic. They were obviously dated; both bore the figures 1619.

According to this, he was approximately twelve thousand years in the past, or, more precisely, in the first half of the seventeenth century (old calendar), if the dates were accurate. At any rate, the papers appeared not to be very old. The energy of the time field had been far from high enough at the time of his departure to transport him this far. Could the machine have had a breakdown? But then it would have been impossible for the field energy to increase. Someone must have had his hand in the matter, and who could it have been but his brother? He wouldn't have thought it possible, but he had to get used to the idea.

He put both letters in his pocket. They were addressed to a certain Weisslinger, as he found out later when he had learned to decipher the handwriting, and were written by the priest of a small town, who begged the man to return home immediately, as his wife was dangerously ill, the household going to ruin, and his children suffering bitter want. In the second letter the priest informed him that in the meantime his wife had died and had been buried at the costs of the community, his workshop had been demolished, and his five children were being seen after by various families, where they had to work for bed and board. They were cared for well enough but the stern hand of a father was obviously lacking, as they had been occasionally caught thieving. Their father was an unscrupulous vagabond whom God would one day punish for his sins and his disgraceful life by allotting him a base and unworthy death. The man had met his fate; he had died of a slit throat.

The prince also found near the dead man one of those primitive firearms which function on the basis of the rapid expansion of gases which develop from the ignition of certain chemical substances, whereby a small piece of metal is set into rapid motion and is aimed at its target through a pipe in which the explosion takes place. He also found a stock of the burning substance and of the little pieces of metal, which fit exactly into the pipe of the weapon. Outfitted with these, he was no longer defenseless and faced the future more calmly.

Then he dragged all the bodies to one spot and piled wood over them. He set the wood on fire and quickly left the site of horror. He hoped to find a larger settlement. But he was to find even more gruesome scenes of devastation.

"Yes, Collins, and so his life went on. That was the beginning of a period of the most varied adventures and dangers. He struggled along, a prey to good and bad fortune, and learned how to use the cut-and-thrust weapon as well as pistols, muskets, and heavier explosive weapons. He learned many different languages. From the first he attracted no attention to himself, because soldiers from all corners of the earth served in the armies. He learned their coarse and savage customs, learned how to fight and how to kill. It is amazing and frightening, Collins, how quickly one can learn such things. He had soon become so well adapted that he could behave like a man of the seventeenth century in all situations without being the least bit conspicuous. He traveled through many lands in which the war was raging—and God knows there were plenty of them. He was witness to nameless misery and himself bore unspeakable adversity; he was often desperate and sometimes happy, but above all he survived. And he had learned. He had learned how to plunder, how to prepare trick-playing dice, how to protect his property with cunning and spite, force and coldbloodedness. At last he had amassed enough money to insure himself of a carefree existence, and he withdrew from the tradings of war, much to the dismay of his generals, for his knowledge of mechanics and ballistics had made him one of the most sought-after artillerymen and he could have easily earned military distinctions as cannoneer or pyrotechnician, cannonsmith or rocket launcher. But this was not his goal; he had in the true sense of the word more far-reaching plans. One thing had always sustained him and helped him overcome all dangers—his brooch. He often slipped his hand into his pocket to reassure himself that he wasn't simply dreaming of returning, but then he felt the crystal screen vibrate and come alive in the time stream, and as long as there was life in this mechanism there was activity on the timeline in the section where he was helplessly floating along, there were time travelers and there was hope for him. He was cut off, for without a mirror he could not construct a time field. Help must come from outside, even if unwillingly or unwittingly; he was clever enough to know that there was at least one man who considered the present solution to be the better one—his opponent in the little game that he wanted to chance. First he needed a permanent location which could satisfy all the requirements of offering relative safety, raw materials, and tools. Then he would have to wait until someone appeared from the future with a mirror.

"After months and years of restless wandering he found a small town in the south which was fortified and pleased him and was far from all battlefronts. Here he decided to settle down. With his gold he bought a small house on the market square and installed a workshop in it. He took advantage of his technical knowledge and established a modest mechanic's shop. At first he made hinges and handles and repaired locks; later he constructed all manner of clever toys, which he sold or gave away to travelers or citizens of the town. He was friendly and open to everyone, always considerate and ready to help, and he soon came to enjoy the reputation of being the most upright member of the community. Nevertheless, he led a secluded life and was seldom seen in the Red Ox Inn, although it stood directly across from his house.

"He waited. No traveler who entered the town and stopped at the Red Ox escaped his eye. Every evening he put out the lamp and peered for hours through the crack in the shutters at the market place, in case anything suspicious should happen. He spent every free moment which his numerous contracts left him pondering over sketches and plans for solving his problem with only the most primitive means which were available to him and with no source of electrical energy. There were two possibilities which seemed feasible. He could build a mechanism that would survive the twelve thousand years and would bring help by means of some clever trick. This would cause a fracture, but it would be a small one. He would be taking no chances, as this solution worked, if at all, only with complete success. When the mechanism gave him a sign, that would mean at the same time that he had won the move, for that was the prerequisite of the help; he would have to return sooner or later to the future. The second possibility was to build an apparatus which would allow him directly to tap the energy of the time field. With its help he could set up a primitive electronic system which would localize activities on the timeline. He could then establish the position of the seal and perhaps even shift it, for on this subject his research was far more advanced than his brother imagined. He decided to try both possibilities and set to work. Then there was nothing to do but wait. He soon had proof that his work would bring results. The first spies soon showed up, and he could quickly tell by their behavior that they were the wrong ones and had no intention of helping Weisslinger out of his predicament. Are we right, Collins?"

"To be sure, Your Majesty, that was not our intention."

"Now, Weisslinger had expected that and had long since taken it into account. He had even made some preparations. His appearance had changed no small amount during his life in this time period. He had grown older, his features were harder and his body stronger. And he had contributed to the effect somewhat too; he looked older than he actually was, his hair was streaked with gray and reached to his shoulders. He wanted to take no risks, for this move was far too important to him.

"Soon the guests from the future were arriving by the dozen. He registered one fracture and anachronism after another. Obviously they had found him. The visitors gave Weisslinger many an evening's entertainment. But we already told you about that. Then the master started his counterattack. Now it was his move. Who the better player was would soon be seen.

"What do you say now, Collins?"

"I almost know it, Your Majesty. It is not difficult to infer, from Your Majesty's manner of choosing his words and reporting out of the distant past, that it was Your Majesty who outwitted me. Your Majesty must have spent much time in that age, otherwise Your Majesty would not have gained such deep knowledge of it. To think that I didn't realize it earlier!" The minister struck his forehead with the flat of his hand. "Many things are becoming clear to me now, Your Majesty. But there is still something missing in the story."

"You are right there, Collins, something is still missing. The last piece of the puzzle, the decisive move."

"By Your Majesty's leave, who is WHITE in reality?"

"That is unfair, Collins. That means giving up the game. Just try and think back! We have told you everything. You have a good head on your shoulders."

Collins pondered and stared in absorption at the doll, which was making a whirlwind chain of pirouettes.

"It could be the inventor, Your Majesty, the old man who devised the time machine and who appeared as the Polish count—"

"He was a pure figment of the imagination, as we already mentioned," interjected the king.

"—to whom Your Majesty or I tell the story," continued the minister without interruption. "He brings the information to Weisslinger. And Weisslinger in turn, by Your Majesty's leave, exchanges . . ."

"Just wait a minute, Collins! What are you trying to do? Your imagination is running away with you. Take things in their turn! Why try to bring another figure into our game? The old man left all questions unanswered. So let us leave him out of the game. He played neither for WHITE nor for BLACK. He was, let us say, GRAY. Perhaps he knows the whole game, has seen all the moves, but is keeping out of it himself. Perhaps he is playing an entirely different game, which requires all his attention. Anything is possible. The future is vast. Perhaps thousands have watched our moves, in order to learn from them for their own games. We don't need any additional figures. Try it from another angle. How would it be if we finished the story together, gave it a happy end, so to speak?"

"Does Your Majesty mean that . . . that I am to play WHITE?"

"What else did you expect, Collins? You've been on our side for a long time, otherwise you would long ago have put an end to Weisslinger and we wouldn't be sitting here. After all, you are our best man. Now, pay close attention! You will take our cloak here and at the appropriate time turn it so that the pale lining is on the outside. The contrast of BLACK and WHITE will be noticed. But you will also give Weisslinger another sign. Upon receiving it he will set the seal in motion and put to rout the crew of Operations Base 7. Later you will get Weisslinger out of the affair. Off with you now! Do exactly what we told you to do. And have a good time!"

"A good time or a good age, Your Majesty?"

"However you prefer to take it, Collins."

"With pleasure, Your Majesty. I am honored to be allowed to finish the game together with Your Majesty."

The minister stepped through the mirror and returned again. He swayed slightly.

"Finished?" asked the king.

"Finished," answered Collins, and rubbed his eyes.

"You took advantage of the occasion to stop in at the Red Ox, we see," laughed the king. "That is our fault, we suppose. We made your mouth water long enough, and you had to stand here over two hours and listen to our stories. We could stand a cool drink too, but first we'll finish the game. The decisive move is still ahead of us. Will you manage, Collins?"

"No question about it, Your Majesty. The long ride through the forest and the cool night air have sobered me up again."

"Very well," said the king. "Now we're going to checkmate you, brother of ours! Collins! Get going now and appear at the critical moment in the throne room, exactly under the seal that is ten seconds long. You will have to make very careful adjustments to accomplish this. You won't be able to see yourself, as you will be working in Zerotime, that is, in complete darkness. This is something which only the seals permit. Here is the equipment you need to get through the mirror. This is an improved model of the brooch. You will cautiously feel your way over to the throne and hoist our brother onto your shoulders. That won't be easy, because he is heavy and of course during Zerotime as stiff as a board. If you were to drop him, you would break all his bones. He won't feel a thing and will think he is still sitting on his little throne. Then you will calmly carry him through the mirror into the carriage and let him smell this excellent essence, which will send him into a deep and beneficial sleep." He handed the minister a small vial. "All the rest you know as well as we do. You did pay extremely close attention to our story, didn't you? A silly question, we see."

"Yes indeed, Your Majesty—that is—I meant, not the question but about the story."

"Then tell it exactly like that to Weisslinger. Teach him how to sit on the throne properly, how to behave—and he had better not make any mistakes! That goes for you too, Collins!"

"Just as Your Majesty commands. But what would happen if I did make a mistake, if I forgot a part of the story or told it incorrectly?"

"We are sure you won't make any mistakes, otherwise we couldn't retell the story to you. How do you think we know it if not from you?"

"But what if I—by Your Majesty's leave, it is just a thought—what if I intentionally twisted the story or told Weisslinger something completely different, which would cause a fracture at the last moment?"

"That, dear Collins, would be damned unfair of you. That would mean changing the rules of the game. That would mean starting all over again from the beginning, and an entirely different story would develop. Neither we two nor anyone else would ever know our story. It would all have been invented in vain. The situation would look like this: you would return to find our brother here and would have no explanation for your absence. The whole game would start again from scratch but you would have a trick card up your sleeve. That could easily cost you your head. But we will take the risk. We trust you. Now, let's get on to the last move! Checkmate the king!"

His Majesty smiled in delight. The doll stopped dancing, sprang into Collins's arms, and clung fast to his cape.

"Checkmate the king!" said the minister, who disappeared into the mirror and stepped out from it again. He was a bit out of breath.

"It all went off as planned, we see."

"At Your Majesty's command. Together we put on pretty fireworks at Operations Base 7, as Your Majesty remembers. Not a stick remained."

"Yes, we remember. And now, how did you like the whole story, Collins?"

"One can imagine it all very well, Your Majesty."

"Quite right, especially as we never did have a brother." The king winked at his minister.

"Especially as Your Majesty never had a brother, as Your Majesty expressly decreed," returned Collins with a smile.

The king stood up and gave his minister a friendly slap on the shoulder.

"We have made a good job of it, the two of us. We have taken many points into consideration, discarded this one, improved that one, added yet another one. Now the picture is complete. The last piece of the puzzle has been fitted in. We think it is rather good. What do you say, Collins?"

"Oh yes, good, Your Majesty, very good. When I think of Weisslinger—he was killed plundering a farmhouse, turns into a dollmaker, and becomes a respected citizen of the town . . ."

"We can afford that fracture. It is insignificant. He had no children, as far as he knew."

". . . One day, that is, one night he awakes with a splitting headache and from that time on is like a different person. He can't put together the simplest clock, is prey to fits of delirium, becomes addicted to the bottle, gets a thrashing at the Red Ox by the young men of the town because of his sudden overbearing behavior, becomes more and more depraved, and all of this, mind you, he can foresee, including the bitter end: one day he will have his fill of it, will put a noose around his neck and will make an end to it all."

"Rather cruel, don't you think?" put in the king doubtfully.

"Hmm," said Collins and nodded. "Hideous."

"But we insist on the sound thrashing at the Red Ox!"

"That he richly deserved, Your Majesty!" smirked the minister.

"We can still grant the poor devil a better fate. But let's let him struggle for a while before we intervene. Do you see, Collins, that is the best part of our story; we can still change any piece of it, if something better occurs to us. But now it is BLACK's move. We shouldn't underestimate him. After all, he went through the same apprenticeship we did. Let us wait and see. It would be a pity if the game were already over. At our leisure we will think through all of the possibilities he has in his position. Agreed, Collins?"

"Agreed, Your Majesty."

They both fell silent and watched the doll as it started an elaborate new dance and tried out the first steps.

"Does Your Majesty permit one last question?"

"But of course, Collins. And we know what is going to come. You are going to say, there is one piece left over."

"Yes, Your Majesty. The picture is complete, but where does the doll fit in? It is useless; I mean, it has absolutely no purpose in our story as it now stands. It was entirely unnecessary."

The king gave a resigned sigh.

"Yes, Collins. You have a good head on your shoulders, but why can't you see that not everything must have a purpose?"

"But, Your Majesty, the question is justified. Why did Weisslinger go to the trouble of making a doll, if he knew from the start that it would have no—"

"Good God, Collins! You and your frightful utilitarian reasoning! You still haven't understood. Do you think we are setting our minds together to solve the problems of the universe when we make up these stories of ours? All day long we have to grapple with this problem. At least a few hours should remain for us to paint our fantasies in the air and do cerebral gymnastics. And we often get a good idea out of it, for free, so to speak, if you are so intent on utility!"

The king glared at him and the minister hastened to appease him: "Certainly, Your Majesty."

"For instance, why do you suppose we made up this story?"

"Out of boredom, perhaps, if I may allow myself to say so, and because Your Majesty delights in the play of thoughts," suggested the minister doubtfully.

"One could put it that way. Isn't it wonderful that in our world, which is so entirely oriented to purpose and utility, profit and efficiency, there are still things which seem to have no purpose or usefulness, because their meaning lies only in the fact that they exist, like the doll in our story? And yet this little doll is delightful—or perhaps it is so for that very reason."

Collins nodded.

"I find it quite nice," he ventured, and pointed to the doll.

"One ought to be able to invent better ones," answered the king disparagingly. "Let us think of something new, Collins."

The king brooded and stared at the empty walls as if he were lost in the contemplation of a picture.

The minister looked pensively at the delicate mechanical figure as it accomplished its last spin and then with a courteous bow announced the end of the performance.

Connie Willis

Connie Willis (1945–   ) began publishing SF stories in the 1970s and became a leading writer in the genre in the late 1980s and early 1990s, following several short fiction awards and the publication of her first collection (*Fire Watch*, 1985) and novel (*Lincoln's Dreams*, 1987). Her humorous science fiction is clever and sophisticated, the work of a frantic garrulous monologuist (she is popular as a humorous speaker at SF events), but her most significant work to date appears to be in the mode of "Fire Watch," concerned with history. Her most ambitious novel to date, *Doomsday Book* (1992), a winner of the Hugo Award for best novel, is a sequel to this story.

Time travel is one of her characteristic literary devices, but her stories cover a broad range of moods and subjects. *The Encyclopedia of Science Fiction* says, "In the best of her stories, and in her novels, a steel felicity of mind and style appears effortlessly married to a copious empathy."

This story uses a standard SF idea, the use of time travel to preserve or retrieve the treasures of the past, in a new way. Willis writes science fiction in the tradition of the 1950s, of Mildred Clingerman, Judith Merril, and Margaret St. Clair, with character foregrounded and technology and the standard tropes of science fiction in the background.

FIRE WATCH

*History hath triumphed over time, which besides
it nothing but eternity hath triumphed over.*
                                                  —Sir Walter Raleigh

September 20—Of course the first thing I looked for was the fire watch stone. And of course it wasn't there yet. It wasn't dedicated until 1951, accompanying speech by the Very Reverend Dean Walter Matthews, and this is only 1940. I knew that. I went to see the fire watch stone only yesterday, with some kind of misplaced notion that seeing the scene of the crime would somehow help. It didn't.

The only things that would have helped were a crash course in London during the Blitz and a little more time. I had not gotten either.

"Traveling in time is not like taking the tube, Mr. Bartholomew," the esteemed Dunworthy had said, blinking at me through those antique spectacles of his. "Either you report on the twentieth or you don't go at all."

"But I'm not ready," I'd said. "Look, it took me four years to get ready to travel with St. Paul. *St. Paul.* Not St. Paul's. You can't expect me to get ready for London in the Blitz in two days."

"Yes," Dunworthy had said. "We can." End of conversation.

"Two days!" I had shouted at my roommate Kivrin. "All because some computer adds an 's. And the esteemed Dunworthy doesn't even bat an eye when I tell him. 'Time travel is not like taking the tube, young man,' he says. 'I'd suggest you get ready. You're leaving day after tomorrow.' The man's a total incompetent."

"No," she said. "He isn't. He's the best there is. He wrote the book on St. Paul's. Maybe you should listen to what he says."

I had expected Kivrin to be at least a little sympathetic. She had been practically hysterical when she got her practicum changed from fifteenth- to fourteenth-century England, and how did either century qualify as a practicum? Even counting infectious diseases they couldn't have been more than a five. The Blitz is an eight, and St. Paul's itself is, with my luck, a ten.

"You think I should go see Dunworthy again?" I said.

"Yes."

"And then what? I've got two days. I don't know the money, the language, the history. Nothing."

"He's a good man," Kivrin said. "I think you'd better listen to him while you can." Good old Kivrin. Always the sympathetic ear.

The good man was responsible for my standing just inside the propped-open west doors, gawking like the country boy I was supposed to be, looking for a stone that wasn't there. Thanks to the good man, I was about as unprepared for my practicum as it was possible for him to make me.

I couldn't see more than a few feet into the church. I could see a candle gleaming feebly a long way off and a closer blur of white moving toward me. A verger, or possibly the Very Reverend Dean himself. I pulled out the letter from my clergyman uncle in Wales that was supposed to gain me access to the dean, and patted my back pocket to make sure I hadn't lost the microfiche *Oxford English Dictionary, Revised, with Historical Supplements*, I'd smuggled out of the Bodleian. I couldn't pull it out in the middle of the conversation, but with luck I could muddle through the first encounter by context and look up the words I didn't know later.

"Are you from the ayarpee?" he said. He was no older than I am, a head shorter and much thinner. Almost ascetic looking. He reminded me of Kivrin. He was not wearing white, but clutching it to his chest. In other circumstances I would have thought it was a pillow. In other circumstances I would know what was being said to me, but there had been no time to unlearn sub-Mediterranean Latin and Jewish law and learn Cockney and air raid procedures. Two days, and the esteemed Dunworthy, who wanted to talk about the sacred burdens of the historian instead of telling me what the ayarpee was.

"Are you?" he demanded again.

I considered whipping out the OED after all on the grounds that Wales was a foreign country, but I didn't think they had microfilm in 1940. Ayarpee. It could be anything, including a nickname for the fire watch, in which case the impulse to say no was not safe at all. "No." I said.

He lunged suddenly toward and past me and peered out the open doors. "Damn," he said, coming back to me. "Where are they then? Bunch of lazy bourgeois tarts!" And so much for getting by on context.

He looked at me closely, suspiciously, as if he thought I was only pretending not to be with the ayarpee. "The church is closed," he said finally.

I held up the envelope and said, "My name's Bartholomew. Is Dean Matthews in?"

He looked out the door a moment longer as if he expected the lazy bourgeois tarts at any moment and intended to attack them with the white bundle; then he turned and said, as if he were guiding a tour, "This way, please," and took off into the gloom.

He led me to the right and down the south aisle of the nave. Thank God I had memorized the floor plan or at that moment, heading into total darkness, led by a raving verger, the whole bizarre metaphor of my situation would have been enough to send me out the west doors and back to St. John's Wood. It helped a little to know where I was. We should have been passing number twenty-six: Hunt's painting of "The Light of the World"—Jesus with his lantern—but it was too dark to see it. We could have used the lantern ourselves.

He stopped abruptly ahead of me, still raving. "We weren't asking for the bloody savoy, just a few cots. Nelson's better off than we are—at least he's got a pillow provided." He brandished the white bundle like a torch in the darkness. It was a pillow after all. "We asked for them over a fortnight ago, and here we still are, sleeping on the bleeding generals from Trafalgar because those bitches want to play tea and crumpets with the tommies at victoria and the hell with us!"

He didn't seem to expect me to answer his outburst, which was good, because I had understood perhaps one key word in three. He stomped on ahead, moving out of sight of the one pathetic altar candle and stopping again at a black hole. Number twenty-five: stairs to the Whispering Gallery, the Dome, the library (not open to the public). Up the stairs, down a hall, stop again at a medieval door and knock. "I've got to go wait for them," he said. "If I'm not there they'll likely take them over to the Abbey. Tell the Dean to ring them up again, will you?" and he took off down the stone steps, still holding his pillow like a shield against him.

He had knocked, but the door was at least a foot of solid oak, and it was obvious the Very Reverend Dean had not heard. I was going to have to knock again. Yes, well, and the man holding the pinpoint had to let go of it, too, but even knowing it will all be over in a moment and you won't feel a thing doesn't make it any easier to say, "Now!" So I stood in front of the door, cursing the history department and the esteemed Dunworthy and the computer that had made the mistake and brought me here to this dark door with only a letter from a fictitious uncle that I trusted no more than I trusted the rest of them.

Even the old reliable Bodleian had let me down. The batch of research stuff I cross-ordered through Balliol and the main terminal is probably sitting in my room right now, a century out of reach. And Kivrin, who had already done her practicum and should have been bursting with advice, walked around as silent as a saint until I begged her to help me.

"Did you go to see Dunworthy?" she said.

"Yes. You want to know what priceless bit of information he had for me? 'Silence and humility are the sacred burdens of the historian.' He also told me I would love St. Paul's. Golden gems from the Master. Unfortunately, what I need to know are the times and places of the bombs so one doesn't fall on me." I flopped down on the bed. "Any suggestions?"

"How good are you at memory retrieval?" she said.

I sat up. "I'm pretty good. You think I should assimilate?"

"There isn't time for that," she said. "I think you should put everything you can directly into long-term."

"You mean endorphins?" I said.

The biggest problem with using memory-assistance drugs to put information into your long-term memory is that it never sits, even for a microsecond, in your short-term memory, and that makes retrieval complicated, not to mention unnerving. It gives you the most unsettling sense of déjà vu to suddenly know something you're positive you've never seen or heard before.

The main problem, though, is not eerie sensations but retrieval. Nobody knows exactly how the brain gets what it wants out of storage, but short-term is definitely involved. That brief, sometimes microscopic, time information spends in short-term is apparently used for something besides tip-of-the-tongue availability. The whole complex sort-and-file process of retrieval is apparently centered in short-term, and without it, and without the help of the drugs that put it there or artificial substitutes, information can be impossible to retrieve. I'd used endorphins for examinations and never had any difficulty with retrieval, and it looked like it was the only way to store all the information I needed in anything approaching the time I had left, but it also meant that I would *never* have known any of the things I needed to know, even for long enough to have forgotten them. If and when I could retrieve the information, I would know it. Till then I was as ignorant of it as if it were not stored in some cobwebbed corner of my mind at all.

"You can retrieve without artificials, can't you?" Kivrin said, looking skeptical.

"I guess I'll have to."

"Under stress? Without sleep? Low body endorphin levels?" What exactly had her practicum been? She had never said a word about it, and undergraduates are not supposed to ask. Stress factors in the Middle Ages? I thought everybody slept through them.

"I hope so," I said. "Anyway, I'm willing to try this idea if you think it will help."

She looked at me with that martyred expression and said, "Nothing will help." Thank you, St. Kivrin of Balliol.

But I tried it anyway. It was better than sitting in Dunworthy's rooms having him blink at me through his historically accurate eyeglasses and tell me I was going to love St. Paul's. When my Bodleian requests didn't come, I overloaded my credit and bought out Blackwell's. Tapes on World War II, Celtic literature, history of mass transit, tourist guidebooks, everything I could think of. Then I rented a high-speed recorder and shot up. When I came out of it, I was so panicked by the feeling of not knowing any more than I had when I started that I took the tube to London and raced up Ludgate Hill to see if the fire watch stone would trigger any memories. It didn't.

"Your endorphin levels aren't back to normal yet," I told myself and tried to relax, but that was impossible with the prospect of the practicum looming up before me. And those are real bullets, kid. Just because you're a history major doing his practicum doesn't mean you can't get killed. I read history books all the way home on the tube and right up until Dunworthy's flunkies came to take me to St. John's Wood this morning.

Then I jammed the microfiche *OED* in my back pocket and went off feeling as if I would have to survive by my native wit and hoping I could get hold of artificials in 1940. Surely I could get through the first day without mishap, I thought, and now here I was, stopped cold by almost the first word that was spoken to me.

Well, not quite. In spite of Kivrin's advice that I not put anything in short-term, I'd memorized the British money, a map of the tube system, a map of my own Oxford. It had gotten me this far. Surely I would be able to deal with the Dean.

Just as I had almost gotten up the courage to knock, he opened the door, and as with the pinpoint, it really was over quickly and without pain. I handed him my letter and he shook my hand and said something understandable like, "Glad to have another man, Bartholomew." He looked strained and tired and as if he might collapse if I told him the Blitz had just started. I know, I know: Keep your mouth shut. The sacred silence, etc.

He said, "We'll get Langby to show you round, shall we?" I assumed that was my Verger of the Pillow, and I was right. He met us at the foot of the stairs, puffing a little but jubilant.

"The cots came," he said to Dean Matthews. "You'd have thought they were doing us a favor. All high heels and hoity-toity. 'You made us miss our tea, luv,' one of them said to me. 'Yes, well, and a good thing, too,' I said. 'You look as if you could stand to lose a stone or two.'"

Even Dean Matthews looked as though he did not completely understand him. He said, "Did you set them up in the crypt?" and then introduced us. "Mr. Bartholomew's just got in from Wales," he said. "He's come to join our volunteers." Volunteers, not fire watch.

Langby showed me round, pointing out various dimnesses in the general gloom and then dragged me down to see the ten folding canvas cots set up among the tombs in the crypt, also in passing, Lord Nelson's black marble sarcophagus. He told me I don't have to stand a watch the first night and suggested I go to bed, since sleep is the most precious commodity in the raids. I could well believe it. He was clutching that silly pillow to his breast like his beloved.

"Do you hear the sirens down here?" I asked, wondering if he buried his head in it.

He looked round at the low stone ceilings. "Some do, some don't. Brinton has to have his Horlich's. Bence-Jones would sleep if the roof fell in on him. I have to have a pillow. The important thing is to get your eight in no matter what. If you don't, you turn into one of the walking dead. And then you get killed."

On that cheering note he went off to post the watches for tonight, leaving his pillow on one of the cots with orders for me to let nobody touch it. So here I sit, waiting for my first air raid siren and trying to get all this down before I turn into one of the walking or non-walking dead.

I've used the stolen OED to decipher a little Langby. Middling success. A tart is either a pastry or a prostitute. (I assume the latter, although I was wrong about the pillow.) Bourgeois is a catchall term for all the faults of the middle class. A Tommy's a soldier. Ayarpee I could not find under any spelling and I had nearly given up when something in long-term about the use of acronyms and abbreviations in wartime popped forward (bless you, St. Kivrin) and I realized it must be an abbreviation. ARP. Air Raid Precautions. Of course. Where else would you get the bleeding cots from?

September 21—Now that I'm past the first shock of being here, I realize that the history department neglected to tell me what I'm supposed to do in the three-odd months of this practicum. They handed me this journal, the letter from my uncle, and ten pounds in pre-war money and sent me packing into the past. The ten pounds (already depleted by train and tube fares) is supposed to last me until the end of December and get me back to St. John's Wood for pickup when the second letter calling me back to Wales to sick uncle's bedside comes. Till then I live here in the crypt with Nelson, who, Langby tells me, is pickled in alcohol inside his coffin. If we take a direct hit, will he burn like a torch or simply trickle out in a decaying stream onto the crypt floor, I wonder. Board is provided by a gas ring, over which are cooked wretched tea and indescribable kippers. To pay for all this luxury I am to stand on the roofs of St. Paul's and put out incendiaries.

I must also accomplish the purpose of this practicum, whatever it may be. Right now the only purpose I care about is staying alive until the second letter from uncle arrives and I can go home.

I am doing make-work until Langby has time to "show me the ropes." I've cleaned the skillet they cook the foul little fishes in, stacked wooden folding chairs at the altar end of the crypt (flat instead of standing because they tend to collapse like bombs in the middle of the night), and tried to sleep.

I am apparently not one of the lucky ones who can sleep through the raids. I spent most of the night wondering what St. Paul's risk rating is. Practica have to be at least a six. Last night I was convinced this was a ten, with the crypt as ground zero, and that I might as well have applied for Denver.

The most interesting thing that's happened so far is that I've seen a cat. I am fascinated, but trying not to appear so, since they seem commonplace here.

September 22—Still in the crypt. Langby comes dashing through periodically cursing various government agencies (all abbreviated) and promising to take me up on the roofs. In the meantime I've run out of make-work and taught myself to work a stirrup pump. Kivrin was overly concerned about my memory retrieval abilities. I have not had any trouble so far. Quite the opposite. I called up firefighting information and got the whole manual with pictures, including instructions on the use of the stirrup pump. If the kippers set Lord Nelson on fire, I shall be a hero.

Excitement last night. The sirens went early and some of the chars who clean offices in the City sheltered in the crypt with us. One of them woke me out of a sound sleep, going like an air raid siren. Seems she'd seen a mouse. We had to go whacking at tombs and under the cots with a rubber boot to persuade her it was gone. Obviously what the history department had in mind: murdering mice.

September 24—Langby took me on rounds. Into the choir, where I had to learn the stirrup pump all over again, assigned rubber boots and a tin helmet. Langby says Commander Allen is getting us asbestos firemen's coats, but hasn't yet, so it's my own wool coat and muffler and very cold on the roofs even in September. It feels like November and looks it, too, bleak and cheerless with no sun. Up to the dome and onto the roofs, which should be flat but in fact are littered with towers, pinnacles, gutters, statues, all designed expressly to catch and hold incendiaries out of reach. Shown how to smother an incendiary with sand before it burns through the roof and sets the church on fire. Shown the ropes (literally) lying in a heap at the base of the dome in case somebody has to go up one of the west towers or over the top of the dome. Back inside and down to the Whispering Gallery.

Langby kept up a running commentary through the whole tour, part practical instruction, part church history. Before we went up into the Gallery he dragged me over to the south door to tell me how Christopher Wren stood in the smoking rubble of Old St. Paul's and asked a workman to bring him a stone from the graveyard to mark the cornerstone. On the stone was written in Latin, "I shall rise again," and Wren was so impressed by the irony that he had the word inscribed above the door. Langby looked as smug as if he had not told me a story every first-year history student knows, but I suppose without the impact of the fire watch stone, the other is just a nice story.

Langby raced me up the steps and onto the narrow balcony circling the Whispering Gallery. He was already halfway round to the other side, shouting dimensions and acoustics at me. He stopped facing the wall opposite and said softly, "You can hear me whispering because of the shape of the dome. The sound waves are reinforced around the perimeter of the dome. It sounds like the very crack of doom up here during a raid. The dome is one hundred and seven feet across. It is eighty feet above the nave."

I looked down. The railing went out from under me and the black-and-white marble floor came up with dizzying speed. I hung onto something in front of me and dropped to my knees, staggered and sick at heart. The sun had come out, and all of St. Paul's seemed drenched in gold. Even the carved wood of the choir, the white stone pillars, the leaden pipes of the organ, all of it golden, golden.

Langby was beside me, trying to pull me free. "Bartholomew," he shouted, "what's wrong? For God's sake, man."

I knew I must tell him that if I let go, St. Paul's and all the past would fall in on me, and that I must not let that happen because I was an historian. I said something, but it was not what I intended because Langby merely tightened his grip. He hauled me violently free of the railing and back onto the stairway, then let me collapse limply on the steps and stood back from me, not speaking.

"I don't know what happened in there," I said. "I've never been afraid of heights before."

"You're shaking," he said sharply. "You'd better lie down." He led me back to the crypt.

September 25—Memory retrieval: ARP manual. Symptoms of bombing victims. Stage one—shock; stupefaction; unawareness of injuries; words may not make sense except to victim. Stage two—shivering; nausea; injuries, losses felt; return to reality. Stage three—talkativeness that cannot be controlled; desire to explain shock behavior to rescuers.

Langby must surely recognize the symptoms, but how does he account for the fact there was no bomb? I can hardly explain my shock behavior to him, and it isn't just the sacred silence of the historian that stops me.

He has not said anything, in fact assigned me my first watches for tomorrow night as if nothing had happened, and he seems no more preoccupied than anyone else. Everyone I've met so far is jittery (one thing I had in short-term was how calm everyone was during the raids) and the raids have not come near us since I got here. They've been mostly over the East End and the docks.

There was a reference tonight to a UXB, and I have been thinking about the Dean's manner and the church being closed when I'm almost sure I remember reading it was open through the entire Blitz. As soon as I get a chance, I'll try to retrieve the events of September. As to retrieving anything else, I don't see how I can hope to remember the right information until I know what it is I am supposed to do here, if anything.

There are no guidelines for historians, and no restrictions either. I could tell everyone I'm from the future if I thought they would believe me. I could murder Hitler if I could get to Germany. Or could I? Time paradox talk abounds in the history department, and the graduate students back from their practica don't say a word one way or the other. Is there a tough, immutable past? Or is there a new past every day and do we, the historians, make it? And what are the consequences of what we do, if there are consequences? And how do we dare do anything without knowing them? Must we interfere boldly, hoping we do not bring about all our downfalls? Or must we do nothing at all, not interfere, stand by and watch St. Paul's burn to the ground if need be so that we don't change the future?

All those are fine questions for a late-night study session. They do not matter here. I could no more let St. Paul's burn down than I could kill Hitler. No, that is not true. I found that out yesterday in the Whispering Gallery. I could kill Hitler if I caught him setting fire to St. Paul's.

September 26—I met a young woman today. Dean Matthews has opened the church, so the watch have been doing duties as chars and people have started coming in again. The young woman reminded me of Kivrin, though Kivrin is a good deal taller and would never frizz her hair like that. She looked as if she had been crying. Kivrin has looked like that since she got back from her practicum. The Middle Ages were too much for her. I wonder how she would have coped with this. By pouring out her fears to the local priest, no doubt, as I sincerely hoped her look-alike was not going to do.

"May I help you?" I said, not wanting in the least to help. "I'm a volunteer."

She looked distressed. "You're not paid?" she said, and wiped at her reddened nose with a handkerchief. "I read about St. Paul's and the fire watch and all, and I thought perhaps there's a position there for me. In the canteen, like, or something. A paying position." There were tears in her red-rimmed eyes.

"I'm afraid we don't have a canteen," I said as kindly as I could, considering how impatient Kivrin always makes me, "and it's not actually a real shelter. Some of the watch sleep in the crypt. I'm afraid we're all volunteers, though."

"That won't do, then," she said. She dabbed at her eyes with the handkerchief. "I love St. Paul's, but I can't take on volunteer work, not with my little brother Tom back from the country." I was not reading this situation properly. For all the outward signs of distress she sounded quite cheerful and no closer to tears than when she had come in. "I've got to get us a proper place to stay. With Tom back, we can't go on sleeping in the tubes."

A sudden feeling of dread, the kind of sharp pain you get sometimes from involuntary retrieval, went over me. "The tubes?" I said, trying to get at the memory.

"March Arch, usually," she went on. "My brother Tom saves us a place early and I go . . ." She stopped, held the handkerchief close to her nose, and exploded into it. "I'm sorry," she said, "this awful cold!"

Red nose, watering eyes, sneezing. Respiratory infection. It was a wonder I hadn't told her not to cry. It's only by luck that I haven't made some unforgivable mistake so far, and this is not because I can't get at the long-term memory. I don't have half the information I need even stored: cats and colds and the way St. Paul's looks in full sun. It's only a matter of time before I am stopped cold by something I do not know. Nevertheless, I am going to try for retrieval tonight after I come off watch. At least I can find out whether and when something is going to fall on me.

I have seen the cat once or twice. He is coal-black with a white patch on his throat that looks as if it were painted on for the blackout.

September 27—I have just come down from the roofs. I am still shaking.

Early in the raid the bombing was mostly over the East End. The view was incredible. Searchlights everywhere, the sky pink from the fires and reflecting in the Thames, the exploding shells sparkling like fireworks. There was a constant, deafening thunder broken by the occasional droning of the planes high overhead, then the repeating stutter of the ack-ack guns.

About midnight the bombs began falling quite near with a horrible sound like a train running over me. It took every bit of will I had to keep from flinging myself flat on the roof, but Langby was watching. I didn't want to give him the satisfaction of watching a repeat performance of my behavior in the dome. I kept my head up and my sand bucket firmly in hand and felt quite proud of myself.

The bombs stopped roaring past about three, and there was a lull of about half an hour, and then a clatter like hail on the roofs. Everybody except Langby dived for shovels and stirrup pumps. He was watching me. And I was watching the incendiary.

It had fallen only a few meters from me, behind the clock tower. It was much smaller than I had imagined, only about thirty centimeters long. It was sputtering violently, throwing greenish-white fire almost to where I was standing. In a minute it would simmer down into a molten mass and begin to burn through the roof. Flames and the frantic shouts of firemen, and then the white rubble stretching for miles, and nothing, nothing left, not even the fire watch stone.

It was the Whispering Gallery all over again. I felt that I had said something, and when I looked at Langby's face he was smiling crookedly.

"St. Paul's will burn down," I said. "There won't be anything left."

"Yes," Langby said. "That's the idea, isn't it? Burn St. Paul's to the ground? Isn't that the plan?"

"Whose plan?" I said stupidly.

"Hitler's, of course," Langby said. "Who did you think I meant?" and, almost casually, picked up his stirrup pump.

The page of the ARP manual flashed suddenly before me. I poured the bucket of sand around the still sputtering bomb, snatched up another bucket and dumped that on top of it. Black smoke billowed up in such a cloud that I could hardly find my shovel. I felt for the smothered bomb with the tip of it and scooped it into the empty bucket, then shoveled the sand in on top of it. Tears were streaming down my face from the acrid smoke. I turned to wipe them on my sleeve and saw Langby.

He had not made a move to help me. He smiled. "It's not a bad plan, actually. But of course we won't let it happen. That's what the fire watch is here for. To see that it doesn't happen. Right, Bartholomew?"

I know now what the purpose of my practicum is. I must stop Langby from burning down St. Paul's.

September 28—I try to tell myself I was mistaken about Langby last night, that I misunderstood what he said. Why would he want to burn down St. Paul's unless he is a Nazi spy? How can a Nazi spy have gotten on the fire watch? I think about my faked letter of introduction and shudder.

How can I find out? If I set him some test, some fatal thing that only a loyal Englishman in 1940 would know, I fear I am the one who would be caught out. I *must* get my retrieval working properly.

Until then, I shall watch Langby. For the time being at least that should be easy. Langby has just posted the watches for the next two weeks. We stand every one together.

September 30—I know what happened in September. Langby told me.

Last night in the choir, putting on our coats and boots, he said, "They've already tried once, you know."

I had no idea what he meant. I felt as helpless as that first day when he asked me if I was from the ayarpee.

"The plan to destroy St. Paul's They've already tried once. The tenth of September. A high explosive bomb. But of course you didn't know about that. You were in Wales."

I was not even listening. The minute he had said "high explosive bomb," I had remembered it all. It had burrowed in under the road and lodged on the foundations. The bomb squad had tried to defuse it, but there was a leaking gas main. They decided to evacuate St. Paul's, but Dean Matthews refused to leave, and they got it out after all and exploded it in Barking Marshes. Instant and complete retrieval.

"The bomb squad saved her that time," Langby was saying. "It seems there's always somebody about."

"Yes," I said, "there is," and walked away from him.

October 1—I thought last night's retrieval of the events of September tenth meant some sort of breakthrough, but I have been lying here on my cot most of the night trying for Nazi spies in St. Paul's and getting nothing. Do I have to know exactly what I'm looking for before I can remember it? What good does that do me?

Maybe Langby is not a Nazi spy. Then what is he? An arsonist? A madman? The crypt is hardly conducive to thought, being not at all as silent as a tomb. The chars talk most of the night and the sound of the bombs is muffled, which somehow makes it worse. I find myself straining to hear them. When I did get to sleep this morning, I dreamed about one of the tube shelters being hit, broken mains, drowning people.

October 4—I tried to catch the cat today. I had some idea of persuading it to dispatch the mouse that has been terrifying the chars. I also wanted to see one up close. I took the water bucket I had used with the stirrup pump last night to put out some burning shrapnel from one of the antiaircraft guns. It still had a bit of water in it, but not enough to drown the cat, and my plan was to clamp the bucket over him, reach under, and pick him up, then carry him down to the crypt and point him at the mouse. I did not even come close to him.

I swung the bucket, and as I did so, perhaps an inch of water splashed out. I thought I remembered that the cat was a domesticated animal, but I must have been wrong about that. The cat's wide complacent face pulled back into a skull-like mask that was absolutely terrifying, vicious claws extended from what I had thought were harmless paws, and the cat let out a sound to top the chars.

In my surprise I dropped the bucket and it rolled against one of the pillars. The cat disappeared. Behind me, Langby said, "That's no way to catch a cat."

"Obviously," I said, and bent to retrieve the bucket.

"Cats hate water," he said, still in that expressionless voice.

"Oh," I said, and started in front of him to take the bucket back to the choir. "I didn't know that."

"Everybody knows it. Even the stupid Welsh."

October 8—We have been standing double watches for a week—bomber's moon. Langby didn't show up on the roofs, so I went looking for him in the church. I found him standing by the west doors talking to an old man. The man had a newspaper tucked under his arm and he handed it to Langby, but Langby gave it back to him. When the man saw me, he ducked out. Langby said, "Tourist. Wanted to know where the Windmill Theater is. Read in the paper the girls are starkers."

I know I looked as if I didn't believe him because he said, "You look rotten, old man. Not getting enough sleep, are you? I'll get somebody to take the first watch for you tonight."

"No," I said coldly. "I'll stand my own watch. I like being on the roofs," and added silently, where I can watch you.

He shrugged and said, "I suppose it's better than being down in the crypt. At least on the roofs you can hear the one that gets you."

October 10—I thought the double watches might be good for me, take my mind off my inability to retrieve. The watched-pot idea. Actually, it sometimes works. A few hours of thinking about something else, or a good night's sleep, and the fact pops forward without any prompting, without any artificials.

The good night's sleep is out of the question. Not only do the chars talk constantly, but the cat has moved into the crypt and sidles up to everyone, making siren noises and begging for kippers. I am moving my cot out of the transept and over by Nelson before I go on watch. He may be pickled, but he keeps his mouth shut.

October 11—I dreamed Trafalgar, ships' guns and smoke and falling plaster and Langby shouting my name. My first waking thought was that the folding chairs had gone off. I could not see for all the smoke.

"I'm coming," I said, limping toward Langby and pulling on my boots. There was a heap of plaster and tangled folding chairs in the transept. Langby was digging in it. "Bartholomew!" he shouted, flinging a chunk of plaster aside. "Bartholomew!"

I still had the idea it was smoke. I ran back for the stirrup pump and then knelt beside him and began pulling on a splintered chair back. It resisted, and it came to me suddenly, There is a body under here. I will reach for a piece of the ceiling and find it is a hand. I leaned back on my heels, determined not to be sick, then went at the pile again.

Langby was going far too fast, jabbing with a chair leg. I grabbed his hand to stop him, and he struggled against me as if I were a piece of rubble to be thrown aside. He picked up a large flat square of plaster, and under it was the floor. I turned and looked behind me. Both chars huddled in the recess by the altar. "Who are you looking for?" I said, keeping hold of Langby's arm.

"Bartholomew," he said, and swept the rubble aside, his hands bleeding through the coating of smoky dust.

"I'm here," I said. "I'm all right." I choked on the white dust. "I moved my cot out of the transept."

He turned sharply to the chars and then said quite calmly, "What's under here?"

"Only the gas ring," one of them said timidly from the shadowed recess, "and Mrs. Galbraith's pocketbook." He dug through the mess until he had found them both. The gas ring was leaking at a merry rate, though the flame had gone out.

"You've saved St. Paul's and me after all," I said, standing there in my underwear and boots, holding the useless stirrup pump. "We might all have been asphyxiated."

He stood up. "I shouldn't have saved you," he said.

Stage one: shock, stupefaction, unawareness of injuries, words may not make sense except to victim. He would not know his hand was bleeding yet. He would not remember what he had said. He had said he shouldn't have saved my life.

"I shouldn't have saved you," he repeated. "I have my duty to think of."

"You're bleeding," I said sharply. "You'd better lie down." I sounded just like Langby in the gallery.

October 13—It was a high explosive bomb. It blew a hole in the Choir, and some of the marble statuary is broken, but the ceiling of the crypt did not collapse, which is what I thought at first. It only jarred some plaster loose.

I do not think Langby has any idea what he said. That should give me some sort of advantage, now that I am sure where the danger lies, now that I am sure it will not come crashing down from some other direction. But what good is all this knowing, when I do not know what he will do? Or when?

Surely I have the facts of yesterday's bomb in long-term, but even falling plaster did not jar them loose this time. I am not even trying for retrieval, now. I lie in the darkness waiting for the roof to fall in on me. And remembering how Langby saved my life.

October 15—The girl came in again today. She still has the cold, but she has gotten her paying position. It was a joy to see her. She was wearing a smart uniform and open-toed shoes, and her hair was in an elaborate frizz around her face. We are still cleaning up the mess from the bomb, and Langby was out with Allen getting wood to board up the Choir, so I let the girl chatter at me while I swept. The dust made her sneeze, but at least this time I knew what she was doing.

She told me her name is Enola and that she's working for the WVS, running one of the mobile canteens that are sent to the fires. She came, of all things, to thank me for the job. She said that after she told the WVS that there was no proper shelter with a canteen for St. Paul's, they gave her a run in the City. "So I'll just pop in when I'm close and let you know how I'm making out, won't I just?"

She and her brother Tom are still sleeping in the tubes. I asked her if that was safe and she said probably not, but at least down there you couldn't hear the one that got you and that was a blessing.

October 18—I am so tired I can hardly write this. Nine incendiaries tonight and a land mine that looked as though it was going to catch on the dome till the wind drifted its parachute away from the church. I put out two of the incendiaries. I have done that at least twenty times since I got here and helped with dozens of others, and still it is not enough. One incendiary, one moment of not watching Langby, could undo it all.

I know that is partly why I feel so tired. I wear myself out every night trying to do my job and watch Langby, making sure none of the incendiaries falls without my seeing it. Then I go back to the crypt and wear myself out trying to retrieve something, anything, about spies, fires, St. Paul's in the fall of 1940, anything. It haunts me that I am not doing enough, but I do not know what else to do. Without the retrieval, I am as helpless as these poor people here, with no idea what will happen tomorrow.

If I have to, I will go on doing this till I am called home. He cannot burn down St. Paul's so long as I am here to put out the incendiaries. "I have my duty," Langby said in the crypt.

And I have mine.

October 21—It's been nearly two weeks since the blast and I just now realized we haven't seen the cat since. He wasn't in the mess in the crypt. Even after Langby and I were sure there was no one in there, we sifted through the stuff twice more. He could have been in the Choir, though.

Old Bence-Jones says not to worry. "He's all right," he said. "The jerries could bomb London right down to the ground and the cats would waltz out to greet them. You know why? They don't love anybody. That's what gets half of us killed. Old lady out in Stepney got killed the other night trying to save her cat. Bloody cat was in the Anderson."

"Then where is he?"

"Someplace safe, you can bet on that. If he's not around St. Paul's, it means we're for it. That old saw about the rats deserting a sinking ship, that's a mistake, that is. It's cats, not rats."

October 25—Langby's tourist showed up again. He cannot still be looking for the Windmill Theatre. He had a newspaper under his arm again today, and he asked for Langby, but Langby was across town with Allen, trying to get the asbestos firemen's coats. I saw the name of the paper. It was *The Worker*. A Nazi newspaper?

November 2—I've been up on the roofs for a week straight, helping some incompetent workmen patch the hole the bomb made. They're doing a terrible job. There's still a great gap on one side a man could fall into, but they insist it'll be all right because, after all, you wouldn't fall clear through but only as far as the ceiling, and "the fall can't kill you." They don't seem to understand it's a perfect hiding place for an incendiary.

And that is all Langby needs. He does not even have to set a fire to destroy St. Paul's. All he needs to do is let one burn uncaught until it is too late.

I could not get anywhere with the workmen. I went down into the church to complain to Matthews, and saw Langby and his tourist behind a pillar, close to one of the windows. Langby was holding a newspaper and talking to the man. When I came down from the library an hour later, they were still there. So is the gap. Matthews says we'll put planks across it and hope for the best.

November 5—I have given up trying to retrieve. I am so far behind on my sleep I can't even retrieve information on a newspaper whose name I already know. Double watches the permanent thing now. Our chars have abandoned us altogether (like the cat), so the crypt is quiet, but I cannot sleep.

If I do manage to doze off, I dream. Yesterday I dreamed Kivrin was on the roofs, dressed like a saint. "What was the secret of your practicum?" I said. "What were you supposed to find out?"

She wiped her nose with a handkerchief and said, "Two things. One, that silence and humility are the sacred burdens of the historian. Two"—she stopped and sneezed into the handkerchief—"don't sleep in the tubes."

My only hope is to get hold of an artificial and induce a trance. That's a problem. I'm positive it's too early for chemical endorphins and probably hallucinogens. Alcohol is definitely available, but I need something more concentrated than ale, the only alcohol I know by name. I do not dare ask the watch. Langby is suspicious enough of me already. It's back to the *OED*, to look up a word I don't know.

November 11—The cat's back. Langby was out with Allen again, still trying for the asbestos coats, so I thought it was safe to leave St. Paul's. I went to the grocer's for supplies, and hopefully an artificial. It was late, and the sirens sounded before I had even gotten to Cheapside, but the raids do not usually start until after dark. It took awhile to get all the groceries and to get up my courage to ask whether he had any alcohol—he told me to go to a pub—and when I came out of the shop, it was as if I had pitched suddenly into a hole.

I had no idea where St. Paul's lay, or the street, or the shop I had just come from. I stood on what was no longer the sidewalk, clutching my brown-paper parcel of kippers and bread with a hand I could not have seen if I held it up before my face. I reached up to wrap my muffler closer about my neck and prayed for my eyes to adjust, but there was no reduced light to adjust to. I would have been glad of the moon, for all St. Paul's watch cursed it and called it a fifth columnist. Or a bus, with its shuttered headlights giving just enough light to orient myself by. Or a searchlight. Or the kickback flare of an ack-ack gun. Anything.

Just then I did see a bus, two narrow yellow slits a long way off. I started toward it and nearly pitched off the curb. Which meant the bus was sideways in the street, which meant it was not a bus. A cat meowed, quite near, and rubbed against my leg. I looked down into the yellow lights I had thought belonged to the bus. His eyes were picking up light from somewhere, though I would have sworn there was not a light for miles, and reflecting it flatly up at me.

"A warden'll get you for those lights, old tom," I said, and then as a plane droned overhead, "Or a jerry."

The world exploded suddenly into light, the searchlights and a glow along the Thames seeming to happen almost simultaneously, lighting my way home.

"Come to fetch me, did you, old tom?" I said gaily. "Where've you been? Knew we were out of kippers, didn't you? I call that loyalty." I talked to him all the way home and gave him half a tin of the kippers for saving my life. Bence-Jones said he smelled the milk at the grocer's.

November 13—I dreamed I was lost in the blackout. I could not see my hands in front of my face, and Dunworthy came and shone a pocket torch at me, but I could only see where I had come from and not where I was going.

"What good is that to them?" I said. "They need a light to show them where they're going."

"Even the light from the Thames? Even the light from the fires and the ack-ack guns?" Dunworthy said.

"Yes. Anything is better than this awful darkness." So he came closer to give me the pocket torch. It was not a pocket torch, after all, but Christ's lantern from the Hunt picture in the south nave. I shone it on the curb before me so I could find my way home, but it shone instead on the fire watch stone and I hastily put the light out.

November 20—I tried to talk to Langby today. "I've seen you talking to the old gentleman," I said. It sounded like an accusation. I meant it to. I wanted him to think it was and stop whatever he was planning.

"Reading," he said. "Not talking." He was putting things in order in the choir, piling up sandbags.

"I've seen you reading then," I said belligerently, and he dropped a sandbag and straightened.

"What of it?" he said. "It's a free country. I can read to an old man if I want, same as you can talk to that little WVS tart."

"What do you read?" I said.

"Whatever he wants. He's an old man. He used to come home from his job, have a bit of brandy and listen to his wife read the papers to him. She got killed in one of the raids. Now I read to him. I don't see what business it is of yours."

It sounded true. It didn't have the careful casualness of a lie, and I almost believed him, except that I had heard the tone of truth from him before. In the crypt. After the bomb.

"I thought he was a tourist looking for the Windmill," I said.

He looked blank only a second, and then he said, "Oh, yes, that. He came in with the paper and asked me to tell him where it was. I looked it up to find the address. Clever, that. I didn't guess he couldn't read it for himself." But it was enough. I knew that he was lying.

He heaved a sandbag almost at my feet. "Of course you wouldn't understand a thing like that, would you? A simple act of human kindness?"

"No," I said coldly. "I wouldn't."

None of this proves anything. He gave away nothing, except perhaps the name of an artificial, and I can hardly go to Dean Matthews and accuse Langby of reading aloud.

I waited till he had finished in the choir and gone down to the crypt. Then I lugged one of the sandbags up to the roof and over to the chasm. The planking has held so far, but everyone walks gingerly around it, as if it were a grave. I cut the sandbag open and spilled the loose sand into the bottom. If it has occurred to Langby that this is the perfect spot for an incendiary, perhaps the sand will smother it.

November 21—I gave Enola some of "uncle's" money today and asked her to get me the brandy. She was more reluctant than I thought she'd be, so there must be societal complications I am not aware of, but she agreed.

I don't know what she came for. She started to tell me about her brother and some prank he'd pulled in the tubes that got him in trouble with the guard, but after I asked her about the brandy, she left without finishing the story.

November 25—Enola came today, but without bringing the brandy. She is going to Bath for the holidays to see her aunt. At least she will be away from the raids for a while. I will not have to worry about her. She finished the story of her brother and told me she hopes to persuade this aunt to take Tom for the duration of the Blitz but is not at all sure the aunt will be willing.

Young Tom is apparently not so much an engaging scapegrace as a near criminal. He has been caught twice picking pockets in the Bank tube shelter, and they have had to go back to Marble Arch. I comforted her as best I could, told her all boys were bad at one time or another. What I really wanted to say was that she needn't worry at all, that young Tom strikes me as a true survivor type, like my own tom, like Langby, totally unconcerned with anybody but himself, well-equipped to survive the Blitz and rise to prominence in the future.

Then I asked her whether she had gotten the brandy.

She looked down at her open-toed shoes and muttered unhappily, "I thought you'd forgotten all about that."

I made up some story about the watch taking turns buying a bottle, and she seemed less unhappy, but I am not convinced she will not use this trip to Bath as an excuse to do nothing. I will have to leave St. Paul's and buy it myself, and I don't dare leave Langby alone in the church. I made her promise to bring the brandy today before she leaves. But she is still not back, and the sirens have already gone.

November 26—No Enola, and she said their train left at noon. I suppose I should be grateful that at least she is safely out of London. Maybe in Bath she will be able to get over her cold.

Tonight one of the ARP girls breezed in to borrow half our cots and tell us about a mess over in the East End where a surface shelter was hit. Four dead, twelve wounded. "At least it wasn't one of the tube shelters!" she said. "Then you'd see a real mess, wouldn't you?"

November 30—I dreamed I took the cat to St. John's Wood.

"Is this a rescue mission?" Dunworthy said.

"No, sir," I said proudly. "I know what I was supposed to find in my practicum. The perfect survivor. Tough and resourceful and selfish. This is the only one I could find. I had to kill Langby, you know, to keep him from burning down St. Paul's. Enola's brother has gone to Bath, and the others will never make it. Enola wears open-toed shoes in the winter and sleeps in the tubes and puts her hair up on metal pins so it will curl. She cannot possibly survive the Blitz."

Dunworthy said, "Perhaps you should have rescued her instead. What did you say her name was?"

"Kivrin," I said, and woke up cold and shivering.

December 5—I dreamed Langby had the pinpoint bomb. He carried it under his arm like a brown-paper parcel, coming out of St. Paul's Station and around Ludgate Hill to the west doors.

"This is not fair," I said, barring his way with my arm. "There is no fire watch on duty."

He clutched the bomb to his chest like a pillow. "That is your fault," he said, and before I could get to my stirrup pump and bucket, he tossed it in the door.

The pinpoint was not even invented until the end of the twentieth century, and it was another ten years before the dispossessed communists got hold of it and turned it into something that could be carried under your arm. A parcel that could blow a quarter mile of the City into oblivion. Thank God that is one dream that cannot come true.

It was a sunlit morning in the dream, and this morning when I came off watch the sun was shining for the first time in weeks. I went down to the crypt and then came up again, making the rounds of the roofs twice more, then the steps and the grounds and all the treacherous alleyways between where an incendiary could be missed. I felt better after that, but when I got to sleep I dreamed again, this time of fire and Langby watching it, smiling.

December 15—I found the cat this morning. Heavy raids last night, but most of them over toward Canning Town and nothing on the roofs to speak of. Nevertheless the cat was quite dead. I found him lying on the steps this morning when I made my own, private rounds. Concussion. There was not a mark on him anywhere except the white blackout patch on his throat, but when I picked him up, he was all jelly under the skin.

I could not think what to do with him. I thought for one mad moment of asking Matthews if I could bury him in the crypt. Honorable death in war or something. Trafalgar, Waterloo, London, died in battle. I ended by wrapping him in my muffler and taking him down Ludgate Hill to a building that had been bombed out and burying him in the rubble. It will do no good. The rubble will be no protection from dogs or rats, and I shall never get another muffler. I have gone through nearly all of uncle's money.

I should not be sitting here. I haven't checked the alleyways or the rest of the steps, and there might be a dud or a delayed incendiary or something that I missed.

When I came here, I thought of myself as the noble rescuer, the savior of the past. I am not doing very well at the job. At least Enola is out of it. I wish there were some way I could send St. Paul's to Bath for safekeeping. There were hardly any raids last night. Bence-Jones said cats can survive anything. What if he was coming to get me, to show me the way home? All the bombs were over Canning Town.

December 16—Enola has been back a week. Seeing her, standing on the west steps where I found the cat, sleeping in Marble Arch and not safe at all, was more than I could absorb. "I thought you were in Bath," I said stupidly.

"My aunt said she'd take Tom but not me as well. She's got a houseful of evacuation children, and what a noisy lot. Where is your muffler?" she said. "It's dreadful cold up here on the hill."

"I . . ." I said, unable to answer, "I lost it."

"You'll never get another one," she said. "They're going to start rationing clothes. And wool, too. You'll never get another one like that."

"I know," I said, blinking at her.

"Good things just thrown away," she said. "It's absolutely criminal, that's what it is."

I don't think I said anything to that, just turned and walked away with my head down, looking for bombs and dead animals.

December 20—Langby isn't a Nazi. He's a communist. I can hardly write this. A communist.

One of the chars found *The Worker* wedged behind a pillar and brought it down to the crypt as we were coming off the first watch.

"Bloody communists," Bence-Jones said. "Helping Hitler, they are. Talking against the king, stirring up trouble in the shelters. Traitors, that's what they are."

"They love England same as you," the char said.

"They don't love nobody but themselves, bloody selfish lot. I wouldn't be surprised to hear they were ringing Hitler up on the telephone," Bence-Jones said. " 'Ello, Adolf, here's where to drop the bombs."

The kettle on the gas ring whistled. The char stood up and poured the hot water into a chipped teapot, then sat back down. "Just because they speak their minds don't mean they'd burn down old St. Paul's, does it now?"

"Of course not," Langby said, coming down the stairs. He sat down and pulled off his boots, stretching his feet in their wool socks. "Who wouldn't burn down St. Paul's?"

"The communists," Bence-Jones said, looking straight at him, and I wondered if he suspected Langby too.

Langby never batted an eye. "I wouldn't worry about them if I were you," he said. "It's the jerries that are doing their bloody best to burn her down tonight. Six incendiaries so far, and one almost went into that great hole over the choir." He held out his cup to the char, and she poured him a cup of tea.

I wanted to kill him, smashing him to dust and rubble on the floor of the crypt while Bence-Jones and the char looked on in helpless surprise, shouting warnings to them and the rest of the watch. "Do you know what the communists did?" I wanted to shout. "Do you? We have to stop him." I even stood up and started toward him as he sat with his feet stretched out before him and his asbestos coat still over his shoulders.

And then the thought of the Gallery drenched in gold, the communist coming out of the tube station with the package so casually under his arm, made me sick with the same staggering vertigo of guilt and helplessness, and I sat back down on the edge of my cot and tried to think what to do.

They do not realize the danger. Even Bence-Jones, for all his talk of traitors, thinks they are capable only of talking against the king. They do not know, cannot know, what the communists will become. Stalin is an ally. Communists mean Russia. They have never heard of Karinsky or the New Russia or any of the things that will make "communist" into a synonym for "monster." They will never know it. By the time the communists become what they became, there will be no fire watch. Only I know what it means to hear the name "communist" uttered here, so carelessly, in St. Paul's.

A communist. I should have known. I should have known.

December 22—Double watches again. I have not had any sleep and I am getting very unsteady on my feet. I nearly pitched into the chasm this morning, only saved myself by dropping to my knees. My endorphin levels are fluctuating wildly, and I know I must get some sleep soon or I will become one of Langby's walking dead, but I am afraid to leave him alone on the roofs, alone in the church with his communist party leader, alone anywhere. I have taken to watching him when he sleeps.

If I could just get hold of an artificial, I think I could induce a trance, in spite of my poor condition. But I cannot even go out to a pub. Langby is on the roofs constantly, waiting for his chance. When Enola comes again I must convince her to get the brandy for me. There are only a few days left.

December 28—Enola came this morning while I was on the west porch, picking up the Christmas tree. It has been knocked over three nights running by concussion. I righted the tree and was bending down to pick up the scattered tinsel when Enola appeared suddenly out of the fog like some cheerful saint. She stooped quickly and kissed me on the cheek. Then she straightened up, her nose red from her perennial cold, and handed me a box wrapped in colored paper.

"Merry Christmas," she said. "Go on then, open it. It's a gift."

My reflexes are almost totally gone. I knew the box was far too shallow for a bottle of brandy. Nevertheless, I believed she had remembered, had brought me my salvation. "You darling," I said, and tore it open.

It was a muffler. Gray wool. I stared at it for fully half a minute without realizing what it was. "Where's the brandy?" I said.

She looked shocked. Her nose got redder and her eyes started to blur. "You need this more. You haven't any clothing coupons and you have to be outside all the time. It's been so dreadful cold."

"I *needed* the brandy," I said angrily.

"I was only trying to be kind," she started, and I cut her off.

"Kind?" I said. "I asked you for brandy. I don't recall ever saying I needed a muffler." I shoved it back at her and began untangling a string of colored lights that had shattered when the tree fell.

She got that same holy martyr look Kivrin is so wonderful at. "I worry about you all the time up here," she said in a rush. "They're *trying* for St. Paul's, you know. And it's so close to the river. I didn't think you should be drinking. I— it's a crime when they're trying so hard to kill us all that you won't take care of yourself. It's like you're in it with them. I worry someday I'll come up to St. Paul's and you won't be here."

"Well, and what exactly am I supposed to do with a muffler? Hold it over my head when they drop the bombs?"

She turned and ran, disappearing into the gray fog before she had gone down two steps. I started after her, still holding the string of broken lights, tripped over it, and fell almost all the way to the bottom of the steps.

Langby picked me up. "You're off watches," he said grimly.

"You can't do that," I said.

"Oh, yes, I can. I don't want any walking dead on the roofs with me."

I let him lead me down here to the crypt, make me a cup of tea, put me to bed, all very solicitous. No indication that this is what he has been waiting for. I will lie here till the sirens go. Once I am on the roofs he will not be able to send me back without seeming suspicious. Do you know what he said before he left, asbestos coat and rubber boots, the dedicated fire watcher? "I want you to get some sleep." As if I could sleep with Langby on the roofs. I would be burned alive.

December 30—The sirens woke me, and old Bence-Jones said, "That should have done you some good. You've slept the clock round."

"What day is it?" I said, going for my boots.

"The twenty-ninth," he said, and as I dived for the door, "No need to hurry. They're late tonight. Maybe they won't come at all. That'd be a blessing, that would. The tide's out."

I stopped by the door to the stairs, holding on to the cool stone. "Is St. Paul's all right?"

"She's still standing," he said. "Have a bad dream?"

"Yes," I said, remembering the bad dreams of all the past weeks—the dead cat in my arms in St. John's Wood, Langby with his parcel and his *Worker* under his arm, the fire watch stone garishly lit by Christ's lantern. Then I remembered I had not dreamed at all. I had slept the kind of sleep I had prayed for, the kind of sleep that would help me remember.

Then I remembered. Not St. Paul's, burned to the ground by the communists. A headline from the dailies. "Marble Arch hit. Eighteen killed by blast." The date was not clear except for the year. 1940. There were exactly two more days left in 1940. I grabbed my coat and muffler and ran up the stairs and across the marble floor.

"Where the hell do you think you're going?" Langby shouted to me. I couldn't see him.

"I have to save Enola," I said, and my voice echoed in the dark sanctuary. "They're going to bomb Marble Arch."

"You can't leave now," he shouted after me, standing where the fire watch stone would be. "The tide's out. You dirty—"

I didn't hear the rest of it. I had already flung myself down the steps and into a taxi. It took almost all the money I had, the money I had so carefully hoarded for the trip back to St. John's Wood. Shelling started while we were still in Oxford Street, and the driver refused to go any farther. He let me out into pitch blackness, and I saw I would never make it in time.

Blast. Enola crumpled on the stairway down to the tube, her open-toed shoes still on her feet, not a mark on her. And when I try to lift her, jelly under the skin. I would have to wrap her in the muffler she gave me, because I was too late. I had gone back a hundred years to be too late to save her.

I ran the last blocks, guided by the gun emplacement that had to be in Hyde Park, and skidded down the steps into Marble Arch. The woman in the ticket booth took my last shilling for a ticket to St. Paul's Station. I stuck it in my pocket and raced toward the stairs.

"No running," she said placidly. "To your left, please." The door to the right was blocked off by wooden barricades, the metal gates beyond pulled to and chained. The board with names on it for the stations was x-ed with tape, and a new sign that read ALL TRAINS was nailed to the barricade, pointing left.

Enola was not on the stopped escalators or sitting against the wall in the hallway. I came to the first stairway and could not get through. A family had set out, just where I wanted to step, a communal tea of bread and butter, a little pot of jam sealed with waxed paper, and a kettle on a ring like the one Langby and I had rescued out of the rubble, all of it spread on a cloth embroidered at the corners with flowers. I stood staring down at the layered tea, spread like a waterfall down the steps.

"I—Marble Arch—" I said. Another twenty killed by flying tiles. "You shouldn't be here."

"We've as much right as anyone," the man said belligerently, "and who are you to tell us to move on?"

A woman lifting saucers out of a cardboard box looked up at me, frightened. The kettle began to whistle.

"It's you that should move on," the man said. "Go on then." He stood off to one side so I could pass. I edged past the embroidered cloth apologetically.

"I'm sorry," I said. "I'm looking for someone. On the platform."

"You'll never find her in there, mate," the man said, thumbing in that direction. I hurried past him, nearly stepping on the tea cloth, and rounded the corner into hell.

It was not hell. Shopgirls folded coats and leaned back against them, cheerful or sullen or disagreeable, but certainly not damned. Two boys scuffled for a shilling and lost it on the tracks. They bent over the edge, debating whether to go after it, and the station guard yelled to them to back away. A train rumbled through, full of people. A mosquito landed on the guard's hand and he reached out to slap it and missed. The boys laughed. And behind and before them, stretching in all directions down the deadly tile curves of the tunnel like casualties, backed into the entranceways and onto the stairs, were people. Hundreds and hundreds of people.

I stumbled back onto the stairs, knocking over a teacup. It spilled like a flood across the cloth.

"I told you, mate," the man said cheerfully. "It's hell in there, ain't it? And worse below."

"Hell," I said. "Yes." I would never find her. I would never save her. I looked at the woman mopping up the tea, and it came to me that I could not save her either. Enola or the cat or any of them, lost here in the endless stairways and cul-de-sacs of time. They were already dead a hundred years, past saving. The past is beyond saving. Surely that was the lesson the history department sent me all this way to learn. Well, fine, I've learned it. Can I go home now?

Of course not, dear boy. You have foolishly spent all your money on taxicabs and brandy, and tonight is the night the Germans burn the City. (Now it is too late, I remember it all. Twenty-eight incendiaries on the roofs.) Langby must have his chance, and you must learn the hardest lesson of all and the one you should have known from the beginning. You cannot save St. Paul's.

I went back out onto the platform and stood behind the yellow line until a train pulled up. I took my ticket out and held it in my hand all the way to St. Paul's Station. When I got there, smoke billowed toward me like an easy spray of water. I could not see St. Paul's.

"The tide's out," a woman said in a voice devoid of hope, and I went down in a snake pit of limp cloth hoses. My hands came up covered with rank-smelling mud, and I understood finally (and too late) the significance of the tide. There was no water to fight the fires.

A policeman barred my way and I stood helplessly before him with no idea what to say. "No civilians allowed here," he said. "St. Paul's is for it." The smoke billowed like a thundercloud, alive with sparks, and the dome rose golden above it.

"I'm fire watch," I said, and his arm fell away, and then I was on the roofs.

My endorphin levels must have been going up and down like an air raid siren. I do not have any short-term from then on, just moments that do not fit together: the people in the church when we brought Langby down, huddled in a corner playing cards, the whirlwind of burning scraps of wood in the dome, the ambulance driver who wore open-toed shoes like Enola and smeared salve on my burned hands. And in the center, the one clear moment when I went after Langby on a rope and saved his life.

I stood by the dome, blinking against the smoke. The City was on fire and it seemed as if St. Paul's would ignite from the heat, would crumble from the noise alone. Bence-Jones was by the northwest tower, hitting at an incendiary with a spade. Langby was too close to the patched place where the bomb had gone through, looking toward me. An incendiary clattered behind him. I turned to grab a shovel, and when I turned back, he was gone.

"Langby!" I shouted, and could not hear my own voice. He had fallen into the chasm and nobody saw him or the incendiary. Except me. I do not remember how I got across the roof. I think I called for a rope. I got a rope. I tied it around my waist, gave the ends of it into the hands of the fire watch, and went over the side. The fires lit the walls of the hole almost all the way to the bottom. Below me I could see a pile of whitish rubble. He's under there, I thought, and jumped free of the wall. The space was so narrow there was nowhere to throw the rubble. I was afraid I would inadvertently stone him, and I tried to toss the pieces of planking and plaster over my shoulder, but there was barely room to turn. For one awful moment I thought he might not be there at all, that the pieces of splintered wood would brush away to reveal empty pavement, as they had in the crypt.

I was numbed by the indignity of crawling over him. If he was dead I did not think I could bear the shame of stepping on his helpless body. Then his hand came up like a ghost's and grabbed my ankle, and within seconds I had whirled and had his head free.

He was the ghastly white that no longer frightens me. "I put the bomb out," he said. I stared at him, so overwhelmed with relief I could not speak. For one hysterical moment I thought I would even laugh, I was so glad to see him. I finally realized what it was I was supposed to say.

"Are you all right?" I said.

"Yes," he said, and tried to raise himself on one elbow. "So much the worse for you."

He could not get up. He grunted with pain when he tried to shift his weight to his right side and lay back, the uneven rubble crunching sickeningly under him. I tried to lift him gently so I could see where he was hurt. He must have fallen on something.

"It's no use," he said, breathing hard. "I put it out."

I spared him a startled glance, afraid that he was delirious and went back to rolling him onto his side.

"I know you were counting on this one," he went on, not resisting me at all. "It was bound to happen sooner or later with all these roofs. Only I went after it. What'll you tell your friends?"

His asbestos coat was torn down the back in a long gash. Under it his back was charred and smoking. He had fallen on the incendiary. "Oh, my God," I said, trying frantically to see how badly he was burned without touching him. I had no way of knowing how deep the burns went, but they seemed to extend only in the narrow space where the coat had torn. I tried to pull the bomb out from under him, but the casing was as hot as a stove. It was not melting, though. My sand and Langby's body had smothered it. I had no idea if it would start up again when it was exposed to the air. I looked around, a little wildly, for the bucket and stirrup pump Langby must have dropped when he fell.

"Looking for a weapon?" Langby said, so clearly it was hard to believe he was hurt at all. "Why not just leave me here? A bit of overexposure and I'd be done for by morning. Or would you rather do your dirty work in private?"

I stood up and yelled to the men on the roof above us. One of them shone a pocket torch down at us, but its light didn't reach.

"Is he dead?" somebody shouted down to me.

"Send for an ambulance," I said. "He's been burned."

I helped Langby up, trying to support his back without touching the burn. He staggered a little and then leaned against the wall, watching me as I tried to bury the incendiary, using a piece of the planking as a scoop. The rope came down and I tied Langby to it. He had not spoken since I helped him up. He let me tie the rope around his waist, still looking steadily at me. "I should have let you smother in the crypt," he said.

He stood leaning easily, almost relaxed against the wooden supports, his hands holding him up. I put his hands on the slack rope and wrapped it once around them for the grip I knew he didn't have. "I've been onto you since that day in the Gallery. I knew you weren't afraid of heights. You came down here without any fear of heights when you thought I'd ruined your precious plans. What was it? An attack of conscience? Kneeling there like a baby, whining, 'What have we done? What have we done?' You made me sick. But you know what gave you away first? The cat. Everybody knows cats hate water. Everybody but a dirty Nazi spy."

There was a tug on the rope. "Come ahead," I said, and the rope tautened.

"That WVS tart? Was she a spy, too? Supposed to meet you in Marble Arch? Telling me it was going to be bombed. You're a rotten spy, Bartholomew. Your friends already blew it up in September. It's open again."

The rope jerked suddenly and began to lift Langby. He twisted his hands to get a better grip. His right shoulder scraped the wall. I put up my hands and pushed him gently so that his left side was to the wall. "You're making a big mistake, you know," he said. "You should have killed me. I'll tell."

I stood in the darkness, waiting for the rope. Langby was unconscious when he reached the roof. I walked past the fire watch to the dome and down to the crypt.

This morning the letter from my uncle came and with it a five-pound note.

December 31—Two of Dunworthy's flunkies met me in St. John's Wood to tell me I was late for my exams. I did not even protest. I shuffled obediently after them without even considering how unfair it was to give an exam to one of the walking dead. I had not slept in—how long? Since yesterday when I went to find Enola. I had not slept in a hundred years.

Dunworthy was in the Examination Buildings, blinking at me. One of the flunkies handed me a test paper and the other one called time. I turned the paper over and left an oily smudge from the ointment on my burns. I stared uncomprehendingly at them. I had grabbed at the incendiary when I turned Langby over, but these burns were on the backs of my hands. The answer came to me suddenly in Langby's unyielding voice. "They're rope burns, you fool. Don't they teach you Nazi spies the proper way to come up a rope?"

I looked down at the test. It read, "Number of incendiaries that fell on St. Paul's————Number of land mines————Number of high explosive bombs———— Method most commonly used for extinguishing incendiaries————land mines————high explosive bombs————Number of volunteers on first watch ————second watch————Casualties————Fatalities————" The questions made no sense. There was only a short space, long enough for the writing of a number, after any of the questions. Method most commonly used for extinguishing incendiaries. How would I ever fit what I knew into that narrow space? Where were the questions about Enola and Langby and the cat?

I went up to Dunworthy's desk. "St. Paul's almost burned down last night," I said. "What kind of questions are these?"

"You should be answering questions, Mr. Bartholomew, not asking them."

"There aren't any questions about the people," I said. The outer casing of my anger began to melt.

"Of course there are," Dunworthy said, flipping to the second page of the test. "Number of casualties, 1940. Blast, shrapnel, other."

"Other?" I said. At any moment the roof would collapse on me in a shower of plaster dust and fury. "Other? Langby put out a fire with his own body. Enola has a cold that keeps getting worse. The cat . . ." I snatched the paper back from him and scrawled "one cat" in the narrow space next to "blast." "Don't you care about them at all?"

"They're important from a statistical point of view," he said, "but as individuals they are hardly relevant to the course of history."

My reflexes were shot. It was amazing to me that Dunworthy's were almost as slow. I grazed the side of his jaw and knocked his glasses off. "Of course they're relevant!" I shouted. "They *are* the history, not all these bloody numbers!"

The reflexes of the flunkies were very fast. They did not let me start another swing at him before they had me by both arms and were hauling me out of the room.

"They're back there in the past with nobody to save them. They can't see their hands in front of their faces and there are bombs falling down on them and you tell me they aren't important? You call that being an historian?"

The flunkies dragged me out the door and down the hall. "Langby saved St. Paul's. How much more important can a person get? You're no historian! You're nothing but a—" I wanted to call him a terrible name, but the only curses I could summon up were Langby's. "You're nothing but a dirty Nazi spy!" I bellowed. "You're nothing but a lazy bourgeois tart!"

They dumped me on my hands and knees outside the door and slammed it in my face. "I wouldn't be an historian if you paid me!" I shouted, and went to see the fire watch stone.

December 31—I am having to write this in bits and pieces. My hands are in pretty bad shape, and Dunworthy's boys didn't help matters much. Kivrin comes in periodically, wearing her St. Joan look, and smears so much salve on my hands that I can't hold a pencil.

St. Paul's Station is not there, of course, so I got out at Holborn and walked, thinking about my last meeting with Dean Matthews on the morning after the burning of the city. This morning.

"I understand you saved Langby's life," he said. "I also understand that between you, you saved St. Paul's last night."

I showed him the letter from my uncle and he stared at it as if he could not think what it was. "Nothing stays saved forever," he said, and for a terrible moment I thought he was going to tell me Langby had died. "We shall have to keep on saving St. Paul's until Hitler decides to bomb something else."

The raids on London are almost over, I wanted to tell him. He'll start bombing the countryside in a matter of weeks. Canterbury, Bath, aiming always at the cathedrals. You and St. Paul's will both outlast the war and live to dedicate the fire watch stone.

"I am hopeful, though," he said. "I think the worst is over."

"Yes, sir." I thought of the stone, its letters still readable after all this time. No, sir, the worst is not over.

I managed to keep my bearings almost to the top of Ludgate Hill. Then I lost my way completely, wandering about like a man in a graveyard. I had not remembered that the rubble looked so much like the white plaster dust Langby had tried to dig me out of. I could not find the stone anywhere. In the end I nearly fell over it, jumping back as if I had stepped on a body.

It is all that's left. Hiroshima is supposed to have had a handful of untouched trees at ground zero. Denver the capitol steps. Neither of them says, "Remember men and women of St. Paul's Watch who by the grace of God saved this cathedral." The grace of God.

Part of the stone is sheared off. Historians argue there was another line that said, "for all time," but I do not believe that, not if Dean Matthews had anything to do with it. And none of the watch it was dedicated to would have believed it for a minute. We saved St. Paul's every time we put out an incendiary, and only until the next one fell. Keeping watch on the danger spots, putting out the little fires with sand and stirrup pumps, the big ones with our bodies, in order to keep the whole vast complex structure from burning down. Which sounds to me like a course description for History Practicum 401. What a fine time to discover what historians are for when I have tossed my chance for being one out the windows as easily as they tossed the pinpoint bomb in! No, sir, the worst is not over.

There are flash burns on the stone, where legend says the Dean of St. Paul's was kneeling when the bomb went off. Totally apocryphal, of course, since the front door is hardly an appropriate place for prayers. It is more likely the shadow of a tourist who wandered in to ask the whereabouts of the Windmill Theatre, or the imprint of a girl bringing a volunteer his muffler. Or a cat.

Nothing is saved forever, Dean Matthews, and I knew that when I walked in the west doors that first day, blinking into the gloom, but it is pretty bad nevertheless. Standing here knee-deep in rubble out of which I will not be able to dig any folding chairs or friends, knowing that Langby died thinking I was a Nazi spy, knowing that Enola came one day and I wasn't there. It's pretty bad.

But it is not as bad as it could be. They are both dead, and Dean Matthews too, but they died without knowing what I knew all along, what sent me to my knees in the Whispering Gallery, sick with grief and guilt: that in the end none of us saved St. Paul's. And Langby cannot turn to me, stunned and sick at heart, and say, "Who did this? Your friends the Nazis?" And I would have to say, "No, the communists." That would be the worst.

I have come back to the room and let Kivrin smear more salve on my hands. She wants me to get some sleep. I know I should pack and get gone. It will be humiliating to have them come and throw me out, but I do not have the strength to fight her. She looks so much like Enola.

January 1—I have apparently slept not only through the night, but through the morning mail drop as well. When I woke up just now, I found Kivrin sitting on the end of the bed holding an envelope. "Your grades came," she said.

I put my arm over my eyes. "They can be marvelously efficient when they want to, can't they?"

"Yes," Kivrin said.

"Well, let's see it," I said, sitting up. "How long do I have before they come and throw me out?"

She handed the flimsy computer envelope to me. I tore it along the perforation. "Wait," she said. "Before you open it, I want to say something." She put her hand gently on my burns. "You're wrong about the history department. They're very good."

It was not exactly what I expected her to say. "Good is not the word I'd use to describe Dunworthy," I said and yanked the inside slip free.

Kivrin's look did not change, not even when I sat there with the printout on my knees where she could surely see it.

"Well," I said.

The slip was hand-signed by the esteemed Dunworthy. I have taken a first. With honors.

January 2—Two things came in the mail today. One was Kivrin's assignment. The history department thinks of everything—even to keeping her here long enough to nursemaid me, even to coming up with a prefabricated trial by fire to send their history majors through.

I think I wanted to believe that was what they had done, Enola and Langby only hired actors, the cat a clever android with its clockwork innards taken out for the final effect, not so much because I wanted to believe Dunworthy was not good at all, but because then I would not have this nagging pain at not knowing what had happened to them.

"You said your practicum was England in 1400?" I said, watching her as suspiciously as I had watched Langby.

"1349," she said, and her face went slack with memory. "The plague year."

"My God," I said. "How could they do that? The plague's a ten."

"I have a natural immunity," she said, and looked at her hands.

Because I could not think of anything to say, I opened the other piece of mail. It was a report on Enola. Computer-printed, facts and dates and statistics, all the numbers the history department so dearly loves, but it told me what I thought I would have to go without knowing: that she had gotten over her cold and survived the Blitz. Young Tom had been killed in the Baedaker raids on Bath, but Enola had lived until 2006, the year before they blew up St. Paul's.

I don't know whether I believe the report or not, but it does not matter. It is, like Langby's reading aloud to the old man, a simple act of human kindness. They think of everything.

Not quite. They did not tell me what happened to Langby. But I find as I write this that I already know: I saved his life. It does not seem to matter that he might have died in hospital next day, and I find, in spite of all the hard lessons the history department has tried to teach me, I do not quite believe this one: that nothing is saved forever. It seems to me that perhaps Langby is.

January 3—I went to see Dunworthy today. I don't know what I intended to say—some pompous drivel about my willingness to serve in the fire watch of history, standing guard against the falling incendiaries of the human heart, silent and saintly.

But he blinked at me nearsightedly across his desk, and it seemed to me that he was blinking at that last bright image of St. Paul's in sunlight before it was gone forever and that he knew better than anyone that the past cannot be saved, and I said instead, "I'm sorry that I broke your glasses, sir."

"How did you like St. Paul's?" he said, and like my first meeting with Enola,

I felt I must be somehow reading the signals all wrong, that he was not feeling loss, but something quite different.

"I loved it, sir," I said.

"Yes," he said. "So do I."

Dean Matthews is wrong. I have fought with memory my whole practicum only to find that it is not the enemy at all, and being an historian is not some saintly burden after all. Because Dunworthy is not blinking against the fatal sunlight of the last morning, but into the gloom of that first afternoon, looking in the great west doors of St. Paul's at what is, like Langby, like all of it, every moment, in us, saved forever.

Poul Anderson

Poul Anderson (1926–   ) has written over sixty novels and published over forty collections of short stories in his long and influential career in science fiction. James Blish called Anderson "the enduring explosion" because of the high quality of his continuing literary production. Distinguished as a fantasy writer (*The Broken Sword* [1954] was his first adult novel) and a mystery writer (his first mystery, *Perish By the Sword* [1959], won the Cock Robin prize), he is nevertheless principally one of the heroic figures of hard science fiction. While a devotee of the hard science approach of Hal Clement, he is given to making his stories vehicles for philosophical and social commentary, in the manner of Heinlein.

Anderson has always defended the traditions of military honor in his fiction, and devoted much of his effort to adventure plots. But he has also turned out a number of colorful, powerful SF stories and novels, from *Brain Wave* (1954) to *The Boat of a Million Years* (1989), that are generally perceived as his major works—the most famous is probably *Tau Zero* (1970). These are marked by astronomical and physical speculation and large-scale Stapledonian vistas of time and space. Even in his swashbuckling adventure stories, Anderson is famous for beginning with calculations of the elements of the orbit of the world to be his setting, and allowing the physics, chemistry, and biology to follow logically, thus generating the parameters in which human beings would have to live and survive.

He is also interested in mythology and often uses myth in his fiction, as in this story. "Goat Song," from the 1970s, is one of his many Hugo Award-winning stories, hard science fiction with an overlay of mythic fantasy.

GOAT SONG

Three women: one is dead; one is alive; One is both and neither, and will never live and never die, being immortal in SUM.

On a hill above that valley through which runs the highroad, I await Her passage. Frost came early this year, and the grasses have paled. Otherwise the slope is begrown with blackberry bushes that have been harvested by men and birds, leaving only briars, and with certain apple trees. They are very old, those trees, survivors of an orchard raised by generations which none but SUM now remembers (I can see a few fragments of wall thrusting above the brambles)—scattered crazily over the hillside and as crazily gnarled. A little fruit remains on them. Chill across my skin, a gust shakes loose an apple. I hear it knock on the earth, another stroke of some eternal clock. The shrubs whisper to the wind.

Elsewhere the ridges around me are wooded, afire with scarlets and brasses and bronzes. The sky is huge, the westering sun wanbright. The valley is filling with a deeper blue, a haze whose slight smokiness touches my nostrils. This is Indian summer, the funeral pyre of the year.

There have been other seasons. There have been other lifetimes, before mine and hers; and in those days they had words to sing with. We still allow ourselves music, though, and I have spent much time planting melodies around my rediscovered words. *"In the greenest growth of the May-time—"* I unsling the harp on my back, and tune it afresh, and sing it to her, straight into autumn and the waning day.

> *"—You came, and the sun came after,*
> *And the green grew golden above:*
> *And the flag-flowers lightened with laughter,*
> *And the meadowsweet shook with love."*

A footfall stirs the grasses, quite gently, and the woman says, trying to chuckle, "Why, thank you."

Once, so soon after my one's death that I was still dazed by it, I stood in the home that had been ours. This was on the hundred and first floor of a most desirable building. After dark the city flamed for us, blinked, glittered, flung immense sheets of radiance forth like banners. Nothing but SUM could have controlled the firefly dance of a million aircars among the towers: or, for that matter, have maintained the entire city, from nuclear powerplants through automated factories, physical and economic distribution networks, sanitation, repair, services, education, culture, order, everything as one immune immortal organism. We had gloried in belonging to this as well as to each other.

But that night I told the kitchen to throw the dinner it had made for me down the waste chute, and ground under my heel the chemical consolations which the medicine cabinet extended to me, and kicked the cleaner as it picked up the mess, and ordered the lights not to go on, anywhere in our suite. I stood by the vieWall, looking out across megalopolis, and it was tawdry. In my hands I had a little clay figure she had fashioned herself. I turned it over and over and over.

But I had forgotten to forbid the door to admit visitors. It recognized this woman and opened for her. She had come with the kindly intention of teasing me out of a mood that seemed to her unnatural. I heard her enter, and looked around through the gloom. She had almost the same height as my girl did, and her hair chanced to be bound in a way that my girl often favored, and the figurine dropped from my grasp and shattered, because for an instant I thought she was my girl. Since then I have been hard put not to hate Thrakia.

This evening, even without so much sundown light, I would not make that mistake. Nothing but the silvery bracelet about her left wrist bespeaks the past we share. She is in wildcountry garb: boots, kilt of true fur and belt of true leather, knife at hip and rifle slung on shoulder. Her locks are matted and snarled, her skin brown from weeks of weather; scratches and smudges show beneath the fantastic zigzags she has painted in many colors on herself. She wears a necklace of bird skulls.

Now that one who is dead was, in her own way, more a child of trees and horizons than Thrakia's followers. She was so much at home in the open that she had no need to put off clothes or cleanliness, reason or gentleness, when we sickened of the cities and went forth beyond them. From this trait I got many of the names I bestowed on her, such as Wood's Colt or Fallow Hind or, from my prowlings among ancient books, Dryad and Elven. (She liked me to choose her names, and this pleasure had no end, because she was inexhaustible.)

I let my harpstring ring into silence. Turning about, I say to Thrakia, "I wasn't singing for you. Not for anyone. Leave me alone."

She draws a breath. The wind ruffles her hair and brings me an odor of her: not female sweetness, but fear. She clenches her fists and says, "You're crazy."

"Wherever did you find a meaningful word like that?" I gibe; for my own pain and—to be truthful—my own fear must strike out at something, and here she stands. "Aren't you content any longer with 'untranquil' or 'disequilibrated'?"

"I got it from you," she says defiantly, "you and your damned archaic songs. There's another word, 'damned.' And how it suits you! When are you going to stop this morbidity?"

"And commit myself to a clinic and have my brain laundered nice and sanitary? Not soon, darling." I use *that* last word aforethought, but she cannot know what scorn and sadness are in it for me, who know that once it could also have been a name for my girl. The official grammar and pronunciation of language is as frozen as every other aspect of our civilization, thanks to electronic recording and neuronic teaching; but meanings shift and glide about like subtle serpents. (O adder that stung my Foalfoot!)

I shrug and say in my driest, most city-technological voice, "Actually, I'm the practical, nonmorbid one. Instead of running away from my emotions—via drugs, or neuroadjustment, or playing at savagery like you, for that matter—I'm about to implement a concrete plan for getting back the person who made me happy."

"By disturbing Her on Her way home?"

"Anyone has the right to petition the dark Queen while she's abroad on earth."

"But this is past the proper time—"

"No law's involved, just custom. People are afraid to meet Her outside a crowd, a town, bright flat lights. They won't admit it, but they are. So I came here precisely not to be part of a queue. I don't want to speak into a recorder for subsequent computer analysis of my words. How could I be sure She was listening? I want to meet Her as myself, a unique being, and look in Her eyes while I make my prayer."

Thrakia chokes a little. "She'll be angry."

"Is She able to be angry, anymore?"

"I . . . I don't know. What you mean to ask for is so impossible, though. So absurd. That SUM should give you back your girl. You know It never makes exceptions."

"Isn't She Herself an exception?"

"That's different. You're being silly. SUM has to have a, well, a direct human liaison. Emotional and cultural feedback, as well as statistics. How else can It govern rationally? And She must have been chosen out of the whole world. Your girl, what was she? Nobody!"

"To me, she was everybody."

"You—" Thrakia catches her lip in her teeth. One hand reaches out and closes on my bare forearm, a hard hot touch, the grimy fingernails biting. When I make no response, she lets go and stares at the ground. A V of outbound geese passes overhead. Their cries come shrill through the wind, which is loudening in the forest.

"Well," she says, "you are special. You always were. You went to space and came back, with the Great Captain. You're maybe the only man alive who understands about the ancients. And your singing, yes, you don't really entertain, your songs trouble people and can't be forgotten. So maybe She will listen to you. But SUM won't. It can't give special resurrections. Once that was done, a single time, wouldn't it have to be done for everybody? The dead would overrun the living."

"Not necessarily," I say. "In any event, I mean to try."

"Why can't you wait for the promised time? Surely, then, SUM will re-create you two in the same generation."

"I'd have to live out this life, at least, without her," I say, looking away also, down to the highroad which shines through shadow like death's snake, the length of the valley. "Besides, how do you know there ever will be any resurrections? We have only a promise. No, less than that. An announced policy."

She gasps, steps back, raises her hands as if to fend me off. Her soul bracelet casts light into my eyes. I recognize an embryo exorcism. She lacks ritual; every "superstition" was patiently scrubbed out of our metal-and-energy world, long ago. But if she has no word for it, no concept, nevertheless she recoils from blasphemy.

So I say, wearily, not wanting an argument, wanting only to wait here alone: "Never mind. There could be some natural catastrophe, like a giant asteroid striking, that wiped out the system before conditions had become right for resurrections to commence."

"That's impossible," she says, almost frantic. "The homeostats, the repair functions—"

"All right, call it a vanishingly unlikely theoretical contingency. Let's declare that I'm so selfish I want Swallow Wing back now, in this life of mine, and don't give a curse whether that'll be fair to the rest of you."

You won't care either, anyway, I think. None of you. You don't grieve. It is your own precious private consciousnesses that you wish to preserve; no one else is close enough to you to matter very much. Would you believe me if I told you I am quite prepared to offer SUM my own death in exchange for It releasing Blossom-in-the-Sun?

I don't speak that thought, which would be cruel, nor repeat what is crueller: my fear that SUM lies, that the dead never will be disgorged. For (I am not the All-Controller, I think not with vacuum and negative energy levels but with ordinary begotten molecules; yet I can reason somewhat dispassionately, being disillusioned) consider—

The object of the game is to maintain a society stable, just, and sane. This requires satisfaction not only of somatic, but of symbolic and instinctual needs. Thus children must be allowed to come into being. The minimum number per generation is equal to the maximum: that number which will maintain a constant population.

It is also desirable to remove the fear of death from men. Hence the promise: At such time as it is socially feasible, SUM will begin to refashion us, with our complete memories but in the pride of our youth. This can be done over and over, life after life across the millennia. So death is, indeed, a sleep.

—*in that sleep of death, what dreams may come*— No. I myself dare not dwell on this. I ask merely, privately: Just when and how does SUM expect conditions (in a stabilized society, mind you) to have become so different from today's that the reborn can, in their millions, safely be welcomed back?

I see no reason why SUM should not lie to us. We, too, are objects in the world that It manipulates.

"We've quarreled about this before, Thrakia," I sigh. "Often. Why do you bother?"

"I wish I knew," she answers low. Half to herself, she goes on: "Of course I want to copulate with you. You must be good, the way that girl used to follow you about with her eyes, and smile when she touched your hand, and— But you can't be better than everyone else. That's unreasonable. There are only so many possible ways. So why do I care if you wrap yourself up in silence and go off alone? Is it that that makes you a challenge?"

"You think too much," I say. "Even here. You're a pretend primitive. You visit wildcountry to 'slake inborn atavistic impulses' . . . but you can't dismantle that computer inside yourself and simply feel, simply be."

She bristles. I touched a nerve there. Looking past her, along the ridge of fiery maple and sumac, brassy elm and great dun oak, I see others emerge from beneath the trees. Women exclusively, her followers, as unkempt as she; one has a brace of ducks lashed to her waist, and their blood has trickled down her thigh and dried black. For this movement, this unadmitted mystique has become Thrakia's by now: that not only men should forsake the easy routine and the easy pleasure of the cities, and become again, for a few weeks each year, the carnivores who begot our species; women too should seek out starkness, the better to appreciate civilization when they return.

I feel a moment's unease. We are in no park, with laid-out trails and campground services. We are in wildcountry. Not many men come here, ever, and still fewer women; for the region is, literally, beyond the law. No deed done here is punishable. We are told that this helps consolidate society, as the most violent among us may thus vent their passions. But I have spent much time in wildcountry since my Morning Star went out—myself in quest of nothing but solitude—and I have watched what happens through eyes that have also read anthropology and history. Institutions are developing; ceremonies, tribalisms, acts of blood and cruelty and acts elsewhere called unnatural are becoming more elaborate and more expected every year. Then the practitioners go home to their cities and honestly believe they have been enjoying fresh air, exercise, and good tension-releasing fun.

Let her get angry enough and Thrakia can call knives to her aid.

Wherefore I make myself lay both hands on her shoulders, and meet the tormented gaze, and say most gently, "I'm sorry. I know you mean well. You're afraid She will be annoyed and bring misfortune on your people."

Thrakia gulps. "No," she whispers. "That wouldn't be logical. But I'm afraid of what might happen to you. And then—" Suddenly she throws herself against me. I feel arms, breasts, belly press through my tunic, and smell meadows in her hair and musk in her mouth. "You'd be gone!" she wails. "Then who'd sing to us?"

"Why, the planet's crawling with entertainers," I stammer.

"You're more than that," she says. "So much more. I don't like what you sing, not really—and what you've sung since that stupid girl died, oh, meaningless, horrible!—but, I don't know why, I *want* you to trouble me."

Awkward, I pat her back. The sun now stands very little above the treetops. Its rays slant interminably through the booming, frosting air. I shiver in my tunic and buskins and wonder what to do.

A sound rescues me. It comes from one end of the valley below us, where further view is blocked off by two cliffs; it thunders deep in our ears and rolls through the earth into our bones. We have heard that sound in the cities, and been glad to have walls and lights and multitudes around us. Now we are alone with it, the noise of Her chariot.

The women shriek, I hear them faintly across wind and rumble and my own pulse, and they vanish into the woods. They will seek their camp, dress warmly, build enormous fires; presently they will eat their ecstatics, and rumors are uneasy about what they do after that.

Thrakia seizes my left wrist, above the soul bracelet, and hauls. "Harper, come with me!" she pleads. I break loose from her and stride down the hill toward the road. A scream follows me for a moment.

Light still dwells in the sky and on the ridges, but as I descend into that narrow valley I enter dusk, and it thickens. Indistinct bramblebushes whicker where I brush them, and claw back at me. I feel the occasional scratch on my legs, the tug as my garment is snagged, the chill that I breathe, but dimly. My perceived-outer-reality is overpowered by the rushing of Her chariot and my blood. My inner-universe is fear, yes, but exaltation too, a drunkenness which sharpens instead of dulling the senses, a psychedelia which opens the reasoning mind as well as the emotions; I have gone beyond myself, I am embodied purpose. Not out of need for comfort, but to voice what Is, I return to words whose speaker rests centuries dust, and lend them my own music. I sing:

"—Gold is my heart, and the world's golden,
And one peak tipped with light;
And the air lies still about the hill
With the first fear of night;

"Till mystery down the soundless valley
Thunders, and dark is here;
And the wind blows, and the light goes,
And the night is full of fear.

"And I know one night, on some far height,
In a tongue I never knew,
I yet shall hear the tidings clear
From them that were friends of you.

"They'll call the news from hill to hill,
Dark and uncomforted,
Earth and sky and the winds; and I
Shall know that you are dead.—"

But I have reached the valley floor, and She has come in sight.

Her chariot is unlit, for radar eyes and inertial guides need no lamps, nor sun nor stars. Wheel-less, the steel tear rides on its own roar and thrust of air. The pace is not great, far less than any of our mortals' vehicles are wont to take. Men say the Dark Queen rides thus slowly in order that She may perceive with Her own senses and so be the better prepared to counsel SUM. But now Her annual round is finished; She is homeward bound; until spring She will dwell with It Which is our lord. Why does She not hasten tonight?

Because Death has never a need of haste? I wonder. And as I step into the middle of the road, certain lines from the yet more ancient past rise tremendous within me, and I strike my harp and chant them louder than the approaching car:

> *"I that in heill was and gladnèss*
> *Am trublit now with great sickness*
> *And feblit with infirmitie:—*
> Timor mortis conturbat me."

The car detects me and howls a warning. I hold my ground. The car could swing around, the road is wide and in any event a smooth surface is not absolutely necessary. But I hope, I believe that She will be aware of an obstacle in Her path, and tune in Her various amplifiers, and find me abnormal enough to stop for. Who, in SUM's world—who, even among the explorers that It has sent beyond in Its unappeasable hunger for data—would stand in a cold wildcountry dusk and shout while his harp snarls

> *"Our pleasance here is all vain glory,*
> *This fals world is but transitory,*
> *The flesh is bruckle, the Feynd is slee:—*
> Timor mortis conturbat me.
>
> *"The state of man does change and vary,*
> *Now sound, now sick, now blyth, now sary,*
> *No dansand mirry, now like to die:—*
> Timor mortis conturbat me.
>
> *"No state in Erd here standis sicker;*
> *As with the wynd wavis the wicker*
> *So wannis this world's vanitie:—*
> Timor mortis conturbat me.—?"

The car draws alongside and sinks to the ground. I let my strings die away into the wind. The sky overhead and in the west is gray-purple; eastward it is quite dark and a few early stars peer forth. Here, down in the valley, shadows are heavy and I cannot see very well.

The canopy slides back. She stands erect in the chariot, thus looming over me. Her robe and cloak are black, fluttering like restless wings; beneath the cowl Her face is a white blur. I have seen it before, under full light, and in how many thousands of pictures; but at this hour I cannot call it back to my mind, not entirely. I list sharp-sculptured profile and pale lips, sable hair and long green eyes, but these are nothing more than words.

"What are you doing?" She has a lovely low voice; but is it, as oh, how rarely since SUM took Her to Itself, is it the least shaken? "What is that you were singing?"

My answer comes so strong that my skull resonates; for I am borne higher and higher on my tide. "Lady of Ours, I have a petition."

"Why did you not bring it before Me when I walked among men? Tonight I am homebound. You must wait till I ride forth with the new year."

"Lady of Ours, neither You nor I would wish living ears to hear what I have to say."

She regards me for a long while. Do I indeed sense fear also in Her? (Surely not of me. Her chariot is armed and armored, and would react with machine speed to protect Her should I offer violence. And should I somehow, incredibly, kill Her, or wound Her beyond chemosurgical repair, She of all beings has no need to doubt death. The ordinary bracelet cries with quite sufficient radio loudness to be heard by more than one thanatic station, when we die; and in that shielding the soul can scarcely be damaged before the Winged Heels arrive to bear it off to SUM. Surely the Dark Queen's circlet can call still further, and is still better insulated, than any mortal's. And She will most absolutely be re-created. She has been, again and again; death and rebirth every seven years keep Her eternally young in the service of SUM. I have never been able to find out when She was first born.)

Fear, perhaps, of what I have sung and what I might speak?

At last She says—I can scarcely hear through the gusts and creakings in the trees—"Give me the Ring, then."

The dwarf robot which stands by Her throne when She sits among men appears beside Her and extends the massive dull-silver circle to me. I place my left arm within, so that my soul is enclosed. The tablet on the upper surface of the Ring, which looks so much like a jewel, slants away from me; I cannot read what flashes onto the bezel. But the faint glow picks Her features out of murk as She bends to look.

Of course, I tell myself, the actual soul is not scanned. That would take too long. Probably the bracelet which contains the soul has an identification code built in. The Ring sends this to an appropriate part of SUM, Which instantly sends back what is recorded under that code. I hope there is nothing more to it. SUM has not seen fit to tell us.

"What do you call yourself at the moment?" She asks.

A current of bitterness crosses my tide. "Lady of Ours, why should You care? Is not my real name the number I got when I was allowed to be born?"

Calm descends once more upon Her. "If I am to evaluate properly what you say, I must know more about you than these few official data. Name indicates mood."

I too feel unshaken again, my tide running so strong and smooth that I might not know I was moving did I not see time recede behind me. "Lady of Ours, I cannot give You a fair answer. In this past year I have not troubled with names, or with much of anything else. But some people who knew me from earlier days call me Harper."

"What do you do besides make that sinister music?"

"These days, nothing, Lady of Ours. I've money to live out my life, if I eat sparingly and keep no home. Often I am fed and housed for the sake of my songs."

"What you sang is unlike anything I have heard since—" Anew, briefly, that robot serenity is shaken. "Since before the world was stabilized. You should not wake dead symbols, Harper. They walk through men's dreams."

"Is that bad?"

"Yes. The dreams become nightmares. Remember: Mankind, every man who ever lived, was insane before SUM brought order, reason, and peace."

"Well, then," I say, "I will cease and desist if I may have my own dead wakened for me."

She stiffens. The tablet goes out. I withdraw my arm and the Ring is stored away by Her servant. So again She is faceless, beneath flickering stars, here at the bottom of this shadowed valley. Her voice falls cold as the air: "No one can be brought back to life before Resurrection Time is ripe."

I do not say, "What about You?" for that would be vicious. What did She think, how did She weep, when SUM chose Her of all the young on earth? What does She endure in Her centuries? I dare not imagine.

Instead, I smite my harp and sing, quietly this time:

> *"Strew on her roses, roses,*
> *And never a spray of yew.*
> *In quiet she reposes:*
> *Ah! Would that I did too."*

The Dark Queen cries, "What are you doing? Are you really insane?" I go straight to the last stanza.

> *"Her cabin'd, ample Spirit*
> *It flutter'd and fail'd for breath.*
> *To-night it doth inherit*
> *The vasty hall of Death."*

I know why my songs strike so hard: because they bear dreads and passions that no one is used to—that most of us hardly know could exist—in SUM's ordered universe. But I had not the courage to hope She would be as torn by them as I see. Has She not lived with more darkness and terror than the ancients themselves could conceive? She calls, "Who has died?"

"She had many names, Lady of Ours," I say. "None was beautiful enough. I can tell You her number, though."

"Your daughter? I . . . sometimes I am asked if a dead child cannot be brought back. Not often, anymore, when they go so soon to the crèche. But sometimes. I tell the mother she may have a new one; but if ever We started re-creating dead infants, at what age level could We stop?"

"No, this was my woman."

"Impossible!" Her tone seeks to be not unkindly but is, instead, well-nigh frantic. "You will have no trouble finding others. You are handsome, and your psyche is, is, is extraordinary. It burns like Lucifer."

"Do You remember the name Lucifer, Lady of Ours?" I pounce. "Then You are old indeed. So old that You must also remember how a man might desire only one woman, but her above the whole world and heaven."

She tries to defend Herself with a jeer: "Was that mutual, Harper? I know more of mankind than you do, and surely I am the last chaste woman in existence."

"Now that she is gone, Lady, yes, perhaps You are. But we— Do you know how she died? We had gone to a wildcountry area. A man saw her, alone, while I was off hunting gem rocks to make her a necklace. He approached her. She refused him. He threatened force. She fled. This was desert land, viper land, and she was barefoot. One of them bit her. I did not find her till hours later. By then the poison and the unshaded sun— She died quite soon after she told me what had happened and that she loved me. I could not get her body to chemosurgery in time for normal revival procedures. I had to let them cremate her and take her soul away to SUM."

"What right have you to demand her back, when no one else can be given their own?"

"The right that I love her, and she loves me. We are more necessary to each other than sun or moon. I do not think You could find another two people of whom this is so, Lady. And is not everyone entitled to claim what is necessary to his life? How else can society be kept whole?"

"You are being fantastic," She says thinly. "Let me go."

"No, Lady, I am speaking sober truth. But poor plain words won't serve me. I sing to You because then maybe You will understand." And I strike my harp anew; but it is more to her than Her that I sing.

> *"If I had thought thou couldst have died,*
> *I might not weep for thee:*
> *But I forgot, when by thy side,*
> *That thou couldst mortal be:*
>
> *"It never through my mind had past*
> *The time would e'er be o'er,*
> *And I on thee should look my last,*
> *And though shouldst smile no more!"*

"I cannot—" She falters. "I do not know—any such feelings—so strong—existed any longer."

"Now You do, Lady of Ours. And is that not an important datum for SUM?"

"Yes. If true." Abruptly She leans toward me. I see Her shudder in the murk, under the flapping cloak, and hear Her jaws clatter with cold. "I cannot linger here. But ride with Me. Sing to Me. I think I can bear it."

So much have I scarcely expected. But my destiny is upon me. I mount into the chariot. The canopy slides shut and we proceed.

The main cabin encloses us. Behind its rear door must be facilities for Her living on earth; this is a big vehicle. But here is little except curved panels. They are true wood of different comely grains: so She also needs periodic escape from our machine existence, does She? Furnishing is scant and austere. The only sound is our passage, muffled to a murmur for us; and, because their photo-multipliers are not activated, the scanners show nothing outside but night. We huddle close to a glower, hands extended toward its fieriness. Our shoulders brush, our bare arms, Her skin is soft and Her hair falls loose over the thrown-back cowl, smelling of the summer which is dead. What, is She still human?

After a timeless time, She says, not yet looking at me: "The thing you sang, there on the highroad as I came near—I do not remember it. Not even from the years before I became what I am."

"It is older than SUM," I answer, "and its truth will outlive It."

"Truth?" I see Her tense Herself. "Sing Me the rest."

My fingers are no longer too numb to call forth chords.

> *"—Unto the Death gois all Estatis,*
> *Princis, Prelattis, and Potestatis,*
> *Baith rich and poor of all degree:—*
> Timor mortis conturbat me.

> "He takis the knichtis in to the field
> Enarmit under helm and scheild;
> Victor he is at all mellie: —
> Timor mortis conturbat me.
>
> "That strong unmerciful tyrand
> Takis, on the motheris breast
> sowkand,
> The babe full of benignitie: —
> Timor mortis conturbat me.
>
> "He takis the campion in the stour,
> The captain closit in the tour,
> The ladie in bour full of bewtie: — "

(There I must stop a moment.)

> "Timor mortis conturbat me.
>
> "He sparis no lord for his piscence,
> Na clerk for his intelligence;
> His awful straik may no man flee: —
> Timor mortis conturbat me."

She breaks me off; clapping hands to ears and half shrieking, "No!"

I, grown unmerciful, pursue Her: "You understand now, do You not? You are not eternal either. SUM isn't. Not Earth, not sun, not stars. We hid from the truth. Every one of us. I too, until I lost the one thing which made everything make sense. Then I had nothing left to lose, and could look with clear eyes. And what I saw was Death."

"Get out! Let Me alone!"

"I will not let the whole world alone, Queen, until I get her back. Give me her again, and I'll believe in SUM again. I'll praise It till men dance for joy to hear Its name."

She challenges me with wildcat eyes. "Do you think such matters to It?"

"Well," I shrug, "songs could be useful. They could help achieve the great objective sooner. Whatever that is. 'Optimization of total human activity'—wasn't that the program? I don't know if it still is. SUM has been adding to Itself so long. I doubt if You Yourself understand Its purpose, Lady of Ours."

"Don't speak as if It were alive," She says harshly. "It is a computer-effector complex. Nothing more."

"Are You certain?"

"I—yes. It thinks, more widely and deeply than any human ever did or could; but It is not alive, not aware, It has no consciousness. That is one reason why It decided It needed Me."

"Be that as it may, Lady," I tell Her, "the ultimate result, whatever It finally does with us, lies far in the future. At present I care about that; I worry; I resent our loss of self-determination. But that's because only such abstractions are left to me. Give me back my Lightfoot, and she, not the distant future, will be my concern. I'll be grateful, honestly grateful, and You Two will know it from the songs I then choose to sing. Which, as I said, might be helpful to It."

"You are unbelievably insolent," She says without force.

"No, Lady, just desperate," I say.

The ghost of a smile touches Her lips. She leans back, eyes hooded, and murmurs, "Well, I'll take you there. What happens then, you realize, lies outside My power. My observations, My recommendations, are nothing but a few items to take into account, among billions. However . . . we have a long way to travel this night. Give me what data you think will help you, Harper."

I do not finish the Lament. Nor do I dwell in any other fashion on grief. Instead, as the hours pass, I call upon those who dealt with the joy (not the fun, not the short delirium, but the joy) that man and woman might once have of each other.

Knowing where we are bound, I too need such comfort.

And the night deepens, and the leagues fall behind us, and finally we are beyond habitation, beyond wildcountry, in the land where life never comes. By crooked moon and waning starlight I see the plain of concrete and iron, the missiles and energy projectors crouched like beasts, the robot aircraft wheeling aloft: and the lines, the relay towers, the scuttling beetle-shaped carriers, that whole transcendent nerve-blood-sinew by which SUM knows and orders the world. For all the flitting about, for all the forces which seethe, here is altogether still. The wind itself seems to have frozen to death. Hoarfrost is gray on the steel shapes. Ahead of us, tiered and mountainous, begins to appear the castle of SUM.

She Who rides with me does not give sign of noticing that my songs have died in my throat. What humanness She showed is departing; Her face is cold and shut, Her voice bears a ring of metal. She looks straight ahead. But She does speak to me for a little while yet:

"Do you understand what is going to happen? For the next half year I will be linked with SUM, integral, another component of It. I suppose you will see Me, but that will merely be My flesh. What speaks to you will be SUM."

"I know." The words must be forced forth. My coming this far is more triumph than any man in creation before me has won; and I am here to do battle for my Dancer-on-Moonglades; but nonetheless my heart shakes me, and is loud in my skull, and my sweat stinks.

I manage, though, to add: "You *will* be a part of It, Lady of Ours. That gives me hope."

For an instant She turns to me, and lays Her hand across mine, and something makes Her again so young and untaken that I almost forget the girl who died; and she whispers, "If you knew how I hope!"

The instant is gone, and I am alone among machines.

We must stop before the castle gate. The wall looms sheer above, so high and high that it seems to be toppling upon me against the westward march of the stars, so black and black that it does not only drink down every light, it radiates blindness. Challenge and response quiver on electronic bands I cannot sense. The outer-guardian parts of It have perceived a mortal aboard this craft. A missile launcher swings about to aim its three serpents at me. But the Dark Queen answers— She does not trouble to be peremptory—and the castle opens its jaws for us.

We descend. Once, I think, we cross a river. I hear a rushing and hollow echoing and see droplets glitter where they are cast onto the viewports and outlined against dark. They vanish at once: liquid hydrogen, perhaps, to keep certain parts near absolute zero?

Much later we stop and the canopy slides back. I rise with Her. We are in a room, or cavern, of which I can see nothing, for there is no light except a dull bluish phosphorescence which streams from every solid object, also from Her flesh and mine. But I judge the chamber is enormous, for a sound of great machines at work comes very remotely, as if heard through dream, while our own voices are swallowed up by distance. Air is pumped through, neither warm nor cold, totally without odor, a dead wind.

We descend to the floor. She stands before me, hands crossed on breast, eyes half shut beneath the cowl and not looking at me nor away from me. "Do what you are told, Harper," She says in a voice that has never an overtone, "precisely as you are told." She turns and departs at an even pace. I watch Her go until I can no longer tell Her luminosity from the formless swirlings within my own eyeballs.

A claw plucks my tunic. I look down and am surprised to see that the dwarf robot has been waiting for me this whole time. How long a time that was, I cannot tell.

Its squat form leads me in another direction. Weariness crawls upward through me, my feet stumble, my lips tingle, lids are weighted and muscles have each their separate aches. Now and then I feel a jag of fear, but dully. When the robot indicates *Lie down here*, I am grateful.

The box fits me well. I let various wires be attached to me, various needles be injected which lead into tubes. I pay little attention to the machines which cluster and murmur around me. The robot goes away. I sink into blessed darkness.

I wake renewed in body. A kind of shell seems to have grown between my forebrain and the old animal parts. Far away I can feel the horror and hear the screaming and thrashing of my instincts; but awareness is chill, calm, logical. I have also a feeling that I slept for weeks, months, while leaves blew loose and snow fell on the upper world. But this may be wrong, and in no case does it matter. I am about to be judged by SUM.

The little faceless robot leads me off, through murmurous black corridors where the dead wind blows. I unsling my harp and clutch it to me, my sole friend and weapon. So the tranquility of the reasoning mind which has been decreed for me cannot be absolute. I decide that It simply does not want to be bothered by anguish. (No; wrong; nothing so humanlike; It has no desires; beneath that power to reason is nullity.)

At length a wall opens for us and we enter a room where She sits enthroned. The self-radiation of metal and flesh is not apparent here, for light is provided, a featureless white radiance with no apparent source. White, too, is the muted sound of the machines which encompass Her throne. White are Her robe and face. I look away from the multitudinous unwinking scanner eyes, into Hers, but She does not appear to recognize me. Does She even see me? SUM has reached out with invisible fingers of electromagnetic induction and taken Her back into Itself. I do not tremble or sweat—I cannot—but I square my shoulders, strike one plangent chord, and wait for It to speak.

It does, from some invisible place. I recognize the voice It has chosen to use: my own. The overtones, the inflections are true, normal, what I myself would use in talking as one reasonable man to another. Why not? In computing what to do about me, and in programming Itself accordingly, SUM must have used so many billion bits of information that adequate accent is a negligible subproblem.

No . . . there I am mistaken again . . . SUM does not do things on the basis that It might as well do them as not. This talk with myself is intended to have some effect on me. I do not know what.

"Well," It says pleasantly, "you made quite a journey, didn't you? I'm glad. Welcome."

My instincts bare teeth to hear those words of humanity used by the unfeeling unalive. My logical mind considers replying with an ironic "Thank you," decides against it, and holds me silent.

"You see," SUM continues after a moment that whirrs, "you are unique. Pardon Me if I speak a little bluntly. Your sexual monomania is just one aspect of a generally atavistic, superstition-oriented personality. And yet, unlike the ordinary misfit, you're both strong and realistic enough to cope with the world. This chance to meet you, to analyze you while you rested, has opened new insights for Me on human psychophysiology. Which may lead to improved techniques for governing it and its evolution."

"That being so," I reply, "give me my reward."

"Now look here," SUM says in a mild tone, "you if anyone should know I'm not omnipotent. I was built originally to help govern a civilization grown too complex. Gradually, as My program of self-expansion progressed, I took over more and more decision-making functions. They were *given* to Me. People were happy to be relieved of responsibility, and they could see for themselves how much better I was running things than any mortal could. But to this day, My authority depends on a substantial consensus. If I started playing favorites, as by re-creating your girl, well, I'd have troubles."

"The consensus depends more on awe than on reason," I say. "You haven't abolished the gods, You've simply absorbed them into Yourself. If You choose to pass a miracle for me, your prophet singer—and I will be Your prophet if You do this—why, that strengthens the faith of the rest."

"So you think. But your opinions aren't based on any exact data. The historical and anthropological records from the past before Me are unquantitative. I've already phased them out of the curriculum. Eventually, when the culture's ready for such a move, I'll order them destroyed. They're too misleading. Look what they've done to you."

I grin into the scanner eyes. "Instead," I say, "people will be encouraged to think that before the world was, was SUM. All right. I don't care, as long as I get my girl back. Pass me a miracle, SUM, and I'll guarantee You a good payment."

"But I have no miracles. Not in your sense. You know how the soul works. The metal bracelet encloses a pseudovirus, a set of giant protein molecules with taps directly to the bloodstream and nervous system. They record the chromosome pattern, the synapse flash, the permanent changes, everything. At the owner's death, the bracelet is dissected out. The Winged Heels bring it here, and the information contained is transferred to one of My memory banks. I can use such a record to guide the growing of a new body in the vats: a young body, on which the former habits and recollections are imprinted. But you don't understand the complexity of the process, Harper. It takes Me weeks, every seven years, and every available biochemical facility, to re-create My human liaison. And the process isn't perfect, either. The pattern is affected by storage. You might say that this body and brain you see before you remembers each death. And those are short deaths. A longer one—man, use your sense. Imagine."

I can; and the shield between reason and feeling begins to crack. I had sung, of my darling dead,

> "No motion has she now, no force;
> She neither hears nor sees;
> Roll'd round in earth's diurnal course,
> With rocks, and stones, and trees."

Peace, at least. But if the memory-storage is not permanent but circulating; if, within those gloomy caverns of tubes and wire and outerspace cold, some remnant of her psyche must flit and flicker, alone, unremembering, aware of nothing but having lost life—No!

I smite the harp and shout so the room rings: "Give her back! Or I'll kill you!"

SUM finds it expedient to chuckle; and, horribly, the smile is reflected for a moment on the Dark Queen's lips, though otherwise She never stirs. "And how do you propose to do that?" It asks me.

It knows, I know, what I have in mind, so I counter: "How do You propose to stop me?"

"No need. You'll be considered a nuisance. Finally someone will decide you ought to have psychiatric treatment. They'll query My diagnostic outlet. I'll recommend certain excisions."

"On the other hand, since You've sifted my mind by now, and since You know how I've affected people with my songs—even the Lady yonder, even Her— wouldn't you rather have me working for You? With words like, 'O taste, and see, how gracious the Lord is; blessed is the man that trusteth in him. O fear the Lord, ye that are his saints; for they that fear him lack nothing.' I can make You into God."

"In a sense, I already am God."

"And in another sense not. Not yet." I can endure no more. "Why are we arguing? You made Your decision before I woke. Tell me and let me go!"

With an odd carefulness, SUM responds: "I'm still studying you. No harm in admitting to you, My knowledge of the human psyche is as yet imperfect. Certain areas won't yield to computation. I don't know precisely what you'd do, Harper. If to that uncertainty I added a potentially dangerous precedent—"

"Kill me, then." Let my ghost wander forever with hers, down in Your cryogenic dreams.

"No, that's also inexpedient. You've made yourself too conspicuous and controversial. Too many people know by now that you went off with the Lady." Is it possible that, behind steel and energy, a nonexistent hand brushes across a shadow face in puzzlement? My heartbeat is thick in the silence.

Suddenly It shakes me with decision: "The calculated probabilities do favor your keeping your promises and making yourself useful. Therefore I shall grant your request. However—"

I am on my knees. My forehead knocks on the floor until blood runs into my eyes. I hear through storm winds:

"—testing must continue. Your faith in Me is not absolute; in fact, you're very skeptical of what you call My goodness. Without additional proof of your willingness to trust Me, I can't let you have the kind of importance which your getting your dead back from Me would give you. Do you understand?"

The question does not sound rhetorical. "Yes," I sob.

"Well, then," says my civilized, almost amiable voice, "I computed that you'd react much as you have done, and prepared for the likelihood. Your woman's body was re-created while you lay under study. The data which make personality are now being fed back into her neurones. She'll be ready to leave this place by the time you do.

"I repeat, though, there has to be a testing. The procedure is also necessary for its effect on you. If you're to be My prophet, you'll have to work pretty closely with Me; you'll have to undergo a great deal of reconditioning; this night we begin the process. Are you willing?"

"Yes, yes, yes, what must I do?"

"Only this: Follow the robot out. At some point, she, your woman, will join you. She'll be conditioned to walk so quietly you can't hear her. Don't look back. Not once, until you're in the upper world. A single glance behind you will be an act of rebellion against Me, and a datum indicating you can't really be trusted . . . and that ends everything. Do you understand?"

"Is that all?" I cry. "Nothing more?"

"It will prove more difficult than you think," SUM tells me. My voice fades, as if into illimitable distances: "Farewell, worshipper."

The robot raises me to my feet, I stretch out my arms to the Dark Queen. Half blinded with tears, I nonetheless see that She does not see me. "Good-bye," I mumble, and let the robot lead me away.

Our walking is long through those mirk miles. At first I am in too much of a turmoil, and later too stunned, to know where or how we are bound. But later still, slowly, I become aware of my flesh and clothes and the robot's alloy, glimmering blue in blackness. Sounds and smells are muffled; rarely does another machine pass by, unheeding of us. (What work does SUM have for them?) I am so careful not to look behind me that my neck grows stiff.

Though it is not prohibited, is it, to lift my harp past my shoulder, in the course of strumming a few melodies to keep up my courage, and see if perchance a following illumination is reflected in this polished wood?

Nothing. Well, her second birth must take time—O SUM, be careful of her!— and then she must be led through many tunnels, no doubt, before she makes rendezvous with my back. Be patient, Harper.

Sing. Welcome her home. No, these hollow spaces swallow all music; and she is as yet in that trance of death from which only the sun and my kiss can wake her; if, indeed, she has joined me yet. I listen for other footfalls than my own.

Surely we haven't much farther to go. I ask the robot, but of course I get no reply. Make an estimate. I know about how fast the chariot traveled coming down. . . . The trouble is, time does not exist here. I have no day, no stars, no clock but my heartbeat, and I have lost the count of that. Nevertheless, we must come to the end soon. What purpose would be served by walking me through this labyrinth till I die?

Well, if I am totally exhausted at the outer gate, I won't make undue trouble when I find no Rose-in-Hand behind me.

No, now that's ridiculous. If SUM didn't want to heed my plea, It need merely say so. I have no power to inflict physical damage on Its parts.

Of course, It might have plans for me. It did speak of reconditioning. A series of shocks, culminating in that last one, could make me ready for whatever kind of gelding It intends to do.

Or It might have changed Its mind. Why now? It was quite frank about an uncertainty factor in the human psyche. It may have reevaluated the probabilities and decided: better not to serve my desire.

Or It may have tried, and failed. It admitted the recording process is imperfect. I must not expect quite the Gladness I knew; she will always be a little haunted. At best. But suppose the tank spawned a body with no awareness behind the eyes? Or a monster? Suppose, at this instant, I am being followed by a half-rotten corpse?

No! Stop that! SUM would know, and take corrective measures.

Would It? *Can It?*

I comprehend how this passage through night, where I never look to see what follows me, how this is an act of submission and confession. I am saying, with my whole existent being, that SUM is all-powerful, all-wise, all-good. To SUM I offer the love I came to win back. Oh, It looked more deeply into me than ever I did myself.

But I shall not fail.

Will SUM, though? If there has indeed been some grisly error . . . let me not find it out under the sky. Let her, my only, not. For what then shall we do? Could I lead her here again, knock on the iron gate, and cry, "Master, You have given me a thing unfit to exist. Destroy it and start over."—? For what might the wrongness be? Something so subtle, so pervasive, that it does not show in any way save my slow, resisted discovery that I embrace a zombie? Doesn't it make better sense to look—make certain while she is yet drowsy with death— use the whole power of SUM to correct what may be awry?

No, SUM wants me to believe that It makes no mistakes. I agreed to that price. And to much else . . . I don't know how much else, I am daunted to imagine, but that word "recondition" is ugly. . . . Does not my woman have some rights in the matter too? Shall we not at least ask her if she wants to be the wife of a prophet; shall we not, hand in hand, ask SUM what the price of her life is to her?

Was that a footfall? Almost, I whirl about. I check myself and stand shaking; names of hers break from my lips. The robot urges me on.

Imagination. It wasn't her step. I am alone. I will always be alone.

The halls wind upward. Or so I think; I have grown too weary for much kinesthetic sense. We cross the sounding river and I am bitten to the bone by the cold which blows upward around the bridge, and I may not turn about to offer the naked newborn woman my garment. I lurch through endless chambers where machines do meaningless things. She hasn't seen them before. Into what nightmare has she risen; and why don't I, who wept into her dying sense that I loved her, why don't I look at her, why don't I speak?

Well, I could talk to her. I could assure the puzzled mute dead that I have come to lead her back into sunlight. Could I not? I ask the robot. It does not reply. I cannot remember if I may speak to her. If indeed I was ever told. I stumble forward.

I crash into a wall and fall bruised. The robot's claw closes on my shoulder. Another arm gestures. I see a passageway, very long and narrow, through the stone. I will have to crawl through. At the end, at the end, the door is swinging wide. The dear real dusk of Earth pours through into this darkness. I am blinded and deafened.

Do I hear her cry out? Was that the final testing; or was my own sick, shaken mind betraying me; is there a destiny which, like SUM with us, makes tools of suns and SUM? I don't know. I know only that I turned, and there she stood. Her hair flowed long, loose, past the remembered face from which the trance was just departing, on which the knowing and the love of me had just awakened—flowed down over the body that reached forth arms, that took one step to meet me and was halted.

The great grim robot at her own back takes her to it. I think it sends lightning through her brain. She falls. It bears her away.

My guide ignores my screaming. Irresistible, it thrusts me out through the tunnel. The door clangs in my face. I stand before the wall which is like a mountain. Dry snow hisses across concrete. The sky is bloody with dawn; stars still gleam in the west, and arc lights are scattered over the twilit plain of the machines.

Presently I go dumb. I become almost calm. What is there left to have feelings about? The door is iron, the wall is stone fused into one basaltic mass. I walk some distance off into the wind, turn around, lower my head, and charge. Let my brains be smeared across Its gate; the pattern will be my hieroglyphic for hatred.

I am seized from behind. The force that stops me must needs be bruisingly great. Released, I crumple to the ground before a machine with talons and wings. My voice from it says, "Not here. I'll carry you to a safe place."

"What more can You do to me?" I croak.

"Release you. You won't be restrained or molested on any orders of Mine."

"Why not?"

"Obviously you're going to appoint yourself My enemy forever. This is an unprecedented situation, a valuable chance to collect data."

"You tell me this, You warn me, deliberately?"

"Of course. My computation is that these words will have the effect of provoking your utmost effort."

"You won't give her again? You don't want my love?"

"Not under the circumstances. Too uncontrollable. But your hatred should, as I say, be a useful experimental tool."

"I'll destroy You," I say.

It does not deign to speak further. Its machine picks me up and flies off with me. I am left on the fringes of a small town farther south. Then I go insane.

I do not much know what happens during that winter, nor care. The blizzards are too loud in my head. I walk the ways of Earth, among lordly towers, under neatly groomed trees, into careful gardens, over bland, bland campuses. I am unwashed, uncombed, unbarbered; my tatters flap about me and my bones are near thrusting through the skin; folk do not like to meet these eyes sunken so far into this skull, and perhaps for that reason they give me to eat. I sing to them.

> "From the hag and hungry goblin
> That into rags would rend ye
> And the spirit that stan' by the naked man
> In the Book of Moons defend ye!
> That of your five sound senses
> You never be forsaken
> Nor travel from yourselves with Tom
> Abroad to beg your bacon."

Such things perturb them, do not belong in their chrome-edged universe. So I am often driven away with curses, and sometimes I must flee those who would arrest me and scrub my brain smooth. An alley is a good hiding place, if I can find one in the oldest part of a city; I crouch there and yowl with the cats. A forest is also good. My pursuers dislike to enter any place where any wildness lingers.

But some feel otherwise. They have visited parklands, preserves, actual wild-country. Their purpose was overconscious—measured, planned savagery, and a clock to tell them when they must go home—but at least they are not afraid of silences and unlighted nights. As spring returns, certain among them begin to follow me. They are merely curious, at first. But slowly, month by month, especially among the younger ones, my madness begins to call to something in them.

> *"With an host of furious fancies*
> *Whereof I am commander*
> *With a burning spear, and a horse of air,*
> *To the wilderness I wander.*
> *By a knight of ghosts and shadows*
> *I summoned am to tourney*
> *Ten leagues beyond the wild world's edge.*
> *Me thinks it is no journey."*

They sit at my feet and listen to me sing. They dance, crazily, to my harp. The girls bend close, tell me how I fascinate them, invite me to copulate. This I refuse, and when I tell them why they are puzzled, a little frightened maybe, but often they strive to understand.

For my rationality is renewed with the hawthorn blossoms. I bathe, have my hair and beard shorn, find clean raiment, and take care to eat what my body needs. Less and less do I rave before anyone who will listen; more and more do I seek solitude, quietness, under the vast wheel of the stars, and think.

What is man? Why is man? We have buried such questions; we have sworn they are dead—that they never really existed, being devoid of empirical meaning—and we have dreaded that they might raise the stones we heaped on them, rise and walk the world again of nights. Alone, I summon them to me. They cannot hurt their fellow dead, among whom I now number myself.

I sing to her who is gone. The young people hear and wonder. Sometimes they weep.

> *"Fear no more the heat o' the sun,*
> *Nor the furious winter's rages;*
> *Thou thy worldly task hast done,*
> *Home art gone, and ta'en thy wages:*
> *Golden lads and girls all must*
> *As chimney-sweepers, come to dust."*

"But this is not so!" they protest. "We will die and sleep a while, and then we will live forever in SUM."

I answer as gently as may be: "No. Remember I went there. So I know you are wrong. And even if you were right, it would not be right that you should be right."

"What?"

"Don't you see, it is not right that a thing should be the lord of man. It is not right that we should huddle through our whole lives in fear of finally losing them. You are not parts in a machine, and you have better ends than helping the machine run smoothly."

I dismiss them and stride off, solitary again, into a canyon where a river clangs, or onto some gaunt mountain peak. No revelation is given me. I climb and creep toward the truth.

Which is that SUM must be destroyed, not in revenge, not in hate, not in fear, simply because the human spirit cannot exist in the same reality as It.

But what, then, is our proper reality? And how shall we attain it?

I return with my songs to the lowlands. Word about me has gone widely. They are a large crowd who follow me down the highroad until it has changed into a street.

"The Dark Queen will soon come to these parts," they tell me. "Abide till She does. Let Her answer those questions you put to us, which make us sleep so badly."

"Let me retire to prepare myself," I say. I go up a long flight of steps. The people watch from below, dumb with awe, till I vanish. Such few as were in the building depart. I walk down vaulted halls, through hushed high-ceilinged rooms full of tables, among shelves made massive by books. Sunlight slants dusty through the windows.

The half memory has plagued me of late: once before, I know not when, this year of mine also took place. Perhaps in this library I can find the tale that— casually, I suppose, in my abnormal childhood—I read. For man is older than SUM: wiser, I swear; his myths hold more truth than Its mathematics. I spend three days and most of three nights in my search. There is scant sound but the rustling of leaves between my hands. Folk place offerings of food and drink at the door. They tell themselves they do so out of pity, or curiosity, or to avoid the nuisance of having me die in an unconventional fashion. But I know better.

At the end of the three days I am little further along. I have too much material; I keep going off on sidetracks of beauty and fascination. (Which SUM means to eliminate.) My Education was like everyone else's, science, rationality, good sane adjustment. (SUM writes our curricula, and the teaching machines have direct connections to It.) Well, I can make some of my lopsided training work for me. My reading has given me sufficient clues to prepare a search program. I sit down before an information retrieval console and run my fingers across its keys. They make a clattery music.

Electron beams are swift hounds. Within seconds the screen lights up with words, and I read who I am.

It is fortunate that I am a fast reader. Before I can press the Clear button, the unreeling words are wiped out. For an instant the screen quivers with form-lessness, then appears

I HAD NOT CORRELATED THESE DATA WITH THE FACTS CONCERNING YOU. THIS INTRODUCES A NEW AND INDETERMINATE QUANTITY INTO THE COMPUTATIONS.

The nirvana which has come upon me (yes, I found that word among the old books, and how portentous it is) is not passiveness, it is a tide more full and strong than that which bore me down to the Dark Queen those ages apast in wildcountry. I say, as coolly as may be, "An interesting coincidence. If it is a coincidence." Surely sonic receptors are emplaced hereabouts.

EITHER THAT, OR A CERTAIN NECESSARY CONSEQUENCE OF THE
LOGIC OF EVENTS.

The vision dawning within me is so blinding bright that I cannot refrain from answering, "Or a destiny, SUM?"

MEANINGLESS. MEANINGLESS. MEANINGLESS.

"Now why did You repeat Yourself in that way? Once would have sufficed. Thrice, though, makes an incantation. Are You by any chance hoping Your words will make me stop existing?"

I DO NOT HOPE. YOU ARE AN EXPERIMENT. IF I COMPUTE A SIGNIFICANT
PROBABILITY OF YOUR CAUSING SERIOUS DISTURBANCE, I WILL HAVE YOU
TERMINATED.

I smile. "SUM," I say, "I am going to terminate You." I lean over and switch off the screen. I walk out into the evening.

Not everything is clear to me yet, that I must say and do. But enough is that I can start preaching at once to those who have been waiting for me. As I talk, others come down the street, and hear, and stay to listen. Soon they number in the hundreds.

I have no immense new truth to offer them: nothing that I have not said before, although piecemeal and unsystematically; nothing they have not felt themselves, in the innermost darkness of their beings. Today, however, knowing who I am and therefore why I am, I can put these things in words. Speaking quietly, now and then drawing on some forgotten song to show my meaning, I tell them how sick and starved their lives are; how they have made themselves slaves; how the enslavement is not even to a conscious mind, but to an insensate inanimate thing which their own ancestors began; how that thing is not the centrum of existence, but a few scraps of metal and bleats of energy, a few sad stupid patterns, adrift in unbounded space-time. Put not your faith in SUM, I tell them. SUM is doomed, even as you and I. Seek out mystery; what else is the whole cosmos but mystery? Live bravely, die and be done, and you will be more than any machine. You may perhaps be God.

They grow tumultuous. They shout replies, some of which are animal howls. A few are for me, most are opposed. That doesn't matter. I have reached into them, my music is being played on their nervestrings, and this is my entire purpose.

The sun goes down behind the buildings. Dusk gathers. The city remains unilluminated. I soon realize why. She is coming, the Dark Queen Whom they wanted me to debate with. From afar we hear Her chariot thunder. Folk wail in terror. They are not wont to do that either. They used to disguise their feelings from Her and themselves by receiving Her with grave sparse ceremony. Now they would flee if they dared. I have lifted the masks.

The chariot halts in the street. She dismounts, tall and shadowy cowled. The people make way before Her like water before a shark. She climbs the stairs to face me. I see for the least instant that Her lips are not quite firm and Her eyes abrim with tears. She whispers, too low for anyone else to hear, "Oh, Harper, I'm sorry."

"Come join me," I invite. "Help me set the world free."

"No. I cannot. I have been too long with It." She straightens. Imperium descends upon Her. Her voice rises for everyone to hear. The little television robots flit close, bat shapes in the twilight, that the whole planet may witness my defeat. "What is this freedom you rant about?" She demands.

"To feel," I say. "To venture. To wonder. To become men again."

"To become beasts, you mean. Would you demolish the machines that keep us alive?"

"Yes. We must. Once they were good and useful, but we let them grow upon us like a cancer, and now nothing but destruction and a new beginning can save us."

"Have you considered the chaos?"

"Yes. It too is necessary. We will not be men without the freedom to know suffering. In it is also enlightenment. Through it we travel beyond ourselves, beyond earth and stars, space and time, to Mystery."

"So you maintain that there is some undefined ultimate vagueness behind the measurable universe?" She smiles into the bat eyes. We have each been taught, as children, to laugh on hearing sarcasms of this kind. "Please offer me a little proof."

"No," I say. "Prove to me instead, beyond any doubt, that there is *not* something we cannot understand with words and equations. Prove to me likewise that I have no right to seek for it."

"The burden of proof is on You Two, so often have You lied to us. In the name of rationality, You resurrected myth. The better to control us! In the name of liberation, You chained our inner lives and castrated our souls. In the name of service, You bound and blinkered us. In the name of achievement, You held us to a narrower round than any swine in its pen. In the name of beneficence, You created pain, and horror, and darkness beyond darkness." I turn to the people. "I went there. I descended into the cellars. I know!"

"He found that SUM would not pander to his special wishes, at the expense of everyone else," cries the Dark Queen. Do I hear shrillness in Her voice? "Therefore he claims SUM is cruel."

"I saw my dead," I tell them. "She will not rise again. Nor yours, nor you. Not ever. SUM will not, cannot raise us. In Its house is death indeed. We must seek life and rebirth elsewhere, among the mysteries."

She laughs aloud and points to my soul bracelet, glimmering faintly in the gray-blue thickening twilight. Need She say anything?

"Will someone give me a knife and an ax?" I ask.

The crowd stirs and mumbles. I smell their fear. Streetlamps go on, as if they could scatter more than this corner of the night which is rolling upon us. I fold my arms and wait. The Dark Queen says something to me. I ignore Her.

The tools pass from hand to hand. He who brings them up the stairs comes like a flame. He kneels at my feet and lifts what I have desired. The tools are good ones, a broad-bladed hunting knife and a long double-bitted ax.

Before the world, I take the knife in my right hand and slash beneath the bracelet on my left wrist. The connections to my inner body are cut. Blood flows, impossibly brilliant under the lamps. It does not hurt; I am too exalted.

The Dark Queen shrieks. "You meant it! Harper, Harper!"

"There is no life in SUM," I say. I pull my hand through the circle and cast the bracelet down so it rings.

A voice of brass: *"Arrest that maniac for correction. He is deadly dangerous."*

The monitors who have stood on the fringes of the crowd try to push through. They are resisted. Those who seek to help them encounter fists and fingernails.

I take the ax and smash downward. The bracelet crumples. The organic material within, starved of my secretions, exposed to the night air, withers.

I raise the tools, ax in right hand, knife in bleeding left. "I seek eternity where it is to be found," I call. "Who goes with me?"

A score or better break loose from the riot, which is already calling forth weapons and claiming lives. They surround me with their bodies. Their eyes are the eyes of prophets. We make haste to seek a hiding place, for one military robot has appeared and others will not be long in coming. The tall engine strides to stand guard over Our Lady, and this is my last glimpse of Her.

My followers do not reproach me for having cost them all they were. They are mine. In me is the godhead which can do no wrong.

And the war is open, between me and SUM. My friends are few, my enemies many and mighty. I go about the world as a fugitive. But always I sing. And always I find someone who will listen, will join us, embracing pain and death like a lover.

With the Knife and the Ax I take their souls. Afterward we hold for them the ritual of rebirth. Some go thence to become outlaw missionaries; most put on facsimile bracelets and return home, to whisper my word. It makes little difference to me. I have no haste, who own eternity.

For my word is of what lies beyond time. My enemies say I call forth ancient bestialities and lunacies; that I would bring civilization down in ruin; that it matters not a madman's giggle to me whether war, famine, and pestilence will again scour the earth. With these accusations I am satisfied. The language of them shows me that here, too, I have reawakened anger. And that emotion belongs to us as much as any other. More than the others, maybe, in this autumn of mankind. We need a gale, to strike down SUM and everything It stands for. Afterward will come the winter of barbarism.

And after that the springtime of a new and (perhaps) more human civilization. My friends seem to believe this will come in their very lifetimes: peace, brotherhood, enlightenment, sanctity. I know otherwise. I have been in the depths. The wholeness of mankind, which I am bringing back, has its horrors.

When one day
    the Eater of the Gods returns
    the Wolf breaks his chain
    the Horsemen ride forth
    the Age ends
    the Beast is reborn
then SUM will be destroyed; and you, strong and fair, may go back to earth and rain.

I shall await you.

My aloneness is nearly ended, Daybright. Just one task remains. The god must die, that his followers may believe he is raised from the dead and lives forever. Then they will go on to conquer the world.

There are those who say I have spurned and offended them. They too, borne on the tide which I raised, have torn out their machine souls and seek in music and ecstasy to find a meaning for existence. But their creed is a savage one, which has taken them into wildcountry, where they ambush the monitors sent against them and practice cruel rites. They believe that the final reality is female. Nevertheless, messengers of theirs have approached me with the suggestion of a mystic marriage. This I refused; my wedding was long ago, and will be celebrated again when this cycle of the world has closed.

Therefore they hate me. But I have said I will come and talk to them.

I leave the road at the bottom of the valley and walk singing up the hill. Those few I let come this far with me have been told to abide my return. They shiver in the sunset; the vernal equinox is three days away. I feel no cold myself. I stride exultant among briars and twisted ancient apple trees. If my bare feet leave a little blood in the snow, that is good. The ridges around are dark with forest, which waits like the skeleton dead for leaves to be breathed across it again. The eastern sky is purple, where stands the evening star. Overhead, against blue, cruises an early flight of homebound geese. Their calls drift faintly down to me. Westward, above me and before me, smolders redness. Etched black against it are the women.

Jack London

Jack London (1876–1916) wrote enough science fiction to fill a substantial collection. This story is one of his best (his other high point is "The Red One") and certainly his most influential. It is in the tradition of the last man on Earth story, a subgenre that extends in fiction from Cousin de Grainville's *Le Dernier Homme* (1805), through Mary Shelley's *The Last Man* (1826) and M. P. Shiel's *The Purple Cloud* (1900), to George R. Stewart's *Earth Abides* (1950) and the many British SF disaster novels of the 1950s and '60s by John Wyndham, John Christopher, J. G. Ballard, and others.

London's story introduces a notable alteration in this tradition. Earlier stories show a Romantic resurgence of nature, crumbling buildings and beautiful natural vistas. London portrays the scientifically possible descent, perhaps devolution, of civilized humans into barbarism. It is an interesting contrast to Forster's "The Machine Stops." It is also one of the ancestors of the large-scale disaster novel, so much a feature of this century.

"There was a hidden side to primitivism," says Richard Gid Powers in his introduction to London's collected science fiction, *The Science Fiction of Jack London* (1975), "and that was a hatred of civilization, an almost pathological longing for a catastrophe that would sweep away civilization and restore the pre-Adamite ceremony of innocence—a will to believe that the future would be a restoration of a past that would eclipse the obscenities of the present." London's twin themes in his science fiction are Social Darwinism and revolutionary socialism. It seems possible that London's character of the Chauffeur (the dark side of J. M. Barrie's admirable Crichton) is a partial inspiration for the Boss in H. G. Wells's *Things to Come*.

THE SCARLET PLAGUE

I

The way led along upon what had once been the embankment of a railroad. But no train had run upon it for many years. The forest on either side swelled up the slopes of the embankment and crested across it in a green wave of trees and bushes. The trail was as narrow as a man's body, and was no more than a wild-animal runway. Occasionally, a piece of rusty iron, showing through the forest-mould, advertised that the rail and the ties still remained. In one place, a ten-inch tree, bursting through at a connection, had lifted the end of a rail clearly into view. The tie had evidently followed the rail, held to it by the spike long enough for its bed to be filled with gravel and rotten leaves, so that now the crumbling, rotten timber thrust itself up at a curious slant. Old as the road was, it was manifest that it had been of the mono-rail type.

An old man and a boy travelled along this runway. They moved slowly, for the old man was very old, a touch of palsy made his movements tremulous, and he leaned heavily upon his staff. A rude skull-cap of goat-skin protected his head from the sun. From beneath this fell a scant fringe of stained and dirty-white hair. A visor, ingeniously made from a large leaf, shielded his eyes, and from under this he peered at the way of his feet on the trail. His beard, which should have been snow-white but which showed the same weather-wear and camp-stain as his hair, fell nearly to his waist in a great tangled mass. About his chest and shoulders hung a single, mangy garment of goat-skin. His arms and legs, withered and skinny, betokened extreme age, as well as did their sunburn and scars and scratches betoken long years of exposure to the elements.

The boy, who led the way, checking the eagerness of his muscles to the slow progress of the elder, likewise wore a single garment—a ragged-edged piece of bear-skin, with a hole in the middle through which he had thrust his head. He could not have been more than twelve years old. Tucked coquettishly over one ear was the freshly severed tail of a pig. In one hand he carried a medium-sized bow and an arrow. On his back was a quiverful of arrows. From a sheath hanging about his neck on a thong projected the battered handle of a hunting knife. He was as brown as a berry, and walked softly, with almost a catlike tread. In marked contrast with his sunburned skin were his eyes—blue, deep blue, but keen and sharp as a pair of gimlets. They seemed to bore into all about him in a way that was habitual. As he went along he smelled things, as well, his distended, quivering nostrils carrying to his brain an endless series of messages from the outside world. Also, his hearing was acute, and had been so trained that it operated automatically. Without conscious effort, he heard all the slight sounds in the apparent quiet—heard, and differentiated, and classified these sounds—whether they were of the wind rustling the leaves, of the humming of bees and gnats, of the distant rumble of the sea that drifted to him only in lulls, or of the gopher, just under his foot, shoving a pouchful of earth into the entrance of his hole.

Suddenly he became alertly tense. Sound, sight, and odor had given him a simultaneous warning. His hand went back to the old man, touching him, and the pair stood still. Ahead, at one side of the top of the embankment, arose a crackling sound, and the boy's gaze was fixed on the tops of the agitated bushes. Then a large bear, a grizzly, crashed into view, and likewise stopped abruptly, at sight of the humans. He did not like them, and growled querulously. Slowly the boy fitted the arrow to the bow, and slowly he pulled the bowstring taut. But he never removed his eyes from the bear. The old man peered from under his green leaf at the danger, and stood as quietly as the boy. For a few seconds this mutual scrutinizing went on; then, the bear betraying a growing irritability, the boy, with a movement of his head, indicated that the old man must step aside from the trail and go down the embankment. The boy followed, going backward, still holding the bow taut and ready. They waited till a crashing among the bushes from the opposite side of the embankment told them the bear had gone on. The boy grinned as he led back to the trail.

"A big un, Granser," he chuckled.

The old man shook his head.

"They get thicker every day," he complained in a thin, undependable falsetto. "Who'd have thought I'd live to see the time when a man would be afraid of his life on the way to the Cliff House. When I was a boy, Edwin, men and women and little babies used to come out here from San Francisco by tens of thousands on a nice day. And there weren't any bears then. No, sir. They used to pay money to look at them in cages, they were that rare."

"What is money, Granser?"

Before the old man could answer, the boy recollected and triumphantly shoved his hand into a pouch under his bear-skin and pulled forth a battered and tarnished silver dollar. The old man's eyes glistened, as he held the coin close to them.

"I can't see," he muttered. "You look and see if you can make out the date, Edwin."

The boy laughed.

"You're a great Granser," he cried delightedly, "always making believe them little marks mean something."

The old man manifested an accustomed chagrin as he brought the coin back again close to his own eyes.

"2012," he shrilled, and then fell to cackling grotesquely. "That was the year Morgan the Fifth was appointed President of the United States by the Board of Magnates. It must have been one of the last coins minted, for the Scarlet Death came in 2013. Lord! Lord!—think of it! Sixty years ago, and I am the only person alive to-day that lived in those times. Where did you find it, Edwin?"

The boy, who had been regarding him with the tolerant curiousness one accords to the prattlings of the feeble-minded, answered promptly.

"I got it off of Hoo-Hoo. He found it when we was herdin' goats down near San José last spring. Hoo-Hoo said it was *money*. Ain't you hungry, Granser?"

The ancient caught his staff in a tighter grip and urged along the trail, his old eyes shining greedily.

"I hope Har-Lip's found a crab . . . or two," he mumbled. "They're good eating, crabs, mighty good eating when you've no more teeth and you've got grandsons that love their old grandsire and make a point of catching crabs for him. When I was a boy—"

But Edwin, suddenly stopped by what he saw, was drawing the bowstring on a fitted arrow. He had paused on the brink of a crevasse in the embankment. An ancient culvert had here washed out, and the stream, no longer confined, had cut a passage through the fill. On the opposite side, the end of a rail projected and overhung. It showed rustily through the creeping vines which overran it. Beyond, crouching by a bush, a rabbit looked across at him in trembling hesitancy. Fully fifty feet was the distance, but the arrow flashed true; and the transfixed rabbit, crying out in sudden fright and hurt, struggled painfully away into the brush. The boy himself was a flash of brown skin and flying fur as he bounded down the steep wall of the gap and up the other side. His lean muscles were springs of steel that released into graceful and efficient action. A hundred feet beyond, in a tangle of bushes, he overtook the wounded creature, knocked its head on a convenient tree-trunk, and turned it over to Granser to carry.

"Rabbit is good, very good," the ancient quavered, "but when it comes to a toothsome delicacy I prefer crab. When I was a boy—"

"Why do you say so much that ain't got no sense?" Edwin impatiently interrupted the other's threatened garrulousness.

The boy did not exactly utter these words, but something that remotely resembled them and that was more guttural and explosive and economical of qualifying phrases. His speech showed distant kinship with that of the old man, and the latter's speech was approximately an English that had gone through a bath of corrupt usage.

"What I want to know," Edwin continued, "is why you call crab 'toothsome delicacy'? Crab is crab, ain't it? No one I never heard calls it such funny things."

The old man sighed but did not answer, and they moved on in silence. The surf grew suddenly louder, as they emerged from the forest upon a stretch of sand dunes bordering the sea. A few goats were browsing among the sandy hillocks, and a skin-clad boy, aided by a wolfish-looking dog that was only faintly reminiscent of a collie, was watching them. Mingled with the roar of the surf was a continuous, deep-throated barking or bellowing, which came from a cluster of jagged rocks a hundred yards out from shore. Here huge sea-lions hauled themselves up to lie in the sun or battle with one another. In the immediate foreground arose the smoke of a fire, tended by a third savage-looking boy. Crouched near him were several wolfish dogs similar to the one that guarded the goats.

The old man accelerated his pace, sniffing eagerly as he neared the fire.

"Mussels!" he muttered ecstatically. "Mussels! And ain't that a crab, Hoo-Hoo? Ain't that a crab? My, my, you boys are good to your old grandsire."

Hoo-Hoo, who was apparently of the same age as Edwin, grinned.

"All you want, Granser. I got four."

The old man's palsied eagerness was pitiful. Sitting down in the sand as quickly as his stiff limbs would let him, he poked a large rock-mussel from out of the coals. The heat had forced its shells apart, and the meat, salmon-colored, was thoroughly cooked. Between thumb and forefinger, in trembling haste, he caught the morsel and carried it to his mouth. But it was too hot, and the next moment was violently ejected. The old man spluttered with the pain, and tears ran out of his eyes and down his cheeks.

The boys were true savages, possessing only the cruel humor of the savage. To them the incident was excruciatingly funny, and they burst into loud laughter. Hoo-Hoo danced up and down, while Edwin rolled gleefully on the ground. The boy with the goats came running to join in the fun.

"Set 'em to cool, Edwin, set 'em to cool," the old man besought, in the midst of his grief, making no attempt to wipe away the tears that still flowed from his eyes. "And cool a crab, Edwin, too. You know your grandsire likes crabs."

From the coals arose a great sizzling, which proceeded from the many mussels bursting open their shells and exuding their moisture. They were large shellfish, running from three to six inches in length. The boys raked them out with sticks and placed them on a large piece of driftwood to cool.

"When I was a boy, we did not laugh at our elders; we respected them."

The boys took no notice, and Granser continued to babble an incoherent flow of complaint and censure. But this time he was more careful, and did not burn his mouth. All began to eat, using nothing but their hands and making loud mouth-noises and lip-smackings. The third boy, who was called Hare-Lip, slyly deposited a pinch of sand on a mussel the ancient was carrying to his mouth; and when the grit of it bit into the old fellow's mucous membrane and gums, the laughter was again uproarious. He was unaware that a joke had been played on him, and spluttered and spat until Edwin, relenting, gave him a gourd of fresh water with which to wash out his mouth.

"Where's them crabs, Hoo-Hoo?" Edwin demanded. "Granser's set upon having a snack."

Again Granser's eyes burned with greediness as a large crab was handed to him. It was a shell with legs and all complete, but the meat had long since departed. With shaky fingers and babblings of anticipation, the old man broke off a leg and found it filled with emptiness.

"The crabs, Hoo-Hoo?" he wailed. "The crabs?"

"I was foolin', Granser. They ain't no crabs. I never found one."

The boys were overwhelmed with delight at sight of the tears of senile disappointment that dribbled down the old man's cheeks. Then, unnoticed, Hoo-Hoo replaced the empty shell with a fresh-cooked crab. Already dismembered, from the cracked legs the white meat sent forth a small cloud of savory steam. This attracted the old man's nostrils, and he looked down in amazement. The change of his mood to one of joy was immediate. He snuffled and muttered and mumbled, making almost a croon of delight, as he began to eat. Of this the boys took little notice, for it was an accustomed spectacle. Nor did they notice his occasional exclamations and utterances of phrases which meant nothing to them, as, for instance, when he smacked his lips and champed his gums while muttering: "Mayonnaise! Just think—mayonnaise! And it's sixty years since the last was ever made! Two generations and never a smell of it! Why, in those days it was served in every restaurant with crab."

When he could eat no more, the old man sighed, wiped his hands on his naked legs, and gazed out over the sea. With the content of a full stomach, he waxed reminiscent.

"To think of it! I've seen this beach alive with men, women, and children on a pleasant Sunday. And there weren't any bears to eat them up, either. And right up there on the cliff was a big restaurant where you could get anything you wanted to eat. Four million people lived in San Francisco then. And now, in the whole city and county there aren't forty all told. And out there on the sea were ships and ships always to be seen, going in for the Golden Gate or coming out. And airships in the air—dirigibles and flying machines. They could travel two hundred miles an hour. The mail contracts with the New York and San Francisco Limited demanded that for the minimum. There was a chap, a Frenchman, I forget his name, who succeeded in making three hundred; but the thing was risky, too risky for conservative persons. But he was on the right clew, and he would have managed it if it hadn't been for the Great Plague. When I was a boy, there were men alive who remembered the coming of the first aeroplanes, and now I have lived to see the last of them, and that sixty years ago."

The old man babbled on, unheeded by the boys, who were long accustomed to his garrulousness, and whose vocabularies, besides, lacked the greater portion of the words he used. It was noticeable that in these rambling soliloquies his English seemed to recrudesce into better construction and phraseology. But when he talked directly with the boys it lapsed, largely, into their own uncouth and simpler forms.

"But there weren't many crabs in those days," the old man wandered on. "They were fished out, and they were great delicacies. The open season was only a month long, too. And now crabs are accessible the whole year around. Think of it—catching all the crabs you want, any time you want, in the surf of the Cliff House beach!"

A sudden commotion among the goats brought the boys to their feet. The dogs about the fire rushed to join their snarling fellow who guarded the goats, while the goats themselves stampeded in the direction of their human protectors. A half dozen forms, lean and gray, glided about on the sand hillocks or faced the bristling dogs. Edwin arched an arrow that fell short. But Hare-Lip, with a sling such as David carried into battle against Goliath, hurled a stone through the air that whistled from the speed of its flight. It fell squarely among the wolves and caused them to slink away toward the dark depths of the eucalyptus forest.

The boys laughed and lay down again in the sand, while Granser sighed ponderously. He had eaten too much, and, with hands clasped on his paunch, the fingers interlaced, he resumed his maunderings.

" 'The fleeting systems lapse like foam,' " he mumbled what was evidently a quotation. "That's it—foam, and fleeting. All man's toil upon the planet was just so much foam. He domesticated the serviceable animals, destroyed the hostile ones, and cleared the land of its wild vegetation. And then he passed, and the flood of primordial life rolled back again, sweeping his handiwork away—the weeds and the forest inundated his fields, the beasts of prey swept over his flocks, and now there are wolves on the Cliff House beach." He was appalled by the thought. "Where four million people disported themselves, the wild wolves roam to-day, and the savage progeny of our loins, with prehistoric weapons, defend themselves against the fanged despoilers. Think of it! And all because of the Scarlet Death—"

The adjective had caught Hare-Lip's ear.

"He's always saying that," he said to Edwin. "What is *scarlet*?"

" 'The scarlet of the maples can shake me like the cry of bugles going by,' " the old man quoted.

"It's red," Edwin answered the question. "And you don't know it because you come from the Chauffeur Tribe. They never did know nothing, none of them. *Scarlet* is red—I know that."

"Red is red, ain't it?" Hare-Lip grumbled. "Then what's the good of gettin' cocky and calling it scarlet?"

"Granser, what for do you always say so much what nobody knows?" he asked. "Scarlet ain't anything, but red is red. Why don't you say red, then?"

"Red is not the right word," was the reply. "The plague was scarlet. The whole face and body turned scarlet in an hour's time. Don't I know? Didn't I see enough of it? And I am telling you it was scarlet because—well, because it *was* scarlet. There is no other word for it."

"Red is good enough for me," Hare-Lip muttered obstinately. "My dad calls red red, and he ought to know. He says everybody died of the Red Death."

"Your dad is a common fellow, descended from a common fellow," Granser retorted heatedly. "Don't I know the beginnings of the Chauffeurs? Your grandsire was a chauffeur, a servant, and without education. He worked for other persons. But your grandmother was of good stock, only the children did not take after her. Don't I remember when I first met them, catching fish at Lake Temescal?"

"What is *education*?" Edwin asked.

"Calling red scarlet," Hare-Lip sneered, then returned to the attack on Granser. "My dad told me, an' he got it from his dad afore he croaked, that your wife was a Santa Rosan, an' that she was sure no account. He said she was a *hash-slinger* before the Red Death, though I don't know what a *hash-slinger* is. You can tell me, Edwin."

But Edwin shook his head in token of ignorance.

"It is true, she was a waitress," Granser acknowledged. "But she was a good woman, and your mother was her daughter. Women were very scarce in the days after the Plague. She was the only wife I could find, even if she was a *hash-slinger*, as your father calls it. But it is not nice to talk about our progenitors that way."

"Dad says that the wife of the first Chauffeur was a *lady*—"

"What's a *lady?*" Hoo-Hoo demanded.

"A *lady's* a Chauffeur squaw," was the quick reply of Hare-Lip.

"The first Chauffeur was Bill, a common fellow, as I said before," the old man expounded; "but his wife was a lady, a great lady. Before the Scarlet Death she was the wife of Van Worden. He was President of the Board of Industrial Magnates, and was one of the dozen men who ruled America. He was worth one billion, eight hundred millions of dollars—coins like you have there in your pouch, Edwin. And then came the Scarlet Death, and his wife became the wife of Bill, the first Chauffeur. He used to beat her, too. I have seen it myself."

Hoo-Hoo, lying on his stomach and idly digging his toes in the sand, cried out and investigated, first, his toe-nail, and next, the small hole he had dug. The other two boys joined him, excavating the sand rapidly with their hands till there lay three skeletons exposed. Two were of adults, the third being that of a part-grown child. The old man hudged along on the ground and peered at the find.

"Plague victims," he announced. "That's the way they died everywhere in the last days. This must have been a family, running away from the contagion and perishing here on the Cliff House beach. They—what are you doing, Edwin?"

This question was asked in sudden dismay, as Edwin, using the back of his hunting knife, began to knock out the teeth from the jaws of one of the skulls.

"Going to string 'em," was the response.

The three boys were now hard at it; and quite a knocking and hammering arose, in which Granser babbled on unnoticed.

"You are true savages. Already has begun the custom of wearing human teeth. In another generation you will be perforating your noses and ears and wearing ornaments of bone and shell. I know. The human race is doomed to sink back farther and farther into the primitive night ere again it begins its bloody climb upward to civilization. When we increase and feel the lack of room, we will proceed to kill one another. And then I suppose you will wear human scalp-locks at your waist, as well—as you, Edwin, who are the gentlest of my grandsons, have already begun with that vile pigtail. Throw it away, Edwin, boy; throw it away."

"What a gabble the old geezer makes," Hare-Lip remarked, when, the teeth all extracted, they began an attempt at equal division.

They were very quick and abrupt in their actions, and their speech, in moments of hot discussion over the allotment of the choicer teeth, was truly a gabble. They spoke in monosyllables and short jerky sentences that was more a gibberish than a language. And yet, through it ran hints of grammatical construction, and appeared vestiges of the conjugation of some superior culture. Even the speech of Granser was so corrupt that were it put down literally it would be almost so much nonsense to the reader. This, however, was when he talked with the boys. When he got into the full swing of babbling to himself, it slowly purged itself into pure English. The sentences grew longer and were enunciated with a rhythm and ease that was reminiscent of the lecture platform.

"Tell us about the Red Death, Granser," Hare-Lip demanded, when the teeth affair had been satisfactorily concluded.

"The Scarlet Death," Edwin corrected.

"An' don't work all that funny lingo on us," Hare-Lip went on. "Talk sensible,

Granser, like a Santa Rosan ought to talk. Other Santa Rosans don't talk like you."

II

The old man showed pleasure in being thus called upon. He cleared his throat and began.

"Twenty or thirty years ago my story was in great demand. But in these days nobody seems interested—"

"There you go!" Hare-Lip cried hotly. "Cut out the funny stuff and talk sensible. What's *interested*? You talk like a baby that don't know how."

"Let him alone," Edwin urged, "or he'll get mad and won't talk at all. Skip the funny places. We'll catch on to some of what he tells us."

"Let her go, Granser," Hoo-Hoo encouraged; for the old man was already maundering about the disrespect for elders and the reversion to cruelty of all humans that fell from high culture to primitive conditions.

The tale began.

"There were very many people in the world in those days. San Francisco alone held four millions—"

"What is millions?" Edwin interrupted.

Granser looked at him kindly.

"I know you cannot count beyond ten, so I will tell you. Hold up your two hands. On both of them you have altogether ten fingers and thumbs. Very well. I now take this grain of sand—you hold it, Hoo-Hoo." He dropped the grain of sand into the lad's palm and went on. "Now that grain of sand stands for the ten fingers of Edwin. I add another grain. That's ten more fingers. And I add another, and another, and another, until I have added as many grains as Edwin has fingers and thumbs. That makes what I call one hundred. Remember that word—one hundred. Now I put this pebble in Hare-Lip's hand. It stands for ten grains of sand, or ten tens of fingers, or one hundred fingers. I put in ten pebbles. They stand for a thousand fingers. I take a mussel-shell, and it stands for ten pebbles, or one hundred grains of sand, or one thousand fingers. . . ."

And so on, laboriously, and with much reiteration, he strove to build up in their minds a crude conception of numbers. As the quantities increased, he had the boys holding different magnitudes in each of their hands. For still higher sums, he laid the symbols on the log of driftwood; and for symbols he was hard put, being compelled to use the teeth from the skulls for millions, and the crab-shells for billions. It was here that he stopped, for the boys were showing signs of becoming tired.

"There were four million people in San Francisco—four teeth."

The boys' eyes ranged along from the teeth and from hand to hand, down through the pebbles and sand-grains to Edwin's fingers. And back again they ranged along the ascending series in the effort to grasp such inconceivable numbers.

"That was a lot of folks, Granser," Edwin at last hazarded.

"Like sand on the beach here, like sand on the beach, each grain of sand a man, or woman, or child. Yes, my boy, all those people lived right here in San Francisco. And at one time or another all those people came out on this very beach—more people than there are grains of sand. More—more—more. And San Francisco was a noble city. And across the bay, where we camped last year, even more people lived, clear from Point Richmond, on the level ground and on the hills, all the way around to San Leandro—one great city of seven million people.—Seven teeth . . . there, that's it, seven millions."

Again the boys' eyes ranged up and down from Edwin's fingers to the teeth on the log.

"The world was full of people. The census of 2010 gave eight billions for the whole world—eight crab-shells, yes, eight billions. It was not like to-day. Mankind knew a great deal more about getting food. And the more food there was, the more people there were. In the year 1800, there were one hundred and seventy millions in Europe alone. One hundred years later—a grain of sand, Hoo-Hoo—one hundred years later, at 1900, there were five hundred millions in Europe—five grains of sand, Hoo-Hoo, and this one tooth. This shows how easy was the getting of food, and how men increased. And in the year 2000, there were fifteen hundred millions in Europe. And it was the same all over the rest of the world. Eight crab-shells there, yes, eight billion people were alive on the earth when the Scarlet Death began.

"I was a young man when the Plague came—twenty-seven years old—and I lived on the other side of San Francisco Bay, in Berkeley. You remember those great stone houses, Edwin, when we came down the hills from Contra Costa? That was where I lived, in those stone houses. I was a professor of English literature."

Much of this was over the heads of the boys, but they strove to comprehend dimly this tale of the past.

"What was them stone houses for?" Hare-Lip queried.

"You remember when your dad taught you to swim?" The boy nodded. "Well, in the University of California—that is the name we had for the houses—we taught young men and women how to think, just as I have taught you now, by sand and pebbles and shells, to know how many people lived in those days. There was very much to teach. The young men and women we taught were called students. We had large rooms in which we taught. I talked to them, forty or fifty at a time, just as I am talking to you now. I told them about the books other men had written before their time, and even, sometimes, in their time—"

"Was that all you did?—just talk, talk, talk?" Hoo-Hoo demanded. "Who hunted your meat for you? and milked the goats? and caught the fish?"

"A sensible question, Hoo-Hoo, a sensible question. As I have told you, in those days food-getting was easy. We were very wise. A few men got the food for many men. The other men did other things. As you say, I talked. I talked all the time, and for this food was given me—much food, fine food, beautiful food, food that I have not tasted in sixty years and shall never taste again. I sometimes think the most wonderful achievement of our tremendous civilization was food—its inconceivable abundance, its infinite variety, its marvellous delicacy. O my grandsons, life was life in those days, when we had such wonderful things to eat."

This was beyond the boys, and they let it slip by, words and thoughts, as a mere senile wandering in the narrative.

"Our food-getters were called *freemen*. This was a joke. We of the ruling classes owned all the land, all the machines, everything. These food-getters were our slaves. We took almost all the food they got, and left them a little so that they might eat, and work, and get us more food—"

"I'd have gone into the forest and got food for myself," Hare-Lip announced; "and if any man tried to take it away from me, I'd have killed him."

The old man laughed.

"Did I not tell you that we of the ruling class owned all the land, all the forest, everything? Any food-getter who would not get food for us, him we punished or compelled to starve to death. And very few did that. They preferred to get food for us, and make clothes for us, and prepare and administer to us a thousand—a mussel-shell, Hoo-Hoo—a thousand satisfactions and delights. And I was Professor Smith in those days—Professor James Howard Smith. And my lecture courses were very popular—that is, very many of the young men and women liked to hear me talk about the books other men had written.

"And I was very happy, and I had beautiful things to eat. And my hands were soft, because I did no work with them, and my body was clean all over and dressed in the softest garments—" He surveyed his mangy goat-skin with disgust. "We did not wear such things in those days. Even the slaves had better garments. And we were most clean. We washed our faces and hands often every day. You boys never wash unless you fall into the water or go in swimming."

"Neither do you, Granser," Hoo-Hoo retorted.

"I know, I know. I am a filthy old man. But times have changed. Nobody washes these days, and there are no conveniences. It is sixty years since I have seen a piece of soap. You do not know what soap is, and I shall not tell you, for I am telling the story of the Scarlet Death. You know what sickness is. We called it a disease. Very many of the diseases came from what we called germs. Remember that word—germs. A germ is a very small thing. It is like a woodtick, such as you find on the dogs in the spring of the year when they run in the forest. Only the germ is very small. It is so small that you cannot see it—"

Hoo-Hoo began to laugh.

"You're a queer un, Granser, talking about things you can't see. If you can't see 'em, how do you know they are? That's what I want to know. How do you know anything you can't see?"

"A good question, a very good question, Hoo-Hoo. But we did see—some of them. We had what we called microscopes and ultramicroscopes, and we put them to our eyes and looked through them, so that we saw things larger than they really were, and many things we could not see without the microscopes at all. Our best ultramicroscopes could make a germ look forty thousand times larger. A mussel-shell is a thousand fingers like Edwin's. Take forty mussel-shells, and by as many times larger was the germ when we looked at it through a microscope. And after that, we had other ways, by using what we called moving pictures, of making the forty-thousand-times germ many, many thousand times larger still. And thus we saw all these things which our eyes of themselves could not see. Take a grain of sand. Break it into ten pieces. Take one piece and break it into ten. Break one of those pieces into ten, and one of those into ten, and one of those into ten, and one of those into ten, and do it all day, and maybe, by sunset, you will have a piece as small as one of the germs."

The boys were openly incredulous. Hare-Lip sniffed and sneered and Hoo-Hoo snickered, until Edwin nudged them to be silent.

"The woodtick sucks the blood of the dog, but the germ, being so very small, goes right into the blood of the body, and there it has many children. In those days there would be as many as a billion—a crab-shell, please—as many as that crab-shell in one man's body. We called germs micro-organisms. When a few million, or a billion, of them were in a man, in all the blood of a man, he was sick. These germs were a disease. There were many different kinds of them—more different kinds than there are grains of sand on this beach. We knew only a few of the kinds. The micro-organic world was an invisible world, a world we could not see, and we knew very little about it. Yet we did know something. There was the *bacillus anthracis*; there was the *micrococcus*; there was the *Bacterium termo*, and the *Bacterium lactis*—that's what turns the goat milk sour even to this day, Hare-Lip; and there were *Schizomycetes* without end. And there were many others. . . ."

Here the old man launched into a disquisition on germs and their natures, using words and phrases of such extraordinary length and meaninglessness, that the boys grinned at one another and looked out over the deserted ocean till they forgot the old man was babbling on.

"But the Scarlet Death, Granser," Edwin at last suggested.

Granser recollected himself, and with a start tore himself away from the rostrum of the lecture-hall, where, to another-world audience, he had been expounding the latest theory, sixty years gone, of germs and germ-diseases.

"Yes, yes, Edwin; I had forgotten. Sometimes the memory of the past is very strong upon me, and I forget that I am a dirty old man, clad in goat-skin, wandering with my savage grandsons who are goatherds in the primeval wilderness. 'The fleeting systems lapse like foam,' and so lapsed our glorious, colossal civilization. I am Granser, a tired old man. I belong to the tribe of Santa Rosans. I married into that tribe. My sons and daughters married into the Chauffeurs, the Sacramentos, and the Palo-Altos. You, Hare-Lip, are of the Chauffeurs. You, Edwin, are of the Sacramentos. And you, Hoo-Hoo, are of the Palo-Altos. Your tribe takes its name from a town that was near the seat of another great institution of learning. It was called Stanford University. Yes, I remember now. It is perfectly clear. I was telling you of the Scarlet Death. Where was I in my story?"

"You was telling about germs, the things you can't see but which make men sick," Edwin prompted.

"Yes, that's where I was. A man did not notice at first when only a few of these germs got into his body. But each germ broke in half and became two germs, and they kept doing this very rapidly so that in a short time there were many millions of them in the body. Then the man was sick. He had a disease, and the disease was named after the kind of a germ that was in him. It might be measles, it might be influenza, it might be yellow fever; it might be any of thousands and thousands of kinds of diseases.

"Now this is the strange thing about these germs. There were always new ones coming to live in men's bodies. Long and long and long ago, when there were only a few men in the world, there were few diseases. But as men increased and lived closely together in great cities and civilizations, new diseases arose, new kinds of germs entered their bodies. Thus were countless millions and billions of human beings killed. And the more thickly men packed together, the more terrible were the new diseases that came to be. Long before my time, in the Middle Ages, there was the Black Plague that swept across Europe. It swept across Europe many times. There was tuberculosis, that entered into men wherever they were thickly packed. A hundred years before my time there was the bubonic plague. And in Africa was the sleeping sickness. The bacteriologists fought all these sicknesses and destroyed them, just as you boys fight the wolves away from your goats, or squash the mosquitoes that light on you. The bacteriologists—"

"But, Granser, what is a what-you-call-it?" Edwin interrupted.

"You, Edwin, are a goatherd. Your task is to watch the goats. You know a great deal about goats. A bacteriologist watches germs. That's his task, and he knows a great deal about them. So, as I was saying, the bacteriologists fought with the germs and destroyed them—sometimes. There was leprosy, a horrible disease. A hundred years before I was born, the bacteriologists discovered the germ of leprosy. They knew all about it. They made pictures of it. I have seen those pictures. But they never found a way to kill it. But in 1984, there was the Pantoblast Plague, a disease that broke out in a country called Brazil and that killed millions of people. But the bacteriologists found it out, and found the way to kill it, so that the Pantoblast Plague went no farther. They made what they called a serum, which they put into a man's body and which killed the pantoblast germs without killing the man. And in 1910, there was Pellagra, and also the hookworm. These were easily killed by the bacteriologists. But in 1947 there arose a new disease that had never been seen before. It got into the bodies of babies of only ten months old or less, and it made them unable to move their hands and feet, or to eat, or anything; and the bacteriologists were eleven years in discovering how to kill that particular germ and save the babies.

"In spite of all these diseases, and of all the new ones that continued to arise, there were more and more men in the world. This was because it was easy to get food. The easier it was to get food, the more men there were; the more men there were, the more thickly were they packed together on the earth; and the more thickly they were packed, the more new kinds of germs became diseases. There were warnings. Soldervetzsky, as early as 1929, told the bacteriologists that they had no guaranty against some new disease, a thousand times more deadly than any they knew, arising and killing by the hundreds of millions and even by the billion. You see, the micro-organic world remained a mystery to the end. They knew there was such a world, and that from time to time armies of new germs emerged from it to kill men. And that was all they knew about it. For all they knew, in that invisible micro-organic world there might be as many different kinds of germs as there are grains of sand on this beach. And also, in that same invisible world it might well be that new kinds of germs came to be. It might be there that life originated—the 'abysmal fecundity,' Soldervetzsky called it, applying the words of other men who had written before him. . . ."

It was at this point that Hare-Lip rose to his feet, an expression of huge contempt on his face.

"Granser," he announced, "you make me sick with your gabble. Why don't you tell about the Red Death? If you ain't going to, say so, an' we'll start back for camp."

The old man looked at him and silently began to cry. The weak tears of age rolled down his cheeks, and all the feebleness of his eighty-seven years showed in his grief-stricken countenance.

"Sit down," Edwin counselled soothingly. "Granser's all right. He's just gettin' to the Scarlet Death, ain't you, Granser? He's just goin' to tell us about it right now. Sit down, Hare-Lip. Go ahead, Granser."

III

The old man wiped the tears away on his grimy knuckles and took up the tale in a tremulous, piping voice that soon strengthened as he got the swing of the narrative.

"It was in the summer of 2013 that the Plague came. I was twenty-seven years old, and well do I remember it. Wireless despatches—"

Hare-Lip spat loudly his disgust, and Granser hastened to make amends.

"We talked through the air in those days, thousands and thousands of miles. And the word came of a strange disease that had broken out in New York. There were seventeen millions of people living then in that noblest city of America. Nobody thought anything about the news. It was only a small thing. There had been only a few deaths. It seemed, though, that they had died very quickly, and that one of the first signs of the disease was the turning red of the face and all the body. Within twenty-four hours came the report of the first case in Chicago. And on the same day, it was made public that London, the greatest city in the world, next to Chicago, had been secretly fighting the plague for two weeks and censoring the news despatches—that is, not permitting the word to go forth to the rest of the world that London had the plague.

"It looked serious, but we in California, like everywhere else, were not alarmed. We were sure that the bacteriologists would find a way to overcome this new germ, just as they had overcome other germs in the past. But the trouble was the astonishing quickness with which this germ destroyed human beings, and the fact that it inevitably killed any human body it entered. No one ever recovered. There was the old Asiatic cholera, when you might eat dinner with a well man in the evening, and the next morning, if you got up early enough, you would see him being hauled by your window in the death-cart. But this new plague was quicker than that—much quicker. From the moment of the first signs of it, a man would be dead in an hour. Some lasted for several hours. Many died within ten or fifteen minutes of the appearance of the first signs.

"The heart began to beat faster and the heat of the body to increase. Then came the scarlet rash, spreading like wildfire over the face and body. Most persons never noticed the increase in heat and heart-beat, and the first they knew was when the scarlet rash came out. Usually, they had convulsions at the time of the appearance of the rash. But these convulsions did not last long and were not very severe. If one lived through them, he became perfectly quiet, and only did he feel a numbness swiftly creeping up his body from the feet. The heels became numb first, then the legs, and hips, and when the numbness reached as high as his heart he died. They did not rave or sleep. Their minds always remained cool and calm up to the moment their heart numbed and stopped. And another strange thing was the rapidity of decomposition. No sooner was a person dead than the body seemed to fall to pieces, to fly apart, to melt away even as you looked at it. That was one of the reasons the plague spread so rapidly. All the billions of germs in a corpse were so immediately released.

"And it was because of all this that the bacteriologists had so little chance in fighting the germs. They were killed in their laboratories even as they studied the germ of the Scarlet Death. They were heroes. As fast as they perished, others stepped forth and took their places. It was in London that they first isolated it. The news was telegraphed everywhere. Trask was the name of the man who succeeded in this, but within thirty hours he was dead. Then came the struggle in all the laboratories to find something that would kill the plague germs. All drugs failed. You see, the problem was to get a drug, or serum, that would kill the germs in the body and not kill the body. They tried to fight it with other germs, to put into the body of a sick man germs that were the enemies of the plague germs—"

"And you can't see these germ-things, Granser," Hare-Lip objected, "and here you gabble, gabble, gabble about them as if they was anything, when they're nothing at all. Anything you can't see, ain't, that's what. Fighting things that ain't with things that ain't! They must have been all fools in them days. That's why they croaked. I ain't goin' to believe in such rot, I tell you that."

Granser promptly began to weep, while Edwin hotly took up his defence.

"Look here, Hare-Lip, you believe in lots of things you can't see."

Hare-Lip shook his head.

"You believe in dead men walking about. You never seen one dead man walk about."

"I tell you I seen 'em, last winter, when I was wolf-hunting with Dad."

"Well, you always spit when you cross running water," Edwin challenged.

"That's to keep off bad luck," was Hare-Lip's defence.

"You believe in bad luck?"

"Sure."

"An' you ain't never seen bad luck," Edwin concluded triumphantly. "You're just as bad as Granser and his germs. You believe in what you don't see. Go on, Granser."

Hare-Lip, crushed by this metaphysical defeat, remained silent, and the old man went on. Often and often, though this narrative must not be clogged by the details, was Granser's tale interrupted while the boys squabbled among themselves. Also, among themselves they kept up a constant, low-voiced exchange of explanation and conjecture, as they strove to follow the old man into his unknown and vanished world.

"The Scarlet Death broke out in San Francisco. The first death came on a Monday morning. By Thursday they were dying like flies in Oakland and San Francisco. They died everywhere—in their beds, at their work, walking along the street. It was on Tuesday that I saw my first death—Miss Collbran, one of my students, sitting right there before my eyes, in my lecture-room. I noticed her face while I was talking. It had suddenly turned scarlet. I ceased speaking and could only look at her, for the first fear of the plague was already on all of us and we knew that it had come. The young women screamed and ran out of the room. So did the young men run out, all but two. Miss Collbran's convulsions were very mild and lasted less than a minute. One of the young men fetched her a glass of water. She drank only a little of it, and cried out:

" 'My feet! All sensation has left them.'

"After a minute she said, 'I have no feet. I am unaware that I have any feet. And my knees are cold. I can scarcely feel that I have knees.'

"She lay on the floor, a bundle of notebooks under her head. And we could do nothing. The coldness and the numbness crept up past her hips to her heart, and when it reached her heart she was dead. In fifteen minutes, by the clock—I timed it—she was dead, there, in my own classroom, dead. And she was a very beautiful, strong, healthy young woman. And from the first sign of the plague to her death only fifteen minutes elapsed. That will show you how swift was the Scarlet Death.

"Yet in those few minutes I remained with the dying woman in my classroom, the alarm had spread over the university; and the students, by thousands, all of them, had deserted the lecture-room and laboratories. When I emerged, on my way to make report to the President of the Faculty, I found the university deserted. Across the campus were several stragglers hurrying for their homes. Two of them were running.

"President Hoag, I found in his office, all alone, looking very old and very gray, with a multitude of wrinkles in his face that I had never seen before. At the sight of me, he pulled himself to his feet and tottered away to the inner office, banging the door after him and locking it. You see, he knew I had been exposed, and he was afraid. He shouted to me through the door to go away. I shall never forget my feelings as I walked down the silent corridors and out across that deserted campus. I was not afraid. I had been exposed, and I looked upon myself as already dead. It was not that, but a feeling of awful depression that impressed me. Everything had stopped. It was like the end of the world to me—my world. I had been born within sight and sound of the university. It had been my predestined career. My father had been a professor there before me, and his father before him. For a century and a half had this university, like a splendid machine, been running steadily on. And now, in an instant, it had stopped. It was like seeing the sacred flame die down on some thrice-sacred altar. I was shocked, unutterably shocked.

"When I arrived home, my housekeeper screamed as I entered, and fled away. And when I rang, I found the housemaid had likewise fled. I investigated. In the kitchen I found the cook on the point of departure. But she screamed, too, and in her haste dropped a suitcase of her personal belongings and ran out of the house and across the grounds, still screaming. I can hear her scream to this day. You see, we did not act in this way when ordinary diseases smote us. We were always calm over such things, and sent for the doctors and nurses who knew just what to do. But this was different. It struck so suddenly, and killed so swiftly, and never missed a stroke. When the scarlet rash appeared on a person's face, that person was marked by death. There was never a known case of a recovery.

"I was alone in my big house. As I have told you often before, in those days we could talk with one another over wires or through the air. The telephone bell rang, and I found my brother talking to me. He told me that he was not coming home for fear of catching the plague from me, and that he had taken our two sisters to stop at Professor Bacon's home. He advised me to remain where I was, and wait to find out whether or not I had caught the plague.

"To all of this I agreed, staying in my house and for the first time in my life attempting to cook. And the plague did not come out on me. By means of the telephone I could talk with whomsoever I pleased and get the news. Also, there were the newspapers, and I ordered all of them to be thrown up to my door so that I could know what was happening with the rest of the world.

"New York City and Chicago were in chaos. And what happened with them was happening in all the large cities. A third of the New York police were dead. Their chief was also dead, likewise the mayor. All law and order had ceased. The bodies were lying in the streets unburied. All railroads and vessels carrying food and such things into the great city had ceased running, and mobs of the hungry poor were pillaging the stores and warehouses. Murder and robbery and drunkenness were everywhere. Already the people had fled from the city by millions—at first the rich, in their private motor cars and dirigibles, and then the great mass of the population, on foot, carrying the plague with them, themselves starving and pillaging the farmers and all the towns and villages on the way.

"The man who sent this news, the wireless operator, was alone with his instrument on the top of a lofty building. The people remaining in the city—he estimated them at several hundred thousand—had gone mad from fear and drink, and on all sides of him great fires were raging. He was a hero, that man who staid by his post—an obscure newspaperman, most likely.

"For twenty-four hours, he said, no transatlantic airships had arrived, and no more messages were coming from England. He did state, though, that a message from Berlin—that's in Germany—announced that Hoffmeyer, a bacteriologist of the Metchnikoff School, had discovered the serum for the plague. That was the last word, to this day, that we of America ever received from Europe. If Hoffmeyer discovered the serum, it was too late, or otherwise, long ere this, explorers from Europe would have come looking for us. We can only conclude that what happened in America happened in Europe, and that, at the best, some several score may have survived the Scarlet Death on that whole continent.

"For one day longer the despatches continued to come from New York. Then they, too, ceased. The man who had sent them, perched in his lofty building, had either died of the plague or been consumed in the great conflagrations he had described as raging around him. And what had occurred in New York had been duplicated in all the other cities. It was the same in San Francisco, and Oakland, and Berkeley. By Thursday the people were dying so rapidly that their corpses could not be handled, and dead bodies lay everywhere. Thursday night the panic outrush for the country began. Imagine, my grandsons, people, thicker than the salmon-run you have seen on the Sacramento River, pouring out of the cities by millions, madly over the country, in vain attempt to escape the ubiquitous death. You see, they carried the germs with them. Even the airships of the rich, fleeing for mountain and desert fastnesses, carried the germs.

"Hundreds of these airships escaped to Hawaii, and not only did they bring the plague with them, but they found the plague already there before them. This we learned, by the despatches, until all order in San Francisco vanished, and there were no operators left at their posts to receive or send. It was amazing, astounding, this loss of communication with the world. It was exactly as if the world had ceased, been blotted out. For sixty years that world has no longer existed for me. I know there must be such places as New York, Europe, Asia, and Africa; but not one word has been heard of them—not in sixty years. With the coming of the Scarlet Death the world fell apart, absolutely, irretrievably. Ten thousand years of culture and civilization passed in the twinkling of an eye, 'lapsed like foam.'

"I was telling about the airships of the rich. They carried the plague with them and no matter where they fled, they died. I never encountered but one survivor of any of them—Mungerson. He was afterwards a Santa Rosan, and he married my eldest daughter. He came into the tribe eight years after the plague. He was then nineteen years old, and he was compelled to wait twelve years more before he could marry. You see, there were no unmarried women, and some of the older daughters of the Santa Rosans were already bespoken. So he was forced to wait until my Mary had grown to sixteen years. It was his son, Gimp-Leg, who was killed last year by the mountain lion.

"Mungerson was eleven years old at the time of the plague. His father was one of the Industrial Magnates, a very wealthy, powerful man. It was on his airship, the *Condor*, that they were fleeing, with all the family, for the wilds of British Columbia, which is far to the north of here. But there was some accident, and they were wrecked near Mount Shasta. You have heard of that mountain. It is far to the north. The plague broke out amongst them, and this boy of eleven was the only survivor. For eight years he was alone, wandering over a deserted land and looking vainly for his own kind. And at last, travelling south, he picked up with us, the Santa Rosans.

"But I am ahead of my story. When the great exodus from the cities around San Francisco Bay began, and while the telephones were still working, I talked with my brother. I told him this flight from the cities was insanity, that there were no symptoms of the plague in me, and that the thing for us to do was to isolate ourselves and our relatives in some safe place. We decided on the Chemistry Building, at the university, and we planned to lay in a supply of provisions, and by force of arms to prevent any other persons from forcing their presence upon us after we had retired to our refuge.

"All this being arranged, my brother begged me to stay in my own house for at least twenty-four hours more, on the chance of the plague developing in me. To this I agreed, and he promised to come for me next day. We talked on over the details of the provisioning and the defending of the Chemistry Building until the telephone died. It died in the midst of our conversation. That evening there were no electric lights, and I was alone in my house in the darkness. No more newspapers were being printed, so I had no knowledge of what was taking place outside. I heard sounds of rioting and of pistol shots, and from my windows I could see the glare of the sky of some conflagration in the direction of Oakland. It was a night of terror. I did not sleep a wink. A man—why and how I do not know—was killed on the sidewalk in front of the house. I heard the rapid reports of an automatic pistol, and a few minutes later the wounded wretch crawled up to my door, moaning and crying out for help. Arming myself with two automatics, I went to him. By the light of a match I ascertained that while he was dying of the bullet wounds, at the same time the plague was on him. I fled indoors, whence I heard him moan and cry out for half an hour longer.

"In the morning, my brother came to me. I had gathered into a handbag what things of value I purposed taking, but when I saw his face I knew that he would never accompany me to the Chemistry Building. The plague was on him. He intended shaking my hand, but I went back hurriedly before him.

" 'Look at yourself in the mirror,' I commanded.

"He did so, and at sight of his scarlet face, the color deepening as he looked at it, he sank down nervelessly in a chair.

" 'My God!' he said. 'I've got it. Don't come near me. I am a dead man.'

"Then the convulsions seized him. He was two hours in dying, and he was conscious to the last, complaining about the coldness and loss of sensation in his feet, his calves, his thighs, until at last it was his heart and he was dead.

"That was the way the Scarlet Death slew. I caught up my handbag and fled. The sights in the streets were terrible. One stumbled on bodies everywhere. Some were not yet dead. And even as you looked, you saw men sink down with the death fastened upon them. There were numerous fires burning in Berkeley, while Oakland and San Francisco were apparently being swept by vast conflagrations. The smoke of the burning filled the heavens, so that the midday was as a gloomy twilight, and, in the shifts of wind, sometimes the sun shone through dimly, a dull red orb. Truly, my grandsons, it was like the last days of the end of the world.

"There were numerous stalled motor cars, showing that the gasoline and the engine supplies of the garages had given out. I remember one such car. A man and a woman lay back dead in the seats, and on the pavement near it were two more women and a child. Strange and terrible sights there were on every hand.

People slipped by silently, furtively, like ghosts—white-faced women carrying infants in their arms; fathers leading children by the hand; singly, and in couples, and in families—all fleeing out of the city of death. Some carried supplies of food, others blankets and valuables, and there were many who carried nothing.

"There was a grocery store—a place where food was sold. The man to whom it belonged—I knew him well—a quiet, sober, but stupid and obstinate fellow, was defending it. The windows and doors had been broken in, but he, inside, hiding behind a counter, was discharging his pistol at a number of men on the sidewalk who were breaking in. In the entrance were several bodies—of men, I decided, whom he had killed earlier in the day. Even as I looked on from a distance, I saw one of the robbers break the windows of the adjoining store, a place where shoes were sold, and deliberately set fire to it. I did not go to the groceryman's assistance. The time for such acts had already passed. Civilization was crumbling, and it was each for himself."

IV

"I went away hastily, down a cross-street, and at the first corner I saw another tragedy. Two men of the working class had caught a man and a woman with two children, and were robbing them. I knew the man by sight, though I had never been introduced to him. He was a poet whose verses I had long admired. Yet I did not go to his help, for at the moment I came upon the scene there was a pistol shot, and I saw him sinking to the ground. The woman screamed, and she was felled with a fist-blow by one of the brutes. I cried out threateningly, whereupon they discharged their pistols at me and I ran away around the corner. Here I was blocked by an advancing conflagration. The buildings on both sides were burning, and the street was filled with smoke and flame. From somewhere in that murk came a woman's voice calling shrilly for help. But I did not go to her. A man's heart turned to iron amid such scenes, and one heard all too many appeals for help.

"Returning to the corner, I found the two robbers were gone. The poet and his wife lay dead on the pavement. It was a shocking sight. The two children had vanished—whither I could not tell. And I knew, now, why it was that the fleeing persons I encountered slipped along so furtively and with such white faces. In the midst of our civilization, down in our slums and labor-ghettos, we had bred a race of barbarians, of savages; and now, in the time of our calamity, they turned upon us like the wild beasts they were and destroyed us. And they destroyed themselves as well. They inflamed themselves with strong drink and committed a thousand atrocities, quarreling and killing one another in the general madness. One group of workingmen I saw, of the better sort, who had banded together, and, with their women and children in their midst, the sick and aged in litters and being carried, and with a number of horses pulling a truck-load of provisions, they were fighting their way out of the city. They made a fine spectacle as they came down the street through the drifting smoke, though they nearly shot me when I first appeared in their path. As they went by, one of their leaders shouted out to me in apologetic explanation. He said they were killing the robbers and looters on sight, and that they had thus banded together as the only means by which to escape the prowlers.

"It was here that I saw for the first time what I was soon to see so often. One of the marching men had suddenly shown the unmistakable mark of the plague. Immediately those about him drew away, and he, without a remonstrance, stepped out of his place to let them pass on. A woman, most probably his wife, attempted to follow him. She was leading a little boy by the hand. But the husband commanded her sternly to go on, while others laid hands on her and restrained her from following him. This I saw, and I saw the man also, with his scarlet blaze of face, step into a doorway on the opposite side of the street. I heard the report of his pistol, and saw him sink lifeless to the ground.

"After being turned aside twice again by advancing fires, I succeeded in getting through to the university. On the edge of the campus I came upon a party of university folk who were going in the direction of the Chemistry Building. They were all family men, and their families were with them, including the nurses and the servants.

"Professor Badminton greeted me, and I had difficulty in recognizing him. Somewhere he had gone through flames, and his beard was singed off. About his head was a bloody bandage, and his clothes were filthy. He told me he had been cruelly beaten by prowlers, and that his brother had been killed the previous night, in the defence of their dwelling.

"Midway across the campus, he pointed suddenly to Mrs. Swinton's face. The unmistakable scarlet was there. Immediately all the other women set up a screaming and began to run away from her. Her two children were with a nurse, and these also ran with the women. But her husband, Doctor Swinton, remained with her.

" 'Go on, Smith,' he told me. 'Keep an eye on the children. As for me, I shall stay with my wife. I know she is as already dead, but I can't leave her. Afterwards, if I escape, I shall come to the Chemistry Building, and do you watch for me and let me in.'

"I left him bending over his wife and soothing her last moments, while I ran to overtake the party. We were the last to be admitted to the Chemistry Building. After that, with our automatic rifles we maintained our isolation. By our plans, we had arranged for a company of sixty to be in this refuge. Instead, every one of the number originally planned had added relatives and friends and whole families until there were over four hundred souls. But the Chemistry Building was large, and, standing by itself, was in no danger of being burned by the great fires that raged everywhere in the city.

"A large quantity of provisions had been gathered, and a food committee took charge of it, issuing rations daily to the various families and groups that arranged themselves into messes. A number of committees were appointed, and we developed a very efficient organization. I was on the committee of defence, though for the first day no prowlers came near. We could see them in the distance, however, and by the smoke of their fires knew that several camps of them were occupying the far edge of the campus. Drunkenness was rife, and often we heard them singing ribald songs or insanely shouting. While the world crashed to ruin about them and all the air was filled with the smoke of its burning, these low creatures gave rein to their bestiality and fought and drank and died. And after all, what did it matter? Everybody died anyway, the good and the bad, the efficients and the weaklings, those that loved to live and those that scorned to live. They passed. Everything passed.

"When twenty-four hours had gone by and no signs of the plague were apparent, we congratulated ourselves and set about digging a well. You have seen the great iron pipes which in those days carried water to all the city-dwellers. We feared that the fires in the city would burst the pipes and empty the reservoirs. So we tore up the cement floor of the central court of the Chemistry Building and dug a well. There were many young men, undergraduates, with us, and we worked night and day on the well. And our fears were confirmed. Three hours before we reached water, the pipes went dry.

"A second twenty-four hours passed, and still the plague did not appear among us. We thought we were saved. But we did not know what I afterwards decided to be true, namely, that the period of the incubation of the plague germs in a human's body was a matter of a number of days. It slew so swiftly when once it manifested itself, that we were led to believe that the period of incubation was equally swift. So, when two days had left us unscathed, we were elated with the idea that we were free of the contagion.

"But the third day disillusioned us. I can never forget the night preceding it. I had charge of the night guards from eight to twelve, and from the roof of the building I watched the passing of all man's glorious works. So terrible were the local conflagrations that all the sky was lighted up. One could read the finest print in the red glare. All the world seemed wrapped in flames. San Francisco spouted smoke and fire from a score of vast conflagrations that were like so many active volcanoes. Oakland, San Leandro, Haywards—all were burning; and to the northward, clear to Point Richmond, other fires were at work. It was an awe-inspiring spectacle. Civilization, my grandsons, civilization was passing in a sheet of flame and a breath of death. At ten o'clock that night, the great powder magazines at Point Pinole exploded in rapid succession. So terrific were the concussions that the strong building rocked as in an earthquake, while every pane of glass was broken. It was then that I left the roof and went down the long corridors, from room to room, quieting the alarmed women and telling them what had happened.

"An hour later, at a window on the ground floor, I heard pandemonium break out in the camps of the prowlers. There were cries and screams, and shots from many pistols. As we afterward conjectured, this fight had been precipitated by an attempt on the part of those that were well to drive out those that were sick. At any rate, a number of the plague-stricken prowlers escaped across the campus and drifted against our doors. We warned them back, but they cursed us and discharged a fusillade from their pistols. Professor Merryweather, at one of the windows, was instantly killed, the bullet striking him squarely between the eyes. We opened fire in turn, and all the prowlers fled away with the exception of three. One was a woman. The plague was on them and they were reckless. Like foul fiends, there in the red glare from the skies, with faces blazing, they continued to curse us and fire at us. One of the men I shot with my own hand. After that the other man and the woman, still cursing us, lay down under our windows, where we were compelled to watch them die of the plague.

"The situation was critical. The explosions of the powder magazines had broken all the windows of the Chemistry Building, so that we were exposed to the germs from the corpses. The sanitary committee was called upon to act, and it responded nobly. Two men were required to go out and remove the corpses, and this meant the probable sacrifice of their own lives, for, having performed the task, they were not to be permitted to re-enter the building. One of the professors, who was a bachelor, and one of the undergraduates volunteered. They bade good-bye to us and went forth. They were heroes. They gave up their lives that four hundred others might live. After they had performed their work, they stood for a moment, at a distance, looking at us wistfully. Then they waved their hands in farewell and went away slowly across the campus toward the burning city.

"And yet it was all useless. The next morning the first one of us was smitten with the plague—a little nurse-girl in the family of Professor Stout. It was no time for weak-kneed, sentimental policies. On the chance that she might be the only one, we thrust her forth from the building and commanded her to be gone. She went away slowly across the campus, wringing her hands and crying pitifully. We felt like brutes, but what were we to do? There were four hundred of us, and individuals had to be sacrificed.

"In one of the laboratories three families had domiciled themselves, and that afternoon we found among them no less than four corpses and seven cases of the plague in all its different stages.

"Then it was that the horror began. Leaving the dead lie, we forced the living ones to segregate themselves in another room. The plague began to break out among the rest of us, and as fast as the symptoms appeared, we sent the stricken ones to these segregated rooms. We compelled them to walk there by themselves, so as to avoid laying hands on them. It was heartrending. But still the plague raged among us, and room after room was filled with the dead and dying. And so we who were yet clean retreated to the next floor and to the next, before this sea of the dead, that, room by room and floor by floor, inundated the building.

"The place became a charnel house, and in the middle of the night the survivors fled forth, taking nothing with them except arms and ammunition and a heavy store of tinned foods. We camped on the opposite side of the campus from the prowlers, and, while some stood guard, others of us volunteered to scout into the city in quest of horses, motor cars, carts, and wagons, or anything that would carry our provisions and enable us to emulate the banded working-men I had seen fighting their way out to the open country.

"I was one of these scouts; and Doctor Hoyle, remembering that his motor car had been left behind in his home garage, told me to look for it. We scouted in pairs, and Dombey, a young undergraduate, accompanied me. We had to cross half a mile of the residence portion of the city to get to Doctor Hoyle's home. Here the buildings stood apart, in the midst of trees and grassy lawns, and here the fires had played freaks, burning whole blocks, skipping blocks and often skipping a single house in a block. And here, too, the prowlers were still at their work. We carried our automatic pistols openly in our hands, and looked desperate enough, forsooth, to keep them from attacking us. But at Doctor Hoyle's house the thing happened. Untouched by fire, even as we came to it the smoke of flames burst forth.

"The miscreant who had set fire to it staggered down the steps and out along the driveway. Sticking out of his coat pockets were bottles of whiskey, and he was very drunk. My first impulse was to shoot him, and I have never ceased regretting that I did not. Staggering and maundering to himself, with bloodshot eyes, and a raw and bleeding slash down one side of his bewhiskered face, he was altogether the most nauseating specimen of degradation and filth I had ever encountered. I did not shoot him, and he leaned against a tree on the lawn to let us go by. It was the most absolute, wanton act. Just as we were opposite him, he suddenly drew a pistol and shot Dombey through the head. The next instant I shot him. But it was too late. Dombey expired without a groan, immediately. I doubt if he even knew what had happened to him.

"Leaving the two corpses, I hurried on past the burning house to the garage, and there found Doctor Hoyle's motor car. The tanks were filled with gasoline, and it was ready for use. And it was in this car that I threaded the streets of the ruined city and came back to the survivors on the campus. The other scouts returned, but none had been so fortunate. Professor Fairmead had found a Shetland pony, but the poor creature, tied in a stable and abandoned for days, was so weak from want of food and water that it could carry no burden at all. Some of the men were for turning it loose, but I insisted that we should lead it along with us, so that, if we got out of food, we would have it to eat.

"There were forty-seven of us when we started, many being women and children. The President of the Faculty, an old man to begin with, and now hopelessly broken by the awful happenings of the past week, rode in the motor car with several young children and the aged mother of Professor Fairmead. Wathope, a young professor of English, who had a grievous bullet-wound in his leg, drove the car. The rest of us walked, Professor Fairmead leading the pony.

"It was what should have been a bright summer day, but the smoke from the burning world filled the sky, through which the sun shone murkily, a dull and lifeless orb, blood-red and ominous. But we had grown accustomed to that blood-red sun. With the smoke it was different. It bit into our nostrils and eyes, and there was not one of us whose eyes were not bloodshot. We directed our course to the southeast through the endless miles of suburban residences, travelling along where the first swells of low hills rose from the flat of the central city. It was by this way, only, that we could expect to gain the country.

"Our progress was painfully slow. The women and children could not walk fast. They did not dream of walking, my grandsons, in the way all people walk to-day. In truth, none of us knew how to walk. It was not until after the plague that I learned really to walk. So it was that the pace of the slowest was the pace of all, for we dared not separate on account of the prowlers. There were not so many now of these human beasts of prey. The plague had already well diminished their numbers, but enough still lived to be a constant menace to us. Many of the beautiful residences were untouched by fire, yet smoking ruins were everywhere. The prowlers, too, seemed to have got over their insensate desire to burn, and it was more rarely that we saw houses freshly on fire.

"Several of us scouted among the private garages in search of motor cars and gasoline. But in this we were unsuccessful. The first great flights from the cities had swept all such utilities away. Calgan, a fine young man, was lost in this work. He was shot by prowlers while crossing a lawn. Yet this was our only casualty, though, once, a drunken brute deliberately opened fire on all of us. Luckily, he fired wildly, and we shot him before he had done any hurt.

"At Fruitvale, still in the heart of the magnificent residence section of the city, the plague again smote us. Professor Fairmead was the victim. Making signs to us that his mother was not to know, he turned aside into the grounds of a beautiful mansion. He sat down forlornly on the steps of the front veranda, and I, having lingered, waved him a last farewell. That night, several miles beyond Fruitvale and still in the city, we made camp. And that night we shifted camp twice to get away from our dead. In the morning there were thirty of us. I shall never forget the President of the Faculty. During the morning's march his wife, who was walking, betrayed the fatal symptoms, and when she drew aside to let us go on, he insisted on leaving the motor car and remaining with her. There was quite a discussion about this, but in the end we gave in. It was just as well, for we knew not which ones of us, if any, might ultimately escape.

"That night, the second of our march, we camped beyond Haywards in the first stretches of country. And in the morning there were eleven of us that lived. Also, during the night, Wathope, the professor with the wounded leg, deserted us in the motor car. He took with him his sister and his mother and most of our tinned provisions. It was that day, in the afternoon, while resting by the wayside, that I saw the last airship I shall ever see. The smoke was much thinner here in the country, and I first sighted the ship drifting and veering helplessly at an elevation of two thousand feet. What had happened I could not conjecture, but even as we looked we saw her bow dip down lower and lower. Then the bulkheads of the various gas-chambers must have burst, for, quite perpendicular, she fell like a plummet to the earth. And from that day to this I have not seen another airship. Often and often, during the next few years, I scanned the sky for them, hoping against hope that somewhere in the world civilization had survived. But it was not to be. What happened with us in California must have happened with everybody everywhere.

"Another day, and at Niles there were three of us. Beyond Niles, in the middle of the highway, we found Wathope. The motor car had broken down, and there, on the rugs which they had spread on the ground, lay the bodies of his sister, his mother, and himself.

"Wearied by the unusual exercise of continual walking, that night I slept heavily. In the morning I was alone in the world. Canfield and Parsons, my last companions, were dead of the plague. Of the four hundred that sought shelter in the Chemistry Building, and of the forty-seven that began the march, I alone remained—I and the Shetland pony. Why this should be so there is no explaining. I did not catch the plague, that is all. I was immune. I was merely the one lucky man in a million—just as every survivor was one in a million, or, rather, in several millions, for the proportion was at least that."

V

"For two days I sheltered in a pleasant grove where there had been no deaths. In those two days, while badly depressed and believing that my turn would come at any moment, nevertheless I rested and recuperated. So did the pony. And on the third day, putting what small store of tinned provisions I possessed on the pony's back, I started on across a very lonely land. Not a live man, woman, or child, did I encounter, though the dead were everywhere. Food, however, was abundant. The land then was not as it is now. It was all cleared of trees and brush, and it was cultivated. The food for millions of mouths was growing, ripening, and going to waste. From the fields and orchards I gathered vegetables, fruits, and berries. Around the deserted farmhouses I got eggs and caught chickens. And frequently I found supplies of tinned provisions in the store-rooms.

"A strange thing was what was taking place with all the domestic animals. Everywhere they were going wild and preying on one another. The chickens and ducks were the first to be destroyed, while the pigs were the first to go wild, followed by the cats. Nor were the dogs long in adapting themselves to the changed conditions. There was a veritable plague of dogs. They devoured the corpses, barked and howled during the nights, and in the daytime slunk about in the distance. As the time went by, I noticed a change in their behavior. At first they were apart from one another, very suspicious and very prone to fight.

But after a not very long while they began to come together and run in packs. The dog, you see, always was a social animal, and this was true before ever he came to be domesticated by man. In the last days of the world before the plague, there were many many very different kinds of dogs—dogs without hair and dogs with warm fur, dogs so small that they would make scarcely a mouthful for other dogs that were as large as mountain lions. Well, all the small dogs, and the weak types, were killed by their fellows. Also, the very large ones were not adapted for the wild life and bred out. As a result, the many different kinds of dogs disappeared, and there remained, running in packs, the medium-sized wolfish dogs that you know to-day."

"But the cats don't run in packs, Granser," Hoo-Hoo objected.

"The cat was never a social animal. As one writer in the nineteenth century said, the cat walks by himself. He always walked by himself, from before the time he was tamed by man, down through the long ages of domestication, to today when once more he is wild.

"The horses also went wild, and all the fine breeds we had degenerated into the small mustang horse you know to-day. The cows likewise went wild, as did the pigeons and the sheep. And that a few of the chickens survived you know yourself. But the wild chicken of to-day is quite a different thing from the chickens we had in those days.

"But I must go on with my story. I travelled through a deserted land. As the time went by I began to yearn more and more for human beings. But I never found one, and I grew lonelier and lonelier. I crossed Livermore Valley and the mountains between it and the great valley of the San Joaquin. You have never seen that valley, but it is very large and it is the home of the wild horse. There are great droves there, thousands and tens of thousands. I revisited it thirty years after, so I know. You think there are lots of wild horses down here in the coast valleys, but they are as nothing compared with those of the San Joaquin. Strange to say, the cows, when they went wild, went back into the lower mountains. Evidently they were better able to protect themselves there.

"In the country districts the ghouls and prowlers had been less in evidence, for I found many villages and towns untouched by fire. But they were filled by the pestilential dead, and I passed by without exploring them. It was near Lathrop that, out of my loneliness, I picked up a pair of collie dogs that were so newly free that they were urgently willing to return to their allegiance to man. These collies accompanied me for many years, and the strains of them are in those very dogs there that you boys have to-day. But in sixty years the collie strain has worked out. These brutes are more like domesticated wolves than anything else."

Hare-Lip rose to his feet, glanced to see that the goats were safe, and looked at the sun's position in the afternoon sky, advertising impatience at the prolixity of the old man's tale. Urged to hurry by Edwin, Granser went on.

"There is little more to tell. With my two dogs and my pony, and riding a horse I had managed to capture, I crossed the San Joaquin and went on to a wonderful valley in the Sierras called Yosemite. In the great hotel there I found a prodigious supply of tinned provisions. The pasture was abundant, as was the game, and the river that ran through the valley was full of trout. I remained there three years in an utter loneliness that none but a man who has once been highly civilized can understand. Then I could stand it no more. I felt that I was going crazy. Like the dog, I was a social animal and I needed my kind. I reasoned that since I had survived the plague, there was a possibility that others had survived. Also, I reasoned that after three years the plague germs must all be gone and the land be clean again.

"With my horse and dogs and pony, I set out. Again I crossed the San Joaquin Valley, the mountains beyond, and came down into Livermore Valley. The change in those three years was amazing. All the land had been splendidly tilled, and now I could scarcely recognize it, such was the sea of rank vegetation that had overrun the agricultural handiwork of man. You see, the wheat, the vegetables, and orchard trees had always been cared for and nursed by man, so that they were soft and tender. The weeds and wild bushes and such things, on the contrary, had always been fought by man, so that they were tough and resistant. As a result, when the hand of man was removed, the wild vegetation smothered and destroyed practically all the domesticated vegetation. The coyotes were greatly increased, and it was at this time that I first encountered wolves, straying in twos and threes and small packs down from the regions where they had always persisted.

"It was at Lake Temescal, not far from the one-time city of Oakland, that I came upon the first live human beings. Oh, my grandsons, how can I describe to you my emotion, when, astride my horse and dropping down the hillside to the lake, I saw the smoke of a campfire rising through the trees. Almost did my heart stop beating. I felt that I was going crazy. Then I heard the cry of a babe— a human babe. And dogs barked, and my dogs answered. I did not know but what I was the one human alive in the whole world. It could not be true that here were others—smoke, and the cry of a babe.

"Emerging on the lake, there, before my eyes, not a hundred yards away, I saw a man, a large man. He was standing on an outjutting rock and fishing. I was overcome. I stopped my horse. I tried to call out but could not. I waved my hand. It seemed to me that the man looked at me, but he did not appear to wave. Then I laid my head on my arms there in the saddle. I was afraid to look again, for I knew it was an hallucination, and I knew that if I looked the man would be gone. And so precious was the hallucination, that I wanted it to persist yet a little while. I knew, too, that as long as I did not look it would persist.

"Thus I remained, until I heard my dogs snarling, and a man's voice. What do you think the voice said? I will tell you. It said: '*Where in hell did you come from?*'

"Those were the words, the exact words. That was what your other grandfather said to me, Hare-Lip, when he greeted me there on the shore of Lake Temescal fifty-seven years ago. And they were the most ineffable words I have ever heard. I opened my eyes, and there he stood before me, a large, dark, hairy man, heavy-jawed, slant-browed, fierce-eyed. How I got off my horse I do not know. But it seemed that the next I knew I was clasping his hand with both of mine and crying. I would have embraced him, but he was ever a narrow-minded, suspicious man, and he drew away from me. Yet did I cling to his hand and cry."

Granser's voice faltered and broke at the recollection, and the weak tears streamed down his cheeks while the boys looked on and giggled.

"Yet did I cry," he continued, "and desire to embrace him, though the Chauffeur was a brute, a perfect brute—the most abhorrent man I have ever known. His name was . . . strange, how I have forgotten his name. Everybody called him Chauffeur—it was the name of his occupation, and it stuck. That is how, to this day, the tribe he founded is called the Chauffeur Tribe.

"He was a violent, unjust man. Why the plague germs spared him I can never understand. It would seem, in spite of our old metaphysical notions about absolute justice, that there is no justice in the universe. Why did he live?—an iniquitous, moral monster, a blot on the face of nature, a cruel, relentless, bestial cheat as well. All he could talk about was motor cars, machinery, gasoline, and garages—and especially, and with huge delight, of his mean pilferings and sordid swindlings of the persons who had employed him in the days before the coming of the plague. And yet he was spared, while hundreds of millions, yea, billions, of better men were destroyed.

"I went on with him to his camp, and there I saw her, Vesta, the one woman. It was glorious and . . . pitiful. There she was, Vesta Van Warden, the young wife of John Van Warden, clad in rags, with marred and scarred and toil-calloused hands, bending over the campfire and doing scullion work—she, Vesta, who had been born to the purple of the greatest baronage of wealth the world has ever known. John Van Warden, her husband, worth one billion, eight hundred millions and President of the Board of Industrial Magnates, had been the ruler of America. Also, sitting on the International Board of Control, he had been one of the seven men who ruled the world. And she herself had come of equally noble stock. Her father, Philip Saxon, had been President of the Board of Industrial Magnates up to the time of his death. This office was in process of becoming hereditary, and had Philip Saxon had a son that son would have succeeded him. But his only child was Vesta, the perfect flower of generations of the highest culture this planet has ever produced. It was not until the engagement between Vesta and Van Warden took place, that Saxon indicated the latter as his successor. It was, I am sure, a political marriage. I have reason to believe that Vesta never really loved her husband in the mad passionate way of which the poets used to sing. It was more like the marriages that obtained among crowned heads in the days before they were displaced by the Magnates.

"And there she was, boiling fish-chowder in a soot-covered pot, her glorious eyes inflamed by the acrid smoke of the open fire. Hers was a sad story. She was the one survivor in a million, as I had been, as the Chauffeur had been. On a crowning eminence of the Alameda Hills, overlooking San Francisco Bay, Van Warden had built a vast summer palace. It was surrounded by a park of a thousand acres. When the plague broke out, Van Warden sent her there. Armed guards patrolled the boundaries of the park, and nothing entered in the way of provisions or even mail matter that was not first fumigated. And yet did the plague enter, killing the guards at their posts, the servants at their tasks, sweeping away the whole army of retainers—or, at least, all of them who did not flee to die elsewhere. So it was that Vesta found herself the sole living person in the palace that had become a charnel house.

"Now the Chauffeur had been one of the servants that ran away. Returning, two months afterward, he discovered Vesta in a little summer pavilion where there had been no deaths and where she had established herself. He was a brute. She was afraid, and she ran away and hid among the trees. That night, on foot, she fled into the mountains—she, whose tender feet and delicate body had never known the bruise of stones nor the scratch of briars. He followed, and that night he caught her. He struck her. Do you understand? He beat her with those terrible fists of his and made her his slave. It was she who had to gather the firewood, build the fires, cook, and do all the degrading camp-labor—she, who had never performed a menial act in her life. These things he compelled her to do, while he, a proper savage, elected to lie around camp and look on. He did nothing, absolutely nothing, except on occasion to hunt meat or catch fish."

"Good for Chauffeur," Hare-Lip commented in an undertone to the other boys. "I remember him before he died. He was a corker. But he did things, and he made things go. You know, Dad married his daughter, an' you ought to see the way he knocked the spots outa Dad. The Chauffeur was a son-of-a-gun. He made us kids stand around. Even when he was croakin', he reached out for me, once, an' laid my head open with that long stick he kept always beside him."

Hare-Lip rubbed his bullet head reminiscently, and the boys returned to the old man, who was maundering ecstatically about Vesta, the squaw of the founder of the Chauffeur Tribe.

"And so I say to you that you cannot understand the awfulness of the situation. The Chauffeur was a servant, understand, a servant. And he cringed, with bowed head, to such as she. She was a lord of life, both by birth and by marriage. The destinies of millions, such as he, she carried in the hollow of her pink-white hand. And, in the days before the plague, the slightest contact with such as he would have been pollution. Oh, I have seen it. Once, I remember, there was Mrs. Goldwin, wife of one of the great magnates. It was on a landing stage, just as she was embarking in her private dirigible, that she dropped her parasol. A servant picked it up and made the mistake of handing it to her—to her, one of the greatest royal ladies of the land! She shrank back, as though he were a leper, and indicated her secretary to receive it. Also, she ordered her secretary to ascertain the creature's name and to see that he was immediately discharged from service. And such a woman was Vesta Van Warden. And her the Chauffeur beat and made his slave.

"—Bill—that was it; Bill, the Chauffeur. That was his name. He was a wretched, primitive man, wholly devoid of the finer instincts and chivalrous promptings of a cultured soul. No, there is no absolute justice, for to him fell that wonder of womanhood, Vesta Van Warden. The grievousness of this you will never understand, my grandsons; for you are yourselves primitive little savages, unaware of aught else but savagery. Why should Vesta not have been mine? I was a man of culture and refinement, a professor in a great university. Even so, in the time before the plague, such was her exalted position, she would not have deigned to know that I existed. Mark, then, the abysmal degradation to which she fell at the hands of the Chauffeur. Nothing less than the destruction of all mankind had made it possible that I should know her, look in her eyes, converse with her, touch her hand—ay, and love her and know that her feelings toward me were very kindly. I have reason to believe that she, even she, would have loved me, there being no other man in the world except the Chauffeur. Why, when it destroyed eight billions of souls, did not the plague destroy just one more man, and that man the Chauffeur?

"Once, when the Chauffeur was away fishing, she begged me to kill him. With tears in her eyes she begged me to kill him. But he was a strong and violent man, and I was afraid. Afterwards, I talked with him. I offered him my horse, my pony, my dogs, all that I possessed, if he would give Vesta to me. And he grinned in my face and shook his head. He was very insulting. He said that in the old days he had been a servant, had been dirt under the feet of men like me and of women like Vesta, and that now he had the greatest lady in the land to be servant to him and cook his food and nurse his brats. 'You had your day before the plague,' he said; 'but this is my day, and a damned good day it is. I wouldn't trade back to the old times for anything.' Such words he spoke, but they are not his words. He was a vulgar, low-minded man, and vile oaths fell continually from his lips.

"Also, he told me that if he caught me making eyes at his woman he'd wring my neck and give her a beating as well. What was I to do? I was afraid. He was a brute. That first night, when I discovered the camp, Vesta and I had great talk about the things of our vanished world. We talked of art, and books, and poetry; and the Chauffeur listened and grinned and sneered. He was bored and angered by our way of speech which he did not comprehend, and finally he spoke up and said: 'And this is Vesta Van Warden, one-time wife of Van Warden the Magnate—a high and stuck-up beauty, who is now my squaw. Eh, Professor Smith, times is changed, times is changed. Here, you, woman, take off my moccasins, and lively about it. I want Professor Smith to see how well I have you trained.'

"I saw her clench her teeth, and the flame of revolt rise in her face. He drew back his gnarled fist to strike, and I was afraid, and sick at heart. I could do nothing to prevail against him. So I got up to go, and not be witness to such indignity. But the Chauffeur laughed and threatened me with a beating if I did not stay and behold. And I sat there, perforce, by the campfire on the shore of Lake Temescal, and saw Vesta, Vesta Van Warden, kneel and remove the moccasins of that grinning, hairy, apelike human brute.

"—Oh, you do not understand, my grandsons. You have never known anything else, and you do not understand.

"'Halter-broke and bridle-wise,' the Chauffeur gloated, while she performed that dreadful, menial task. 'A trifle balky at times, Professor, a trifle balky; but a clout alongside the jaw makes her as meek and gentle as a lamb.'

"And another time he said: 'We've got to start all over and replenish the earth and multiply. You're handicapped, Professor. You ain't got no wife, and we're up against a regular Garden-of-Eden proposition. But I ain't proud. I'll tell you what, Professor.' He pointed at their little infant, barely a year old. 'There's your wife, though you'll have to wait till she grows up. It's rich, ain't it? We're all equals here, and I'm the biggest toad in the splash. But I ain't stuck up—not I. I do you the honor, Professor Smith, the very great honor of betrothing to you my and Vesta Van Warden's daughter. Ain't it cussed bad that Van Warden ain't here to see?'"

VI

"I lived three weeks of infinite torment there in the Chauffeur's camp. And then, one day, tiring of me, or of what to him was my bad effect on Vesta, he told me that the year before, wandering through the Contra Costa Hills to the Straits of Carquinez, across the Straits he had seen a smoke. This meant that there were still other human beings, and that for three weeks he had kept this inestimably precious information from me. I departed at once, with my dogs and horses, and journeyed across the Contra Costa Hills to the Straits. I saw no smoke on the other side, but at Port Costa discovered a small steel barge on which I was able to embark my animals. Old canvas which I found served me for a sail, and a southerly breeze fanned me across the Straits and up to the ruins of Vallejo. Here, on the outskirts of the city, I found evidences of a recently occupied camp. Many clam-shells showed me why these humans had come to the shores of the Bay. This was the Santa Rosa Tribe, and I followed its track along the old railroad right of way across the salt marshes to Sonoma Valley.

Here, at the old brickyard at Glen Ellen, I came upon the camp. There were eighteen souls all told. Two were old men, one of whom was Jones, a banker. The other was Harrison, a retired pawnbroker, who had taken for wife the matron of the State Hospital for the Insane at Napa. Of all the persons of the city of Napa, and of all the other towns and villages in that rich and populous valley, she had been the only survivor. Next, there were the three young men—Cardiff and Hale, who had been farmers, and Wainwright, a common day-laborer. All three had found wives. To Hale, a crude, illiterate farmer, had fallen Isadore, the greatest prize, next to Vesta, of the women who came through the plague. She was one of the world's most noted singers, and the plague had caught her at San Francisco. She has talked with me for hours at a time, telling me of her adventures, until, at last, rescued by Hale in the Mendocino Forest Reserve, there had remained nothing for her to do but become his wife. But Hale was a good fellow, in spite of his illiteracy. He had a keen sense of justice and right-dealing, and she was far happier with him than was Vesta with the Chauffeur.

"The wives of Cardiff and Wainwright were ordinary women, accustomed to toil with strong constitutions—just the type for the wild new life which they were compelled to live. In addition were two adult idiots from the feeble-minded home at Eldredge, and five or six young children and infants born after the formation of the Santa Rosa Tribe. Also, there was Bertha. She was a good woman, Hare-Lip, in spite of the sneers of your father. Her I took for wife. She was the mother of your father, Edwin, and of yours, Hoo-Hoo. And it was our daughter, Vera, who married your father, Hare-Lip—your father, Sandow, who was the oldest son of Vesta Van Warden and the Chauffeur.

"And so it was that I became the nineteenth member of the Santa Rosa Tribe. There were only two outsiders added after me. One was Mungerson, descended from the Magnates, who wandered alone in the wilds of Northern California for eight years before he came south and joined us. He it was who waited twelve years more before he married my daughter, Mary. The other was Johnson, the man who founded the Utah Tribe. That was where he came from, Utah, a country that lies very far away from here, across the great deserts, to the east. It was not until twenty-seven years after the plague that Johnson reached California. In all that Utah region he reported but three survivors, himself one, and all men. For many years these three men lived and hunted together, until, at last, desperate, fearing that with them the human race would perish utterly from the planet, they headed westward on the possibility of finding women survivors in California. Johnson alone came through the great desert, where his two companions died. He was forty-six years old when he joined us, and he married the fourth daughter of Isadore and Hale, and his eldest son married your aunt, Hare-Lip, who was the third daughter of Vesta and the Chauffeur. Johnson was a strong man, with a will of his own. And it was because of this that he seceded from the Santa Rosans and formed the Utah Tribe at San José. It is a small tribe—there are only nine in it—but, though he is dead, such was his influence and the strength of his breed, that it will grow into a strong tribe and play a leading part in the recivilization of the planet.

"There are only two other tribes that we know of—the Los Angelitos and the Carmelitos. The latter started from one man and woman. He was called Lopez, and he was descended from the ancient Mexicans and was very black. He was a cowherd in the ranges beyond Carmel, and his wife was a maidservant in the great Del Monte Hotel. It was seven years before we first got in touch with the Los Angelitos. They have a good country down there, but it is too warm. I estimate the present population of the world at between three hundred and fifty and four hundred—provided, of course, that there are no scattered little tribes elsewhere in the world. If there be such, we have not heard from them. Since Johnson crossed the desert from Utah, no word nor sign has come from the East or anywhere else. The great world which I knew in my boyhood and early manhood is gone. It has ceased to be. I am the last man who was alive in the days of the plague and who knows the wonders of that far-off time. We, who mastered the planet—its earth, and sea, and sky—and who were as very gods, now live in primitive savagery along the water courses of this California country.

"But we are increasing rapidly—your sister, Hare-Lip, already has four children. We are increasing rapidly and making ready for a new climb toward civilization. In time, pressure of population will compel us to spread out, and a hundred generations from now we may expect our descendants to start across the Sierras, oozing slowly along, generation by generation, over the great continent to the colonization of the East—a new Aryan drift around the world.

"But it will be slow, very slow; we have so far to climb. We fell so hopelessly far. If only one physicist or one chemist had survived! But it was not to be, and we have forgotten everything. The Chauffeur started working in iron. He made the forge which we use to this day. But he was a lazy man, and when he died he took with him all he knew of metals and machinery. What was I to know of such things? I was a classical scholar, not a chemist. The other men who survived were not educated. Only two things did the Chauffeur accomplish—the brewing of strong drink and the growing of tobacco. It was while he was drunk, once, that he killed Vesta. I firmly believe that he killed Vesta in a fit of drunken cruelty though he always maintained that she fell into the lake and was drowned.

"And, my grandsons, let me warn you against the medicine-men. They call themselves *doctors*, travestying what was once a noble profession, but in reality they are medicine-men, devil-devil men, and they make for superstition and darkness. They are cheats and liars. But so debased and degraded are we, that we believe their lies. They, too, will increase in numbers as we increase, and they will strive to rule us. Yet are they liars and charlatans. Look at young Cross-Eyes, posing as a doctor, selling charms against sickness, giving good hunting, exchanging promises of fair weather for good meat and skins, sending the death-stick, performing a thousand abominations. Yet I say to you, that when he says he can do these things, he lies. I, Professor Smith, Professor James Howard Smith, say that he lies. I have told him so to his teeth. Why has he not sent me the death-stick? Because he knows that with me it is without avail. But you, Hare-Lip, so deeply are you sunk in black superstition that did you awake this night and find the death-stick beside you, you would surely die. And you would die, not because of any virtues in the stick, but because you are a savage with the dark and clouded mind of a savage.

"The doctors must be destroyed, and all that was lost must be discovered over again. Wherefore, earnestly, I repeat unto you certain things which you must remember and tell to your children after you. You must tell them that when water is made hot by fire, there resides in it a wonderful thing called steam, which is stronger than ten thousand men and which can do all man's work for him. There are other very useful things. In the lightning flash resides a similarly strong servant of man, which was of old his slave and which some day will be his slave again.

"Quite a different thing is the alphabet. It is what enables me to know the meaning of fine markings, whereas you boys know only rude picture-writing. In that dry cave on Telegraph Hill, where you see me often go when the tribe is down by the sea, I have stored many books. In them is great wisdom. Also, with them, I have placed a key to the alphabet, so that one who knows picture-writing may also know print. Some day men will read again; and then, if no accident has befallen my cave, they will know that Professor James Howard Smith once lived and saved for them the knowledge of the ancients.

"There is another little device that men inevitably will rediscover. It is called gunpowder. It was what enabled us to kill surely and at long distances. Certain things which are found in the ground, when combined in the right proportions, will make this gunpowder. What these things are, I have forgotten, or else I never knew. But I wish I did know. Then would I make powder, and then would I certainly kill Cross-Eyes and rid the land of superstition—"

"After I am man-grown I am going to give Cross-Eyes all the goats, and meat, and skins I can get, so that he'll teach me to be a doctor," Hoo-Hoo asserted. "And when I know, I'll make everybody else sit up and take notice. They'll get down in the dirt to me, you bet."

The old man nodded his head solemnly, and murmured:

"Strange it is to hear the vestiges and remnants of the complicated Aryan speech falling from the lips of a filthy little skin-clad savage. All the world is topsy-turvy. And it has been topsy-turvy ever since the plague."

"You won't make me sit up," Hare-Lip boasted to the would-be medicine-man. "If I paid you for a sending of the death-stick and it didn't work, I'd bust in your head—understand, you Hoo-Hoo, you?"

"I'm going to get Granser to remember this here gunpowder stuff," Edwin said softly, "and then I'll have you all on the run. You, Hare-Lip, will do my fighting for me and get my meat for me, and you, Hoo-Hoo, will send the death-stick for me and make everybody afraid. And if I catch Hare-Lip trying to bust your head, Hoo-Hoo, I'll fix him with that same gunpowder. Granser ain't such a fool as you think, and I'm going to listen to him and some day I'll be boss over the whole bunch of you."

The old man shook his head sadly, and said:

"The gunpowder will come. Nothing can stop it—the same old story over and over. Man will increase, and men will fight. The gunpowder will enable men to kill millions of men, and in this way only, by fire and blood, will a new civilization, in some remote day, be evolved. And of what profit will it be? Just as the old civilization passed, so will the new. It may take fifty thousand years to build, but it will pass. All things pass. Only remain cosmic force and matter, ever in flux, ever acting and reacting and realizing the eternal types—the priest, the soldier, and the king. Out of the mouths of babes comes the wisdom of all the ages. Some will fight, some will rule, some will pray; and all the rest will toil and suffer sore while on their bleeding carcasses is reared again, and yet again, without end, the amazing beauty and surpassing wonder of the civilized state. It were just as well that I destroyed those cave-stored books—whether they remain or perish, all their old truths will be discovered, their old lies lived and handed down. What is the profit—"

Hare-Lip leaped to his feet, giving a quick glance at the pasturing goats and the afternoon sun.

"Gee!" he muttered to Edwin. "The old geezer gets more long-winded every day. Let's pull for camp."

While the other two, aided by the dogs, assembled the goats and started them for the trail through the forest, Edwin stayed by the old man and guided him in the same direction. When they reached the old right of way, Edwin stopped suddenly and looked back. Hare-Lip and Hoo-Hoo and the dogs and the goats passed on. Edwin was looking at a small herd of wild horses which had come down on the hard sand. There were at least twenty of them, young colts and yearlings and mares, led by a beautiful stallion which stood in the foam at the edge of the surf, with arched neck and bright wild eyes, sniffing the salt air from off the sea.

"What is it?" Granser queried.

"Horses," was the answer. "First time I ever seen 'em on the beach. It's the mountain lions getting thicker and thicker and driving 'em down."

The low sun shot red shafts of light, fan-shaped, up from a cloud-tumbled horizon. And close at hand, in the white waste of shore-lashed waters, the sea-lions, bellowing their old primeval chant, hauled up out of the sea on the black rocks and fought and loved.

"Come on, Granser," Edwin prompted.

And old man and boy, skin-clad and barbaric, turned and went along the right of way into the forest in the wake of the goats.